STALIN'S MUSIC PRIZE

STALIN'S MUSIC PRIZE

SOVIET CULTURE AND POLITICS

MARINA FROLOVA-WALKER

YALE UNIVERSITY PRESS
NEW HAVEN AND LONDON

For information about this and other Yale University Press publications, please contact:
U.S. Office: sales.press@yale.edu   www.yalebooks.com
Europe Office: sales@yaleup.co.uk   www.yalebooks.co.uk

Typeset in Minion Pro by IDSUK (DataConnection) Ltd
Printed in Great Britain by Gomer Press, Llandysul, Ceredigion, Wales

Library of Congress Cataloging-in-Publication Data

Names: Frolova–Walker, Marina, author.
Title: Stalin's music prize / Marina Frolova–Walker.
Description: New Haven : Yale University Press, [2016] | Includes
    bibliographical references and index.
Identifiers: LCCN 2015040942 | ISBN 9780300208849 (alk. paper)
Subjects: LCSH: Stalin prizes—History. | Music—Awards—Soviet Union. |
    Music—Soviet Union—History and criticism.
Classification: LCC ML76.S725 F76 2016 | DDC 780.79/47—dc23
LC record available at http://lccn.loc.gov/2015040942

A catalogue record for this book is available from the British Library

10 9 8 7 6 5 4 3 2 1

To Ekaterina Mikhailovna, with love and gratitude

CONTENTS

NOTE ON THE TEXT

The system of transliteration I have adopted is based on the system used in Grove Music Online, which has been widely used by anglophone music scholars (*http://www.oxfordmusiconline.com/public/page/transliteration*).

Surnames are given in the most common transliteration (e.g. as in Wikipedia: Prokofiev, Myaskovsky); first names are mostly given in the familiar anglicized form (Sergei, Nikolai). In the notes, however, where Russian sources are cited, the same names are spelled in accordance with the transliteration system used in Grove (Sergey Prokof'yev, Nikolay Myaskovskiy).

Appendices not included in the printed book are available at: http://yalebooks.co.uk/frolova_walker_appendix.asp

ACKNOWLEDGEMENTS

A Major Research Fellowship from the Leverhulme Trust (2011–13) allowed me to devote two years to full-time research and immerse myself fully into my archival studies in Moscow. If not for their generous support, this book would have taken much longer to write. I am also grateful to my colleagues at the Music Faculty, University of Cambridge, and in particular to its Senior Administrator, Sue Round, for the support they have given me in organizing periods of leave. Warmest thanks are also due to Malcolm Gerratt and Robert Baldock from Yale University Press, for their interest in my work and for making this volume's path to publication short and smooth.

I have been fortunate to benefit from the help of many colleagues and friends who volunteered information, answered questions, provided me with additional sources, read parts of the script, or gave broader encouragement and advice: John Barber, Kevin Bartig, Maria Belodubrovskaya, Margaret Bent, Elena Chugunova-Paulson, Olga Digonskaya, Evgeny Dobrenko, Olga Dombrovskaya, Oleg Dorman, David Fanning, Laurel Fay, Leah Goldman, Yoram Gorlizki, Oleg Hlevniuk, Jana Howlett, Catriona Kelly, Olga Khvoina, Olga Kushniruk, Gulnara Kuzbakova, Urve Lippus, Leonidas Melnikas, Simon Morrison, Zhanna Murzabekova, Joan Neuberger, Dmitry Neustroyev, Vladimir Orlov, Daniil Petrov, John Riley, Saulus Sondeckis, Rūta Stanevičiūtė, Živilė Stonytė, Natalya Strizhkova, Richard Taruskin, Ekaterina Tsareva and Patrick Zuk. I am also grateful to the staff of the archives and libraries that I frequented: RGALI, RGANI, RGASPI, GARF, the Glinka Museum (VMOMK), the Goldenweiser Museum and the Music Department of the Russian State Library – many pleasant hours were spent in all of these institutions.

This book would not have been possible without the love and dedication of my family members, first and foremost my late mother, Alla Krylova, who made my numerous archival trips to Moscow logistically possible. My

wonderful in-laws, John Walker and the late Edna Walker, contributed generously to childminding. I thank my son Alexander Walker for enduring (and
enjoying) his periods of study in Moscow, as well as for his day-to-day understanding and patience. And, of course, my deepest gratitude goes to Jonathan
Walker, my best reader and editor, whose selfless work on the text of this book
has been invaluable. I treasure the memory of those long hours we spent in
conversation about the Stalin Prizes, and all the laughs we had together.

I dedicate this book to Ekaterina Mikhailovna Tsareva, whom I met in the
spring of 1981, when I was only beginning to dream of a music-related career.
I am immensely grateful to her as a teacher, for shaping my professional core,
and as a friend, for watching over my life.

INTRODUCTION

In '46, when I was a delegate to the Congress of Antifascist Women, I happened to speak with an English actress, who had been forbidden to approach our delegation. But she boldly made her way over to us regardless, and struck up a conversation with the Soviet women. While she was talking to me about the arts, she couldn't keep herself from looking downwards, at my chest, and eventually she asked me: 'What did you get that medal for?' I told her that it was a medal given to Stalin Prize laureates. 'For what?' she asked. 'For my work in the role of Nadezhda Durova,' I replied. 'I was also awarded something for my theatre work,' she went on. 'What did they give you?' I asked her. After a moment's hesitation, she dipped into her handbag and pulled out something drab-looking, small and flat, a kind of powder box. 'That's how they reward us performers.'

Comrades, this is dreadful. They reward their artists with powder boxes. This shows that as far as they're concerned, the arts are a mere distraction, a kind of amusement, a decadent form of escapism. But on our tunics, we proudly bear the medal of Stalin Prize laureates, a medal portraying our great leader, Stalin – Stalin who is leading all the peoples forward, Stalin the fighter for peace. We feel that we are people of the state, if I can put it like that. We carry out the tasks of the state and we build up that state.

That actress smiled at me, with a hint of envy, realizing that we were a different kind of people.

– Vera Maretskaya[1]

On the same day that *Pravda* was filled with articles marking Stalin's sixtieth birthday, it would have been very easy to miss the announcement that a new state prize for excellence in the arts and sciences was to be established. The day was 21 December 1939, and over the following months, the picture gradually came into focus: there were to be ten prizes made available in the arts, four of them reserved for literary works, to the value of 100,000 roubles each. Only works that had been presented to the public for the first time in 1940 were eligible for nomination, and the deadline for submissions was 15 October. It was not yet entirely clear how the awards process would work out in practice, and it would have been hard to anticipate the crucial role the prizes would soon play in reshaping the Soviet cultural scene.

Finally, on 16 March 1941 the country was informed of the first 'Stalin Prize laureates', as they were officially called, through a lengthy list of their names and achievements that covered the first two pages of *Pravda*. Notably, the first category on the front page was 'Music', and the first artist depicted in the row of portraits on page one was none other than Dmitry Shostakovich (fig. 1). *Pravda* readers far and wide were probably more likely to recognize his bespectacled face than any of the other faces on display, because only five years earlier, in very different circumstances, he had been a target of a strident personalized campaign that targeted his opera *Lady Macbeth of Mtsensk*. All those misdemeanours had evidently been forgiven, and Shostakovich's name was now forever tied to Stalin's: he was now Shostakovich the Stalin Prize laureate. Of all the honours made available by the Soviet state, this one in particular seemed to bear the stamp of Stalin's personal approval.

Prizes were awarded on eleven occasions over the course of the years 1940–54, but what seemed an exceptional honour in the first round of awards eventually became more routine, and in the later years, enormous numbers of new laureates were created. Yet, even with thousands of prizes awarded after a decade had gone by (and hundreds in music), no other honour carried quite the same degree of prestige. The individual awards were also great windfalls: the amount of money awarded was far beyond the earnings of ordinary workers. The ritual of the awards now shaped the annual cycle for the Soviet artistic intelligentsia: the completion of works and their premieres were often timed to fit with nomination deadlines. On the day of the prize list, artists opened their copies of *Pravda* and perused the list of the fortunate with a gamut of feelings from joy to dismay, from mild curiosity to *Schadenfreude*. Despite the many rumours circulating in advance, no one could be certain of anything until they saw *Pravda*'s printed page.

And then in March 1953 Stalin died. 'The machine suddenly faltered, and with a sudden jolt, came to a standstill. A few days later, it seemed as if everything was running again just as before, *but not quite* – it only looked that way.'[2] The Stalin Prize was a part of the machinery that stopped and restarted, and in spite of many hours of meetings, voting and perusal of prize lists, there were never to be any further *Pravda* pages devoted to the winners. Soon the very

Постановление Совета Народных Комиссаров Союза ССР

О ПРИСУЖДЕНИИ СТАЛИНСКИХ ПРЕМИИ ЗА ВЫДАЮЩИЕСЯ РАБОТЫ В ОБЛАСТИ ИСКУССТВА И ЛИТЕРАТУРЫ.

Во исполнение Постановления Совета Народных Комиссаров Союза ССР от 20 декабря 1939 г. и 20 декабря 1940 г. о присуждении Сталинских премий за выдающиеся работы в области искусства и литературы в период последних 6—7 лет, Совет Народных Комиссаров Союза ССР постановляет:

Присудить Сталинские премии за выдающиеся работы в области:

а. Музыки.

Премии первой степени в размере 100.000 рублей

в. Скульптуры.

Премии первой степени в размере 100.000 рублей

Премии второй степени в размере 50.000 рублей

г. Архитектуры.

Премии первой степени в размере 100.000 рублей

Премии второй степени в размере 50.000 рублей

Премии второй степени в размере 50.000 рублей

д. Театрально-драматического искусства.

Премии первой степени в размере 100.000 рублей

Д. Д. Шостакович.   А. М. Герасимов.   В. И. Мухина.

Fig. 1. *Pravda*, 16 March 1941, fragments of the front page.

name of the award would become unprintable; former Stalin laureates became winners of the 'State Prize' and were encouraged to exchange their medals for replacements that lacked the now unspeakable leader's profile (although they also lacked most of the gold or silver content of the originals).

In recent years, I have become progressively fascinated, engrossed and possessed by this story. My earlier researches into the history of Soviet music had often led me towards the study of the transcripts of official meetings that were left to posterity by the efficient bureaucratic machine. From the transcripts of the

Composers' Union, I almost accidentally drifted into those of the Stalin Prize Committee (the main, or at least, the publicly visible jury panel for the Stalin Prizes), and I found these particularly revealing. These raw transcripts of stenographic notes, astonishing in their completeness, transmitted voices from the past, and those voices were arguing, debating, at times smoothly insulting each other behind euphemistic veneers. I knew most of the judges from their own works and reputation, among them the legendary theatre director and friend of Stanislavsky, Nemirovich-Danchenko, and the leading Soviet sculptor Vera Mukhina, as well as my old research interests Shostakovich and Myaskovsky. Among them was also the celebrated actor Mikhail Tsarev, whom I saw live as King Lear and who happened to be the father of my own research supervisor, Ekaterina Tsareva. Now I knew something about her father that even she didn't know: what he said on a particular day, down to the precise hour, about a certain novel, play or painting. I found this kind of time travelling and eavesdropping irresistible.

At first, I tried to confine myself to the debates on music, then found that there was essential contextual material in many of the other debates, and finally I became a voracious reader of debates across all the arts, for their intrinsic interest. Having been born and raised in the Soviet Union, I heard many of the prize-winning symphonies and songs as part of the background cultural hum; during my schooldays, I studied several of the prize-winning novels, and through all my commuting back and forth across Moscow, I knew intimately the décor of prize-winning Moscow Metro stations. These layers of the Soviet artistic landscape were laid down in the decades before my birth, but were still everywhere visible or audible, often familiar to the point of neutrality or even tedium, sometimes already taking on a tinge of exoticism from the historical peculiarities of their times. All of this was now coming fully alive, animated by the people who had produced, judged and validated these artworks, performances and buildings. This personal dimension, and the fact that the Stalin Prize discussions mixed the arts together, made this book what it is. The primary focus is on music and musicians, but on composers of art music above all. At the same time, I cover discussions of all the rest of Soviet musical life, whether popular song composers, the Red Army choir, balalaika ensembles or Kirghiz music dramas, and retain many interesting or significant items from the broader context of the other arts. This context, I feel, helps us realize just how odd it actually was to bestow an award of such magnitude on a quartet, a symphony or a singer's operatic role when these are placed next to gigantic tower blocks or statues of Stalin seen by whole cities, or patriotic films watched by millions.

Studies of Soviet music in the West have, in recent years, engaged with the theme of 'music and power' in many productive ways. Initially, Shostakovich was the only constant focus of attention, his life and his music continually cross-examined to serve either the narrative of his persecution by the state or the counter-narrative of his co-option and reward.[3] Prokofiev, once seen as a more neutral, apolitical figure, has now joined him on that intersection.[4] And while the personal stories of such familiar names as Khachaturian, Khrennikov or Kabalevsky still remain in the shadows for Western readers, this deficit has been partially remedied by studies of Soviet music's institutional structure, such as Kiril Tomoff's excellent volume on the Union of Composers.[5]

The present book attempts to address both the institutions and the individuals. Its first goal is to write another page into the institutional history of Soviet culture by viewing Soviet music through the lens of the Stalin Prize awards. Much of this undertaking is narrowly micro-historical, but it also leads us to a new perspective on the very broad field of Soviet musical life between 1940 and 1954, which includes not only 'academic' composition but also popular song, not only opera but also state folk ensembles. The award process allows us to contemplate a multi-tiered structure of professional, state and Party bodies that controlled and managed this broad field, and examine the power relationships within this structure. This promises us a better understanding of *how things were done* in the musical sphere, and more broadly, in the surrounding culture.

The second goal of the book is to populate this institutional narrative with individuals and trace the effects of their personal agency within this great bureaucratic game. Shostakovich has proved, indeed, an inescapable focus yet again (he begins and ends the book), not for external reasons, but precisely because of the unrivalled dominance his music exercised over prize discussions in music. On the basis of the wealth of materials available to me, I believe I was able to approach Shostakovich's role largely freed of any prejudices picked up from more recent discourse, whether the Shostakovich debates of the late twentieth century, or the various memoirs written years after the events (and filtering them through later perspectives). What I was surprised to find was that his contemporaries actually thought of him in very similar terms: not just as an artistic genius, but as someone who created controversy. Whenever his music came up for discussion in the Stalin Prize Committee, the members tensed up 'as if in a nuclear lab', as one of them put it.[6] Beyond Shostakovich, I also wanted to provide insight into the prize trajectories of Prokofiev, Myaskovsky and some of Myaskovsky's most important pupils, such as Khachaturian and Kabalevsky, who also won multiple prizes. And beyond these, as far as the format of the book allowed, I wanted to include other personalized vignettes, with the expectation that even if readers were hitherto unaware of this or that composer, let alone familiar with his music, they could use the Internet to go beyond the nuggets of information I offer. I have likewise attempted to humanize the jury panels, giving a sense of distinct and powerful personalities:

Myaskovsky appears in a new light, the centre of a network of influence, while Shostakovich is seen treading on toes for the sake of upholding quality. They are joined by the pianist Goldenweiser, who said whatever he wanted, by the composer and administrator Khrennikov, formidable but often losing his battles and bringing trouble upon himself, and also the state folk ensemble director, Zakharov, who took the role of Khrennikov's comic sidekick.

This humanizing aspect of my narrative was prompted by something that has always been a part of Soviet studies: a desire to glimpse subjectivities, a thirst for authenticity, for the knowledge of *what people actually thought*. In some of the transcripts, I found that elusive understanding of human behaviour tantalizingly close, whereas the many colourful anecdotes I found in the memoir literature often turned out to be untrue (even if they revealed something important about their tellers).

There is, however, a third goal, too, which as a musicologist I could not leave aside. The Stalin Prize was the only honour awarded for particular works (or in the sciences, particular research projects) rather than being awarded only to individuals for their career-long achievements. This stipulation was inherited from the Nobel Prize rules, although it was suspended in many cases where a worthy individual would not otherwise have been able to receive a prize. The attempt to define Socialist Realism in music has seemed an all but impossible task for scholars in recent decades, but my work on the Stalin Prizes offers us, I believe, a way out of the impasse. Since the Stalin Prize jurors avowedly attempted to shape the Socialist Realist artistic canon, we are able to see from their discussions not only *which works were awarded* but also *why*. Whenever possible, then, I touch upon the music (as received by the jurors and as heard by myself), although for reasons of space, I am regretfully unable to launch into long, affectionate descriptions of masterworks, or of lesser works that still have the power to delight. The reasons for awarding or withholding a prize for a given work were always complex: aesthetic considerations were mixed not only with ideology, but also with matters of prestige, patronage, previous awards, personal issues, practicalities of the voting system and various other ingredients. Even so, we are still able to draw conclusions on how musical Socialist Realism was institutionally practised.

As I have already stated, my core sources are archival. The Stalin Prize awards are very well documented where the Stalin Prize Committee itself is concerned (every plenary session and some section meetings were transcribed verbatim). But the mists descend over the higher bodies that oversaw the Committee's work, modifying or even overturning its hard-won decisions: there are no verbatim transcripts at these levels, and the complex network of discussions has to be worked out from a large quantity of correspondence between these bodies, and from the ever-proliferating lists of nominees attached to the letters. This correspondence is dispersed through multiple collections in several archives[7] and, even after my considerable efforts, it still offers a picture that is in some respects incomplete. One of the most interesting archival finds was a batch of materials amassed in preparation for the Politburo sessions where the final decisions were made. These contain Stalin's own marginalia on the nomination lists and, importantly, the lists of people present at these sessions. Some further clarification of what took place at those higher levels can be gleaned from the memoirs of Dmitry Shepilov and Konstantin Simonov, which, upon comparison with the Politburo materials, I found strikingly accurate.[8]

The body of archival materials I describe is, of course, not entirely *terra incognita*, but in my view it remains lamentably underused by scholars, and a full picture of this complex enterprise has not yet been revealed. Even the purely factual and statistical side has not been fully sorted out: Wikipedia (particularly in Russian) often offers accurate information on the who-what-when of a prize, and yet even serious publications are still sometimes littered with mistakes and misconceptions (confusions often arise because there could be a one- or two-year gap between initial nomination and the awarding of a prize). A very useful volume devoted specifically to Stalin Prizes in the arts was published in Russia in 2007: it managed to bring the lists from different years together and usefully ordered the information according to different categories (I spotted only a few mistakes there). However, most of the other materials in the book were from secondary sources, while some of the transcripts were copied from printed publications and Internet sites (most of the references to the latter are no longer valid).[9] A complete reference book where all the factual information will finally be verified is in the making, and, in one of the archives, I met its dedicated compiler, Vladimir Ivkin, a retired military man. The larger part of his projected four-volume work will be devoted to the prizewinners in sciences and technology.[10]

But factual accuracy is only the beginning of the matter. It has fallen to individuals working on related topics to provide interpretation of the names, figures and bureaucratic procedures of the Stalin Prize saga. So far, two books have been particularly illuminating: Tomoff's *Creative Union*, which devotes a chapter to the Stalin Prizes and explains the working of the system using a few case studies, and Vladimir Perkhin's (Russian-language) publication of letters to the culture minister Khrapchenko, which contains many quotations from the transcripts of the Stalin Prize Committee accompanied by a penetrating commentary.[11] Archival sources informed Oliver Johnson's discussion of Stalin Prize winners in painting and Joan Neuberger's case study of the film *Ivan the Terrible* by Sergei Eisenstein.[12] Despite these efforts, I must emphasize that the archival materials have remained underused and could potentially arm many more scholars with powerful explanations of Soviet culture's inner workings.

While scholars are gradually exploring this treasure trove, popular literature entertains its readers with elaborate yarns that travel unchallenged from source to source. Here is one colourful example, which suddenly cropped up in the middle of my project and left me at first perplexed and then bemused. It was, apparently, received wisdom that the pianist Maria Yudina, an imposing if rather mysterious figure in Soviet music history, defiantly and courageously gave the full sum of her Stalin Prize to the Russian Orthodox church. I knew of Yudina's deep religious beliefs, which she chose not to hide even when state atheism was at its most militant, and I knew about the many troubles this brought on her head. I was also well aware that not only had Yudina never won a Stalin Prize, but she was never nominated for one, nor, in any of the discussions that I have read, was she even so much as mentioned. As an eccentric figure, languishing in the shadows of the Soviet music world, she was, in fact, the most unlikely candidate for a nomination (I will further clarify the reasons for this in Chapter 9). But although the story was undoubtedly a fiction, it was being spread globally through Wikipedia articles, and so I finally decided that I had to trace it back to its source.

This took little effort – indeed, I found the culprit in seconds. The most complete version of the yarn was in a book whose author styles himself 'Blazhennïy Ioann' (John the Blessed).[13] According to this writer, the decision to award Yudina a Stalin Prize was taken by Stalin, who decided to give her 20,000 roubles in cash (the price of a new car at the time was 16,000 roubles, but the writer tells us it was about two million dollars by today's standards). Why? Supposedly because he found himself profoundly moved by a broadcast of a Mozart piano concerto he heard on the radio, performed by Yudina. In the afternoon of the same day, according to John the Blessed, a courier handed over the award to the impoverished Yudina, who did not even own a piano at the time. But Yudina, 'supported by the Holy Mother of God', was not to be bought. She wrote Stalin a letter, as quoted by John the Blessed: 'Day and night I will pray for the forgiveness of the monstrous atrocities that you have perpetrated against your people. I reject the Stalin Prize, and am sending the money for the renovation of a church and the salvation of your soul.'[14]

The text of this letter seemed vaguely familiar, and soon, with help from colleagues, I found it in Solomon Volkov's *Testimony*, the purported (and, in many eyes, discredited) memoir of Shostakovich.[15] Everything was there already, even the sum of 20,000 roubles – everything but the key reference to the Stalin Prize. Another Google search returned a further puzzling reference from a 1950 German newspaper, in which Yudina was named a Stalin Prize laureate during her concert series in Leipzig and Berlin for the J. S. Bach tercentenary celebrations.[16] The newspaper could have made a mistake, but where did John the Blessed get his information from? I never received a reply to an email I sent him, but by happy chance, I was approached a few months later by two disciples of John, who wanted to enlighten me about the activities of their religious sect (they claimed to be the spiritual heirs of the Cathars). To my question about John the Blessed's historical sources, they replied that he must have drawn the story from his visions. Which would certainly add a touch of colour to his footnote references.

This is not an isolated case: I have observed even the most respectable popularizers of cultural history demonstrate a cavalier attitude to the notion of the Stalin Prize which, it seems, Stalin could simply pull out of his pocket on a whim. In a public talk for Cambridge University in the summer of 2014, a friend of Svyatoslav Richter (I shall allow him to remain nameless here) said that the pianist once played for Stalin at a Kremlin banquet and 'woke up the next day to find he was a Stalin Prize laureate'. The fact that the speaker knew Richter personally would seem to lend this anecdote some additional credibility, but we should not be too quick to accept it; if the impossible Stalin Prize detail is removed from the anecdote, the account of Richter's performance at the banquet could already be found in Yury Lyubimov's memoirs, so it would seem that the anecdote was merely an embellishment of a story already in the public domain.[17] The background belief that leads to such embellishments is the assumption, as I said, that the award was Stalin's own, to hand out as he pleased. I won't deny that a very successful Kremlin-banquet performance might well have been of assistance if the same artist happened to be nominated for a prize at a later date (in fact, I explore such issues in Chapter 9), but the primary assumption of the anecdotalists is wrong, and to undermine it is another aim of this book. As we shall see, Stalin's whims had a direct effect in only a handful of cases, while the hundreds of other music prizes were the result of collective decisions.

This, of course, complicates the story and spoils the attractive simplicity of the anecdote. Oleg Khlevniuk, who has done some exemplary work on interpreting the newly declassified materials on the workings of Soviet Party and government structures, remarked on the longevity of various legends: they persisted because they give simple, palatable answers to complex historical questions.[18] Just as his detailed scholarly work and refutations would not stop these legends from continuing to proliferate in popular writing, I do not expect my researches to sink the various Stalin Prize yarns either. I have noticed, however, that after the various public lectures I have given on the present topic, I have never been asked the standard naive questions such as 'did Shostakovich believe in Communism?' that I would be asked if I was lecturing on, say, his Fifth Symphony or Eighth Quartet. When given the chance, my listeners seemed to enjoy their Soviet history complicated, and hearing received wisdom punctured, which gives me hope that this book will interest a broader audience.

A few words on the structure of the book: it does not proceed chronologically, but in a series of thematic cross sections, in order to make the text more useful and more engaging. This, however, means that readers less familiar with the subject may need to adopt a less linear approach. In particular I would recommend those unfamiliar with the effects of the 1948 Resolution against formalism in music to read the beginning of Chapter 10 before starting Chapter 3.

Before we narrow our focus mainly to music, Chapter 1 explains in general terms how the award system worked. Chapter 2 illustrates this with examples from the first year of the awards, using one of the more unusual cases – Shostakovich's Piano Quintet – to acquaint readers with some of the twists and turns of the process. Chapters 3, 4 and 6 are devoted to the prize histories of individual composers, respectively Prokofiev, Shostakovich and Myaskovsky, and thus span the whole period from 1940 to 1954. The Myaskovsky chapter also includes smaller studies of three composers in his circle of former students: Khachaturian, Kabalevsky and Shebalin. Chapter 5 looks at Shostakovich as a Stalin Prize Committee member, overturning the familiar image of him as a reluctant performer of his many official duties, a stuttering reader of speeches written for him – here he often performs with relish, and sees it as his duty to defend the institution of the prizes from lax practices.

Chapters 7 and 8 deal with music that largely falls outside the scope of the previous chapters. Chapter 7 covers the awards given to the non-Russian 'national' republics forming the Soviet Union, while Chapter 8 looks at various musical genres that lie outside highbrow art music. Chapter 9 focuses on performance rather than composition, with prizes both for individuals and for production teams in opera. Chapter 10 picks up the chronological thread, dealing with the new environment in which the Stalin Prize Committee worked from the beginning of 1948 onwards. Chapter 11 deals with the Committee's afterlife once Stalin had died. The Conclusion addresses issues of *listening* in the Stalin Prize Committee and demonstrates how the Stalin Prize can illuminate the concept, or better, the practice of Socialist Realism in music. The Appendices offer further possibilities for reference by offering lists of prize-winning individuals and works in several formats, together with coverage of the shifting membership of the Stalin Prize Committee.

It only remains for me to say that this volume could not absorb all the information I have managed to gather. Further reference material, musical and pictorial illustrations, as well as corrections to any mistakes lurking within the book, will appear on the associated website, to which all readers are warmly invited.

CHAPTER ONE

HOW IT ALL WORKED

Or take the issue of Stalin Prizes (movement in the audience).
Even the Tsars didn't institute prizes named after themselves.

*– Nikita Khrushchev, Speech at the 20th Party Congress
on 25 February 1956[1]*

Stalin's Own

How did the Stalin Prize come about? There is a colourful story that offers a possible answer, and it is worth retelling even if we must exercise some scepticism.[2] It runs as follows: at one point in 1939, Stalin discovered that a metal safe in his office contained piles of banknotes and, on enquiring, he was told that these were his royalties on his published works, translated and printed around the world. He then wanted to know whether other Politburo members were also receiving such royalties, angered by the thought that they might be profiteering from their Party work. He immediately convoked an extraordinary meeting of the Politburo, which led to the decision that royalties from Party publications abroad should be used to fund prizes for the highest achievements in science and technology, as well as literature and the other arts. One Politburo member piously suggested that the prize could bear Stalin's name and the awards held on his birthday.

And so it is possible that Stalin Prizes were indeed Stalin's prizes, funded at least in part from his own earnings. But whatever the origins and source of funding, each year's prizewinners wrote letters to Stalin, thanking him personally, and promising him that the prize would spur them on to new triumphs.[3] The composer Zakharov, for example, when given his prize for wartime songs, sent Stalin a telegram in which he thanked him and all the government for the honour, and promised to write songs that would undermine the enemies of humanity.[4] In any case, the ministry of finance was instructed to open a credit account for the Stalin Prize Committee; there is nothing documented to say whether or not this was from royalties earned abroad by Stalin or other Politburo members.[5] The money was generous, and became ever more so with every coming year. There was something extraordinary in how easily requests for increasing the number of prizes were honoured, creating the image of a munificent leader.

Despite the colourful story about its origins, the Stalin Prize had a precedent. After Lenin's death, a Lenin Prize for outstanding scientists was instituted (in June 1925), and prizewinners were to receive the sum of 100,000 roubles. Thirty-two scientists had been granted the award between 1925 and 1934, when this prize system petered out.[6] In 1936, the Communist Academy, which had been choosing the winners, was reorganized into the Academy of Sciences, and it was decided that the new body would take over the awards process. Oddly, the relevant documentation never actually reached the Academy, and a phone call from the government informed them that the issue had been taken off the agenda.[7] With hindsight, we can see that the Purges threw everything up in the air: it would have been pointless giving awards to scientists who, for all the Academy knew, might the next day be indicted for sabotage.

Once the Purges had run their course, and some stability returned to the upper echelons of Soviet society, the new Stalin Prize emerged in a form that was quite similar to the defunct Lenin Prize. The same round sum of 100,000 was envisaged,[8] and the number of annual awards for scientists was only slightly higher. The main difference was that the new prize would also recognize achievements in the arts.

How Much was 100,000 Roubles?

Compared to the salaries of ordinary workers, this was an astonishing sum of money. Manual workers were paid, on average, 300 roubles a month, so for them, the value of a single prize would not be far short of their own lifetime earnings. Higher up the social scale, heads of university departments commanded 1,500 roubles a month, so even for them such a prize would also be an extraordinary windfall.[9] It would seem that the prizes were designed to create an elite among scientific and artistic intelligentsia whose remuneration was far out of reach for the rest of society.

And yet such an elite was already in place. If we compare the prize with the earnings of a select few artists, the sum no longer looks extraordinary. Ivan Kozlovsky, a celebrity tenor, was rumoured to earn 80,000 to 90,000 a month, mostly from privately organized concerts (his Bolshoi salary was only good enough to pay his driver).[10] Some of the best earners were popular plays, where authors or translators received generous royalties from every performance (and the more acts the play contained, the more they received). Thus, playwright and poet Konstantin Simonov received 2.5 million roubles in the four years after the war (the equivalent of more than six Stalin Prizes annually!).[11] Compared to that, Shostakovich's cantata *Song of the Forests* earned him only 144 roubles in the first year, plus 10,000 for its publication.[12] In his case, receiving a Stalin Prize for it later must have seemed only fair. The new system of paying art workers, introduced in 1949, effectively capped their royalties at 200,000 roubles annually, but even this was still the equivalent of two Stalin Prizes a year.[13]

The money awarded was only part of the value of the prize. Collateral benefits included huge print runs, productions nationwide, performances and, importantly, spin-offs: if a novel was awarded a Stalin Prize one year, the following year was likely to bring a play based on the story, and the year after a film or an opera. If an opera was awarded in the nomination for Music, the following year's productions in opera houses across the Soviet Union were likely to garner further nominations in the theatrical performance category. Winners were thus likely to see their fame and fortune increase further in the wake of the initial prize.

The value of a small, elegant medal pinned to the jacket was incalculable in a society where prestige and connections could assure extravagant social privileges. At fifteen paces, all medals looked the same and only closer inspection would reveal either the gold sheen of the first-class one or the silver shades indicating lesser degrees. Even then one could not say whether the winner had received an individual award (say, for single-handedly crafting a perfect Socialist Realist novel) or had struck it lucky by being included in the film cast list for a prize despite a relatively minor role. The first would have received the 100,000 roubles, the second perhaps only about 5,000 (since collective prizes were of the same value, but shared between members according to the importance of their contribution). Even so, both could call themselves 'laureates' (a specially established title for Stalin Prize winners) and both could use the prestige of the medal to procure desirable goods, whether railway tickets in season or theatre passes for a performance that was sold out as far as the general public was concerned. At the absurd end of this spectrum, we find a report on the levity of two much-praised film stars, Nikolai Bogolyubov and Yevgeny Samoilov, who pawned their laureate cards in order to cover a post-shoot drinking session. They were much too slow to buy them back, and word eventually reached the authorities.[14]

Together with the title, laureates received tremendous bargaining power. A young actress, once she had played a minor role in an award-winning film, would never again have to settle for modest parts in provincial theatres. There were various scandals created by aggrieved artists when eagerly awaited prizes failed to materialize: for example, the Bolshoi mezzo-soprano Vera Davydova, already a Stalin Prize laureate, threatened to resign after the prize for singing Marina Mniszek in *Boris Godunov* went to her rival Maria Maksakova. The Bolshoi's artistic director Nikolai Golovanov dried her tears with the promise of a part in *Sadko*, which, in his reckoning, would definitely earn her another prize.[15] In the end, she received not just one, but two in a row, for *Sadko* and then for *Khovanshchina*.

The high prestige of the Stalin Prize was clearest to those artists who were excluded from consideration. One of these was the poet Boris Pasternak, whose work was considered too decadent for Soviet tastes. In 1943, his candidature for the prize was actually debated at the Stalin Prize Committee but it fell through: while his poetry was too controversial a choice, he was also rejected even for the more neutral work that had been proposed – his translations of Shakespeare.[16] Following this misfortune, which must have been leaked to him, Pasternak wrote a letter to Alexander Shcherbakov, a Party Central Committee (CC) member who was directly involved in overseeing the Stalin Prize selection process: he complained of his invisibility as an artist, worrying that it would be perceived by his colleagues as a sign of censure. 'It seems to me,' he continued, 'that I have done no less than today's prizewinners and order-bearers, but I am placed in a lowly position in comparison to them.'[17] His plea was disregarded. In 1947, after his new book of poetry was banned, Pasternak wrote yet more desperately to the new Prize Committee chairman (and literary detractor) Fadeyev: 'If I, too, could be elevated to the status of laureate, like so many of the artists and musicians of my age, then there wouldn't be any need for my confessions and there wouldn't be any more cause for talk about me.'[18] By 1949, realizing that he would never be accorded this status, he adopted a tone of bitter mockery when writing about another detractor, Mikhail Lukonin: 'It was foolish, by the way, to allow the young laureate Lutokhin [Pasternak's careless and perhaps contemptuous distortion of Lukonin's surname] to measure my "greatness" against his own stature. This is not fair, because out of the two of us only he, the laureate, has been recognized as great, while I have never contended for this kind of scale.'[19] After 1943, Pasternak's name never resurfaced in any Stalin Prize discussions, even though it must have been in the members' thoughts when they selected the other great translator of the time, Mikhail Lozinsky, for his rendition of Dante.

But the prestige of the prize was eventually undermined, even though it held its monetary value. As the number of laureates increased to industrial scales, the prize started to become a target for mockery. One mordant satirical play from 1953, which greatly amused the Moscow public, repeatedly referred to 'laureates' as most desirable, eligible men for the golden girls of the Soviet elite. One passage is particularly striking. Here, a disgraced minister is listing his misfortunes: 'One of my daughter's suitors was sent to prison as a thief and speculator. Another one became a laureate.'[20] What might appear to us as a non sequitur implied, for contemporary audiences, that being a laureate was almost equally disreputable as being a petty speculator (as throwaway humour, rather than serious analysis). The play might even have won a Stalin Prize itself, had the awards not been discontinued shortly afterwards.

The Stalin Prize Committee

Soviet artists were already used to receiving state awards such as Order of Lenin and titles such as People's Artist, which were often tied to anniversaries, whether of individuals or institutions. The procedure for both kinds of honour was the same: lists of candidates were usually worked out between the levels of cultural administration (say, an artistic union and the relevant ministry) and then approved by the Politburo. With Stalin Prizes, another element was introduced into the system – a panel of expert judges under the name of the Stalin Prize Committee for Literature and the Arts (and a parallel committee meeting separately for the sciences and technology). These well-respected judges, generally at the top of their professions and some of them household names, would take their decisions by secret ballot.

Let us dwell a little on the pleasant moment when the *Komitet po Stalinskim premiyam* (the Stalin Prize Committee – we will refer to it as the KSP from now on) entered for the first time the plush interiors of the Moscow Art Theatre (MKhAT) in a quiet lane just off the bustling Gorky Street. MKhAT ended up hosting the KSP for many years, even though the connection was established by chance: the theatre's legendary director and co-founder, Vladimir Nemirovich-Danchenko, was chosen as the KSP's chairman, and he offered not only his home institution as the Committee's venue, but also his administrative support team at the theatre for KSP work (the principal secretary of the KSP in the first few years was Olga Bokshanskaya, who had been Nemirovich's personal assistant since 1919).[21]

Thus, on 16 September 1940, most of the forty chosen members[22] stepped into the hallowed Lower Foyer of the Art Theatre, the place where *The Cherry Orchard* had first been read out to the troupe, nearly four decades earlier. It was not an official Soviet space designed for efficient meetings but, on the contrary, an artistic space in the art nouveau style, with drapes, palm trees and old-fashioned armchairs inviting more relaxed conversation. Few of the members would have been overawed by the setting: most of them only had to make a short walk from their equally well-appointed and spacious apartments in central Moscow, and those in higher administrative positions would have been driven by chauffeurs from their comfortable dachas. By 1940, the Soviet artistic elite was well ensconced. For those who had travelled from afar, the representatives of the other republics, this would have been a more striking change of scene, but we shouldn't imagine that they lived in a yurt for the rest of the year. The general level of privilege for artistic celebrities in the republics could be even higher than in Moscow, but many of them also had previous experience of the very grandest dining and entertainment the country had to offer: namely, a banquet in the Kremlin.

Who were the lucky forty, and how had they been chosen? Some of the names were truly illustrious, like those of the writers Mikhail Sholokhov and Alexei Tolstoy. Sholokhov, it has to be noted, never bothered to attend a single meeting, preferring to stay put in his native village, but his name remained on the KSP list until the very end. Some appointments were sure to cause debate and disruption, such as the poet Nikolai Aseyev, known for his quick tongue, or the outspoken literary critic Alexander Gurvich, or the controversial film director Alexander Dovzhenko (none of them managed to hold onto their places for long).[23] Others, conversely, were known to toe the Party line, such as Alexander Fadeyev, a rising star both in the literary and bureaucratic firmaments, and the Stalin hagiographer, the filmmaker Mikhail Chiaureli. Disputes were likely to arise between the two leading painters, Igor Grabar, a post-Impressionist, and Alexander Gerasimov, who created huge Socialist Realist canvases; despite this difference, both were senior administrators. The composers Yury Shaporin and Nikolai Myaskovsky, highly respected figures in high-art music, found they had little to say to Isaak Dunayevsky, the star of Soviet popular song.

There was, of course, a sizeable representation from the republics, including writers from Ukraine and Belorussia and singers from Central Asia. The two sopranos, Kulyash Baiseitova from Kazakhstan and Khalima Nasyrova from Uzbekistan, improved the ratio of women (the only other woman was the formidable sculptor Vera Mukhina), but they hardly ever spoke in the meetings. Another kind of national representation, non-territorial in this instance, was to be found in the appointment to the KSP of Solomon Mikhoels, director of the State Jewish Theatre. An avid contributor to music discussions, he will appear many times during our narrative, until the business of the KSP would lead him to Minsk, the place of his fatal traffic 'accident' (staged by the NKVD).[24]

Finally, there were the senior cultural administrators: the chairman of the Committee for Arts Affairs Mikhail Khrapchenko (effectively the minister of culture, as we will refer to him for brevity), and the chairman of the Cinematography Committee (from 1946, minister) Ivan Bolshakov. Both, as we shall see, played a huge role in the KSP and behind the scenes, unlike Georgy Aleksandrov, a supposed overseer from Agitprop (propaganda department of the Party CC), who was another absentee from KSP meetings.

Regarding the selection process for the forty members, while no direct evidence has yet come to light, the list is remarkably similar to the membership of the Artistic Council of the Committee for Arts Affairs, so it should be safe to assume that the culture minister Khrapchenko had a hand in the selection.[25] Thus, for many Artistic Council members, the KSP was simply another occasion for their participation in a high-level artistic jury, with some extra prestige. They were now given a generous hourly fee and, of course, enjoyed the best seats at the theatre and freshly printed books delivered to their desk so that they could carry out their assessment of new works. So although the members of the KSP would have been conducting familiar tasks in familiar settings, their new role must have been felt as a promotion, and a sense of occasion pervaded the opening meeting.

From the beginning, members of the Committee saw their role as something greater than the mundane distribution of honours. Tolstoy suggested that the Committee needed to play a substantial part 'in raising the level of aesthetic culture' of the Soviet people – he even envisaged that transcripts of KSP meetings would be published for their edification (failing to see that the discussions could be so free precisely because they were not public). Nemirovich-Danchenko, too, agreed that the people would expect from the Committee some kind of direction in matters of aesthetics and taste.[26] This initial emphasis on aesthetics (rather than ideology) is typical of the KSP in its early phase: it seems that for a while, its members were lulled into feeling as if they formed an autonomous elite artistic circle (perhaps the atmosphere of the Lower Foyer helped this perception). Together, they attended drama and opera premieres, held discussions in the Tretyakov Gallery or in the newly built Metro stations, or invited composers and performers to play for them. Their discussions, a conversation between equals, were conducted with considerable freedom – the stenographers' transcripts were not seen as a potential threat. All in all, it was a highly pleasurable activity, the Soviet state paying and empowering them to do what they liked best: after the first round of discussions, Nemirovich-Danchenko light-heartedly proposed that if the Committee were disbanded, its members should continue to meet informally, and volunteered to continue as chair in such circumstances.[27] Gerasimov, despite his differences in outlook and background from Nemirovich-Danchenko, continued in the same genial manner, musing that 'here, for the first time, we spoke only about art'.[28]

In his more official speech at the first award ceremony, on 21 April 1941, Nemirovich-Danchenko drew a connection between his own desire to see a synthesis of all the arts, which he had entertained since the turn of the century, and this newly emerging *Gesamtkunstwerk*, brought forth by the wave of Stalin's hand:

> I have always sensed that there are deep inner connections between all the arts. [...] I think that the archive of the former director of the Imperial Theatres holds more than several of my letters saying, 'Could we not invent a form of social life that would allow opera, drama and ballet people to meet and influence each other?' I believe we undoubtedly influence each other's respective arts. [...]
>
> Indeed, I have never seen this unification of the arts so vividly realized in practice as it is now. [...] The great task that lies ahead of us is to see how we can influence [each other], not only through articles and discussions, but through face-to-face meetings, so that we can unify all the arts to meet the highest goals of all human culture.
>
> [...] Sometimes we used to meet together – at banquets. But only today, only in our times, has it become possible for the representatives of all the arts to be brought together at a single stroke, by that bold stroke of genius that is the mark of a true leader. [...] It is with the greatest delight that I say: how can we not thank Comrades Stalin and Molotov for all of this![29]

The Overseers

The creation of such a body as the KSP must seem at first sight most unusual within the Stalinist command system. Was Stalin really delegating decision-making powers to the experts – powers, that is, over prizes awarded in his own name? Was he happy to encourage free debate among the fractious members of the artistic intelligentsia and respect the unpredictable results of their secret ballots? The KSP was meeting, after all, outside of the constraints of both Party structures and state administration. There were already bodies with competence in this area, namely, the governmental Committee for Arts Affairs (effectively the ministry for culture) and the artistic unions. Were these now to lose some of their power?

The short answer is 'no': the statutes of the KSP clearly restricted its remit to 'the preliminary examination of works'. In other words, the KSP was set up as a consultative body, not an executive body, while the awarding body was the government, which had the right to make the final decisions.[30] But we will see that this is insufficient: the very presence of the KSP altered the balance of power and made the cultural power games ever more complicated. Leaving this aside until later, it is time to look at the overseers who controlled the KSP's work.

Casual commentators on Stalin Prizes often presume that Stalin was the only arbiter, and when they occasionally show an awareness of the KSP, they presume that it had no independence from Stalin. In reality, the system of approving awards was much more complex, and became ever more labyrinthine as the years rolled by. Most of the nominations were submitted by artistic unions, theatres, philharmonic societies and also the Party organizations in the republics. Once these were received, individual members of the KSP often exercised their right to nominate artists and works themselves. After they had discussed all of these nominations and voted on them by secret ballot, their decisions were sent to the government, and the KSP collectively had no further influence on the details of the final prize list. Most of them were quite unaware that their list still faced up to five further stages:

KSP → Ministries → Agitprop → Politburo Commission → Politburo → Stalin

Thus, after the KSP had voted and sent the paperwork to the government, the ministries also received a copy; these were the Committee for Arts Affairs and later also the Committee for Cinematography and the Committee for Architecture which branched out from their parent committee in 1943. The respective ministers (most importantly, Khrapchenko for the arts ministry and Bolshakov for cinema) had their own ideas on the nominations and circulated their proposed corrections to the KSP list within government departments, together with a draft resolution that took these changes for granted (presumptuously, since this was not the end of the matter). Either simultaneously with this or slightly later, was a similar letter and draft resolution issued by the Agitprop Department of the Party Central Committee (it changed its name several times over our period, so we will refer to it simply as Agitprop).[31] It was initially debatable whether Agitprop correctives carried more weight than their ministerial counterparts, but during the post-war years, Agitprop enjoyed a gradual increase in power within the award process.

At the next stage, there was input from a select group of CC and Politburo members, which in some years was formally organized as a Politburo Commission (a subcommittee with some external members). They usually had a few days to take in all three sets of suggestions (KSP, ministerial and Agitprop) and to compile their own list. Then there was a meeting of the Politburo itself (again, usually with some external invitees), at which all this information would be taken into account. Such meetings were, curiously, never recorded in the

Politburo agendas,[32] but for most years we can confirm their existence through the official documentation and through memoirs of the participants. After the Politburo meeting, yet another draft resolution was prepared and sent to Stalin for signing, so potentially he could still make final changes despite having been present at the Politburo (and he occasionally did so).

If we were to present this narrative hierarchically, it would look something like this:

or, in later years, when Agitprop's power increased and it took over the role of the Politburo Commissions:

From the extant documentation, it is not clear whether the decision-making process always went through all these stages. The record of the process is haziest for the first year, since procedures had not been worked out in advance, and the various interested parties improvised. During the war, some shortcuts were inevitably taken, and in the bleakest year of 1942, the KSP couldn't even form a quorum, so it fell to the minister, Khrapchenko, to shape a plausible list out of two separate ballots of KSP members, one taken in Kuybyshev, the other in Tbilisi; he also had to decide whether the successful nominations were to be granted first- or second-class prizes. The higher-level overseers in 1942 were Andrei Andreyev (member of the CC, member of the Politburo), Alexander

Shcherbakov (CC Secretary and candidate for the Politburo) and Nikolai Voznesensky (Molotov's first deputy); all three reported to Stalin and Molotov. A similar scheme was employed in 1943, and Andreyev and Shcherbakov (this time without Voznesensky) once again performed their duties as overseers of the process.

Who were these people and what stakes did they have in the artistic sphere? The most involved with the arts was, of course, Khrapchenko. He was a highly cultured man, a literary scholar whose wife was a musicologist,[33] and he had served as minister for the arts since 1939. He knew everyone in the arts and took a deep interest in every corner of his domain. The higher-level overseers were a different mater. The darkest figure among them was Andreyev, who had collaborated in sending many to their deaths in 1937 during the Purges. With only two years of village school behind him, he was a creature of Stalin's Party; of his artistic interests we know nothing. But even then, the nimbus of power performed its magic: Fadeyev's first impression of Andreyev was that of a charming man with intelligent and 'very clear' eyes, who seemed to know already everything Fadeyev was going to tell him about some trouble at the Writers' Union.[34]

Shcherbakov and Voznesensky were much more highly educated, both having passed through the Communist University and the Institute of Red Professors in the 1920s. Shcherbakov was involved in the formation of the Writers' Union, and watched over its activities for a while; importantly, perhaps, he was Andrei Zhdanov's protégé (and brother-in-law). Even so, Shcherbakov had his limitations, and it was doubted that he had any genuinely independent opinions on literary or artistic matters; in the dismissive words of the writer Kornei Chukovsky, 'his cultural level was that of a senior janitor'.[35] Voznesensky was both intellectually superior and able to think critically and independently. He was an economist and won a Stalin Prize himself in 1947 for his book on Soviet economy during the war years. Remembered for his fearless attitude and his unusual directness even when speaking to Stalin, he fell victim in the Leningrad Affair and was executed in 1950. While we can assess the contribution of the Andreyev/Shcherbakov/Voznesensky team in the decisions of 1942, their individual contributions cannot easily be disentangled; Andreyev, it appears, preferred to doodle on his own copy of the draft resolution rather than make notes, so it can fairly be supposed that his contribution was the least.[36]

In 1944, we see documented input from Agitprop for the first time. Prior to this, Aleksandrov, the Agitprop chairman, seems to have shown no interest in the awards process, even though he was a member of the KSP himself. Agitprop was usually well stocked with educated people who had to combine their cultural capital under the lid of exemplary ideological zeal. Aleksandrov may not have been quite the right person for the job: a scholar of Aristotle, he himself fell into an ideological trap with his book on Western philosophy in 1944, and was demoted.[37]

The 1944 prize round was, however, postponed and then coupled with the following year's: it seems that the top-level overseers did not find enough time to attend to the list. This disruption of the annual cycle, which had previously been kept running even when the war had been in the balance, was not welcomed (Molotov initially opposed the idea of coupling the two years),[38] and perhaps it was in order to avoid such an embarrassment in future that the role of the top-level overseers was formalized in 1945. By special government decree, a Politburo Commission was formed, consisting of Georgy Malenkov (chairman), Aleksandrov, the two relevant ministers Bolshakov and Khrapchenko, and Nikolai Tikhonov, a poet, who represented the KSP as its deputy chairman (the chairman Moskvin was too ill to run the KSP at the time). The constitution of this commission shows a clear intent to unite the representatives of all strata of the system for the final determination of winners. In principle, this should have increased the KSP's influence and made the higher-level deliberations more transparent – at last the KSP would find out about the dealings upstairs, and the changes to their list would no longer be shrouded in mystery. Perhaps the KSP chairman would even be able to defend the experts' decisions in this higher forum?

At this juncture, however, a subtle power shift occurred in the system: Andrei Zhdanov became a member of the Politburo Commission and quickly took the reins.[39] It is well known that Zhdanov became the country's chief ideologue in 1946, but he involved himself in cultural matters immediately after his move from Leningrad to Moscow, in early 1945. Zhdanov was a powerful figure with a keen interest in culture, and strong opinions on music in particular (he was known to entertain Politburo members by singing their favourite folk songs and accompanying himself on the piano or accordion).[40] He had been involved in shaping the two great cultural shifts of the 1930s, the First Writers' Congress in 1934 and the anti-formalist campaign of 1936 initiated by criticism of Shostakovich's opera *Lady Macbeth of Mtsensk*. Now, back on the ideological front (as a CC curator of Agitprop), he carved out an important role for himself in the Stalin Prize system. For the next two years, he chaired the commission, which still consisted of Aleksandrov, Khrapchenko, Bolshakov, and the newly appointed KSP chairman, Fadeyev.[41]

During these years, Zhdanov became central to the prize system, presiding over the ministerial and Agitprop stages, so that both bodies had to send their lists to him, and he would collate and revise as he wished, before passing his version on to the Politburo. Dmitry Shepilov, head of Agitprop, gives us a glimpse of the system under Zhdanov in his memoirs:

> Before sending Agitprop's corrections [to Stalin] every single proposal was discussed and assessed at Zhdanov's. We discussed literary works that had been published over the past year and we watched a number of films. Puzin, the chairman of Radiokomitet [radio ministry], organized auditions, where we listened to recordings of the symphonies, concertos and songs nominated for prizes, all of this taking place in Zhdanov's office.[42]

Shepilov, who was in awe of his superior, admired the level of attention Zhdanov paid to every single work with his customary critical astuteness. And, we should remember, he devoted such attention not only to the arts, but also to many of the science nominations.

Due to Zhdanov's influence, the role of Agitprop in the process was magnified: Shepilov and his culture experts' involvement was spread over a longer time. Now they not only submitted their own opinions, but also prepared a tidy table for the Politburo, allowing easy comparison of the three lists – those of the KSP, the Committee for Arts Affairs and Agitprop itself. Agitprop also now provided short blurbs for every single work, and relevant biographical details for the artists concerned. As intermediate lists went back and forth between officials, Agitprop's opinion on certain works occasionally changed, which implies that even more discussion took place in the background than we can trace from surviving documents. From this time onwards, Agitprop immersed itself in the details of every nomination as much as the KSP did and sometimes, it could be argued, they did their job even more conscientiously.

Now let us take a look at those unminuted Politburo sessions, the *sanctum sanctorum* of the prize system. While it appears that discussions of prizes at the Politburo took place each year (aside from the missed year 1944), we can only picture them in any detail from 1947 onwards. The writer Konstantin Simonov was present at the 1947 meeting and he tells us the attendance was larger and the discussion shorter than at the meetings he attended in the following years.[43] Indeed, 1947 was the last year when the Politburo discussed the arts and sciences prizes together, but the pace of discussion was brisk. Simonov reports a great number of scientists in the room, and does not mention any other invitees from the arts, so it is possible that he was alone in this respect that year.

So from 1948 onwards, the arts were discussed separately from sciences, and the discussion was more leisurely, sometimes spread over two sessions. Greater numbers of guests were invited, since Stalin was turning these annual gatherings into his private parties. As Simonov remarked, Stalin lavished his time and attention on them even when other matters did not seem to reach him in the seclusion of his late years.[44]

The meetings took place at the long table in Stalin's office suite, or, later, in the Politburo Meeting Room. For some of them we have precise lists of attendees, written out either in Stalin's own hand (as in fig. 2) or by a secretary. For example, on 19 March 1949, at 10 p.m. (everyone had to conform to Stalin's night-owl routine), such a meeting was attended by twelve persons who were either Politburo members or CC secretaries,[45] and seven invitees. The latter included Khrapchenko's replacement Polycarp Lebedev (Committee for Arts Affairs), Bolshakov (Committee for Cinematography), Shepilov (Agitprop), Fadeyev (KSP) and, importantly, three people from the Writers' Union (Tikhonov, Simonov and Anatoly Sofronov) whose presence had been requested by Fadeyev (he specified these three writers).[46] This was a session devoted to literature and cinema, and Fadeyev came well prepared. According to Shepilov, the meeting was not considered particularly long: it ended at 11.50 p.m.; the sciences meeting that followed was a little longer, and continued past 2 a.m.[47]

Exactly one week later, a session on the remaining arts took place, with the same number of invitees but a differing selection of names. Lebedev and Tikhonov were there again, while the arts on the agenda were represented by their top administrators: Tikhon Khrennikov (head of the Composers' Union), Vladimir Pimenov (head of the Drama Theatres Administration at the Committee for Arts Affairs), Pyotr Sysoyev (head of visual arts there); Grigory Simonov (head of the Architecture Committee) was ill, so architecture was represented by the vice president of the Architecture Academy, Arkady Mordvinov.[48]

The meetings in 1950, '51 and '52 ran along similar lines.[49] The largest took place on 25 February 1952, with twelve Politburo members and seventeen invitees in attendance. It is likely that this further broadening resulted from the loss of both Khrapchenko and Zhdanov in 1948 (the former was sacked, the second died), leaving no one with a comparable range and depth of cultural knowledge. The practice of relying on the Politburo Commission petered out around the same time, while these broad discussions increased in importance. Did Stalin feel that without Zhdanov there was no one competent (either politically or artistically) to digest the list of nominations? Perhaps it was simply his enjoyment of these annual shows that motivated him. Or, as Simonov suggests, did these sessions enable Stalin 'to check the pulse of the intelligentsia'[50] and (implicit in Simonov) carefully shape his image in the eyes of the intelligentsia?[51] These reasons are not mutually exclusive, and it is most likely that all were contributing factors.

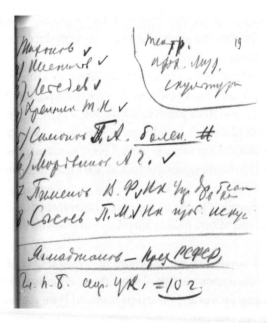

Fig. 2. List of invitees to the Politburo meeting (March or April 1949). In Stalin's hand: Theatre, Architecture, Music, Sculpture. 1) Tikhonov; 2) Shepilov; 3) Lebedev; 4) Khrennikov; 5) Simonov G. A. is ill; 6) Mordvinov A. G.; 7) Pimenov V. F., head of the Drama Theatres Administration of the C[ommittee for Arts Affairs]; Sysoyev P. M., head of visual arts [Administration of the Committee for Arts Affairs]. Yagmadjanov – Pres[idium?] RSFSR. Members of the Politburo, CC secretaries =10 people. RGANI, fond 3, op. 53, ye. kh. 18, l. 19.

Stalin's Hand

Now it is time to tackle the key question: what role did Stalin himself play in the decision-making?

We can approach this question from three directions: first, through the memoir literature, and especially through the colourful descriptions of Politburo sessions by Shepilov and Simonov, which we have already sampled. Second, through the painstaking examination of multitudinous markings in coloured pencils made in Stalin's handwriting on the lists of nominees which he carefully inspected. These markings often corroborate claims made in the memoirs, while the memoirs shed light on many such scribbles. The third way is to look 'between the documents', so to speak: to surmise, for example, that if a certain change is made in the 'final, final' draft of the Resolution (after the Politburo debates), then only Stalin can have made it. Similar deductions are prompted at those rare dramatic junctures in the awards process, for example, when a prize was granted and then withdrawn.

Let us begin with the memoirs. Shepilov attended those 'open' meetings of the Politburo in 1948 and '49; Simonov in 1947, '48, '50 and '52. Although their memoirs were written up decades later, both had made notes or dictated their record immediately after the event. Comparisons with documentary evidence reveal an impressive level of accuracy.

Shepilov claimed that Stalin came to the Politburo meetings better prepared than anyone else. A voracious reader with a daily average of 300 pages,[52] he kept a pile of books and thick journals on the left side of his desk which even literati found intimidating: he could easily put them to shame.[53] Simonov believed that if Stalin did not manage to read every nominated work, then from his contributions to the meetings, he had at least read all that were likely to raise a debate.[54]

According to Shepilov, it was in the field of literature that Stalin made his most dramatic interventions, pulling surprises out of his sleeve:

Stalin: Here is a novella that was published in *Zvezda* at the end of last year (he mentioned the author and title). I think this is a fine novella. Why hasn't it been nominated for a prize? (Everyone is silent.) Have you read it?
Me [Shepilov]: No, I haven't.
Stalin: I understand. You don't have the time. You're busy. Well, *I've* read it. Anyone else? (Everyone is silent.) Well, I've read it. I think we can give it a second-class prize.[55]

Shepilov gives twelve more instances of Stalin's interventions in literature, and four in painting, sculpture or architecture, and he talks at length about Stalin's passion for cinema. There is only one reference to music – Stalin's defence of Glazunov's ballet *Raymonda*, despite objections that it was based on a medieval plot remote from Soviet realities.[56]

Simonov, of course, has a more biased perspective than Shepilov: he cared most about literature and wrote almost exclusively about literary debates. Yet he does make an interesting comparison: these debates arose almost exclusively between Stalin and the writers; other members of the Politburo remained silent. This is easy to understand: no one else bothered to read new fiction. With painting it was different – photos of the works were available at the meeting, and the other Politburo members did occasionally offer an opinion. They were more active when theatre productions and especially films were discussed, since everyone was well acquainted with the cinema of the day. Stalin even called for votes to determine the class of the prize, although he never raised his own hand. Simonov insists that this procedure was only used for films.[57] How discussions of music were held, Simonov does not tell us.

What Simonov's memoirs allow us to imagine much better than Shepilov's is the atmosphere of the meetings. He describes them as gentler and friendlier than the meetings on political matters he was also privileged to attend (he became a member of the CC). Stalin, who kept pacing the room while sucking on his pipe, often inserted acerbic comments into the discussion, but was never rude or aggressive, as he was in political meetings. In fact, the only example of aggressive behaviour mentioned by Simonov was on the part of Lavrenty Beria, who was outraged by Simonov's objections to a piece of writing by a Georgian author.[58] On the contrary, Stalin enjoyed showing generosity, approving longer lists of contributors for collective nominations than anyone else desired. As for invited guests, they came to the proceedings with a mixture of awe and fear, and despite daring to raise objections from time to time, they were always ready to desist if their points were not accepted. Only once, according to Simonov, did Fadeyev, having a severe hangover, argue with Stalin about the literary qualities of a novel with some persistence and, seeing that Stalin had no intention of changing his mind, he grumbled, 'A eto uzh vasha volya' (somewhere between 'Well, that's your prerogative' and 'Well, suit yourself').[59] Everyone knew that Fadeyev, who had proven his loyalty to Stalin over many years, was forgiven much.

Tikhon Khrennikov, who represented Music on several of these Politburo meetings, unfortunately left us only a single paragraph describing them:

> I saw Stalin only at the meetings of the Committee for Lenin and Stalin Prizes [sic], during the discussion of nominated candidates. This only took place on four occasions, the last in 1952. He participated in the discussions of musical works and other artistic and literary works, as well as work in the area of science and technology. I always listened very attentively to what he said and how he said it. Stalin revealed a complete knowledge of the subject; he must have found the time to familiarize himself with the nominated works, because I witnessed several times how he caught out [sazhal v luzhu] celebrated academics when scientific studies were discussed. Stalin sometimes agreed to accept proposals that were at odds with his own. He was a most intelligent man, and never entered into long polemics with anyone except Fadeyev, who dared to argue with the leader. Let us be frank: we feared and worshipped him together with the rest of our people, who had won such a terrible war. Our eyes were opened a little after the 20th Party Congress, but many still doubted and disbelieved those atrocities that had been allegedly committed by Stalin. Once, I too stood up to defend the virtuoso balalaika player Pavel Necheporenko, who was even called 'the Oistrakh of the balalaika'. But the chairman of the Committee for Arts Affairs, N. Bespalov, knowing that Stalin dismissed all non-classical art as mere fairground amusements [balagan], said that the balalaika is not a real

musical instrument at all and that the balalaika player shouldn't be granted
any award, since that would debase the prize itself. Stalin was ready to agree
with Bespalov when I asked for the floor and spoke with great passion,
saying that the balalaika is an instrument now studied at the conservatoire,
that it has glorified Russian instrumental performance, and that such
virtuosi as Andreyev and Troyanovsky visited Tolstoy in Yasnaya Polyana,
and the old man wept from their playing. Stalin concluded briefly: 'Then we
must give [him] a prize.'[60]

Tea-stained sheaves of paper with Stalin's distinctive markings in coloured
pencil (mostly blue, sometimes red, on rare occasions brown or green)[61] clearly
show where his interests lay. We can usually see that he carefully perused the
whole document, marked out by underscores or ticks, but pages pertaining to
literature and film are usually thick with corrections: arrows when the class of
the prize is changed, exclamations like 'No!' or additional names in the margins.
Other sections of the list usually contain fewer substantive corrections, and at
times are left unmarked. This is not to say that there are no markings of interest
in Music nominations; we shall discuss some of these in subsequent chapters.

It is not always possible to establish from the evidence whether the changes
and deletions were made by Stalin in private or in the course of the Politburo
meeting. The example below (fig. 3) shows how the ambiguities arose. Here we
see a KSP list of nominees on the left and Agitprop's comments in the right
column with Stalin's handwritten notes on top. These markings could well be
the result of his preliminary work, but they could equally be a combination
of this preliminary work with the outcome of the Politburo discussion.
Khrennikov's memoir of Necheporenko's prize makes us look at his name
particularly closely, and one possible interpretation is that Stalin first put a tick
of agreement on top of Agitprop's proposal 'not to grant an award' in his case,
but after Khrennikov's interjection at the Politburo, Stalin must have changed
this decision to '3rd' (a third-class prize).

Where we find no direct evidence of Stalin's input, we would have to use our
third, comparative, method. In 1946, for example, when comparing the draft
resolution prepared by the Politburo Commission with the final, published list,
we only find a single change: the addition of a novel by the Latvian writer
Andrejs Upīts (Stalin was especially generous towards the Baltic republics at
this time, for obvious political reasons). Most written evidence (markings)
comes from the years 1949–52, which reinforces our earlier suggestion that
after the death of Zhdanov, Stalin's personal role in the award process increased
dramatically, and so did the proportion of changes to the original KSP lists. On
rare occasions, he would make a change even after the Politburo discussion, but

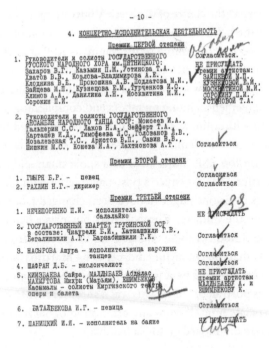

Fig. 3. Stalin's marginalia on the list of nominations prepared by Agitprop (1952). Top right: an instruction to 'leave in full' ('оставить полн[остью]') the list of members of the Pyatnitsky Folk Choir (Agitprop had sought to reduce the list). Middle right: he wants a '3rd' for Necheporenko instead of Agitprop's 'no award' ('не присуждать'). Penultimate comment: 'to postpone' (отл[ожить])the nomination of the soloists of the Kirghiz Opera; bottom right: a redundant instruction to 'delete' ('снять') the nomination of the accordion player Panitsky (Agitprop had already said: 'no award').

normally, when he wanted any changes, he would argue his point in the Politburo and win agreement there.

Interactions, Frictions, Scandals

How were the dealings upstairs viewed by the KSP? In the first five years of its existence, the KSP chair was not drawn into any higher-level discussions. The only person who shuttled between levels was Khrapchenko, but in the absence of any evidence that he reported back to the KSP, it would seem that other members were left none the wiser.

The situation changed radically in 1946. After the death of Moskvin, a new chairman, Alexander Fadeyev, was appointed. While Nemirovich-Danchenko had been eighty-two at the time of his appointment, and Moskvin sixty-five, Fadeyev was only forty-five and thus much more dynamic, despite the notorious drinking binges that occasionally put him out of action. Crucially, he had for many years been at the centre of the literary bureaucracy, and in 1946 finally took his place at the helm of Soviet literature as the Union of Writers' general secretary. From the very beginning of his tenure as KSP chairman, we can see where his loyalties lay. Even before the ballot was taken, he wrote to the CC Secretariat giving advance warning of the likely outcomes, and even divulging some of the disagreements among members and complaining about the group interests pursued within the KSP.[62] This had never happened before, and was indeed unthinkable under Nemirovich or Moskvin. Fadeyev acted more like an agent reporting on the KSP, rather than as a spokesman and defender of the body. Five days later, Fadeyev wrote a post-ballot letter with his own thoughts on how the KSP's decisions ought to have been changed (something that was routinely done by the minister Khrapchenko, but never before by the KSP's chairmen).[63] The flavour of these changes can be gleaned from one example: Fadeyev suggests that the colourful landscapes by Martiros Saryan, chosen by the KSP, should be replaced by a work of another Armenian painter, Dmitry Nalbandyan – his portrait of Stalin. This was a shrewd move to prove his loyalty and also to dissociate himself from any promotion of Saryan's modernism. In the event, the prize did indeed go to Nalbandyan.

A few months later, Fadeyev proposed a shake-up in the KSP's member-ship.[64] The main result of this reorganization was a significant expansion (the number rose from thirty-seven to fifty-two) but there were also some removals from the list.[65] On 22 February 1947, the Politburo approved the new member-ship of the Committee, which included, among others, Shostakovich. Georgy Aleksandrov (of Agitprop), using a supposed conflict of interests as a pretext, asked to be kept off the KSP, otherwise he would feel hampered in the task of overseeing that committee's work.[66] Khrapchenko had no such worries–as we know, he was happy to participate at three levels of decision-making: in the KSP (in 1947 he became deputy chairman), then as the Committee for Arts Affairs chairman (minister) and as a member of the Politburo Commission. His days as a minister were numbered, however: he became one of the prime targets of Zhdanov's reshuffle of the cultural scene in 1948, following the Party resolution on the opera *The Great Friendship* (see Chapter 10).

The KSP sessions of 1947 and '48 were, of course, greatly affected by the hardening ideological line of the *Zhdanovshchina*. Fadeyev did not allow members to lose sight of 1946 Party resolutions on culture, and the atmosphere thickened further after the 1948 Resolution on Music, when most of the Music Section personnel were replaced overnight.[67] But then Fadeyev went on government-approved leave in order to rework his novel *The Young Guard* (which, bizarrely, had come under criticism despite the fact that it had already received a Stalin Prize of the first class). Feeling that the KSP was losing its direction without him, he wrote to Stalin in March 1949 about some serious shortcomings in the Committee's work.[68] Fadeyev complained that the members did not trouble themselves to follow cultural life in the other republics, and so their awards in this area had become noticeably random. He also criticized some members of the Visual Arts section for 'formalist' and 'aestheticist' views. Although in 1947 Fadeyev had succeeded in expanding the KSP, he now wanted it reduced from its current fifty-four members – he felt that music was over-represented and that there were too many elderly members. It was certainly true that the 1948 resolution had led not only to a change in the musical membership, but also an increase, since music was the art then at the centre of attention. The proposed reduction was rejected. He even ventured that the KSP no longer had 'the interests of the state' at heart and suggested that its processes should be treated more bureaucratically, proposing to Suslov that four ex-officio deputy chairs should be appointed, and they would be able to oversee and manage discussion under Fadeyev (and in his absence).[69] This proposal was likewise rejected, but Fadeyev had enough power within the KSP to implement it informally, calling upon the most senior members in cinema (Bolshakov), the visual arts (Gerasimov) and music (Khrennikov) to marshal the process. There was still a secret ballot, but Fadeyev and his deputies were generally able to ensure that a given nomination appeared (or did not appear) on the voting sheets.

Fadeyev's letter also revealed one startling fact: the KSP was short of funds even for such essentials as buying the nominated books and paying for trips to see the nominated theatre productions. In other words, he both criticized the KSP as too wayward, and also lobbied the government to provide it with better resources. A year later, the members themselves voiced their discontent over the conditions of their work, feeling that they were less of an elite artistic circle now, and more an overworked, frustrated and unglamorous corner of Stalinist bureaucracy. This outpouring of dissatisfaction was prompted by a scandal that had erupted in the spring of 1950: the unprecedented withdrawal of a Stalin prize after it had been publicly awarded.

The scandal concerned an academic work by Heydar Huseynov, *From the History of Social and Philosophical Thought in 19th-century Azerbaijan*. Strictly speaking, this was a work of social history and should not have even been considered by the Literature and Arts subcommittee of the KSP; it was properly in the remit of the separate Sciences committee. Nevertheless, it was assigned to the arts, and found a vigorous advocate in Fadeyev himself. The book aimed to demonstrate that there had been a significant influence from Russian culture on Azeri thinkers, and was being promoted primarily for this reason. In its assessment of the book, the KSP relied mainly on a report from the Literature

Institute, and only one KSP member claimed to have read it himself.[70] Even so, Huseynov was nodded through, and passed for a second-class prize. After the ballot Agitprop belatedly pointed out that book should have been considered instead by the Science Committee. In spite of this, the transfer was not made (probably through mere inertia, given the absence of evidence for any more concrete reason), and Agitprop eventually advocated that only a third-class prize should be awarded, due to some 'serious shortcomings' of the book.

Only after the awards had been made was it was determined that these 'serious shortcomings' were not simply faults in scholarship, but included a political error. At one point in the narrative, Huseynov spoke positively of Shamil, who had once led the highlanders of the Caucasus in an uprising against the Russian Empire. Huseynov had failed to keep up to date with the shifting perspective of Soviet historical scholarship on the national policies of the Tsarist Russian Empire: it was no longer to be condemned as a 'prison-house of the peoples', nor were those who resisted the Empire to be given automatic praise. Even though Shamil only received one or two mentions, the offence was deemed too serious. The KSP was instructed to gather for an extraordinary plenary session in May 1950, where they obediently voted to withdraw the prize. Huseynov was then sacked from his job and expelled from the Party; he committed suicide in August.

It was at this humiliating meeting of 11 May 1950 that a wave of pent-up frustration broke through. KSP members felt overworked, underappreciated and at the same time ashamed that they had not carried out their work conscientiously in this instance. The volume of nominations had soared and was beginning to overwhelm the KSP, not least because the new category of third-class prizes, introduced in 1949, meant that work of lower quality was now eligible for consideration. In 1949, the Writers' Union made eighty nominations, with no attempt to separate out the best from the mediocre and the downright bad.[71] Most of the books remained unread by KSP members, simply because there was insufficient time, and members were further discouraged from reading them when they found out that they had to pay for the books themselves (the price was now being deducted from their committee pay).[72] The assessment of provincial drama and opera theatres was left to hired assistants who often produced contradictory reports. The Music Section also tended to vote without getting to know the pieces, or hearing them only through poor-quality recordings rather than through special auditions.[73] The KSP was gradually succumbing to boredom, and this would lead them into trouble.

Just as the KSP was recovering from the Huseynov affair, it suffered another humiliating blow to its self-image. Less than a month later, on 5 June 1950, another extraordinary session was convoked, and extraordinary it was indeed.

At this point in the early summer, artists were normally preparing to leave for their dachas, for a return to their own work in tranquil surroundings. Now they had to set aside their preparations. The chairman, Tikhonov, opened the meeting:

> We've had one extraordinary plenary session already, which was devoted to a regrettable business – we had to withdraw a prize. The case before us today is of a different nature. I would even call it a joyful occasion, because we are about to add another to our family of laureates.[74]

So the dacha was delayed, but at least they were not about to be chastised. The cinema minister Bolshakov unveiled the nomination: a Georgian-made film, *Jurgai's Shield*.[75] The mystery deepened. This was not a new film at all: it had been made in 1944, but had not been distributed widely at the time. In May 1950, however, it had been re-released and according to Tikhonov had been warmly received by the Soviet public this time round. The members were astounded. Goldenweiser was the first to articulate the question that was on everyone's mind:

> [I]f we are about to vote, we need to have some motive and justification for so doing. Whose was the initiative, and what organization or which member of our Committee gave it the necessary approval? Suddenly, in the middle of the year, we are nominating a particular item. Clearly, some kind of approval had to be granted for this?[76]

Tikhonov was evasive. Everyone *knew* the answer, or at least they knew how the probabilities stacked up. In this case, probing with further questions would be embarrassing and imprudent. But one member decided to set caution aside, namely, the poet Alexander Tvardovsky, author of a controversial wartime hit *Vasily Tyorkin*. His next hour of fame was to come during Khrushchev's Thaw, when he, in his role of *Novy mir* editor, would dare to publish Solzhenitsyn. At this tense moment in 1950, we could just about begin to guess at the measure of this man:

> [T]he question which has been left unanswered was by no means frivolous. I find myself in a particularly difficult situation. I have not seen this film. I do trust the conscience of the highly placed men in whose company I find myself. But it must have been on someone's initiative, at someone's behest. Nothing untoward would happen if the members of the Committee were informed of this. If it had been a proposal from the cinematography

ministry, it would be kept until the end of the year. If it were some other initiative, why shouldn't we know of it?

[...] The atmosphere at the ballot would then be rather more natural.[77]

The others preferred to dissipate the tension. We have a right to meet whenever we like, said one. Let Comrade Tvardovsky see it, and then we will vote, said another. This is not an ordinary feature film, it wouldn't be right to judge it within the normal run, said someone else. It wouldn't go among the documentaries, either, said another. The picture has brought together all the riches of Georgian culture, said the previous speaker.

The scene would be still more delectable if only we could hear the intonation of the speakers and see their body language. Did they exchange knowing glances and half-smiles? Were they poker-faced? Did their evaluations of this 'new genre' betray a shade of irony? For this was, indeed, neither a feature film nor a documentary, but more a loosely threaded revue of folk and popular numbers performed by famous Georgian artistes. Someone had taken a sudden liking to it – now who on earth could that be? The memoir of Grigory Maryamov, film editor, who was often present at the nocturnal film showings in the Kremlin, reveals all (if we are to rely on him): he tells us that Stalin had not seen the film when it first came out, and when he eventually saw it six years later, he asked whether it had received a Stalin Prize.[78] This, according to Maryamov, set in motion the extraordinary chain of events we have described above. As for documentary evidence, all we know is that Malenkov gave the minister for cinema the awkward task of massaging *Jurgai's Shield* on its way to an extra Stalin Prize. On 11 May 1950 (coincidentally, the day of Huseynov's fall), Bolshakov laid out his plan: first, the film was to be re-released, second, reviews in the central press were to be arranged, and third, it would then be seemly for a nomination be made from the ministry. Malenkov approved the plan and sent Bolshakov's letter on to Suslov, who then unleashed the press campaign. The whole process took only a few weeks. The KSP passed the film for a prize (need it even be said?), and three days later, on 8 June, it was settled at a Politburo meeting that the prize would indeed be awarded.

Although the outcome was comedy rather than tragedy, it was no less of a dent in the KSP's prestige, which then sustained a further battering in 1951, when another prize had to be withdrawn. This time, the unfortunate winner-cum-loser was the Ukrainian composer Herman Zhukovsky. A detailed account of this affair will be provided in Chapter 10, but at this point it will suffice to say that this third humiliation for the KSP was enough to prompt even the hardnosed Fadeyev to give his KSP charges a pat on the back, lest their mounting frustration should lead to a scandal. He confided in them, lifting a little the veil of secrecy that had previously shielded post-ballot deliberations from the curiosity of the KSP:

> Do remember that the Committee has considerable authority. Many corrections are proposed, some by the directors of institutions, others by departments of the CC, or by members of the government, and they may criticize this or that point,
>
> [...] but special attention is always paid to the Committee's opinion. As far as possible, they try not to change [the Committee's decisions], only doing so where there are clear, unassailable and convincing reasons.
>
> [And then, adopting a patronizing tone on behalf of the government:] They really did have to give it a good talking-over, you know [*Oni ved' tam obsuzhdali, reshali*].[79]

But Fadeyev's pep talk was too little, too late. The KSP was now a sinking ship. In February 1952, yet another humiliation came their way. The twist this time was that the KSP's papers, after a quick lookover by Stalin, were sent back to them, with demands for changes. Previously, the committee's recommendations had been discreetly modified upstairs, but now, like kittens in toilet training, they had their noses rubbed in their own mess. Having received the requested changes made by the KSP, Stalin wrote a triumphant 'Ha-ha!' opposite the name of Vilis Lācis, a Latvian writer, an old Party member and now prime minister of his republic.[80] Under duress, the KSP agreed to give him a third-class prize for the novel *Towards a New Shore*, but Stalin was already resolved to promote him to the first class. When the final prize list was published, Goldenweiser, in his diary, called it 'a crushing defeat for the KSP'.[81]

After all this, it was hardly surprising that, on 27 May 1952, Vladimir Kruzhkov of Agitprop wrote a damning report on the practices of the KSP and effectively proposed that this weak link should be removed from the chain. Why, he wondered, could the nominations from creative unions and the ministry not simply be sifted through by Agitprop?[82] True enough, Agitprop was duplicating the KSP's work and was now able to do the job more thoroughly: unlike the KSP, they went to the Composers' Union concerts to hear every nominated musical work, and followed a tight schedule of trips to the provincial theatres.[83]

Fadeyev, in his response to Kruzhkov, agreed with many of the complaints against the membership of the KSP. But he resolutely objected to the insinuation that the KSP could simply be disbanded, warning that Kruzhkov's proposed reforms, which would eliminate the KSP filter, would inadvertently introduce a much greater class of arbitrariness to the selection, with an increase in pressure from local, group and personal interests. In other words, a much higher proportion of prizes would be awarded on the basis of personal connections and lobbying. But most importantly, Fadeyev stressed, without the participation of the KSP the selection process would become purely bureaucratic rather than public (*obshchestvennïy*).[84] Whatever he thought of the KSP, his own reputation was at risk now: it would not look good if his six years in charge of the KSP were to end in its disbandment. But to defend his position, Fadeyev highlighted a contradictory element in the awards process: the public nature of the KSP's selection, however desirable in itself, had always been a hindrance to the bureaucratic structures and had gradually been eroded, with considerable assistance from Fadeyev himself.

Fadeyev managed to stave off the KSP's disbandment, but within a year events took their course. Kruzhkov's damning report was consigned to the archives on 7 March 1953: action now seemed superfluous after Stalin's death, and the Stalin Prize Committees could be disbanded without controversy. Even though the KSP's list of nominations had been sent to the government at the end of February, no more Stalin Prizes were awarded. This turbulent chapter of Soviet cultural life was over.

CHAPTER TWO

THE FIRST YEAR

Shostakovich's Piano Quintet

Among the first to take an interest in the vagaries of the Stalin Prize for music was Solomon Volkov. One particular award intrigued him: the 1941 prize earned by Shostakovich's Piano Quintet. The piece was neither monumental, nor had it been given any Soviet programme or subtitle, and accordingly, Volkov thought it reasonable to assume that the prize must have been awarded on the basis of Stalin's personal choice.[1] This was in line with the title of his book, *Shostakovich and Stalin: The Extraordinary Relationship between the Great Composer and the Brutal Dictator*, and with its main conceit, his view of this relationship as the quintessential confrontation between poet and Tsar.

The award is indeed puzzling, especially if we set the first-class winners in the other arts alongside the Quintet, with its subtle play of colours and its graceful, elusive ending. By contrast, we have Gerasimov's enormous cityscape-cum-portrait, *Stalin and Voroshilov in the Kremlin*, Mukhina's iconic statue, *Worker and Kolkhoz Woman*, and the baroque décor of the Kievskaya metro station. How then, in 1941, did the Quintet receive a first-class award in the inaugural round of prizes in the midst of all this grandeur? The combination could hardly provide Soviet artists with a coherent model for Socialist Realist art.

Volkov supported his argument with a letter to Stalin from one Moisei Grinberg, which came to scholarly attention on its publication in Russia in 1995.[2] In his letter, Grinberg protests at the KSP's selection of Shostakovich's Quintet, proving, Volkov argues, that Stalin could not have been unaware of the matter. For Volkov, this can only mean that Stalin must have decided to reject Grinberg's complaint and keep the Quintet. As Volkov puts it: 'We know that they tried to talk Stalin out of this decision. Why can't we imagine that Stalin listened to Shostakovich's music and liked it?'[3]

Indeed, why can't we? The evidence presented in this chapter does not so much refute Volkov's claim, but rather places it in a different and to a large extent unexpected context, in effect, prompting us to change the question. At any rate, the evidence provided here does much to explain away the apparent anomaly of this award. The whole inaugural round was tentative, and the path towards the final list of laureates quite tortuous. Taking the Quintet as our leading thread, we shall explore the events of this first prize season in this chapter – events running from September 1940 to April 1941.

The Music Section

It is important to remember that at this point, in 1940, Shostakovich was not yet a member of the KSP himself – he would be appointed for the first time in 1947. His official standing was not yet as high as it would become two years later, after the Seventh Symphony. Compared to him, the 1940 members of the Music Section were, on balance, more conservative, and perhaps had enjoyed a smoother path to the top of the Soviet music scene. Let us make ourselves better acquainted with them.

The first chairman of the Music Section was Reinhold Glière, an avuncular figure, sixty-five years old, who represented the Composers' Union. Glière was a highly professional composer, who early in his career had the makings of a Russian Richard Strauss, but was now stylistically conservative. He had thrown himself energetically into the Soviet system, both artistically and bureaucratically, but he was well respected by his colleagues and was held in genuine affection by many of them. He had a hand in teaching many composers, both the younger generation and those already in their middle age: Myaskovsky and Prokofiev, for example, had both taken lessons from him as private pupils. Glière was versatile above all: his pre-Soviet Third Symphony was adventurous and monumental (it won international acclaim, particularly in the USA), but he also wrote the first popular ballet on a Soviet theme (*The Red Poppy*, 1927) and pioneered the genre of 'national' opera written to commission (the first of these, *Shah-Senem*, he wrote for Azerbaijan, while *Gyulsara*, 1937, was for Uzbekistan). As early as 1930, he envisaged a single union of composers that would operate according to some clear official guidelines (neither the union nor the guidelines at that time were yet in view),[4] so when such a system was established, he did not feel that he was being unduly restricted as an artist. In the photo (fig. 4) he is seen decorated with two orders: the Red Banner order he received in 1937, specifically for the Uzbek drama *Gyulsara*, and the Badge of Honour from 1938.

Fig. 4. The Music Section at work: Shaporin, Myaskovsky, Dunayevsky and Glière, *Sovetskoye iskusstvo*, 8 December 1940. Photo by A. Gornshteyn.

In the same league of seniority was Alexander Goldenweiser (not in the photo), who, as its director, represented the Moscow Conservatoire. His career as a pianist was in the past, but he was one of the leading piano professors and a tireless editor of piano repertoire. Importantly, he was also a relatively conservative composer but, unlike Glière, completely unrecognized and unperformed. Throughout this volume, we will often hear his distinctive voice, as he generally spoke on every musical issue. He often reiterated his dislike of musical modernism, emphasized his links with pre-revolutionary culture and even liked to pepper his contributions with religious metaphors and references to the Bible, which were simply tolerated as a harmless eccentricity – in the end, he was too good a committee man for objections to be raised. He was a useful organizer, and knew how to balance and compromise.

Another heavyweight was Nikolai Myaskovsky, the top composition teacher in the country. He seemed to have taught almost every younger Soviet composer, at least before Shostakovich began teaching. Although he was a highly prolific symphonist, he managed to find the time for many administrative activities, usually involving what he did best: evaluating other people's music. Whether in his private letters, in his reports to the Union of Composers, or in his contributions to KSP meetings, he could produce an astute and frank review of any new work. His colleagues would turn to him for advice when trouble came their way, but he was certainly not as smooth a *komitetchik* as Glière or Goldenweiser. Some of his remarks were perhaps too frank, and he lacked the will or the ability to cultivate the ideological veneer that the other two had mastered.

Yury Shaporin is the only figure in the photo to gaze confidently into the camera. He was a striking man: tall, bald and with round glasses, he was famed for his love of life's pleasures, and he could well afford them, thanks to his many theatre and film commissions. He worked more slowly on his more serious works, famously taking most of his life over his only opera, *The Decembrists*, which for decades was 'almost ready' (to the extent that it featured in the Bolshoi's lists of forthcoming productions years before it was finally ready). His own rather conservative musical style was as unimpeachable as Glière's, with a solid base in the Russian classics. From the transcripts, however, it becomes clear that he was not so dedicated to the KSP as the previous three.

While Glière, Goldenweiser, Myaskovsky and Shaporin formed a solid core of highbrow musical elite, Isaak Dunayevsky, the leading popular composer, could not feel at home in the KSP. His field was too marginal for the committee, and a certain tension must have been apparent. Dunayevsky was one of the very few members to be removed from the committee in 1943, allegedly for not commanding sufficient respect from his fellow members. Another outsider was Alexander Aleksandrov, the director of the Red Army Ensemble, who was clearly too busy even to attend the meetings. Uzeyir Hajibeyov, the venerated Azeri who won all-Union fame with his opera *Koroğlu*, did attend when he could fit in a trip to Moscow, but his prestige was clearly lower than that of the 'core' musicians, and his interjections less polished.

Beside the seven composers, there were five other members. The Bolshoi conductor Samuil Samosud was well respected, but he only participated intermittently. The only two women were both leading sopranos, Kulyash Baiseitova from Kazakhstan and Khalima Nasyrova from Uzbekistan. They had achieved fame in Moscow during their respective national *dekadas* (festivals devoted to a particular republic). When they were able to attend, they usually kept silent, except when they wished to lobby for a particular 'national' work. Finally, there were two officials: the forever absent Georgy Aleksandrov from Agitprop, and the forever present Khrapchenko, the culture minister. Khrapchenko sat on three out of the four sections (music, theatre/cinema and fine arts), overseeing the whole of his territory, while literature fell outside his remit.

Music's Ballot 1

Out of the ten initial prizes, music was allotted one. The remit only covered works made public during the course of 1940. The system of nominations from across the entire Soviet Union still lay in the future, leaving the KSP with shortlists that were indeed short, and plenty of time to acquaint themselves well with the nominated works. On 12 November 1940, Shostakovich performed his Quintet for the KSP in a special audition, together with the members of the Beethoven Quartet; as soon as it was finished, they were asked to play it again, in its entirety (not necessarily for the sake of prolonging the pleasure, but for arriving at a thorough and informed assessment).[5] Some of the KSP members also went to hear it again at the Union of Composers on 19 November. The KSP plenary session on 21 November could thus rely on fresh impressions of the piece, memorable for its abundant references to baroque and classical idioms. This all took place before the Quintet's official premiere on 23 November.

Goldenweiser, summarizing the opinion of the Music Section, put the Quintet in second place after Myaskovsky's Symphony No. 21. He took care to remind those present that Shostakovich had 'messed up' earlier (srïvï), but the ill effects, he said, had been dispelled by the Fifth Symphony. Various other negative notes crept into his generally positive assessment of the work:

> This work is interesting for its strange vitality, a kind of 'renaissance' aspect, as Samosud called it. This means the use of particular devices, the formal methods, one might say, of the old masters, [combining] the old language with a new, contemporary idiom. This synthesis produces some very interesting results. This work has moments that leave a very deep impression.
>
> I should give special mention to the second movement, a fugue, which is notable for its great complexity, but even so, the listener is able to perceive this technical mastery without [consciously] noticing it, and at the same time, the songful character of the music is immediately accessible and gripping.
>
> A similar impression, just as deep, is left by the fourth movement, the Intermezzo. But alongside this, in the Scherzo [the third movement], we suddenly begin to notice some intonations of the [old] Shostakovich, who was alien to us. There are some deliberately grotesque passages there, a fascination with formalist feats, which sets this movement at odds with the general tone of deep significance that typifies the work. The Finale, although exquisite in many ways, is not quite so successful in addressing the 'renaissance' issue that I mentioned earlier: it is possible to detect some artificiality here in the filling of old forms with the new idiom.[6]

Goldenweiser, of course, had his own axe to grind: he was rooting for Myaskovsky's Symphony No. 21, which had been premiered a few days earlier in a reportedly rather colourless performance conducted by Alexander Gauk. But it seems that none of the Music Section members was prepared to place the younger Shostakovich above the long-established Myaskovsky, who was about to celebrate his sixtieth birthday. Although both works were of similar length (about twenty minutes), a symphony suggested something of greater seriousness than a quintet. Note that slight ambivalence about the 'renaissance' aspect of the piece – its neoclassicism; Goldenweiser, as we shall see, was not the only one to place a question mark over it.

Representatives of other arts were, as a rule, unwilling to challenge the opinion of musical experts. And yet one after another, they cautiously admitted that they had enjoyed Shostakovich's piece much more than Myaskovsky's (in fairness, the deeply serious character of this symphony meant that it had to eschew any of the surface attractions that were available to Shostakovich for his Quintet). The poet Aseyev spoke about his 'emotional affinity' for Shostakovich's piece, even though he wasn't prepared to challenge Myaskovsky's candidacy. Nor did the sculptor Mukhina dare to put Shostakovich ahead of Myaskovsky, but she reported that she had experienced the same kind of 'inner shivering' that could normally be induced only by Beethoven or Tchaikovsky.[7]

It took the outspoken patriarch of the Russian art scene, Igor Grabar, to change the direction of the discussion forcefully:

> We have heard the opinions of the highly authoritative Music Section, and they are carefully considered, and deeply thought through. It is very hard for us to speak, as mere dilettantes, after such clearly defined opinions have been voiced. And if I dare to take the floor, it is only because I am concerned that we are making a mistake.
>
> When I was listening to Shostakovich's Quintet, I had the feeling that I was not among contemporary composers but among the great masters. I was completely shaken – no, I was crushed. I had the feeling that I was back in Mozart's time. [...] This work is stamped with the seal of genius, in the best sense of that word. How could we not give it a prize! At the dawn of my life, I was lucky to have known Tchaikovsky [...], and at my life's sunset, I live in the time of Shostakovich.[8]

No one had spoken in such terms about Myaskovsky's Symphony: some complained of occasional longueurs, even though all agreed that the work was masterful, serious and moving. Their unshakeable respect for Myaskovsky played its role, too.

This was exactly what Nemirovich-Danchenko had predicted from the start: that one music prize would be inadequate. How was it possible, he argued, to choose between Tchaikovsky's *Queen of Spades*, for example, and his Sixth Symphony?[9] Although it embarrassed him to ask for more prizes to be provided even before any had even been awarded, he decided nevertheless that it was right to request three prizes for music, one each for large-scale vocal works (operas or cantatas), for symphonies and for chamber works. A precedent was ready to hand: in Literature, there were four separate prizes to accommodate prose, poetry, drama and even literary criticism. Nemirovich-Danchenko, fortunate to secure an audience not just with Molotov but also with Stalin, extracted from them a firm promise of at least one more music prize.[10] With this knowledge, the KSP went to the ballot box.

In the ballot that took place on 25 November 1940 (we will refer to it in future as Ballot 1), Shostakovich lost to Myaskovsky only by a single vote (twenty-four against twenty-five),[11] and the two potential music prizes were thus decided. The other contenders, Khachaturian's Violin Concerto and Prokofiev's opera *Semyon Kotko*, were far behind, with six and four votes respectively, although not necessarily because the members liked them so much less, but more probably because they were reluctant to split the vote between the front runners.

Everything seems straightforward here: 'respect' for Myaskovsky and 'love' for Shostakovich were reconciled in the ballot because the members now knew that a second prize would be made available. The vote was so close that the committee reported to the government that it 'could not give preference to either one or the other'.[12] We should take note of the strong support Shostakovich received from non-musicians, won over to his cause by the direct impact of his music. This was not the last time such a thing would happen.

Together with the KSP's support, there was a measure of support within government circles. On 25 November, two days after the public premiere, a short but emphatic endorsement of the Quintet ('the best work of 1940') appeared on the fourth page of *Pravda*, written by the prominent critic Alexander Shaverdyan. At the time, Shaverdyan sat on the editorial board of *Sovetskoye iskusstvo*, the house publication of the arts ministry, so readers of the review would have been able to assume that such opinions were endorsed by the ministry and indeed by Khrapchenko personally.[13] The date of publication looks a little suspect: the KSP members would have received this issue of *Pravda* on the morning of Ballot 1. Goldenweiser was obviously troubled, and he phoned the editorial board of *Pravda* to protest that the review was gravely prejudicial to the KSP's imminent vote (remember that his choice was Myaskovsky's symphony). Khrapchenko responded, reassuring the KSP that the discussion of nominated works by the press was perfectly normal (that is, the review had no further implications).[14]

What should we make of this? Volkov interprets the appearance of the *Pravda* review as a sign of Stalin's interference (which is highly speculative, especially since Volkov had scant acquaintance with the award process, apparently knowing nothing of the ballot, and very little about the KSP). But there is an important distinction to be drawn here, lest we be led astray. On the one hand, there were *Pravda* editorials, such as the condemnation of *Lady Macbeth* in 1936, which set out Party policy. On the other hand, there were reviews of new works, which, in the case of the Quintet, appeared in *Pravda* as normal features. From Khrapchenko's reaction to Goldenweiser's complaint, we can gather that he was a Quintet supporter, and it is likely that we can read Shaverdyan's review as the voice of the ministry. But the ministry was one thing, and Stalin quite another. The government and Party were large enough to embrace a range of conflicting opinions (certainly on non-essential matters) on a given topic. When we see that Khrapchenko had a particular opinion on such a matter, we cannot infer that Stalin was the source of the opinion, that he had the same opinion, that he cared about the matter or that he was even aware of it. In any case, let us not forget that this publication appeared *after* the KSP members had already aired their almost unanimously positive opinion of the Quintet; only the vote remained to be taken, and that was a secret ballot. If the ministry had really wanted to influence the vote, the review should have been placed a few days earlier, and even then, a routine review could be ignored without any serious consequences.

No One is Watching

To understand the significance of the success of Myaskovsky and Shostakovich in Ballot 1, let us put them into the context of other winners. Unexpectedly, there were only three of them: Mikhail Sholokhov, *And Quiet Flows the Don* (a multi-volume novel); Friedrich Ermler, *The Great Citizen* (a film); Vladimir Nemirovich-Danchenko, *Three Sisters* (a production of Chekhov's play at the Moscow Art Theatre).

While more prizes had to be requested for Music, it is startling to see that in the other arts, six available prizes were not even going to be awarded. In Literature, a huge debate raged around Sholokhov's novel. All were agreed that this was a towering masterpiece, but the ending of the novel was clearly at odds with Socialist Realism. Alexei Tolstoy and Nemirovich-Danchenko defended the novel for its depth and outstanding literary qualities, while Fadeyev (characteristically) spoke in favour of ideological considerations:

> We have all found our best Soviet feelings offended by the way this work ends. We have waited fourteen years for the ending, and Sholokhov has led his hero to complete moral destruction. For fourteen years, he was writing about people cutting off each other's heads, and nothing [edifying] has emerged from this carnage.[15]

Gurvich summed up the general feeling in the debate by saying that Sholokhov 'had no business ending the novel like this, and yet it was impossible to end it otherwise'.[16] Ideological necessity, he implied, was trumped by aesthetic necessity. In the debate, too, ideological considerations were moved aside to award the best novel of the past twenty years, not just of the year 1940. Having voted for *Don*, the members couldn't find any poetry, drama or criticism of comparable stature – and three prize places were left empty.

In the visual arts, things went especially badly: nothing submitted in Painting, Sculpture or Architecture was considered worthy of a prize. The KSP gave serious consideration to a rather original, rough-surfaced bust of Stalin by Grigor Kepinov, but in the end it was too controversial: Gerasimov even suggested that it looked more like the head of a dictator than that of a 'friend, teacher and father'.[17] The sprawling, star-shaped Red Army Theatre building, however impressive its exterior, was found to be too impractical inside, and so it went on. Another three prize places went to waste.

In the category of Theatre, on the contrary, there were several serious contenders for the single prize that was available. Galina Ulanova had thrilled audiences as Juliet in Prokofiev's ballet. The revered actor Alexander Ostuzhev, although at the end of his career and increasingly deaf, created a searing image of Uriel Acosta in the Russian version of Karl Gutzkow's tragedy of the same name. Nemirovich-Danchenko had launched a new and highly acclaimed production of Chekhov's *Three Sisters*. In the end, Nemirovich-Danchenko was chosen. He was, of course, the KSP chairman, but his artistic stature was so high, and this production so clearly deserving of recognition, that there was no reason to think this had any bearing on the vote (which, once again, was by secret ballot).

In film, most KSP members favoured Ermler's *Great Citizen*, a film about the life and violent death of the old Bolshevik, Sergei Kirov. Politically *engagé*, this film seems to have produced sincere admiration in members for its mastery, although perhaps from our perspective it hasn't aged as well as the other chosen nominations (many scenes are dominated by weighty discussions).

So, here we have it – the list received by the government as a result of Ballot 1:

Myaskovsky, Symphony No. 21
Shostakovich, Piano Quintet
Sholokhov, *And Quiet Flows the Don*
Ermler, *The Great Citizen*
Nemirovich-Danchenko, *Three Sisters*

In the context of the times, this list is particularly striking for one thing: of the five selected works, only one even approaches Socialist Realism, namely, the Ermler film, which has a Soviet topic and was politically impeccable, although it lacked the demotic qualities expected of core Socialist Realist pieces. Sholokhov's *Don*, as we have seen, may have conformed in some ways to Socialist Realism (although the earlier volumes pre-dated the artistic doctrine), but the ending fundamentally disqualified it. *Three Sisters* is, of course, a pre-revolutionary play, and it was produced by a major figure of pre-revolutionary theatre – still perfectly legitimate, but not Socialist Realist. Myaskovsky's Symphony is elegiac from beginning to end, and even if we take Shostakovich's Quintet as life-affirming (as did the members), its Socialist Realist credentials can be easily thrown into doubt, as Goldenweiser had hinted and as we will soon find out. In this very first KSP session, the aesthetic prevailed over the ideological.

The selection makes it clear that there was still much great art being produced in the Soviet Union of 1940. The lack of ideological concerns in the list was due to a particular confluence of circumstances which left KSP members on their own for a while, free from direct supervision. Within the Soviet administrative hierarchy, the KSP met under the aegis of the Council of Ministers, which meant that it was Vyacheslav Molotov, the prime minister, who was supposed to set up and direct the KSP's work. Molotov, however, had recently acquired another portfolio: he was now also the foreign minister, and immersed in matters of great moment (Britain and France having rejected a proposed alliance, the Soviet government had entered into a non-aggression pact with Hitler to stave off the inevitable for a while longer). Nemirovich-Danchenko, now in his eighties, was still obliged, as the KSP's chairman, to work things out on his own in the absence of any movement from Molotov's deputies.[18] Eventually, after his November trip to Berlin, Molotov made himself available, and quickly became very active. He received complaints (some of them addressed to Stalin), re-directed them to the relevant officials and, when necessary, took organizational decisions himself. Like Stalin, he remained a continuous presence throughout the whole period, and certainly invested more time in the day-to-day running of the award system than his superior.

For a brief period, though, a bubble of freedom emerged: what, indeed, would an elite group from the artistic intelligentsia do without direct interference from above? Normal service was to resume shortly.

Ballot 2

Even before Nemirovich-Danchenko solemnly handed the papers directly to Molotov on 2 December 1940, a worried Khrapchenko sounded the alarm. The thinness of Ballot 1 results implied that his own ministry had fallen short of expectations, and he hurried to put things right. On 30 November, he wrote a letter to Stalin and Molotov, in which he protested his disagreement with the KSP's decisions.[19] He quoted the KSP's conclusions: the visual arts could not boast anything comparable to Sholokhov, *The Three Sisters*, Myaskovsky or Shostakovich; they had also insisted that the first year of prizes called for strict standards (as opposed to balance across the arts). They could say what they wanted, but Khrapchenko filled out the prize list with his own proposals: to give a prize to the designer of the Lenin monument in Ulyanovsk (Matvei Manizer), to the architects of the Tchaikovsky Concert Hall and to the cartoonists of the Kukryniksy group for their series of drawings illustrating the history of the Party.[20]

Not that the KSP had overlooked these works: they rejected them after a thorough discussion with a sprinkling of mockery. Grabar called the Lenin monument 'a symphony of the overcoat', remarking that it was hardly right for the flailing overcoat to overwhelm its wearer, Lenin.[21] The Tchaikovsky Concert Hall was a conversion of the building that had originally been intended for the Meyerhold Theatre (the ensemble was disbanded by decree in 1938). The Kukryniksy, KSP members thought, treated a highly serious subject in their habitual cartoon style and produced something that, in their opinion, was not art at all.

Something needed to be done about Ballot 1, and Molotov's deputies gathered for a meeting, but they decided it was best to leave the business to Khrapchenko, since only he could add (and defend) any concrete proposals beyond those of the KSP.[22] Khrapchenko had second thoughts about the Kukryniksy cartoons, and replaced them with a sculpture, a Stalin statue by Sergei Merkurov. He was content, though, to leave the five KSP choices unchanged.[23] Now it was time for final approval to be granted, and Molotov requested that the Politburo discuss the nominations. On 20 December, finally, the Politburo gathered to consider the results of Ballot 1 plus Khrapchenko's additional proposals.

Unfortunately, we have no access to what happened beyond those closed doors. Was Khrapchenko present? Did tempers fly? When the doors opened, Ballot 1 was no more than a distant memory. The KSP was to be sent back to work with a completely new set of rules. Given the tight deadline, their New Year's holiday was going to be severely curtailed.

The Politburo's logic in changing the rules can be deduced easily enough: if there were not enough suitable candidates from 1940, then widen the remit back to 1935, giving the KSP six years to choose from. The number of prizes would have to be increased accordingly, since this was to be a summation of the art of the period. Now the task was broader: it would set in stone the canon of Soviet art, and thereby codify Socialist Realism. It was the KSP's turn to panic: they had only ten days until the new deadline of 5 January 1941. With no time to receive extra nominations from institutions and unions, they now had to mine their own memories for suitably outstanding works from the previous six years. Arguments raged. This was truly a mess, but the KSP members felt their prestige had increased with the weightiness of the new task, which made them forget to complain about the encroachment on their holiday season.

Now that the Music Section had five prizes to play with, they could easily accommodate the variety of genres they so desired. The Myaskovsky and Shostakovich nominations stayed on the list as unanimous and uncontroversial, even though they could have easily been replaced by more established, canonical pieces. The committee could have selected one of Myaskovsky's earlier and more obviously Socialist Realist pieces such as the Sixteenth Symphony (with its standard four-movement form and its mass-song theme in the finale), but instead it adhered to its original decision to give the award to the melancholy Twenty-first. Similarly, it would have made sense to drop Shostakovich's new Quintet in favour of the weightier and historically more significant Fifth Symphony from three years earlier, but again the committee stood by its original decision. Goldenweiser summarized the argument:

> The possibility of replacing Shostakovich's Quintet with his Fifth Symphony was considered, but because the Quintet contains a more noticeable shift away from the positions that had brought sharp public condemnation upon Shostakovich, we decided to stick with the Quintet, although the Fifth Symphony is certainly a work of high stature.[24]

In other words, in the collective memory of the Music Section, Shostakovich's Fifth was still associated too closely with the scandal over *Lady Macbeth*, and thus remained controversial.

A clearer gesture towards a Socialist Realist canon was the inclusion of Shaporin's patriotic cantata of 1939, *On the Field of Kulikovo*: it chimed both with Stalinist historical obsessions and with the worship of Russian classics – Shaporin's music was reminiscent of these to the point of sounding vaguely familiar.[25] Next to this stood another cantata, Prokofiev's *Alexander Nevsky*, which seemed to boast the same credentials, but still had a maverick character when placed next to Shaporin. The trickiest problem was to find an opera deserving of inclusion on the list. One canonic title that was not overlooked but deliberately avoided was the opera *And Quiet Flows the Don* by Ivan Dzerzhinsky. It had become an overnight success when Stalin attended a performance and endorsed it in January 1936, two weeks before the condemnation of Shostakovich's *Lady Macbeth*. By 1941, however, the laurels had wilted, especially since Dzerzhinsky's second Sholokhov opera, commissioned by the Bolshoi, had been a spectacular failure (it was *Virgin Soil Upturned*, 1937). Dzerzhinsky's poor grounding in compositional technique (he had never managed to graduate from the Leningrad Conservatoire), was the main reason given by Goldenweiser:

> [...] if we were to give a prize to this work now, we would convey a strong message that Soviet composers should write operas on Soviet themes in just this way. But we need to say that Soviet composers require mastery. No one should imagine that a lesser degree of mastery is needed for writing on Soviet themes. On the contrary, it demands the highest level of mastery from Soviet composers.[26]

One other possible title was the opera *Into the Storm* by Tikhon Khrennikov, which had only recently been pitted against Prokofiev's *Semyon Kotko* in a debate on whether Soviet opera should be founded on a song-based idiom (Khrennikov) or declamation/recitative (Prokofiev). The KSP showed no great enthusiasm for *Kotko*, but Khrennikov's opera was never even mentioned at the plenary, since the Music Section had already dismissed it, considering it too close to Dzerzhinsky (even if Khrennikov's overall competence was not in doubt). In order to grant the prize, they had to turn to 'national operas', which became known through the festivals of national republics held in Moscow every few months. These festivals (*dekadas*) were lavish, showy affairs with no expense spared, including the commissioning of operas from scratch and sending musicians to the republics en masse to help the locals learn and rehearse them. They were crowned by a grand banquet at the Kremlin, where Stalin presided and Voroshilov was toastmaster.

Of these 'national' operas, the Music Section chose, somewhat reluctantly, Uzeyir Hajibeyov's *Koroğlu*, which had received much praise at a *dekada* in 1938. Where the music alone was concerned, they would have preferred another national opera, *Enkhe Bulat Bator* ('Enkhe, Warrior of Steel'), which was shown at the Buryat-Mongol *dekada* in 1940. However, this was an opera written by a Russian composer Markian Frolov, a student of Glière, by way of 'friendly assistance' to the Buryat-Mongol Autonomous Republic, and was therefore only national by proxy. There was yet another such work in the running, Glière's *Gyulsara* (shown at the Uzbek *dekada* of 1937), but here the idea was to award the distinguished composer rather than the piece, which was less of an opera then a play with songs and dances, as befitting the nascent Uzbek operatic tradition.

In the concerto genre, Khachaturian held sway, although his Piano Concerto from 1937 was now seen as a more deserving piece, more serious and ingeniously constructed than the Violin Concerto, despite the exciting performance of the latter by David Oistrakh. The Music Section also showed its breadth of mind by suggesting Dunayevsky's mass songs to represent small forms. The Section nominated four of its own members, but since its members were drawn from the Soviet musical elite, this was not implausible.

One notable aspect of the music nominations was the absence of any works dedicated to Stalin, or indeed any kind of occasional work for the state. There was even a ready candidate, Khachaturian's *Stalin Poem* (*Poema o Staline*), a cantata that had received an overwhelmingly positive response in the press. And yet Goldenweiser put forward a strong argument against any award for the piece:

> Despite its undoubted worth, we didn't submit the Stalin Poem because by granting it a prize, we would be saying: here is a work which offered a fine rendition of this huge theme in the language of its art. But we don't consider this work to be on the scale of the finale in *Ivan Susanin*, or the finale of Beethoven's Ninth Symphony. This is why we are submitting [Khachaturian's] Concerto.[27]

An ingenious dismissal: the work is good, but not good enough for its theme. Even so, such an argument could only pass muster in music; for painting, sculpture and film, it was much harder to avoid the iconography or narratives of the state. Everyone could see whether Stalin was painted or sculpted well, or whether Lenin was well acted. But who could judge what quality of music was required to satisfy the impossibly high demands that the Stalin theme presented? (This also relied on the greater deference of the KSP to its musicians, whereas everyone felt competent to assess work in the other arts.) Interestingly, no one put forward Prokofiev's cantata *Zdravitsa* ('Toast to Stalin'), although it, too, had received excellent press. Perhaps even in those years, KSP members felt embarrassment over this piece, and preferred to reward Prokofiev for something else. For several years to come – until the watershed of 1948 – not a single Stalin cantata would receive an award.

Most musical nominations were put forward without any major discussion, and even Dunayevsky's songs generated no debate, despite the fact that the genre itself wasn't taken very seriously by most KSP members, who preferred to deal with operas and symphonies. The only argument arose from Prokofiev's nomination. The more the Music Section pushed Prokofiev forward, the more resistance his candidature met from Khrapchenko (a detailed account of these debates will follow in Chapter 3). It is not clear at this point whether Khrapchenko was personally unconvinced by Prokofiev's music, or whether he made his objections from a ministerial viewpoint; nor is it yet possible to assess how widespread a suspicion of Prokofiev there was within the Soviet political elite. The core of Khrapchenko's argument was that Prokofiev had not yet become a composer 'for the people', although he conceded that *Alexander Nevsky* was a step in the right direction. It is true that the cantata (and the film of the same name) had not yet reached the peak of their popularity: the film had to rest on the shelves as part of a general effort to avoid creating friction with Germany after the Molotov–Ribbentrop Pact. As for the cantata, it existed to secure an audience for the music in the absence of the film, which Khrapchenko must have understood. In any case, Khrapchenko's opinion (to KSP members he was just like them, a member with a single vote) did not sway the other members to drop Prokofiev from the ballot.

The new ballot (we will refer to it as Ballot 2) took place on 4 January 1941, and the results were as follows:

Myaskovsky, Symphony No. 21	30 votes
Shostakovich, Piano Quintet	30 votes
Shaporin, *On the Field of Kulikovo*	26 votes
Prokofiev, *Alexander Nevsky*	22 votes
Khachaturian, Piano Concerto	21 votes

These top five were now in contention, while the other three fell well below the line: Glière received thirteen votes, Dunayevsky eleven and Hajibeyov only four.

Having performed their duty, the members of the KSP could go home with a clear conscience. They had taken their important decisions on the future development of Soviet culture. Their opinion mattered. What they did not know was that two days later one of their apparently rank-and-file members, Khrapchenko, would exchange his KSP hat for his ministerial hat and override these collective decisions. Perhaps it was always intended that the work of the KSP would be overridden by the ministry, but the KSP had been told nothing of this.

The Discontented

On 6 January 1941, Khrapchenko wrote a letter to Stalin and Molotov commenting on the KSP's decisions. Only one of his suggested changes concerned Music: Prokofiev's *Alexander Nevsky* was to be removed from the list and replaced by one of the failed candidates, either Dunayevsky or Hajibeyov. Khrapchenko thought little enough of eighteen KSP votes that he could cancel them with a stroke of his pen. His objections to *Nevsky* were as follows:

> I consider it wrong to award the Stalin Prize to S. S. Prokofiev [...] The *Alexander Nevsky* suite is not an outstanding musical work. Created on the basis of the film score for *Alexander Nevsky*, the suite has failed to achieve any wide popularity. Prokofiev lived abroad for a long time. And even now, he still remains largely alien to Soviet reality, and alien to the ideas that inspire true Soviet artists.
>
> Among the Stalin Prize candidates, there are much more deserving composers, such as I. O. Dunayevsky, who has written a widely acclaimed set of songs, or U. Hajibeyov, the author of the opera *Koroğlu*, which is the most important of the works shown at the *dekadas* of national arts in Moscow. In our opinion, a Stalin Prize should be given [instead] to one of these composers.[28]

Khrapchenko was not the only one dissatisfied with the results of Ballot 2.[29] Despite remaining confidential, the results were immediately leaked, and this is why just a day after Khrapchenko sent his own letter to Stalin and Molotov, another letter questioning the KSP's decisions arrived with Stalin's Secretariat. This letter, dated 7 January 1941, was devoted exclusively to the musical selection, and was signed by Moisei Grinberg, a Party member from 1930, with Party card number 1234451.[30]

Letters to Stalin are generally colourful affairs, but we have added reason to pay attention to this particular letter, because it becomes a crucial piece of evidence in Volkov's argument. A denunciation of the Quintet should (supposedly) have destroyed Shostakovich's chances of a prize if it were not for Stalin's (supposed) defence. The first problem with Volkov's argument is his assumption that Stalin would actually have read Grinberg's letter. True, Grinberg insisted that his letter be read by Stalin personally, or returned to him if this was not possible. But the letter went down the steps of the bureaucratic ladder: from Stalin's Secretariat to Molotov, and then to Khrapchenko. Thus Khrapchenko suddenly found on his desk a list of complaints and, moreover, a programme of action put together by someone who was evidently well informed, and no stranger even to the undercurrents of the Soviet music world.

So who was Moisei Grinberg? An official report on him from 1949 gives us an intriguing, if necessarily biased, picture (it was written as part of the anti-cosmopolitanism campaign, of which Grinberg fell foul):[31] Moisei Abramovich

Grinberg, born 1904, Jewish. Joined the Party while in Rostov, where he studied as a pianist (his education ended at secondary level). From 1926, he began a career as an arts administrator, first in Rabis (the non-state arts trade union), then in local cinema administration. Party membership clearly gave him a boost: he moved to Moscow as a higher Rabis official in 1931 (immigration to Moscow had to be justified for career reasons). In 1936, he began moving up the bureaucratic ladder, eventually to be appointed head of the State Administration of Music Institutions (GUMU), a body within the ministry. This was the job he lost in 1939 as a result of the Purges; apart from knowing closely some of the 'enemies of the people' – who didn't? – he was found to have concealed the fact that his brother had been in the White Army. Grinberg could count himself very lucky that he suffered nothing worse than demotion and a caution. He was able to remain a Party member, and continued in appropriate employment, albeit at a lower level. At the time of the letter, he was deputy artistic director at the Stanislavsky Opera House, and also worked as a junior editor at *Sovetskaya muzïka* (apart from his ministry post, he had previously been editor in chief for the state music publisher, Muzgiz).

Grinberg, then, was no random malcontent. We might think of him, rather, as a boyar in disgrace, hoping that his noble standing would be restored as a result of this letter (to fast-forward, it was, and in June 1941 he received a more senior post on the Radio Committee). He was certainly known to Khrapchenko. The previous minister, Platon Kerzhentsev, had been ousted in April 1938, during the Purges, but Grinberg remained as head of his department for several more months under the leadership of Khrapchenko. Whether or not Khrapchenko had known of Grinberg's intention to write a letter to Stalin, he was dealing with a former colleague whose motives he could understand, and with whom he shared much common ground.

Now let us examine the contents of Grinberg's letter:

My decision to turn to you is based on my deep conviction that certain unhealthy tendencies are emerging in our music at present, and these can prevent music from developing in the right direction. In my opinion, these tendencies have revealed themselves most clearly in the nominations of musical works for the prize awarded in your name.[32]

If we didn't know the date, we could easily have supposed that such a letter was written on the eve of the anti-formalist campaign of 1948. Grinberg is ready to begin such a campaign now, in 1941, and he sets out his arguments with some panache. This is a broad attack with multiple targets (an aspect of the letter that

Volkov does not take into account). Let us take these in turn, starting with Shostakovich:

> [... S]o much of the Quintet is contrived, and there are so many abstract formal quests, and so little of genuine beauty and strength. [...] The Quintet may stand out for its formal perfection, but this form is nourished by rationalism and the air of the hothouse, rather than by any living human energy. This is music that lacks any connection with the life of the People.[33]

In case we might imagine otherwise, the letter makes it clear that Grinberg was opposed to an award for this particular piece, and had no wider animus against its composer. Grinberg even supported the idea that Shostakovich should receive a prize, but that the Fifth Symphony would be a much more appropriate recipient than the Quintet. His problem with the Quintet was its neoclassicism, even though this aspect of the work had contributed much to its great public success, had endeared it to many of the KSP members and had singled it out for praise by Shaverdyan in his *Pravda* article.[34] Grinberg, on the contrary, saw this neoclassicism as a sign of the Quintet's 'deeply Western orientation' and opposed the work's 'abstract formal quests' to the 'live human energy' that should mark a worthy recipient of the prize. We must concede that Grinberg was very perceptive, and at various points during the Stalin period there was indeed controversy over the acceptability of musical neoclassicism within Socialist Realism, given the Western origins of the style. At this juncture, anti-neoclassical polemic was at a low ebb,[35] but criticism intensified during the war years (particularly in relation to Shostakovich's Eighth Symphony), and in 1948 neoclassicism was declared unacceptable. As for the contrasting 'live human energy' that Grinberg mentioned, this was customarily associated with more conservative styles "that" relied on Romantic idioms and pacing. In fact, if we go back to Goldenweiser's account of the Quintet, we can see that he and Grinberg are of the same opinion (whatever their social differences).

Grinberg's second complaint was that Khachaturian's brilliant and popular Violin Concerto had been overlooked in Ballot 2, while the nomination had gone instead to the more harmonically complex and demanding Piano Concerto (1937). Once again, we must agree that Grinberg's ear is well attuned to stylistic subtleties. Grinberg saved up some heavier weaponry for his third target, Prokofiev. It is worth quoting the whole paragraph devoted to him:

> S. Prokofiev is a master of great significance who has received wide recognition abroad. But for several decades, this outstanding composer had been under the influence of contemporary Western music. In a number

of his recent works, including the cantata *Alexander Nevsky*, it is very clear that Prokofiev has made considerable efforts to overcome these influences. Such efforts deserve every support, but it is still doubtful whether the highest prize should be given to Prokofiev's cantata, a kind of suite compiled from film music.[36]

As we can see, Grinberg's opinion here fully coincides with Khrapchenko's. We should not be surprised: Grinberg knew first-hand about the ministry's rejection of Prokofiev's 20th-Anniversary Cantata (1937), information that would have been confined largely to ministry insiders.[37] Grinberg concludes this part of his letter by saying that he fully supports both the Myaskovsky symphony and the Shaporin cantata, and that the contrast between these two works and the three he wants rejected could not be more apparent.

Now on to Grinberg's other grudges.[38] He poses a series of strident questions (as if he still held his former position of power): why was Marian Koval's *Pugachev* oratorio passed over? Why wasn't a single Soviet opera honoured? He concedes that Dzerzhinsky's *And Quiet Flows the Don* had probably 'lost its significance', which was an interesting point to make to Stalin, who had once promoted it.[39] But if not Dzerzhinsky, then what about Khrennikov's *Into the Storm*? Or if not a Soviet-themed opera, then what of the national operas? There was Hajibeyov's *Koroğlu* and Glière's 'national' operas – why had they not been considered either? Finally, where is the mass-song genre on the KSP's list? Grinberg's selection here, once again, is prescient: mass song, patriotic oratorio and opera, all written in a populist, 'democratic' style, were encouraged above other genres in the 1948 campaign. Koval and Khrennikov, who had cultivated this populist style, would indeed come out on top in 1948.

With a certain daring, Grinberg uncovers the reasons for what was, in his opinion, such a poor selection of nominations: the KSP was clearly influenced by the choices made by the most authoritative composers, both inside the KSP itself and in the Composers' Union. In Grinberg's view, these composers of the older generation were constrained by their narrow professionalism; worse still, their tastes were determined by Western trends of the previous two decades. These influences made them 'view form as a self-sufficient constituent of a musical work, and deliberate formal complexity as a sign of innovation', and so 'the music of the young composers who have stepped onto the broad democratic path is organically alien to them'. This is the culmination of Grinberg's forceful argument. The argument is familiar: it had been much used by the RAPM group in the 1920s and early '30s, but lost traction when RAPM was disbanded in 1932.[40] The 'narrow professionals' had triumphed back then, but Grinberg now sought a reversal. Indeed, Grinberg's letter allows us to understand the continuity between the debates broken off in 1932 and the debacle of 1948, showing that the great opposition between the believers in high art and the pursuers of a more demotic middlebrow never went away.

When, at the end of his letter, Grinberg begs Stalin to lend his own ear to the music nominated for prizes, he implies that Stalin would be capable of noting these stylistic and ideological distinctions:

> In order to confirm the correctness of my evaluations of the above works, I can only ask of you one thing: listen to these pieces and you will be able to figure them out perfectly. For you are familiar with works of all the other arts, with literature, painting, architecture and dramatic theatre.[41]

Thus, at the end of his letter, Grinberg seems to suggest that music is the only art that Stalin does not personally oversee.

The next question then arises: was Grinberg's letter simply ignored, or did it have some oblique effect on the ensuing deliberations? It is, in fact, very difficult to give an answer to this. The difficulties arise not only because the letter contained a variety of criticisms, but also because, as I hinted earlier, many of Grinberg's suggestions coincided with Khrapchenko's own opinions, and Khrapchenko hardly needed Grinberg to tell him what he wanted to do already. Thus, Grinberg argued against an award for Prokofiev, as Khrapchenko had already done, and in almost the same formulations. On the candidatures of Hajibeyov and Dunayevsky, again Grinberg and Khrapchenko were of like mind. Grinberg's suggestion that Khachaturian's weighty Piano Concerto should be replaced with the lighter and more accessible Violin Concerto may prefigure the final decision of the government, but again, it is entirely possible that the same decision would have been taken without the letter: the Violin Concerto had initially been in the running, and certainly had a lot of support from the people who had recently been struck by Oistrakh's premiere. On Shostakovich's Quintet, however, Grinberg and Khrapchenko differed, and the latter was too confident of his opinion to be swayed by the letter.

Ballot 3

Let us now return to the timeline of the award process. On 12 January 1941, the government made a further change to the rules, again in the direction of increasing the total number of awards: the KSP was now also to consider works for a second-class prize, worth 50,000 roubles. Music was to be allocated eight prizes – three first-class and five second-class. The KSP was once again running short of time and by this stage it was also depleted in numbers, since its non-Moscow members

had already left for home. The remainder of the KSP decided on the most efficient solution, which was simply to award the first-class prize to the three works
with the highest number of votes, while the five remaining candidates would
receive the second. The first-class list now looked like this:

Shostakovich, Piano Quintet
Myaskovsky, Symphony No. 21
Shaporin, *On the Field of Kulikovo*

The second-class list would have comprised Prokofiev, Khachaturian, Glière,
Dunayevsky and Hajibeyov if the KSP had continued moving down the Ballot
2 list. Khrapchenko, however, now demanded that the KSP consider new candidates, claiming that the second prize had been created for the purpose of
encouraging younger talent. The younger talents he had in mind were Frolov
and Koval, whose work had earlier been rejected by the KSP. Khrapchenko got
his way. The only other change after Ballot 3 was the replacement of Hajibeyov,
who had received fewest votes in Ballot 2, with the relatively young Koval,
thereby replacing a national opera with a populist oratorio, *Yemelyan Pugachev*.

Now the KSP's task was truly over. Summing up the process, Myaskovsky
noted in his diary, 'Reconsidered nominations for Stalin Prizes twice – the
quantity kept going up, the quality kept going down'.[42] All that was left was to
wait for the results of their work to be published in the central newspapers. The
wait was all the more anxious for those potential prizewinners to whom the
results of Ballot 3 were, no doubt, leaked.

The Aftershock

It was another two months before the results became public. On 16 March
1941, *Pravda* published a list that was, in parts, unrecognizable. No one outside
government knew what had happened in the interim or why, neither the KSP
nor the would-be prizewinners who had disappeared from the list. Others,
equally in the dark, were much happier, having suddenly appeared on the list
even though the KSP had rejected them or not even considered them. A bumper
crop was gathered by the film industry, as their category won ten first and
fifteen second prizes, producing eighty-six laureates (bearing in mind that
rewards were shared out among the principal contributors in film). Great
surprises were also in store for the musicians: while the three first-class prizes
were unchanged from Ballot 3 (Shostakovich, Myaskovsky, Shaporin), the
second-class bracket looked very different, as can be seen from Table 1.
Myaskovsky left us a reserved reaction in his diary: he fell ill the day before the

Table 1. Second-class awards in 1941.

Ballot 3	Published list
Prokofiev,	Hajibeyov [Azerbaijan],
cantata *Alexander Nevsky*	opera *Koroğlu*
Khachaturian,	Khachaturian [Armenia],
Piano Concerto	Violin Concerto
Dunayevsky,	Kiladze [Georgia],
mass songs*	symphonic poem *The Hermit*
Glière,	Bogatyrev [Belorussia],
opera *Gyulsara*	opera *In the Forests of Polesye*
Koval,	Revutsky [Ukraine],
oratorio *Yemelyan Pugachev*	Symphony No. 2

*awarded in the Film category

announcement, then left for a sanatorium, and so 'observed the whole commotion from a distance'.[43]

The most prominent casualty was Prokofiev. The disappearance of Glière's semi-opera and Koval's undercooked oratorio were of much lesser significance, having been in and out at various stages of the KSP's deliberations. Hajibeyov's reappearance was no great surprise either. But what were the new names doing on the list? Who had added the lucky three – Bogatyrev, Kiladze and Revutsky?

The available information on the list's transformation is meagre and hard to interpret,[44] but some dates and facts can be established with certainty. On 16 January, the day after the final plenary session of the KSP, Khrapchenko wrote another letter to Stalin and Molotov, giving them his comments on Ballot 3. He granted that compared to their earlier attempts, the KSP had now managed to 'correct certain mistakes'. Even so, Prokofiev was still on the list, and Khrapchenko wished to replace *Alexander Nevsky* with a national opera, either Hajibeyov's or Frolov's. Khrapchenko proposed similar corrections for the other arts.

On 21 January, Molotov's deputies gathered for another meeting, but once again found themselves out of their depth and passed the matter up to the Party CC.[45] It was most likely discussed at the Politburo, and Khrapchenko was asked to come up with new names to give the republics more representation – the dearth of 'national' candidates must have been seen as the most pressing problem at this point. Khrapchenko responded with a letter on 8 March, in which he suggested that Prokofiev and Koval could be replaced by Hajibeyov (Politburo members would remember him from the Azeri *dekada*) and

Revutsky, 'a composer popular in Ukraine, whose Second Symphony has been performed in Kiev and Lvov'.[46] This clears up part of the mystery.

We can only reconstruct what happened next on the basis of the two extant intermediate documents presented in figs 5 and 6. The first contains markings in Khrapchenko's handwriting: we can see here that some of his changes have already been established (such as the exclusion of Prokofiev and Glière), while others are still pending, such as the new names appearing on the left side.

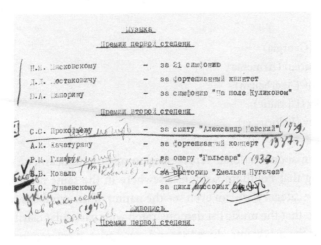

Fig. 5. Comments in Khrapchenko's hand (red pencil in the original): 'исключить' ('exclude', referring to Prokofiev and Glière); 'снять' ('remove', referring to Dunayevsky and Koval). Marian Koval's original name (Vitold Viktorovich Kovalev) is added (blue in the original). On the left there are the names of the proposed replacements, [Gadzhi]bekov, [Rev]utsky Lev Nikolayevich, Kiladze, and Bogatyrev. RGALI, fond 962, op. 10, ye. kh. 44, l. 18a.

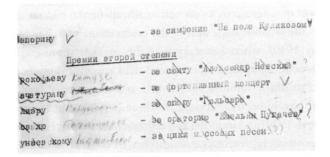

Fig. 6. The replacement names are now added more neatly (in an unknown hand), but two of them have not been spelled in their standard form: Ревутский instead of Ревуцкий and Гаджи-Беков instead of Гаджибеков. RGALI, fond 962, op. 10, ye. kh. 44, l. 7.

In the second document, which has the new names added neatly in an unknown hand, the slight misspelling of two names suggests they were taken down by ear rather than checked against records. Both documents seem to summarize discussions, most likely a Politburo meeting, which must have included Stalin, Molotov and Khrapchenko, and we also know from marginalia in another document that Beria and Khrushchev were also present. (There may have been others.)[47]

The final result speaks for itself: the second-prize list now presents a neat parade of the five national republics that were recognized as most culturally advanced:

Kiladze (Georgia)
Khachaturian (Armenia)
Hajibeyov (Azerbaijan)
Revutsky (Ukraine)
Bogatyrev (Belorussia)

This concern about 'national' representation must have been one of the foremost during that Politburo session: elsewhere in the same document, in the Architecture category, we can even see the names of the republics written in. It so happened that the music list demonstrated with particular clarity one of the purposes of the newly introduced second-class prize: it catered for the highest achievements at the level of the republics (with some Union-wide exposure), while the first degree was reserved for work of Union-wide or even international importance. The one composer who was badly served by this division was Khachaturian who already had Union-wide renown, but who was needed to represent Armenia in the prize system.

It is most likely that Khrapchenko supplied all the newcomers' names. He knew Lev Revutsky, a fifty-one-year-old professor at the Kiev Conservatoire and former student of Glière; only a year earlier Khrapchenko had sat together with Revutsky on the Bolshoi stage during the celebrations of Tchaikovsky's centenary (7 May 1940), when Revutsky was the speaker representing Ukraine. Revutsky's Second Symphony was a post-Kuchka work (*Moguchaya kuchka* – the Mighty Handful),[48] quite accomplished and attractive, if lacking in originality. It had largely been composed in the mid-1920s, but it was revised for performance in 1940 (and sounded as if it might have been written in the 1890s).

The Belorussian representative, Bogatyrev, by contrast, was very young. He made himself known through the Belorussian 1940 *dekada*, when his freshly completed opera *In the Forests of Polesye* (*V pushchakh Polesya*) was performed at the Bolshoi Theatre. He was only twenty-eight at the time. He had studied with Vasily Zolotarev, who was himself a student of Rimsky-Korsakov, and at this point he had hardly moved beyond the Kuchka style. His opera, with a standard 'love across the front line' story set in the Civil War, was transparent and unpretentious. It was hurriedly published in fragments to satisfy the Stalin Prize eligibility criteria after the event. Myaskovsky had attended the Belorussian *dekada*, and referred to the opera as 'childish' at the time. On seeing Bogatyrev's name on the prize list in March 1941, he could no longer even remember who this was.[49]

The most mysterious nomination was for Grigor Kiladze's symphonic poem, *The Hermit*. The Composers' Union, which nominated musical works to be passed on to the KSP, had considered and rejected Kiladze's piece, so the KSP was unaware of it. Its Orientalist style and legendary topic made it acceptable stylistically, but the religious undertones of its literary source, a poem by Ilya Chavchavadze, could have raised doubts (if this was noticed at the time). Kiladze, it should be added, also had one foot in Russian musical culture, since he was a student of Mikhail Ippolitov-Ivanov (a Rimsky-Korsakov pupil who had an interest in Georgian music).

Casting our parting glance at the prizewinning music of 1941, we cannot fail to notice that Shostakovich's Quintet continues to stand out among music influenced by the Kuchka's *style russe* and its Orientalist variants. Its neoclassicism distinguished it stylistically from the prizewinning mainstream. Volkov was, of course, right to notice this oddity. And yet we find no evidence that Stalin ever listened to the Quintet or other musical nominations, or that at any point of the process he felt the need to do so. The Grinberg letter was not a turning point in a story of The Poet and The Tsar, as Volkov argued, but a marginal matter that affected neither Shostakovich nor Stalin, but merely reminded Khrapchenko that his former junior colleague Grinberg was still around and had not lost his edge.

The story assembled here from a multitude of documents is certainly not as exciting as Volkov's. By way of compensation, it has the modest advantage of actually being supported by the evidence, which cannot be said of the more exciting story. The Quintet did not have to be favoured by Stalin in order to win – he did not even need to hear the work. It was brought to the top of the list (jointly with Myaskovsky) after a successful audition for the KSP, which left members in raptures, and it kept its place there thanks to the staunch support of Khrapchenko, who for years continued to cite the work as an example of 'the good Shostakovich'.[50] The press reaction (not unrelated to Khrapchenko's support) and the (independent) enthusiasm of the public must have also played their role. And Stalin? Well, simply by signing the final list he showed that he knew of no reason why the Quintet should be stopped.

We should remember that the Quintet, of course, was not the only work that had to brave the squalls and undercurrents of the award process. The other leading nomination in Music, Myaskovsky's Twenty-first Symphony, also survived – a fact that is in some ways no less surprising (we shall return to this story in Chapter 6). These two original music nominations, as already mentioned, shared the stage with Sholokhov's novel, Ermler's film and Nemirovich-Danchenko's Chekhov production. Of these, however, only Sholokhov's novel remained at the top together with the music nominations. Ermler's film was demoted to a second-class prize, while Nemirovich-Danchenko in the end received no award at all for his *Three Sisters* (he won the prize the following year, for his production of an explicitly Socialist Realist play, *The Kremlin Chimes*). This suggests to us that Music, despite the upheavals in the second-class list, suffered from less interference from above than the other arts – the bloated final lists for Film and Literature are eloquent testimony to Stalin's enthusiasms in these arts. Even the rewriting of the second-class list reveals only an extraneous political agenda, a kind of equal-opportunities effort to ensure representation from the national republics. In general, composers were added or deleted for the purposes of creating a more balanced list, whether for more young composers, more national composers, more demotic works and so on; they were not being endorsed or censured on any personal basis.

With one exception: Prokofiev. His exclusion was pointedly personal, justi-fied by the purported flaws in his curriculum vitae, his artistic personality and the music itself. Even here, there is no indication that Stalin played a part in the story: Prokofiev's exclusion, as we have seen, was argued for and arranged by Khrapchenko. Unlike the Shostakovich–Stalin story refuted earlier in this chapter, the Prokofiev–Khrapchenko story stands on firmer ground. This is the subject we will investigate in the next chapter.

CHAPTER THREE

PROKOFIEV: THE UNLIKELY CHAMPION

'It's likely that *Semyon Kotko* won't run: the minister of fine arts didn't like it. As with any work of genius, this seems to be its inevitable lot.'[1] Myaskovsky made this remark in his diary when the fate of Prokofiev's first Soviet opera was hanging in the balance. His reference to Khrapchenko as the *ministr izyashch-nykh iskusstv* (the minister for fine arts) sounds quaintly old-fashioned in the Soviet context, but with sarcastic intent. At this point, Khrapchenko was still new to his post, an unknown quantity, but Myaskovsky expected nothing good from this encounter between genius and bureaucracy. Was he right? At first, it seemed he was vindicated, but after a time, it turned out that he was far off the mark. Khrapchenko was not a philistine functionary, but a passionate and powerful manager of culture, who chose to be deeply involved in Prokofiev's career, even entering into a kind of co-authorship in the case of *War and Peace*.

And Prokofiev, rather than fulfilling the role of the great misunderstood artist that Myaskovsky predicted, went on to win six Stalin Prizes – more than any other composer, and among the very highest across all the arts and sciences. Does this mean that, after all, his music fulfilled the ideological demands of the state perfectly and completely? As far as success is concerned, his counterpart in literature would be the six-times winner Konstantin Simonov, who obediently reflected every twist and turn of state propaganda in his topical plays. But the comparison is otherwise grotesque. Many lovers of Prokofiev's music would baulk even at the suggestion that it could be considered Socialist Realist – its spirit seems freer, its beauty more absolute, its appeal more universal. We would be well advised, then, to be cautious and, as with Shostakovich's Quintet, to refrain from any easy assumptions: Prokofiev's Stalin Prize history is particularly tortuous and even paradoxical, and his wins and misses are entangled in an intricate web of personal relations and unpredictable circumstances.

Kotko and *Nevsky*

Contrary to Myaskovsky's pessimistic prediction, Prokofiev was allowed to see *Semyon Kotko* through to the premiere, overcoming not just Khrapchenko's apparent 'dislike', but a dangerous brush with high politics. The formidable Andrei Vyshinsky, at that point one of Molotov's deputies, saw the opera in a private audition on 11 June 1940 and reported to Molotov that the episodes featuring Austro-German invaders needed to be removed from the libretto – such were the unspoken consequences of the Molotov–Ribbentrop Pact.[2] The offending scenes were duly adapted, presumably with Molotov's acquiescence, and the opera went ahead on 20 September at the Stanislavsky Opera House (one of Moscow's smaller stages). Myaskovsky was in raptures about *Kotko*'s 'extraordinary music'; in fact, he had nominated the opera for a Stalin Prize before the premiere.[3] This was his very first act as a KSP member – an act of support for a lifelong friend whose music he ardently admired.

In that very first season, the KSP's business was conducted with the utmost thoroughness, so the members were able to see *Kotko* in a specially organized matinee (11 November 1940). But the reaction, even within the Music Section, was mixed, and from the beginning, ideological considerations were brought into play. This is how Goldenweiser reported the Music Section's deliberations to the plenary meeting:

> This is a work by a composer of undoubted talents, one of the most remarkable of our time. Prokofiev's mastery is exceptional, at an international level, but he has a further virtue that is not always found among gifted composers: he has his own style. Some may find it to their liking, others may not, but no one could deny that he has a very striking style of his own. [. . .]
>
> But is this opera the kind of work that could unhesitatingly be nominated for a Stalin Prize? Some doubts arise here. Alongside some very vivid scenes – the *pogrom*, or [Lyubka's] madness – the opera contains some rather limp moments: the scene with the cannon, for example. He [Prokofiev] displays a certain coldness. Nor could one say that the revolutionary plot is used in such a topical way as to grab the audience's attention. The opera is not meeting with a very warm response. It continues on its run, but without having any great impact on the public.
>
> With all due deference to Prokofiev's talents, we have to consider the opera as staged, in its entirety, and then we have to take into account the fact that this opera would not command the sympathy of the wider public if we were to nominate it for a Stalin Prize.[4]

Ostensibly, Goldenweiser simply pitted Prokofiev's superb music against certain dramatic weaknesses of the opera, but for those versed in 'Sovietese', the terms he used suggested graver, ideological deficiencies. His suggestion that Prokofiev treated his revolutionary plot with 'coldness' was damaging, and his lament over the lack of public support seemed to refer not so much to the audience's behaviour in the theatre, but to the lukewarm press the opera was receiving.[5] For an old Tolstoyan, Goldenweiser had acquired a curious mastery of the Stalinist language of veiled insinuations.

There didn't seem to be anyone who wished to argue with Goldenweiser, especially since at this point there was only one Music prize to award. And yet *Kotko* found unexpected support from the Azeri composer Uzeyir Hajibeyov, who said he would be prepared to reward Prokofiev's innovative yet accessible operatic language if there were more prizes available (that was rather generous of him, since his own opera was also in the running). However, on dramatic weaknesses Hajibeyov had to agree with Goldenweiser: 'What is so heroic about Kotko? That he threw a bomb into the church and everyone came out whole, just one wounded?'[6] With only four votes in Ballot 1, *Kotko* fell at the first hurdle, predicting troubles that would inevitably befall any opera on a Soviet topic.

When earlier works became eligible for Ballot 2, a stronger Prokofiev offering was selected, and Myaskovsky, fearing that *Alexander Nevsky* might also prove contentious, decided to support his friend much more forcefully. This was not as effective as Myaskovsky intended, since he preferred simply to speak his mind rather than calculate what kind of argument would best suit the context. He began setting out his case by claiming that Prokofiev was among the five leading composers in the world today. And who were the other four? Rachmaninov, Stravinsky, Medtner and Richard Strauss – that is, three Russian émigrés and one Western 'decadent', as any ideologically minded critic would have noted.

Fortunately, Myaskovsky then switched tack, and proceeded to enumerate Prokofiev's specifically Soviet credentials:

> In his most recent work, we find him quite acceptable. *Alexander Nevsky* is a patriotic national work displaying a high level of musical mastery and inspiration.
>
> Some have reproached Prokofiev for not saying enough to the people. I must ask 'what kind of people?' To lovers of *estrada* music, Prokofiev has nothing to say. But neither does our [Myaskovsky's own] Symphony or [Shostakovich's] Quintet. The chorus 'Arise, ye Russian people', from *Alexander Nevsky*, has been arranged for a military band and this is performed

everywhere with great success. Another chorus from the cantata has been performed by the Red Army Ensemble and is also very successful.

Prokofiev makes an astonishing impact in his presentation of musical material and in giving it character. In these respects, we can consider his work to be on the same level as the Russian classics. If Maksakova or another, still finer singer performed his song 'On the Field of the Dead', Glinka would have been happy to attach his name to it. It has the most remarkable depth, sincerity and warmth of feeling.[7]

Myaskovsky ended with an exhortation: without Prokofiev among the winners, musicians would feel beheaded. This moved other members to utter similarly strong statements. Grabar appealed to the conscience of his fellow members to correct 'the mistake that hovers over this huge musician, Prokofiev' (he presumably meant the lack of official recognition), and even Goldenweiser warned that Prokofiev's omission from the list would be seen as 'an unjustifiable step'.[8]

And at this point, for the first time in musical discussions, a rift opened up between the minister Khrapchenko and other members of the KSP, a rift that we will encounter repeatedly. Khrapchenko outlined a position that was essentially his bureaucratic perspective (which may or may not have coincided with his personal view):

> I would like to say a few words about Prokofiev as a candidate for a Stalin Prize. I am not going to discuss Prokofiev's talent, since it seems to me that Stalin Prizes are not awarded on the basis of talent per se, but for talent that serves the people, for talent that is used in a way that enables the people to feel joy and strength, to feel empowered. [They are awarded] for talent that encourages the people to exercise its own creativity, assisting in the development of socialist culture.
>
> If we approach Prokofiev's oeuvre from this point of view, then, it seems to me, his works do not deserve a Stalin Prize in spite of his talents.
>
> If we take a particular work, *Alexander Nevsky*, then we must say that it lacks the great virtues of a work that would win a wide following among the people; no, we cannot claim that it has been recognized by the people and therefore deserves an honour such as the Stalin Prize.
>
> I would say that Prokofiev is only setting out on the path that will lead him to become a composer who dedicates all his abilities to the people, a composer who directs his work towards the broad masses. It would be premature to guess at his further development, at the kind of work that will prove to be significant in the future. This is why I don't think it would be beneficial to award him a Stalin Prize.[9]

Note here that Khrapchenko is not formulating objections particular to *Nevsky*, but rather a general perspective on Prokofiev as a Soviet composer, as seen from the high towers of the culture ministry. It is too early, he says, and Prokofiev is as yet unproven. Other KSP members could have pointed out that he was twisting the evidence: as Myaskovsky mentioned, some choruses from *Nevsky* had already reached much deeper into the masses than his own Symphony or Shostakovich's Quintet. They chose not to argue but expressed their disagreement with the minister through Ballot 2: Prokofiev received twenty-two votes, a respectable number that eventually placed him at the top of the second-class category in Ballot 3. We already know what happened next: Khrapchenko attempted to block Prokofiev's nomination in his letter to Stalin and Molotov – and succeeded. The blow to the composer was all the greater because the final list also included a collective award for the film *Alexander Nevsky*, in which Prokofiev would have been justified to expect a share – but he was not named among the film crew. It was not as if there was any general policy at the time against shared film awards including composers: Dunayevsky, one of Stalin's favourite song composers, benefited from this after losing his chance of a prize in the Music category. Prokofiev remained unrewarded. An invisible wall was standing between him and the prize.

The Second Quartet

Twelve months later, life changed beyond all recognition. After the beginning of the war, most cultural personnel were evacuated eastwards. The KSP was itself split into two parts by evacuation: some members were sent to the city of Kuybyshev (now Samara), on the Volga, others to the Georgian capital Tbilisi. Those who met in Kuybyshev had no chance to hear and assess any Prokofiev works, while those in Tbilisi, on the contrary, included many of his supporters, such as Myaskovsky, Shaporin and Goldenweiser (Prokofiev was also in Tbilisi at this point, so everyone there became acquainted with his latest works).

At first, the supporters considered playing the 'topical' card, and looked to nominate Prokofiev's 'war' pieces forming the *1941* Suite. But they found the suite disappointingly 'superficial', and transferred their hopes to the Second Quartet, which used folk themes from the region of Kabardino-Balkaria (Prokofiev was initially evacuated to Nalchik, the capital of this region, spending three months there before moving to Tbilisi). This looked like a sure winner: the piece could be seen as exemplifying Stalin's slogan of art that is 'national in form, socialist in content', which since the early 1930s had shaped cultural development in the republics.[10] Furthermore, the Quartet was a persuasive demonstration that wartime migration had its benefits, in this case, a mutually enriching encounter between an internationally known composer and a distant national culture.

It fell to Myaskovsky to present the work, a task he performed, again, with good intentions but rather awkwardly. Myaskovsky made a habit of studying every Prokofiev score as soon as it was available, and he always took his friend's music very seriously. His letters often contain frank assessments of the latest piece, with admiration and delight often interspersed with disappointment or bemusement. While this was all very well in private, it was not suited to public advocacy, but such distinctions eluded Myaskovsky. And so, among all his praise for the work, he told his audience that he found the first movement of the Quartet a little dry, and that the finale perhaps contained one folk theme too many. The second and third movements, on the other hand, were 'amazing'. His concluding comments were not very helpful: he suggested that the scale of the Quartet was perhaps greater than the Kabardins' and Balkars' present level of musical appreciation, and that they might need to school themselves in the music of the wider world in order to appreciate it.[11]

At this point, no one had yet heard a performance of the Quartet, although they were able to form an impression from Prokofiev's own solo-piano rendition. Khrapchenko, who came to Tbilisi specially to attend the KSP meetings, had managed to hear this, leading Shaporin to caution that 'Mikhail Borisovich [Khrapchenko] might have formed a false impression on the basis of the composer's performance, which was not particularly good'. Neither Prokofiev nor Shostakovich, he said, present their works very well, and Prokofiev, especially, tended to spoil the effect with his dry articulation ('*bezumno vïstukivayet*').[12] If performed by a real quartet, Shaporin thought it might well sound wonderful. Nemirovich-Danchenko supported this, contending that such a musician as Prokofiev could not be left without a prize, and Myaskovsky reminded KSP members of the unfair treatment Prokofiev had received the previous year:

I remember last year how Mikhail Borisovich was saying that [Prokofiev] had done little for the people. He works like a man possessed, and he composes a mind-boggling quantity of music that is never less than first-class. After *Alexander Nevsky*, he managed to write *Zdravitsa*, then a grandiose piano sonata (the Sixth), the opera *Duenna*, two acts of a ballet, and then this Suite [*1941*] and the Quartet.[13]

Khrapchenko, ignoring Myaskovsky, took issue with Nemirovich-Danchenko, pointing out that the latter had failed to argue in favour of the work itself, as opposed to its composer. And that work had left scant impression on Khrapchenko: 'It is on the level of his usual work – if we went with this, he'd receive a prize every year.'[14] The conservative Goldenweiser, surprisingly, came to the Quartet's defence. As he explained, he certainly was not automatically in favour of Prokofiev's works (his colleagues knew that he held Rachmaninov and Medtner in greatest esteem). Taste aside, Goldenweiser said that Prokofiev was certainly one of the most outstanding composers alive, and this Quartet was striking and likeable, so why not award it a prize? Goldenweiser also had a shrewd point to make about this work: there was a need for 'cultivated music' for the republics, which lacked it, and this Quartet certainly answered this need for Kabardino-Balkaria.[15] Even Hajibeyov felt prompted to speak positively about the Quartet, which said much, since this grand man of Azeri music was usually quite scathing about other composers' attempts to write 'national' music for the republics (he was particularly jealous of Khachaturian).[16]

Khrapchenko then decided to move the goalposts:

> Allow me to digress a little. We must explain to the people, why, in 1941, in the midst of such terrible events, this piece ought to be commended – because it is musically superior? Or because it helps the people? What has a greater resonance with the people? We cannot allow the public aspect to slip out of sight. From the standpoint of pure art, I would award a prize to *Romeo and Juliet*, but what would the people say? Could we really give a prize to a beautiful painting of lilacs?[17]

The reference to lilacs was immediately understood by everyone present: the KSP had more than once debated the work of the eminent painter Pyotr Konchalovsky and, in particular, his still lifes featuring lilacs. Reinforcing his point with a less pretty subject, Khrapchenko also recalled Konchalovsky's masterly painting of a hanging carcass, a classic still-life theme. It was also difficult to see the significance of this painterly tour de force when the war was in full swing. The parallel drawn between Prokofiev and Konchalovsky was loaded: the painter was well known not only for his technical mastery, but also for his avoidance of Soviet themes. The pairing was unfair to Prokofiev, since he had certainly not avoided Soviet themes in his work. At the same time, we can perhaps detect a hint of Khrapchenko's inner struggle between his ministerial voice and the personal opinion that can only be found between the lines. Let us hear one of his statements again: 'From the standpoint of pure art, I would award a prize to *Romeo and Juliet*, but what would the people say?'

Prokofiev's ballet *Romeo and Juliet*, it has to be said, was never considered for a nomination on the basis of its score, although the leading ballerina Galina Ulanova had received a Stalin Prize largely because of her Juliet. From the KSP transcripts, we can sense that Ulanova's Juliet – shaped, of course, by Prokofiev's music – provided audiences with some of the most sublime, heart-stopping moments that could ever be experienced in the theatre.[18] Although it can be difficult for us to understand today, Soviet musicians of the time heard the orchestral suites in concert first, and only afterwards came to know the complete score through the ballet, which seemed less gripping from a purely musical point of view. This might well be the reason why the ballet score failed to pick up a nomination. Khrapchenko, however, seems split between what he personally likes and what he thinks is right for 'the people': he could appreciate *Romeo*, along with the rest of the cultivated audience for high art, but the rest of the population should be offered something else. Such sentiments were by no means unique to Khrapchenko; other KSP members would likewise admit to comprehending and enjoying artworks which they still felt duty-bound to decry as 'formalist' for the sake of the people. One of the more extreme cases was the literary editor Pyotr Tarasenkov, who privately collected first editions of symbolist poets while in public he was a vigorous detractor of symbolism.[19]

If Prokofiev's Quartet or Konchalovsky's lilacs were not significant enough as public art, then what was? Mass songs appeared on the list of nominations for the first time, and two composers, Alexander Aleksandrov (the author of the stirring and sombre iconic song 'Holy War') and Matvei Blanter (the author of the celebrated 'Katyusha') were competing not just against each other, but with composers of symphonies and operas – separate nominations by genre hadn't yet been introduced within the Music category. Members of the KSP met this novelty with suspicion, especially with regard to Blanter, whose music was often sneered at as lowbrow. It took Khrapchenko some effort to convince them that the mass song was a valid genre, eligible for nomination:

> I can't agree with this division between real music that has grandeur and respectability, and, on the other hand, light music that is defective in some way, that fails to be 'real music'. The issue here is not respectability, but something else entirely: the force of the emotional impact on the listener. If a song has feelings, emotions, if there is life in it, if the song excites people, fires them up and calls them to noble deeds, then it is true art. [...] At the front and in the rear these days, they are not singing [symphonic] poems, but mass songs rather, and so I insist that mass songs should take their proper place on the Stalin Prize list.[20]

Nemirovich-Danchenko, however, continued to grumble:

> This is what we'll end up doing: Aleksandrov will be a prizewinner, and
> Prokofiev won't. It turns out that Aleksandrov judged the time and the place
> for his little gift very well. [...] If we give a prize to Aleksandrov, but not to
> Prokofiev for his Quartet, then it is not actually the music that we are
> judging.[21]

The incompleteness of transcripts for 1942 prevents us from knowing whether
any further KSP discussion of music candidates took place. Members were
expecting a final vote in Moscow, but this did not take place because of logis-
tical difficulties, and in the end, Khrapchenko collated the results of two separate votes, in Kuybyshev and Tbilisi. All Prokofiev managed to garner was five
votes in Tbilisi (the five individuals can be deduced from the quotations above),
while in Kuybyshev his work was neither heard nor balloted. Aleksandrov beat
him with nine votes (among his songs was the Bolshevik Party anthem, which
was later to become the national anthem of the USSR), while Shostakovich's
unassailable Seventh Symphony received twenty-one in total, the maximum
possible. Another mass-song writer, Vladimir Zakharov, managed to receive an
award without ever passing through the ballots of the KSP in either location:
his name, as we can establish from the documents, was added by Khrapchenko.[22]
It is worth taking note of the name Zakharov, who will return several times
during the course of this chapter, becoming a kind of personal nemesis for
Prokofiev. Despite receiving the award as a composer, Zakharov had likely
benefited from the great symbolic value of the Pyatnitsky Choir's fourteen-
month tour of unoccupied Soviet territories. Although the choir never
performed at the front, their songs reached the front line through documentary reels.[23] Zakharov's songs displaced one of the 'national' nominations, an
Armenian opera *David Sasunsky* by Haro Stepanian. The fourth and final
award went to another 'national' work, by the Georgian composer Shalva
Mshvelidze, whose work was well received by the KSP: a four-movement
'symphonic poem' *Zviadauri*, based on a folk-style epic by the classic Georgian
poet Vazha Pshavela.[24]

What did this second snub mean to Prokofiev? Amidst the general hard-
ships of evacuation, a composer's official status could mean the difference
between starvation and a decent ration. Prokofiev's partner, Mira Mendelson,
noted in her diary that his lack of a 'special' ration meant a condescending attitude from the administrator of the evacuees in Tbilisi. 'Sometimes,' she wrote
with bitterness, 'Seryozha receives a laureate's meal: although he is not a laureate,
this means that we then have some meat, which we cannot afford to buy at the

market.'[25] But this unhappy situation was about to change. Although Khrapchenko had just sunk another Prokofiev nomination, this was to be his last démarche: from now on, his attitude would change to one of unquestionable support. Why, then, did Khrapchenko's attitude to Prokofiev undergo a fundamental change at this point? The key, it seems, lies in the very trip to Tbilisi we have just discussed.

While in Tbilisi during February 1942, Khrapchenko attended to business beyond the KSP's duties. Nemirovich-Danchenko reported that the minister had made quite an impression on the evacuated intelligentsia: 'he is energetic, active, attentive, simple, he inspires trust, doesn't flatter, and he is neither too formal nor overfamiliar [ne amikoshonstvuyet]'.[26] Khrapchenko visited Prokofiev twice to hear the music of the new opera War and Peace,[27] and afterwards, in April, as soon as he learnt the opera was ready, he summoned Prokofiev to Moscow for an audition.[28] Well attuned to the demands of the time, Khrapchenko immediately saw the potential of War and Peace to become a project of national importance, one that he could not afford to let slip.

Prokofiev, however, did not travel to Moscow, and the audition at the ministry took place without him on 12 May 1942 (the opera was heard in a four-hands arrangement played by Svyatoslav Richter and Anatoly Vedernikov). Prokofiev anxiously awaited the results of the audition, but Khrapchenko only wrote back on 19 June. This letter, containing Khrapchenko's personal evaluation of the opera at some length, was coupled with a detailed analysis produced by the musicologist Semyon Shlifshteyn, Khrapchenko's assistant in this matter.[29] These two letters are unique, striking documents that reveal the extent of the government's intervention into Prokofiev's creative process at this point. While both letters contained much praise, especially of the lyrical scenes of the opera, they also offered strong criticisms and an array of constructive suggestions showing how the mass scenes of the opera could be improved. Shlifshteyn's letter even proposed certain concrete musical solutions to the opera's problems. If ever the government directed a composer's pen in the most literal sense of the phrase, this was a case in point.

Prokofiev was indignant at the outset, but he acquiesced, accepting, step by step, nearly all of the suggestions for revision. Khrapchenko, Shlifshteyn and later also Eisenstein and the conductor Samosud all became Prokofiev's collaborators in the shaping of dramatic structure of the mass scenes in War and Peace.

On 16 January 1943, Prokofiev played the opera, partially revised, at a Bolshoi Theatre audition, where the premiere was being planned. At this point, on the threshold of producing an epic national opera, he was receiving every kind of encouragement from state officials, and a Stalin Prize, which was well overdue, was to become one of the incentives. Another was Khrapchenko's promise, in January, of a new apartment in Moscow for Prokofiev.[30] And indeed, these tokens of attention were much needed, since Prokofiev was easily offended, and in the absence of incentives would become bogged down in arguments about the changes, or simply procrastinate.

We can also speculate that Khrapchenko's closer acquaintance with Prokofiev's music and the man himself simply won him over on a personal basis. Through his work on the revisions he became, to some extent, a collaborator in the opera. As a literary scholar with a particular interest in Tolstoy (he later published a monograph on him), Khrapchenko would have been well aware of the impossible challenge Prokofiev had taken upon himself in *War and Peace*. Let us not forget that Khrapchenko's wife, the musicologist Tamara Tsytovich, was (or perhaps at this point became) an ardent admirer of Prokofiev, and eventually produced a reverent essay on him, in 1945.[31] And even though *War and Peace* was to be derailed more than once and in the end never brought Prokofiev the status of a national artistic hero during his lifetime, it greatly advanced his Soviet reputation, from the early stages of the project onwards.

Success! The Seventh Sonata

The backstage goings-on over *War and Peace* were perhaps the most important reason why Prokofiev finally received a prize in the spring of 1943. The nature of the winning piece itself seems to have been less important, hence Prokofiev's own surprise when the Seventh Sonata won him the prize: '[W]hy would they give [the prize] to such a convoluted piece when it had been denied to pieces that were simpler and more transparent?'[32] In January 1943, Prokofiev played his Seventh Sonata for invited composers and musicologists at the ministry and received a very good review in the ministry-run paper, *Literatura i iskusstvo* (Literature and the Arts). The lyrical and impassioned slow movement and the frantic toccata finale prompted most of the praise, but it was remarkable that the challenging, more-or-less atonal first movement did not sink the nomination – much milder fare was dismissed as 'formalist' on other occasions. This was the first piano sonata of Prokofiev's Soviet years, and it was noted and welcome that the Seventh was grander and more serious than his earlier essays in the genre; one critic wrote of the work's 'epic scale'.[33] On 18 January, Richter gave the sonata a powerful and memorable premiere in the October Hall of the House of the Unions in Moscow: as he himself remembered, after the applause died down he repeated the entire sonata for the musicians, including Oistrakh and Shebalin, who did not want to leave.[34]

The Music Section originally wanted to nominate Prokofiev for lifetime achievement (an option that was now being made available for the first time), but it decided instead to nominate two specific works, the Seventh Sonata and a new set of piano pieces (most likely the *Cinderella* piano arrangements of op. 95). The discussion was very brief, with Shaporin simply stating that had the KSP heard Richter's performance, they would have granted a prize to the Sonata straight away.[35] It was passed for a first-class prize (it received fifteen votes in all, eleven for a first and four for a second). Khrapchenko, at long last, desisted from meddling, although Agitprop later reduced the award to the second class.[36]

On 10 March, Levon Atovmyan[37] wrote to Prokofiev:

> The Stalin Committee completed its work. Waiting for the confirmation. You must know the preliminary results: you, Shebalin, Khachaturian, Koval, Sedoi, Ashrafiy, Ivanov-Radkevich.[38]

On 24 March, after the results were out, Atovmyan was at last able to send Prokofiev a congratulatory telegram,[39] and two days later, a letter. In the letter, the matter is referred to euphemistically and with a curious slant:

> [...] I feel somehow that my conscience is not clear (as would many who realize what role you play in music), because you are the first who had the right and who should have been the first to receive what has been fulfilled only today. And in a sense, we need to apologize to you for the fact that our congratulations are slightly belated. But, as they say, 'the [river] ice has broken up', and now we can and must expect the way ahead to be clear in accordance with the scale of your oeuvre and your significance in music.[40]

The use of 'we' here is not fanciful. Not that there is any reason to suspect that Atovmyan had any influence on the awards – the reason for his contrition lies

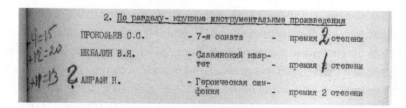

Fig. 7. Shcherbakov's copy of the KSP list of nominations, presumably with his markings: Prokofiev's Sonata receives a second-class prize instead of the first; Shebalin's Quartet the reverse; Ashrafiy's nomination has a question mark next to it. RGASPI, fond 17, op. 125, ye. kh. 127, l. 26.

deeper. It was Atovmyan who a decade earlier played an important part in bringing about Prokofiev's move to the USSR, attracting him with promises of an illustrious career and elite social status.[41] Atovmyan, even though he had then been acting on higher instructions, was implicated in the whole business of Prokofiev's repatriation. He could not help feeling guilty that the promises had not been fulfilled until now.

Yet Atovmyan was right: the ice *had* been broken. Prokofiev hurried to order new letterhead paper with the word 'laureate' on it, the key to new privileges. A few months later, Prokofiev was further reassured that this first success was not a flash in the pan, and that he was now officially in favour. On 23 July 1943, Khrapchenko proposed to Stalin and Molotov that Prokofiev should be awarded the Order of the Red Banner of Labour and the title of Merited Art Worker, and in his letter of support, he already designated Prokofiev as a Stalin Prize laureate.[42] Now Prokofiev was going to find out how true a popular Russian saying was: *den'gi k den'gam* (money goes to money).

The Windfall

The following year, 1944, Prokofiev once again provided the KSP with an array of possible nominations. His cantata, *The Ballad of an Unknown Boy*, is sometimes expressionistic in style, and it is hardly surprising that this harrowing work failed to command universal support in the Music Section. They switched their attention to the Flute Sonata, a piece that is bright and melodious, and superbly crafted – perfect fare for a prize. An audition for the KSP was set up in the Beethoven Hall (the former royal foyer of the Bolshoi Theatre). Afterwards, KSP members were convinced that the flautist, Nikolai Kharkovsky, had failed to do justice to the sonata.[43] The sculptor Sergei Merkurov could hardly contain his anger:

> I was sitting in the Beethoven Hall, listening, and such ennui [*toska*] possessed me. I thought of my own childhood, of sheep and imagined a [shepherd] fellow sitting down next to me and playing the flute. That would have been great in comparison. This is my opinion.
>
> Now they say that the flautist was poor. Was he by any chance drunk? He simply floored Prokofiev. What I heard in the Beethoven Hall was impossible.[44]

Another audition was held. Oddly, Myaskovsky was pointedly negative, finding the work marred by its use of 'Western-European technique, so that the music is assembled rather than created'. By contrast, Khrapchenko was happy to throw his support behind the piece.[45] The tables had turned, and he now appeared as a loyal admirer of Prokofiev – to the detriment of Shostakovich, as it happens (this will be taken up on Shostakovich's side in the next chapter).

In the end, the Sonata missed the target by just one vote, whereupon Shaporin, Samosud, Glière, the KSP chairman Moskvin and (somewhat perversely) Myaskovsky, wrote a joint letter asking the government to make a special dispensation and award the Sonata a prize.[46] Whether this would have happened, we cannot tell, because the awards were postponed and then doubled up with the following year's harvest.

By the time the KSP gathered to discuss this double list in 1945, Prokofiev had provided two weightier pieces that took precedence over the Flute Sonata, namely, the monumental Fifth Symphony and the equally grand, but much more private and demanding Eighth Piano Sonata. They were jointly nominated for a prize, and, surprisingly, both were passed. There was a minimum of discussion, limited to the following brief exchange:

> *Glière:* Those who have heard these wonderful works know that there is no argument here on the grounds of accessibility or inaccessibility [*dokhodit ili ne dokhodit*]. The music is wonderful both in terms of musical content and orchestration [*sic*]. I think the value of these works is incontrovertible.
> *[Alexander] Aleksandrov:* Is he nominated for two works: both the Sonata and the Symphony?
> *Goldenweiser:* The Music Section considers these to be the most outstanding symphonic [*sic*] works of Prokofiev, very vivid and strong from a technical point of view. The musicians are unanimous on this count.
> *Mikhoels:* The symphony is wonderful.[47]

When we realize that this brief exchange took place after a lengthy two-season battle over Shostakovich's Eighth Symphony (to be witnessed in the next chapter), we cannot fail to be struck by this extraordinary contrast. Somehow Prokofiev managed to shed entirely his dubious émigré status in the space of two years, to become a safe pair of hands, an artist who could be nodded through at a KSP meeting – and all this without artistic compromise. While the Symphony successfully combined wide appeal with a high level of artistry, the Sonata would surely have been found highly problematic if any of Shostakovich's detractors had troubled themselves to listen to it. The problems had even been flagged up in a review by Izrael Nestyev, who complained of lyrical episodes that were 'too cryptic', and elsewhere he found 'a harsh discordance of structural layering'.[48] But the public profile of a piano sonata is very slight compared to that of a symphony (particularly in the Soviet Union, where new symphonies could win a large audience), and it seems most likely that the Sonata slipped through without being heard by most KSP members – which only underlines how much trust was now placed in Prokofiev. And so, the Symphony and Sonata received thirty votes out of a possible thirty-two (twenty-six for the first degree, four for a second).

But this was not the end of Prokofiev's good fortune: he managed to win another prize in the same round (the awards for 1943/4, which were given out in January 1946).[49] This was the shared first prize for the music to Eisenstein's legendary film *Ivan the Terrible* (Part I). Two prizes in one year? Prokofiev's name did indeed appear in two places on the published list, even though prose descriptions referred to him as having received *a* prize, in the singular, for three musical works. Indeed, it would have seemed improper to emphasize his double award, since this was simply not supposed to happen. It turns out that the KSP had been aware of this possibility, and had actually made a provision that if the film was passed, then Prokofiev's soundtrack should be combined with the Fifth Symphony and the Eighth Sonata for a single prize.[50]

How did it happen? Eisenstein's *Ivan* was much anticipated: it was set to be the most significant response to Stalin's appeal for Ivan the Terrible to be portrayed as a national hero.[51] Various novels and plays about Ivan appeared in the wake of this appeal, but Eisenstein's project carried official status from the start, to the extent that some KSP members raised the issue of giving a prize to Eisenstein simply for the newly published scenario, before a single camera had been set up in the film studios. This was unprecedented, since a film scenario is not an independent literary work. Yet, when the film itself came out, the KSP members took fright. Even to the most broad-minded of them the film seemed formalist because it was calculated and operatic, with no concern for historical verisimilitude. Prokofiev's music was also controversial.[52] Not that dislike can always be written off as purely ideological: Myaskovsky, for example, wrote in his diary that the film was 'giftless', and Prokofiev's music consisted of 'grunting' (*khryukayushchaya*).[53]

In any case, *Ivan the Terrible* failed to receive enough votes. But what the KSP rejected, the Politburo Commission rewarded, most likely because Stalin's personal approval of the film was much clearer to them.[54] And because this was a high-level decision, no one in the KSP was informed and able to check the details. By this circuitous route, Prokofiev's name showed up in two award categories. In this round of awards, made public in January 1946, he must have received 100,000 roubles for the Symphony and the Sonata, and around another 10,000 as a member of the *Ivan the Terrible* team. A windfall, indeed!

Only a few months later, the following round of awards was rushed through, for works of 1945; the short interval was to ensure that the Stalin Prize would not continue running a year or two behind. Prokofiev was again at the forefront, thanks to his new ballet, *Cinderella*, which was already running both at the Bolshoi and at the Kirov. And once again, there was no discussion: Glière referred to this nomination as 'music everyone knows',[55] while Fadeyev, in his report to the government, said its status was 'incontrovertible'.[56] In the papers distributed to the Politburo Commission, *Cinderella* appeared with the following blurb, as safe and bland as can be imagined:

> The ballet *Cinderella* was written during the Great Patriotic War on the plot of a well-known folk fairy tale. The music of the ballet is vivid and melodic. The work represents a significant landmark in Soviet music theatre. The composer takes the best traditions of Tchaikovsky's and Glazunov's classical ballets a step further.[57]

Once again, a first-class prize was assured, and this time there is no cause for surprise, since *Cinderella* was indeed very much a ballet for the Soviet court. Prokofiev had clearly acted upon the dancers' criticisms levelled at *Romeo and Juliet*: that the music was undanceable. Compared to *Romeo*, *Cinderella* is both more danceable and incomparably grander, so the references to Tchaikovsky and Glazunov in the blurb were not merely an idle puff – Prokofiev was indeed making a contribution to this tradition, even though the music is very much his own.

Compare this, however, with the award received by Prokofiev the following year, in 1947, for his sombre and introverted Violin Sonata. The Sonata was played in an audition called by the KSP on 4 April 1947, by the great duo of David Oistrakh and Lev Oborin. In spite of this, we find no spontaneous excitement in the transcript, either for the work or for this performance. Instead, we have a brief reference to the work from Glière, which is entirely positive, but also entirely matter of fact: 'I can state that it suffers from no low spots [*provalov*]. It sounds like a unified work, very significant and serious, and it will probably be performed everywhere.'[58]

The Politburo Commission received a description that was again positive, but only slightly more concrete: 'An outstanding work. The imagery of the Sonata is vivid, sincere and emotional. The music of the Sonata is steeped in Russian national colouring.'[59] Behind this bland endorsement lies an edgy, tormented and, some would say, profoundly tragic work in which Prokofiev himself imagined 'autumn evening wind blowing across a neglected cemetery grave'.[60] If a similar piece had been written by Shostakovich, it would have been taken apart, competing narratives would have been imposed and, after much argument, it would most likely have been rejected for pessimism, or at best, scraped in for a second prize. By contrast, the Prokofiev of the mid-1940s needs no discussion: he is a Soviet classic who can be nodded through by the KSP without the need for careful listening. The Violin Sonata received its first-class prize, carried through by Prokofiev's reputation.

Throughout this happy patch in Prokofiev's Soviet career, his music helped others to win further prizes that further enhanced his prestige. The Bolshoi production of *Cinderella* and its new production of *Romeo and Juliet* both received first-class prizes. Turning from Moscow to Leningrad, a first-class prize was awarded to the Kirov production of *War and Peace*, Part I. Prokofiev's score for *War and Peace* was not being considered at the time for a nomination, since the completion of the full opera was still pending.

Tragedy and Farce

As Richter recalled, musical life in Moscow during the first post-war years was unimaginable without Prokofiev's music: 'Prokofiev worked tirelessly. He tirelessly replenished the treasury of the latest classical works, so to speak.'[61] But a constant stream of awards received by a single individual could become unnerving and eventually intolerable even for his colleagues – even for some who had previously taken his side. Goldenweiser, for example, had ardently defended Prokofiev's music back in 1942. Now, in the autumn of 1947, we hear something else entirely:

> We have [, for example,] Prokofiev, an important composer. He is fifty-two or fifty-three years old. He can continue writing music for another thirty years, and every year he will produce a symphony or a concerto. Even today there's hardly room enough on his jacket for all the medals; he has five of them, and he will have twenty-five. Perhaps it would be easier simply to grant him a pension of 100,000 roubles a year for his great international artistic achievements.[62]

Goldenweiser was making a general point about prize inflation here, and only mentioned Prokofiev by way of illustration (he also mentioned Myaskovsky). Still, it is hard to hear these words as anything other than mockery aimed at Prokofiev personally. This seems to be borne out a few months later, when Goldenweiser eagerly jumped on the anti-formalist bandwagon (see Chapter 10).

With the debacle of 1948, Prokofiev's luck was over, and his status as a Soviet classic would not return within his lifetime. His music suddenly came under scrutiny, and his detractors woke up to its modernism. The new chairman of the Composers' Union, Tikhon Khrennikov, who had once attended Prokofiev's composition seminars,[63] now picked out his works one by one and demolished them with gusto in his speeches. Every turn of the melody and every harmonic modulation was now aesthetically and morally suspect.

It could be argued that, of all the victims of the 1948 campaign (which I discuss in more detail in Chapter 10), Prokofiev suffered the most protracted and cruel castigation, its devastating effect further aggravated by the arrest of his first wife Lina[64] and a catastrophic deterioration of his health. Those branded 'formalists' could not, of course, be nominated for a Stalin Prize in the aftermath (although they were not stripped of the prizes they had received). But after a two-year hiatus, the offenders were forgiven. Prokofiev's turn came in 1951, when the Music Section considered some of his new music for passing up to the KSP. There were two pieces, one a 'penitent' work, the oratorio *On Guard for Peace*, the other a suite for children, *Winter Bonfire*.[65] The Music Section had undergone an almost complete change in personnel in keeping with the 1948 resolution (see Appendix VIII) but it was now unanimous in its wish to support Prokofiev, quite possibly out of concern for his declining health. Nevertheless, there was disagreement over the value of the nominated works. Khrennikov, who was now chairman of the Music Section, worried whether the oratorio might prove controversial because, as he put it, there was 'a certain disorder in the music', but Khrennikov's friend Zakharov reassured him that the 'old Prokofiev' in the oratorio was redeemed by the presence of the 'new Prokofiev': the finale might not have come out well but the lullaby was just right. The musicologist Tamara Livanova, while speaking in support of the oratorio, warned that the *Bonfire* was weak. Khrennikov, too, thought that the *Bonfire* was 'rather pale', while Zakharov thought it pleasant enough.[66]

Although the KSP passed both works for a second-class prize, Agitprop did not consider the oratorio suitable for an award. In his report, the Agitprop official Vladimir Kruzhkov concluded that 'in many episodes the music does not fit the text and contains elements of formalism'. Agitprop's proposal was to give an award to the *Bonfire* Suite only, since it had received good press and was uncontroversial, but because it was a relatively slight work, Prokofiev would only receive a third-class prize in the category of 'small forms'.[67] This new class of prize, introduced in 1950, was never intended for artists of Prokofiev's stature, and so the award was going to seem more like another humiliation rather than a message of encouragement. One way to avoid this was simply to drop Prokofiev from that year's list, which is indeed what happened in one of the later Agitprop lists.[68] The final decision, however, reverted to the KSP's preference, which was to award a second-class prize for the two works together. Khrennikov later took credit for this:

When Prokofiev wrote *On Guard for Peace*, there was a lot of formalism there, but the government asked [*v pravitel'stve sprosili*]: 'Has he taken a step towards regeneration?', and I said, yes, and not just one step, but two. And I was told: 'If so, he has to be supported.'[69]

This conversation, if it actually took place, must have occurred during one of the expanded Politburo meetings to which Khrennikov was invited. If so, the voice we hear could very well be Stalin's.

This 'consolation prize' of 1952 proved to be Prokofiev's last Stalin award. Our story, however, continues, stretching a little beyond the lifetimes of both Prokofiev and Stalin. Prokofiev's health deteriorated steeply at the beginning of 1953, when the KSP began its deliberations on his Seventh Symphony. On 8 January, the Music Section broached the issue for the first time, and Khrennikov gave the discussion a positive impetus, with comments on the Symphony that indicated sincere enjoyment on his part.[70] Livanova, however, although not hostile, was condescending: the Symphony was playful and theatrical, in her eyes only a 'light' work. A week later, members of the plenary session listened to a recording of the Symphony, and a lively exchange of views ensued. Goldenweiser was the first to express delight in the melodiousness and lyricism of the music (now that Prokofiev was an underdog once more), and his comments immediately received support from two non-musicians, the choreographer Konstantin Sergeyev and the film director Mikhail Chiaureli.[71] Chiaureli was particularly effusive:

I think there is such obvious power in this music, and it is put together so brilliantly that we can undoubtedly consider it for a Stalin Prize. It is written magnificently, simply and melodiously, and it has been orchestrated in such a way that the music simply astonishes. From my point of view, it is an utterly incredible piece of music, and Prokofiev must be congratulated. [E]very movement has a clear structure. [...] [N]ational melody is always perceptible.[72]

The painter Vasily Yefanov lamented the fact that some of the members had not been able to hear the Symphony in concert. He said that he had always found Prokofiev's music beautiful in a lace-like, intricate way and yet somehow elusive – but this time, he relished the Symphony's broad and memorable melodies.[73]

Still, the Symphony also had its detractors. The secretary to the KSP, Vladimir Kemenov, and the composer Andriy Shtoharenko both claimed that they could not perceive the clarity and organic unity of form that others were talking about; the symphony was not equal to Tchaikovsky's, and they generally doubted its national roots. Shtoharenko failed to see how the finale was related to the first movement (even though Goldenweiser had pointed out the return of the broad lyrical theme of the first movement in the finale).[74] In response to these criticisms, Shostakovich took the floor and spoke at length and with enthusiasm. In fact, this may have been his most passionate speech in support of Prokofiev's music (if we discount what he said years earlier as a star-struck youth). Shrewdly, Shostakovich stressed that the work revealed the rich lyrical side of Prokofiev's gift, which had in the past been overshadowed by irony, sarcasm and the grotesque. For the doubters, he emphasized the contrast and unity of the four movements and even named the Russian symphonies the Seventh was following: Tchaikovsky's First, Kalinnikov's G minor and Borodin's unfinished Third. Like some of the preceding orators, he also spoke of the melodies:

> The melodies are very lengthy, but one listens to them with great interest, and they are easy to recall [...]. But perhaps this is not the main thing: some poor melodies can also be easily recalled, but these are very original, and their musical imagery has been perfected to the highest degree. [...] Just like *Romeo and Juliet*, this work presents the best side of Prokofiev's gift. This trend in Prokofiev's music is dear to me, and I hold this symphony in my affections.[75]

Given Shostakovich's dislike of much of Prokofiev's music, we could easily imagine that he chose to speak more out of common decency in the face of Prokofiev's physical frailty, rather than wholeheartedly. But the final flourish seems to be more personal. Perhaps he genuinely liked the music? Or perhaps again, he was cannily playing on the right strings for his audience, underplaying the grotesque in the Symphony and emphasizing its lyrical melody? He was, after all, an experienced and sophisticated player, unlike Prokofiev's friend Myaskovsky.

If the latter, then he anticipated an attack, which duly came from Livanova, who further developed the remarks she had made at the Music Section meeting. She saw the Symphony as toy-like, theatrical and buffoonish, a mere playing at symphonies rather than a real symphony, and certainly not a serious represen-tation of the 'typical images' and 'central ideas of our era' – in short, it was neither Realist nor Socialist.[76] This was Livanova's attempt to draw the bounda-ries of musical Socialist Realism in such a way as to exclude Prokofiev's playful-ness, no matter how benign it had become. Goldenweiser, remaining true to his reawakened support for Prokofiev, seemed offended by Livanova's remarks, and complained that instead of celebrating a great musical work, some colleagues attempted to tarnish it. 'Even Beethoven's Ninth is not free of faults,' he exclaimed.[77]

A couple of weeks later the Music Section went over the nominations once again, and this time another member was present, one quite capable of dragging the discussion down to the level of farce: Vladimir Zakharov, the director of the Pyatnitsky Folk Choir, whom we met on an earlier occasion when he joined his friend Khrennikov in Prokofiev's defence. This time, although Zakharov liked the work, he had a bee in his bonnet:

> I find Prokofiev's symphony more and more interesting every time, but much of it remains controversial. What of all these young people dancing the *galop*? They are running along the streets and pulling faces at everyone.[78]

If this comment seems cryptic to us, it was less so to the other members of the Music Section. The 'young people' Zakharov refers to were the hypothetical protagonists of the piece – it was only a rumour that Prokofiev's Seventh was inspired by 'our Soviet Youth'.[79] The *galop*, that fast 2/4 dance of French provenance, is indeed the musical topos used for the main theme of the finale. Zakharov, perhaps remembering that the cancan was one example of this dance, constructed a narrative of irreverence to use against Prokofiev. He went on to clarify:

> The ideological side of this work is controversial to say the least. We cannot ignore the fact that this is an inspired work, but neither should we close our eyes to the fact that Prokofiev's earlier pernicious direction, which represented his separation from life, can be felt here quite clearly. Our young people are not like that.[80]

Goldenweiser came to the Symphony's defence again, without directly addressing Zakharov's contention: 'If you take other Prokofiev works, such as his Sixth or Seventh Sonatas, they are full of formalist, modernist moments, while this symphony is written differently, with clear harmony.' The conversation drifted to the other new work by Prokofiev the KSP had heard: the Symphony-Concerto for cello and orchestra. Zakharov found it technically superb, but gloomy. Goldenweiser didn't like the Concerto either, finding it a striking but paradoxical work. The Symphony, he insisted, did not have these problems.[81] But Zakharov was not about to back down:

> There [in the Concerto] we have some kind of hopelessness, while here there is satire. Why should the merry-making young people make merry with the help of a *galop*? We have a huge number of means to portray

merry-making youth besides the *galop* – some other dances perhaps, but just not the *galop*.

'What about that little carillon in the finale?' enquired Livanova, perhaps provocatively, switching attention to the mysterious chimes of the finale's coda. Or was she, perhaps, only attempting to wean Zakharov off his *idée fixe*? 'They are showing their tongues,' he maintained, still taking offence at those insolent young people who supposedly inhabited the finale.

The discussion drifted on, and Zakharov, feeling he was on a roll, offered his prediction that Prokofiev's music would be played little in the future. What would survive, he told his fellow committee members, was the music of another candidate on the list, and that was ... Chistyakov.[82] The day drew to a close on a note of uncertainty.

Next day, however, Zakharov was eager to return to his *galop*-induced worries (like the dog to his own vomit, as Goldenweiser would have put it):

If we portray our youth in such a manner, *galop*ing along, pulling faces, etc., this is not our youth. [...] In the first three movements there are no such grimaces, but in the fourth the young people are represented by some kind of *galop*. One can show young people dancing, young people singing, young people marching in the streets, but young people dancing a *galop* with all that 'brl, brl', with those harps, with so many decorations, these are grimaces of some sort, which elicit a kind of protest. [...][83]

Fig. 8. Vladimir Zakharov speaking (the event is most likely connected with the Pyatnitsky Choir, Zakharov's assistant director Pyotr Kazmin is also present, at the far left of the picture). RGALI, fond 2628, op. 1, ye. kh. 35, l. 1.

The 'brl, brl' of the harps needs a little explaining. Here they are in the score:

Livanova, who had not yet declared her hand the previous day, now sided firmly with Zakharov. She certainly admired the work, and yet something made her uneasy, preventing her from enjoying it fully. She sensed an undercurrent of sarcasm, or some other vestige of the old Prokofiev. The discussion once again ended unresolved:

Shostakovich: I [. . .] consider it a superb work. [. . .]
Shaporin [to Zakharov]: I don't hear sarcasm. Why can't we imagine a skating-rink in the fourth movement – that the young people are skating. This is how I perceive those harps [see fig. 9].
Zakharov: They are just showing their tongues.
Khrennikov [evidently tiring of Zakharov]: We're leaving [the Symphony] on the list.[84]

On this grotesque note, alas, ended the last KSP discussion of Prokofiev's music in the composer's lifetime. Before they could settle the matter, Prokofiev died, as did Stalin. After a long hiatus, the Music Section returned to the issue of the Seventh Symphony on 30 March 1954:

Khrennikov: At our meeting [at the Composers' Union], he was passed for the second class.
Goldenweiser: The master is dead. The Symphony is enjoying great success. We need to award it a first-class prize. This is his swan song. I propose a first.
Zakharov: And I would support a second. [. . .][85]

The votes were split again: five for a first, four for a second. A similar dialogue continued in the plenary session, until someone threw in a fresh idea: why not add *The Stone Flower*, Prokofiev's last ballet, to the Symphony, and boost the nomination that way?[86] This, in the end, proved a winning strategy, and the symphony/ballet combination received an overwhelming vote for a first-class prize with thirty-nine votes for a first, eleven for a second and four for a third.[87]

A Tale of Two Endings

In one of Mstislav Rostropovich's interviews[88] we find an intriguing story that would explain why the published score of the Seventh Symphony includes an

Fig. 9. Fragment from the finale of Prokofiev's Seventh Symphony, the passage referred to by Zakharov: 'a galop with all that "brl, brl", with those harps'.

alternative ending: as in the better-known version, there is the same slow coda, with mesmerizing bell-like sonorities, but instead of fading away, the *galop* theme returns briefly, giving the Symphony an energetic close. The poignant mystery of the original ending is put aside for a few brilliant, applause-inducing final bars. Conductors could choose which way to conclude the Symphony. According to Rostropovich, the idea for the alternative ending came from the conductor Samuil Samosud, who persuaded Prokofiev that the planned ending would ensure that the Symphony could only rise to the second class, whereas the return of the *galop* theme at the end would be enough to raise it to the first class (Samosud was speaking here for himself only, since he was no longer a KSP member). Whatever scruples Prokofiev might have had, they were outweighed by the prospect of an extra 50,000 roubles. The original idea could still be preserved in the score, and according to Rostropovich, Prokofiev still preferred it and hoped that it would eventually establish itself. The story finds corroboration in the documents of Prokofiev's last year of life, as Simon Morrison has shown: the conversation with Samosud took place immediately after he conducted the Symphony's premiere on 11 October 1952, which was attended by members of the KSP. But Morrison gives the story a slightly different twist: the new ending was a stipulation of the KSP, to render the work eligible for a prize.[89]

But if the idea came from the KSP, then it is very strange indeed that the KSP transcripts do not contain a single reference to the issue of the two endings. Most of the debate, as we have seen, circled around the nature of the finale as a whole (Zakharov's *galopshchina*), that is, whether a light-hearted and playful representation of exuberance and joy was convincing after the other, more serious movements. Similar concerns had already arisen with Shostakovich's *galop*-like finales (in his Sixth and Ninth Symphonies), and even with the care-free but elusive ending of the Quintet. Those critics most attuned to Socialist Realism felt that such finales, while certainly optimistic, avoided the challenge of an emphatically positive, monumental and visionary ending – Socialist Realism's Beethovenian ideal for large-scale music. This line of reasoning would make it all the more bizarre for the KSP, after some strangely undocu-mented discussion, to require a repetition of the *galop* theme after the chiming coda, since this could not have helped the Symphony's prospects for a prize, and might even have damaged them.

And yet the score undeniably contains the alternative ending with the return of the *galop*. Taking into account all the direct and lateral evidence discussed above, the most plausible explanation would seem to run along the following lines: the members simply did not get a chance to hear the altered ending (which Samosud performed on 6 November 1952) and they were not aware of it. They would either have heard the premiere of the Symphony live, with the quiet ending, or in recording, again with the quiet ending (this recording is still available to us, so there is no doubt about the ending). If, by any chance, some members of the KSP had heard both endings prior to the March 1954 meeting, they said nothing about it. The lack of evidence for any stipulation from the KSP leaves us with one culprit: Samosud was in all prob-ability the source of the idea for an alternative ending. This returns us to Rostropovich's version of events, but we would have to treat with scepticism the claim that the change was motivated by the prospects of a higher award, since this is not only lacking in logic but was never put into use in prize discussions before or after the composer's death.

That said, one sympathetic KSP member did express deeper concerns about the Symphony's (original) outcome – it was the painter Gerasimov, who identified himself as an ardent music lover. He had heard the Symphony in concert, and was deeply moved by it. Yet, he had his own, personal account to settle with Prokofiev. 'To me,' he said, 'in the finale the music begins to fall apart and grow difficult. The coda, those final chords, poses a difficulty for me, and I don't see that final exhalation, when the artist's arms embrace the world.'[90] There is an interesting ambiguity here. 'Final exhalation' suggests a final accept-ance, a submission to 'fate', like the end of Mahler 9. 'The artist's arms embrace the world' seems like a clear reference to the end of Beethoven 9, which would fit Socialist Realist aesthetics better. But whichever possibility Gerasimov had in mind, it is clear that the perfunctory return of the *galop* would not have satis-fied him. He neither knew of it, nor would he have accepted it.

We have to agree that at the end Prokofiev, or his authorial persona in the Symphony, does not welcome us with outstretched arms in a universal embrace. Those 'difficult' chords, disjointed and disorientating, set a strict limit to the exciting whirlwind of life, as at the end of Cinderella's ball, and in the percus-sion, empty time ticks away. Prokofiev's illness certainly would have made him reflect on mortality, even if he might have hoped the Seventh Symphony was not to be his last. The KSP musicians would have been aware of how precarious Prokofiev's health was by the time of the January 1953 meeting, but few of the non-musicians would have, although, as we have just seen, Gerasimov very perceptively characterized the ending when he expressed his unease. An arbi-trary petering out after a life of overflowing vitality, an end without reconcilia-tion – in these terms and with that music, we can see Prokofiev's own untimely death. Who knows? If his health had held up a little longer, the post-Stalin dispensation might have raised his morale sufficiently to pull him out of danger, and he could have flourished in the Thaw years.

Epilogue

The post-Stalin round of prizes never yielded anything, whether in the form of money or medals, but the saga of the prize for the Seventh only reached its end in 1957, when the work was awarded a Lenin Prize. The new Lenin Prize Committee, which included some of the KSP veterans, had to share out eight (*only* eight between all the arts!) awards for the works of the past five years. The late Prokofiev's greatness seemed finally to have come into full focus, enhanced by recent productions of the complete *War and Peace*, and this was the last award that could be granted to him. Khrennikov's tone with regard to Prokofiev was transformed: he spoke of Prokofiev as 'a phenomenon of grandeur',[91] 'a great Russian composer' and 'a national artist'.[92] In the light of the 20th Party Congress, which officially turned the country away from Stalinism, the shadows of the 1948 Resolution were fast fading – in fact, its revocation, initiated by the same Khrennikov, was only a year away.

Since the Lenin Prize rules made no provision for a lifetime award, the Seventh Symphony effectively represented Prokofiev's whole oeuvre. Khrennikov now described it as 'an amazing work – very life-affirming and melodious, very youthful in sentiment'.[93] Five years earlier, some found rhythms in the symphony that were incompatible with 'our Soviet youth', but now it became the repository of 'our life', especially since the comparable piece under consideration at the time was Shostakovich's Tenth, which still remained controversial. Shostakovich, moved by the radio broadcast of *War and Peace*, even insisted that his own symphony be taken off the list to allow Prokofiev more votes. And so Prokofiev's Seventh graced the 1957 award list, which, as the chairman Tikhonov said, 'we are not ashamed to publish and display to the whole world'.[94] Thus, together with other deserving winners of 1957, Prokofiev's Seventh Symphony ushered in the Thaw.

CHAPTER FOUR

SHOSTAKOVICH: HITS AND MISSES

Shostakovich has a unique profile among twentieth-century composers. Most of his musical contemporaries are little known to the wider educated public in the West today, but Shostakovich is not only a regular feature in concert programmes and radio schedules, but he and his music have generated public polemics that are usually absent from musical discourse. Since this has much to do with our intense interest in Stalinism and the weight of extramusical associations that have accumulated around Shostakovich's work over the years, we may find it difficult to imagine how his music was received by its first audiences. How did Shostakovich's Soviet audience hear this music before anyone could associate it (at least openly) with the strictures of life under Stalin, before anyone had read Volkov's *Testimony*? I must admit that the extent and intensity of Shostakovich discussions in the KSP transcripts came as a surprise to me. No other composer comes close – the continuous debate around Shostakovich stands as absolutely central in Soviet music discourse. What is particularly revealing is how much of their own personalities the speakers were tempted to uncover, how Shostakovich's music touched their own raw nerves, and how persistent some of them were in listening to those demanding scores, fighting tedium in expectation of great rewards. If this wasn't music for the people (as the officials so often insisted), then it was definitely music for the Soviet intelligentsia.

The roller coaster of Shostakovich's prize trajectory was no less extreme than Prokofiev's; it merely swerves and dips at different times. We have already had a chance to witness the reception of the Piano Quintet (first-class prize No. 1 for Shostakovich), which reflected both popular enthusiasm and official approval. In the next prize round, Shostakovich received his first-class prize No. 2 for a very different work, the Seventh Symphony. Unlike the Quintet, the Symphony had no audition and no discussion before the vote, and was nominated for the prize even before its public premiere on 5 March 1942. Those members of the KSP who had been evacuated to Kuybyshev, the place of the premiere, had an opportunity to hear it in rehearsal, while those in Tbilisi either had to rely on their own score-reading skills (even Goldenweiser found it hard to grasp the whole)[1] or on Alexei Tolstoy's glowing report from the rehearsals, published in *Pravda*.[2] At the Tbilisi plenary meeting of 19 February, Khrapchenko simply said: 'I think there is no need to discuss it, since everything is perfectly clear.'[3] The Symphony followed in the wake of its fame, thanks to Shostakovich's press interviews and the performances of individual movements (in piano arrangements at the ministry).

Eighth Symphony (I)

It was a different story with the next symphony, the Eighth, which prompted an extraordinarily long and tense debate on various musical issues. Due to the break in the award cycle, the debate of 1944 had to be picked up again in 1945; what is most remarkable, though, is that the two phases of the debate had the opposite outcomes – the work truly tested the boundaries of musical Socialist Realism. By drawing many non-musicians into fierce plenary discussions, the Symphony staked a claim on its extraordinary importance for society as a whole.

The Eighth was written in 1943 and first came up for consideration in the spring of 1944, when the war had already passed its turning point but was still far from over. Shostakovich's status at the time was extremely high: he was a heroic figure who had served his country and its Allies with his Seventh Symphony. The Eighth was markedly different, not so clearly programmatic and more demanding of the listeners' concentration, swinging between austere stasis and expressionist assaults on the senses. Notably, it had a muted ending, perhaps of quiet affirmation, but certainly not a standard Socialist Realist apotheosis: one critic compared it to Chekhov's 'We shall rest'.[4] The Symphony's language was also found trying by many, even by Myaskovsky, who came to enjoy it fully only on the third listening.[5]

The discussion was led by Goldenweiser, whose initial statement was similar to Alexei Tolstoy's 1941 assessment of Sholokhov's *And Quiet Flows the Don*, balancing the ideological shortcomings with compensating aesthetic virtues:

> [...] I regard the Eighth Symphony to be one of Shostakovich's most brilliant achievements: in terms of the music, it stands much higher than the Seventh, not to mention the Sixth. It contains plenty of musical material that's strong, vivid and original. It's presented with great mastery and the handling of the orchestra is almost unsurpassed, the last word.

There are no purely musical faults in this work. Perhaps there are some longueurs, and perhaps the language is not laconic enough. It has extraordinarily powerful moments. In any case, this is a wonderful work from a musical point of view.

I'll give my impression as a music lover, rather than as a musician (and in listening to music, I always distinguish between professional listening and the times when I'm transformed into a music lover): then I must say that this work made a great impression on me, one that lasted a long time. I listened to the symphony four times through.

But there are, in my view, certain ideological shortcomings: there's the fact that this work is extremely pessimistic. In our days, although we are going through much hardship, we still expect something that will rise up over our painful experiences. But the Eighth Symphony gives the impression that it portrays with huge power all the darkness and pain that undoubtedly have a place in our experiences.[6]

This conflict between aesthetics and ideology was complicated in Shostakovich's case by the issue of accessibility. This point was introduced into the discussion by the leading Socialist Realist painter, Alexander Gerasimov, creator of the enormous cityscape-cum-portrait *Stalin and Voroshilov in the Kremlin*. Gerasimov said that he could understand Beethoven (and we have previously seen that he was sensitive to Prokofiev's virtues), but Shostakovich, for him, was quite another matter. Gerasimov's statement of personal opinion sparked a more general debate on the comprehensibility of music:

> *Gerasimov:* [. . .] For whom, essentially, are we producing our works?
> *Moskvin [chairman]:* For the People, with a capital letter.
> *Gerasimov:* We shouldn't include just the people . . .
> *Mikhoels:* . . . but its immediate future as well. I can't remember whether it was Baratynsky or Vyazemsky who said *à propos* of Glinka: 'I am told that this is the music of the future. That may be so, but why must I listen to the music of the future right now?' With the passing of time, it has been proven that there really was a point in making people listen to Glinka then.
> [. . .] People need to study music. They are not receptive to [new works] in the other arts either, so accessibility and comprehensibility cannot be the only criterion. As for various leftist deviations and formalist contrivances, that is another matter, and these do, of course, need to be exposed.[7]

Goldenweiser, acting in Shostakovich's defence, reminded his listeners of the failure of *Carmen*, which became a great success just a year later. Khrapchenko raised a laugh with his quick reply: 'So what should we do? Postpone it for a year?'[8] His wisecrack was perhaps rather more complicated than it appears to us. The KSP did, in fact, sometimes postpone the consideration of various works: this was a ruse applied to mediocre work that had been placed in the running for some external reason (such as intense lobbying by a national republic for one of its local stars), in the hope that the unwanted work would be forgotten a year later. Shostakovich's Eighth, of course, was a work at the highest level of artistry, and it would not be forgotten.

Khrapchenko, however, was not in attendance as a mere comedy turn. From this moment on, he would give Shostakovich the status he had previously reserved for Prokofiev before 1943: namely, a candidate whose remarkable abilities could not be allowed to mask his ideological deficiencies, and who must be prevented from winning a prize:

> We need to consider that we are discussing Stalin Prizes. We don't simply determine the worth of this or that work [in the abstract]. The concept of the Stalin Prize includes recognition by the people, and we cannot overlook this issue. If we are arguing about this work in the Stalin Prize Committee, and many of the members need it to be explained to them [why this work merits a prize], then our intelligentsia will need to be persuaded, too, that this is a work of genius and that it will be recognized as such in the future.[9]

And if the intelligentsia would need persuading, then the work would be all the more forbidding to a mass audience. Vera Mukhina, the great sculptor, then addressed the meeting with a strong statement of support for the Symphony. She recounted her own struggles with Shostakovich's symphonies – struggles that many members would have recognized, just like anyone today who is becoming acquainted with Shostakovich for the first time:

> I heard the Eighth twice and the Seventh twice and I would like to compare them. The Seventh makes a very strong impression; why so? Because you are beaten down by Fate, beaten down by some kind of terrifying march, and you don't know how you can possibly escape from this thing. This makes a colossal impression. They say that there used to be a form of torture when drops of water fell on a person's head, and he would go mad. This is the same. Perhaps this is how the German jackboot ought to feel.
>
> The Eighth, to me, is much more diverse. [...] I would say that the two marches which follow one another [the second and third movements],

make a colossal impression. The last movement seems over-expansive, and there are moments when you wonder 'Is the end close?' – that is how impatient you become.

In my opinion, the Eighth Symphony is not at all lower than the Seventh. But there is one feature in Shostakovich's music, which, for me personally, is difficult: I can't take it home with me after the concert. [...] Perhaps this is because of fearsome complexity. But the impression is colossal. The Eighth Symphony is a huge work. There might be drawbacks, but there are always some of these. The two marches are quite exceptional.[10]

Mukhina's statement even convinced the KSP that they had to listen to the Symphony again. Khrapchenko noticed that the Music Section had only presented four works for the KSP's consideration, and there were four prizes available for music. There was a genuine point of principle here, since the Music Section had effectively removed any decision-making powers from the KSP plenary session. Khrapchenko, of course, was interested in the leverage this could give him against Shostakovich's Symphony, and he proposed an alternative: Gavriil Popov's Symphony No. 2. The Music Section were attracted by the proposal, but they felt that Popov's work lacked a certain coherence: the whole was perhaps worth less than the sum of its parts. This reflected the external origins of some of the music, which came from Popov's soundtrack to the film *She Defends the Motherland*. But it was a shrewd choice on Khrapchenko's part, since Popov's Symphony was far from being a mere piece of Socialist Realist hackwork, while its virtues were more readily apparent than those of the much more forbidding Shostakovich Symphony. There was no known rivalry between the two composers, and they did not in any way represent opposing camps, so Khrapchenko's proposal seemed, on the face of it, to lack any ideological motivation. He now made himself a passionate advocate for Popov:

I personally think that this symphony has great emotional force, it has great breadth, great inner pathos: the composer has something to say, and he says a lot indeed, in an expressive and accessible manner. This symphony has something that others don't have: a combination of accessibility with a complex musical idiom. This is by no means a simplistic musical symphony [sic], its musical idiom is very complex and the author is entirely in control of the contemporary musical language, and yet both in content and in form, it is very accessible to listeners. My impression is that this symphony is of very high quality, even outstanding, and I insist that it should be included in the list.[11]

Although the KSP agreed to postpone further discussion of the Shostakovich Symphony until they had heard it once more, Khrapchenko was determined to pre-empt this at the next plenary session, on 24 March, when he launched into a long disquisition on why this symphony could not be awarded a Stalin Prize:

> On the last occasion, the musicians and a good many other comrades spoke positively of Shostakovich's Eighth Symphony and evaluated it highly. As far as musical technique is concerned, this work probably does indeed have great potential. But I am approaching this work as an ordinary listener. I listened to it three times, and gained the impression that in his Eighth Symphony, Shostakovich returns to themes that he had addressed earlier. Here we see, I think, an idiom that is deliberately complicated, and the kind of refinement that is not accessible to ordinary cultured listeners. This is the first point.
>
> Secondly, it seems to me that this work lacks some kind of objective element, some broad public element that every large-scale symphonic work possesses. Shostakovich is speaking on his own behalf here, rather than on behalf of the many. His work is individualistic, or [at least] too individual.
>
> And finally, as other colleagues have already said here, it is an extremely pessimistic work.
>
> My feeling, as one who cannot be considered an expert in music, is that here we have a piece that leads Shostakovich away from the path he had taken in the Quintet and the Seventh Symphony. It is something that lies outside this course. It is, I say again, a return to the past for Shostakovich. I like Shostakovich very much, and value his talent very highly, and so it's hard for me to say this, but I cannot refrain from doing so if I want to remain honest. [...]
>
> I will say it again: perhaps the composers are right when they tell us that it is an outstanding work in terms of compositional technique, but it remains a fact that for a cultured listener who may even have undergone some preparation in the musical sphere, this work is still not one that can be heard with an open heart and soul, it is not comprehensible and accessible, it does not take hold of you, touch you or move you. No, it's not very comprehensible, and it doesn't touch or move us a great deal.[12]

This time, Khrapchenko found some support: Aleksandrov, the composer of the Soviet national anthem, agreed that the Eighth was a step backwards in Shostakovich's oeuvre. The Seventh 'had shaken him to the core', while the Eighth merely 'gave him a headache'. And furthermore, he said, just because Shostakovich happened to be writing symphonies all the time, this does not mean that every one of them should get an award. 'This is individual music, not programmatic, and you can't tell what the composer of this symphony wanted to say. In the Seventh, you can tell, but here it's not clear.'[13] Aleksandrov was joined by Dunayevsky, and then by the KSP chairman, the venerable actor Ivan Moskvin, who (without having heard the piece) insisted on the principle that the Stalin Prize should give artists guidance, not send them off in the wrong direction: 'If we give him a prize, he'll write the Ninth the same way. And if we don't, he'll start thinking. This is not a punishment, but he'll begin to wonder what the problem might be.'[14]

The committee was split down the middle, and it was decided that Shostakovich should come and provide a rendition of his Symphony on the piano as soon as possible (accordingly, he was scheduled to appear before the KSP on 25 March). After Shostakovich had played, Shaporin called members to reconsider one of their concerns about the work, namely that it was pessimistic:

> I'd heard the symphony performed by the orchestra, and now, here, on the piano. After I heard Shostakovich play, I think that Mravinsky's interpretation doesn't quite correspond to the author's conception. [. . .] Shostakovich is reproached for his pessimism. But I didn't find any pessimism in his own performance. Perhaps there was deep tragedy, but not pessimism.[15]

As a result of this discussion, the committee arrived at a compromise: by twenty votes out of twenty-nine, it passed the Symphony, but only for a second-class prize. Khrapchenko, of course, was still not satisfied, and he behaved just as he had done at the beginning of the 1940s, when faced with unwelcome Prokofiev nominations: he called upon the government to reverse the KSP's decision. In his letter to Stalin and Molotov of 1 April 1944, the formulation was harsher than anything he had said at the KSP meetings:

> Deliberate over-complication and a lack of clear melody make the Symphony No. 8 incomprehensible to a wide layer of listeners. In this work, Shostakovich repeats the same formalist errors that had been typical of some of his earlier works.[16]

A very similar formulation was also used in the Agitprop letter to the government: 'This symphony is a step backwards compared to the Seventh Symphony, and it contains throwbacks to Shostakovich's old formalist errors.'[17] With the ministry and Agitprop in agreement, the Symphony was doomed to fail.

Eighth Symphony (II), Second Quartet and Trio

This was not the end, however. Due to wartime conditions, the government did not find the time to confirm the awards for 1943 until one award cycle started running into the next. It was then decided to make combined awards for the years 1943 and '44, and the KSP gathered again in the spring of 1945 to revise their earlier nominations and add some new items. This was not a straightforward task: some of the previous year's decisions now had to be reconsidered in the light of the new selection available. Some works required a new vote, while others were to be left standing on the list.

The situation with Shostakovich now looked different: by this stage, he had composed another two substantial works that were considered prize material: the Second String Quartet and the Piano Trio (No. 2), which were both performed for the members on 19 March 1945 by the Beethoven Quartet and the composer at the piano. Opinion had also been shaped, to some degree, by Shaporin's published review of all three works: he was quite acerbic about the Symphony but claimed that the Quartet and the Trio broke new ground in a more promising way.[18] There was now more room for manoeuvre, especially since the Trio (like the Quintet before it) seemed to have fired the KSP members' imagination.

Shostakovich's supporters saw this as an opportunity to get rid of the embarrassing second-class: the Eighth Symphony and the Trio together, they were sure, were worth a first prize. Khrapchenko, on the contrary, saw this as an opportunity to dispense with the Eighth altogether, and for the Trio to go to the ballot as an alternative. Had the KSP members known about Khrapchenko's and Agitprop's earlier attempts to block the Symphony's progress, they would not have wasted time debating the issue further. But since these events had been concealed from them, they continued to put up a struggle to retain the Symphony.

Fadeyev felt that swapping the Symphony for the Trio was somewhat embarrassing, since the two works were so different in scale. The conductor Samosud, a long-standing advocate for Shostakovich, spoke in defence of the Symphony on the same grounds that the defenders of Sholokhov's novel had once chosen: that a towering artistic achievement simply cannot be turned down, whatever the ideological considerations:

> The Eighth Symphony is a work of a very high order, indeed an extraordinarily high order. But it happens to be controversial. It is somehow improper to withhold the prize. It was even said that only passing it for the second class was also rather awkward.[19]

But at this point, the tone and direction of the discussion changed dramatically. The architect Arkady Mordvinov, who designed some of the most iconic Stalin-period buildings in central Moscow,[20] launched an extraordinary attack on Shostakovich, in the style of 1936. He began, however, with an easier target, the young Moisei Weinberg (Vaynberg), who, everyone knew, was Shostakovich's disciple. It so happened that Weinberg's Quintet, although rejected by the Music Section, was still auditioned by the plenary session (at the prompting of Myaskovsky and Samosud). A recent refugee from Nazi-occupied Poland, Weinberg quickly began to establish himself as a composer in his new country, and he was much talked about. Weinberg's highly dramatic forty-minute Quintet was played by Emil Gilels and the Beethoven Quartet on 20 March and, unusually, the composer was present at the audition too. This attempt to promote Weinberg backfired badly: Mordvinov, who had already been grumbling about both of Shostakovich's new works, now launched into a full-scale attack:

> Some youth brings us a piece of utterly unbearable rubbish. [...] It is an outrageous thing, the most incredible cacophony, just a lot of caterwauling. There were some attempts at technical innovation: now you do it with a finger, now with a bow![21] We were laughing about it, that maybe he should get something attached to his back, so he could drum on it. How did this come about?
>
> In this regard, I must raise an issue of principle here. The Stalin Prize Committee has a certain criterion of evaluation. It approaches every work from the point of view of Socialist Realism. If we were offered some kind of futurist smear as a painting, we would not even look at it. If we were offered some *zaum'* ['transrational' poetry] in literature, we wouldn't listen to it. So why in music do we have to listen to these formalist scams?

At this point the KSP chairman Moskvin interjected: 'Music is obscure' (*Muzïka – samoye tyomnoye delo*). Mordvinov, ignoring him, went on:

> Some say, with regard to Shostakovich, that they understand nothing about music. But this music is supposed to be written for the masses. We heard Shostakovich's [Second] Quartet. How does this differ from the Weinberg Quintet? Of course, one is a teacher, the other a pupil, but it's unbearable cacophony [again], and it's the most you can do just to stay put in your seat. And we say about Shostakovich that he is a genius, he's a genius, a genius. We give it our encouragement. [...] After this Quartet, this incredible chaos and cacophony, we heard some rounded phrases in the Trio, and people said that it's very good. But if you take it by itself, there is nothing particularly good about it. People liked it because they heard it after the cacophony. I think we pay too much attention to Shostakovich, and by doing so, we open the way for mainstream formalism like this. They say that he's won recognition in America. But how many leftist artists of various trends are

recognized by English and American artists! That doesn't mean for a moment that we should encourage this formalism. This is not the main line of development – it's not the path along which music will develop. It will develop from world classics, and this is just a sideline, pure technique [...].

When the Eighth Symphony is performed, there is a lot of cacophony there, but people hear something in it that reminds them of the cannons firing and the Katyusha rocket launchers squealing, but in the Quartet and the Trio this justification is not present.[22]

This attack from Mordvinov tipped the earlier balance between aesthetic and ideological considerations; the type of discourse Mordvinov introduced was aggressive and demagogical. When such shifts occurred in the committee's deliberations, they were usually initiated by people who belonged to a certain social type–the Soviet intelligentsia, usually from humble roots, with a background either in Party work or in the 'proletarian' artistic organizations of the 1920s, which had pioneered this brand of aggressively ideological stance in the arts. Mordvinov came from a small village and lacked the benefits of a full formal education; he had joined the Party in 1919 and was an active member of VOPRA, the proletarian organization for architecture that had harassed constructivists and eclectics at the end of the 1920s. He had made a name for himself in developing and supervising the faster method of construction used in the residential buildings that grace the centre of Moscow. It became very clear to everyone that his exposure to art music was much lower than that of his fellow committee members. Even so, his rhetoric was full of the right phrases, and his colleagues would have been reluctant to challenge it head on, however much they privately disdained it. For this reason, every speaker after Mordvinov felt constrained to agree with the general direction of his thoughts, with any departures introduced as qualifications rather than refutations. Fadeyev, for example, had to express himself thus, whatever he had originally intended to say:

I am quite sympathetic to the direction of Mordvinov's attack, to his main ideas, because it is true that in such spheres as literature and painting we are better able to discern what formalism is – we can spot it straight away. In the sphere of music, however, we are too timid, and when specialists tell us something, we fall into a respectful silence, not following the living voice of our hearts, which is very important in this area.[23]

However, Fadeyev chose to separate Shostakovich from Weinberg, and Shostakovich's Trio from the Symphony, although not in a way that anyone could have predicted even five minutes earlier:

[The Trio] impresses people who know very little about specific musical issues. It grips those whose souls are alive. It is an outstanding work. I'm a person without any musical education, but I was greatly impressed by this work, and it left a lasting impression upon me. [...]

As for the Eighth Symphony, [...] it found no response in my innermost being, it leaves me cold and sometimes it unsettled and angered me, making me want to walk out, so that my nerves could recover.[24]

Mordvinov hoped to capitalize on his provocation, pressing for a full-scale discussion of Socialist Realism in music. Goldenweiser, however, decided to launch into a small condescending lecture on how music differs from the other arts due to its abstract language. He deflated Mordvinov's argument by insisting that 'calling a musical work formalist just because one doesn't understand it, is not always correct'. Mordvinov, perhaps sensing that he was losing ground, retreated to his initial attack on Weinberg, asking Goldenweiser to concede that at least Weinberg's work was definitely formalist. Goldenweiser eagerly obliged.[25]

By this stage, many KSP members probably realized that a vote for the Trio alone would be most likely to resolve the deadlock, but since the results of the previous year's vote could not be simply disregarded, the Symphony still appeared on the ballot paper, although separately from the Trio. The results of the ballot were as follows: the Trio received twenty-five votes out of a possible thirty-two (fifteen for the first class, ten for the second), while the Symphony earned only twelve. The KSP as a whole was therefore far from hostile to Shostakovich, but appreciation for what he could do at the peak of his powers was probably limited to the twelve who voted for the Symphony.[26]

Thus the Piano Trio, like the Piano Quintet before it, won over the majority of the members through tunefulness, especially in the Finale, which, arguably for the first time in Shostakovich's oeuvre, introduced material in the style of Jewish folk music. It is worth pointing out here that while today's Shostakovich scholars make much of the Jewish elements in Shostakovich's music, seeing them, more often than not, as a sign of subversion,[27] in 1945 they were actually a hook that drew Stalin Prize Committee members to favour the work for its simple, memorable and instantly effective moments, which concentrated their attention and made them tap their feet. It was a compromise: the Trio was a work of lesser significance, but also less controversial. In the end, it missed a first-class prize by only one or two votes (seventeen for first class would have been needed – one more than half of the total number of voters).

The Ninth Symphony and the Third Quartet

The Ninth Symphony, judging by the first press reactions, had a happy start in life. The directorate of the Moscow Philharmonia organized an audition for conductors and music critics: Shostakovich and Svyatoslav Richter played the symphony in a four-hand arrangement, while the conductors Nikolai Anosov, Alexander Gauk and Samuil Samosud followed the score. Those present concluded that the symphony was an outstanding work, even though at least one participant recalled his disbelief when the expectation for a monumental work was undercut by an array of cheeky tunes.[28] An early review by Izrael Nestyev in the Agitprop paper *Culture and Life*, however, already reflected unease about the Symphony: Nestyev lamented the appearance of a TASS notice which misleadingly advertised the Symphony as dedicated 'to the celebration of our great Victory'.[29] Without being overtly hostile, the article subtly raised doubts about Shostakovich's connection to Stravinsky and his method of 'stylization', which Nestyev considered 'soulless'. In other words, the kind of neoclassicism that Shostakovich explored in the Ninth was received very differently from similar writing in the Quintet five years earlier. During these early auditions, Shostakovich let slip that this symphony was not the original Ninth he had planned. The truth of this statement was corroborated only recently, by the discovery of the sketches for the original, monumental Ninth, which had indeed been abandoned by the composer.[30]

Shostakovich's defenders among the critics did their best to gloss over the embarrassment. A review by Semyon Shlifshteyn (still based on the piano version) in the arts ministry newspaper *The Soviet Arts* was overwhelmingly positive.[31] The Moscow and Leningrad orchestral premieres by Mravinsky only confirmed the generally positive impression, according to a review by Daniil Zhitomirsky.[32] When composers and musicologists gathered to discuss the Ninth at a December meeting of the Composers' Union, the musicologist Lev Mazel sang the Symphony's praises in his position paper. There was no immediate response, but eventually another musicologist, Yury Keldysh, sparked a row. He had listened to Shostakovich's defenders praising the Symphony for its supposed light-heartedness and joyful brilliance, but he evidently felt this was only a ruse, and he insisted that the Symphony was actually a complex work, but also a provocation. Most importantly, the Symphony should have expressed the feelings of the Soviet people in the wake of the war, but it did no such thing. In the climate of 1945, Shostakovich supporters had little trouble making Keldysh retreat, but unease over the Symphony became ever harder to suppress.[33]

Five months later, the Ninth was introduced to the KSP by Shaporin in a benign yet ambivalent way: he claimed that although normally a symphony would be expected to contain a dramatic conflict, there is none here: 'This is an entertaining symphony of grotesqueries. It is put together with the brilliance and wit that are typical of Shostakovich. It sounds very good too.'[34] Khrapchenko thought this was too positive:

> The Ninth Symphony, in my opinion, does not belong among Shostakovich's best works. It is masterfully written, but without any particular brilliance or depth, as it seemed to me. I think it is most likely intermediate in character, assembled during a breathing space between large-scale works [...].[35]

Goldenweiser hastened to agree. Mikhoels, who had defended the Eighth the previous year, sincerely wondered whether the Ninth was on the same level. Unexpectedly, Dunayevsky came out on the side of the Ninth, defending the lighter symphony's right to exist as a genre. Ermler agreed with Dunayevsky, but Shaporin still grumbled that Shostakovich's Ninth was no match for Prokofiev's 'Classical' Symphony. Despite all the doubts, the Ninth scraped through with enough votes for a second-class prize (the minimum of seventeen votes for the second class).

But the Ninth was never going to reach the finishing line: it received a thumbs-down from the new KSP chairman Fadeyev, who claimed in his letter to the government that the Symphony was not a step forward for the composer,[36] and similar negative comments followed from Khrapchenko and Agitprop. As for the Politburo Commission (under Zhdanov), its rejection of the Symphony was formulated thus:

> The symphony is not of significant artistic value; it was performed in several concerts and public opinion held it to be a none-too-successful work within Shostakovich's symphonic oeuvre. The symphony was not widely performed, and it has not been heard anywhere for more than a year now.[37]

Having seen its decision on the Ninth overturned, the KSP was more cautious the following year (1947), when Shostakovich's Third Quartet came up for discussion. The Music Section actually turned it down, and yet because of Shostakovich's standing, the Quartet resurfaced in a plenary discussion. Glière warned that the Music Section had found it 'narrowly individualistic', aloof from 'universal human feelings', and expressing this individualism through over-refined, modernist language. Khrapchenko even mentioned Myaskovsky's comment: 'solipsistic' – a word Myaskovsky came to regret.[38] However, everyone agreed that these descriptions could only apply to the first three movements, while the fourth and fifth moved listeners deeply.

Fig. 10. Plenary session of the KSP, 1947(?). Glière is speaking, behind him, seated, are, from left to right, Goldenweiser, Zavadsky, Myaskovsky, the actor Mikhail Tsarev, and Alexei Popov (?). With permission from the Shostakovich Archive in Moscow.

Myaskovsky described the trajectory of the Quartet as moving from the very light through more serious moods reminiscent of the Eighth Symphony, and on to great heights: 'The fourth and fifth movements made an impression on me that this was music of genius, something absolute, something beyond doubt.'[39] Ermler, Shostakovich's long-standing film collaborator, formulated it thus: 'If you have to think and feel [for yourself] through the first three [movements], then the last two take possession of the listener. This is superb. And that is why it would be a great crime to take this work off the list.'[40]

Listening to the Quartet today, we can interpret this distinction in the following way: the members preferred to shy away from the faux naive neoclassicism of the first movement and from the searing grotesque of the two scherzos that follow. In the Eighth Symphony, scherzos quite similar in character were the members' favourites, and they were able to detect the sounds of war there. But now that the war was over, the intensity of the new scherzos was perceived as dubiously individualistic – the public motivation for such music had gone. What gripped members most in the Quartet was the tragic passacaglia of the fourth movement, one of the most powerful in Shostakovich's whole oeuvre, but their endorsement of the finale is more notable: the finale's narrative trajectory is far from straightforward, and the faux naive style, to an extent, makes a return there. Perhaps it was the haunting, irresistible coda with its endlessly held major chord in the celestial register that made such an impact on the members.

Conversations about Shostakovich often tended to move beyond direct discussion of the music and on to more dangerous ground. Ermler, for example, piqued by the charge of 'individualism' thrown at Shostakovich, qualified his own comments as being made 'from an individual's position'. The 'universal feelings' that were supposed to be lacking in the Quartet, he argued, are, after all 'made up from the feelings of individuals'. Sensing that the discussion could become bogged down in philosophical ruminations, Khrapchenko decided that it was time to rehearse his master argument:

> In the Committee here, we have all been observing Shostakovich's artistic development over the past few years, and I think that Shostakovich has two different sides to his artistic biography and oeuvre. On the one hand, we have the Quintet, the Seventh Symphony and the Trio [Khrapchenko is careful to name only prizewinning works] – these are works which have a common theme, as in the Seventh Symphony – a very clear world of human feelings. [...] And then there are the works in which Shostakovich reveals himself as a deeply individualistic artist. This is the Eighth Symphony, which had been discussed and balloted for here, and other works which are charac-terized by their stepping away from the human, from the vivid perception of the world, by their withdrawal into some closed world of sensations. Perhaps Nikolai Yakovlevich [Myaskovsky] was right to speak about a kind of solip-sistic perception of the world. It seems to me that this Quartet belongs to the second side of Shostakovich's oeuvre. In my view, the range of feelings there is extremely narrow and separated off from life and reality. Finally, the very language is modernist; as Alexander Borisovich [Goldenweiser] said, this is not the kind of living and lucid language that is spoken by musicians who are addressing a wide audience. It was said at the Music Section that every artist has the right to express his own world by his own means, but what has the Stalin Prize to do with that? It is not just given for the artist's individu-ality but for a particular quality: for a work in which *narodnost*[41] is reflected. The Stalin Prize emphasizes that our art has the qualities of *narodnost'*. And a work which lacks these qualities cannot lay claim to a Stalin Prize.[42]

Shostakovich had been made a laureate three times, but with this following upon the previous year's difficulties, it was now clear to KSP members that the tide had turned against him. They agreed that Shostakovich's next award would have to wait until he produced a truly great masterpiece that would not provoke such fundamental doubts.

Birthday Gifts: *Song of the Forests* and *The Fall of Berlin*

Two years later, Shostakovich managed to produce not one, but two works that no one could fault, but neither of these could have been expected from the composer in 1947. The root of this transformation lies in the events of January and February 1948, when Shostakovich's career hit a new low. In the wake of the anti-formalist Resolution, the Eighth and Ninth Symphonies and many of his other works were banned from the concert platform.[43] The transformation also perhaps owed much to that famous phone call from Stalin inviting Shostakovich to travel to the USA for a peace conference. In that phone call, reportedly, Shostakovich held his ground, reminding Stalin that he could hardly represent the Soviet Union abroad while his music was still banned at home.[44] The ban, in any case, was immediately rescinded, and Shostakovich travelled to New York at the end of March 1949. He endured that stressful circus together with the other members of the Soviet delegation, which included two Stalin hagiographers, the filmmaker Mikhail Chiaureli and his scenario writer Pyotr Pavlenko.[45] It is hardly a coincidence that, by early May of that year, Shostakovich had already signed a contract to provide the film score for Chiaureli's and Pavlenko's forthcoming *Fall of Berlin*, another piece of Stalin hagiography.[46] The score ends with a grand 'Glory to Stalin' chorus – Shostakovich's first direct participation in the Stalin cult. By July, Shostakovich was already sketching his oratorio *Song of the Forests* (about Stalin's post-war reforestation plan), which expanded a number of musical ideas from the film, but shrewdly avoided outright quotation so that it could be presented as an independent work. Thus, Shostakovich had not one, but two gifts for Stalin's seventieth birthday, and as events turned out, Stalin was bound to lend his ear to at least one of them (and hear rumours about the other).[47]

Without delving into the mixture of pride and turmoil within Shostakovich's mind in this period, we can certainly say that as a result of composing these two works, Shostakovich overcame his enemies and flew up so high again as to become unreachable. Khrennikov, the new, post-1948, chairman of the KSP Music Section, seems to have had some difficulty swallowing his own pride, and introduced the oratorio to the KSP in a somewhat patronizing manner, commending Shostakovich for his decisive move onto the path of realism, but also criticizing him for some supposed 'shortcomings'.[48] Khrennikov's sidekick Zakharov had less baggage to carry and so moved more swiftly with the times. He spoke now with an appropriate degree of awe:

> I think that Shostakovich, of course, ought to receive a Stalin Prize, but I am afraid of one circumstance. As it happens, a very important film is being put forward for the Stalin Prize, and as far as the audience was concerned, this

is the best we've ever seen in Soviet cinema. That film is *The Fall of Berlin*. The music is by Shostakovich. I am very sure that Shostakovich will receive a Stalin Prize for this music.[49]

Sergei Mikhalkov, the writer of the text for the Soviet national anthem, was still more adoring of Shostakovich's new work: 'Let him get two!', he called out, no doubt, sarcastically. The supposed problem here was very tenuous, since the government had not yet nominated the film, and it could easily have been sorted out once they did so. It is highly unlikely that Zakharov was genuinely vexed about this problem, which would seem to have been a mere pretext for his true purpose: he wanted to present himself as an insider who could bring fresh news to the KSP that had previously been confined to higher levels. Fadeyev was not about to indulge Zakharov in another of his games, and he moved the discussion on with this blunt remark:

> It's not up to us to make decisions on *The Fall of Berlin*. The deadline for nominating films has passed. If this film is ready, the Government has the right to abrogate the deadline, but we have to stick to it.[50] [In other words, the KSP has no business discussing the matter prematurely.]

A few meetings later, the film was confirmed as legitimately in the running, and Zakharov wanted to ensure that Shostakovich was nominated for both scores (jointly for a single prize), despite Khrennikov's previous concerns about their similarity: 'We absolutely need to add [the film score]. If we don't add it, this will mean that we consider this music undeserving of attention.'[51]

Whatever we think of Shostakovich's Stalin eulogies, they succeeded at least in forcing his former detractors to change their ways. And Zakharov was right: Stalin *did* check that Shostakovich was due to receive an award for *The Fall of Berlin*, a film in which he had taken great pleasure. Noticing that the list of names in the nominated film crew did not include the composer, Stalin was puzzled, and added 'Shostakovich?' in the margins. At this stage, Shostakovich was listed in the Music category as a nominee for both works, the film score having been added by Agitprop (see fig. 11). When the confusion was clarified in the Politburo meeting, Stalin struck the name out again, satisfied now that Shostakovich's contribution to the film was receiving due recognition (fig. 12).

Ten Choral Poems and After

The Ten Poems on texts by revolutionary poets, op. 88, ostensibly continued along Shostakovich's 'realist' path: choral writing was in fashion, and the prov-

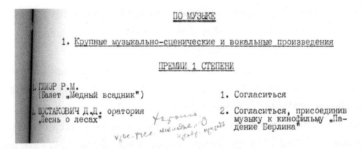

ПО МУЗЫКЕ

1. Крупные музыкально-сценические и вокальные произведения

ПРЕМИИ 1 СТЕПЕНИ

ГЛИЭР Р.М.
(Балет „Медный всадник")   1. Согласиться

ШОСТАКОВИЧ Д.Д. оратория   2. Согласиться, присоединив
„Песнь о лесах"   музыку к кинофильму „Па-
                                                         дение Берлина"

Fig. 11. On the right, opposite the nomination for Shostakovich's *Song of the Forests*, we see Agitprop's additional nomination of *The Fall of Berlin* score. The handwritten comment (by Suslov?) reads: 'Good. A beautiful Russian melody. On the transformation of nature'. RGASPI, fond 17, op. 132, ye.kh. 272, l. 76.

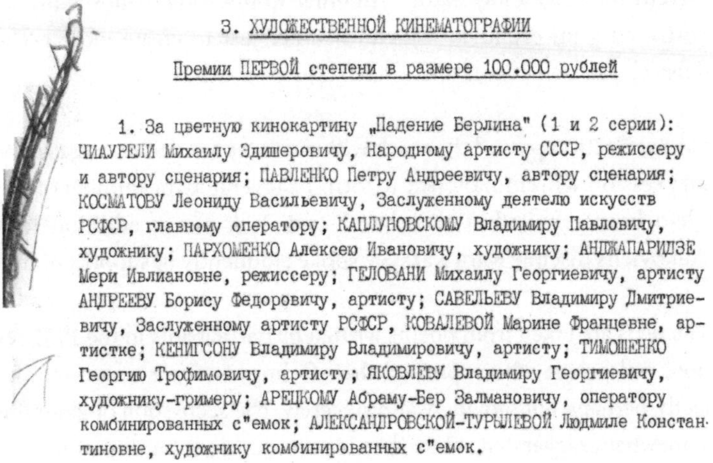

3. ХУДОЖЕСТВЕННОЙ КИНЕМАТОГРАФИИ

Премии ПЕРВОЙ степени в размере 100.000 рублей

1. За цветную кинокартину „Падение Берлина" (1 и 2 серии):
ЧИАУРЕЛИ Михаилу Эдишеровичу, Народному артисту СССР, режиссеру
и автору сценария; ПАВЛЕНКО Петру Андреевичу, автору сценария;
КОСМАТОВУ Леониду Васильевичу, Заслуженному деятелю искусств
РСФСР, главному оператору; КАПЛУНОВСКОМУ Владимиру Павловичу,
художнику; ПАРХОМЕНКО Алексею Ивановичу, художнику; АНДЖАПАРИДЗЕ
Мери Ивлиановне, режиссеру; ГЕЛОВАНИ Михаилу Георгиевичу, артисту
АНДРЕЕВУ Борису Федоровичу, артисту; САВЕЛЬЕВУ Владимиру Дмитрие-
вичу, Заслуженному артисту РСФСР, КОВАЛЕВОЙ Марине Францевне, артистке; КЕНИГСОНУ Владимиру Владимировичу, артисту; ТИМОШЕНКО
Георгию Трофимовичу, артисту; ЯКОВЛЕВУ Владимиру Георгиевичу,
художнику-гримеру; АРЕЦКОМУ Абраму-Бер Залмановичу, оператору
комбинированных с"емок; АЛЕКСАНДРОВСКОЙ-ТУРЫЛЕВОЙ Людмиле Констан-
тиновне, художнику комбинированных с"емок.

Fig. 12. Stalin's marginalia: 'Shostakovich?' next to the list of award-winners for the film *The Fall of Berlin*. RGANI, fond 3, op. 53a, ye.kh. 33, l. 13.

enance of texts, contemporary with the unsuccessful Russian revolution of 1905, could hardly be faulted, even though most of them spoke of prison, exile and death. But the two leading advocates of 'music for the people', Khrennikov and Zakharov, who could easily see that this was not another *Song of the Forests*, threw their recent circumspection to the wind and went on the attack. The other members of the Music Section came to the cycle's defence, most importantly including experts on choral music like Sveshnikov and Shaporin. The exchange was sharp and with undertones of mutual contempt:

Zakharov: Three or four songs are good there. But I must say that I do meet the masses, and the masses see this work as a negative phenomenon.

Khrennikov (chairman): There is a general tone of pessimism.

Zakharov: The implied perspective on events in this work is not ours, it is not of today. And we are talking here about the most serious side of the work, the political side. [. . .] We wouldn't want to make a mistake here.

Sveshnikov: This is not primitive music, and the masses accept only the primitive. [. . .] And as for the perspective on 1905, we shouldn't have any worries. I don't know which comrades had suggested this to you [namely, that the work is politically unsafe], but I was told that it [the text] is almost like an appendix to the Short Course [an official account of Party History, set reading in schools].[52]

Shaporin [to Khrennikov and Zakharov]: Do you mean to say that the beginnings of the revolution that didn't succeed had joyful aspects to them? Weren't they incredibly hard?[53] [In other words, should Shostakovich have portrayed grim events in a joyful manner just to create more accessible music?]

The Music Section passed the work with six votes for and two against, yet at the plenary session, Khrennikov, true to form, exaggerated the number of complaints that had been directed at the choral cycle.[54] A recent addition to the KSP, Shostakovich's disciple Kara Karayev spoke eloquently in support of his mentor:

The texts are taken from poems written by participants in the 1905 revolution, real people who expressed their feelings in verse, sometimes imperfectly, perhaps, but movingly and sincerely. The accusation of gloominess is somewhat exaggerated, while the epic and severe colouring of that time is expressed very convincingly and clearly by the composer. Those gloomy and pessimistic choruses alternate with rousing ones, and in compositional terms, this is done very persuasively. In melodic terms, the composer used the intonations of revolutionary songs of the era and did this very realistically: this is fully conveyed to the listener. And the writing is on a very high technical level.[55]

But others *did* have some reservations on the technical side regarding Shostakovich's command of choral writing. Even Shaporin, while admitting that there were some 'astonishing' numbers in the cycle (including the famous '9 January' section), generally disliked the syllabic setting and suggested that Shostakovich could have produced more interesting melodies had he allowed himself to set some syllables to two or three notes instead of always one. Anatoly

Novikov, a composer of mass songs, went further: he claimed that Shostakovich did not actually know how to write for choir, that his writing was restricted to a single device and the textures were overcomplicated, putting the piece beyond the reach of amateur choirs (which was an important consideration at the time).[56] Novikov also thought the choice of texts revealed flaws in Shostakovich's own thinking:

> The cycle does not reveal all the forces which came to the revolution, it does not show the motive forces behind the revolution. Shostakovich picked up some verses by poets of this period. But why did he choose such a one-sided topic as a funeral meeting in memory of the victims? Why didn't he find another topic and other poets? It would have been possible for him to have found different poets and verses. You leave [the concert hall] without knowing how this revolution turned out.[57]

Perhaps, in the heat of the moment, Novikov had forgotten that the 1905 revolution did indeed turn out badly. Shostakovich's supporters were particularly frustrated because the class of the prize in question had already been decided as second, but it was being argued over as if it were a candidate for the first class. The opinion of non-musicians was called for. Fadeyev came out strongly in favour, with praise that was both intelligent and heartfelt:

> I can't see that listeners, after hearing this piece, would descend into gloom and start crying over the revolution's failure. They will understand that there were great losses and that the struggle was hard. The fact that we are living happily now, this has been achieved through the great determination of the people, who stood next to tragedy and death. I am not denying that perhaps the work would have been stronger had the composer found among these texts something that would provide for a triumphant hymn or the prospects for future action. [...] Yet there is no sourness or whining here – everything is elevated to the heights of tragedy. These are powerful passions and powerful feelings. [...] This is not at all formalist music. It is heroic music, music that makes you want to sing together with the choir.[58]

The discussion rolled to a close with Sveshnikov's quip: 'Novikov wasn't there to witness it, but after 1905 people did have a bad feeling' (Sveshnikov was born in 1890). 'To put it mildly,' agreed Fadeyev. Shostakovich's fifth (and last) Stalin Prize was in the bag.

Since there was some vociferous support for the 'realist' Shostakovich over the 'formalist' in those heady years, it is worth asking whether this was insincere and merely politically motivated, or whether those involved really found his 'realist' music more enjoyable and considered it more valuable than his old 'formalist' scores. We have some pointers towards the answer in the KSP's discussions of early 1953, when Shostakovich was close to being nominated again for the combination of a cantata and a film score. The new cantata, *The Sun Shines over Our Motherland*, was shorter, less elaborate and generally much less ambitious than *Forests*, and the new film score was much slighter than the score for *Berlin* (the film this time was another contribution to the Stalin hagiography, *The Unforgettable 1919*, by the same team of Chiaureli and Pavlenko). The cantata was discussed first, and the session soon took an absurd turn – the case against the cantata being considered for a prize was made by Shostakovich himself. He insisted that 'he had not taken any steps forward' in this work and it should not therefore earn him a sixth Stalin Prize (he emphasized that it would be the sixth, as if to put off anyone who was still vacillating). This attack by the composer on his own piece was repeatedly rejected by Shostakovich's defenders (or should we say his critics?). Shtoharenko, for example, argued that there were, on the contrary, new developments in this cantata. Considering the cantata was dedicated to the Communist Party, Shostakovich could not go too far in his criticisms, since this would not have been mere self-deprecation but an implied insult to the Party. Shostakovich therefore repeated to his defenders/critics that 'since it exists, since it has been written, [the cantata] has the right to be performed in concert and on the radio', that he did not consider it unsuccessful, but merely not good enough to bring him a sixth Stalin Prize.[59]

Perverse as it may seem, no sooner was Shostakovich out of the room than the criticisms of his piece began (the very criticisms he had tried to elicit a moment earlier). Goldenweiser said that such commonplace music could not be given a prize, and Zakharov seconded this.[60] The mood swung against the cantata, and it was replaced on the nomination list with the *Unforgettable 1919* score. When the time came for the discussion of the new score, the same strange scene replayed, with Shostakovich protesting against the nomination and others defending it. Zakharov, for example, a consistent supporter of Stalin films, was unhappy at the prospect of the score failing to win a prize:

> We cannot accept this withdrawal, because the music is very good. It's not the right argument, that he has five Stalin Prizes already. Let him have ten more, and let him write only good music – this score is outstanding.[61]

Zakharov had shown himself to be a shrewd operator in the past, and we may wonder if he had some ulterior motive, but let us turn to someone who had no stake in this fight, the film director Sergei Gerasimov (not to be confused with the painter Alexander Gerasimov, whom we have encountered previously). We would have trouble explaining why his praise for the score was anything other than sincere:

> Those who remember Shostakovich's music [to the film] can't get it out of their heads. One such episode, the piano concerto, is Dmitry Dmitriyevich's great triumph.[62]

Let us explain: Shostakovich's score included a passage scored for piano and orchestra, and very much in the style of a Rachmaninov concerto. This continued at great length as the accompaniment to an intense battle scene, and it is indeed memorable music, although barely recognizable as Shostakovich and not even very appropriate to the onscreen action. The non-musician Gerasimov, it can well be believed, took delight in the music, but how many other KSP members would, if asked in confidence, have valued this pleasing little earworm over the unwieldy and unmemorable, yet terrifying and sublime Eighth Symphony? Had Zakharov and Shtoharenko really assimilated the notion of 'music for the people' so thoroughly that it had displaced all their musicianship? And surely Khrennikov's superior talents and musical intelligence would have told him better?

At this point, it is worth looking at Shostakovich's behaviour in this episode, which may seem strangely masochistic. The KSP was proposing him for a prize that could have brought him up to 100,000 roubles, while he wanted no prize (and therefore no money). Why did he feel a surge of pride at this moment, rather than before he composed the new cantata and the film score? The mystery can be dispelled, even if the answer is not simple. Firstly, Shostakovich had dashed off various official pieces during this period, but their fleeting time in the public eye was one matter, while it was quite another matter to draw long-term attention to such trifles if they were awarded a prize. Regarding the financial aspect, Shostakovich had fully recovered from the career setbacks of 1948, and since the Soviet Union did not have a straightforward money economy in the way that was normal in the West, there were limited opportunities to use extra money after all creature comforts had been met. Regarding prestige, Shostakovich was one of the very few artists to have a string of Stalin Prizes to his name, and accepting another prize for the Party Cantata or the *Unforgettable 1919* score would not only have added nothing to his prestige, but could have damaged it, given their very slight artistic value. There was also the warning from 1948, which was in part motivated by petty jealousies; if Shostakovich were to accept rewards too easily, he might conceivably be setting himself up for another fall. Lastly, Shostakovich had the precedent of

Myaskovsky rejecting the offer of a prize in 1946, when he withdrew his Eleventh Quartet and then attempted to withdraw his Cello Concerto when these were nominated (see Chapter 6).

The battle for the 'realist' Shostakovich that we have observed in this chapter seems strangely unreal, akin to the game of croquet played by Alice in Wonderland, where mallets and balls disobeyed the players, the players disobeyed the rules and there was a vague air of threat hanging over the proceedings. The officially approved and generously awarded Good Shostakovich of old, the Shostakovich of the Quintet, the Seventh Symphony, the Trio – was he really so very different from the Bad Shostakovich of the rejected works, the Eighth and Ninth Symphonies and the Third Quartet? Who could plot out the arbitrary zigzagging line that separated them? By contrast, there was a yawning chasm between the old Good Shostakovich and the new Good Shostakovich, the composer of 'realist' cantatas and film scores.

KSP members were evidently worried and confused when they set out to discuss pieces by Shostakovich that were controversial or which might later be taken to mean something they had not anticipated. The discussions were accordingly constrained. Even so, various individuals broke out of these constraints at times, and debated in earnest, even passionately, as we have seen with Mikhoels, Fadeyev and Goldenweiser. There were many uncontroversial KSP decisions, particularly for music, and when disagreement arose, it was often over issues whose political dimension was small. But Shostakovich heightened the tension far more than any other composer, convincing some members that it was best simply to play the game in a detached manner in order to avoid trouble, while others acted as thinking and feeling human beings who took a vital interest in the music, both for its personal and public dimensions. It may not always be possible to tell where the authentic behaviour ends and where the simulacrum begins, but it is vital to acknowledge that the two co-existed within discussions, and even for individual KSP members. In the next chapter we will find out more about how Shostakovich attempted both to play the game and to remain true to himself.

CHAPTER FIVE

SHOSTAKOVICH AS A COMMITTEE MEMBER

After the newspapers published a resolution on establishing the Stalin Prize for outstanding works of art, I had a conversation with Shostakovich in a hotel room. He expressed serious doubts about these awards, which, he said, would have a detrimental effect on music and other arts: composers would now begin to hanker after prizes and write pompous official music, forgetting the true purpose of their art.

– *Levon Atovmyan*[1]

The Golubev Incident

'Shostakovich speaks his mind, while Myaskovsky and Shaporin always choose their words carefully. Glière never expresses his own opinion but joins the majority.'[2] These were Goldenweiser's comments on the changed atmosphere once Shostakovich started attending meetings of the Music Section in March 1947. In April, the plenary sessions of the KSP began, and Shostakovich again spoke as he saw fit, which led Myaskovsky to record his behaviour as unfair and tactless.[3] Myaskovsky was mainly offended on behalf his former student, Yevgeny Golubev (1910–1988), whose oratorio *The Immortal Heroes* (*Geroi bessmertnï*) was under discussion. Shostakovich's criticism of Golubev, it seems, had further consequences, and the incident became part of Soviet musical lore.[4] Overlapping but conflicting accounts of the Golubev incident were left by Levon Atovmyan, a long-time friend of Shostakovich and the arranger of his symphonies for piano, and Yury (later Georgy) Sviridov, who had been Shostakovich's student and also numbered among his friends; both accounts were given decades later when, as we shall see, the distorting prism of time had done its work. We shall first consider these mythologized versions, keeping in mind that Shostakovich might himself have contributed to this collective mythmaking.

Here are the two accounts, the first by Sviridov:

There was once in Moscow a composer. A fine, talented composer. But for some reason Dmitry Dmitriyevich [Shostakovich] did not like his music. And when the composer was put forward for a Stalin Prize, Shostakovich wrote a letter to Stalin himself. In any case, this is how Dmitry Dmitriyevich recounted it to me. The letter said: I consider the Committee's decision unfair: the work is weak in its form, its thematic material is of little interest, and the orchestration is inexpressive [...]. At that time Shostakovich was not even a member of the Stalin Prize Committee, and the Committee, led by Zhdanov, had already taken the decision, which only had to be approved at the Politburo. And now at the very end of the Politburo's deliberations, when everyone had already agreed with the Committee's nominations, Stalin took the floor: 'Comrade Zhdanov, I've got a letter here ...' And he reads 'To Comrade Stalin from Comrade Shostakovich'. Everyone is at a loss, and Stalin says: 'Comrade Zhdanov! I think that Shostakovich knows more about music than you and me. I suggest that we take his opinion into account.' I swear on the holy cross, this is how Dmitry Dmitriyevich himself told this to me.[5]

Atovmyan's version, however, is significantly different:

Once Zhdanov came to a performance of Golubev's oratorio at the Conservatoire, and applauded demonstratively after every section. Discovering that Golubev wasn't present, he asked his assistants to bring him, sending his car for him and then sitting him in his box. Everyone understood that the oratorio would receive a Stalin Prize and indeed the Committee decided that it was worth a first-class prize. But when Zhdanov gave the Committee's decision to Stalin for signing, Stalin asked whether this decision was unanimous. Zhdanov answered, 'yes, but one person abstained'. Stalin asked for the transcript and saw that the one who had abstained (or, more precisely, the one who spoke against) was Shostakovich. He struck out Golubev's name and told Zhdanov: 'Shostakovich voted against and his opinion is more important than your decision and the resolution of the Committee.' This is how Shostakovich unwittingly heightened Zhdanov's hostility towards him.[6]

Entertaining as these accounts are, the conflicting details prevent us from accepting them at face value, and both, indeed, are at odds with confirmable events. The first and most glaring mistake is made by Sviridov, who claims that

Shostakovich was not, at this juncture, a member of the KSP – we know this to be untrue. Zhdanov, on the contrary, was not a member of the KSP, although he did oversee its work through Agitprop. Sviridov is correct, however, when he says that Shostakovich had already shown a dislike for Golubev's music before this incident, since we find that in 1938, Myaskovsky had complained about Shostakovich's 'merciless and unfair' criticism of another of Golubev's works, in this instance, his Second Symphony.[7]

But what were the offensive things that Shostakovich allegedly said about Golubev's oratorio in April 1947? The transcript tells us he said this:

> To me, this is a weak piece from the oeuvre of a gifted composer – I wouldn't say he was a great talent, but he *is* gifted. The musical language [of this piece] is impoverished and inexpressive. While I had allowed myself to reproach [Anatoly] Aleksandrov for a lack of musical dramaturgy [in his Lermontov-based opera *Bela*], here I found nothing that met the requirements of a large-scale musical work. It is very imperfect in this respect. It is lacklustre, giving a grey, monotonous impression.[8]

These words may be harsh, but in the context of the discussion they do not seem tactless: Myaskovsky himself defended Golubev only half-heartedly, admitting the work's dramatic flatness and lapses in orchestration; few others at the plenary session had a good word to put in.[9] Goldenweiser rose to the occasion with one of the biblical metaphors he liked to use in Soviet official meetings; in this case, he took a lurid image from Revelations and applied it to Golubev: 'So then because thou art lukewarm, and neither cold nor hot, I will spew thee out of my mouth' (Rev. 3:16 – admittedly, Goldenweiser stopped short of the 'spewing' clause). The film director Ermler complained that he could not even tell whether the organ (present in the score) was playing at all, so poor was the orchestration. The only person who came out strongly in defence of the work was Khrapchenko – his approval would have been a clear sign that his ministry was promoting Golubev's piece (notice that this is contrary to both Sviridov and Atovmyan, who erroneously place Zhdanov in this role). Goldenweiser even commented in his diary on Khrapchenko's ire at the Music Section's stubborn refusal to support Golubev, and eventually was driven to write an explanatory and apologetic note to the minister.[10]

Once the discussion was finished, KSP members voted on the work, as normal, by secret ballot. Atovmyan had said that Shostakovich had cast the only vote against, but the transcripts show no such thing: if Shostakovich, as we could expect from his statement to the KSP, voted against, he was only one of twenty others – precisely half of those who cast votes.[11] This placed the piece just below the qualifying line and so Golubev was not included in the list the KSP sent upwards, but even so, Khrapchenko used the fact that the vote was split to argue that Golubev should be included, as he said in his customary post-ballot letter to Stalin.[12] It was decided that Zhdanov should hear the piece himself, as we find out from a tangential source: on 14 May 1947, Lavrenty Beria forwarded Zhdanov a letter from the composer Vano Gokieli, who complained of unfair treatment at the hands of the KSP, and requested that his own piece should be auditioned once more, just like Golubev's (Gokieli claims to have heard from an unnamed source that Zhdanov had scheduled Golubev's cantata for an audition).[13] On the basis of this evidence, Atovmyan's tale of the audition at the Conservatoire begins to ring true: Zhdanov could have indeed sent a car for Golubev and sat him in his box.

We now come to a major first-hand source: a memoir by Golubev himself, which tells us that the audition did indeed take place and the car was indeed sent. But contrary to the rumours we examined earlier, Golubev certainly did not consider his meeting with Zhdanov to be a triumph. Although Zhdanov was genial in his manner, Golubev found some of his questions loaded and unnerving. Zhdanov enquired whether Golubev had composed the final chorus before or after the victory, whether he had any complaints regarding the poets, and, most puzzlingly, whether he was able to work on more than one work simultaneously.[14] Very helpfully for our purposes, Golubev also points out that Moscow's musicians and music officials jumped to the conclusion that the special audition for Zhdanov meant a first-class prize was on the way. Atovmyan's version is again corroborated on this point.

What Golubev might have sensed, *we* know for certain: contrary to both Sviridov's and Atovmyan's accounts, Zhdanov's verdict on the oratorio was negative. At a meeting of the Politburo Commission on the Stalin Prizes, Zhdanov spoke about the work in detail, after making a comment on his personal musical tastes:

> I'm not on the side of cacophonous music. In this respect, I'm a conserva-
> tive. I was raised on the Mighty Handful, on Beethoven, Chopin, Mozart
> and Verdi. But perhaps I've fallen behind the newest trends in the music
> world – perhaps these days it's the cacophonous music that's valued?
>
> I think that Golubev's *Immortal Heroes* oratorio is weak specifically in
> the area of melody. In its second part, the music is cacophonous; the first
> and second parts are both repetitious, and the second fails to develop the
> first. I advised Golubev to rewrite the oratorio in the following way: the first
> part would, in effect, summarize the whole conception; the second would be
> 'the moan of the earth', the third 'the moan of mothers and wives', then in the

fourth part, the theme of victory would enter, while in the fifth, there would be a victory apotheosis.

The content of the oratorio [as Golubev wrote it] displays deep pathos throughout, but there is no unity between form and content. Admittedly, the granting of an award to this oratorio would have encouraged a positive tendency in music, and the oratorio itself is somewhere 'near a prize', but even so, it would still make more sense to withhold the prize here.[15]

Zhdanov's analysis of the music is not at all inept: the 'cacophonous' second part indeed relies on the use of some strikingly dissonant harmonies (for example a D-minor triad over a C-sharp pedal note); the first and second parts do share the funeral march topos and are indeed very similar. Whether his own perceptions were acute, or whether he took sound advice, Zhdanov produced a credible assessment of the piece after the audition.

We find, then, that Zhdanov and Shostakovich reached the same conclusions on the oratorio, albeit from very different aesthetic positions. We do not have to make any assumptions about Stalin's personal interference, since the matter was resolved within the existing institutional processes. Khrapchenko's desires might have remained unfulfilled, but since Zhdanov had been given oversight of Agitprop in 1946, the minister often found himself overruled on cultural matters. Golubev, in the end, was left empty-handed, although he later consoled himself with the notion that the oratorio had failed 'for the right reason', namely that it included no references to Stalin in the text.[16] Here, however, we encounter yet another failure of memory, since Stalin's name does indeed appear in the oratorio's opening number (only the once, and in a rather perfunctory manner, but it is there nonetheless).

Although Sviridov's and Atovmyan's accounts differ in details, the general thrust is the same: that Shostakovich had a direct line to Stalin at the time. Rather than putting this down to a chance convergence of random errors, we should understand why Sviridov and Atovmyan should both believe such things. They were well aware that Shostakovich, at this point in his career, enjoyed a very amicable and lucrative relationship with the state. The kudos he had earned during the war with his Seventh Symphony allowed him to make certain demands with regard to his re-settlement in Moscow. On 3 May 1945, he wrote to Khrapchenko rather bluntly: 'For me and my family to have a decent life I would need 150,000 roubles a year, so about 12,000 a month.'[17] From the two personal letters of thanks Shostakovich sent to Stalin in 1946 and 1947, we know how the government responded. One of his letters concerned the promise of a five-room apartment in Moscow, a private dacha outside the city and, most astonishingly, 60,000 roubles for fixtures and fittings (more than the value of a second-class Stalin prize).[18] The second letter was written once he had moved into the new apartment, which he found very comfortable.[19] But while such letters acquaint us better with the degree of privilege he enjoyed, the fact of their existence doesn't increase the likelihood that Shostakovich had written a letter to Stalin about Golubev: this was a very different category of communication, and Shostakovich was not known for pestering Stalin with trivial requests.

Sviridov reported (swearing 'on the holy cross') that Shostakovich himself had told him the story, although even if we trust Sviridov, we do not know what embellishments from other sources Sviridov might have heard and unwittingly added; at any rate, Sviridov's version contains elements we know to be untrue, together with the implausibility and sheer redundancy of the supposed letter to Stalin. The errors over basic details mean that Shostakovich could hardly have been the only source of the story (and it is not as if he had anything to gain by saying that he was not on the KSP in 1947, or that Zhdanov was). It seems that the imagination of several observers was fired up by the fact that Golubev did not win the prize despite having had an extra audition and even an audience with Zhdanov (and it was not in Golubev's interests to divulge the content of that meeting). Even four years later, Shaporin recalled the events of 1947 when he urged the KSP to look more kindly on Golubev's Second Quartet: 'I think that we really ought to be considerate towards this composer, who was strangely ill-starred, since he had even been invited to see Comrade Zhdanov, and we were all counting on him getting a prize, but it didn't happen ...'[20]

Strange turns of fate like this were often assumed to be intervention from Stalin in the absence of any more mundane evidence. And, since leaks would have pointed to Shostakovich as Golubev's main detractor, it is easy to see how the story could have emerged about Shostakovich prompting Stalin to intervene. And yet, in this case, judging from our more reliable perspective based on documents, no such skulduggery was even needed: Golubev disappeared from the lists well before the Politburo session, and there is no reason to think he was discussed there at all, let alone in such a dramatic fashion.

Points of Principle

Aside from the Golubev episode, which set Shostakovich up as a difficult, if authoritative colleague, there was much in his behaviour that could irritate his peers. It is as if the well-established balance of power among the older musicians (Goldenweiser, Myaskovsky and Shaporin) was suddenly thrown out of joint. Ever more often, Goldenweiser recorded the atmosphere of the meetings as being 'unpleasant', not only on account of Khrapchenko's heavy presence, but also because of Shostakovich's undiplomatic behaviour.

Fig. 13. Shostakovich at a KSP plenary session, sitting alongside the sculptor Sergei Merkurov. 27 March 1947 (as dated by Olga Dombrovskaya). Reproduced with permission of the Shostakovich Archive in Moscow.

At the very same time as he sent down Golubev, Shostakovich caused much greater distress to his older colleagues when he passed judgement on Anatoly Aleksandrov's opera *Bela*. Aleksandrov was a generation older than Golubev, a well-established and respected composer whose career was already under way a decade before the Revolution; he was an old friend of Myaskovsky's and commanded greater overall sympathy in the KSP than Golubev. Aleksandrov's lyrical opera after Lermontov, *Bela*, was his magnum opus, and it opened up real prospects for a Stalin Prize (he had not previously won a prize). Not only Myaskovsky, but also Glière and Goldenweiser believed that *Bela* was a work of lasting value, which would stay in the repertoire and make its mark in music history.[21] And there was apparently nothing to block its way: the opera's plot was taken from a classic novella, while the music was smooth, intelligent, pleasant and professional – what was there not to like?

Shostakovich, however, decided unilaterally that the bar must be set higher (and never mind that less accomplished work had received prizes in previous years). There were some weaknesses in the libretto, due to the inexperience of the librettist, but this was only tangential to Shostakovich's line of attack. He said that it was the composer who ultimately had to shoulder the responsibility for dramatic shortcomings:

Here is the criticism I want to level at the composer. For all the excellent musical language, good technique, expressiveness and the undoubted talent of the composer, the weakest aspect of the opera lies in the lack of any well-defined and expressive characterization. And so Bela sings in more or less the same [musical] language as Pechorin and the others. I am not insisting on the use of Wagner's leitmotivic principle. There are operas where such leitmotives are lacking, but the characters are still well defined – Carmen and Don José are vivid figures, but here everything is flattened out by the same fine writing of good quality. The main shortcoming here is the lack of definite musical characteristics, and this is exactly what makes an opera, in that high sense of the word which we should demand, a musico-dramatic work.[22]

That settled that: for Shostakovich, *Bela* was not a proper opera. Knowing how musically distinct the characters are in Shostakovich's own *Lady Macbeth*, we can see that here he was stating his own operatic credo. He knew how good his own musico-dramatic skills were, and we can well understand that he was most likely very frustrated that, out of prudence after the debacle of *Lady Macbeth*, he now had to abandon this side of his musical genius. Shostakovich's intervention was a departure from the good manners of KSP debate, usually only abrogated for the occasional ideological skirmish. This intervention was harsh, but also devoid of ideological motivation, leaving experienced members of the KSP in a quandary. Did they feel that Shostakovich was being unfair to Aleksandrov, who had produced a good work that had managed deftly to be both officially acceptable for performance while suggesting nothing of Socialist Realism? Or did they feel that Shostakovich's behaviour could be put down to his ignorance of KSP etiquette? Or on the contrary, might he have been acting knowingly in an attempt to undermine the power of Myaskovsky, his main rival at the Moscow Conservatoire?

Goldenweiser's abiding memory of the meeting, as recorded in his diary, was what he perceived as Shostakovich's deeply unfair intervention against Aleksandrov's opera. Even so, the KSP passed it for a second-class prize (the degree that could have been expected even if Shostakovich had not intervened). Unfortunately for Aleksandrov, Shostakovich was not his only problem, and his opera disappeared from the list after some pruning by the Politburo Commission. The motivation could hardly have been Shostakovich's objection; instead, while the opera was perfectly performable, its lack of any Socialist Realist qualities left it without any strong claim on a Stalin Prize. The opera's plot was neither contemporary nor historical – it had no significance beyond the love story it presented. To award *Bela* a prize would hardly provide composers or librettists with a suitable model for genuine Soviet opera (the genre that was so eagerly awaited, but never quite emerged). Aleksandrov worked as a composer outside the fray, and little in his output suggested that anything had significantly changed for him since the early 1910s; he was not a problematic composer for the authorities, but nor were they rushing to encourage him either. In the end, he received a second-class prize, four years later, in 1951, although not for an opera, but for a more modest collection of Pushkin romances together with a set of piano pieces for children.

On many other occasions during his 1947 debut in the KSP, Shostakovich behaved as a self-appointed quality inspector, exposing what he saw as sloppy or shoddy practices. He objected, for example, to the practice of awarding whole production teams (for example, opera conductor/director/main soloists) without judging how valuable the contribution of each individual was. This, however, was the normal and hitherto uncontroversial approach to team nominations, and Shostakovich's objections to the practice in particular cases caused some confusion. While, for example, he supported the nomination of the Bolshoi production of Prokofiev's *Cinderella*, he objected to the inclusion of the house ballet conductor Yury Fayer, who, he said, had done no more than his usual job (and he had already won two prizes anyway).[23] Still more controversially, he objected to the team nomination for the Leningrad production of Prokofiev's *War and Peace*: he proposed instead that the award should be made to the conductor Samosud alone, since he had not noticed anything outstanding in the contributions of the director Boris Pokrovsky or the lead soprano Tatyana Lavrova (Natasha Rostova).[24] Shostakovich objected even more insistently against the mediocre composers who were receiving a share of team prizes in nominations for large film crews: the composer Nikolai Kryukov, for example, was about to receive a Stalin Prize for what Shostakovich considered a merely routine soundtrack for the film *Admiral Nakhimov*.[25]

Shostakovich created a flap, but in each case he was overruled. The KSP was accustomed to a certain degree of latitude and diplomacy, and the members knew well the offence such exclusions would cause: there would be letters of complaint from the Bolshoi and Maly companies, and expressions of outrage from the cinematography minister Bolshakov. On a pragmatic level, they also knew that if they excluded various individuals, they were most likely to be reinstated by the government (we have already commented on Stalin's perhaps over-generous approach to large teams). By himself, Shostakovich could not change the practice of awarding everyone involved 'in one sneeze' – *chokhom* – to use a colourful Russian expression. Such habits were strengthening the inflationary trend in the awards system, so Shostakovich had a point in principle, but he lacked the diplomacy and networking skills to have any effect beyond making a splash in meetings.

As we have seen, Shostakovich positioned himself in the KSP as a discerning expert rather than an ideological whip. The sole exception was his contribution to the discussion of the Kirghiz opera *Manas*, composed by the trio of Vlasov/Fere/

Maldybaev, who had enjoyed previous successes (more on this in Chapter 7). There was concern over the libretto, which on scrutiny was not only of a low literary standard but also showed poor judgement on the ideological level. It was a tale of feudal power struggles, which should have been welcome, but the serfs were only granted a token presence, and the overall effect was an aestheticization of feudal life, which the Party had already instructed artists to avoid.[26] Shostakovich, on this occasion, did what was often left to the reliable Fadeyev – he spoke as an ideological watchdog:

> Here it's not simply the case that the libretto has various trivial faults. Yevgeny Mikhailovich [Kuznetsov] has reported to us that the libretto goes against the latest CC Resolution on the arts. If this is indeed so, we need to sort out the issue and then the musicians should suffer too [i.e. not only the librettist], because they should have seen this clearly.[27]

This proved to be both Shostakovich's first and last ideological pronouncement in the KSP, since he was removed from his position in February 1948 – not because he had stepped on too many toes the previous year, but because of the following CC Resolution on Music, which attacked him for his formalism. His intervention on the Kirghiz opera hints that Shostakovich might have set himself on a very different trajectory before the 1948 Resolution put him on the wrong side of the authorities once more.

Fighting for Friends and Disciples

Once Shostakovich had regained official favour, he was reinstalled on the KSP, and took up his duties again in December 1951. This time he desisted from his former displays of rosy-cheeked enthusiasm and shiny principles. He was in some ways a greater success than ever, but he was also more jaded and compromised. It did not help that the new Music chairman was Khrennikov, his chief tormentor in 1948, although Khrennikov, in turn, had to be more diplomatic towards Shostakovich now. This time round, Shostakovich made himself useful to those he respected and loved, and sometimes even to more distant acquaintances who could use a helping hand. This, in fact, was only normal for KSP members, and like his colleagues, he must also have had his assistance solicited at various times. But although he was no longer trying to deprive anyone of a prize – quite the opposite – he still stood out from his colleagues. While most KSP members would simply give up on those occasions when they could raise little or no support for their protégés, Shostakovich continued his hopeless fights to the point of embarrassment and beyond. It is as if he wished to register his opinion emphatically even when he knew that he could achieve nothing more. Once again then, he was seen as rocking the boat, even if his reasons were much more benign, but in the transcripts, there is no sign that he let emotions get the better of him: his words are passionate but rational.

It is true that Shostakovich was capable of looking after his friends in earlier years: a marginal note in the sketches for his opera *The Gamblers* is a memo that he should put his old friends Boleslav Yavorsky and Vissarion Shebalin forward for a Stalin Prize (and indeed, Shebalin received a first-class prize for his 'Slavonic' Quartet in 1943).[28] He rooted for Shebalin again during the 1947 session, describing the mood of his cantata *Moscow* as ardent, with no suggestion of indifference, implying that it rose above the level of the standard official cantata (this work also received a first-class prize). But these, after all, were safe choices, clear winners. Now Shostakovich was repeatedly standing up for clear losers.

In 1952, at the height of the anti-cosmopolitanism campaign, Shostakovich put forward Weinberg's Moldavian Rhapsody, a work on Jewish themes. Weinberg, as we know, had featured in the KSP auditions before, without any success, but this nomination was close to a provocation, and Shostakovich received an unambiguous retort:

> *Shostakovich:* A very good piece, it sounds marvellous.
> *Golovanov:* In technical terms, it was very well orchestrated, but I'm worried about the topic: it is all based on Jewish tunes.[29]

Golovanov had the reputation of being anti-Semitic after he was heavily criticized for his behaviour in 1928,[30] but during the anti-cosmopolitanism campaign, he felt that the restraints were off. Khrennikov was more circumspect, saying he disliked the piece only for its 'coolness'. Shaporin found the version for violin and piano cooler and drier than the orchestral version, despite Oistrakh's brilliant rendition. Zakharov, evidently not up to speed, suggested that if that was the problem, then it was the orchestral version that should be considered for a prize. Khrennikov, having been put on the spot by his closest comrade, now had to state the matter more plainly: 'This orchestral work has been subjected to some very strong public criticism, owing to the fact that its national spirit wasn't conveyed well enough, among other things.'[31] He was clearly signalling that there was no point in continuing with Weinberg's piece, and the message was received, since no one but Shostakovich supported the piece when it came to the Music Section's vote (only one vote in the secret ballot was cast in favour, which must have been his). This, according to the rules, meant that the piece still had to go forward to the plenary session, when it was auditioned before everyone in a live performance by Oistrakh.[32] 'It came out rather on the cool side,' Khrennikov remarked, improbably, sensing that he could retreat to his blander argument in this meeting. And indeed, no one at the plenary session wished to associate himself with these dangerous goods. They must have felt their caution was well judged a year later, when Weinberg was arrested shortly after another of Oistrakh's performances of the same Moldavian Rhapsody, given in the Tchaikovsky Hall.[33] He spent seventy-eight days in a prison cell, awaiting the expected charge of 'Jewish nationalism', but after Stalin's death the victims of the anti-cosmopolitanism campaign (together with most other political prisoners) were freed in waves. Shostakovich wrote a letter to Beria, lobbying for Weinberg's swift release. It was not, of course, the Moldavian Rhapsody that landed Weinberg in prison, since he had been under close surveillance for five years after the death of his father-in-law, Mikhoels, but the timing of the arrest would have seemed symbolic for KSP members.

True to form, Shostakovich tried his luck with Weinberg's music again in 1954, putting forward an innocuous radio play for children, *The Invisible Dimka* (*Dimka-nevidimka*).[34] But that failed, too, for whatever reason, leaving Weinberg as one of the very few significant Soviet composers of the time who had not only failed to win a Stalin Prize, but had never even gone as far as the plenary ballot.

Shostakovich was more fortunate with another protégé of his, his former student Yury Levitin, in 1952. Levitin's oratorio *Lights upon the Volga* (on the great construction sites of the Stalin period) was heard by the whole plenary session in recording and met with approval.[35] Even Khrennikov was upbeat: '[The work] has a good many positive features: the choice of topic is a daring one, the technical level is high, and the composer's nationality is clear – this is a Russian work.'[36]

Shostakovich, scenting success, suggested moving Levitin's piece up a class, putting it ahead of the cantata *Song of Joy* by the Uzbek composer Mukhtor Ashrafiy.[37] But this was a step too far, and drew objections: Ashrafiy, he was told, stood out because he was engaged in a heroic struggle for polyphonic music in Uzbekistan against the prevailing 'unison' singing; Levitin was fine, but nothing made him stand out – he was not even particularly original. Shostakovich said that Ashrafiy should be given no special consideration: he was an educated, experienced, serious musician, and a Stalin Prize winner already.[38] In the end, both received third-class prizes.

Levitin's submission the following year was his Seventh Quartet, based on Ukrainian folk songs, which many considered a step up from the cantata. Unexpectedly, though, the Quartet sparked some controversy. Its troubles started when one of the members of the quartet decided to enhance the impact of the audition by reading out the dedication: to the memory of the partisan girl Lyalya Ubiyvovk, executed by the fascists during the Great Patriotic War.[39] The KSP members, as they agreed afterwards, enjoyed the music and appreciated the composer's masterly treatment of the folk material, but their knowledge of the dedication made them listen to it as a programmatic piece, and as such, it was clearly found wanting. The dramatic climax of the slow movement was understood as the scene of the girl's execution, and Livanova complained that the writing here was over the top, verging on expressionism. Shtoharenko took issue with the choice of songs: why choose old, traditional songs rather than those specifically commemorating Lyalya's heroic deeds? Such songs (according to him) were in circulation and available to the composer. Doubts also arose over the use of particular songs at certain points in the programme, even though this programme was only being constructed for the first time in the minds of the listeners. Why was a drinking song 'Chorna khmara' (Dark Cloud) used to represent the Ukrainians' attack? Worse still, one of the songs was identified by Shaporin as Polish and thus unfit for the purpose.

Shostakovich sensed that the unforeseen consequences of the dedication were going to sink a good piece by his former pupil, and so he attempted to distance the piece from its supposed programme:

> I am not entirely sure that this is a programmatic work. Comrade Karayev
> says that there is an execution scene in it. I listened twice, but I didn't notice
> that. The work is dedicated to the memory of a national heroine, but I didn't
> get the impression that it was programme music.[40]

Khrennikov disregarded Shostakovich: 'Does it convince as a programmatic piece? For its programmatic nature is indeed declared.' 'It is only a dedication …,' Shostakovich kept protesting, but he was silenced by Livanova: 'Dedicated – that already means it has a programme, [especially in] the context of folk music.' And Khrennikov further strengthened the point: 'Every folk theme is a programme, which gives the idea to the whole work.'[41]

Shostakovich's line of defence may seem reasonable today, but at the time it was clearly disingenuous. He knew very well that for his contemporaries in Stalin's Soviet Union, a dedication was a powerful way of suggesting a programme without a wholesale commitment to a detailed narrative. He himself had taken advantage of this convention in his Seventh Symphony, which was only 'dedicated to the city of Leningrad'; he had not published or announced any programme, but audiences perceived such a programme nevertheless (the 'invasion episode' in particular cried out for a programmatic explanation). It was precisely this perceived programme that made the impact of the Symphony so powerful and earned Shostakovich his international wartime celebrity. He used the trick again in his Eighth Quartet, dedicated 'to the victims of fascism and war', sending commentators on a false trail and masking the Quartet's autobiographical nature. For Levitin, though, the same strategy backfired: partly because he lacked Shostakovich's authority, but also because the Music Section members were wise to the ruse, and not pleased to find that the composer had failed to work through the implications seriously. Shostakovich's sole vote in favour of the piece[42] kept it on the list of nominations only for a few days: its detractors regrouped and came out with much more stringent accusations. Shaporin dismissed the Quartet as 'a false work in principle', while Khrennikov, worse still, accused the composer of 'an opportunistic [*prisposoblencheskaya*] treatment of the theme'.[43]

In the following year, 1954, Shostakovich became embroiled in a far greater row, now on account of his former student Sviridov. A few weeks before his own Tenth Symphony appeared on the agenda, the KSP auditioned Sviridov's vocal cycle, *My Fatherland* (*Moya Rodina*, later reworded as *Strana otsov*) for tenor and bass, on texts by the Armenian poet Avetik Isaakian (1875–1957). According to Sviridov himself, Shostakovich took a particular liking to the piece and was instrumental in bringing it to the concert stage, acting through the new minister of culture, Panteleimon Ponomarenko. Shostakovich spoke in support of the piece at the Moscow Composers' Union audition, and then, as Sviridov remembered, came up to him and thanked him for allowing him 'to have passed the day in an atmosphere of the beautiful'.[44]

Despite Shostakovich's strong support, the work's 'gloominess' was bound to make its progress difficult; it was noted straight away by the KSP Music Section.[45] By this stage, the cycle had already come under a barrage of criticism at the Leningrad Composers' Union, where Shostakovich had failed to convince the majority that the work was of great merit. At the KSP, the work failed to win sympathy on two counts: because of its challenging, uncompromising style and because of its content. Despite a very Socialist Realist title, the poetry spoke of poignant and tragic things: of oppression by another nation, of exile, sadness and death. This made the members of the committee apprehensive: what was the piece really about? One perceptive KSP member noticed that one of the Isaakian poems alluded to a poem by Hristo Botev.[46] He asked a pointed question: what is this Bulgarian reference doing here? It would be safe to assume that in 1954, the censor would be worried by anything that could be construed as casting doubt on the legitimacy of the Moscow-aligned Bulgarian state. (As it happens, Sviridov did indeed write another work of a similar hue, *Three Bulgarian Songs*, at around the same time.) There was also the immediate impact of the performance: the cycle was sung for the KSP by the two soloists who had only just arrived from Leningrad (the tenor Ivan Nechayev and the bass Vladimir Andriyanov), in a small, unsuitable room with an out-of-condition piano. Even if they had sung it as well as they had back in Leningrad, the force of two powerful male voices singing highly intense music, often at the top of their ranges, with the hindrance of both the acoustic and the piano, must have been uncomfortable and intimidating for the KSP audience.

My Fatherland was voted down. Shostakovich, who could not influence the decision due to his absence, was unwilling to accept it, and sent a telegram to the committee, to be read out at the plenary session:

> It is with great regret that I have learnt of the plenary session's decision to reject Sviridov's vocal cycle, in agreement with the [Music] Section's report. I assume that this must have happened due to the rather unsatisfactory performance of the piece. If it is possible to organize another performance urgently, under normal musical conditions, I request that this be done.[47]

The members were somewhat shocked by the telegram – or shock, at least, is what they decided to express. Goldenweiser admitted that the performance had indeed been unsatisfactory, but tentatively suggested that the piece might not be worth as much as Shostakovich thought. Khrennikov said that it would be impossible to carry out Shostakovich's request. Why? – asked the others, their puzzlement increasing. Because the singers are refusing to sing the piece again, claimed Khrennikov, because they say it is too uncomfortable for the voice. The two singers, moreover, had originally been told that they would only have to perform it for the Leningrad Composers' Union plenary session, which they had done, albeit reluctantly, only to find they had to perform it again in Moscow. A third performance was asking too much of them, Khrennikov claimed. Alexei Popov, uncertain whether the music was really so ill-suited to the voice, suggested that the singers among the KSP members should offer their opinion on the matter. The KSP's two singers, Larisa Aleksandrovskaya and Georgy Nelepp,[48] did as requested, but this only made matters worse for Sviridov's bid. Aleksandrovskaya corroborated Khrennikov's account of the performers' reluctance, and she herself wondered how the tenor Nechayev had ever managed to find his entry notes (intended as a criticism of Sviridov's accompaniment, not Nechayev's musicianship). Nelepp agreed, and said that he could never fathom a piece with such incomprehensible harmonies, and it would give him no pleasure to learn it (admittedly, Nelepp's own preferences were for classical repertoire).[49] The KSP thus decided not to act on Shostakovich's telegram, only to receive a letter from him expanding on the telegram's message, and asking them to postpone the nomination of Sviridov's cycle to the following year rather than rejecting it outright now.[50] Shaporin thought this was downright egocentric of Shostakovich (as if the rest of the KSP was incompetent to assess the matter in his absence) and expressed embarrassment and shame over this inappropriate behaviour on his colleague's part.[51]

It is worth quoting some passages from the offending letter, in which Shostakovich clearly uses formulations that were stronger than anything he would have written before Stalin's death:

> Things have turned out rather complicated for this work. Sviridov wrote his cycle *My Fatherland* in 1949. Then some influential Leningrad musicians strongly criticized it so that it could receive no public performances. It was only in 1953, due to the insistence of some musicians who valued the work highly, that it ever came before the public. I don't want to condemn a negative evaluation of Sviridov's work merely because I disagree with it; it is because I am *firmly against administrative measures and categorical judgements in the sphere of art.*
>
> [...]
>
> The criticisms made by the [Music] Section members did not convince me. Comrades Zakharov and Novikov, in particular, claimed that such a work 'is not needed by the people', that 'the people are not looking forward to such works'. [...] I cannot agree with these remarks because I think that neither Comrade Zakharov, nor Comrade Novikov, *nor any other musician, even those occupying high positions, has any right to speak categorically on behalf of the people.*[52] [italics added]

All the KSP rows we have covered, this one included, can tell us much about the pieces concerned, as well as the power games in which they were enmeshed. *My Fatherland* was incomparably higher in its artistry than so many works destined for a third-class or even a second-class prize. It was substantial, even monumental, and emotionally demanding. But it also tested the KSP in several ways: their openness to modernism (those 'strange chords' and 'difficult vocal entries'), their tolerance of darker emotional hues and their courage to accept a text that was much deeper than the easy-going doggerel that was so often accepted in song texts of the time. On a more general level, it was a test of the distance covered since January 1948, or even from March 1953. Shostakovich's forceful language challenged the KSP (and the Council of Ministers) to demonstrate that the country had moved on, that new winds had shaken apart the old patterns of behaviour. Musically, his own Tenth Symphony provided another such challenge, as we shall see in Chapter 11.

Weinberg, Levitin and Sviridov were recognized as disciples of Shostakovich. That association might have hindered them more than it helped them, although Sviridov had managed to win a prize for his Shostakovich-infused Piano Trio in 1946, at a time when Shostakovich's own Ninth Symphony and Third Quartet were sidelined. Karayev, whom Shostakovich always supported (and who, in his turn, tirelessly supported his mentor), did not even need Shostakovich's voice: he was counted among the most talented and professional of the 'national' composers, and he had won two prizes and was in line for a third when the business folded. But besides these three, Shostakovich propped up many lesser names, and finding common threads among them is a fascinating task.

A case in point is Shostakovich's support, in 1952, for a rather modest work by Yury Kochurov, his *Five Romances*, op. 17.[53] The prize at stake might have been only the third class, but Khrennikov opposed the work on grounds of principle: the work, and in fact the whole of Kochurov's oeuvre, evinced a profound disconnectedness from Soviet life. Looking at the songs, we can only agree with the assessment: despite using Soviet poetry, the romances managed to retain a decidedly non-Soviet look and feel. With their simplicity, but also with a degree of elegance, they are reminiscent sometimes of Schubert songs, at other times of Russian Orientalist songs, but they steer clear of any recognizably Soviet patterns. The texts were also rather peculiar: 'Life's Joys' (by Iosif Grishashvili), for example, painted pictures of peaceful life at a balmy seaside resort, a child sleeping sweetly to the rustling of the leaves in the garden. The child's slumbers were not even being watched over by Father Stalin!

From the musical qualities alone, it is not possible to say why Shostakovich would wish to root for Kochurov's songs. But some biographical details suggest an explanation: Kochurov graduated from the Leningrad Conservatoire in 1931, and at one stage had belonged to the 'progressive' class of Vladimir Shcherbachev, whose students were part of Shostakovich's regular circle of friends during the good times of his Conservatoire years. Now Kochurov was teaching there, not yet a full professor and, perhaps most importantly, gravely ill (a fact Shostakovich mentioned in the meeting). He died two months after his prize was announced. An award out of sympathy, perhaps? At this point in his life, Shostakovich was no stranger to such sentiments.

Another composer whose music Shostakovich championed was Georgy Kreitner, a former diplomat. His eagerness and *personal* involvement became obvious when, in 1951, he mentioned that he would not only support Kreitner's Suite on themes from Czechoslovakia and the Baltic republics, but would also nominate his opera *The Stormy Year* (*V grozniy god*, based on Lermontov's *Vadim*) when it was ready. Here, again, Shostakovich mentioned that the composer was at the time seriously ill (unlike Kochurov, he lived on until 1958).[54] Shostakovich went so far as to publish a sharp retort to Marina Sabinina's criticism of the opera, which prompted the bemused critic to write an 'open letter', in which she said the music of the opera was clichéd, the work of an epigone of the Russian classics.[55] In principle, non-national composers were expected to draw from the Russian classics, so Kreitner's fault was one of degree – he had gone too far in his use of backward-looking elements. Even Marian Koval found the music of the opera 'too traditional'.[56]

The following year (1953), Shostakovich spent a disproportionate amount of energy defending Leon Khodja-Einatov's *Symphonic Dances*; the composer was an Armenian who spent much of his career in Leningrad and belonged to Shostakovich's wider circle (he was a friend of Sviridov). The *Dances* were written solidly as Soviet 'national' music, but they displayed some flair even so. When they came up for consideration, opinion was split on grounds of taste. Shostakovich spoke first, commending the work's fresh melodic material and excellent orchestration, and addressing the salient issue of its position in the hierarchy of serious music:

> [T]his music may not lay any claim to profundity or philosophizing, but it is so well written, delectable, graceful, undoubtedly pleasing to the listener, and put together without the least hint of anything vulgar or cheap.[57]

Shaporin and Golovanov, from the older generation, disagreed: the work's lightness, in their eyes, clearly worked against it, and they also pointed out that it did not work as light music for dancing either. Shostakovich replied:

> If we accept this work, it will drive out much of that vulgarity [*poshlyatina*], that inappropriate stuff that can be heard in every public space, on every train and so on. But, comrades, the seeds of musical culture can be sown on trains too, where certain records are played over and over again.[58]

His argument even won support from both the mass-song composer Anatoly Novikov and from Zakharov. These general points may remind us of the younger Shostakovich, who, it seems, had sincerely pondered the issue and even contributed to the genre himself in the form of his 'Jazz suites' of the mid-1930s (not jazz in our sense, but light, popular and danceable orchestral music). Whether Shostakovich made his argument in all sincerity, or produced it for the sake of a close colleague, he still took an interest in a wide range of music: he showed his admiration for the Voronezh Folk Choir and for the folk performer

Tamara Khanum; he recommended his old friend, the harpist Vera Dulova to the KSP, and also the military-band conductor Ivan Petrov. Far from being completely immersed in his own work, the Shostakovich of KSP meetings is clearly an avid follower of all kinds of music, a theatre- and cinemagoer, and a reader of diverse literature. Of all the musicians on the committee, only Goldenweiser displays a comparable degree of voracity for culture. Shostakovich is passionate about the Kirov production of *Sleeping Beauty*,[59] recommends the film *Village Doctor* (*Sel'skiy vrach*), and admits to reading, and taking some pleasure in middlebrow adventure books such as *The Arsonists* and *The Conspirators* by Nikolai Shpanov. His interest in Gogol is well known, but is here corroborated both by his attraction to the Kukryniksy group's illustrations for Gogol's *Portrait*,[60] and also by his excitement over the Pushkin Drama Theatre's production of *The Government Inspector* in Leningrad, when others were dismissing it as too 'grotesque' (the director Leonid Vivien was a disciple of Meyerhold).[61]

One of Shostakovich's acts of advocacy must strike us as absurdly out of place, and yet we have it on record: he was passionate in his promotion of a collection of Stalin songs by the composer Iona Tuskiya (Tuskia). Against the Music Section's better judgement, Shostakovich brought this set of five songs to the table in February 1953. The songs did not even have any catchy tunes to recommend them, and in fact they were clearly written for professional choirs, with harmony that drew from Georgian folk polyphony. With Shostakovich's vote behind them, the songs went forward to the plenary session, where KSP members heard four out of the five songs in a very poor-quality recording. The following dialogue ensued:

Fadeyev: This is somehow less than captivating.

Goldenweiser: They're very monotonous songs.

Fadeyev: If no one is put out, let's not listen to the fifth song.

Shostakovich: In my opinion these are very good songs, written with great sincerity and passion. The combination of heroic and lyrical elements is very good, especially in the last song, and they are written in a way that is both original and very national. I've been able to hear them live, not just through this poor recording, and I think that the songs work very well.

Khrennikov: [Sarcastically] You've heard yourselves how good they are. I would say that a song about Stalin must be trans-national in character, which would enable it to address the whole of the Soviet people. But these songs aren't even popular in Georgia, so other peoples are still less likely to accept them.

Shostakovich: In Georgia, they're very popular indeed.

Fadeyev: My immediate impression: they're a bore.

Pudovkin: They're very monotonous.

Fadeyev: Obviously, Dmitry Dmitriyevich, you've suffered a defeat. We're not going to put these songs forward at the present time [a euphemism for 'never'].[62]

At first sight, Shostakovich seems to be enjoying some kind of private joke, making ridiculous statements with a poker face. And yet the evidence shows that there is some logic to Shostakovich's support of Tuskiya. Throughout his career, he paid special attention to composers of the Georgian school, and often supported its representatives in the press[63] or at Stalin Prize meetings. Back in 1947, he had given high praise to Mshvelidze's opera *The Tale of Tariel* (it received a second-class Stalin Prize). In 1952, he attempted, in vain, to have Otar Taktakishvili's Piano Concerto promoted to a first-class award, arguing with Khrennikov about the value of non-programmatic instrumental music (the piece was everyone's favourite that year, but this was not enough).[64] In 1953, he made a similar attempt to promote Balanchivadze's Third Piano Concerto from a third-class to second-class prize, and also supported a trio by Alexander Shaverzashvili (a student of Balanchivadze), exercising such persistence that even after Khrennikov had established that it was rejected, Shostakovich managed to have it reinstated behind Khrennikov's back.

The roots of this special relationship lie in his lifelong friendship with Andrei Balanchivadze, his classmate at the Leningrad Conservatoire. Three more Georgian composers, Kiladze, Mshvelidze and Tuskiya, came to Leningrad for postgraduate study in the years either side of 1930, and they too were old acquaintances of Shostakovich. These connections were reinforced during several trips he made to Georgia, and Tuskiya, for example, figures prominently in at least three photos with Shostakovich from 1952.[65] Shostakovich's impassioned promotion of Tuskiya's Stalin songs followed only three months after the photos had been taken, and was most likely in response to a request from his friend.

In one case, however, Shostakovich was suspected by colleagues of trying to deprive another composer of a prize for personal reasons, an old animosity. The composer in question was Alexander Mosolov, who was proposed for a lower-degree prize in 1953. Mosolov had been a leading modernist in the 1920s and the only other Soviet composer to rival Shostakovich on the international music scene in the latter part of that decade. Now, however, he was a broken man with a tame, bland style. Persecution from RAPM in the early 1930s drove him to write a letter to Stalin in which he begged him either to stop the persecutors or to let him emigrate. RAPM was disbanded in April 1932 (some musicians even imagined that Mosolov's letter had played a role in this), but unlike Shostakovich, Mosolov could not find himself a place in the newly reorganized world of Soviet culture, and in 1937 even endured several months in the camps (ostensibly because of drunken brawling, but his plight as an artist most likely contributed to his degraded state). Afterwards, he tried to rebuild the remnants of his career in the provinces.

While some of his former colleagues might have been happy to vote for Mosolov out of sympathy, the reason for his appearance on the list in 1953 was a bright idea of Khrennikov's: Mosolov could be presented as a perfect case of the repentant modernist turning his hand to worthy and useful Socialist Realist music. Khrennikov nominated Mosolov for a suitable work, a suite for an orchestra of folk instruments (this was a Soviet genre) based on folk songs from the Kuban' region. But the choice was perhaps not so ingenious on Khrennikov's part. Not only was there no touch of originality in the music, but Mosolov had precious little to do as a composer in order to produce the suite. It was simply a transparent and pleasant set of folk-song arrangements that managed to pick up a few votes in the Music Section. The reappearance of Mosolov's name after such a long interval must have set off some regretful reminiscing: as Sveshnikov remarked of Mosolov's truncated career: 'He is a master, but is [now] afraid to write in an extra note.'[66] At the plenary session, however, Mosolov's history was not an issue; the members enjoyed the piece, saw no reason to reject it, and voted for it to receive a third-class prize (uncontroversially, since it was an unambitious 'national' work). Khrennikov was satisfied: 'This is grand positive music, beautiful and of good quality, and it will serve our art well.'[67]

Since no prizes were actually awarded in 1953, the KSP returned to the list the following year, and this time Mosolov's modest piece gathered more votes in the Music Section (probably more compassionate than musically convinced). In the interim, the *Kuban' Village* had become a popular item on Soviet radio, so the vote was no longer for something utterly obscure. Zakharov, harking back to Khrennikov's original sales pitch, tried to persuade his colleagues that the path to Mosolov's redemption as a composer was precisely through the worthy activity of folk-song collecting, making the Kuban' work a particularly apposite choice. Shostakovich alone had harsh words for Mosolov:

Zakharov: What corrected Mosolov? Folk songs. He travelled, transcribed them himself, and that corrected him. If he continues to work in this way . . .

Shostakovich: ... then nothing will happen, due to his very modest talents as
a composer.

Zakharov: But at least this is a work that is bound to meet success with the
broader public.

[...]

Shostakovich: Perhaps as a folk-song collector [he could be successful], but
I don't believe in his talent. And his modernist excursions were just as
talentless as this.[68]

To speak dismissively of Mosolov's later work was perhaps unpleasant, but
frank. Dismissing his earlier work was another matter, and perhaps Shostakovich
himself had a little of the spirit of January 1948 lurking within him. Having
delivered his dismissal, Shostakovich went back to his fruitless defence of
Levitin.

In the light of the revival that Mosolov's earlier music has enjoyed since the
1990s (and Levitin's descent into obscurity), many listeners today would
strongly disagree with Shostakovich's choices. *Kuban' Village* may have indeed
been ephemeral, but many of Mosolov's 'modernist excursions' have withstood
the test of time. Was Shostakovich, the composer of the First Piano Sonata, the
Second Symphony and *The Nose*, really completely impervious to Mosolov's
modernism? It seems rather unlikely, and Shostakovich was in any case no
longer wearing his quality-control hat. This prompts us to wonder if there was
once some friction between the two composers, great enough to leave
Shostakovich with a merciless grudge a quarter of a century later, a grudge
which could not be set aside even for such an obvious underdog. There is no
evidence to say so, and Mosolov was never in any position of official power
over Shostakovich. We may never know, but for all his good deeds, Shostakovich
had his darker moments.

Hearing Shostakovich's voice at the KSP meetings can leave us asking
the same questions that we pose after listening to his music. Was he being
sincere or ironic? Principled or cynical? Fearless or cautious? It seems he was,
at various times, all these things. But the one thing he never did was to keep
silent. He could have done so: Glière, for example, was a stalwart of the
committees, but he never ventured a controversial word. Shostakovich's
interventions at the KSP give us a glimpse of a fiery public temperament
that could not conform to professional etiquette or delicacy, nor to
hypocrisy or tedium. Shostakovich clearly had a strong desire to participate in
public life, and following this compulsion sometimes allowed him to make a
principled stand, or to help out friends, and at other times drew him into
shabby compromises, or indeed into joining the Communist Party. Once

he had accepted the mantle of a public figure, he could not slip it off and on at will. But it was surely that same public temperament that shaped much of his music. Without that innate need to speak up, to interfere, whether to take a stand or to find official approval, we wouldn't have had either the Seventh or the Thirteenth Symphony, nor, on the other side, *Song of the Forests* or the Twelfth Symphony.

CHAPTER SIX

MYASKOVSKY AND HIS SCHOOL

Myaskovsky and his 'Clan'

While Prokofiev and Shostakovich have received copious coverage, both academic and popular, Myaskovsky remains an enigmatic, if indubitably powerful, presence in Soviet music. The weightiness of his presence is borne out by his five Stalin Prizes, four of them first class in comparison to Shostakovich's three. It was only an administrative oversight that enabled Prokofiev to outstrip Myaskovsky, when he received two prizes in one year (they should have been combined). The debate around Myaskovsky's works was minimal; they usually sailed through the committees smoothly. To those who know little or nothing of Myaskovsky's work, these facts would be enough to place him at the very centre of musical Socialist Realism. Yet, the predominance of melancholy and elegiac moods makes this impossible: even Myaskovsky's prizewinning works are all in minor keys.

Myaskovsky's new pieces were also assisted by his unassailable reputation. Once again, it is hard to believe that such an introvert, who held fast to certain aesthetic constants and shied away from demagoguery, could possibly have come to occupy such a pivotal position in the Soviet music scene. One way to explain this would be to see Myaskovsky as the ultimate 'expert' (*spets*), who had been co-opted by the Soviet system by the early 1930s, and set down such deep roots that he seemed indispensable. Myaskovsky's voracious appetite for all new music and his broad tastes led him to become one of the fairest and most reliable appraisers of music. His matchless professionalism in every aspect of composition, from large-scale structure to minuscule details, was highly valued by colleagues and audiences alike.

One of Myaskovsky's seats of power was his position at the State Music Publishers, which he occupied from the creation of that institution up to the end of his life. Before the rise of the Composers' Union in the late 1930s, this was the main financial base for composers. Thousands of musical works passed through Myaskovsky's hands before they went into publication: he assessed them and often lent his keen eye to editing and proofreading. The other position of influence was his twenty-seven-year professorship at the Moscow Conservatoire, during which generations of grateful pupils passed into the ever-growing pool of his supporters. It was not the length of his tenure that was most impressive: more importantly, most of Myaskovsky's pupils, no matter how mature and distinguished, continued to visit their former master and ask for his advice on their new works.

Myaskovsky's clan consisted of several circles. There was a circle of old friends, cemented by weekly music-making at Pavel Lamm's[1] – among them, for example, was the composer Anatoly Aleksandrov. There were former students who became close friends, such as Vissarion Shebalin and Lev Knipper or, at slightly greater distance, the eminent Khachaturian and Kabalevsky, or the lesser-known Yevgeny Golubev and Nikolai Peyko. Students of friends and close colleagues, and students of his own students were also drawn into Myaskovsky's orbit. Even Shostakovich's disciples (such as Weinberg), who were usually seen as a rival camp, took Myaskovsky's advice on board, and we should not be surprised, because Shostakovich occasionally did the same. On 30 November 1948, for example, the younger 'formalist' visited the older 'formalist' in order to play him the Jewish cycle and the Violin Concerto, which the public would not hear until several years afterwards.[2]

From around the mid-1920s, Myaskovsky began showing tolerance for colleagues who were, so to speak, more Sovietized than himself, such as those of his students who were active in RAPM, like Marian Koval and Viktor Bely, and he even allowed himself to be influenced and led by them up to a point.[3] To his mind, people did not lose the right to be considered intelligent, talented or likeable, even if they adopted the new jargon and curried favour with the Soviet regime, like his old friend Boris Asafyev. Only if they overstepped certain boundaries of trust and respect, as Asafyev eventually did in 1948 by supporting the anti-formalist Resolution, did Myaskovsky break off relations.

Myaskovsky's tolerant nature also manifested itself in his attitude to other people's music. He was prepared to engage with even the most hopeless scores, to find a few grains of musical value in them and to formulate some useful advice on how to improve them. To the KSP, his expertise was crucial: the task of ploughing through vocal scores of national operas and other obscure submissions fell mainly on his shoulders (although Goldenweiser and Shaporin did help at times). His quiet but authoritative voice helped many of his clan over the KSP hurdle, although he never held his tongue when he had criticisms to make. The harvest of prizes is impressive: Khachaturian won four, Kabalevsky three, Shebalin, Muradeli, Knipper and Peyko two each, and so on. And we have already discussed the hopes and failures of Aleksandrov and Golubev in earlier chapters.

Myaskovsky's Twenty-first and a Glimpse Backstage

Had Myaskovsky posthumously acquired his own Solomon Volkov, then today we would probably be puzzling over the prize for his Symphony No. 21, and supposing that the only explanation was that Stalin himself had listened to the Symphony and liked it. As in the case of the Shostakovich Quintet, there was a letter of denunciation in the background that could have derailed the nomination – and the piece itself, as we shall see, was hardly Socialist Realist.

One surprise lies in the fact that No. 21 was actually a commission from the Chicago Symphony Orchestra to celebrate its fiftieth anniversary. This already gives us a measure of Myaskovsky's international fame, which may not have been as great as that of Prokofiev or Shostakovich, but was long-standing and steady (his symphonies had regularly been published and performed in the West from the early 1920s). It is not known whether the length was stipulated in the contract, but the Symphony ended up being, unusually for Myaskovsky, a single-movement, twenty-minute piece. He drafted it within twelve days and orchestrated it within a month. When Goldenweiser heard the Symphony for the first time, in an eight-hand piano rendition at Lamm's, he was moved by its intimate character and wrote in his diary: 'Excellent music, but of a kind that is not needed by anyone these days. It's the opposite of Dunayevsky.'[4] And yet he was proved wrong: the audition at the Composers' Union was a success (this time it was a four-hand version played by Svyatoslav Richter and Anatoly Vedernikov), and the Symphony became one of the centrepieces of the Soviet music *dekada* of 1940.

A positive review of the work, penned by Semyon Shlifshteyn in *Sovetskoye iskusstvo*, gave it the nickname 'Symphonic Elegy'.[5] Shlifshteyn compared it to the graceful, balanced and profound elegies by Russia's favourite poet, Alexander Pushkin. Contrary to standard narratives of Myaskovsky's progress, which involved the overcoming of his earlier, pessimistic self, this review dared to assert that in this symphony Myaskovsky once again turned to the personal, and even reminded readers of his Sixth, Myaskovsky's major tragic canvas from 1918 which was read as a comment on the Revolution.[6] We have to see 1940 as a very open-minded year in Soviet music history, if the Sixth was viewed then as Myaskovsky's finest achievement, while the Twelfth (the proto-Socialist Realist work of 1932) had now lost its prestige and was considered a creative failure.[7]

Listening to the music of No. 21 today, one wonders how it came to be such an uncontroversial choice for a Stalin Prize. It is certainly attractive, with its compact and very clear, rounded structure, where the slow, mournful beginning and ending frame a sonata allegro with clear outlines. Myaskovsky's usual contrapuntal complications are present, but not overbearing, and the orchestration, too, is on the transparent side. And yet the darkness of the Symphony cannot be willed away; the return of the introductory material, rather than being given any brighter twist, is just as lugubrious as before. Even in its most dynamic moments, such as the main allegro theme, this elegiac quality is not completely dispelled.

Despite his deep admiration for the work, Goldenweiser gave it a rather subdued introduction at the plenary session of the KSP: he was worried that the bland, lacklustre orchestral premiere under Alexander Gauk had spoiled the impression. Despite this, he made it clear to his colleagues that this was a profound and significant work, drawing on the melodiousness of Russian song and distinguished by an exquisite handling of texture. But rather than staking everything on this symphony, Goldenweiser moved quickly on to Myaskovsky's general virtues:

> [I]t should be said that Myaskovsky is the principal founder of our school of composition: the absolute majority of our most talented young composers are his students. And so the public resonance of Myaskovsky's work as an artist is less than he deserves. I think that if he were to receive a Stalin Prize, it would be the crowning achievement of his splendid career.[8]

Indeed, Myaskovsky was about to turn sixty, and anniversaries like this usually entailed some sign of recognition from the government. Should we presume, then, that in the minds of the members this was a 'lifetime achievement' award, rather than a prize for a twenty-minute 'symphonic elegy'? The KSP placed it ahead of Shostakovich's Quintet, and yet the comparison with Shostakovich perturbed them: Shostakovich's work was brilliant and gripping, which could not be said of Myaskovsky's symphony, even though most listeners perceived in his music a reflection of profound human experiences. The actor Ruben Simonov, particularly moved by the 'calming down' at the end of the finale, said that there was some essential humanity behind the music. He even suggested that, like Shostakovich's Fifth (as was the common perception), Myaskovsky's Twenty-first Symphony was autobiographical. And yet he added that for a wider audience, the Symphony would perhaps be too complex (he had overheard some listeners muttering that it was 'boring') and he suggested that the KSP would have to make a special effort to explain to the people its decision to award a prize to such a work.[9] Even so, the award would serve to raise the general cultural level, Simonov continued: '... recently masters have tended to lower their art in order to be accessible. But now we will put forward works of high art without taking into account whether they are accessible or not. And by this means, we will stimulate the growth of art and the growth of our public.'[10]

Myaskovsky's worthy and sometimes demanding works would thus keep the bar of musical standards raised high. The nomination remained unchallenged throughout the process, and the announcement of the awards, which roughly coincided with Myaskovsky's sixtieth birthday, prompted further positive press.[11] Myaskovsky had the honour to receive the very first laureate's card: it happened that Music was first in the list of categories, and his name came first alphabetically in the Music list (the card was a proof of laureateship, sent to laureates before they received their medals).[12] Unlike some card-flashers who used their title to impress, Myaskovsky must have left his card in the drawer: he neither bothered to attach a photograph to it nor did he sign it.[13]

Given the exceptionally smooth passage of the Symphony through the KSP and the higher echelons, it is startling to find that there was in fact a behind-the-scenes scandal. An anonymous informant contacted the KSP to remind them that the Symphony had been commissioned by the Chicago Symphony Orchestra. This could indeed have derailed the nomination: the top Soviet prize, sanctified by Stalin's good name, was about to be granted to a symphony that was dedicated to an American orchestra. But given the invisibility of this issue in the transcripts, it seems that the KSP simply shrugged the news off and did not bother to keep the letter in its files or comment on it. We only know of the matter because it gained wider attention within the Composers' Union, where it was said that the informant was none other than Khachaturian. Myaskovsky immediately broke off all contact with Khachaturian, while some other composers, performers and even Khachaturian's own Conservatoire students also started boycotting him.

Myaskovsky was so upset that he attempted to withdraw his Symphony from the list of nominations (at the Union of Composers level), while Khachaturian took the matter of the boycott to the Orgkomitet of the Union. Eventually, Myaskovsky and Khachaturian were reconciled through the ministrations of Levon Atovmyan, who wrote about it in his memoirs.[14] At the next meeting of the Orgkomitet presidium (25 January 1941), Myaskovsky had to apologize for alleging that Khachaturian was the culprit, while Shaporin was reprimanded for spreading the rumour.[15] Khachaturian also required his colleagues to hold a discussion on composers' morals and ethics. This is how he presented his plight to them:

For two months I was in a terrible state. The fact is, there were conscious or unconscious attempts to create a rift between Nikolai Yakovlevich and me, a permanent rift, and breaking off relations with Myaskovsky means breaking off relations with the whole of our musical milieu. [...] I was described as a traitor, because I, like Myaskovsky, was a [rival] candidate for a Stalin Prize, and allegedly wrote a letter [to destroy his chances].[16]

Then, with a seemingly throwaway phrase, Khachaturian makes us wonder again what the facts actually were: 'Although of course every honest Soviet citizen can write [a letter] or pass on the information if needed, and this cannot be considered a betrayal.'[17] If he had written the letter, but thought it merely the action of any 'honest Soviet citizen' and that it could not be 'considered a betrayal', then why such sustained indignation and denial? Why not simply admit to what is not a betrayal at all? But if he had not written the letter, and his indignation was sincere, then these words make no sense.

One accidental phrase can sometimes shed light on the hidden lining of the Soviet intelligentsia's existence – such letters, 'passing on information', could make or break careers on a daily basis. But the composers at the meeting preferred to concentrate on the more superficial moral failures of their institution, although, even then, they painted a picture that is worse than anything that would emerge from a reading of public documents.

We find out that at the level of the Composers' Union, the process of nominating works for the Stalin Prize was a sordid affair (making sense of Goldenweiser's disgusted remark describing the composers as 'troglodytes ready to go for each other's throats'[18]). There was a noticeable discrepancy between the opinions expressed in a given discussion and the results of the (secret) ballot that followed: certain 'Georgian composers' would receive general support in the discussion, and then fail to pick up a single vote. Although they were left unnamed, these 'Georgian composers' must have included Vano Muradeli, an active member of the Orgkomitet, whose Cantata for Molotov's sixtieth birthday was not nominated. Muradeli took offence at this two-faced behaviour and suspended his activities in the Orgkomitet by way of revenge.[19] On another occasion, Kabalevsky tactlessly told his colleagues that one of them (unnamed) voted for the Twenty-first Symphony purely out of respect for Myaskovsky, despite admitting that he disliked the piece.[20] Long-standing rumours were aired that Shaporin did not orchestrate his music himself, and that his cantata On the Field of Kulikovo had been written as far back as 1915 (Shaporin denied both allegations).[21] A ministry representative, Vladimir Surin, present at the meeting, identified a militant group (consisting of Ivan Dzerzhinsky, Khrennikov, Vladimir Yurovsky and the critic Georgy Khubov), who were sharply opposed to their colleagues.[22] From this discussion, it appears that the rooms of the Union building, where the composers indulged in drinking and billiards, were thick not only with cigarette smoke but with poisonous gossip and intrigue.

Yet, Myaskovsky, while certainly affected by this gossip and poison pens, continued to stand tall. Once again, as in the case with Grinberg and Shostakovich's Quintet, we have to note that not every denunciation was acted upon or even reached its intended audience. In this case, the powerful informal network around Myaskovsky was able to exonerate him for the American dedication and protect him.

First Class is the Norm

The generally acknowledged consistent quality of Myaskovsky's work could have led to almost any of his more ambitious works being nominated. After Symphony No. 21 came No. 22, the 'Symphonic Ballad', with a subtitle 'On the Patriotic War of 1941'. Myaskovsky himself admitted that it was 'very gloomy',[23] although the finale contained passages of victory music. The new symphony was premiered in Tbilisi in 1942 under Abram Stasevich, an effort that made the best of less than ideal resources and circumstances (Stasevich even paid for the copying of parts from his own pocket).[24] But in spite of the character of the music, and in spite of this rough-hewn premiere, the Symphony was received very well, and some members of the Composers' Union even expressed a preference for No. 22 over No. 21.[25] Still unknown in Kuybyshev, the Symphony was balloted only in Tbilisi, and received six votes for the first class and two for the second. This was enough to see it through the KSP vote, but when the nominations reached Khrapchenko, he argued (in his usual letter to the government) against awarding Myaskovsky a prize for two consecutive years, suggesting that some deserving works from the republics might be considered instead.[26]

In 1944, the members of the Music Section thought it was time to award Myaskovsky again, and it seemed that almost any piece would do. Goldenweiser summed up the discussion to the KSP:

[The Ninth Quartet] is one of his most successful works, a superlative piece, and his finest quartet. The second movement makes its impression on the first hearing, and there is no need for debate here. At the same time we could point to the wonderful 24th Symphony. But because only one work can go forward, we put the Quartet in first place. The Section's opinion is unanimous here.[27]

It is curious, perhaps, that the second movement, singled out by Goldenweiser, is the most dramatic in the cycle: its mournful slow themes are contrasted with an agitated *moto perpetuo* middle section. The finale, however, can be described as determined and even heroic, with a folk (or folk-like) theme as a foil, and is more populist than the other movements. A few dissonant chords do not disturb its recognizably Socialist Realist tone, which Myaskovsky himself identified as 'solemn and a little vulgar' (*torzhestvenno-poshlovatïy*).[28] The members were convinced, if not overenthusiastic: seventeen voted for the first class, eight for the second. Thus, Myaskovsky received his second first-class prize at the beginning of 1946.

When just a few months later a new round began, the main difficulty for Myaskovsky's supporters was persuading the composer himself that he deserved a third Stalin Prize. He withdrew his Eleventh Quartet from the list, claiming that it suffered from imperfections, and then did the same with his Cello Concerto, arguing that it was time for him to make way for others. Shaporin, whether sincerely or not, insisted on including the Cello Concerto on the list against the composer's wishes. He maintained that if the KSP failed to grant an award to the best large-scale work of the season, then their standards were bound to slip.[29] Once again, Myaskovsky's work was cited as a touchstone for high standards in music.

The members agreed: no one objected to the funereal beginning, nor indeed to the melancholy, elegiac nature of the Concerto as a whole. It was Romantic in style, serious and elevated, with mild allusions to the Russian style of the Kuchka, all of which constituted core characteristics of ambitious instrumental works eligible for award. The Concerto's solid dependability was clearly going to win out over the disturbing playfulness of Shostakovich's Ninth Symphony, its main rival. We should also keep in mind that the war was still very much in the minds of listeners, and the Concerto was likely to have been heard as yet another 'war piece'. In any case, Shaporin chose to praise Myaskovsky's art of weaving slowly evolving music, rather than criticize it. The virtuosic, brilliant moments in the second (and final) movement were, of course, even more welcome, although even there, the lyrical element clearly predominated.

The Concerto received a very similar spread of votes to the Ninth Quartet: eighteen for the first class, eight for the second. Once again, the support was very respectable, but not overwhelming. This was now Myaskovsky's third prize, and all three were first-class – which made him one of the most highly honoured artists of the time. Unfortunately for the composer, much of his prize money was lost during the money reform of December 1947, which wiped out any substantial savings of individuals.[30] This reform explains why the 'formalists' of 1948 found themselves in financial trouble so soon after the Resolution: the

savings they had amassed during their lucrative period of glory were now largely
gone.

Myaskovsky and 1948

Many musicians wondered how Myaskovsky's name could possibly appear
among the six 'formalists'. It seemed somehow unfair: he had done nothing to
earn Shostakovich's controversy, nor had he spent years abroad like Prokofiev,
and he held no high official post like Shebalin or Khachaturian, so he could
not have earned himself resentment that way either. The only real reason
for Myaskovsky's inclusion on the blacklist was that he was clearly a leading
member of the ruling musical elite and partook of all its privileges. In 1948, this
ruling group was to be displaced by musical populists who could not wait any
longer for a taste of prestige and power.

Although Myaskovsky's name had already been included in some pre-
Resolution documents,[31] it is possible to imagine that he could still have escaped
the 'formalist' epithet, were it not for one Nikolai Sherman, who lent his poison
pen to the heightening of the anti-formalist campaign of 1948. Sherman's letter,
dated 13 January 1948, was addressed to Polycarp Lebedev, then of Agitprop, who
would in a few days become Khrapchenko's successor.[32] It is unclear from the
evidence whether it was solicited by the CC, or written on Sherman's own initiative. In any case, while ostensibly devoted to the general state of affairs in Soviet
music, it quickly homed in on Myaskovsky's oeuvre and made it a primary target.

Sherman's main claim was that Myaskovsky's music was little known to the
wider audience, and that this was true even for his prizewinning works. This
was not the fault of concert organizations, but resulted from the nature of the
music itself, which displayed a vice that Sherman labelled 'intellectualism'. The
social roots of this vice, according to Sherman, lay in the pre-revolutionary
intellectual milieu, of which he singled out the most preposterous element, the
decadent Symbolism of Zinaida Gippius, on whose texts Myaskovsky had once
written some songs.[33] Maintaining that Myaskovsky's style had not undergone
any radical change since those days, Sherman implied that the noxious air of
Symbolist decadence still hung around Myaskovsky's music.

Sherman was particularly eloquent on the extent and nature of Myaskovsky's
influence. He called him 'the most influential and authoritative composer' on
the Soviet music scene, but emphasized that this influence did not spread to
'the people', but was limited to his own school of composers, which had come
to occupy the leading position in Soviet musical institutions and dominated
the musical press. In Sherman's remarkable description, Myaskovsky becomes
a kind of Mafia don, operating from the shadows:

The basis of Myaskovsky's influence lies in his significant organizational skills, which have enabled him to gather around himself all those he needed, to maintain firm discipline among them, to put them in right places and permanently direct their activities, while staying out of the limelight.

One characteristic feature of Myaskovsky's public face is his reticence. He does not speak at [public] meetings, and does not write articles. His only means of expression is the music that he creates in the silence of his study.[34]

The music, Sherman insists, is 'silent', too. Most of his symphonies, quartets and other works are not performed, and those that are receive no more than one or two airings a year. And yet, Sherman states, 'Myaskovsky is the only Soviet composer no one dares to criticize.'

The emphasis markings in the margins of Sherman's letter, which could belong to Lebedev or Zhdanov, tell us that his letter was read very carefully, and his arguments found convincing. Sherman's animosity towards Myaskovsky would in all probability have dated back to the late 1920s and early '30s, when they were on opposing sides of the musical-ideological debate: Myaskovsky belonged to ASM,[35] Sherman to RAPM. Even so, this is not scattershot abuse, and Sherman's accusations contain recognizable elements of truth. Myaskovsky was indeed elusive and reticent, and he did indeed manage to exercise great influence (musical and organizational) through his loyal pupils across the generations. His music was accorded great respect in professional circles but, as Sherman says, this was out of proportion to the relatively few performances he was able to secure. The roots of his music did indeed lie in parts of the pre-revolutionary cultural scene and, owing to the complexity of its textures and contrapuntal elements, it could often be called 'intellectualist' by anyone who wished to adopt such a term. In other words, Sherman's letter was malicious not through mere invention, but by elaborating on a carefully drawn picture of reality.

Myaskovsky's reaction to the Resolution differed markedly from that of his fellow 'formalists': he did not write or sign any statement of repentance and, pleading illness, absented himself from public discussions.[36] He remained completely silent, as Sherman would have expected, but was not secretly pulling strings to reverse the situation: he was now powerless to do anything but maintain his personal dignity. Together with the other victims, he lost his post in the KSP, and now Khrennikov, the powerful newcomer to that forum, could castigate the same works for which Myaskovsky had once been lauded. The Cello Concerto certainly looked different from the new perspective: Khrennikov said that this work was 'not simply substandard', but 'dreadful'. He even insinuated that the prominent cellist Svyatoslav Knushevitsky had failed to win a prize because he was associated with this piece,[37] while the piece itself was allowed to win a prize. This supposedly revealed the old KSP's double standards.[38]

Forgiven

Despite Myaskovsky's lack of public repentance and his withdrawal from public discussions, there is evidence to suggest that he was still considered, for a while at least, as a valuable figurehead. We may be surprised to discover that the same Khrennikov included Myaskovsky's name in the draft membership list for the new Orgkomitet of the Composers' Union, alone of all the 'formalists'.[39] His name passed the vetting of Shepilov, who acted as Zhdanov's closest subordinate in the business of 1948, and it was only Zhdanov who tore up the whole list as premature and suggested waiting until the first Congress of the Union, due in April 1948.[40] At the Congress, which Myaskovsky did not attend, neither he nor any other 'formalists' were elected to the ruling structures of the Union. But when the new academic year loomed, the new director of the Conservatoire instructed Myaskovsky to resume his composition teaching – they simply could not do without him.[41]

Knowing that Myaskovsky was writing his next symphony in the summer of 1948, Khrennikov pressed him to finish it in time for the Union of Composers' plenary session at the end of the year: none of the 'formalists' was in a hurry to increase the size of Khrennikov's harvest. Myaskovsky obliged, but this, his Symphony No. 26, based on old Russian chants, was considered too gloomy and was shelved. The spring of 1949, however, brought brighter news: Myaskovsky's previously banned works were allowed back into circulation at the same time as Shostakovich's.[42] And less than a year later, Myaskovsky found his Second Cello Sonata on the list of Stalin Prize nominations; he believed that this happened despite Khrennikov, and that the Sonata must have made an impression on someone at the top of the KSP.[43] Perhaps it was simply decided that a full official rehabilitation of the hapless 'formalist' was due.

The Cello Sonata, premiered by Rostropovich, did not advertise itself as an act of repentance or of trying to curry any favours (unlike Shostakovich's Stalin tributes of 1949). The Sonata may be more transparent and melodic than many of Myaskovsky's works, but its predominantly elegiac tone and its abundance of slow music remain true to his habitual mode of expression. Myaskovsky's contemporaries might have heard greater differences than we perceive today: Khachaturian, for example, wrote Myaskovsky a congratulatory letter after the Sonata's audition at the Composers' Union, in which he twice applied the word 'realist' to the piece. The bleakness of the Soviet musical landscape in 1949 also made the piece stand out. Khachaturian complained that Myaskovsky's Sonata found itself in the midst of music that was so poor that its composers should have been expelled from the Union.[44]

In spite of Myaskovsky's doubts, the transcripts show that Khrennikov actually spoke briefly but warmly in the Sonata's favour when the KSP began its discussion of the music nominations: 'This work by Nikolai Yakovlevich is very poetic, melodic and inspired; the Music Section gives its full support and asks other members to support it during the vote.'[45] Goldenweiser seconded the motion, but made some reference to Myaskovsky's recent difficulties:

> The name of Myaskovsky does not arouse any doubts. He is a major composer. Essentially, he lacked the formalist aspect, but he did have a certain academic dryness that he has left behind. This work is very sincere and very songful, and it is distinguished by great talent and technical skill.[46]

The KSP voted the Sonata through for the first prize, but both the minister, Lebedev and Agitprop were in favour of downgrading the prize. Agitprop lamented the fact that Myaskovsky failed to create something weightier than a cello sonata whose 'range of thoughts and feelings' was limited.[47] They would have preferred to see a large-scale work on Soviet themes marking Myaskovsky's return to favour.[48]

The full Agitprop comment on Myaskovsky's nomination summarized his career thus:

> N. Myaskovsky is the composer of a little under thirty symphonies and various quartets, sonatas, concertos and other works. Many of these works suffered from serious formalist errors.
>
> After the CC Resolution, Myaskovsky strove to overcome these shortcomings in his artistic work, although he did not manage to do so in full measure. In 1948, he wrote a Symphony on Russian themes [No. 26] and a Dance Suite [Divertimento op. 80] for orchestra. Both these works demonstrate the significant progress he was making as he tried to distance himself from formalist thinking and to approach a realist embodiment of our reality.
>
> Myaskovsky's Second Cello Sonata, written in 1949, is distinguished for its bright lyricism, its clear and accessible melodic writing, and its optimistic character.[49]

It is also likely that the speed and ease of Myaskovsky's rehabilitation was due to the news that he was seriously ill, which could well have prompted Khrennikov to decide that enough was enough. On 8 March 1950, when the

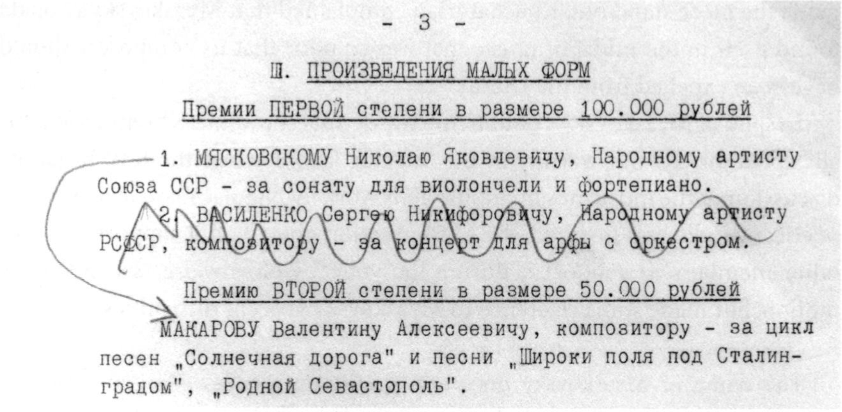

- 3 -

Ⅲ. ПРОИЗВЕДЕНИЯ МАЛЫХ ФОРМ

Премии ПЕРВОЙ степени в размере 100.000 рублей

1. МЯСКОВСКОМУ Николаю Яковлевичу, Народному артисту
Союза ССР - за сонату для виолончели и фортепиано.

2. ВАСИЛЕНКО Сергею Никифоровичу, Народному артисту
РСФСР, композитору - за концерт для арфы с оркестром.

Премию ВТОРОЙ степени в размере 50.000 рублей

МАКАРОВУ Валентину Алексеевичу, композитору - за цикл
песен „Солнечная дорога" и песни „Широки поля под Сталин-
градом", „Родной Севастополь".

Fig. 14. The markings on this KSP list are most likely Molotov's: Myaskovsky's Cello Sonata demoted to the second class, Vasilenko's Harp Concerto deleted. RGASPI, fond 82 (Molotov), op. 2, ye.kh. 467, l. 106.

news of the prize came out, Myaskovsky was receiving visitors, telegrams and phone calls from morning till night.[50] Friends and supporters, the whole of Myaskovsky's great 'clan', breathed a sigh of relief. Three days later, Myaskovsky's Thirteenth Quartet was also given official approval at the union and the ministry, confirming that the period of disfavour was now consigned to the past.

Within six months, however, Myaskovsky had died of cancer, and it seems that his colleagues were still left with the sense of guilt or regret for the humiliation that could have brought forward his demise. When, in the spring of 1951, a posthumous prize was considered, Shaporin made a brief memorial speech:

> I would like to remind you that this man, who had worked on the Stalin Prize Committee, wrote a work at the end of his life that I found deeply moving. I think that his Symphony No. 27 will enter the repository of classic Russian symphonic music. It was written shortly before his death, when the composer sensed that the end was looming. This work came from his very heart. I think it is a testament, a confession, and when, after the wonderful Andante, he moves on to the marches [the finale], he says: 'I am with you in the business of constructing a new society!'

To this, Goldenweiser replied squeamishly, 'I don't think this needs to be spelled out, but it is [indeed] a superb work.'[51] The last symphony and the last quartet (No. 13) jointly garnered a posthumous first-class prize.

Even so, there was something of Myaskovsky's damaged reputation that lingered beyond his death. In 1953, the minor writer, Osip Chorny, published his roman-à-clef *Snegin's Opera* (*Opera Snegina*), which presented in fictionalized form the pre- and post-1948 events in Soviet music. The novel's characters include the formalist composer Gilyarevsky, who is clearly based on Myaskovsky, a cold, solitary man to whom, nevertheless, throngs of composers came for advice and who was considered 'for fifteen years or more' a leader of the Soviet school. His music, passionless and mathematical, is described in the novel as 'vicious' and 'awful', and the composer himself is portrayed as almost an *otshchepenets*, a renegade. When the storm descends on formalism, Gilyarevsky, like Myaskovsky, strikes an aloof pose and says nothing. Gilyarevsky also contains a large dose of Prokofiev, and even some elements of Shostakovich, but the author was evidently eager to cast aspersions on Myaskovsky two years after his death.[52]

Khachaturian: A National or International Composer?

As we saw in Chapter 2, Khachaturian's Violin Concerto was his first musical work to appear on the original 1940 list, and it received a high evaluation from the Music Section. Its performance by Oistrakh was so irresistible that Goldenweiser was prepared to forgive what he saw as the rather light character of the music and some formal defects.[53] Behind Khachaturian's idiom, it seemed, there was a solid core of folk-based musical language, which earned the music the ideological prestige of national authenticity. This was strenuously denied from an unexpected quarter: the rival national composer Uzeyir Hajibeyov, of Azerbaijan:

> What kind of music is he writing? If he is a national composer, we have to make one set of demands of him, but if he is a Moscow composer, then the demands are different. In order to write Armenian music, a good knowledge of Armenian folk music is needed. But that is what interests him least of all. And if he has some folk aspects, they're merely a smokescreen. The music he writes has nothing to do with [true] folk music.[54]

There is undoubtedly a hint of sour grapes here: Hajibeyov seems to resent Khachaturian's Moscow training and a technical polish that he himself could not match. He therefore turns to the issue of authentic folk expression, where he could credibly claim to outdo Khachaturian. And yet Hajibeyov touched upon a crucial issue of Khachaturian's dual role as a composer, which was indeed a defining feature of his career and, as we shall see, was reflected in the spread of Stalin Prizes he received. The Violin Concerto won him a second-class prize, followed by three first-class prizes – for the ballet *Gayaneh* in 1943, for the Second Symphony in 1946 and for his 'rehabilitation' work, the film score for *The Battle of Stalingrad*, in 1950.

The ballet *Gayaneh* is a useful case in point. This was a reworking of Khachaturian's earlier ballet, *Happiness*, which had been performed at the 1939 Armenian *dekada*. *Happiness* was presented as the work of a 'national' composer representing one of the non-Russian republics. The Kirov Ballet decided to produce the ballet during the war; they had been re-housed in the city of Molotov (now Perm), where Khachaturian was now summoned, and he began fresh work on the ballet under the supervision of the theatre. As a result, more than half of the music in *Gayaneh* was new, and Khachaturian was overwhelmed by the quality of the production, especially when the star ballerina Galina Ulanova stepped into the main role. Khachaturian felt that his triumph was in danger of passing unrecognized in the midst of war and in the provincial city of Molotov; in better circumstances, the production would have moved him into quite another orbit.[55] He was unhappy to find that the ballet was treated with condescension from some of his Moscow colleagues, as he reported in a letter: 'I am very offended by the fact that many regard my ballet as an old work, as a kind of *dekada* work [*chto-to dekadnoye*] – the use of that word implies everything.'[56] Khachaturian was anxious to correct this impression, and fortunately the KSP members were immediately struck by the passages they heard performed on the piano (since they had not been able to see the Kirov production). Glière now characterized Khachaturian as a European composer first and foremost, with only 'a shade' of the national about him.[57]

This matter was of great moment to Khachaturian, and in one letter he produced the following formulation of the reception he desired for his music:

> No matter how much I switch between my musical languages, I will still remain an Armenian, but an Armenian who is European rather than Asian, an Armenian who will make Europe and the whole world listen to our music. And as they hear the music, listeners will surely have to say: tell us about these people, show us the country that has such music. This is my life's dream.[58]

The Second Symphony, premiered a year before this statement, was one further step towards his acceptance as a European composer. Of course, the habit of viewing Khachaturian as a 'national' did not disappear overnight, and one of the KSP members, Moskvin, exclaimed with delight: 'He is national – this is wonderful!'[59] A stereotype of Khachaturian gained some traction: he was, supposedly, an emotional, intuitive composer guided by his Southern temperament, and this led some members to doubt whether he had mastered the vaguely defined but all-important art of 'symphonic thinking'. Myaskovsky, although he agreed that the Symphony fell into large but separate episodes, still gave Khachaturian the benefit of the doubt, insisting that a symphony does not have to be written according to any particular template.[60] Goldenweiser also thought that the Symphony had flaws, namely the preponderance of slow music and 'viscous' material that tended to lead towards stasis,[61] but he also insisted that none of this was grave enough to disqualify the work. There was some prestige attached to the notion of amalgamating musical nationalism with international developments in music, and this also helped to strengthen Khachaturian's case. In the Second Symphony, indeed, the familiar idiom of Russian Orientalism is intensified and elevated to the heights of tragedy. Something new is forged from its habitual triplets and dance rhythms, something that leaves connotations of exoticism and eroticism far behind. In his Third Symphony (Symphony-Poem, 1947), he was still more determinedly searching for a new style (its extravagant sonority featured fifteen extra trumpets and a soloistically treated organ), but the result fell between the grinding stones of the 1948 Resolution, blocking off the territory he wanted to explore, and leaving him the safe 'song and dance' music of the stereotypical 'exuberant Armenian' which he had tried to leave behind.

The Resolution hurt Khachaturian badly, and some would claim that he never recovered his stride, that he 'was broken, lost his voice, lost himself', as Rodion Shchedrin put it.[62] He received his 'consolation prize' for the film score of *The Battle of Stalingrad*, a film that unusually featured the Russian actor Alexei Diky in the role of Stalin, which he rendered with polished Russian drama-school tones. Just as Diky dispensed with the usual Georgian flavour of Stalin's speech, Khachaturian largely dispensed with the Oriental flavour of his music, which can only be detected in a couple of cues (notably in the requiem-like lament for the dying soldiers). The rest of the music is generic: beyond arrangements of Russian and German folk songs, we have music in the style of the Soviet national anthem together with marches and battle music. There is also a tender violin solo in a passage of lyrical beauty for a scene in which Stalin is at work late at night in the Kremlin.

Kabalevsky on the Edge

Dmitry Kabalevsky, a major force in Soviet music, was an accomplished and diverse composer. Once bitten by the Prokofiev bug, he never quite recovered, although at various stages of his career his Prokofievian bent had to be concealed or diluted. He was a prolific composer of opera, and courageously tackled the most challenging of contemporary topics. His first Stalin-Prize-nominated work, in 1943, demonstrated just how difficult it was to write such operas at the time. The opera in question was *In the Fire* (*V ogne*, also known as *Near Moscow – Pod Moskvoy*), set during the 1941 defence of Moscow, and the KSP voted for it to receive a second-class prize; it fell short of the first class because of the weakness of the libretto and the unevenness of the music (according to the KSP's discussion).[63] Act I was considered particularly deficient, and it is not difficult to see why: the whole of Scene 1 is both action-free and very gloomy (characters talk to each other about the devastation of their land and those about to fight as partisans leave amidst painful farewells); Scene 2, in the partisan camp, is livelier, but still devoid of dramatic action. However, when the list passed through the hands of Agitprop and the Politburo (just after the end of the war), *In the Fire* was deleted from the list. At this stage, it is unlikely that the decision was taken on the grounds of dramatic weakness. The problem now was that the opera clearly belonged to that first stage of the war, when individual initiative and heroism were valued. The opera presented ordinary people making their decisions for themselves, and the atmosphere of grief, resolve and revenge is far from the monumentality that was encouraged once victory was assured. The 'role of the Party' is not discernible in the opera, and the references to Stalin in the final chorus seem quite perfunctory. An opera written in the darkest period of the war (most of it in the autumn of 1942) was unwanted after the victory, and Kabalevsky was prudent to shelve it, recycling only individual numbers in his next opera.

Compared to this trouble, Kabalevsky had a relatively easy ride with his Second String Quartet, which was nominated in 1946. The KSP voted to give it a second-class prize, but Khrapchenko suggested that it should be raised to a first, and Zhdanov agreed (at the same time as they removed Shostakovich's Ninth Symphony from the list).[64] The documents were sent up to the Politburo, where the Quartet was now strangely billed as a victory piece:

> The Quartet, influenced by the victory of the Soviet people over fascist Germany, is distinguished for its profoundly optimistic content, and it has been written with masterful technique; it is an outstanding instrumental work of 1945, as Soviet critics have remarked. It therefore makes good sense to award Kabalevsky a first-class prize.[65]

The Quartet is a substantial work, running from a serious and densely written opening movement to a finale whose main material is lightweight, in the 'pioneer' style. The reasons for its elevation to the first-class are not obvious from the score alone, but an explanation emerges when we look at the context in which the Quartet appeared. It was completed in the victory year of 1945, and with some prodding and pushing, the piece can be fitted to a narrative of struggle and triumph, with the Russian folk song of the variation movement even adding the requisite patriotic aspect. The cheery finale is preceded by a long funereal slow introduction – the burying of the dead. Once the war narrative has been suggested, it is easy to find 'confirmation' for it unless the work is designed to resist such interpretations, as was Shostakovich's Ninth Symphony. And yet, the same Kabalevsky was writing war operas before and after this quartet, all of them problematic and none of them winning him such praise and recognition. If Kabalevsky's colleagues were to draw a lesson from his experiences (which were far from unique), they would seek to write more instrumental pieces that could be linked to whatever topical theme was being encouraged; writing an opera, by contrast, soaked up more time for a poorer return or even trouble.

In 1948, a shadow hung over Kabalevsky. Among his past misdeeds were the 24 Preludes for piano, op. 38 (1944), which Goldenweiser singled out as formalist pieces, because they offered a modernist, Prokofievian treatment of Russian folk songs.[66] At one point Kabalevsky was even named by Zhdanov as formalist, but his place on the Resolution's list of offenders was eventually taken by Gavriil Popov.[67] Kabalevsky's reputation sustained some damage but he escaped outright condemnation. Before long, Kabalevsky began to find himself nominated for administrative positions, and it was clear that he was in better official standing than ever. An explanation seemed to be required, and Alexander Ogolevets, a writer of various malicious letters, claimed in a new letter that the strange turn in Kabalevsky's fortunes could be traced to the composer's personal friendship with Lebedev, the new arts minister, and Vladimir Kemenov, the secretary to the KSP.[68] The oddest show of official favour for Kabalevsky was his nomination for election to the USSR Academy of Sciences, to fill the seat left vacant on the death of the musicologist Asafyev; Kabalevsky was not a scholar at all, not even as an adjunct to his activities as a composer, so he was simply not eligible for such a post. In the end, the problem was noticed, and Kabalevsky was not elected, but in the meantime, the musicologist Tamara Livanova tried to denounce Kabalevsky for his connections to a supposed Jewish conspiracy (the 'anti-cosmopolitanism' campaign was already underway).[69]

Kabalevsky became, in a sense, the first composer to be 'rehabilitated' in the wake of the 1948 Resolution. Although he had not, in the end, been condemned by name, he knew that he had come close, and he found himself in the large grey area of composers who had seen some of their previous work labelled in the press as formalist. He decided, then, that it was prudent to strike a repentant pose, reportedly saying that although his name was not in the CC Resolution, it was true that his work displayed formalist tendencies.[70] He showed his good will by composing an easy-going Violin Concerto targeted at accomplished younger performers, eschewing both high intellectual and technical demands. Myaskovsky humorously referred to it as a 'children's concerto', judging it in his diary to be 'lightweight, but not at all bad'.[71] Indeed, the Concerto sings and sparkles without any pretensions to profundity; it still teases the ear with devices reminiscent of Prokofiev, but takes the edge off these with a more conventional lyricism, and a suggestion of Russian or Ukrainian folk songs (as well as *galops* and Hungarian dances). Exciting harmonic shifts rush past in a flurry of virtuosity, but they pass by too quickly for the hostile listener to detect any formalist tendencies (the whole Concerto lasts only fifteen minutes). Traces of Prokofiev are found almost everywhere: in the opening theme, in the slow movement (even the scales in the accompaniment to the return of the main lyrical theme can be traced back to Prokofiev's First Violin Concerto) and in the great excitement of the closing coda. But the 'pioneer music' that dominates the Finale is a more perfect fit with Socialist Realism than Prokofiev ever managed – and indeed, we have seen what happened to Prokofiev's own 'pioneer' finale in the Seventh Symphony during the KSP's discussions (Chapter 3). The present author, as an insider to musical Socialist Realism (having grown up with its sounds), can recommend this Kabalevsky movement as an example of the purest Socialist Realism, not the drudgery of hack music, but the product of a composer of genuine talent who was a keen observer of the general musical environment.

In spite of all this, there was still an objection raised during the KSP's discussions of the Concerto. Khrennikov's was the dissenting voice:

> This work is not bad – it's even good – but he already has a prize. Apart from that, he's recently been linked to the formalist trend in music. He was named as a formalist in Comrade Zhdanov's speech [to the Orgkomitet of the Composers' Union, prior to the Resolution]. This work doesn't have any formalist features, but let him write another few works of this sort, and then we can start talking about awarding him a Stalin Prize.[72]

The KSP was prepared to follow Khrennikov's lead in music, since he was general secretary of the Composers' Union, with backing from above. The Concerto, accordingly, was absent from the KSP's final list, and Agitprop, which was at this point hostile to Kabalevsky, was hardly going to restore it. In the end, it was thanks to the intervention of Lebedev (allegedly Kabalevsky's friend, as we saw above) that it received a prize, at the second-class level.[73]

At the same time, Kabalevsky's new opera, *Taras's Family*, was in production in Moscow at the Stanislavsky Theatre. After the premiere, in December 1947, Myaskovsky had commented in his diary: 'Excellent music (much Prokofiev), but the libretto is dreadful (for the third time! Even though he's an intelligent man).'[74] Since then, Kabalevsky had received advice on ideological issues, and made revisions accordingly, but there were still major problems. When the revised version came before the KSP in 1950, Kabalevsky's opera was recognized as superior to any of the other works under consideration (discussed further in Chapter 10), but it was not beyond reproach. The members described it as lacking in melody because of its emphasis on *recitativo* writing. It was also criticized for lacking the expected Ukrainian national colouring, and some thought it was possibly 'too intense' at times.[75] Unmentioned, but probably not altogether unnoticed, were the echoes of Prokofiev: *War and Peace* in the overture, *Semyon Kotko* in its comic representations of the Germans. But in general, the Prokofievian idiom was sufficiently diluted with elements of Tchaikovsky, Rimsky-Korsakov and Glinka (Taras's memorable address to Andrei followed in the footsteps of Susanin's farewell aria). The Soviet mass-song genre also made appearances.

While the music was acceptable on the whole, there were serious doubts about the libretto. The story follows the fortunes of a Ukrainian family during the Great Patriotic War, but it is laced with allusions to the classic work of Nikolai Gogol, *Taras Bulba*. In Gogol's novella, the Cossack Taras has two sons: the loyal Ostap is killed in battle with the Poles, while the other, Andrei, turns traitor, and is killed by Taras himself. Kabalevsky's opera (based on a novel by Boris Gorbatov, *The Unconquered*) seems at first to be a retelling of the story in modern times. The loyal Stepan goes off to fight with the partisans. The other, Andrei, has been absent for unexplained reasons (with the partisans, with the army, collaborating with the Germans?) but turns up at his father's house in rags and a shaggy beard, claiming that he had been captured by the Germans, but now that he has escaped, he wants only to sit out the rest of the war. Taras calls him a deserter and throws him out of the house (instead of killing him). The updated story has a very different ending: after spending most of the opera offstage, Andrei finally returns as a decorated hero on top of a Soviet tank.

Andrei's sudden transformation outraged the musicologist Livanova; she saw it as a lamentable failure of censorship. She also wondered about the larger problem in the story: why had a family of able-bodied people remained on occupied territory in the first place, including Taras himself? True, they resisted at a later stage, but people worthy of celebrating should have retreated to join the Red Army.[76] There was no answer to this, as Livanova well knew, but the other KSP members vacillated. Kabalevsky was their best hope for an opera award, and the primary motivation for Livanova was much more likely to be long-standing animosity than ideological purity.[77] The result was another second-class prize for Kabalevsky.

Shebalin and Concluding Thoughts

Vissarion Shebalin's two first-class prizes were, moneywise, equal to Kabalevsky's first and two seconds, but his official standing was far below Kabalevsky's in the years following the 1948 Resolution. Not only had he been mentioned in the Resolution by name, but he also failed to win any 'rehabilitation' prize. Worse, he was sacked from his position as director of the Moscow Conservatoire, and banned from teaching at any institution in Moscow. For some years, his career lay in ruins. His Seventh String Quartet appeared too early, at the end of 1948, to be considered as grounds for a rehabilitation prize; instead, it was criticized as the work of a man who sat in his study, shut off from real life.[78] The following year's Piano Trio failed to bring him any attention, and the 1951 Sinfonietta was withdrawn by Shebalin himself after an unsuccessful premiere. Shebalin, now too lacking in confidence to produce further major works, threw himself into editing other people's music, and writing for stage and screen.

Back in 1943, Shebalin had come dramatically to the forefront of Soviet music when he received a first-class prize for his Fifth String Quartet, the 'Slavonic'. The Quartet received the initial push, at the Union of Composers stage, from Shostakovich (see Chapter 5; Shebalin was not only part of the Myaskovsky circle, but also a close friend of Shostakovich). The KSP heard the work in an audition given by the prestigious Beethoven Quartet. Myaskovsky introduced the work to the KSP as 'first-rate', claiming that Shebalin had overcome a certain reticence in musical expression and had produced something in this Quartet that was genuinely emotionally affecting. Shaporin, however, suggested slyly that this was not a proper quartet but a series of 'novelettes', akin to Glazunov's five *Novelettes* for quartet from 1886. The Shebalin Quartet, to his mind, lacked all sense of dramatic conception.[79] The reference to Glazunov was unlikely to have bothered Shebalin (Glazunov, after all, was the first to write a 'Slavonic' quartet, in 1888). Indeed, the idea of arranging folk songs from several Slav nations should have resulted in a suite. Nevertheless, the war context made the Quartet topical and lent it a sense of drama: the notion of a Slavic brotherhood, propagated in the nineteenth century by the Pan-Slavist movement, was now resurrected in the Soviet press as Russia joined the other victims of Hitler in Eastern Europe and struggled to free them from Nazi occupation.

Shebalin's Quartet competed directly with Prokofiev's Seventh Sonata, a much more turbulent and modernist work, although it also prompted listeners to make a wartime connection (see Chapter 3). The result of voting for them side by side was interesting: the Shebalin received twenty votes, the Prokofiev only fifteen. But while Shebalin had a preponderance of second-class votes (eight for first, twelve for second), Prokofiev had eleven firsts against only four seconds. Despite Shebalin's greater number of votes overall, he had to take second place after Prokofiev by the rules of the ballot. Myaskovsky reported to a mutual friend: 'I hope that Vissarion will have a joyful year as a great artist – he has recognition (his Fifth Quartet made a very good impression on the Stalin Prize Committee) and this will make things easier in his various paths [strands of his career, perhaps].'[80] Agitprop decided to give Prokofiev a second-class prize instead, and the two were simply swapped around, so that Shebalin now received the first class.

Shebalin's next quartet, No. 6, also came up for discussion in 1944, but met with a lukewarm response. Myaskovsky only had praise for the middle movements, especially the Andante, while he found the outer movements 'intellectual, rather than emotional' and even generalized that such intellectualism was in fact characteristic of the composer. Samosud agreed that the Quartet was 'rather dry'. Goldenweiser, who had been displaced by Shebalin as the director of the Moscow Conservatoire, was not particularly well disposed towards him, and he rounded off the discussion on a dismissive note: 'Shebalin is still a relatively young composer, so what's the point of awarding him for a quartet the second time in a row? Let him write a symphony or something else.'[81]

That 'something else' proved to be Shebalin's cantata, *Moscow*, written for the widely celebrated octocentenary of the city in 1947. Most members missed the chance to hear it, since the choir that had given the premiere had disbanded shortly afterwards.[82] Voting blind (or deaf, rather), they had to take on trust an endorsement from Glière and praise from Shostakovich (he was very sparing with his praise at this time, as we saw in Chapter 5). Shostakovich addressed the issue of Shebalin's dryness, and insisted that 'this work has been written in an ardent language, without the slightest hint of indifference'.[83]

All four of the composers featured in this chapter were top professionals, dazzling peers with their compositional technique, and all four were well versed in the nineteenth-century idiom of the 'Russian classics', which they could rely upon to temper their occasional modernist urges. Each had his own supposed vice, exposed in 1948: for Shebalin it was an intellectual 'dryness', for Kabalevsky it was his Prokofievisms, for Khachaturian a tendency towards excess or eccentricity (revealed in his Symphony-Poem), and for Myaskovsky his pessimism. Their levels of individuality differed widely. Myaskovsky remains recognizable even in his blander works. Khachaturian inherited the Russian Orientalist idiom but, almost uniquely, he managed to bend it to his own talents and purposes. Kabalevsky and Shebalin are considerably more difficult to distinguish from larger groupings of their contemporaries, but Kabalevsky has a certain verve of his own in addition to his Prokofievisms, while Shebalin gave his own subtle twist to Shostakovich's language.

The Stalin Prize histories of the composers featured in this chapter support the view that they represent the mainstream of Soviet music. While it is tempting to suppose that their styles must therefore qualify as Socialist Realism, the relationship is more problematic, and we shall have to return to this issue in the Conclusion. It should become obvious, however, that the standard Western picture of Soviet music, focused on Shostakovich and Prokofiev, does not quite make sense without this mainstream, which contains much ambitious and expertly crafted music (some of which was known in the West in its own time much better than it is now). And it is hardly possible to conceptualize the workings of Soviet music culture without the composer who was clearly at the institutional epicentre: namely, Myaskovsky. The Stalin-Prize angle of our narrative undeniably points to Myaskovsky as the key figure in the Soviet musical landscape – a key that may in future open up more of the secrets of Soviet music history.

CHAPTER SEVEN

CHECKS AND BALANCES

No one had a firmer grasp of the national question, and no one organized our national republics with more foresight than Stalin. He alone was responsible for the formation of the Central Asian Republics – it was Stalin's thing! Both the [drawing up of] borders and even the discovery of whole peoples the centre had never taken any interest in, and no one really knew about, because all of us, Lenin included, had never managed to find the time to deal with the matter, but he [Stalin] got to grips with it very well. But, as you know, there was a bitter struggle underway. The Kazakh big shots, for example, were busy fighting for Tashkent so that it could be their capital. Stalin assembled them, talked the matter over, looked at the borders, and said, 'Tashkent can go to the Uzbeks, but Alma-Ata to the Kazakhs'.

– *Molotov[1]*

Centre and Periphery

As a huge multinational state, the Soviet Union needed a successful national policy to stay in one piece, as it did for seventy years. This policy was shaped with much input from Stalin. The multitude of ethnicities was organized into a complex administrative system consisting of several tiers: national republics, autonomous republics within national republics and autonomous regions (*oblasti*) as the smallest ethno-territorial units within national or autonomous republics. Once these units were established, any further levels of ethnic diversity within them were largely ignored, and minorities were co-opted to represent the titular nationality. All these ethno-territorial units were subjected to a thorough Sovietization (rather than Russification, as was the case before the Revolution). That meant that while national languages were supported, Soviet cultural structures were uniformly imposed. Stalin's slogan of 1929, that art should be 'national in form, socialist in content', was not just empty bluster: individual cultures were allowed to display and even develop their national traits.[2] As for the socialist element, this was more nebulous; among other things, it could be the adoption of Western institutions (we shall expand on this later in the chapter).

For music, the imposition of Soviet cultural norms meant: the introduction of a standardized system of music education; the construction of opera houses, conservatoires and concert halls where previously there had been none; the spread of Western/Russian repertoires combined with the building of national ones; modification of folk instruments in the direction of Westernization; the creation of uniform outlets for folk music-making such as folk orchestras and song-and-dance ensembles; and the discarding of those parts of the folk traditions that were identified as 'courtly', 'feudal' or 'bourgeois-nationalist'. These changes remain controversial today, and the Soviet institutions, such as conservatoires or opera houses, have been celebrated, tolerated or abandoned depending on the political and cultural mix that has developed over the post-Soviet period.

In the ideal Soviet future that cultural administrators were trying to bring closer, the republics would all meet on the same cultural level. But now, at the beginning of the process, they fell into distinct groups that required very different approaches. The three republics of the Caucasus (Georgia, Armenia, Azerbaijan) were much further along the path of Westernization than the Central Asian republics. In the Caucasus, Georgia and Armenia already had a solid tradition of national opera, for example, while Azerbaijan was only beginning to catch up. In Central Asia, opera and symphonic culture had to be created from scratch. The Baltic republics with their highly developed, German-influenced culture presented different challenges as latecomers, once they had been dragged into the Soviet family.

Here are the statistics on how many prizes were awarded to national composers, from high to low (Khachaturian and Muradeli are included in this count, although their 'national' status was dubious):

Table 2. Music awards by national republic.

Republic	Number of individual composers' awards	Number of composers' awards within production teams	Total
Ukraine	12	1	13
Georgia	11	2	13
Azerbaijan	7	2	9

Armenia	6	2	8
Estonia	6	1	7
Uzbekistan	3	1	4
Lithuania	3	1	4
Latvia	3	1	4
Kazakhstan	2	1	3
Belorussia	1	2	3
Turkmenia	2	0	2
Moldavia	1	0	1
Tajikistan	0	1	1
Kirghizia	0	0	0

The position of Ukraine and Georgia at the top seems fair: both republics had strong schools of composition. Georgia, it must be said, also benefited from the presence of two of its countrymen (Stalin and Beria) in the Politburo: the republic was always insistent in promoting its candidates, knowing that they were likely to find support from the top. The other Caucasian republics also did predictably well, and so did the Baltics, whose appearance in the upper middle part of the table is all the more striking, since they had four years fewer to amass their prizes. The stragglers were left behind for very different reasons: Turkmenia, Tajikistan and Kirghizia were slow to Westernize, while Moldavia (the former Bessarabia, annexed in 1940) suffered heavy cultural losses from the de-Romanization policy and took longer to develop its Sovietized national identity. Belorussia's unexpectedly low count might have something to do with its closeness to Russia, to the point that its national distinctiveness was difficult to perceive (even today, while the Belorussian language has joint official status with Russian, the latter is used by the majority of the population and in state institutions). It would be impossible to trace every aspect of the national awards here (although some that are not covered by the main text are summarized in Appendices 4 and 5), so we shall concentrate on a few threads that will help to illuminate the broader issues. First, let us look at the chain of events that led to Kirghizia's unfortunate *nul points*.

Dekada Music

From the spring of 1936 and up to the beginning of the war in 1941, Soviet artistic life was regularly shaken up by the ten-day festivals of national art, the *dekadas*, as they were called. These were events on a monumental scale, which involved the mass transport of artistic forces around the country, first into the chosen republic for preparations, and then to Moscow for the actual perform-ances and accompanying celebrations (the number of participants ranged from about 350 to 1,300). The propaganda value of the *dekadas* was extremely high, since they were the visible evidence of Stalin's overall national policy. Each *dekada* ended with a grand reception and banquet in the Kremlin, where national artistic cadres had a chance to mix with the artistic elite of Moscow, and with members of the government. The singer Khalima Nasyrova and the dancers Tamara Khanum and Mukarram Turgunbaeva, for example, were invited to sit at Stalin's table during the Kremlin banquet that crowned the Uzbek *dekada* on 31 May 1937.[3]

Altogether, ten *dekadas* took place before the Nazi invasion of the USSR:

1936: Ukraine and Kazakhstan
1937: Georgia and Uzbekistan
1938: Azerbaijan
1939: Kirghizia and Armenia
1940: Belorussia and Buryat-Mongolia
1941: Tajikistan

The choice of a particular republic at a particular time was sometimes motivated by political considerations. Hence the choice of Belorussia in 1940, since that republic was dangerously close to war-torn territories. Similarly, Buryat-Mongolia, which was also chosen in 1940, even though it was not a full republic, but an autonomous republic within the Russian Federation; it bordered on Manchuria, the part of China which was under full Japanese control during that country's war on China.[4] Preparations for three Baltic *dekadas* in the newly acquired republics were well under way when the rapid Nazi advance put an end to any such plans.

It is hardly surprising that many of the *dekada* names later found their way onto the Stalin Prize lists: those festivals were the most direct and efficient way of familiarizing Moscow with the art of the republics. The Kazakh festival was the making of Kulyash Baiseitova, who sang in an opera by the Russian-born Yevgeny Brusilovsky, *Kyz-Zhibek*. By 1940, Baiseitova's fame was such that she was invited to join the KSP, and she received two Stalin Prizes herself. Nasyrova, the Uzbek soprano, followed the same path, also becoming a KSP member and winner of two prizes. National composers, where they already existed, were also rewarded: both of Hajibeyov's works popularized by the 1938 Azerbaijani *dekada* received prizes–the opera *Koroğlu* in 1941 and a film production of the operetta *Arşın mal alan* in 1946 (the operetta actually dates back to 1913).[5] As we have already seen in Chapter 2, the hitherto unknown Bogatyrev also had to thank a (Belorussian) *dekada* for his fame and for his unexpected prize in 1941.

However, a large proportion of *dekada* music was not home-grown, but provided through fraternal help sent from Russia, and these contributions, although eagerly hailed in the press, met a cooler reception from the KSP. It was no secret that opera in the Central Asian republics was previously unknown, and had to be created through the work of dozens of Moscow and Leningrad composers, who began new careers on the outskirts of the Soviet cultural empire.

Opera in Kirghizia

In August 1936, the playwright and novelist Vsevolod Ivanov happened to share a train compartment with one of these migrant workers, Vladimir Vlasov, and his visibly upset wife. They were heading to Kirghizia, which, according to the 1936 Constitution, had just been turned into the eleventh national republic. As Ivanov relates in his diary,

> [P]robably envying Kazakhstan and its theatrical successes in Moscow, they [in Kirghizia] decided to produce operas and ballets by 1938, when there would be a [Kirghiz] theatre *dekada*. [...] It must be a 'gold rush' for musicians now. The musician's wife does not approve of her husband's plans in the least, but the fellow hankers after glory – a perfectly legitimate desire – and he complains that operas, even after being passed [by the censor] and accepted [by theatres] in Moscow, don't reach the stage until two or three years later, and he is tired of taking random commissions [*khalturit'*] and composing little songs [...].[6]

Vlasov did indeed strike gold with this appointment. He stayed in Kirghizia for six years and wrote several national operas and ballets in collaboration with Vladimir Fere (stressed 'Feré') and the local composer Abdylas Maldybaev. He collected honours and awards in recognition of these efforts, and returned to Moscow to take a solid administrative post as director of the Moscow Philharmonia, the concert agency. Even after their return to Moscow, Vlasov and Fere continued collaborating with Maldybaev on still more works – it became a lifetime niche. And yet, although Vlasov and Fere were the architects of Kirghiz operatic success at the 1939 *dekada*, the Stalin Prize eluded them. They, and the other ghostwriters who lent their voices to a friendly neighbour, were sidelined in favour of native talent as soon as it appeared. Brusilovsky, a prolific author of Kazakh operas, was luckier, although he only managed to receive a prize in the lean year of 1948, and not for an opera or a ballet, but rather for a cantata, *Soviet Kazakhstan*. Even Reinhold Glière, whose talent had fertilized Azerbaijani, Uzbek and Buryat soils, only received a Stalin Prize for these efforts after concerted pleading on his behalf.[7] To probe this apparent ambiguity over Russian-made national operas, let us follow the course of two discussions of Vlasov-Fere-Maldybaev operas, *Manas* (1946) and *On the Shores of Issyk-Kul* (1951).

Manas was submitted for consideration by the KSP in 1947. An envoy was sent to Frunze to report on the production, and he returned with mixed impressions. On the one hand, Kirghiz opera as a genre seemed to be developing. The earlier efforts, under the name 'music dramas', had only used familiar folk material; this is where Vlasov and Fere needed Maldybaev, who provided them with suitable folk melodies. *Manas* was different, a fully-fledged opera with original melodies. This gave rise to a temporary problem: even though the new melodies were written in the manner of Kirghiz folk song, the audiences were used to hearing melodies that they already knew. The appearance of unfamiliar melodic material initially put off even the most enthusiastically Westernizing part of the Kirghiz audience, and the opera struggled for a while to gain public recognition. But, the envoy reported, the public gradually became accustomed to the new melodies and 'the atmosphere at performances became festive'.[8] Subsequent Kirghiz operas were accepted more easily, because *Manas* had already introduced the audience to the idea that a collection of new melodies could suddenly appear from nowhere.

The audience still saw its familiar epic heroes on stage, which made the Western aspects tolerable. The voice production was based on Western operatic practice. Kirghizia, in this respect, was at the forefront in Central Asia, with singers who had been scouted out several years before and given conservatoire training in Moscow or Leningrad. The dancing in Kirghiz opera was Westernized ballet, although at this stage, the dancers were using demi-pointe shoes.[9] The luxurious sets must have been a major part of the attraction, since they pushed the cost of the production up to 1.5 million roubles,[10] which was well in excess of any Bolshoi production. But the Moscow envoy wasn't so easily seduced: the high quality of the sets was not matched by the weak sound of the orchestra or by the singers, whose intonation was not adequate, except for their great star, the soprano Sayra Kiizbaeva.[11]

The KSP was prepared to give the opera the benefit of the doubt in spite of several reservations. The libretto provided was a poor translation from the Kirghiz, which gave a very bad impression, especially since some members had already read a much smoother version in the recently published Russian edition of the *Manas* epic.[12] The criticisms they levelled at the libretto were quite standard for any Soviet opera based on history or epic: they thought the episode chosen from the epic was too insignificant, and they regretted that the libretto emphasized the love interest to the detriment of any dramatic potential in the plot.[13] In the end, the KSP still thought that *Manas* merited a second-class prize, but the opera was then bluntly dismissed in Khrapchenko's letter to the government, saying that the work was of no artistic value,[14] and the Politburo Commission followed suit. This was a clear signal that the criteria for a successful 'national' opera were being tightened, and also showed that the non-native 'helpers' could not take the government's support for granted any more.

This attitude of the centre was, predictably, very much at odds with the desires of regional governments in the republics. A long and arduous discussion accompanied the 1952 nomination of *On the Shores of Issyk-Kul*, again by the Vlasov-Fere-Maldybaev trio, which was being promoted vigorously by the Kirghiz Party leadership. Within the KSP, the opera's main advocate was one Kasymaly Bayalinov, who was an interested party, being the author of its literary source and a collaborator on the libretto. This time, the plot was modern: a hydro-electric power plant was being built in the mountains, but the construction work was beset by difficulties due to the harsh environment. The opera had been praised in the press and by the Union of Composers, but Khrennikov had other ideas. At this point, he preferred to err on the side of caution, since he had brought trouble on himself with his tendency to endorse any worthy-looking new Soviet opera. When such operas turned out to be riddled with flaws or poor writing, Khrennikov had to answer for his premature approval. *Issyk-Kul* even had a plot that reminded him of his most costly mistake (Zhukovsky's *Heart and Soul*, which we will discuss in Chapter 10), and he decided that he would not risk trouble this time. He launched his attack, saying that the music was weak and the dramatization not merely poor but frivolously poor. The composers' attitude to their folk sources he found equally frivolous, since they had simply harmonized the folk material in a Western fashion, without any attempt to devise harmonizations more sympathetic to the material.[15]

To pacify Bayalinov, Fadeyev attempted to salvage the production in Frunze, which could still be given a prize without the composers appearing on the list. His only worry was that the music might contain formalist elements, in which case he would be prepared to withdraw his support. Shostakovich considered this tactic inappropriate for an opera: without the music, an opera lacked its very foundation, and therefore the production could not properly receive an award. In any case, Shostakovich had no words of praise for the trio of composers: he thought the music was often at odds with the dramatic situation, criticized the lack of connective material between numbers, found the handling of dramatic crises to be primitive and concluded that 'the music induces an extraordinary level of boredom, displeasure and irritation'.[16] He was just as scathing about the libretto, which placed the most important dramatic events offstage: the natural disaster (the falling of a huge rock) is not seen, but everyone on stage sings at length that urgent measures must be taken. (If the falling rock had actually been presented on stage, we can easily imagine that Shostakovich would have been scathing about that too.)

Bayalinov insisted that the Music Section had only heard fragments of the opera, and he arranged for the entire KSP membership to listen to the opera in a complete recording. He warned that a rejection would be a great moral blow for his republic.[17] The second listening, however, changed little, apart from the mounting irritation in the committee at the fact that the members had now devoted about twelve hours of auditioning and discussion time to a piece that was not heading for a prize, whichever way it was packaged and presented. *Issyk-Kul* was taken off the list, although the KSP decided to nominate the Kirghiz soloists for a prize each to honour their careers rather than their work in this opera specifically (unfortunately for them, no more Stalin Prizes were ever awarded in the arts). The trio of composers, by contrast, faced humiliation: the KSP expressed its regret that 'people who have spent so much effort in attempting to raise the level of Kirghiz music culture have proven completely inadequate', and that they had lost even the national charms of their first *dekada* opera *Ai-churek*.[18]

Westernization and the Case of Uzbekistan

The rapid Westernization imposed on the Central Asian republics could hardly fail to meet with some resistance. However, this resistance, which often led to a split among the local intelligentsia and protracted struggles between factions, was almost never reported in the press. The KSP papers and other archival documents shed some light on this matter.

One of the first homegrown composers to receive the Stalin Prize was Mukhtor Ashrafiy, remarkably, not for an Uzbek national opera (he co-authored his first two with Sergei Vasilenko), but something that was even higher up the Soviet scale of cultural development: a symphonic work, the first to emerge from Central Asia. When this work, his 'Heroic' Symphony, was discussed by the KSP in 1943, its landmark status was its highest recommendation. A provocative question was put to Mikhoels, who was acting as an advocate for the work (he had acquainted himself with Ashrafiy's music during his evacuation to Tashkent): 'If you were to take Shostakovich as an RSFSR [national] composer and you gave his work 12 points, how many points would this work get?' Mikhoels replied diplomatically that since

Shostakovich was an exceptional case, such a comparison would reflect unfavourably on almost any composer.[19] Despite this note of doubt, Ashrafiy's work seemed to be appreciated on its own merit: his studies in Moscow were rounded off by a period of study with those Leningrad professors who, like Mikhoels, had found themselves in Tashkent during the war. At the age of thirty-one, Ashrafiy became the director of the Tashkent Opera, and to this he soon added the directorship of the Conservatoire and a high position in the Uzbek Union of Composers.

A scandal that erupted around Ashrafiy a few years later allows us to see the background to his rise. In 1949, the Party Central Committee in Uzbekistan attempted to remove Ashrafiy from his post as Conservatoire director and even to expel him from the Party (by this stage he had already lost his Opera directorship in a reshuffle brought about by the 1948 Resolution). Among his alleged offences were a lack of discipline and other unnamed moral failings, misdirection of funds and even physical violence. The actual trigger for the scandal was risible (Ashrafiy allegedly failed to perform in some concert), and was nothing more than an arbitrary pretext. The matter was referred first to the ministry, where the deputy minister supported the case against Ashrafiy, failing to notice that one of the charges clearly opposed the cause of Westernization, namely that Ashrafiy was in error when he 'wilfully renamed the Department of Uzbek Folk Instruments as the Department for Symphonic Conducting and Uzbek Folk Instruments'.[20] But the minders from Agitprop were more alert, and they were able to present the case to Mikhail Suslov (Zhdanov's replacement as Agitprop's overseer),[21] explaining the background in the following terms:

> In Uzbekistan, there are at present two groups of art workers espousing different views on the development of Uzbek music. One group thinks that the development of national music should take place exclusively on the basis of the study and use of the Uzbek national tradition, which means that a distinctive vocal and musical school should be created, etc. The other group (including Ashrafiy and others) has adopted more progressive positions, supporting the attempt to bring Uzbek music closer to the forward-looking Russian culture, and to assimilate the best achievements of [Western] classical music. Thus, Ashrafiy plays a certain progressive role in the development of Uzbek music [...].[22]

In the end, an intervention from Moscow saved Ashrafiy's career, and it was the Uzbek CC that received a dressing-down. Moscow sent a team of investigators to report on dangerous separatist tendencies, and a number of administrative measures were taken in the wake of this report.[23] Ashrafiy soon received his second Stalin Prize – a third-class award for his cantata *Song of Joy*.

Establishing an outpost of Westernization in a given republic was not enough: it needed continuous maintenance and defence. The nominations sent by the governments of the republics were not fully trusted by Moscow: Uzbekistan, for example, kept putting forward one of its most celebrated musicians, To'xtasin Jalilov, and yet every single time the nomination failed. Jalilov was a so-called 'melodist', a composer of melodies who was not familiar with notation or any Western music theory; even so, his were the melodies that 'the people' chose to sing in Uzbekistan. He sang, played an array of folk instruments, taught his craft to younger musicians and also headed the Music Drama theatre in Uzbekistan. Nasyrova, the KSP member who passionately advocated Jalilov's candidature, presented him as the master of a dying art that didn't seem to be supported by the state in any way. She also spoke of many other former musicians who became kolkhoz workers or cobblers because they were now unable to make a living from their music.

For the KSP, the problem with Jalilov was that there was no category that accommodated his art. As a folk performer, he also lacked the kind of Union-wide fame that might have allowed some bending of the rules. It was not even clear, moreover, what kind of artist he was: Glière, who had been much involved in Uzbek music, assured KSP members that Jalilov was regarded primarily as a creator of songs rather than a performer of existing repertoire. But to award him a prize as a composer seemed impossible, since, as Shaporin remarked, a prize for a 'melodist' would discourage young Uzbek musicians from studying other aspects of composition that were being offered to them in conservatoires.[24] The only other option, the catch-all lifetime award, had been discontinued.

In 1949, four years after this conversation, Jalilov's name surfaced again during a discussion of the Tashkent production of the opera *Takhir and Zukhra*, composed by Jalilov in collaboration with Boris Brovtsyn. The experts sent by the KSP to Tashkent came back to report that the show was an enormous popular success, partly riding on the back of the eponymous film. The experts rated the spectacle highly, but raised concerns that it was still just a compilation of folk songs and dances rather than an opera.[25] This was a more serious shortcoming at the end of the 1940s than it had been a decade earlier; the requirement for coherent, unified artworks was also applied by the KSP outside the context of music from the republics. Jalilov had contributed to the film too, although his name did not appear in the title sequence. For the live show, he provided the basic material, which apparently received only a rather thin arrangement. The singers were employing the non-operatic, 'open' sound (*belïy*, literally, 'white'). While the experts were ready to accept that this kind of musical entertainment was as legitimate as proper opera, Khrennikov proposed that *Takhir* should be rejected, since it was only holding Uzbek music back, especially in comparison with Kazakhstan. The Kazakh soprano Baiseitova agreed: the success of *Takhir* had disheartened some conservatoire-student singers in Central Asia, who had started to wonder whether they really needed to bother learning music notation or change to Western vocal production.[26]

Indeed, *Takhir and Zukhra* seems to have been taken up as a banner for those who wanted to follow a 'separate path' in Uzbek music: during the premiere there were shouts of 'down with Russian opera!' in the audience.[27] This and other concerns were listed in reports sent to Suslov over the course of 1950: the opera house in Tashkent was sliding back to the performance of 'music dramas' while performances of proper operas remained ill-attended; singers with Western voice production were sidelined while 'illiterate' singers were promoted (Nasyrova among them). The rot went all the way to the top: the head of the Uzbek Radio Committee (ministry) made the 'pan-Islamist' statement that in the fourteenth century, musical culture separated into Eastern and Western branches, the Eastern branch reaching its pinnacle of perfection in the genre of *maqam/mugam*. New energy was poured into the study and performance of *maqam*, while its Westernization was rejected: a performance of Amirov's Symphonic Mugams (a work from Azerbaijan) in Tashkent in 1950 was met with boos and catcalls. Uzbek musical Westernizers, including Ashrafiy, seemed to be demoralized and, having collected advances for new operas, reneged on their obligations (with shrinking chances of performance, this was understandable). Thus *Takhir and Zukhra* got nowhere with the KSP, which had heard about the state of musical life in Uzbekistan, and decided it would be best to avoid any involvement. Musical Westernization had stalled, and Moscow needed to take urgent measures in order to restart it.

Kazakhstan's Transitions

As the most advanced of the Central Asian republics, what did Kazakhstan have to offer? The first award issued to a Kazakh composer was still to come (in 1948, see Appendix V), but one remarkable opera production was nominated in 1946: the Alma-Ata staging of *Eugene Onegin*. Kazakh Opera had pulled off something quite astonishing, taking just a decade to make the journey from hybrid, semi-spoken folk-style 'music dramas' to the successful staging of a Russian classic. The KSP members reacted with appropriate amazement on hearing the report of their envoy just back from Alma-Ata (this envoy happened to be Moisei Grinberg whom we met in Chapter 2).[28] Grinberg gave the KSP members a fascinating account of how *Onegin* had sprung to life on Kazakh soil. The celebrated Abai Kunanbaev (Qunanbayuli), a nineteenth-century Kazakh cultural reformer, had not only translated Pushkin's novel in verse into

Kazakh, but had also set the episode of Tatyana's Letter to music, and this song had become widely known in Kazakhstan. This meant that long before the first Soviet efforts to introduce opera, Kazakh audiences already perceived *Eugene Onegin* as part of their culture, and Tchaikovsky's version was an interesting extension to their knowledge of Pushkin's masterpiece, rather than an alien imposition.

Grinberg also gave his insights on various aspects of the production, which, for all its success, was still in a kind of transitional state, although one with its own intrinsic interest. Onegin and Lensky were played by younger Kazakh singers who, as graduates of the Moscow Conservatoire, used academic, 'covered' vocal production, and Lensky was even a competition winner. But next to them on stage stood older singers who continued to use the 'open' sound, including the star of the show, Baiseitova.

Baiseitova, at the age of thirty-six, was already a legend (her debut *dekada* performance had taken place twelve years earlier). Her unique voice, with exquisite top notes, was much admired, as was her stage presence as an actor-singer. Extant recordings prove that her voice was eminently adaptable, and she would change it considerably when switching from Kazakh folk songs to singing in Western or Westernized music. In *Onegin*, she proved particularly charming and convincing as Tatyana, the innocent country girl, and her inter-action with the Nanny (who was played by another 'open'-voiced singer, Turdunkulova) was particularly moving. Admittedly, Baiseitova was less persuasive as Tatyana, the grande dame of the later scenes in St Petersburg, but that was a very forgivable shortcoming beside her overall achievement.

But if anything, the most impressive participant of all was to be found in the pit – the conductor Grigory Stolyarov, who taught the chorus their complex polyphonic numbers by ear (they could not read music) through endless memorization sessions with the piano. So, even though the *mise en scène* had been copied from Stanislavsky's famous production and the set design was not sophisticated, the general impression was that of a credible opera production, which was also a genuine success with Kazakh audiences. One Moscow envoy noted that the Kazakhs in the audience initially tried to clarify their perception of the music by tapping out the rhythms on the arms of their chairs, but from the Letter Scene onwards, they were completely immersed in the music and spectacle.[29] Despite all those positive reports, however, the KSP decided to restrict the award to Baiseitova (in fact, she only received it two years later),[30] while the first national production of *Onegin* to receive a prize was Estonian (second-class in 1950).

Another case of a transitional, semi-Westernized outfit was the Kurmangazy Kazakh Folk Orchestra, and the 1953 KSP debate around it is telling. Friedrich

Ermler, who had had long-standing ties with the republic since his wartime evacuation, described the orchestra thus:

> This orchestra, a great favourite in the republic, was formed in 1933 [...].
> This was the first string orchestra they had organized, and at first they didn't
> even play from printed music. This really was a genuine folk phenomenon:
> the nomads came together and began to play. Today this orchestra plays
> Beethoven, Glinka and Mozart, not to mention their own old folk songs and
> the songs of Soviet composers. I must say that listening to the orchestra lifts
> you into a state of ecstasy. And they also have singers with the orchestra.
> [...] What didn't I like? This orchestra consists of two or three types of
> instrument: the dombra, the three-stringed qobyz [no third type is
> mentioned], and when they start to play Rachmaninov's Prelude No. 6
> [presumably from op. 23], this doesn't sound at all jolly, because the instru-
> ments don't seem to hold their tuning. But they think that this is the only
> way to familiarize [the Kazakhs] with classical music, because this orchestra
> has extraordinary authority.[31]

Anatoly Novikov and Khrennikov, however, reckoned that the Kazakh orchestra was not only lagging behind Russian folk instrument orchestras, but also behind their counterparts in the other republics. The spread of such orchestras took place under Russian influence, and in the 'Eastern' republics it was one more step along the path of Westernization. The Kazakh instruments, despite Ermler's impression of primitivism, had already been modified by the orches-tra's founder Akhmed Zhubanov: the ancient *qyl-qobyz*, for example (which was associated with shamanistic practices) had been altered to produce a stronger and brighter sound. By 1953, however, these steps were no longer considered adequate.

Further objections were mainly directed at the orchestra's core repertoire:

> *Novikov:* This is very limited national music. It is monophonic music.
> [...] I can't see any desire here to step beyond the confines of national
> music.
> *Zakharov:* [...] We need to make it known that as a matter of principle, we
> cannot support monophony!
> *Khrennikov:* This is what was said in the [1948] CC Resolution.
> *Zakharov:* Yes, unison music is primitive. We need to support some kind of
> development, some kind of polyphony, etc. But what we've just heard, espe-
> cially at the beginning, was monophonic music, in octaves, without any
> climaxes, without any form. This is a composition without a beginning or

an ending. I think that if we award a prize to this orchestra, it would legitimize the path it has taken.[32]

Khrennikov and Zakharov, as we might expect, knew the text of Zhdanov's
resolution well. There is indeed a passage in the 1948 Resolution on monophonic music that a casual reader could easily misunderstand. It is little helped
by the fact that it makes no mention of the republics and is wedged between
two paragraphs condemning standard formalism – bourgeois, Western and
cacophonous. This is how the passage in the middle reads:

> Another unfailing sign of the formalist trend is the rejection of polyphonic
> music, which is based on the simultaneous development of independent
> melodic lines. The tendency shows how these composers have become
> obsessed with the monotony of unison lines, often sung without words. This
> violates the norms of the polyphonic musical culture that is characteristic of
> our people, and the result is a further impoverishment and deterioration in
> music.[33]

The discussion around the Kurmangazy orchestra allows us to understand this
otherwise obscure passage, which, it turns out, is concerned with an Eastern
variety of formalism: a kind of music that is not at fault for its excessive
complexity but, on the contrary, for its stubborn insistence on remaining
underdeveloped and primitive. This passage marks a new stage in the relationship between the centre and the peripheries: rather than the 'everything goes'
attitude towards *dekada* art before the war, when the humblest moves towards
Westernization were lavishly rewarded, we now have the Zhdanovshchina
climate of suspicion and censure, when all national art that was not sufficiently
Westernized could easily fall into the category of 'bourgeois nationalism'.[34] It
might seem that this was stretching the concept of 'formalism' to breaking
point or beyond, but this is only because we know the term from the context of
attacks on modernism. It would be possible to reply, simply, that this was how
Zhdanov and others applied it at the time, and that is the end of the matter. But
we can reconstruct the logic of this apparently arbitrary usage. Looking again
at the maxim 'national in form, socialist in content', we can see that the national
form in monophonic music was everything, and the socialist content nowhere
to be seen. 'Socialist content' may also seem obscure here, but it was understood
to mean an embrace of Western institutions and styles, or modern technology,
as appropriate.

Khrennikov and Zakharov could not have failed to know that Akhmed
Zhubanov, the founder of the orchestra, had fallen victim to a targeted attack
from his colleague Mukhat Tulebaev two years earlier: he was accused of

nationalism, expelled from the Party and sacked from all his positions.[35] Tulebaev had taken over the orchestra, but under his artistic direction the orchestra had again stagnated, Khrennikov claimed: they failed to make progress in developing the Kazakh part of their repertoire, although the Russian part they played reasonably well. Now even Uzbekistan, which used to be considered well behind Kazakhstan in modernization, was surging ahead with a similar orchestra, led by Ashot Petrosiants, and a newly created a cappella choir was mastering polyphonic works by Mutal Burkhanov.[36] The project had been spurred on by a special resolution of the Uzbek Party CC (a corrective after the separatism reported in 1950). Now, it seemed, Kazakhstan needed a similar intervention from the centre.

A Boon for the Baltics

In the wake of the war, when the Baltic republics were brought back into the Soviet Union, they received special attention from Moscow – both the iron fist and the velvet glove were in evidence. There was a final push to defeat armed resistance from groups left over from the Nazi occupation, and to remove, through deportations, Nazi collaborators and other undesirable elements. For the rest of the populations, there was a very different struggle to win over their loyalty. Let us begin with one small but powerful example of Stalin's interference in the prize process, seen in fig. 15. Looking through the lists of nominations in February 1951, Stalin wrote a satisfied 'Ha-ha!' next to the name of Vilis Lācis, author of the novel *Towards a New Shore*. His satisfaction came from the KSP's decision to recommend Lācis for a third-class prize; they had originally rejected the nomination, but Stalin had put pressure on them to rethink. From all we have seen so far, we know this was abnormal, and Stalin was clearly determined to see recognition for the Baltic republics in the prize list. His 'Ha-ha!' may also be his reaction to the third class, since he had every intention of promoting Lācis further. In the end, the novelist received a first-class prize (his second, the same award having been made for his 1949 trilogy, *The Storm*).

But there was more afoot here. Lācis, we should know, was not only a writer, but had become prime minister of the Latvian Republic. Rewarding him in this way was a very direct and highly public show of benevolence and encouragement (the KSP's third-class prize would have been taken as an insult, so it simply was not a possibility). There was a further subtle twist. We might jump to the conclusion that the KSP wanted to reject a substandard novel, while Stalin wanted to reward a political ally regardless of his literary stature. If anything, we find the opposite. Lācis was a good writer, recognized in the literary world, and

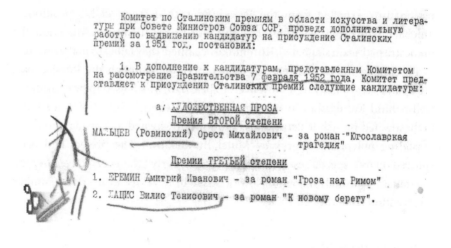

Fig. 15. Stalin's marginalia on a list of nominations for Literature in 1951. Beside Vilis Lācis's novel 'Towards a new shore', Stalin wrote in red pencil: 'Ha-ha!' Another marking (made in blue pencil) indicates his objection to the use of Maltsev's real name, Rovinsky (see Chapter 1, n. 53). RGANI, fond 3, op. 53a, ye. kh. 30, l. 42.

also popular with the wider Latvian public. The KSP's rejection was on ideological grounds: Lācis's portrayal of Latvian 'kulaks' seemed suspiciously sympathetic; some members would have rejected the work in earnest, others out of timidity. But Stalin had another chance to teach everyone his favourite lesson: one has to see the wood for the trees, and larger political goals are more important than petty ideological nitpicking. At the same time, he could reinforce his image as the enlightened and progressive leader in the eyes of the upper intelligentsia.

Stalin's personal patronage of Baltic cultural achievements throws more light on the Music-prize tales that follow. Although we do not have such direct evidence of Stalin's personal involvement, a couple of unexpected first-class prizes reinforce the idea that Stalin was overseeing some kind of affirmative action.

In music, the Baltic republics presented very different problems from those of Central Asia. The level of music culture was very high: they already had opera houses, symphony orchestras and highly educated professional composers, even though the cultural cadres were in need of replenishment due to massive emigration from the region. KSP members repeatedly mentioned their satisfaction that no special allowances had to be made when awarding the Baltics, since their professional standards were impeccable. Yet there was also a general perception in Moscow that the majority of the intelligentsia in the Baltics was hostile to the Soviet regime, and so the choices needed to be made carefully. The Baltics still needed to be won over, brought back into the fold, as the first attempts at Sovietization, begun in 1940, had been knocked off course by the Nazi invasion. On the other hand, the Baltic states had only been out of Russian control (as opposed to Soviet control) for little more than twenty years, and the older generations of the Baltic intelligentsia had preserved their many ties with Russian culture. These were now to be revived and nourished.

One case in point is the Kapp family – father Artur and son Eugen – who carried off four Stalin Prizes between them. Artur was a one-time student of Rimsky-Korsakov, and he had worked in Russia for many years before returning to Estonia in 1920. He was a Russian-speaking, Russian-sympathizing member of the Estonian intelligentsia who could be relied upon in the rebuilding of those broken cultural ties. But it was the son, Eugen Kapp, who turned out to be an even stronger candidate for support and encouragement: he was Soviet-leaning from the start, and had an instinctive feeling for finding good plots for the new times – his ballet *Kalevipoeg* had even been chosen for the 1941 Estonian *dekada*, but this could not take place after the Nazis had taken Estonia. Most importantly, the younger Kapp had spent the war years in Russia and so the KSP had no need to worry that charges of collaboration might surface to embarrass them. His music had been played in Moscow during the war on several occasions, including a whole evening of his work in 1944.[37] He was, then, a tried and tested friend who, by the end of the war, had managed to produce an opera about a fourteenth-century uprising of the indigenous Estonians against their Danish and German overlords (*Tasuleegid*, or *The Flames of Revenge*) – an ideologically astute treatment of history. Admittedly, this astuteness might have passed unnoticed at the time, since Myaskovsky and Goldenweiser, who were entrusted with the task of playing through the score, could not follow the Estonian text. But they found the music emotionally expressive and well constructed, even if not particularly individual (the music seems more Italian than Russian, but with some folk-style touches). Ermler, who was himself born in Latvia and knew more than others about the situation in the Baltic republics, urged his colleagues to think of the great political resonance an Estonian Stalin Prize would have.[38] And so, a second-class prize for *The Flames of Revenge* started melting the ice.

The story surrounding the second music prize for the Baltics is much more exciting. It came in the crisis year of 1948, when the anti-formalist resolution left Khrennikov and the other new members of the Music Section clutching at straws to produce a credible list of nominations. It is easy to imagine that the ever-growing ranks of formalists and their supporters awaited the publication of awards with a grim satisfaction at the prospect of non-entities absurdly taking the places of all the best composers who were now blacklisted. The government, in its embarrassment, would then see that the formalists were indispensable.

But the result was a surprise. Heading the list of music prizes was a composer whose name was as yet unknown outside Lithuania: Juozas Tallat-Kelpša. Another unexpected touch was the fact that the award went to a Stalin Cantata – until then, there had been no work of this kind on the Music prize lists. It seemed to stretch credulity that a Lithuanian composer would even produce a cantata about Stalin, let alone gain a first-class prize for it. It was also unprecedented for a national award to reach the first-class level (we can exclude Khachaturian, whose fame stretched across the Soviet Union and abroad).

Who was this man with a name the newspapers kept misspelling? Like the older Kapp, he had studied at St Petersburg Conservatoire before the Revolution (with Liadov and Steinberg), and he made his name both as a choral and symphonic conductor, and also as a composer of vocal and choral music. He conducted the very first opera production in Lithuania in 1920, and wrote a few songs that became truly popular in his country. In other words, he was a well-respected master, now in his late fifties. Only one line in his earlier biography indicates pro-Soviet leanings: in 1918, during the short life of the Lithuanian–Belorussian Soviet Republic, he was a member of the Music Collegium of the Lithuanian Narkompros (ministry of culture).

We do not yet know how and why Tallat-Kelpša came to write his Stalin Cantata and how sincere the gesture was. We can be more confident of the sincerity of the text that he used, the Stalin Poem by Salomėja Nėris: this much-loved Lithuanian poetess, whose socialist views had been well known, naively allowed herself to be adopted as a figurehead. At the top of the stairs of the Grand Kremlin Palace, where she was to read out her Stalin Poem at the session of the Supreme Soviet in August 1940, she told her audience that she felt as if she were entering a fairy tale, a brighter world that was promised by the leader.[39] This symbolic moment when the young and beautiful Nėris read her ode in Lithuanian and Russian was widely publicized through the newsreels.

Kelpša set this by all accounts finely crafted poem with some care (this was after Nėris's untimely death in 1945). The music is by no means simplistic: the numbers are through-composed, there is a lot of colourful harmony (with echoes of Wagner and Rimsky-Korsakov) and there is even, in a couple of places, a level of dissonance that could have been easily considered formalist in 1948 (for example, the wildly chromatic passages depicting the 'serpent of war'). Stalin, of course, could see the Baltic wood and was not distracted by the formalist trees, if he was ever even aware of them.

The final section, with the glorification of Stalin, is more transparent and folk-like. But perhaps this hardly mattered, since the KSP did not hear the work. The nomination was a last-minute suggestion made by two new members, the conductor Nikolai Golovanov and song composer Anatoly Novikov, who raised the matter in telephone conversations with Khrennikov. Despite the protests of 'too late!' from KSP members, Fadeyev stressed the political importance of a prize for Kelpša, while Khrennikov emphasized Kelpša's authority as a composer in the Lithuanian Republic. Nineteen votes were cast for a first-class prize, twenty-four for a second.[40] The Cantata was performed in Moscow and Leningrad during the following concert season as a result of the award.[41]

There was vacillation in the upper tiers. In one document Agitprop suggested that the prize should be raised to the first class, in another it expressed agreement with the KSP and the ministry that the prize should be second-class. In the list that was presented to Stalin for perusal, Kelpša is still in the second class: Stalin simply ticked the name (his usual indication of agreement).[42] It is likely that Stalin held a special meeting with Zhdanov to discuss the music prizes that decisive year,[43] and it must have been during this meeting that the prize for the Cantata was raised to the first class. This killed two birds with one stone: the glaring absence of first-class awards in the music list was fixed (Glière's Fourth Quartet was also promoted to the first class despite Agitprop's objections), and the cultural elite of Lithuania was also given prestige, and an incentive to further co-operation.

The prize was a great boost to Kelpša's career: he became chair of the Lithuanian Composers' Union, he was invited to Moscow to deliver the required speech at the Composers' Union Congress in April 1948,[44] and he was elected to the Board of the Composers' Union of the USSR. The Cantata was frequently played, and it was reportedly during one of its rehearsals, in February 1949, that Kelpša collapsed, dead at the age of sixty. Across a large swathe of the Lithuanian intelligentsia the news was met with whispers that it was God's punishment.[45] To put the prize and this reaction in its local context, it came at a time when deportations to Siberia had begun. These may not have been as open and terrifying as the mass deportation in mid-June 1941, which took place in full view of Vilnius residents, but they became an annual affair, usually in March–April, of which Lithuanians were very much aware, some keeping packed bags at the ready. Vilnius Conservatoire was then named after Tallat-Kelpša. While this could easily have been changed in post-Soviet times, the name has been retained through to the present day.

The next Lithuanian work to win a prize, again first class, took a rather different course. This was Balys Dvarionas's Violin Concerto of 1948, one of the two works nominated for a prize by the Lithuanian Composers' Union (the other was the oratorio *Soviet Lithuania* by Antanas Račiūnas).[46] This nomination, confirmed only on 18 December 1948, came through almost too late for the piece to be heard at the Composers' Union plenary session in Moscow, and some string-pulling was needed to ensure it was performed there. The flurry of last-minute organizing came from the Concerto's first performer and dedicatee, the Odessan violinist Alexander Livont, a student of Oistrakh's who had recently moved to Lithuania, where he was styled Aleksandras Livontas. Livont was eager to enhance his already flourishing career by playing new Lithuanian works. Livont took Dvarionas to Moscow and, using his connections, managed to pressure the ministry into organizing an audition of the Concerto with piano accompaniment. The audition was a great success, and twenty-five minutes of rehearsal time was found in the full schedule of orchestra rehearsals for the Composers' Union plenary (admittedly, this was not quite enough even for a single, uninterrupted play-through, but this was already a big concession to such a latecomer). Now it was Dvarionas's time to shine: his personal charisma and the instant attractiveness of the music won over the initially reluctant orchestral musicians. Dvarionas was now further rewarded with a full rehearsal, and his Concerto went on to make a great impression at the Composers' Union plenary and was passed up enthusiastically to the KSP.

At the KSP, Dvarionas's Concerto came into direct competition with Kabalevsky's and was deemed better. Khrennikov supported it, but knew that he had to push Kabalevsky out of the way first. He reminded members that Kabalevsky was still under the shadow of the 1948 Resolution, and his Concerto was rejected. Khrennikov moved on to Dvarionas with a glowing recommendation:

> Dvarionas is a Lithuanian composer in his late 30s, a very talented composer. This work displays his talent, and it's written on the basis of genuine folk music, brilliantly put together in a professional way. The violin part plays marvellously well. And, incidentally, this work was written after the Resolution of the Party CC. It is a response to this Resolution, and we take pride in this work.[47]

The KSP passed Dvarionas for a second-class prize, but the ministry suggested moving him up to the first class and giving Kabalevsky a second, a change that was supported by the Politburo. Dvarionas and Livont were feted as heroes back in Lithuania: *this* prize, in contrast to Tallat-Kelpša's, seemed to have a different value. This time they considered it to be a prize based on the music, rather than political considerations. Dvarionas was something of a bon viveur who was known for occasional unguarded statements, so he was certainly not being rewarded for any personal worthiness. We could construct a partial rebuttal of this, with, as we have seen, political aspects to Dvarionas's prize and musical talent evident in Tallat-Kelpša's case, but the point broadly stands.

Let us, then, cast a glance at Dvarionas's music. In comparison with Kabalevsky's now well-known piece, Dvarionas's Concerto seems formally looser, but at the same time more serious and ruminative (Kabalevsky, fully aware that his Concerto was very light in mood, shrewdly dedicated it to the thirtieth anniversary of the Komsomol, thereby creating an association with younger performers and listeners). In Dvarionas, the slow introduction, with its 'epic' horn call at the beginning, sets up more symphonic expectations, which are only partly realized. What is most astonishing is that this Lithuanian composer, a graduate of Leipzig Conservatoire (in the early 1920s), had managed to tap into the Kuchka style so easily: his music, which is indeed based on a handful of folk songs, re-creates a familiar modal style of harmonization (with IV-I progressions in the minor) that gives the music a Russian sound, especially for those who do not know the Lithuanian tunes. The lyrical passages where the violin dominates unchallenged are warm and, indeed, beautifully written for the instrument, thanks in part to the collaboration of Livont (Livont accordingly felt free to alter the violin part further, and created a new version of the Concerto, but Dvarionas disowned this). In the slow movement, the composer's ability to maintain long lyrical phrases is impressive and, curiously, his lyrical idiom slips into the style of Soviet popular song for a moment. One of the passages drew criticism from Dvarionas's own Lithuanian colleagues: a fiery folk dance in the middle section included some prominent unresolved seconds, which they must have considered too 'formalist'.[48] The rather brief finale is brilliant and based on folk tunes again, as could be expected, but the use of the Aeolian mode in the melodic writing prevents it from sounding too light for the work, and with an emphasis on the flat seventh degree, many passages would have sounded well in a Balakirev or Glazunov score, a point Khrennikov would have appreciated.

An exploration of the Kuchka's legacy proved to be just as natural a passage into Socialist Realism for the Baltic composers as it did for those from the Caucasus and Central Asia. If the republics of the Caucasus and Central Asia often produced something that could be described as a reclaiming of the Kuchka's Orientalism, the Baltic republics' diatonic modality took up the Kuchka's devices for representing Russia.

Safe Harbours

Anyone looking at the chronological list of 'national' awards in Music (Appendices 5 and 6) would notice a disproportionate bulge towards the end. The government always encouraged a healthy number of such awards but in the years 1941–47, the matter was generally left in the hands of the KSP (with the exception of the first year, as we saw in Chapter 2). The majority of musical awards given to the republics during this period were given with conviction: there was enough inspired and well-crafted music to create a national presence.

The proportion of national works changed in 1948 because of the dearth of works by major composers that could escape all suspicion of formalism. Music from the republics was now a much more reliable choice, especially when it was seen to be following the model of 'national in form, socialist in content'. The introduction of third-class prizes in 1950 opened the floodgates: Khrennikov's desire to rely on the generally trouble-free national works coincided with the revival of the government's interest in such awards, as we can see, for example, in the post-ballot inclusions of 1951 (see Appendix IV). Khrennikov was well aware of this: 'We have few Russian works,' he said, by which he did not mean works that happened to be written by Russian composers, but works that advertised their Russianness, much as a Kazakh work could advertise its Kazakhness. The example he gave was Vladimir Bunin's Symphony No. 2, which he considered a suitable counterpart to the national music of the other republics (see more on this in Chapter 10). Russian composers had previously seen themselves as central, of Soviet-wide or even international importance, and simply unmarked in nationality; now they often found that they had to look up to the other republics and follow their lead.

Terry Martin notes that 'affirmative action turned nationality into a valuable form of social capital' in Stalin's Soviet Union.[49] As we have seen in this chapter, this was true of music, where national styles became a valuable attribute that could make a career, or save a career that had been going nowhere. The examples given in this chapter are representative of important aspects of national music under Stalin, but they could have been replaced by hundreds of others from the huge pool of national music that was produced in the Soviet Union during this period. It is difficult, indeed, to find a single composer who remained completely aloof from this trend. National music, it is true, does not exhaust the application of the label 'Socialist Realist' to music, but it does offer the clearest, most incontrovertible example. This music's *narodnost'* and 'realism' were assured by its basis in folk material, while the 'socialist' aspect was supplied, as we have seen, by shunning the parts of traditional culture that were regarded as backward, and embracing Western institutions such as through-composed opera, or harmony and counterpoint. Accessibility routinely came from familiar Glinkian and Kuchkist recipes, or when that was not appropriate, from the use of familiar folk melodies or legends and familiar (if modified) folk instruments. If the tone was optimistic and the level of professionalism acceptable, such music was hard to fault. Yet another Kazakh overture or Tatar cantata was far less controversial than a Shostakovich symphony. That does not mean we should regard all national music of these years as a mere pretext for avoiding Shostakovich. There is music that stands on its own merits for its beauty, or excitement, as well as blandly generic work and downright incompetence. Recognizing the aesthetic centrality of national music within Soviet musical culture may help to bring those hidden gems out of the shadows.

CHAPTER EIGHT

HIGH AND LOW

In the Committee's view, even a symphony of middling quality will always be higher and more deserving than the best of songs, and perhaps only a couple of dozens of 'songs of the Motherland' would be comparable in their eyes to Shostakovich's Quintet.

– Dunayevsky to Khrapchenko[1]

Socialist Realism was often understood as the place where higher and lower varieties of art could meet on an equal footing. High art would descend from its ivory tower, while the folk and the popular art would be raised and ennobled. Their meeting in the middle would result in that highly prized 'music for the people'. But what was 'high' and what was 'low'? The Stalin Prizes tell us much about the Soviet hierarchy of artistic genres, and while the prize lists were always weighted towards the high end of the spectrum (which is, of course, the primary focus of this book), the proportion of prizes awarded to the lower genres gradually increased. It is fitting, therefore, that we devote a chapter to lighter music, whose place on the prize lists was hotly debated and constantly redefined.

This 'lighter' music will span several disparate genres: mass songs, popular songs and folk-style songs, military marches, operettas, light orchestral music, light choral music and music for orchestras of folk instruments. Whatever separated the composers of each genre, they were united in creating unease among high-art composers and other more purist KSP members. Still, they could not be ignored: for ideological reasons, their presence was required. It was different in the case of film composers: their nominations and awards took place within the Film category, removing them from direct competition with high-art composers. Film composers often received their awards without any detailed discussion of their film scores, because they won as members of the nominated crew for a given film, and their individual eligibility was rarely an issue. Thus, if we may be curious about how Dunayevsky's, Pokrass's or Khrennikov's best-known songs fit in the general pattern, the KSP transcripts give us no clues, because in each case, the songs appeared within prize-winning films. In the Music category, on the contrary, popular or middlebrow genres had to rub shoulders with symphonies and operas, and that always produced tension.

A Song Hierarchy

If we single out the song awards within the Music category (that is, the popular, mass and folk-style varieties), a clear pattern emerges (see Appendix VII). Although they were rarely absent from the lists, their normal place was the second class; later, when the third-class division was created, they were largely relegated there. In the history of the Stalin Prizes, there were only two exceptions to this pattern: a first-class prize given to Alexander Aleksandrov in 1942, for Red Army songs together with the Party anthem that would soon become the anthem of the Soviet Union; and the first-class prize given to Vladimir Zakharov in 1946, for a collection of folk-style songs. There was no element of chance in these two awards. The Red Army Song and Dance Ensemble and the Pyatnitsky Choir, directed by Aleksandrov and Zakharov respectively, were the USSR's signature cultural institutions: held in great regard within the country as staples of official variety shows and Kremlin banquets, they were also used as prized cultural ambassadors, especially after the Second World War.[2] They were also reproduced in less glamorous versions all over the country: every army division and every collective farm could, in principle, set up their own ensembles based on these models. The music they purveyed seemed to be the safest, free of all suspicion and doubt: it was the right music for the people. At the same time, the two state ensembles were genuinely popular, and thus managed to outlive the Soviet Union, and to continue flourishing up to the present day, both in Russia and touring internationally.

Although both institutions were the epitome of Stalinist art, their roots go much further back and their genesis is complex. Aleksandrov belonged to the large ranks of church choir directors who successfully transformed themselves to serve the Soviet state. His career is quite exceptional, though, because until 1922, he occupied the highest office in Russian Orthodox church music, namely Chief Precentor/choir director (he served at Moscow's Cathedral of Christ the Saviour until it fell into the hands of church 'modernisers' who supported the Borshiviks). He switched only when he had to, and was able to secure a post at the Conservatoire, where he quickly became an eminent professor, but his rise to wider fame began in 1928, when Voroshilov chose him to direct what became the Red Army choir, with small-scale beginnings as a group of only twelve singers.[3]

Thanks to its patronage at the highest level, the ensemble had grown to 274 singers, instrumentalists and dancers by 1937, when it won a Grand Prix at the Paris Exposition. In 1939, Aleksandrov boasted that Stalin and Voroshilov frequently offered their advice on repertoire, and even on the details of the music and dance. He claimed that it was Stalin's own idea to add domras and balalaikas to the accordions that were used for accompaniment at an early stage.[4] The result was a highly engaging mix of folk, military and church sounds. The church element comes from the default vocal production that was at the core of Aleksandrov's training for his singers, who were trained in the 'covered' classical sound production of church choirs (their 1937 performance of the *Marseillaise* in Paris took this approach), but, when desired, they could modify it in the direction of the untutored delivery typical of folk choirs.

In a parallel development, the pre-revolutionary folk choir founded by Mitrofan Pyatnitsky in 1910 also became a Soviet institution. It had begun life as a group of peasants singing their own native songs, to which they later added the songs collected by their founder. They went professional in the 1920s and survived the death of Pyatnitsky in 1928, when Pyatnitsky's nephew, Pyotr Kazmin, took over. In 1931, Kazmin was joined by a dynamic Vladimir Zakharov, who changed the emphasis of the repertoire from traditional songs to Soviet 'fakelore', which he himself either co-produced or arranged. This was a winning idea: Zakharov's shameless overtures to the Party leaders soon paid off. Unlike the Red Army choir, the Pyatnitskys continued to sing in the Russian folk style, although they reduced the shrillness somewhat to widen their appeal. The addition of a folk-instrument orchestra and a dance group in 1938 took them further from their roots in peasant singing, but placed them in the mainstream of Stalinist entertainment. One symbolic change was their move from oral tradition to notation, which led to the removal of an improvisational element that, by 1938, was only entrusted to three soloists (one of whom was Zakharov's wife).[5]

The 'folk orchestra' component that unites both the Red Army Ensemble and the Pyatnitsky Choir has its own exciting history. This was the sound of the Great Russian/Imperial/Court Orchestra founded by Vasily Andreyev in 1887 and patronized by Alexander III and Nicholas II. In many respects, Andreyev's orchestra is an important predecessor to the Soviet star ensembles: it was fed by a continuous supply of talent from the military (Andreyev managed to introduce balalaika teachers into the Russian Army), it received a generous subsidy from the state, and inspired the creation of similar ensembles both inside Russia and abroad. Even the Soviet practice of cultural diplomacy was already practised in late Tsarist Russia: when the ensemble came to England, Andreyev was only half-jokingly called 'a diplomat without portfolio'.[6] Andreyev's fund-raising strategy had both spiritual and material aspects: on the one hand, the balalaika could be presented as giving workers an ennobling, constructive leisure activity, keeping them away from the vodka and preserving national culture in the cities; on the other hand, the manufacture of the modified bala-laikas Andreyev had designed became a sizeable industry and retail sector. His critics argued that the fashion for balalaika playing displaced interest in more noble instruments and was detrimental to musical tastes, but Andreyev pointed to his modifications in reply.[7] The instrument was no longer a crude and limited homemade contraption; Andreyev's balalaika (and the domra) now came in four to five sizes, down to the double bass, and together the instruments could serve as the basis of an orchestra just as well as the earlier enno-bled instruments of the violin family.

Andreyev had managed to anticipate that fine balance between high and low art that the Soviet cultural authorities sought in their 'music for the people' from Stalin onwards. It is quite possible that he even had some direct influence on the aesthetic; he lived until 1918, and the ensembles he had created or inspired continued to play through the 1920s and into the Stalin years. This kind of art, alongside the Red Army Ensemble and the Pyatnitsky Choir, was highly professionalized, and often virtuosic (it most certainly was not untu-tored), and yet it was rooted in spontaneously emerging talent that appeared outside the conservatoire-based, academic route to musical excellence. It also appealed to a very broad audience, which could be multiplied in Soviet times through the power of broadcasting and recording technology.

Now let us return to the music of the star ensembles and their prize-winning composers, Aleksandrov and Zakharov. Their repertoires overlapped in content and even more in style: both sang arrangements of folk songs or folk-style pastiches, and both also sang more dynamic, march-like mass songs. Of the two composers, Aleksandrov seems the more gifted tunesmith: although he only had a limited bag of tricks, he produced many rousing and memorable songs. One of these, 'The Holy War' (*Svyashchennaya voyna*), a peculiar triple-time march written immediately after the Nazi invasion, became a powerful symbol of that grim period. The KSP voted him through for his 'wartime songs', to which the Party anthem was added, most likely at the Politburo stage. Since this later became the national anthem, with minimal reworking, the addition points to Stalin's liking for the song.

The appeal of Zakharov's music was not so broad. He often set embarrass-ingly sycophantic 'fakelore texts' (such as 'One falcon is Lenin, and the other Stalin', in his song 'Falcons') to music that can be described as rather academic folk-song pastiche with well-developed heterophonic textures (undervoices – *podgoloski* – is the Russian term). The result is unimpeachably 'Russian' but not especially engaging, and the real popularity of his choir owed more to catchier numbers by other composers which were sometimes mistakenly attributed to Zakharov (many such mistakes still persist on the web, for example, Isaak Lyuban's more popular setting of the lyric 'Bud'te zdorovi' – Be Healthy – is often attributed to Zakharov, while Zakharov's own setting is little known).[8] It is possible that Stalin himself imagined that Zakharov had written some of these more popular songs: unlike the songs by other prizewinners, Zakharov's were almost completely resistant to arrangement in other styles, and could only be taken up by other folk-style choirs.

Although the Red Army Ensemble and Pyatnitsky Choir were openly patronized by the Kremlin, this official favour did not transfer automatically to others working in the same genres, which could not climb higher than second-class prizes (and later third-class). Even this degree of recognition was often thought too generous by high-art composers, who resented the imbalance between whole symphonies and collections of catchy tunes, both in terms of the requisite expertise and the amount of time and effort required. This kind of resentment surfaced, for example, in KSP discussions of Vasily Solovyov-Sedoi, the composer of some of Russia's most popular songs (even today); some of his songs are well known internationally, especially his 'Moscow Nights' (from the late 1950s). During the war, his 'Evening Patrol' (*Vecher na reyde*) was already sung in America; the song softens its underlying march rhythm with a nostalgic lyricism. This was noted at the 1943 discussion by the filmmaker Alexander Dovzhenko: such songs matched the tender feelings that were needed so much in wartime. Khrapchenko supported Solovyov-Sedoi, too: he claimed that the composer had taken the genre of mass song away from the foxtrot – the ever-present shadow of Western degradation – and given it healthier roots in rural and urban folk song. Myaskovsky was not interested: 'Well as for me, when I listen to these songs, I seem to have heard it all before ...'[9] In 1947, when Solovyov-Sedoi came to the KSP plenary session in person to perform some of his songs, the high-art composers, who would usually have been allowed to dominate musical discussions, fell silent, leaving the filmmakers, painters and actors to their own devices. Lacking the composers' professional rivalries, the non-musicians chatted happily about which songs were their favourites.[10]

One step down from Solovyov-Sedoi was Matvei Blanter, who also produced songs of great popularity (he is internationally known as the composer of 'Katyusha'); even the song composers argued about his worth. In 1945, he was in direct competition with Anatoly Novikov, whose more sober style had won him both popularity and respect. Aleksandrov (the director of the Red Army Ensemble) supported Novikov, claiming that his songs were included in the repertoire of every ensemble at the front line. Khrapchenko and even Goldenweiser were also happy to vote for Novikov.[11] But Blanter's candidature elicited an angry tirade from Aleksandrov, who accused him of plagiarism and banality.[12] The great army favourite, 'In a Forest at the Front' (*V lesu prifrontovom*), he said, was actually nothing more than a rehash of an old waltz. Blanter lost to Novikov on this occasion, but he won a prize in 1946, the following year, when the tone of the discussion was much more positive, and even Aleksandrov reversed his opinion. Mikhoels recalled that during his trip to the United States he was astonished to hear favourite songs by Blanter and Dunayevsky sung in the streets (!), and he urged members to admit that they were also sung at every house party in their own country.[13] Dunayevsky himself spoke ardently in Blanter's support:

> By nominating Blanter, we are nominating one of the most popular composers, one much loved by the people. The art of song-writing is very demanding: of particular importance here is the precise targeting of these works to their intended audience. Blanter has proven himself exceptionally able in hitting that target. While some composers have assistance from cinema [Dunayevsky could have had himself in mind here], Blanter's songs have spread very quickly without any need for this. He is able to produce melodic patterns that reach out to the hearts of millions.[14]

A little further down the ranks was Sigizmund Kats, whose songs were marked by a more pronounced 'operetta style', or a whiff of 'gypsiness' typical of popular songs in the 1910s and '20s. This prompted Shtoharenko to dismiss Kats as representing an older, outdated stage in the development of Soviet song, and his idioms were not to be encouraged. Members then moved from a discussion of the songs to a discussion of Kats's personal morality, calling him a time-server (*obïvatel'*) and a careerist.[15] The chairman Fadeyev had to interfere: 'Let's not talk about the impression he makes, otherwise he'll regret being put forward for a prize. We are not here to pass moral judgements.'[16] It seems that Kats was viewed more benignly by Zhdanov, since we find Kats's name appearing in Agitprop's list of nominees for 1948 (at the time, Zhdanov was in charge there). Going over that list with a pencil (on his own or at the Politburo meeting), Stalin vacillated as Kats was struck out, reinstated and then struck out again.[17] In the end his turn for a prize only came in 1950, when the newly introduced third class seemed to fit his stature perfectly.

Below the level of Kats and a few other like-minded composers were the undifferentiated composers of mere *estrada*, or variety and show songs for popular entertainment. This does not mean that *estrada* went unrecognized, but it was the performers rather than the composers who came up for discussion (singers sometimes wrote their own songs, but here they were being considered for their performing). One of these was Lidia Ruslanova, a singer with a gripping folksy voice whose interpretations could be compelling, but for the purposes of her prize bid her varied repertoire included some 'dubious' material. (One favourite painted a picture of a desperate woman rowing herself and her faithless lover into the open sea seeking death for them both: he is busy with the sails while she steers, and when he realizes they are too far from the shore she stabs him and throws herself into the waves – not the kind of edifying story Socialist Realism was looking for.) In the KSP, her candidature was rejected outright: the eminent painter Grabar dismissed her art as hackwork (*khaltura*), while Shaporin elaborated: 'To give a prize to Ruslanova would be to legitimize the illegitimate.'[18] Goldenweiser often used Ruslanova as a stock example of the debased musical tastes of 'the people'. Ruslanova might have sung at the front and in Berlin, she might have sold millions of records and earned a fortune for herself, but she would not have a Stalin Prize added to her list of successes.[19]

A more persistent candidate was Leonid Utyosov, a chansonnier, actor, comedian and leader of the most popular Soviet jazz band of this period. Having come to Soviet-wide prominence together with his band in the celebrated film *The Merry Fellows*, his fame seemed to have no bounds, and yet no Stalin Prize was in sight. By 1944, Utyosov, tired of waiting, penned a personal letter to Stalin: his *estrada* colleagues, he wrote, found it hurtful that their art seemed to be excluded from the remit of the prize. Khrapchenko had to explain the situation to Molotov: in principle, the possibility of such a nomination did exist for performers (he cited the puppet artist Sergei Obraztsov, a staple of Kremlin banquets), but he stressed that there were other ways of rewarding people like Utyosov – through honorary titles and government awards.[20] The immediate result of Utyosov's complaint was the award of a Banner of the Order of Red Labour. But the following year, 1945, his name was put forward to the KSP.

At the KSP discussion, Khrapchenko reminded members that Utyosov had recently received a government award, and that this should be taken as a sign of *estrada*'s legitimacy. He need not have bothered. Here is the discussion in full:

Glière [announcing the nomination]: ... Utyosov, artistic director of the VGKO Jazz Band.
[VGKO stood for the State Defence Committee, no less.]

Goldenweiser: The artistic level here is . . . not up to a Stalin prize.
Moskvin (chairman): I agree.[21]

Goldenweiser's hesitation, marked in the transcript, is most unlikely to have been due to uncertainty – he was probably holding back a more insulting evaluation.

Opinions had moved on by 1946, when a broader discussion of Utyosov was possible. After the Music Section had rejected this candidate on the grounds that he 'had nothing to do with music', indignant non-musicians in the KSP objected.[22] The film director Ivan Pyryev spoke up:

> It is strange to be sitting here listening to the Music Section's arguments while they treat Utyosov and his genre so condescendingly. This is one of the original musical performers who created the genre of staged song, which is much loved by the people. In recent years, it has been said that his style of performance is to some extent borrowed from abroad. And yet we can remember the moment when jazz music reached us, and it was this man who created a very interesting genre much loved by the people. So I think it is not at all right to speak of him with condescension [. . .]. I understand the great significance of such a musician as [the cellist] Knushevitsky, or the Glazunov Quartet, they have their own place, but we can't simply ignore this merry, pleasing, amusing genre. [. . .] The 'light genre' is vital for us at this time.[23]

But the members, on balance, were not prepared to choose between Utyosov and the Glazunov Quartet; they would only accept him if there was a special *estrada* nomination. Even Dunayevsky, of all people, accused Utyosov of occasional vulgarities in his repertoire. Goldenweiser courted controversy (not that he cared) by claiming that Soviet jazz bands were lagging behind their Western counterparts, but he hoped that the introduction of a special *estrada* nomination would stimulate their development (this should not be taken too seriously, since he was prepared to say anything to ring-fence the existing prizes for classical performers). Khrapchenko's reply was convoluted and obscure, but he evidently had no desire to challenge the consensus and he postponed Utyosov for another year (given his predilection for changing his colleagues' decisions, we can assume that he was in agreement with them this time).[24] In 1947, Utyosov duly resurfaced for discussion, but still without success. There was now strong support from Mikhoels, Kuznetsov, Ermler and even Shaporin, but not nearly enough to pull the consensus in their direction. It was Khrapchenko who blithely dismissed the candidature by suggesting that Utyosov's latest show wasn't as good as those of previous years (we might like to think that this comment was not conveyed to Utyosov).[25]

Times moved on, but in the stormy 1948 meetings, Utyosov's candidature still bobbed up to the surface. The new minister Polycarp Lebedev suggested including him to replace a nomination which in those xenophobic years seemed particularly dubious – that of the tenor Mikhail Aleksandrovich, whose great popularity across the Soviet Union was tempered by the oddity of his career. Born in Latvia and already famous at the age of nine, his early career was spent outside Soviet borders. He took some lessons from the celebrated Italian tenor Beniamino Gigli, worked as a cantor in British and Lithuanian synagogues, and his vocal production always sounded Western – Italianate rather than Russian. After Latvia became Soviet, he was not able to travel abroad again, but became a major Soviet star. A Westerner or not, his repertoire of Neapolitan songs, lighter operatic fare and some Soviet music, was more middlebrow and 'tasteful' than Utyosov's. And his *bel canto* delivery contrasted sharply with Utyosov's hoarse comedy voice. Perhaps more to the point, Aleksandrovich brought to life some hit numbers by Khrennikov (from his *Much Ado about Nothing*), who was now happy to return the favour, overriding the new minister's choice.

A few months later, Utyosov's ensemble was due to celebrate its twentieth anniversary. Lebedev approached Malenkov with a proposal to give state awards to the ensemble and make Utyosov himself a People's Artist of the RSFSR – nothing particularly unusual when such a jubilee cropped up in the career of a significant artist or artistic institution. This was a comparatively modest proposal: no Stalin Prize, and People's Artist not of the USSR but only the Russian Republic. Even so, it was blocked by Agitprop: Shepilov and Kuznetsov managed to convince Malenkov that the anniversary should not be given any official recognition due to the ensemble's 'impoverished repertoire' and 'low quality of performance'.[26] There are reasons for Agitprop's decision other than artistic snobbery: Utyosov's sharp tongue meant that he was no longer invited to Kremlin banquets (at least that was his own explanation),[27] while his celebration of Odessan Jewish culture, and also of jazz, put him on the wrong side during the anti-cosmopolitanism campaign. In any case, the fate of *estrada* was now sealed as far as the Stalin Prizes were concerned, because if Utyosov couldn't win a prize for *estrada*, then no one could.

Operetta

If popular songs with hints of operetta were scorned by KSP members, what hope was there for operetta itself? Work on specifically Soviet operetta, like work on specifically Soviet opera, continued, and the list of ideologically solid titles was growing longer. But it was a difficult task indeed to meld a solid Socialist Realist plot to a genre that was designed as an unabashedly hedonistic entertainment. A precedent was set in 1946, when an operetta production was accepted for a second-class prize (note, a production rather than a score). This was a production of the operetta *The Tobacco Captain*, by Vladimir Shcherbachev, in Sverdlovsk (now Yekaterinburg). The theme (given comic treatment) was historical and patriotic, namely social mobility in the times of Peter the Great, and the librettist Nikolai Aduyev was commended for a most professional job, while the production was pronounced by Khrapchenko the best of any Soviet operetta spectacle. Shcherbachev's score, however, was not one of the attractions: it was described as 'extremely weak', and the composer was not included in the list of nominations. Those who know Shcherbachev as a 1920s modernist and an important Leningrad composition professor may be surprised to hear that he was writing an operetta two decades later, but it was a commission that he had been given during the wartime evacuation. The music was, of course, most professionally put together and historically aware, using eighteenth-century Russian opera idioms and some French colour from a minuet, a pavane and a courante. It seems to have lacked a wider popular appeal, however, and made scant reference to familiar operetta styles. Most KSP members voted for the production without hearing it, and they promptly forgot about the matter.[28]

The 1948 appearance of Dunayevsky's *Free Wind* on the list (as a production at the Moscow Operetta) was a case of much greater importance. On the wave of its huge success in the capital, the Theatre Section labelled it a new and exciting development in the operetta genre. But this was the beginning of the Khrennikov dispensation, and a different wind was now blowing through Soviet music. Xenia Derzhinskaya, a Bolshoi Theatre soprano at the end of her career and a newly appointed member of the KSP, explained to the plenary session that the Music Section was not prepared to support the nomination of *Free Wind*. It very soon became clear, however, that it was mainly Khrennikov who was against it (he was not present at this plenary session). Derzhinskaya herself was an admirer of Dunayevsky's operetta, but as spokesperson for the Music Section she dutifully recited the points that had been raised against the nomination. There was no precedent, she said, for an operetta being awarded a prize. She was immediately corrected, being informed of the prize two years earlier for *The Tobacco Captain*. This mattered little, since the other objection was much more weighty: there was a Western influence in both plot and music; the play was set in an unidentified Mediterranean port, with a cast whose names suggested a mix of nationalities, leading a vague struggle against some vague imperialists.[29]

Unexpectedly, Goldenweiser (of all people) came to *Free Wind*'s defence, recalling how he had attended a performance together with the late Mikhoels. They had both enjoyed the evening, finding the production dynamic and absorbing. As for the music, he continued,

> [B]ecause the plot of the operetta is taken from life outside Russia, it is clear that it wouldn't contain any Russian songs. Dunayevsky is the most talented master of song we have, and I have to say that the music is very melodic and very pleasant to listen to. I simply cannot understand why some colleagues are judging it so severely.[30]

Even the ideology-conscious Fadeyev had to agree:

> The plots of our operettas don't have to be taken from Soviet life. The theme of this piece is truly international. We can imagine that the action is taking place somewhere like Greece. I'd say that here, without straining the genre, the unity of a people in the face of occupation is portrayed, so the theme is connected with the issue of a new democracy and the national liberation movement in a country such as Greece. So the plot is completely acceptable on ideological grounds.[31]

Fadeyev and Derzhinskaya (now free to speak for herself) began to chat merrily about their enjoyment of the powerful mass scenes and the striking set design, but their fun was spoilt by the formidable musicologist Tamara Livanova, who now launched an attack on Dunayevsky:

> We have decided unanimously that the music of *Free Wind* cannot receive a prize. [...] First of all, this operetta [...] has nothing Russian about it. All this music is written in a Western manner, and all the music repeats what the composer has already done in his previous works, which were undoubtedly better.

The discussion stalled. Fadeyev pointed out that, in any case, the music was not being singled out, and Dunayevsky would only be awarded as one member of the team responsible for the production, but conversely, it was unthinkable to exclude him. Livanova, undaunted, said that she did not favour awarding the performers either, who were just a bunch of 'free and easy [*razvyaznïye*] girls'.[32]

Three days later, on 21 February 1948 (eleven days after the publication of the anti-formalist resolution), Khrennikov finally found the time to attend a plenary session and suggested that Dunayevsky could indeed be included in the production list, in recognition of his professionalism, but on no account was he to receive an individual award, since the music was 'not very progressive', and was 'tied to the traditions of Viennese operetta'.[33]

The operetta was passed by the KSP for a second-class prize, but it must have caused controversy again at the next stages. Lebedev agreed with the second-class prize, but removed the set designer Grigory Kigel from the list; Agitprop's Shepilov and Ilyichev, however, rejected the work altogether as 'based on models from run-of-the-mill Western operettas'. Someone above, however, decided to put it back onto the list – this was most likely Zhdanov.

The good news was leaked to Dunayevsky, who wrote on 11 April 1948: '*Free Wind* has been confirmed for a Stalin Prize which will be published in a few days' time'.[34] But when the list of laureates was published, *Free Wind* was no longer there. The composers of the KSP were startled (most of them were present at the First Congress of the Composers' Union). Dunayevsky was presumably dismayed, but he retained his composure, and gave a touchingly light-hearted account of the affair:

> By the way, despite the Resolution of the Stalin [Prize] Committee on the operetta *Free Wind*, the government didn't give me a prize. My frustration lasted no more than five minutes, and gave way to a more philosophical outlook. I don't know anything about the causes of such an unexpected

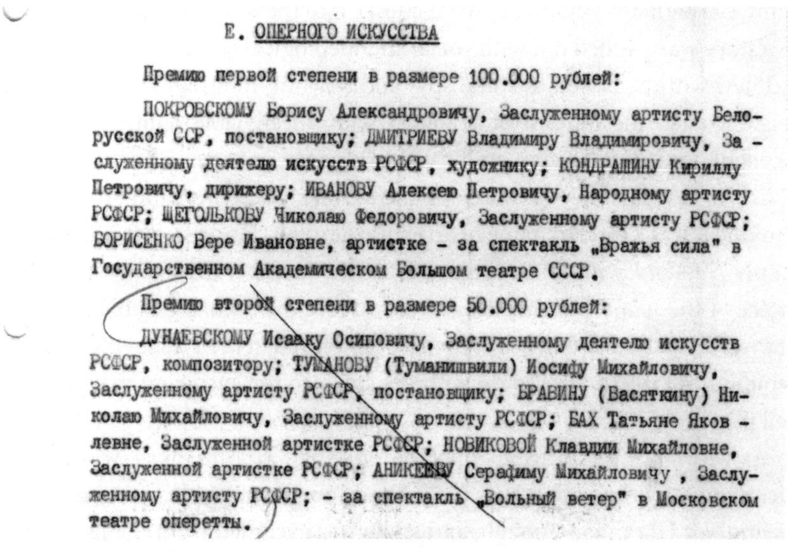

Е. ОПЕРНОГО ИСКУССТВА

Премию первой степени в размере 100.000 рублей:

ПОКРОВСКОМУ Борису Александровичу, Заслуженному артисту Белорусской ССР, постановщику; ДМИТРИЕВУ Владимиру Владимировичу, Заслуженному деятелю искусств РСФСР, художнику; КОНДРАШИНУ Кириллу Петровичу, дирижеру; ИВАНОВУ Алексею Петровичу, Народному артисту РСФСР; ЩЕГОЛЬКОВУ Николаю Федоровичу, Заслуженному артисту РСФСР; БОРИСЕНКО Вере Ивановне, артистке - за спектакль „Вражья сила" в Государственном Академическом Большом театре СССР.

Премию второй степени в размере 50.000 рублей:

ДУНАЕВСКОМУ Исааку Осиповичу, Заслуженному деятелю искусств РСФСР, композитору; ТУМАНОВУ (Туманишвили) Иосифу Михайловичу, Заслуженному артисту РСФСР, постановщику; БРАВИНУ (Васяткину) Николаю Михайловичу, Заслуженному артисту РСФСР; БАХ Татьяне Яковлевне, Заслуженной артистке РСФСР; НОВИКОВОЙ Клавдии Михайловне, Заслуженной артистке РСФСР; АНИКЕЕВУ Серафиму Михайловичу, Заслуженному артисту РСФСР; - за спектакль „Вольный ветер" в Московском театре оперетты.

Fig. 16. Agitprop's deletion of Dunayevsky's *Free Wind*. RGASPI, fond 82, op. 2, ye. kh. 462, l. 32.

outcome, and it would be next to impossible to find out. But we can make a guess. The funniest thing is that on the 19th [of April], the chairman of the Arts Committee [Lebedev] congratulated me on the prize, and the newspapers had already asked for my photo, when suddenly … Well, it doesn't matter. Let those who lack creative spirit be sad. I don't work for a prize. For as long as I have my head on my shoulders, I won't succumb to gloom. *Free Wind* is a huge success – isn't that a prize in itself?[35]

When did the decisive removal of *Free Wind* take place? If it was at the Politburo meeting, then it was quite a routine matter in the awards process, especially after the amount of controversy the nomination had generated at each of the earlier stages. Then again, it would have been rather rash of Lebedev to congratulate Dunayevsky before the Politburo meeting, in which case only Stalin could have made the deletion; after accepting it at the Politburo, he still had time to reflect on the matter and change his mind. Still, the latter scenario was very rare, and the balance of probabilities lies in favour of the former. It was Lebedev's first experience of the awards process as the new minister, so he might well have made some minor errors.

It now seemed to be settled: the 1946 prize was an aberration, and operetta was simply not eligible for Stalin Prizes. But the 1949 nominations (confirmed in 1950) contained an operetta once again. This was *The Trembita* at the Moscow Operetta, a production that rivalled the public success of *Free Wind*, but which could boast a more ideologically pointed libretto: it was a story set in Trans-Carpathian Ukraine, a recent addition to the Soviet Union. A traditional love story was padded out with social and ideological conflicts between the old and new worlds, as well as some spy- and treasure-hunting. The dialogue and music carried the burden of ideology with an enviable lightness, and with excellent performances, the public was easily won over. *The Trembita* managed to live up to its sonorous name, which could easily fool the audience into thinking it was a foreign name of an exotic heroine (in Russian, it was, of course simply *Trembita*, without an article). One KSP member even suggested that the choice of the name was precisely a ruse to lure the ignorant public. The *trembita* was, in fact, an alphorn-like instrument played in the West of the Ukrainian Republic, but it had little to do with the story, so the suspicion may have been well placed.[36]

As with both the previous operetta nominations, the music was problematic: Yury Milyutin's score was considered too generic (too operetta-like, that is), and not Ukrainian enough, and so he was excluded from the list of nominees. There were also concerns about weaknesses in the libretto and the rather trivial, even 'vulgar' scenery, but the director Iosif Tumanov, it was agreed, had energized the actors into producing a gripping and enjoyable spectacle. This time, Khrennikov suggested authoritatively that the Moscow Operetta was becoming a progressive theatre, leaning towards Soviet composers (Milyutin, Dunayevsky, Boris Mokrousov), and it would be possible to give it a prize. Ermler, remembering the previous year's failure, was sceptical, and suggested that such a theatre could never hope to win, simply because operetta was operetta. He was wrong: neither the ministry nor Agitprop objected to *The Trembita*, and they both even wanted to include Milyutin in the list. But the Politburo sided with the KSP and Milyutin did not receive a prize for his contribution to the operetta (it is likely that the Politburo recalled that Milyutin had already won a prize the previous year for popular songs, and didn't consider him outstanding enough for another so soon).[37]

These remarkable goings-on confirm to us that operetta was a borderline genre in the Stalinist hierarchy of the arts, enjoyed even by the most discerning, and yet thought to be of dubious worth. And even as the ideological libretti and tight directing seemed to be bringing the genre into the Soviet fold, the music was seen as pulling it away again. Khrennikov expressed the hope that some genuinely Russian green shoots would appear in operetta music (he might have hoped to produce them himself), but for now, they were conspicuously absent.

Light Classical and the Hybrids

The 'small forms' subcategory of Music, initially created specifically to legitimize awards to wartime songs and marches in 1943, eventually grew in scope to catch everything that did not already have a subcategory of its own, from serious chamber works to single songs. Between these extremes there was room for more unusual nominations that sought, once again, to occupy the elusive middle ground between high and low. A couple of prizewinning pieces – Lev Knipper's Serenade for Strings (1946) and Sergei Vasilenko's Ballet Suite – could be described as 'light classical', but the prizes they received tell us nothing about the value of the genre, since the composers, rather than the works, were being favoured in both these cases. By 1946, the celebrated Knipper, author of the internationally known song 'Meadowlands' (*Polyushko-pole*) was overdue for a prize, but hadn't produced anything on a sufficiently large scale. Not that he had been lazy: during the war, he was busy living his other life as a top-calibre spy, at one point chosen to assassinate Hitler, until this particular plan was abandoned.[38] His composer colleagues, it seems, knew nothing of this and would have been more astounded than readers of this paragraph. While they were told that Knipper was simply going about his musicianly work collecting Persian folk melodies, he was actually preparing the ground for the Tehran

Conference of Stalin, Roosevelt and Churchill. As if his double life were not impressive enough, he was also an expert and passionate mountaineer, and his Mountain Serenade was written as a glorification of the view from high peaks, but the picturesque part of the title was lost during the award process.

Sergei Vasilenko was simply a distinguished superannuated composer for whom the prize was essentially a lifetime award (at the age of 75). His Ballet Suite, a commission from the Bolshoi, was described as masterful, beautifully orchestrated, but without any pretence to profundity.[39] Glière's Concerto for Voice and Orchestra also ended up in the small-forms category: although concertos were generally considered large forms, this example was regarded as a kind of suite and garnered epithets such as 'pleasant' and 'delightful'.[40] In this case, too, it was respect for the composer's distinguished name that brought the piece onto the list, but the process of discussion revealed that some (Mikhoels and Ermler in particular) were genuinely swept away by this highly unusual piece filled with Italianate coloratura brilliance. Glière's Concerto became genuinely popular, broadcast to the furthest corners of the Soviet Union, and pieces like that form a peculiar lining to musical Socialist Realism that is surprisingly free of ideology. Only twice in the KSP discussions did someone try to theorize, or, rather, justify this phenomenon. Once it was Myaskovsky, in an (unsuccessful) attempt to give a helping hand to some light pieces for cello by his student Nikolai Rakov:

> This is a 'forgotten genre', so-called salon music, i.e. music which could be played in any situation, and everywhere it would produce a winning impression for the performers and on the listeners. [...] You have the feeling that you've received great pleasure, although you realize that it's salon music, slightly sweet. But there's nothing bad about that. This is comfortable music.[41]

Despite Khrapchenko's objection that a Stalin Prize for a piece like this would be something shocking, Myaskovsky continued to insist that this kind of music, which he said was 'missing from our life', was the musical equivalent of a novella in literature. The other occasion was when Shostakovich, in a similar situation, attempted to save a composer he supported. The composer was Khodja-Einatov (we encountered this episode in Chapter 5), and Shostakovich offered more appropriate (less nostalgic) arguments than Myaskovsky about serving the needs of rail passengers. And although it proved impossible to create an ideologically solid defence of this leisure music, it continued to exist amidst more openly ideological staples of Socialist Realism. It was performed and enjoyed, and even stole the occasional prize.

A subtly different tone characterized the discussion of Nikolai Budashkin, who wrote music for an orchestra of Russian folk instruments in the manner of Andreyev. His pieces, such as the Russian Rhapsody, or the Fantasy on Russian Folk Themes, were virtuosic arrangements of folk themes. He managed to win two prizes (in 1947 and 1949) without provoking disputes in the Committee, and they were awarded on grounds of high professionalism and flair, since he was recognized as the pinnacle of the medium. And yet it is obvious from little nuances in the discussion that the KSP members themselves considered this kind of music beneath them. In 1947, Glière described the pieces as 'written in their own genre', and Goldenweiser added that it was a 'genre much needed by the broad masses'. Khrapchenko stamped his seal of approval, 'no doubts about this'.[42] In 1949, however, with a different personnel and different expectations, the treatment was less patronizing.

Repertoire for military bands had a much harder time at the KSP, with the exception of marches by Nikolai Ivanov-Radkevich (awarded in 1943), which 'could be marched to, but combined this with the highest artistic form'.[43] A case in point are the suites by Valentin Kruchinin, who strung together marches and songs. Kruchinin's suites were among the first works submitted to the KSP in 1940, and the Music Section rejected them after glancing over the scores. Someone leaked the decision to Kruchinin, who complained to Molotov that only three members of the KSP had actually heard his work (and reminded Molotov that he himself had once had a chance to hear Kruchinin's music at some army celebration). The KSP were outraged by the leak and the complaint, and did not change their decision. In 1944, two Kruchinin suites turned up again, now riding a wave of popular support at the fronts.[44] Regardless, the members assumed a derogatory tone, labelling the suites as 'music adapted to the common understanding' and 'music for undeveloped tastes'. It fell to Myaskovsky, who was not only an upholder of high-art standards, but also doubled up as an authority on military music, to explain that Kruchinin's suites had strong popular appeal, and that other composers, more talented overall, had nevertheless failed to match Kruchinin in this respect. In the interests of fairness, he defended Kruchinin, saying that 'in his own genre and for a particular audience he's doing a great job'. But Samosud insisted that the people's tastes needed to be educated, and Kruchinin's music hindered that process – if it was his call, he would simply ban it.[45] Was it the actual quality of the music under consideration that the KSP objected to, or was it perhaps other parts of Kruchinin's oeuvre – operettas, romances, even 1920s foxtrots and tangos – that sowed moral panic?[46]

The story with Kruchinin was repeated and even amplified in the case of Vladimir Sorokin's oratorio *Alexander Matrosov*, written specifically for army song-and-dance ensembles. This was a large-scale work that had grown from a single successful song of the same name, which, by itself, had already garnered mass support among army music ensembles. In the post-1948 KSP, this unusual nomination polarized the discussion, as in the following representative exchange:

> *Novikov:* The army listens to the Sorokin. The generals listen to the Sorokin as well, and they value it highly.
> *Golovanov:* They listened to Ruslanova, too, but that was a national catastrophe.[47]

Interestingly, *Matrosov* not only ran against the tastes of the high-art composers, but at the same time managed to break several tacit rules of musical Socialist Realism. The part of the heroic soldier who threw himself on a gun-port to save his friends was sung, unsuitably, by a lyrical tenor; his death was then followed by music of poignant farewell rather than heroic uplift; finally, and probably most seriously, the text of Stalin's order was actually set to music. The argument is familiar: the music was too weak and undeserving of the shining text, and this time it was used by the members with particular delight (even Shostakovich joined in), because it allowed them to get rid of this troublesome nomination.[48] But Sorokin was quick to produce a revised version, and so *Matrosov* came back again ... and again. The pressure from army circles was so intense that the KSP ended up listening to the oratorio no less than four times, and every time with the same result. Goldenweiser, fed up with this, allowed himself to question the very notion that 'the people', in uniform or out, gave the piece their unanimous support: he himself volunteered to write a dozen letters to the Radio Committee and sign them with various names (implying that *Matrosov* obtained its support by similar methods). What kind of 'people' is this? – he demanded. We are the people, too, Mikhalkov added in agreement.[49]

Kruchinin's suites and Sorokin's oratorio can be categorized as hybrids between popular (in this case military) and classical music – these pieces aspired to elevate the popular by means of larger-scale forms and certain 'classical' procedures. Below these hybrids in prestige were the stage shows of the NKVD (Secret Police) Song and Dance Ensemble, which also, peculiarly, found their way onto the list of nominations, supplying a sparkling array of big names as producers. The show *Motherland* (*Po rodnoy zemle*), for example, discussed in 1943, boasted the participation of the film director Sergei Yutkevich, the ballet master Kasyan Goleyzovsky, the set designer Pyotr Vilyams and the composers Nikolai Chemberdzhi and Shostakovich. Having attended the show,

Shaporin and Glière reported, however, that this was nothing more than a string of concert numbers, clumsily linked together by the master of ceremonies. The star production team was also rather bogus: Chemberdzhi had only written one song, while Shostakovich was represented only by a theme from his Seventh Symphony.[50]

Another programme by the same ensemble, entitled *A Russian River*, received even more scathing comments from the KSP (in their discussion of 1945). Aleksandrov, always alert to competition, would not even allow that the NKVD group was a 'song and dance ensemble' similar to his own Red Army ensemble. The show, in his estimation, was a mere revue, a variety show, with badly sung folk songs and crudely choreographed dances. The acting was poor, and so were the sets and costumes. Goldenweiser sensed there was bias behind this wretched picture, and hastened to contradict Aleksandrov: 'They sing and dance well there. I am a rather jaded man, and yet I too was able to derive some pleasure from Act I.' But scoring a point against Aleksandrov was not the same as seeking a prize for *A Russian River*, and so Goldenweiser delivered the *coup de grâce*: 'Act II is a pure divertissement, and so the prize is out of the question.'[51] Let us enjoy the freeze-frame: the silver-haired, religious Goldenweiser, once a friend of Tolstoy, a 'jaded' connoisseur of the arts, taps his foot to the merry jig of Stalin's secret police.

Since these variety shows were being nominated or considered as productions (alongside productions of plays, operas and ballets), they failed each time on the grounds that they were not bound together by any coherent narrative or theme, and this consideration did not change after 1948. But from 1950, awards could be given to large performing ensembles, not for a particular song or production, but for their work as a whole, with the prize shared between the director and leading soloists. The first of these went to the Red Army Ensemble, now under the direction of Aleksandrov's son, Boris, with a first-class prize. In 1952, both the Pyatnitsky Choir and the Moiseyev Dance Ensemble received first-class prizes. Although individual songs performed by such ensembles had won awards before, the new ensemble awards after 1948 tilted the balance a little further in favour of the middlebrow. One important motivation for these ensembles was their role as cultural ambassadors in a new context, namely the new Soviet-aligned countries of Eastern Europe. None of this impressed the more highbrow KSP members. It was not just the fact that such ensembles received awards, but the fact that they did so when so many worthy high-art musicians had still not been recognized through the prize system. It rankled with them, for instance, that Samson Galperin, the conductor of the Moiseyev Dance Ensemble, could now pin a first-class medal to his lapel, while many distinguished symphonic conductors either made do with second-class prizes or were still waiting in the queue (Shostakovich and Golovanov were particularly aghast,[52] and this uncomfortable comparison was later cited in official papers as a sign of the Stalin Prize's degradation). No symphony orchestra, not even the Leningrad Philharmonic, was deemed to have deserved a similar honour. Golovanov complained: surely the status of Soviet musical culture was sustained by symphony orchestras, rather than choirs or dance ensembles![53] By this stage, however, Golovanov's objection seemed outdated.

And yet, we should not overestimate the extent of the shift to the demotic in the post-1948 Music awards. Although the performers' lists included more directors of folk-style choirs, orchestras and dance ensembles, the rapid increase in the overall number of awards made them additions, rather than displacements. And although more 'light classical' and hybrid works found their way onto the lists, they were largely fuel for the ever-expanding second- and third-class categories. By contrast, first-class awards for musical works shrank to almost nothing, the last being granted, posthumously, to Myaskovsky for his last symphony and last string quartet. This tells us that the KSP, despite the change in climate, held on to their aesthetic preferences. The space at the top for music remained temporarily vacant until something worthy was produced again.

And, of course, it is important to keep in mind the general rule: Stalin Prizes were only supposed to be awarded to professional or professionalized art, and never to performers or craftsmen who could be described as 'folk' (rather than 'folk-style'). Almost every year, there were nominations for Soviet-themed rugs woven in the Central Asian republics which were routinely dismissed: in 1943, for instance, a gigantic Uzbek rug with portraits woven into it and entitled 'the Politburo' was seen by the KSP as perverse and anti-artistic.[54] However, in 1950, an Azerbaijani rug for Stalin's seventieth birthday did actually receive a first-class prize, but that was only possible because it had been made under the direction of Letuf Kerimov, a carpet-weaver who was by that stage already a professor of fine arts in Baku and had developed a technologically modernized industry of rug production. A musical equivalent to this was Pavel Necheporenko, who, it is true, had learnt the balalaika from his father in his native village, but by the time of his Stalin Prize, he had a conservatoire education behind him, and was a popular recording artist. According to his memoirs, Khrennikov defended Necheporenko's right to a Stalin Prize (see Chapter 1), precisely on the grounds that the balalaika was now a legitimate professional instrument taught at the conservatoire.

In the same passage, Khrennikov mentions something of great importance to the argument in this chapter: that Stalin dismissed all kinds of (unrefined) folk art as mere fairground shows (*balagan* – see Chapter 1). To satisfy his tastes, folk or amateur performers (such as the earliest membership of the Pyatnitsky Choir or the Red Army Ensemble) had to professionalize, learn notation and reach a level of virtuosity comparable to that of classical performers. Such groups also increased in size and eventually received the status of 'State' or 'Academic' institutions. This must stand as a corrective to the misunderstanding of Socialist Realism as a process of 'deindividualization ... deprofessionalization (rejection of 'literate' learning) and [...] destruction of corporate ties [...]'.[55] Quite the reverse: 'folk' and amateur art could only be co-opted by Socialist Realism when the traditionally collective choirs acquired individual 'named' directors and soloists, rejected an oral tradition for the written one and then finally earned a respectable position within the Soviet institutional system.

CHAPTER NINE

AWARDS FOR PERFORMERS

I saw the new opera *Almas*[t], where Maksakova gave an absolutely extraordinary performance of the (Armenian) lezghinka – I haven't seen a dance performed with such artistry in a long time. I think you'll enjoy this dance a lot, and the opera too.

– Nadezhda Alliluyeva to Stalin, 12 September 1930[1]

Opera and Politics

Nothing speaks more eloquently about the genre hierarchy in Soviet culture than the attention lavished on opera. While the absolute numbers of opera awards and dramatic theatre awards did not differ significantly, there was a startling difference in proportions that left the drama artists feeling less favoured. The theatre director Yury Zavadsky, speaking in 1949, gives a very clear account of the problem:

> There are only 16 opera and ballet theatres in the [Soviet] Union, and if each gives three [opera] productions on average annually, we have about 50 productions. If, however, we took [just the more important] 300 drama theatres out of the 600 which we have in the [Soviet] Union, this would [still] yield 1,500 productions. But we have four prizes for each category [Opera and Dramatic Theatre]. This is disproportionate, especially since the drama theatres fulfil more urgent political tasks.[2]

Zavadsky's last point shows that the imbalance was still more striking than the numbers indicated: surely it was dramatic theatre that could convey contemporary political messages with a fast turnover in new plays, whereas opera lumbered on with a repertoire that was largely pre-revolutionary. Drama was indeed faster-moving and more flexible, able to respond quickly to changes in the political environment: Oleksandr Korniychuk's play *The Front* (1942), for example, served to provide the earliest answers to the Soviet people about why their army had to retreat so far before the first victories were won. It ran in twenty-two theatres, but not for long: the play fulfilled its 'urgent political task' until the daily advance of Soviet troops made it feel out of date. Paradoxically, opera, which offered decadent plush interiors and a hedonistic abandon to the musical power of the voice, often played a more enduring political role.

Opera fulfilled political tasks more effectively, but not '*urgent* tasks' – that one word prejudiced the comparison. Its much slower turnover and dependence on repertoire classics determined its different function (the effort to introduce contemporary Soviet subjects largely failed): it was called upon to produce monumental pillars of ideology and identity that could stand firm for many decades. Opera proved to be an effective tool of cultural and ideological expansion into the more distant and reluctant corners of the Soviet empire, as we have already seen in Chapter 7. The opera house was also the grander venue for the celebration of power. It was the entertainment of choice for Party leaders, including those sincerely passionate operagoers, Stalin and Voroshilov.

The first batch of awards in the category 'Opernoye iskusstvo' (operatic art) indicated very clearly what was considered most valuable. The essential award was for the first of those great monumental pillars, the 1939 production of Glinka's *Ivan Susanin* at the Bolshoi, which was a thorough ideological reworking of *A Life for the Tsar* carried out under Stalin's personal supervision.[3] The only question concerned the proper recipient of the award. It was initially suggested that the prize should be granted solely to the conductor Samuil Samosud. This might seem a rather extravagant show of support for this individual, but Samosud was rumoured to be the instigator of the project of turning Glinka's insistently monarchist opera into a national epic for all times, and he had not only conducted for the Bolshoi's production, but had also collaborated with the poet Sergei Gorodetsky on the new libretto. Samosud, however, out of generosity of spirit, or perhaps worried that a personal award might stoke resentments, reportedly said that the award ought to be granted to the entire 3,000-strong team that brought the project to completion.[4] However, there was a rival production at the Kirov Opera in Leningrad running concurrently with the Bolshoi's, and conducted by Ary Pazovsky; moreover, many of those who had managed to see both productions considered Pazovsky's to be musically superior to Samosud's. This introduced doubts about the correct allocation of the prize (at first, more than one prize for the same opera was thought excessive). But a more fundamental doubt was voiced by the theatre director Ilya Sudakov, who questioned *Ivan Susanin*'s credentials as a piece of Soviet theatre:

the score was, after all, already over a century old in 1940. Khrapchenko had to step forward and explain:

> The production of *Ivan Susanin* is the main thing. The opera had been written on a certain text and meant certain things before the Revolution. And now with great tact and skill, it has been produced in such a way as to become a stirring patriotic work which mobilizes the Soviet people. This is a work on a very large scale. The production has played an important role in the general development of theatre. We need only recall that our composers had previously been unable to hear this opera. I know the reactions of some young composers, for whom this production of *Ivan Susanin* was a complete revelation.[5]

KSP members would have understood perfectly well that Khrapchenko was stating the official view of the matter, and not merely throwing his personal thoughts into the debate. And so this reworked opera by Glinka was to be treated as a cornerstone of the Socialist Realist canon, and in some ways as a model for Soviet composers. On this basis, the KSP's list nominated Samosud and Pazovsky jointly for a first-class prize (balancing the rival Bolshoi and Kirov theatres was their foremost consideration), and granted another first prize to the soprano Valeria Barsova, who performed the role of Antonida in the Bolshoi production. There were also two Susanins on the KSP list (Maxim Mikhailov and Alexander Pirogov, both from the Bolshoi), but both were nominated for second-class prizes.

In the hands of the Politburo, this list was significantly modified, indicating, in all probability, the strongly held preferences of the Kremlin's own opera enthusiasts. Pirogov was replaced by Mark Reizen, the third of the Susanins in the Bolshoi's run. Mikhailov was promoted to a first-class prize, and the same was eventually done for Reizen. Barsova was allowed to keep her first-class prize. All the nominated singers – Barsova, Mikhailov, Reizen (plus the tenor Ivan Kozlovsky) – were now awarded simply for 'outstanding achievements', without specifying the production in question, because the period under consideration had been extended to the previous five years, and each of the singers had made excellent contributions to other productions during that time. Samosud and Pazovsky, instead of sharing a single first prize, were now to receive a second-class prize each. This made a subtle distinction: they would receive exactly the same sum of money either way, but they lost some prestige. And so the Bolshoi's star singers were allowed to take precedence over the two conductors. As for Gorodetsky, who had provided all the versification in the new libretto, he never even came up for consideration.

Those Bolshoi stars would become repeated recipients of Stalin Prizes, and for some of them it was enough just to sing another major role. Mikhailov, for example, followed his first-class prize for Susanin with another the following year for singing the comic part of Chub in Tchaikovsky's *Cherevichki*. Pirogov, although he ultimately failed to receive a prize for his Susanin, went on to win first-class prizes in 1943 and 1949. The mezzo-sopranos Vera Davydova and Maria Maksakova managed to build up impressive runs of three first-class prizes each. By contrast, the singers from the Kirov Opera and from provincial theatres appeared on the lists much more rarely. This was in recognition of the fact that while good productions could appear almost anywhere (and were recognized when they did), the very best vocal talent was concentrated in Moscow, on the stage of Stalin's court.

Favourite Singers

The star singers of the Bolshoi were feted by Stalin and the government and became Kremlin intimates. Many sources show how Stalin enjoyed the voices of particular singers and their interpretation of particular pieces, and the most persuasively concrete of these are the programmes of Kremlin banquets, in which we see the pack of favourites shuffled and re-shuffled:

> 23 August 1937: Lemeshev, Kruglikova, Nortsov, Mikhailov, Davydova, Barsova
>
> 20 January 1938: Mikhailov, Barsova, Zlatogorova, Kozlovsky, Nortsov
>
> 2 May 1938: Mikhailov, Kozlovsky, Nortsov, Barsova, Reizen
>
> 17 May 1938: Reizen, Kruglikova, Nortsov, Lemeshev, Pirogov, Barsova
>
> 5 May 1939: Kozlovsky, Reizen, Barsova, Mikhailov
>
> 4 November 1939: Lemeshev, Maksakova, Mikhailov, Barsova
>
> 17 June 1940: Shpiller, Reizen, Davydova, Kozlovsky, Mikhailov
>
> 22 April 1941: Shpiller, Reizen, Barsova, Lemeshev, Mikhailov, Kozlovsky.[6]

Some of these singers kept coming back with the same hit numbers: Mikhailov with his Varangian Guest and Kozlovsky as the Indian Guest (both from *Sadko*), Barsova as Rosina and Nortsov as Figaro (from Rossini's *Il barbiere*). At these banquets, Stalin made no effort to hide the great pleasure he took in acting as the patron of the Bolshoi singers: they often sat at his table, and his conversations with them were reportedly full of mirth. There were even rumours that Stalin treated the Bolshoi as his harem: Barsova, Shpiller, Davydova and Maksakova were at various times named as his lovers (no one has yet suggested that about the Bolshoi men!). However, no credible evidence of this has ever emerged.[7]

When we set the list of the banquet regulars alongside the list of Stalin Prizes, some insights emerge. The bass Pirogov was notably absent from the banquets after 1938 (in contrast to the two other basses, Reizen and Mikhailov), and this corresponds to the deletion of Pirogov's Susanin from the KSP's list. Barsova's 1941 prize remained her only one, in spite of her frequent appearances at the Kremlin, but this was hardly surprising, since her career was at its end when the prize was awarded. Nortsov, another regular at the banquets, also received only one prize; in his case, although his career at the Bolshoi continued, he played no major roles for most of the 1940s. Lemeshev, with the sweetest of tenor voices, who drew one of the largest claques, remarkably won just a single second-class prize, and even that was not for his operatic work, but for his appearance in the musical comedy film *A Musical Story* (1940), where he re-created his own embellished biography. The reason was the same as Nortsov's: he did not play any major new roles during the 1940s.

Thus, Stalin Prizes had to be earned, and although Stalin's personal love for opera did translate into favourable treatment that might have been considered 'disproportionate', it still did not mean that his personal favourites would automatically gain prizes. Perhaps the other way round: it was those extraordinary three-prize runs that caused the public to imagine Shpiller, Maksakova and Davydova in Stalin's bed.

From the existing recordings and even the occasional film clip, we can appreciate just how good these Soviet stars were: Barsova, the least graceful of

Fig. 17. Stalin's marginal comment next to a rather unflattering portrait of Vera Davydova by K. Yuon: 'Rubbish' (*chepukha*). This portrait appeared in *Iskusstvo* (1948), no. 1. RGANI, fond 3, op. 53a, ye. kh. 13, l. 14v.

them, enticed by the silver tones of her coloratura; Shpiller had a commanding voice and a sweet face that could express every shade of emotion; Davydova had the reputation of being a striking beauty among the Bolshoi's women (she was even called the *tsar'-baba* of the Bolshoi – more or less the 'first lady' of the Bolshoi, but more jocular and less respectful) and her interpretation of Carmen was particularly memorable. From recordings, it is clear that she possessed a classic voice that has lost little of its appeal across the decades.

Best Productions

Beyond the glorification of star singers, Stalin Prizes could also elevate entire opera productions. This had not yet fallen into place with *Susanin* (Samosud's suggestion came closest), but did become a standard part of the awards from 1942 onwards. Some of the decisions speak for themselves and provide a very clear window on the workings of the Soviet operatic world. The celebrations of Tchaikovsky, initiated by the state on account of his centenary in 1940, included high-profile productions of lesser-known Tchaikovsky operas: *Cherevichki* at the Bolshoi and *The Enchantress* at the Kirov, the latter with the libretto revised by the same Gorodetsky. By awarding both of them, the desired balance between Moscow and Leningrad was preserved, although Leningrad's team included fewer singers. As mentioned above, no one contested the fact that the best vocal talent was concentrated in Moscow.

The next year of awards preserved the same balance despite the exigencies of wartime: both the Bolshoi and Kirov produced winning productions in evacuation, one in Kuybyshev, the other in Molotov (now Perm). This time the works awarded were slightly more 'risky' than the unassailable Russian classics: the Bolshoi's *William Tell* was a Western opera relatively unfamiliar to the audience, while the Kirov's *Yemelyan Pugachev* was a Soviet opera, which its composer Marian Koval reworked from his earlier oratorio of the same name. Giving a prize to *Tell* was Khrapchenko's idea, and his deputy Solodovnikov spoke at the KSP in its support.[8] This was hardly prompted by the opera's earlier status in Russia as 'revolutionary' (it was much performed immediately after 1917), but more likely by the desire to keep awarding the Bolshoi, which in evacuation had continued its work in the most adverse conditions, its celebrities sharing makeshift dorms.

The story of *Pugachev* is rather different. Koval received a separate, first-class prize for the opera, which compensated him for narrowly missing a prize for the eponymous oratorio two years earlier (see Chapter 2). Reworking the oratorio for a grand stage (if necessarily reduced) revealed the holes in Koval's compositional technique: in his conservatoire years he had skimped on his studies with

Myaskovsky in favour of earning political capital through his activism with RAPM.[9] This proved an astute move in the long run, Now, when criticism of RAPM had been deeply buried and the need for a 'democratic', accessible opera rose again, Koval was kept afloat by the practice of 'brigade method' in Soviet opera houses. Whatever the shortcomings of a new opera, the opera house in charge would take an active role in reshaping and polishing it. In this case the task fell on the shoulders of the conductor Pazovsky in the first instance, and he appointed the experienced Dmitry Rogal-Levitsky who provided all of the orchestration. This wasn't even a secret: an article in *Sovetskoye iskusstvo* of 6 March 1943 divulged the details and expressed some sympathy towards Rogal-Levitsky for his toils in producing a 1,200-page full score.[10] At a KSP meeting, Rogal-Levitsky was even called the joint composer, but in the end Koval was still declared the sole prizewinner for the opera (Koval then became one of several prizewinners to donate his money to the war effort).[11]

Koval's unmerited good luck ran out the next time one of his operas was on the lists: the production of his *People of Sevastopol* (*Sevastopoltsy*) received a second-class prize in 1947, but Koval was pointedly kept off the list of joint recipients. It was an honour turned humiliation: at a KSP meeting, the director Yevgeny Sokovnin was credited with transforming a poor opera into a viable spectacle, which he did by removing excessively melodramatic stretches and foregrounding the 'monumental epic style' which he managed to 'extract from the musical seeds provided by Koval'.[12] This type of prize was a useful device for encouraging opera houses (particularly in the provincial cities) to continue taking risks with new and untested scores. The best scores earned the composer an individual prize; scores that did not stand out left the composer a share in a joint prize for the production team, and if the composer's work was considered poor, as in Koval's *People of Sevastopol*, he could find himself without even so much as a share.

As the number of prizes in the Opera category gradually increased, the national republics began to expect that they would receive a proportion of these. Their hopes often rested on presenting a national epic, a version of *Susanin*, perhaps, their own mighty pillar of ideology. A fascinating solution emerged in Armenia: they rediscovered their own Glinka counterpart, the composer Tigran Tchoukhajian (1837–98), who in 1868 had written an opera about the fourth-century Armenian king, Arshak II, for an Italian troupe in Constantinople (it was left unperformed). This Milan-educated composer who served at the Ottoman court composed in a style inspired by middle-period Verdi, but his story from Armenia's distant past inspired a project to turn his opera into Armenia's own *Susanin*, and the process of modernizing it even outdid *Susanin* in complexity. Not only was the libretto thoroughly rewritten, but a major overhaul of the music was also undertaken, including the addition of newly written numbers.[13] In the original plot, King Arshak was surrounded by conspiracies, infatuated with a murderous woman and entangled with supernatural forces; the new version transformed him into a much more clean-cut national hero who placed Armenians on the path to national unity. There was still some dissatisfaction expressed over the retention of one less worthy action of the king in the finale: he becomes engaged to his mistress while his dead wife's corpse is still to be seen on stage. The 1945 production in Yerevan was expensive and opulent, and it was awarded a second-class prize.[14]

Other republics failed to discover any dormant national operas of their own, and had to create them from scratch. A Georgian offering that proved to be a unanimous success was Shalva Mshvelidze's *Tale of Tariel*, based on Shota Rustaveli's *Knight in a Panther's Skin*. The opera, Goldenweiser noted, was oratorio-like, but it was a suitable rendition of a national epic, enhanced with stylish national costumes. Shostakovich offered his personal endorsement of Mshvelidze's music, and the composer was given the higher honour of an individual prize, second class.[15]

The Trouble with Musorgsky

Meanwhile at the Bolshoi, a growing number of old Russian classics took on a new Soviet form, which became the standard repertoire version for decades to come. None of them seemed as problematic as Glinka's *A Life for the Tsar*, and so the process of reworking was more modest. The most difficult was Musorgsky, whose operas proved more recalcitrant to Stalinization than the other classics. Given Musorgsky's bitter and unflinching treatment of his historical subjects, we should perhaps be surprised that his operas were staged at all in Stalin's times, and yet they went on to feature frequently in the Bolshoi's programmes, and the productions won prizes, reminding us that Soviet artistic policy could sometimes be flexible and capacious.

We shall begin with the post-war production of *Boris Godunov*, which had a long and chequered history. The production's first incarnation dates back to 1946: welcomed by the ministry in the spring, it was delayed due to Pazovsky's illness so that a second preview had to wait until October. This time, the ministry's reaction was markedly cooler: there was surprise at the choice of Rimsky-Korsakov's version of the opera (rather than Musorgsky's original material which had already been used for a 1920s Leningrad production). There was also an assortment of criticisms levelled at the director Leonid Baratov and the singers.[16] The production team wrote to Zhdanov, who sent Grigory Aleksandrov of Agitprop to see the opera. Aleksandrov eventually reported on the new production in February 1947, putting the ministry's reservations in even stronger terms. He complained that the Russian people were presented on stage as poor and pitiful, while the people of the Polish-Lithuanian Commonwealth shone in their luxurious costumes. Aleksandrov also questioned the portrayal of Boris Godunov as a murderer above all, even if he was tormented by his conscience. He insisted on treating Boris as 'Ivan the Terrible's comrade-in-arms', a powerful tsar with a positive historical record.[17] Given the amount of effort invested in the monumentalization of Ivan the Terrible, this can be seen as part of the same trend.

The main sticking point, however, was the scene in the forest near Kromy, which Baratov, the director, simply omitted from the 1946 production – with reason, as we shall see. This scene, which Musorgsky wrote for the 1872 revision of his opera, portrayed the people in revolt, which could have been just the kind of positive revolutionary material that was wanted, but the details undermined that possibility by portraying the revolt as mere rioting, chaotic and violent. Still worse, the people were both gullible and unpatriotic enough to accept the False Dimitry, who was a puppet of the Poles, greeting him as 'the people's tsar'.

On 6 May 1947, the editors of the Agitprop weekly paper, *Culture and Life*, organized a discussion in which the Kromy Scene issue emerged as the main, and seemingly insoluble, problem.[18] The musicologist Boris Yarustovsky, employed by Agitprop, insisted that the Kromy Scene had to be included, but only after receiving a *Susanin*-like reworking of the libretto. Someone recalled that back in 1928, when Boris Asafyev and Pavel Lamm presented their 'original version' of *Boris*, members of the audience, especially those in the Red Army, were outraged, complaining at the lavishly staged procession of False Dimitry. Shaporin, however, warned that rewriting the libretto would be nonsensical in the case of Musorgsky, whose approach to word-setting was very elaborate, a defining characteristic of his art.

A high-level debate continued: while on 15 May *Pravda* published Georgy Khubov's appeal for the restoration of the Kromy Scene, a few days later the editors of Agitprop's *Culture and Life* responded with a harsh criticism of Khubov, who was accused of pushing the Bolshoi down the wrong path,

> [...] using the theatre to stage a scene in which the crowd praises the Pretender and the Polish invaders – a scene whose libretto is based on long-outdated ideas about the Time of Troubles, which stem from the aristocratic historian Karamzin and which have since been overturned by scholarship. It is known also that praise for the Pretender was characteristic of the anti-Marxist Pokrovsky school.[19]

Pravda retaliated, declaring the *Culture and Life* article to be in error, and offered their own attempt at a coherent historical narrative worthy of presentation on the Bolshoi's stage. Indeed, *Pravda* said, the Pretender cunningly used the peasants' revolts for his own ends; the people were temporarily deluded; and the Holy Fool's lament at the end of the opera predicts a dark period for Russia under foreign domination.[20] Other than the word 'temporarily', there was little here that Musorgsky would have disagreed with.

Even after this clarification from above, the Bolshoi did not resume work on *Boris* until a year later, under new management, since Nikolai Golovanov had returned to the directorship of the Bolshoi in 1948, on Pazovsky's retirement. The Kromy Scene, controversial in its absence, was duly restored. Instead of following *Pravda*'s supposed solution, which would have done little or nothing to damp controversy, Baratov found a more elaborate way forward. In Musorgsky, the wandering monks Varlaam and Misail call on the people to riot and later call on them to greet the Pretender. Allowing these immoral drunkards and traitors to appear as leaders of the people would hardly look edifying on the Soviet stage, and so they were replaced by Mityukha and his friends (these characters emerged from the chorus in the Prologue). After these changes, it was only necessary to replace the greeting of the Pretender with six lines of new text (provided by the anthem-writer Sergei Mikhalkov), in which Mityukha and his friends curse Boris.[21]

Agitprop made further strenuous objections, rejecting Baratov's attempt to resolve the Kromy problem and complaining again about the glamorization of the Pretender and the opera's pessimistic ending. Their letter to Malenkov reveals a very detailed knowledge of the several versions of the opera and Musorgsky's correspondence on the subject (it was presumably Yarustovsky, the musicologist, who conducted or supervised this meticulous research at Agitprop).[22] It is striking that such a level of technical expertise was being thrown at the government in this struggle between the Bolshoi and Agitprop (or, perhaps, between Musorgsky and Soviet ideology, although no one wanted to say that). In the end, for all Agitprop's cleverness and industry, the desire, at the highest levels, to continue staging such a recognized masterpiece prevailed, and the production remained on the Bolshoi stage in its 1948 form.

One of the most gripping performances in the new version was given by the eminent tenor Ivan Kozlovsky, who sang the Holy Fool. An expert actor, Kozlovsky gave this relatively small part a new prominence, turning the Fool's final lament into the highlight of the opera. The KSP members felt the power of Kozlovsky's performance, but they experienced some unease, on ideological grounds, which they traced to Baratov's *mise en scène*: 'Kozlovsky, who is vocally magnificent in his role, has been pushed to the foreground on the decision of the director, turning him into a representative of the people, which distorts the general conception [of the production].'[23]

Further unease, articulated by Shaporin, stemmed from the fact that the new *Boris Godunov* had yet to garner any press responses which, we might surmise, indicated that Stalin had not yet seen it and the critics had no inclination to raise their heads above the parapet. Goldenweiser only had scorn for this attitude: why should they be waiting on clues from above, when the KSP had its own authority (as he saw it)?[24] Another bout of nerves came when they looked over the list of nominees proposed by the ministry, only to find that Baratov was missing. Baratov's tribulations over his first attempt at *Boris* and especially his initial defiance in the face of criticism were well remembered, but the KSP did not feel that misgivings over the dubious finale should be allowed to negate all his work on *Boris*. Accordingly, the KSP voted to include Baratov on the list. They also argued that whatever Kozlovsky's great merits, the part of the Holy Fool was too small for him to share in a prize. When it came to the ministry's turn, this was reversed, with Kozlovsky replacing Baratov on the list.[25] At the highest stages of the process, however, the list, in its final form, was more generous than the KSP or the ministry had contemplated, running to nine names: the conductor Golovanov; the director Baratov; the set designer Fyodor Fedorovsky; the choirmaster Mikhail Shorin; the singers Pirogov, Maksakova, Kozlovsky, Khanaev and even Reizen, although he had only sung Boris in the 1946 production.

This story of the *Boris* productions shows us that the Bolshoi's special status[26] could work towards a broadening of permissible ideological space, and that no one in the government was particularly worried by all the possible implications of classical operas despite the narrow-minded concerns of their timid subordinates. (To be fair, it was the timidity that probably produced the narrow-mindedness.) The same message was transmitted with even greater clarity in the case of the Bolshoi's next triumph, Musorgsky's *Khovanshchina*. As with *Boris* four years earlier, the 1950 staging of *Khovanshchina* encountered various problems. On 26 April 1950, Kruzhkov and Tarasov of Agitprop sent a report to Mikhail Suslov (who stepped into Zhdanov's shoes to oversee Agitprop's ideological work), in which they complained that the theatre had not reworked the opera sufficiently, having lacked the imagination to move further away from the old Rimsky-Korsakov version.[27] They welcomed the shift of attention away from the leader of the Old Believers, Dosifey (who had been particularly prominent in Chaliapin's legendary interpretation), and thus away from the religious and self-sacrificial strand of the opera. Equally welcome to them was the expansion of the role of Prince Golitsyn, a 'progressive' character in their view. But the important 'role of the people' remained negligible, and their place was often taken by the *streltsy* who, Agitprop emphasized, should in no way be identified with the people (as in the *narod*), but were instead a reactionary force. Agitprop advocated the inclusion of two particular episodes from Musorgsky's material that had been omitted by Rimsky-Korsakov (the musicologist Yarustovsky hard at work again, no doubt): an episode in which the angry crowd picks up the Scribe's booth (with the Scribe inside), and Kuzka's song from Act III. Agitprop was satisfied that these modifications could be made in the middle of the production run.[28]

When *Khovanshchina* came up for discussion at the KSP, the name of the director Baratov was once again absent from the list of nominees, again as a result of the ministry's interference. Some of the KSP members did not actually care much for Baratov's direction, which they thought 'invisible': they saw the production principally as another of Golovanov's musically luxuriant masterpieces coupled with Fedorovsky's stunning design. Still, as before, Baratov's absence was considered awkward, and a more principled discussion ensued. Vladimir Kemenov, art historian and secretary to the KSP, gave a long speech on the distortion of historical events in *Khovanshchina*, insisting that this gave the Bolshoi every right to submit the libretto to a radical overhaul, but they nevertheless failed to exercise that right. Goldenweiser responded to this with a sarcastic dismissal:

> We have just heard a lecture in Russian history that was most likely redundant, because we know it all. It tells us that *Khovanshchina* is an outdated work that contains a number of serious historical errors, and that these errors cannot be corrected. In *Ivan Susanin* much was corrected. He sacrificed himself for the people, rather than to save the Tsar – this [change] was easy to make. But here the contradictions cannot be smoothed out. We cannot make Golitsyn different, we cannot remove the whole scene with the *streltsy* [...]. But because we know that *Khovanshchina* is a great work, we have to reconcile ourselves with these historical mistakes and see that it is staged regardless. The Bolshoi has done this superbly and we have the right to give them a prize; but the notion that we can dispense with *Khovanshchina* because of Musorgsky's and Stasov's mistakes is impossible, just as it is impossible to patch them up.[29]

Shaporin added a specifically musical point that we saw him applying to *Boris* earlier: 'The moment we alter the recitatives by substituting different words, they will cease to live, and this will mean that the characters uttering these recitatives will also cease to live.'[30] Not everyone present would have realized that changing the words in Musorgsky was a very different matter to changing the words in Glinka. Indeed, these composers represented two extremes in opera where the relationship between music and text was concerned: Glinka often wrote his music first, and the words had to be fitted to his melodies afterwards; Musorgsky, by contrast, staked his identity as a composer on his musical counterparts to the rich variety of speech patterns. If Musorgsky's principles were taken seriously, then every change in the text would necessitate a re-composition of the vocal lines and possibly more. But this clearly went beyond what Soviet aesthetics permitted for a composer as revered as Musorgsky.

Khovanshchina proved to be another vindication for the Bolshoi's vision: this time the list of prizewinners comprised twelve people, with Golovanov, Fedorovsky and the controversial Baratov jointly receiving their fourth Stalin Prize (first class in all four cases). The number itself tells us that to be part of a Bolshoi production team was as sure a way to win a prize as membership in the production team for propaganda documentaries that were addressed to the whole world.[31] The winning teams were responsible for the creation of the monumental style of opera production that we associate with late Stalinism and which continued to dominate the rest of the Soviet period; those who were not around to see them in Soviet times can still find occasional revivals of these productions on the Bolshoi stage today.

But although such lavish productions came to be seen as the epitome of the grand Soviet style, some KSP members still found their virtues debatable at the time. A sense of aesthetic unease pervaded the KSP's discussion of the 1949 Bolshoi production of Rimsky-Korsakov's *Sadko*. The majority of the theatre section found the style of production wanting, and its chair, Zavadsky, summarized the problems:

> [The objections] were mainly raised over the overloading of the production, which was weighed down by superfluous staging effects. The *féerie*-like character of the spectacle fails to develop the poetic element in the opera, and instead serves to create an impression of unwieldy, overdressed eclecticism. This, more than anything else, leads to fatigue in the audience. Comrades have told me that it was tedious and tiring to watch.[32]

Not only the director Boris Pokrovsky,[33] but also the unassailable Fedorovsky (who had designed the stars on the Kremlin's towers) came under criticism here. Korniychuk (a playwright) accused Fedorovsky of lapses in two different directions: naturalism and also a stylized archaism typical of the 'World of Art' group in the pre-revolutionary years.[34] He particularly decried the first curtain in the style of folk woodcuts. The painter Gerasimov, however, who probably understood the nature of Soviet monumentalism better than anyone else, came to the rescue of his older colleague. The *bylinas*, those epic songs from which *Sadko* had grown, are by nature hyperbolic, he reminded his colleagues, and although set designers are powerless to give singers extra height, they can compensate for that by creating hyperbolic sets. He pointed to the harmony between Fedorovsky's sets and Golovanov's monumental musical presentation, which led Gerasimov onto some romantic ruminations about Russia, recruiting the plot of *Sadko* to his purposes: 'This is where these brave freemen [*vol'nitsa*] came from, those who spread their influence almost from one ocean to another [by sailing] in what were little more than tubs.'[35] Perhaps in the politically tame, glorificatory *Sadko*, Fedorovsky's trademark pretty peasants were more apt than in his earlier production of *Yemelyan Pugachev* – there, the KSP wondered then whether it was likely that such finely clad men and women would have lent their support to Pugachev's uprising.[36]

Instrumentalists

By comparison with those for opera singers, Stalin Prizes for instrumental performers were something of an afterthought, and it was some time before they were accepted by the government as a normal part of the system. Although it became obvious at an early stage, in November 1940, that it was only fair to grant prizes to performing musicians by analogy with theatre actors, Nemirovich-Danchenko, who had already secured Molotov's 'very firm' promise of additional Music prizes to cover different genres, was reluctant to go begging for more and set his hopes on a more radical change in the rules. In January 1941, on the insistence of Goldenweiser, the KSP prepared a letter to the Council of Ministers pointing out that the country could boast a great number of instrumental performers deserving of a prize. A small group of KSP members suggested the names of worthy performers off the tops of their heads, and the resulting list was to accompany the letter. There were a handful of conductors: Konstantin Ivanov, Yevgeny Mravinsky and Nathan Rakhlin were definitely to be included, while they had trouble deciding whether to add the controversial Golovanov. There were twelve pianists: Goldenweiser, Konstantin Igumnov, Heinrich Neuhaus, Leonid Nikolayev, Samuil Feinberg, Grigory Ginzburg, Lev Oborin, Vladimir Sofronitsky, Emil Gilels, Yakov Zak, Rosa Tamarkina and Yakov Flier. There were three string players, the violinists David Oistrakh and Miron Polyakin, and the cellist Daniil Shafran. There was no point in adding opera singers to the list, since they were already catered for, but they included the singer Debora Pantofel-Nechetskaya, who now only performed on the concert stage. Since the list had been prepared by a small group of members, it was immediately queried by several others, and eventually it was agreed that there should not be any list of names appended to the letter. 'The Government itself knows the best musicians,' as the playwright Korniychuk put it, with a mixture of prudence and sycophancy.[37]

The issue, however, moved nowhere in the first year and, despite resurfacing in 1942, was buried yet again due to the wartime disruption of KSP operations. It was only in March 1943 that a special category for performers was finally created, effectively for lifetime achievements. This was a great improvement for instrumental performers, but it still did not put them on the same level as opera singers, who could be awarded repeatedly in the opera category as well as once in the performer category.

The selection process for instrumental performers was quite arbitrary: there were generally no special auditions, so KSP members had to rely on their own memories to make a judgement. It is not possible to say how many of them would have been regular concertgoers and record-buyers, but we can safely surmise that the lack of an audition greatly reduced the number of members who could make any useful contributions to the discussion. Those who did express their opinion usually did so forcefully, using inflated rhetoric: in the absence of any hard evidence on the table, flourishes like 'the Chaliapin of the bassoon' or 'better than Casals' could make all the difference to a favoured performer's chances. Given these problems, can we take the discussion of instrumentalists seriously and use the transcripts, as we have elsewhere, to ascertain how ideological and aesthetic concerns were balanced? Can we discern any pattern that would allow us to deduce what the ideal Soviet performer would look like?

A very small number of performers prompted little or no discussion because their candidatures were so obviously well deserved – Oistrakh and Gilels were two prime examples. The ideal Soviet performers, as in the case of these two, would balance their soaring virtuosity with the depth of their artistry, their repertoire would be broad, their health excellent (no record of frequent cancellations) and they would perform at a consistently high level. In their approach to performance they would also project a stage personality that could engage the audience – a counterpart to the accessibility of musical works. Precisely because such artists were never discussed at any length, this portrait of the ideal Soviet performer has to be constructed negatively, as an absence of all the flaws attributed to all the controversial performers.

One such controversial figure was the pianist Samuil Feinberg, once a student of Goldenweiser, but now in his fifties and rather less in public demand than during his heyday in the 1920s. Myaskovsky, his old friend, cautiously brought his name before the committee:

> Feinberg is extraordinarily gifted both as a performer and as a composer. I don't even know which is his greater talent. But everything he does has a touch of the individual about it. His is a rather unusual gift. His interpreta-

tions are rather highly strung, even whimsical, but he is astonishingly lively. If you take some classical piece that would normally send you to sleep, he'll present it in such a way that you'll sense there's life in it.

Aside from this, his memory and culture are astonishing. He is a phenomenon. He can easily perform the whole cycle of Bach's 48 or all of Beethoven's 32 sonatas. And all this is full of life – he is always a huge success. The first concert [in a series] might be attended by comparatively few people, because the interpretation could seem extravagant, but the further on [in the series], the more people will come.[38]

Other KSP members were able to confirm that even when they did not agree with aspects of Feinberg's interpretations, they still left his recitals excited and moved. In Khrapchenko's view, however, Feinberg was a pianist who appealed only to a narrow audience of musical connoisseurs, and he insisted that the wider public was simply unaware of him. Myaskovsky offered mitigating circumstances: Feinberg suffered from agoraphobia which made concert tours difficult for him (he required a kind of chaperone when travelling). Even so, Khrapchenko insisted, the main issue was that performers should have a 'broad public range' (*shirokiy obshchestvenniy diapason*) in repertoire and general appeal, which held true for performers like Oistrakh, Gilels and Oborin, but not Feinberg. Khrapchenko was set on this course, and after the KSP had finished its deliberations, his letter to the government sank Feinberg's nomination.[39] He argued against Feinberg again when the pianist's name re-emerged in 1945. In the end, it proved easier to celebrate Feinberg as a composer than as a pianist, and he received a prize for his Second Piano Concerto, a pleasant and virtuosic work which we could even describe as Socialist Realist (in contrast to most of his compositional output, which was complex and highly distinctive).[40]

Another exciting but unusual candidate who generated controversy was the soprano Debora Pantofel-Nechetskaya. Although she had devoted seven years of her career to singing at the Sverdlovsk (now Yekaterinburg) Opera, her true fame came when she won an *estrada* competition in Moscow in 1940. She was allowed to relocate to Moscow (a special privilege for those not born in the city), but she sang only in concerts. A report by Golovanov, which dates from much later (1950), attempts to explain why she did not continue in opera:

She auditioned for the Bolshoi twice, under Samosud and under Pazovsky, but wasn't accepted. She has a light concert voice with high coloratura but a weak middle and low register. She is a cultured singer, she can play the piano well, and she sings rhythmically and musically. But her timbre just does not cut through the orchestra, even when it is the delicate and transparent orchestra of Verdi in *Rigoletto* and *La traviata*.[41]

On the concert stage, however, Pantofel-Nechetskaya shone with some very unusual repertoire: she sang highly virtuosic arrangements of Chopin's waltzes and became the most famous performer of Glière's Concerto for Voice. Connoisseurs recognized the true *bel canto* quality of her voice, and Nemirovich-Danchenko compared her with Adelina Patti (he was indeed old enough to have heard Patti live).[42] But her odd career profile and unique repertoire were seen as drawbacks higher up in the awards process. Khrapchenko rejected Pantofel-Nechetskaya's candidature in his letter to the government in 1944.[43] Agitprop (Shcherbakov) also deleted her name, as can be seen in fig. 18, noting that her repertoire consisted largely of Western music. Eventually she managed to win a second-class prize, in June 1946.

The conductor Yevgeny Mravinsky, in the discussions of 1944, was initially penalized for the unevenness of his performances. Although his interpretations of Shostakovich were universally held in high regard, his Beethoven 9 was badly received, and as for his interpretation of Bruckner 7, Shaporin said that he performed it like a bootmaker (*sapozhnik*), a common Russian insult reserved for poor musicianship. Even Tchaikovsky 6, the work that would become Mravinsky's calling card later in his career, was seen as evidence of his decline. KSP members even placed him below Alexander Gauk, whom they habitually denigrated. But unlike Feinberg and Pantofel-Nechetskaya, Mravinsky found a powerful advocate in Khrapchenko:

Mravinsky is known as one of the most talented of symphonic conductors; he is Leningrad's darling, someone truly adored and indulged by musical Leningrad, or rather by the whole intelligentsia, or, indeed, not just by them

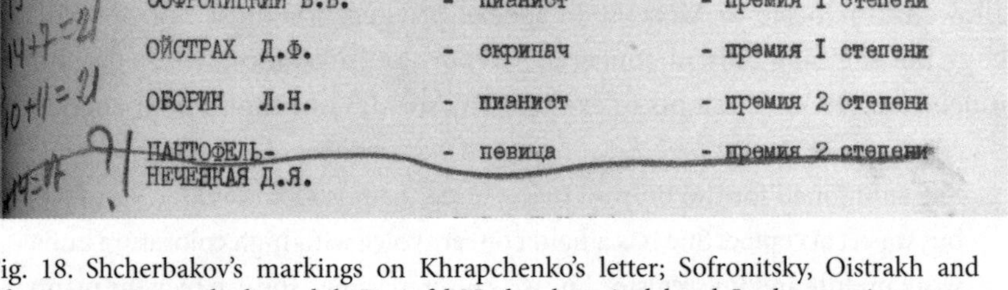

4. По разделу - концертно-исполнительская деятельность

СОФРОНИЦКИЙ В.В.   - пианист   - премия I степени

ОЙСТРАХ Д.Ф.   - скрипач   - премия I степени

ОБОРИН Л.Н.   - пианист   - премия 2 степени

ПАНТОФЕЛЬ-   - певица   - премия 2 степени
НЕЧЕТКАЯ Д.Я.

Fig. 18. Shcherbakov's markings on Khrapchenko's letter; Sofronitsky, Oistrakh and Oborin remain on the list, while Pantofel-Nechetskaya is deleted. In the margins we see his calculations of the KSP vote. RGASPI, fond 17, op. 125, ye. kh. 127, l. 27.

but by the general public too. He's very well known in Moscow. Mravinsky's pre-war concerts were always sold out, and they even used to bring Mravinsky to Moscow to raise the box-office takings in fallow times. [...]

Insofar as I can be the judge of Mravinsky's expertise and artistry, I must say that he is one of the most important of conductors, and a man of great temperament and great musical culture.[44]

This endorsement must have seemed strange from Khrapchenko, who had shown such a strong dislike for Shostakovich's Eighth Symphony, which Mravinsky had premiered, but it helped persuade the KSP to nominate him, although only for a second-class prize (perhaps because of the novelty of awarding prizes to performers). Because a year was skipped, Mravinsky's candidature had to be put to the vote again in 1945, which worked to his advantage, since he was now awarded a first-class prize. By that stage the Leningrad Philharmonic was the pride of the Soviet Union's second city: it was the one thing that was decidedly better than its Moscow counterpart, and some now thought that Mravinsky easily stood out as the Soviet Union's greatest conductor. But Mravinsky's period of official favour was limited, the seeds already sown by his unyielding support for Shostakovich's Eighth Symphony. What settled his reputation as a maverick was his vocal support for Shostakovich in the wake of the 1948 Resolution, when not even Shostakovich supported Shostakovich. When Mravinsky's name appeared on the list of candidates for the title of People's Artist of the USSR, the minister Lebedev wrote to Zhdanov:

It has been established that Mravinsky adopts exactly the same position as the composers of the formalist tendency. In 1947, a performance of Shostakovich's Eighth Symphony in Prague was Mravinsky's condition for his participation in the tour. Despite the negative assessment of this work even by Shostakovich's own supporters, Mravinsky performed the Eighth Symphony in Leningrad during the October festivities [the thirtieth anniversary of the October Revolution in 1947]. After the promulgation of the CC Resolution on Muradeli's opera *The Great Friendship* [i.e. the anti-formalist resolution], Mravinsky spoke in defence of formalist music-workers at the meeting of Leningrad composers, where he argued that it is not the talented Shostakoviches who present most danger, but amateurs like [Ivan] Dzerzhinsky, who, he said, was only omitted from the CC Resolution by some error.[45]

But as far as the Stalin Prize was concerned, Mravinsky's behaviour had no effect, simply because as a symphony conductor (as opposed to an operatic conductor), he was on the same footing as instrumental performers, and so he could only ever win one Stalin Prize for his work, and this he had already done. This pattern was never written down as a rule for the prizes, but it was followed meticulously. Since it was not an express rule, it was not discussed, but we can guess that it was based on the feeling that instrumental performers continue doing the same kind of things throughout their careers, and cannot make significant advances in the way that is possible in the other performing worlds of opera, dramatic theatre, ballet and cinema.

Generally, symphony conducting in Russia was seen by the KSP members as relatively weak, especially beside the world-class standard of instrumental performance. This surfaced in the discussion of Alexander Gauk's candidacy in 1944. Myaskovsky introduced him positively, citing such achievements as his work on Berlioz and Beethoven, and, from recent premieres, Khachaturian's Second Symphony. Even his own Twenty-first Symphony, Myaskovsky said, would not have made such an impact if it had not been for Gauk, although this comment may not have been sincere, since the KSP's consensus was that Gauk had all but murdered the symphony. Mikhoels forcefully disagreed with Myaskovsky, claiming that there were no good conductors in Russia, even though Gauk might be the best of them and certainly the most experienced. Chiaureli interjected laconically: 'We have no Suk', and Mikhoels continued that Gauk was definitely not on the same level as Suk, Nikisch or Klemperer.[46] Grabar was even more disparaging, calling Gauk 'talentless', and claiming that with Russian reper-toire, he could only manage the classic favourites that the orchestral musicians knew by heart anyway. He also questioned the rationale behind nominating a German during a war with Germany (Gauk = Haug). Despite being nominated a few more times, Gauk did not in the end receive a Stalin Prize, and he was certainly one of the most prominent omissions among performers. Gauk's name is still a well-remembered and honoured part of Soviet culture, both through historical record, his own recordings and his many students, but his successful Stalin Prize candidature came too late: he was voted through in 1953 for a prize that was never confirmed or awarded, due to Stalin's death. He soon won recog-nition of a different kind: he was made a People's Artist of the RSFSR in 1954.

One further gripe against certain performers was their apparent disrespect for Soviet music. Among them was the conductor Nathan Rakhlin, whom Shtoharenko accused of allocating so little rehearsal time to a piece by the Ukrainian composer Maiboroda that the performance broke down and came to a halt. Another was the pianist Yakov Zak, who was capable enough to be considered an excellent Rachmaninov interpreter, but yet, according to Livanova, was reduced to 'composing on the spot' instead of playing the right notes in a piece by Koval.[47] Zak never received a prize, while Rakhlin, who had been prominent for many years and had even been on that original list of performers of 1940, finally won a second-class prize at the last opportunity, in 1952. Even this cost Rakhlin a lot of effort: he was consistently blocked by Ukrainian officials (he worked in Odessa), and he attempted to lobby KSP members personally, but one of these members, Shtoharenko, mentioned in the discussion that Rakhlin had done so (it was normal, but officially considered improper). Eventually, with the support of Shostakovich, and despite the boycott of the Ukrainian Party organization, Rakhlin succeeded.[48]

A similar reluctance was shown to other performers. The pianist Grigory Ginzburg was criticized for limiting himself to a narrow range of virtuosic repertoire, but he was eventually given a second-class prize in 1949. The cellist Svyatoslav Knushevitsky was principally employed in the Bolshoi orchestra, where he led the cello section until 1943; only then could he devote himself fully to his solo career. KSP members thought he had not proven himself for long enough, and he was only given a third-class prize in 1950.[49] The pianist Yakov Flier, although held in great affection by his Moscow audience, was criticized for 'exploiting his gift' and 'playing rather carelessly', and failed to win a prize.[50] To be fair, the competition for prizes in performance was fierce. In 1950, for example, when the number of candidates sharply rose, there were around seventy performers chasing only eight prizes. The introduction of third-class prizes did not help either, since performers of high standing tended to consider a third-class prize an insult rather than praise (even if the money was not unwelcome).

From all the criticisms levelled at these contentious prize candidates, we can form a clear picture of the archetypal well-rounded Soviet star performer. Although performers such as Gauk and Flier were major figures in Soviet musical life, the Stalin Prize remained out of their reach. To return to the myth discussed in the Introduction, there was simply no point in nominating a performer who lived a shadowy existence at the margins of Soviet musical life, such as the pianist Maria Yudina, with her strange, dishevelled appearance, her fervent religious beliefs and her routine cancellation of concerts. The myth of her Stalin Prize was therefore based on nothing – not only is the story backed by no evidence, but it lacks the slightest shred of plausibility.

CHAPTER TEN

1948 AND KHRENNIKOV'S RULE

... a new era for the overlooked.[1]

The Great Friendship and the 1948 Resolution

At the KSP plenary session of 12 January 1948, Khrapchenko's chair remained empty. The whole of the Music Section was absent, too, since they had all been called to a more pressing meeting organized by the Party Central Committee. A huge, unprecedented storm over the state of Soviet music was raging there, and a major new ideological campaign was in the making. Not everyone was going to weather it: Khrapchenko, for one, would never be back. Neither would Myaskovsky or Glière. Shostakovich would only reappear a few years later, and what a different Shostakovich that would be. All change: we are approaching the infamous anti-formalist Resolution of 1948.[2]

The story of the 1948 Resolution on music is long and complex, and this book is not the place for retelling it in every detail. But we will examine the parts of the story that cast light on the Stalin Prize awards, which will in turn cast some new light back on the story. Omitting the preamble–all the underground currents preceding the dramatic unfolding of the events–we will start at the usual place, on 5 January, when Stalin and other members of the Politburo went to the Bolshoi for a performance of Muradeli's opera *The Great Friendship*. Khrapchenko, in particular, had taken great pride in seeing this opera through to performance, and considered it to be the principal musical offering for the thirtieth anniversary of the October Revolution. There could hardly have been a more promising Socialist Realist work. It ticked all the boxes: it was a genuinely Soviet opera, at last, with a story of the Revolution and Civil War; it was by a composer who proudly represented a national republic, Georgia; and this composer used an appropriate, well-spiced 'Oriental' style to glorify Stalin.[3] Nothing could possibly go wrong.

We lack documentary evidence for the cause of Stalin's anger that night at the Bolshoi, but there is more oblique evidence that allows us to assess the probabilities. The most likely cause was the opera's lionization, or even deification, of Sergo Ordzhonikidze. Although Ordzhonikidze was one of Stalin's old friends and political allies during his rise to the top during the 1920s, he was due to be arrested in the Purges of 1937, but shot himself rather than undergo torture, trial and execution. This also saved his posthumous reputation, and official historical accounts continued to present him as a heroic figure. However, Stalin, by some accounts, privately viewed him with hatred.[4] Beyond the figure of Ordzhonikidze, Stalin may have had other objections to the opera's chosen narrative regarding the struggle for Georgia during the Civil War period. The music might also have added to the poor impression. The opera's 'Georgian' style is unrelenting, and Stalin might have felt it outstayed its welcome. The opera's Lezghinka dance was not based on any tune Stalin knew, but was created freshly by the composer, and this too might have caused annoyance. But we have descended far enough down the list of probabilities; what is certain is that Stalin wanted action, and that it was Zhdanov who had to plan and execute a response to this embarrassment. This he did quickly and decisively. It was most likely on the same night of 5 January that he jotted down the following memo in his notebook: 'summon Khrapchenko, Mdivani [the librettist], Melik-Pashayev [the conductor] and the leading singers: Mikhailov, Nelepp, Lemeshev, Ivanov, Ivanova, Gamrekeli, Maslennikova, [M]chedeli ...'[5] The following day he was already questioning the bemused Bolshoi performers, trying to make them disown their wretched offering.

But then something grander hatched in Zhdanov's mind: 'to call a meeting ... to say that it will be on musical issues ... connected to such-and-such an opera'.[6] Preparations for some kind of reform in music policy had already been in the making, and Zhdanov's own dissatisfaction with the 'cacophonic' trend in music was at last able to blossom:

[T]o call a composers' meeting ... to make an introduction ... then open a free discussion ... what positions do they [presumably 'formalist' composers] hold at the Conservatoire? Talk about atavism ... perhaps [old music] has been exhausted? Died out? Remind them about *Lady Macbeth of the Mtsensk District*. Agitprop should be sitting on the Radiokomitet [radio ministry]. To install Shepilov instead of Puzin [the then director of the Radiokomitet] [...] To disperse them ... who should be fired from their positions? ... the Caucasians must be dispersed [presumably he is referring to Khachaturian, Atovmyan and Muradeli, who were in charge of the Orgkomitet of the Composers' Union] ...[7]

[...]

Khrapchenko's double-dealing has spoiled a lot of things ... prepare for publication ... remove Bondarenko [the current director of the Bolshoi], bring Golovanov back to the Bolshoi Theatre ... cancel Khrapchenko's financial arrangements ... inspect the whole set-up ... perhaps someone should be punished ... Punish Mdivani and Muradeli financially ... Khrapchenko should be brought under Party discipline. A separate investigation of Muradeli's opera ...[8]

From these jottings one can see how Zhdanov is turning a disagreeable night at the opera into a broad-ranging campaign to shake up all the leading musical institutions: the Bolshoi, the Union of Composers, the Moscow Conservatoire and, at the governmental level, the ministry for radio (Radiokomitet) and the arts ministry. For Zhdanov, it was likely that Khrapchenko's dismissal was the greatest prize, above the banning of 'cacophony', and far, far above the condemnation of Muradeli's opera, which was beginning to disappear from view.

But could we be wrong in assigning central agency to Zhdanov? In a recent monograph, Yoram Gorlizki and Oleg Khlevniuk argue that it is misleading to refer to the cultural purge as *Zhdanovshchina*. They even go so far as to say that 'in matters relating to culture and the arts, Zhdanov appears to have had very few ideas of his own'.[9] They cover four campaigns led by Zhdanov in the second half of the 1940s. There was the 1946 resolution against the literary journals *Zvezda* and *Leningrad*, with censure focused on the poet Anna Akhmatova and the satirical short-story writer Mikhail Zoshchenko. In 1947, there was the campaign against Georgy Aleksandrov's history of Western philosophy. The sciences were also affected: there was a campaign against the scientists Klyueva and Roskin, who were charged with selling secrets of cancer research abroad. Gorlizki and Khlevniuk demonstrate convincingly that Stalin bullied Zhdanov into taking a leading role in these campaigns, which worked against Zhdanov's own interests, isolating him from his friends and diminishing his power base. The fourth campaign, in 1948, moved on to genetics and Lysenko, and here Stalin even forced Zhdanov to turn against his own son.[10] The only prominent campaign that Gorlizki and Khlevniuk do not analyse or even mention is the 1948 anti-formalist Resolution on Music, but it is precisely here that Zhdanov was able to pursue his own bureaucratic interests (such as the removal of Khrapchenko) and passions (his dislike of modernist music). But the anti-formalist resolution fits in very neatly with Stalin's attempt to 'drive the intelligentsia into an ideological war with the West',[11] and those notebook jottings, as Gorlizki and Khlevniuk have shown, could easily be a record of Zhdanov's meetings with Stalin rather than his own thoughts. Khrushchev's memoirs steer us in the same direction when he speaks of the intelligentsia's dislike of Zhdanov for the resolutions on literature and music: 'Of course, Zhdanov played the role he was given, but he was following direct instructions from Stalin. I think that if Zhdanov had been able to decide the policy in these areas [of culture], the result would not have been so harsh.'[12]

The expansion of Zhdanov's plans led to a fundamental flaw in the reasoning that he and Stalin might have overlooked, but which was obvious to every music professional: the deficiencies of Muradeli's opera, whatever they were, had nothing at all to do with the 'formalism' and 'cacophony' that was to be exposed and condemned in the music of Shostakovich and the others who were targeted by the Resolution. Many found this completely baffling. One orchestral musician was reported as wondering why everyone was attacking Muradeli's opera: he had rehearsed and played it several times and thought it was an excellent theatre piece. The worries of a Leningrad composer were also reported:

> I'm in the process of writing an opera and I don't know where I can go from here. In my opinion, there isn't any formalism in Muradeli's opera *The Great Friendship*. I write my music so that it's singable. In Muradeli, the music is also singable. So does that now make me a formalist as well?[13]

Moisei Grinberg, well known to us from his 1941 letter to Stalin (see Chapter 2), also acknowledged this incongruity:

> It is important to take into account the fact that the musical language of Muradeli's opera, its means of expression, was something we all considered to be very moderate, remote from the kind of language composers identify with so-called 'serious' contemporary Soviet music. [...]
> [N]o one considered this opera to be a modernist work, or one that reflected the influence of contemporary Western music [...].[14]

Muradeli's opera was indeed a melodious creation, and couched in that composer's normal 'national' style, which had not given rise to problems before. Had he been a naif, he would simply have protested that he and his opera had nothing to do with formalism, but that was only likely to bring greater trouble upon him. He was shrewder than that, and entered the fast lane to rehabilitation: he immediately agreed that the opera was indeed a modernism-influenced piece, and laid the blame on the culture of 'formalism' that had supposedly sent him in the wrong direction. As far as his career was concerned, this worked, but it meant that instead of being regarded as the first victim of the anti-formalist campaign, he was seen as a participant in the campaign.

The festival of ideological censure began at the CC on 10 January;[15] the Resolution was finally published on 10 February prompting a stream of articles in the press, and endless rounds of further meetings. In parallel with the disciplining of composers was a series of administrative measures. The Orgkomitet of the Composers' Union was 'dispersed' (Atovmyan also lost his position in Muzfond and had to submit to a rigorous audit and a failed attempt at prosecution after financial irregularities were allegedly discovered).[16] The ambitious young Tikhon Khrennikov became 'General Secretary' of the Union, and Khrapchenko had to clear out his desk by 4 February (he was demoted to the editorship of a literary journal); his ministerial portfolio was taken over by Polycarp Lebedev, previously of Agitprop. A wave of dismissals rolled across the music world for several months. The careers of the six composers named in the Resolution (Shostakovich, Prokofiev, Myaskovsky, Khachaturian, Shebalin and Popov) were badly dented, their music no longer to be heard on concert platforms or seen at the printing presses, and their teaching positions lost or restricted. As the campaign widened, the list of formalists grew in the press, and new music largely disappeared from concert halls and opera houses.

At the top of the music hierarchy, Khrennikov made full use of his power as head of the Composers' Union and chairman of the KSP Music Section. He transformed the Music Section, which now included his trusted sidekick Vladimir Zakharov; there was also Andriy Shtoharenko, a Ukrainian colleague of similar persuasion; the formidable musicologist (and writer of denunciations) Tamara Livanova; the unsinkable conductor Nikolai Golovanov (once again at the helm of the Bolshoi); the Bolshoi singer Xenia Derzhinskaya; the choral conductor Alexander Sveshnikov (he would soon replace Shebalin as director of the Moscow Conservatoire); and the composer of mass songs Anatoly Novikov. Only two former Music Section members, Goldenweiser and Shaporin, earned the right to remain on the KSP, since their conduct in early 1948 showed that they were reliable.

Zhdanov must have had the impression that Shaporin would co-operate with the anti-formalist campaign. Shaporin was the only prominent composer with no taint of modernism, and he had written mockingly about Shostakovich's pupils in the press;[17] he might also have given some assurances in private discussions, but of this we have no information. In any case, he was asked to speak at the CC meeting, with the prestige of following immediately after Zhdanov himself.[18] The speech that Shaporin gave must have seemed lacklustre to Zhdanov, who interrupted him with attempts at encouragement. Zhdanov reminded Shaporin that he had been dismissed by the formalists as an 'epigone', but Shaporin was too embarrassed even to confirm this. His speech was vague (although this was characteristic of the man), and he largely avoided naming individuals. Even when he singled out Shostakovich, the only works he specified were *The Nose* and *Lady Macbeth*; this changed nothing, since the two operas already had no prospect of performance, having been condemned over a decade earlier. He preferred to concentrate on the positive content of his speech, which exhorted composers to defend the Russian tradition stemming from Glinka. Zhdanov may have been disappointed, but certainly not to the point of taking offence, and Shaporin benefited significantly: having only recently ascended to a full professorship at Moscow Conservatoire, he was able to inherit students from Shebalin, who had been dismissed, and even some from Myaskovsky, who was temporarily prevented from teaching at the Conservatoire. As a result, Shaporin became Moscow's leading teacher of composition.[19]

For Goldenweiser's conduct in 1948, the record is more extensive. Before the Resolution itself, but during the period when Zhdanov was soliciting support from composers and musicologists, Goldenweiser sent him a document entitled 'Issues on the Music Front', dated 19 January 1948.[20] Goldenweiser had never hidden his opposition to musical modernism (excepting some post-Scriabinist writing), so we can hardly accuse him of insincerity. Indeed, less than a year earlier, having just returned from a performance of Myaskovsky's Twenty-fifth Symphony, he noted his reactions down in his diary:

> Wonderful music – singable, Russian, sincere like a [heartfelt] song. I liked it very much ... From all the fans of Prokofiev and Shostakovich, there was only backhanded praise. Music without wrong notes doesn't satisfy them. All the same, this ('wrong notes') trend is altogether Western and was born from the same source as fascism ... One day, this will be understood here.[21]

Even so, Goldenweiser's aesthetic preferences did not oblige him to declare his support for Zhdanov, and the recent publication of the 'Issues on the Music Front' has certainly damaged his posthumous reputation.[22] In this document, he compared the beautiful pages of his favourite Russian music – Tchaikovsky, Rachmaninov and Scriabin – with the offensive creations of young composers like Weinberg and Meyerovich,[23] with the older Kabalevsky and Sviridov, and with Prokofiev. To Goldenweiser's ears, even Platon Karatayev, the archetypal Russian peasant in *War and Peace*, still spoke the language of international modernism. But Goldenweiser's primary motivation was not aesthetic conservatism in itself (no one was forcing him to perform modernist piano works). At the end, he reveals that he was writing not as a pianist or KSP member, but as a composer, a very frustrated composer tormented by a lifetime of indifference towards his work. He reminds the government that his three operas based on Russian classical literature had never been staged, and that his Cantata for the

30th Anniversary of the Revolution remained unperformed. His rightful place as a Soviet composer had been robbed by modernists, half-modernists, quarter-modernists – anyone could gain access to the public except a true conservative like Goldenweiser. And so he saw the anti-formalist campaign as a chance to put this right, and put himself at the service of Zhdanov and Khrennikov.

But Zhdanov did not have long to enjoy the bracing new world he had created: he died at the end of August 1948. With Khrapchenko and Zhdanov both removed from the picture, there was no one of similar stature to take a close and sustained interest in musical affairs, benign or otherwise. To an extent, musicians were now left to their own devices, and governmental control over them was patchy. But the death of Zhdanov did not result in any immediate relaxation, because the lack of interest from above meant that the new musical administration would be left unaltered even after the loss of Zhdanov's patronage.

A Blank Page of Nominations

When the Resolution was finally published on 10 February, it had an immediate effect on the discussion. Gerasimov, a staunch advocate of Socialist Realism in painting, was heartened that the Resolution gave further support to his own views: 'I will take direction from the latest CC resolution on music, which stresses that an artwork should be comprehensible to the people and capable of winning their affection.'[24] Even before the discussion touched upon the music nominations, the Resolution had already ruled out several opera productions. *Taras's Family* by Kabalevsky could not be considered because its composer had been on the list of formalist composers in the planning stages of the Resolution, and he was named in the press as a formalist. In fact, he shrewdly withdrew the opera, saying that it needed revision, hoping, no doubt, that it might have better prospects a year or two later. A production of *The Great Friendship* in Yerevan, which had been tipped for a prize, obviously had to be shelved. Even the nomination of the ballerina Marina Semyonova foundered because that would have meant awarding her for her role as Cinderella in Prokofiev's eponymous ballet.

Without the anti-formalist campaign and the Resolution, the music nominations would have included various significant works that were now unperformable, with Prokofiev's Sixth Symphony and Khachaturian's Symphony-Poem heading the list. The Resolution was published when the KSP was already in session, and so the members now found themselves deprived of all the obvious candidates for prizes in music, and the schedule gave them little time to search out acceptable alternatives. The theatre director Gulakian suggested that consideration of large-scale musical works (potential first-class prize candidates) should be postponed until the following year, since even if suitable nominations were made, it would not be possible to organize auditions in time for KSP members to hear them before the vote. As far as symphonies were concerned, Khrennikov informed members that there were simply none to consider. He outlined the problems with various symphonies from outside the group of leading formalists. Here, for example, is his comment on a symphony by the Georgian composer Alexei Machavariani: 'This is typical of the kind of symphonic writing that has been condemned by the CC Resolution. It was written under strong influence from Shostakovich, and it is thoroughly formalist.'[25]

In the past, the Music Section had often been faced with too many large-scale works to consider and sometimes shifted them to the small-scale category (a certain number of prizes was available in each category, but the boundary between the categories was not rigidly observed). Now, with too many large-scale works out of the running, a chamber work had to be placed in the large-scale category. Glière's Fourth Quartet was the only safe piece of instrumental music the Music Section could find; this had actually been written in 1943 and published in 1946, so it should not have been eligible, but clearly the Section was desperate. The popular lyrical songs of Boris Mokrousov were also passed, with hearty support from Khrennikov and Zakharov. At the last moment, two new members of the Committee, Golovanov and Novikov, suggested the nomination of a Stalin Cantata by the Lithuanian composer Juozas Tallat-Kelpša – but we have already recounted this story in Chapter 7.

Even with this late addition, the music list signed off by the KSP was very thin, and it fell to the conscientious staff of Agitprop to pad it out. A key role in the process was played by Dmitry Shepilov, Zhdanov's first deputy, although it is likely he delegated at least part of the task (one of the relevant letters is signed by Leonid Ilyichev as well as Shepilov).[26] One of the beneficiaries was the Azerbaijani composer Karayev, for his symphonic poem *Leyli and Majnun*, a work 'in the spirit of Tchaikovsky's *Romeo and Juliet*', which found its way onto the list despite protestations from the Azerbaijani Party chief Bagirov, who considered Karayev too young to receive a second Stalin Prize (in 1946, he had shared in a second-class prize for his national opera, *Veten*). The Karayev award was perhaps decided in haste: Agitprop might have taken Karayev as a convenient national composer, failing to notice that he was a student of Shostakovich. In fact, by the time his nomination had been passed upwards, he had already been exposed as a formalist in the press. In an article by Yury Keldysh, he was accused of musical 'pointillism', for allegedly writing a symphony without a single slur.[27] In the light of this, the prize that Karayev went on to receive was most probably an oversight, but the error was made at a high enough level to become a binding decision. It allows us to deduce one substantial piece of information, however: Khrennikov may have been in official favour, but at this point, he must still have been considered too lowly for Agitprop (or anyone more senior) to bother consulting – he could easily have pointed out the relevant facts about Karayev. The documentary evidence points to a likely meeting of Stalin with Zhdanov in 1948, to discuss the now sensitive issue of the music prizes after the Resolution.[28] Karayev's piece was passed, while another Azeri work, Fikret Amirov's Symphony 'in memory of Nizami' (also proposed by Agitprop), was rejected. Similarly, of the two song nominations proposed by Shepilov, one was upheld but the other was struck out: Anatoly Novikov unprecedentedly received a prize for a single song, the 'Anthem of the world's democratic youth' (although this had shot to fame and did much to help create a semblance of fraternal relations at the Prague Youth Festival in 1947), while Sigizmund Kats was deleted from the list. Two 'national' works nominated by Agitprop were also successful: Yevgeny Brusilovsky's cantata *Soviet Kazakhstan* and the Tatar composer Nazib Zhiganov's opera *Altyn Chach*. Both were ambitious works that gave some much-needed weight to the Music list – after all, the thinner the list, the stronger the implication that the only art music of any worth in the Soviet Union of 1948 was formalist music. This was indeed the moment when 'the overlooked' came into their own.

Reactions, Relaxation and Comebacks

When the official listing for that year's Stalin Prizes was published on 20 April 1948, the First Congress of the Composers' Union was well under way.[29] In spite of the care Khrennikov and his team had taken over the preparations for the congress, it was not running as smoothly as they had hoped. At times, it looked as if two discussions were running simultaneously: one, formal, empty and tedious, took place in the main audience hall, while the other, ardent and lively, continued in the corridors. The air was thick with dissent.

The conduct of the formalist composers was not as humble as could have been expected after more than three months of continuous castigation. Only Shostakovich was masochistically sitting in the hall through each session, with Khachaturian only appearing sporadically; the others were nowhere to be seen after the opening day. Prokofiev came, demonstratively, to hear Boris Asafyev's paper only, although Asafyev himself was not able to read it, since he was terminally ill. Even so, Prokofiev must have been gratified to hear that Asafyev had spared him, channelling all his obligatory anti-formalist fury towards his old adversary Shostakovich instead (a speech on some neutral topic was not an option).[30] Shebalin and Myaskovsky both excused themselves on grounds of illness, although informers reported that an alternative gathering took place at Myaskovsky's apartment on the occasion of his birthday. Worst of all, none of the formalists was planning to speak (Muradeli hardly counts) and this 'conspiracy of silence'[31] disappointed and worried the Agitprop team in attendance, who arranged for some of the speakers to demand a response from the black sheep. This resulted in a brief and formal letter from the absent Shebalin, an apology deemed 'inadequate' from Khachaturian and, finally, at the close of the discussion, Shostakovich's set-piece penitent speech.[32]

Further dissent revealed itself in question slips passed from the floor to the stage where the presidium was sitting. These were supposed to be folded to conceal the question, but some were deliberately left open, inviting the addition of further comments from those who passed them on. One read: 'Time will pass the Kovals and Khrennikovs by, while Shostakovich and Prokofiev will keep their place in history.' Some joker sent Zakharov a pass for the cemetery.[33] The seething hatred and rage materialized in the number of black balls the new Board received: there were seventy to eighty each for Khrennikov, Zakharov, Koval and also for Yarustovsky, the Agitprop musicologist. A row broke out over the inclusion of Shostakovich's name on the list, and even though this was disallowed, at least thirteen chose to write him in on their ballot papers.

On 21 April, the composer Konstantin Dankevich congratulated the new Stalin laureates from the congress podium. The usual leaks had revealed the list in advance, and so there were no surprises apart from the absence of Dunayevsky's *Free Wind*, which had failed to live up to the rumours (see Chapter 8). The 1948 prize list told composers of a shift in the genre hierarchy: in the previous year each main genre tidily received one prize, but in 1948 there were no prizes for symphonies or concertos, while cantatas and mass songs received two each (clearly, the first two genres were more attractive to formalists). This was the furthest the pendulum swung, and the symphonies and concertos reappeared in the following years, but the cantatas and mass songs remained the genres most likely to win an award – a reminder that the Resolution was still in effect (see Appendix I, Table 1). Awards for national music also increased, blurring former distinctions between the centre and periphery. A noticeable shift also took place within awards for performance: starting in 1949, folk choirs and song-and-dance ensembles made their mark, with their directors (sometimes together with their main soloists) taking prominent places next to the usual pianists, violinists and singers.

One year after the Resolution, the tension had not yet dissipated. Formalists were still formalists, although some of them had already made steps to shake off this status (Shostakovich's score for the film *The Young Guard*, released in August 1948, put him firmly onto the path of recovery). But they still needed to do more, as Khrennikov's remarks on Kabalevsky's Violin Concerto indicated (also quoted in Chapter 6):

> This work is not bad – it's even good – but he already has a prize. Apart from that, he's recently been linked to the formalist trend in music. He was named as a formalist in Comrade Zhdanov's speech [to the Orgkomitet of the Composers' Union, prior to the Resolution]. This work doesn't have any formalist features, but let him write another few works of this sort, and then we can start talking about awarding him a Stalin Prize.[34]

To make matters worse, there were still unreconstructed formalists around. Khrennikov dismissed Shcherbachev's Fifth Symphony outright and said that he had had 'a row' with the Leningrad Composers' Union for daring to put it forward.[35] To form an idea of how a 'non-formalist' symphony of the period sounded, we need only turn to Vladimir Bunin's Symphony No. 2, which received a prize in 1949. Golovanov, who heard two of the Symphony's movements on the radio, thought them rather weak, but Khrennikov blamed the recording quality. He insisted:

> This symphony may have some shortcomings, but at the same time, among all the symphonies written after the CC Resolution, Bunin's is the most successful in creating a national colouring. This is a true Russian symphony. Aside from this, the man's personal qualities demand our support. He was once a street-urchin, and is [now] a sick man. He works hard, heroically even. To write such a large-scale piece as a symphony, and to cultivate this area within our musical art, an area that is currently falling behind – this is heroic. We have very few Russian works. That is why our support for this young composer would be a good thing. Perhaps this symphony is not ideal, but it is of great significance for the development of our music.[36]

The year 1950 proved to be one of some major comebacks (see Table 3), even though the preceding plenary session of the Composers' Union still had elements of the witch-hunt about it. As Myaskovsky reported, auditions for the best works, Shebalin's Trio and Prokofiev's Cello Sonata, were hidden away in small unsuitable rooms;[37] neither of these works was nominated. And yet most of the other major formalists emerged as winners: a very reformed Shostakovich took a first-class prize for two scores that took Stalin as their subject; Myaskovsky managed to take a second-class prize for a chamber work that sounded rather unreformed; and Khachaturian shared in a second-class prize for a film score. Their contributions may be very different in weight and style, but it had clearly been decided that all three of them could be brought back in from the cold. The last of the Resolution's six formalists, Popov, was also given encouragement. His choral symphony, *Glory to the Fatherland*, was presented to the KSP by Khrennikov in glowing terms, and it missed a prize only by a narrow margin, probably because a complete performance had not yet been organized.[38] Prokofiev had to wait another year before his next prize, and the reason for this is clearly the spectacular failure of his opera, *The Story of a Real Man*, at the end of 1948. This failure was too fresh in everyone's mind, especially since it had been interpreted as a sign of Prokofiev's persistence in his formalist ways.

Muradeli also had to wait until 1951, and even then there was some resistance on ideological grounds. Here is Shaporin, for example, putting on a show of fair-mindedness at first, but then arguing against Muradeli's nomination:

> I'd very much like to see the accusation that still hangs over Muradeli lifted at last. Because he was the central, the main figure of the Resolution. But

Table 3. Awards given to the works by the official formalists (Kabalevsky is included here, as someone who only narrowly escaped being branded a formalist – a fact that was widely known).

Year	Class	Composer	Awarded for
1949	II	Kabalevsky	Violin Concerto
1950	I	Shostakovich	*Song of the Forests* and *The Fall of Berlin*
1950	II	Myaskovsky	Cello Sonata
1950	II	Khachaturian (in a team)	Film score for *The Battle of Stalingrad*
1951	II	Kabalevsky	*Taras's Family*
1951	II	Prokofiev	*Winter Bonfire* and *On Guard for Peace*
1951	I	Myaskovsky	Symphony No. 27 (posthumously)
1951	II	Muradeli	Songs
1952	II	Shostakovich	Ten Poems for Choir

while even a man of a respectable age, 70 years old, I mean the late Myaskovsky, managed to respond to this Resolution – some people responded better, some at a lower level, but in any case they did respond to the best of their ability – I don't think that these [Muradeli] songs, which we are now discussing, could possibly be seen as a response to the CC Resolution. If we make a mistake, the Government will correct us, but I have to ask myself in good conscience: could these songs, many of them based on clichés, truly be an answer to the CC Resolution?[39]

Despite Khrennikov voicing his support for Muradeli, Shaporin's speech worried some of the non-musicians. The painter Sergei Grigoryev recalled Muradeli's notoriety, and the architect Vladimir Zabolotny echoed this:

Muradeli's name is known to the whole world; we, culture workers in the most remote corners, have discussed his opera – and after that, we would have given him a Stalin Prize only three years later, and for just four little songs? Comrades, I don't understand that.[40]

Just as Muradeli seemed to have lost all hope, he received a boost from the Georgian actor and director Akaky Khorava, who pleaded:

[W]e cannot deal Muradeli another blow, three years afterwards, especially since he has made some good efforts, and these songs are successful, we can see a shift, and so on. [...] The party never said that Muradeli is talentless, or that he must be thrown out of the music world.[41]

The KSP decided to postpone Muradeli's offering until the following year. Not only was he not on the main list they passed up to the government, but he was also missing from the additional list suggesting further candidates the Politburo might wish to consider. But the KSP's rejection of Muradeli was disregarded at the higher levels, and he was awarded a prize. It is probable that Khrennikov interceded for Muradeli when he was able to sit in as one of the expert guests at the Politburo session (his status had been rising in higher circles since 1948).

Because the formalist composers were only gradually coming back into the fold and the prize places still needed to be filled, attention shifted to the younger generation. The works were usually chosen by Khrennikov and automatically accepted by the Music Section. At the plenary session, he introduced them in a uniformly positive manner – each one was 'outstanding' – and what he said generally went unchallenged. As for the higher levels of the process at this stage

(1951), the prize for the symphonic poem by Alexei Muravlev, *Azov Mountain*, allows us some insights. This was a programmatic work based on Pyotr Bazhov's fairy tales, which were a popular literary source at the time (Bazhov himself had received a Stalin Prize for them in 1943). It had passed smoothly through the KSP part of the process, emerging with a nomination for a first-class prize, but encountered obstacles when the prize list was passed upwards. The post-ballot letter signed by the minister, Lebedev, described the work as 'devoid of anything vivid or melodic, and chaotic at times'.[42] Agitprop elaborated on the work's shortcomings, listing them thus:

> [T]he somewhat gloomy character of the music, the excessive harmonic harsh-
> ness in the characteristic of the evil old people, and in particular the [symphonic]
> poem's flawed finale, where the composer did not provide a complete picture of
> the new man, the triumph of the forces of light and progress.[43]

Despite this, Agitprop was still prepared to give it the consolation prize of the third class (they probably preferred to refrain from rejecting a Khrennikov candidate altogether). In a discussion with Suslov, Khrennikov conceded that the work was gloomy at times, but thought that it deserved better overall, and proposed that it should receive a second-class prize, which was upheld at the Politburo's discussion of the prize list.[44] It was not common for a nominated work to overcome such serious criticisms from Agitprop, and so it would be fair to suggest that Muravlev enjoyed Khrennikov's personal protection. (Later Khrennikov even wrote the introduction to an edition of Muravlev's works.) Most surprisingly, this symphonic poem was not even new: its premiere had taken place back in 1945.[45]

The effect of the award lists on the musical community was monitored care-fully. In March 1950, for example, an Agitprop employee, Vladimir Kruzhkov, sent Suslov (Zhdanov's replacement) a report on the response to the new laure-ates in Moscow Conservatoire circles and beyond.[46] There had been an unex-pected prize for an undergraduate student, Sulkhan Tsintsadze, and Muravlev was still a graduate student. This was welcomed by the respondents as a sign that the teaching at the Conservatoire was improving – that is, moving away from formalism. Certain students and teachers, however (Kabalevsky was the sole name here), showed interest only in the prizes given to the (ex-)formalist composers, or to the 'academic' performers, in other words, to Shostakovich and Myaskovsky, and to the pianist Richter and the cellist Knushevitsky. As for the prizes given to the song composers Makarov and Kats, they were greeted with some 'scepticism'. The composer held in most contempt, it seems, was Khrennikov: some unnamed individuals in the Theory Faculty rejoiced that Khrennikov's

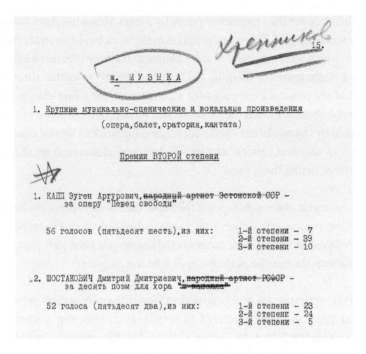

ж. МУЗЫКА

1. Крупные музыкально-сценические и вокальные произведения

(опера, балет, оратория, кантата)

Премии ВТОРОЙ степени

1. КАШП Эуген Артурович, народный артист Эстонской ССР –
за оперу "Певец свободы"

56 голосов (пятьдесят шесть), из них: 1-й степени – 7
2-й степени – 39
3-й степени – 10

2. ШОСТАКОВИЧ Дмитрий Дмитриевич, народный артист РСФСР –
за десять поэм для хора "a капелла"

52 голоса (пятьдесят два), из них: 1-й степени – 23
2-й степени – 24
3-й степени – 5

Fig. 19. A testimony to Khrennikov's power: on the Agitprop copy we see his name next to 'Music', which presumably means that he is being (or is to be) consulted. We can also see that there was a plan to transfer Shostakovich's Ten Poems to the first class, but this was later rejected. RGASPI, fond 17, op. 133, ye. kh. 344, l. 218.

comic opera *Frol Skobeyev* was not to be found on the prize list. As for opinions among the musical public, there was regret that the memorable operetta *The Trembita* had been rejected and a feeling that operetta was generally undervalued. Finally, there was widespread consternation over the prize given to Sergei Mikhalkov for his play *Ilya Golovin*, which was regarded as being laughably poor.

The story of Mikhalkov's play is worth recounting as one of the most perverse twists to the events of 1948.[47] The play was an attempt to extract a stage drama from the 1948 Resolution, and it had been produced in haste while the topic was still fresh. The protagonist, Ilya Golovin, is a formalist composer surrounded by the adulation of false friends. A *Pravda* article castigating his work sends him into a bout of depression. A general who happens to pay a visit to Golovin's dacha (where he had stayed during the war with his soldiers) is introduced to the composer and reminds him of a mass song he had once written. This is a turning point in the plot: Golovin manages to break his writer's block by writing a piano concerto that shows he has reformed himself. Golovin seems to be a composite image, but he comes closest to Shostakovich: not for nothing is one of Golovin's most offensive works his Fourth Symphony. Shostakovich's Fourth, it should be

Fig. 20. Scene from *Ilya Golovin* at the MKhAT: the composer versus the people. Golovin (in front of the table) is played by Vasily Toporkov. RGALI, fond 2959, op. 1, ye. kh. 27, l. 13.

pointed out, was now finally public knowledge, since a four-hand piano arrangement had been published in 1947, and the score, in this form, drew many hostile comments in 1948. A reference to Hindemith, whose style Golovin emulates, makes the allusion even more pointed – for the main target audience of musicians, at least (some of the references would have been above the heads of the rest of the audience).

Mikhalkov may have been a cultured man, but the play is an embarrassing piece of hackwork, as anyone reading the script today can confirm. In those days the general opinion was not much different, yet the topicality of Mikhalkov's play led it to the prestigious stage of the Moscow Art Theatre (MKhAT).[48] The strangest aspect was perhaps the choice of Khachaturian as the composer of the incidental music, which includes, of course, music attributed to the fictitious formalist, Golovin. Mikhalkov, who had clearly been a close observer of events in the music world, was obviously aware of Khachaturian's formalist credentials, and perhaps there was a twisted generosity in the commission: Khachaturian could signal his own reform by setting the reform of Golovin to music.

The perversity of the situation was further enhanced by the prospect of Khachaturian sharing in the production team's Stalin Prize when the play was nominated. But in the discussion of his incidental music, KSP members came to the conclusion that Khachaturian had given better music to the formalist Golovin, while the reformed Golovin of the piano concerto was embarrassingly bad. It looked as if Khachaturian had postponed his rehabilitation instead of hastening it. Goldenweiser, perhaps trying to be charitable, suggested that the curtain should fall at the moment when Golovin sits at the piano, leaving the audience to imagine for themselves the music of the reformed composer.[49] In the end, the KSP decided to spare Khachaturian further misfortune, and nominated him for his soundtrack to *The Battle of Stalingrad* instead. As for the production of Mikhalkov's play, it won a second-class prize, although it was given a rough ride by the KSP, which found the play 'empty', and even Fadeyev dragged his feet, and could only commend the play for its 'political importance'. The play might well have failed if it were not for the actors of MKhAT, who gave it some undeserved polish.[50]

The Chickens Come Home to Roost

The failure of Khrennikov's comic opera *Frol Skobeyev* to win a prize in the spring of 1950, which was met with such glee at the Moscow Conservatoire, offers another story worth recounting, not least because it shows the limit of Khrennikov's powers, or more precisely, how his success as an administrator led to his failure as a composer.[51] Now that he was the general secretary of the Composers' Union, Khrennikov's own music was bound to be subject to the most stringent scrutiny. After 1948, everyone knew Khrennikov's thoughts on his fellow composers, but what did he himself have to offer in these anti-formalist times?

An opera was his answer, but not a Soviet opera. Indeed no, this was a frothy comic opera featuring the picaresque adventures of a loveable rogue in the seventeenth century, with an odd combination of the bawdy and the bizarre, including an appearance of the hero in drag.[52] In the abstract, an interesting if insubstantial project, but as the first anti-formalist offering of the mighty man of Soviet music, it was astonishingly, jaw-droppingly off the mark. The idea, it seems, came from Nemirovich-Danchenko a decade or so earlier, when Khrennikov was a promising young composer. At first, he was rather modernist, with hints of Shostakovich, Prokofiev and various Western composers, such as Bartók, but he had already begun to mine a more populist vein. When bringing the project to fruition in the late 1940s, Khrennikov and his librettist would have realized that the plot needed enhancing, and they attempted to add a little social criticism to the story, but this proved to be far too thin. Khrennikov, having long since moved away from his youthful predilections, was now a master of light, sparkling and melodious music, but this time, he arrived at a stylistic cocktail that was considered noxious by some: Myaskovsky, in his diary, defined it as 'a mixture of pre-Verstovsky with Kálmán', dismissing the opera as 'very poor, vulgar and without talent'.[53]

A routine discussion of the opera at the Moscow Conservatoire was turned by some bold professors and students into a kind of carnivalesque inversion of

power: they read out Khrennikov's anti-formalist pronouncements and illus-
trated them immediately with fragments from his own opera, which they
declared 'a product of bourgeois decay'.[54] On 24 March 1950, the minister
Lebedev attended the opera, which had already been running for a month, and
promptly issued a ban on it. The ban, however, lasted for no more than a week,
since Khrennikov sprang to his own defence. A letter was organized from his
supporters to the CC, who complained about the unfairness of the ban. Agitprop
was only too happy to enter the brawl on Khrennikov's side, since they reckoned
they could score a few points against Lebedev, in their perennial rivalry with the
arts ministry. The gloves soon came off, and the charge of cosmopolitanism was
levelled against the revelry at the Conservatoire: Viktor Berkov, the professor
who led the celebrations, had already been named a rootless cosmopolitan,
while the Jewish surnames of the leading students were supposed to speak for
themselves. The Agitprop officials used all their ingenuity in constructing the
story of an anti-Khrennikov conspiracy: they informed CC members of some
anonymous telephone calls made to Khachaturian and Muradeli in which the
anonymous callers had enticed those formalists to speak against Khrennikov at
the next public discussion of the opera, scheduled to take place at Moscow
University.[55]

Khrennikov even wrote a letter to Stalin asking him to watch the opera and
offer his verdict.[56] It seems that this did not take place, but Agitprop now offered
Khrennikov some more public assistance by publishing a positive article about
his opera in *Culture and Life*, with a selection of grateful letters from members
of the public who had attended performances.[57] Despite the revocation of the
ban, the opera was now tainted by the scandal, and it was soon dropped from
the repertoire. Only selected arias from *Skobeyev* were published (they are
entertaining but very slight operetta-like pieces), until 1966, when Khrennikov
brought out a second version under the title *Bezrodniy zyat'* (The Low-Born
Son-in-Law). The *Skobeyev* scandal caused Khrennikov great distress, and he
suffered a nervous breakdown that landed him in a Kremlin sanatorium.
Perversely, Khrennikov himself belatedly fell victim to the climate of 1948 that
he had assisted so industriously. Once recovered, he concentrated on his administrative work, producing only two film scores over the next few years, although
he was working slowly and quietly on a serious opera, *Mat'* (Mother, based on
Gorky), which he did not complete until 1957.

The open opposition between the ministry and Agitprop began with the
Khrennikov case, but continued to intensify through the summer of 1950, and
musical issues once again became a political football. The competition between
state and Party organizations in the USSR is certainly known to scholars, but
the conflicts were largely overlooked by Soviet citizens, for whom Party and

state seemed to be the same for all practical purposes. In the summer of 1950, the disputes between the minister Lebedev and the Agitprop staff developed to the point where relations could not be patched up. On 1 July, Pyotr Tarasov of Agitprop addressed a letter of denunciation to Suslov, with no less than Lebedev as the target.[58] We learn from this that Tarasov, together with his Agitprop colleague Kruzhkov, had sent an earlier letter complaining that Lebedev's oversight of Soviet opera was an utter failure, and that he would have to take steps to improve matters. In their follow-up letter of 1 July, they told Suslov that Lebedev had failed to take the criticism 'in a Bolshevik way': at a meeting attended by both Kruzhkov (of Agitprop) and Khrennikov, Lebedev flew into a rage, directing a barrage of insults at Agitprop. The atmosphere of mutual suspicion and surveillance thickened in both institutions. Agitprop's Pavel Apostolov blamed the ministry for allowing the publication of substandard Stalin songs; in response, Lebedev conducted an investigation into Agitprop's oversight of Musfond (the main funding body for composers), and revealed that Apostolov (together with his colleagues Yarustovsky and Vartanian) had been receiving (illegal) payments from this source. He reported this in the hope that a prosecution would ensue.[59]

The weightiest accusation directed against Lebedev looked back two years to the *Great Friendship* affair. Agitprop claimed that they had warned Lebedev (who was one of their members at the time) about the opera's serious problems, but Lebedev failed to act until the storm had already broken. Then, according to Agitprop's version of the story, Lebedev hurriedly signed and backdated his resolution, claiming that the report approved by him had been filed away in Agitprop's offices for ages, with no action taken (Lebedev claimed the report was in fact his own, and that Aleksandrov of Agitprop had sat on it).[60] In trying to win these battles, Lebedev was failing to see that he was gradually losing the war; he lost whatever ministerial dignity he had once possessed, and emerged badly weakened. But there were problems even if Agitprop had remained quiescent. Compared to his predecessor, Khrapchenko, Lebedev generally gave the impression that he was much less in control of his portfolio. As one illustration among many, the ministry's letter on the Stalin Prizes of 1950 was not even signed by Lebedev, but by his deputy Nikolai Bespalov. When the *Frol Skobeyev* scandal broke, Agitprop was able to deliver the *coup de grâce*, and Lebedev resigned from his post in April 1951, to be replaced by Bespalov.

The Trouble with Soviet Opera

Lebedev was gone, but Khrennikov still managed to hold on to his position (although his de facto leadership was interrupted by his spell in the sanatorium).

It is a moot point whether Khrennikov's greatest problem was now the failure of his own opera, or the failure of Soviet opera as a whole on his watch. The latter certainly posed a greater obstacle to his hold on power: there had to be at least one worthy Soviet opera that responded to the criticisms of *The Great Friendship*, but if this requirement remained unfulfilled for much longer, it would seem that Khrennikov was unworthy of his appointment in 1948, and simply not up to the job. He fretted, urging composers to produce operas, despairing over the quality of the results, caught between the need to slap down inadequate work and the need to give his endorsement to something. It was not an enviable position.

Golovanov put it bluntly: 'During the entire Soviet period, six hundred operas have been written, and out of these, not a single one is adequate.'[61] Khrennikov, of course, was only responsible for the past three years, but one of his primary tasks was to reverse this sorry situation. In 1949, he could be excused: it was still too early to expect a considered 'response to the Resolution' – operas are not created in a day. But this excuse was wearing very thin in 1950, when there was still nothing to show. The KSP kept mulling over Vladimir Enke's *Lyubov Yarovaya* and Yuly Meitus's *The Young Guard* (which had already undergone two revisions), but felt in the end that they had to be rejected. In 1951, there were at last a few hopeful productions, and these drove the KSP into a lengthy and rather circular debate.

Four offerings were on the table: *Taras's Family*, by Kabalevsky, at the Kirov Opera; *The Young Guard*, by Meitus, at the Leningrad Maly; *Heart and Soul* (*Ot vsego serdtsa*), by Herman Zhukovsky, in Saratov; and *Ivan Bolotnikov*, by Lev Stepanov, in Molotov (now Perm). All of the productions were theatrical successes: *Taras* and *Heart and Soul* both won praise for their casts of talented younger singers;[62] *The Young Guard* was an exciting production by Nikolai Okhlopkov, who based it on his earlier drama staging (which had won a first-class Stalin Prize in 1947); and *Bolotnikov*, too, was an enjoyable piece.

Where the music was concerned, Kabalevsky was clearly in the lead, but doubts over the libretto (which we have witnessed in Chapter 6) prevented it from being considered for a first-class prize. The problem was quite the reverse in the case of Meitus's *Young Guard*, where an ideologically solid and dramatically gripping production was let down by the music. With the exception of Zakharov, no one was prepared to defend Meitus's score, which did not commit any particular offence, but was simply too weak. The opera was in flux, undergoing revision as it continued to play, but it was somehow proving a considerable success: it had already been staged in several opera houses, and in some it had already been running for three seasons. There were long deliberations over Meitus: should he simply be excluded from the prize altogether, or should he be allowed a share with the rest of the production team, or should he be awarded separately? Khrennikov insisted on a separate third-class prize, arguing that the opera was very 'patriotic'.[63] The KSP agreed to request an extra third-class prize to accommodate Meitus,[64] and then the higher powers promoted him to the second class.

Another Ukrainian composer, Zhukovsky, provoked even stronger doubts among the KSP than Meitus had, and now even Zakharov thought that revisions were needed. Not a single member of the committee had seen the Saratov production of *Heart and Soul*, relying on a report from two assistants. In the end, the KSP reluctantly placed Zhukovsky into the nominated production team, and Fadeyev bleakly concluded: 'Obviously, the musical side of [Soviet] opera is still on such a [low] level that we can't even pull it up to the third class, but even so, we need to give encouragement to the art as a whole.'[65] Despite this verdict, the post-KSP part of the process promoted Zhukovsky up to an individual third-class nomination.[66]

In contrast to Meitus and Zhukovsky, Stepanov's music was pleasing to the ear, and Novikov even gave *Bolotnikov* a great compliment: for once, he said, here was an opera that could be enjoyed when performed from the vocal score, unlike so many others that failed to impress without the help of stage action.[67] But the pleasing score was dragged down by the opera's historical plot about the peasants' revolt led by Ivan Bolotnikov from 1606 to 1607. Soviet artists had previously been encouraged to use historical topics in their work, but the device was losing its value through overuse. Even Khrennikov, as we have seen, had recently chosen a historical topic for his ill-fated *Frol Skobeyev*, but Stepanov had made matters still easier for himself by relying on a stock character (Stepanov's Irina, Khrennikov claimed, was drawn from Musorgsky's Marina Mniszek). Khrennikov startlingly decided to point out that: 'It is, of course, considerably easier to write an opera that draws from the past than one based on the events of our times.' It would have been interesting to see whether he delivered this with a sheepish grin, or poker-faced.[68] Shaporin objected that an opera about a peasant uprising could not have been written in the Tsarist period and so it was an essentially Soviet choice (Shaporin had long been working on an opera about the Decembrist uprising, and must have felt that Khrennikov was pulling the rug out from under his feet). Shaporin also spoke about the music with surprise and admiration, noting that Stepanov's characterization was more sophisticated than Kabalevsky's.[69] Khrennikov's response to that was to call Stepanov an epigone.[70] This move was well designed to silence Shaporin, whose music sometimes blurred the line between respect for tradition and epigonism.

After everything had been weighed up, the KSP felt that none of these operas could be considered a proper response to the 1948 Resolution, and left the first-class prize for opera unawarded. Even the lower awards given out that year (1951) were regretted in the longer term. The following year, Khrennikov lamented that the award to Meitus set musical standards too low. And when another production of *Taras* came up for discussion in 1952, the painter Sergei Grigoryev complained about the quality of the music and the 'unpleasant', 'unattractive' words, admitting that it was a struggle to stay in his seat.[71]

As for *Heart and Soul*, regrets came to haunt the members even sooner, and the torment they brought were on quite another level.

Heart, Soul and Tears

Khrennikov might well have been the first to set Zhukovsky's *Heart and Soul* on the road to a prize.[72] Agitprop sent a report to Suslov on the 1949 plenary meeting of the Composers' Union, and in the margin there is a handwritten list of operas on Soviet themes that Khrennikov had brought to Agitprop's attention. Zhukovsky's appears as number one.[73] By February 1950, Agitprop was aware that Zhukovsky's opera had been completed, and they blamed both the ministry and the Union of Composers for ignoring this and failing to support a young talented composer (as they supposed him to be).[74] This gave the opera a further boost.

Fragments from *Heart and Soul* were next presented at the composers' plenary session in May, which fortuitously took place in Kiev. Indeed, Ukraine seemed to be taking the lead in the campaign for Soviet opera, as it could also boast Konstantyn Dankevych's *Bohdan Khmelnytsky* (which was to be denounced in *Pravda* in July 1951)[75] and, of course, Meitus's *Young Guard*.[76] The rise of the Ukrainians was not hindered even by a denunciation sent to Agitprop in the wake of the Kiev plenary meeting, describing endless parties thrown by Ukrainian hosts for their Moscow guests (at the expense of the state), where contacts were made and future Stalin Prizes allegedly decided. Zhukovsky was not accused of throwing parties, but far worse, he was named in the denunciation as an 'occupant', together with Anatoly Svechnikov and Platon Maiboroda; that is, all three composers stayed on under the Nazis during the occupation of Ukraine.[77] Since all three of these Ukrainian 'occupants' were already Stalin laureates, Party organizations would have been well aware of their dossiers: in Agitprop's obligatory response to the denunciation, we read that there were no compromising materials on these three despite their stay on the occupied territories. In other words, their status as 'occupants' was not considered enough in itself to prevent them from receiving prizes.[78]

In October 1950, Agitprop reported to Suslov that the new Soviet operas were not well positioned to make an impact on the people: *Bohdan Khmelnytsky*, for example, had been planned for staging only in Ukraine. The only exception was *Heart and Soul*, which was being prepared for production in *seven* opera houses simultaneously. By this stage, it had clearly been chosen as the one golden hope, to be given much greater promotion than its rivals.[79] It would seem that the lessons of Muradeli's *Friendship* had still not been learned: a trial run in a single opera house would surely have been more prudent.

Among the seven venues was the Saratov Opera House, whose production of *Heart and Soul* would soon be nominated for a Stalin Prize. Crucially, however, the Bolshoi was also among them; just as in the case of *The Great Friendship*, the principal Soviet opera house did not want to miss its chance. Zhukovsky, apparently, came and sang his opera in an audition with accompaniment on two pianos. He charmed everyone there, and absurd rumours of a new Tchaikovsky spread around the theatre.[80] The Bolshoi director, Alexander Solodovnikov, took the composer under his own wing and even became his co-author, correcting the freshly written verses that regularly came through the mail from the Bolshoi's assistant librettist.[81] The Bolshoi did not intend to perform exactly the same opera as the provincial houses, but wanted a thorough reworking under its supervision. As with the inexperienced (and incompetent) Dzerzhinsky's *And Quiet Flows the Don* of 1936, a 'brigade' system was set up: Zhukovsky was asked to cut some numbers, rewrite others and add new ones, while help with orchestration would be provided ('brigade' was a euphemism with spurious socialistic associations to cover up the fact that neither composer was good enough). Eventually, the score would meet with the Bolshoi's approval.

What made this opera stand out? Why all the commotion? The literary source was a novel by Yelizar Maltsev, itself already a prizewinner (second class in 1949). Although far from a masterpiece, it is a gripping story about a soldier, Rodion, who returns home after the war but experiences a difficult transition back into civilian life. During his wartime absence, his wife Grunya has become a powerful kolkhoz leader, overturning Rodion's ideas about a woman's role in life. Competing bitterly both at work and at home, they go through much misery before they learn to respect each other, thanks to the help of friends and colleagues. The story rang true in its unflinching portrayal of post-war traumas of displacement and loss of identity. This psychological depth and the rich language of the novel, though it can be overwrought and awkward, compensated for the various clichés that brought it into line with Socialist Realism. The novel was then successfully adapted to the stage (*Second Love*), so an opera seemed like the next step for this durable story.

The novel was long, and the action had to be thinned out considerably to turn it into an opera libretto. Perhaps in better hands it might have been possible, but the libretto Zhukovsky had to work with was very flawed as a story. The action was transferred from the Altai mountains in Siberia to the steppes of Ukraine, which drained the story of its original and rather unusual local colour. The story received various ideological props. A new character, Novopashin, was introduced (Mr Newplough, we might say, if we treat it as an allegorical name); he was a useful Communist figure who could illustrate the role of the Party in the action. Since the original discussion of agricultural difficulties was rather limited as a source of dramatic tension, the setting was enhanced: a new power station was under construction, and the opera would end when it came to life and began generating electricity. This, however, had nothing to do with the original Rodion-Grunya story, but was connected instead with a newly introduced strand that offered another new character, Yarkin (Mr Bright), who is in love with the lively Klanya. Because of the many changes to the score, the Bolshoi rehearsal schedule was altered sixteen times; the singers had to relearn various passages three or four times, and they were sometimes even entrusted with tidying up their own lines.

A run-through with the piano at the end of November 1950 left a poor impression, but the Bolshoi's director, Solodovnikov, stifled all criticism, insisting that 'the music contains a great truth'.[82] Still more adjustments were made while morale fell further and singers started calling in sick. At another run-through in mid-December, ministry and Agitprop staff were present. Lebedev seemed satisfied, suggesting only a few improvements to the *mise en scène*, a change to the finale of one of the acts and to the music of one of the dances. Agitprop, by contrast, recommended a thorough overhaul: among other things, the Prologue (in which Grunya saves crops from the storm) should be dropped, and some embryonic melodies developed into full-blown arias. Agitprop also made some major ideological criticisms: the mass of *kolkhozniks*, they said, were no more than a background to Rodion's story and were never integrated with it. Worse still, there were now three Communist organizers (including the added Novopashin), who were all stale figures, and too reminiscent of the Commissar in *The Great Friendship*. In some scenes, the organizers did nothing, merely walking silently across the stage. Agitprop suggested that the number of organizers should be reduced, while the one or two remaining should be made more human. If Lebedev's main concern was to ensure the opera was actually seen by Bolshoi audiences in the near future, Agitprop was worried instead about a potential repetition of the *Great Friendship* disaster.[83]

It is hard to say how many of these revisions the Bolshoi managed to implement over the following ten days, although we know for sure that they dropped the Prologue. At the end of the year, the opera was shown to select cultural figures including Khrennikov. Most were lukewarm in their responses, but

Khrennikov had turned against it completely. By this time, he was probably able to foresee a resounding failure, but it was clear that preparations had gone too far, and there was no point in demanding that the premiere be called off. The only option for Khrennikov was to wash his hands of the affair, and so he criticized the music with a barely disguised contempt: its dramatic qualities and characterization were weak, it lacked individuality and it was emotionally flat. This was only a counsel of despair, since correcting such fundamental flaws would mean rewriting the opera (yet again). Release it now, others said, and the Union of Composers can criticize it; Zhukovsky can then do better in his next work.[84]

Khrennikov's position was not good, but at least he had his shrewdness to help him through the trouble to come. Lebedev, however, could not sense that anything was amiss, and he rejected all criticisms, congratulating Zhukovsky on 'the first Soviet people's (*narodnaya*) opera'.[85] Zhukovsky, buoyed by the minister's support, felt brave enough even to kick out at Khrennikov:

> I'd love to hear an opera that was better than mine. But I have to say that, much as I hold T. N. Khrennikov in great affection both as a composer and a man, I find little to agree with in his opera *Frol Skobeyev*. I think that the creation of Soviet opera is our common task and we need to help each other in every way. In the Union of Composers' criticisms, I notice a rather tendentious attitude towards my opera, instead of any desire to help. The Union of Composers still harbours some formalists, and they don't like the *narodnost'* and the democratic musical language of my opera.[86]

With Lebedev's blessing, the opera went through. On 18 January 1951, Lebedev wrote Stalin an entirely positive letter about *Heart and Soul*, and requested permission to start running it from the next day.[87] On 24 January, Zhukovsky, the director Boris Pokrovsky and the conductor Kirill Kondrashin jointly sent Stalin an invitation to attend the opera: 'We ask you to express your opinion on whether the opera house is on the right path in its search for a representation of the contemporary kolkhoz theme on the operatic stage.'[88]

But Stalin was in no great hurry to express his opinion on whether the Bolshoi was on the right path. This was most unfortunate for the Music Section, which was due to discuss the opera on 30 January, completely in the dark about the correct line on paths, searches, kolkhozes and all the rest. A few rather critical responses had already appeared by that date, but these were to be found only in the Bolshoi's internal newspaper. There were growing doubts about the viability of the Bolshoi production, and other opera houses started deleting the opera from their production plans. Curiously, most of the KSP members did not even manage to see the opera, since it was the Saratov production that had been nominated. Accordingly, they did not receive tickets for the Bolshoi production. What they did know was that the discussion of the opera at the Composers' Union was positive, even 'panegyric', but it was not generally known that Khrennikov had not been present at that discussion, nor how differently the discussion would have gone in his presence.

Neither was he present at the KSP plenary discussion of the opera nominations. In his absence, Zakharov praised the opera's folk-style choruses, but others directed criticisms at the confused dramatization and the undifferentiated vocal writing. The members of the Music Section who knew Zhukovsky as a pleasant, inoffensive, perhaps even weak-willed man, had some sympathy for him, as, for example, Khrennikov's friend Shtoharenko:

> [W]hatever he was told to do, he carried out. At the Bolshoi they gave him a whole brigade [of assistants/supervisors], and everyone was offering different advice. He listened to everything, then ran home, sat up night after night and composed, without knowing whether he was doing the right thing, and the next day he brought it to the theatre. Then another version appeared, and so on. [...] He's not very experienced, and it seems this brigade approach wasn't well suited to him.[89]

But even as a fellow Ukrainian, Shtoharenko did not support Zhukovsky for the prize, and neither did Shaporin, Goldenweiser, nor Livanova. They pitied Zhukovsky for his predicament, since he was now in the spotlight without being ready for it. Still, they thought (like Khrennikov earlier) that no revision could improve the music sufficiently. Again, the hope was expressed that Zhukovsky would learn from the experience and his next opera would come out better. Xenia Derzhinskaya, one of the few who had seen the Bolshoi production, expressed her impressions quite colourfully:

> He is melodious, and the choruses are good, but it is so boring, boring from the very first moment, and not at all interesting dramatically, so that even the [Bolshoi] theatre couldn't do anything with it. There is no dramatic conflict. When the female partisan appears [with the potential for creating a love triangle], I was expecting that at last there would be some conflict. But no such thing [...].[90]

The central character of Rodion, it seemed, was least satisfactory, in libretto, music and performance. The singer Grigory Bolshakov had a noticeable paunch which immediately undermined his plausibility as a lean and hungry returning soldier. In the grand finale, where the stage was lit up by myriad light bulbs (representing the power station come to life), Rodion seemed superfluous, aloof from the celebration, only seen through a window. (We might also note that he and Grunya still were not completely reconciled by the end of the opera, so that even this one rather weak element of dramatic conflict was not properly resolved.)

Zakharov made an energetic bid to ensure that the opera remained on the list:

> The opera requires revision – serious corrections. Perhaps the composer shouldn't really shoulder the blame here; perhaps the Bolshoi Theatre was more at fault for putting pressure on him (they invented the 'brigade' method there, and seriously confused the composer). So our proposal is for the author to revise the opera. However, it is already running in two cities, Stalino [Donetsk] and Saratov, and it's been a great success there. In Stalino, the collective farmers buy out whole performances so that everyone from their farms can come to see it.[91]

This claim ran contrary to all they had previously heard, and so the KSP dispatched two assistants to Saratov. When they reported back to the KSP, their account was positive enough for the Saratov production to be put forward for the prize. Not that there was any genuine enthusiasm. It was a weary decision by people who no longer saw much point in their activity, but it seemed harmless.

On 5 April, the opera was performed at the Bolshoi as part of a continuing run, but never appeared on stage again. It would be fair to assume that Stalin attended that performance, given the uniquely catastrophic consequences.[92] On 19 April, *Heart and Soul* was roundly criticized in a *Pravda* editorial, entitled bluntly, 'An unsuccessful opera'.[93] Two days after the editorial, the distressed composer wrote Stalin a scrappy little note, asking for the prize to be withdrawn (see fig. 21).

> Dear Comrade Stalin!
>
> For the music of my opera *Heart and Soul*, I received a Stalin Prize of the third class.
>
> Having read the article in *Pravda* and given its contents my careful consideration, I consider the prize undeserved and am asking you to revoke it.
>
> I will try to win your approval in my future operas on contemporary themes.
>
> Composer H. L. Zhukovsky
> 21.04.51

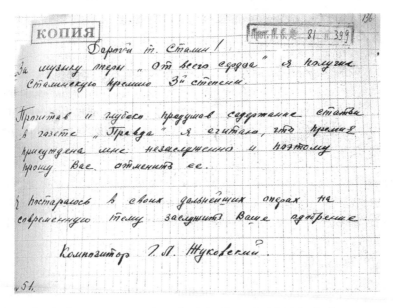

Fig. 21. Zhukovsky's letter to Stalin of 21 April 1951. RGANI, fond 3, op. 53a, ye. kh. 27, l. 136.

It is hard to say whether this letter was the composer's own initiative or written under pressure – either is possible. Another two days passed, and both Lebedev and Solodovnikov lost their posts, just as their predecessors had three years earlier. The matter of Zhukovsky's prize was referred back to the KSP.

This was, of course, a great blow to the KSP's credibility. Goldenweiser, who had recently developed the habit of corresponding with the CC, chose to write again with a personal comment on the *Heart and Soul* matter.[94] After reminding the Party leadership that he, Goldenweiser, was now one of the last musicians who had a living connection back to Russia's great nineteenth-century composers, he poured criticism on the Music Section of the KSP, claiming that the section had effectively been usurped by the Secretariat of the Composers' Union, and that its decisions were usually voted through by an organized majority (something that was indeed true and probably well known to Agitprop). He emphasized that both he and Livanova had spoken against Zhukovsky's wretched opera.[95]

On 8 May, when the KSP was called into special session, giving its members the opportunity to confess to their gross errors of judgement, Goldenweiser did not hesitate to make his thoughts public, and he blamed the poor decisions of the Music Section on undue pressure from the leadership of the Composers' Union, just as Khrennikov and Zakharov walked into the room, late:

> The Music Section has become a complete fiction recently. We are never called for meetings. We assemble literally an hour before the plenary sessions [...] we make important decisions on the go, and there is an attempt, whether deliberate or not, to replace the Music Section with the Secretariat of the Composers' Union.[96]

Khrennikov, no doubt happy that he had avoided dismissal, readily repented, explaining that his 'rotten liberalism' had led him to support almost any opera on a Soviet topic. A hilarious exchange ensued on the subject of Meitus's opera, *The Young Guard*:

> *Zakharov:* But sometimes we make a mistake in the opposite direction [...]. We had put Meitus forward for the third class, for example, but this was corrected [by the government] and he was given a second-class prize. This was also [our] mistake.
>
> *Livanova:* That [the Meitus] is even worse than Zhukovsky's opera.
> *Zakharov:* You may think it's worse, but the *government* thinks it's better.
>
> *Livanova:* Iosif Vissarionovich [Stalin] hasn't seen it.[97]

By which she implied: had Stalin chosen to see *The Young Guard* instead (unlikely because of its lower profile), Meitus would probably have been handing back a prize instead of Zhukovsky.

The committee then passed the following resolution, partly lifted from the earlier *Pravda* editorial:

> The Stalin Prize Committee notes that the music of Zhukovsky's opera is primitive and colourless. In an opera that should have shown the life of Ukrainian *kolkhozniks*, the composer failed to use the riches of the Ukrainian people's culture, especially Ukrainian folk song.
>
> The characters are not individuated nor portrayed with any realism. As a result, Zhukovsky has created unattractive schematic figures instead of showing us the progressive Soviet people with its rich spiritual world and strong feelings.
>
> The arias and ensembles are generally bland in their musical themes. Not only does the music in many of the arias fail to complement the characters' feelings, but it can even conflict strongly with them. The orchestra doesn't assist in revealing the ideas, and doesn't enrich the opera's vocal lines.

Zhukovsky's opera *Heart and Soul* is therefore both ideologically and musically weak, and does not deserve a Stalin prize.[98]

It is interesting to note that the KSP resolution does not address the libretto's ideological faults, even though they were discussed at the meeting and featured prominently in the *Pravda* editorial. Perhaps we can detect a hint of mercy towards the librettist, whose castigation was not required from the KSP.

Still, such a penalty for a piece that was merely bland and clichéd seemed out of proportion. Unlike the Muradeli scandal three years earlier, the government this time was not trying to impress any significant ideological point on Soviet artists. Or perhaps the absence of a Zhdanov meant that no one could formulate any such point. After a while, everyone stopped trying to guess what the point might have been, and remembered the affair simply as an individual misfortune. Two years later, in February 1953, the painter Gerasimov referred back to the affair, casually dropping a remark that 'the chairman of the Music Section [...] should have known that Zhukovsky had worked for the Germans'.[99] (The job in question was his appointment as conductor of the Kharkov Opera during the German occupation.) Our evidence tells us that this could not have been the main reason (remember that exonerating clause in Zhukovsky's dossier), and yet the fact of his employment during the occupation could have been dredged up from the files and used against Zhukovsky if Stalin had demanded to know who the offender was.

It is, of course, also possible and indeed tempting to look for a deeper political reason behind the condemnation of the opera. Leonid Maximenkov makes an imaginative suggestion here: that a scandal was created around *Heart and Soul*, an opera by a Ukrainian composer about Ukrainian collective farms, as a kind of proxy attack on Khrushchev, who had recently annoyed Stalin because of his contentious proposals for new agricultural policies in Ukraine.[100] The chronology, it must be said, fits Maximenkov's hypothesis perfectly:

4 March 1951: Khrushchev's article 'On the Construction and Improvement of Collective Farms' is published in *Pravda*

6 March 1951: Khrushchev writes an apologetic letter to Stalin asking him to forgive the mistakes made in the article

2 April 1951: The Politburo adopts the decision 'On the Challenges of Collective Farm Construction'

5 April 1951 (most likely date): Stalin attends a performance of *Heart and Soul* at the Bolshoi, after which the opera never runs again

18 April 1951: the Politburo releases a closed letter to Party organizations that contains criticisms of Khrushchev's 'agri-town' idea[101]
19 April 1951: The *Pravda* article against *Heart and Soul* is published

In the opera, life on a collective farm finds its consummation in the opening
of an electric power station nearby, and Maximenkov rightly says that this
seemed like a perfect illustration of Khrushchev's ideas on the amalgamation
of smaller farms for the purpose of creating prosperous and comfortable
'agri-towns'. Further grist to Maximenkov's mill can be found in an article by
Pokrovsky, the director of the Bolshoi production. Well before the premiere, he
described the research trip of Bolshoi artistes to just such an amalgamated
collective farm where electricity was plentiful. This kolkhoz was even named
after Khrushchev.[102]

It all fits together wonderfully, but it is still quite possible that the debacle
may not have had anything to do with Khrushchev and his 'agri-towns'. The
opera could easily have annoyed Stalin much earlier than the closing illumina-
tions, for the same reasons that it had annoyed others before him – it was boring
and ineptly constructed. And if it was a warning shot to Khrushchev, or indeed
if there was any political or ideological point to the scandal, why was the winning
team for the Saratov production not also deprived of its prize? The issue was
raised, of course, at the KSP extraordinary session, but the chair Fadeyev, that
consummate insider, dismissed it so confidently (how are the actors to blame?)
that it must be suspected that he had been given clear instructions to limit the
punishment to Zhukovsky personally. The public noticed the discrepancy, and
wrote letters of complaint against the Saratov production team.

In comparison with the 1948 Resolution, with its long-term consequences
and a tinge of tragedy, the Zhukovsky affair may look farcical. Zhukovsky
survived the blow, and the hiatus in his career was short-lived. And yet we
should not underestimate the damage to the morale of Soviet artists. There is
little direct documentary evidence of this (although much that can be read
between the lines) but one valuable exception is a letter written by Dunayevsky
that tells us much about the general mood:

It is becoming harder and harder to work in the creative field. Things are
bad not because the work is hard. Not because new tasks keep arising,
demanding fulfilment and creative expression. No!

What is bad and painfully impossible is that no one knows which path
is right, that everyone is confused, fearful, over-cautious, mean, that they
indulge in intrigues, become provocateurs, change their opinions every day,
and then beat their chests, confessing to mistakes both real and fictitious.

It's something dreadful and quite intolerable that a creative failure should be viewed as some kind of crime. Is this the kind of criticism that we are told to receive calmly and thoughtfully? Can you take this kind of criticism calmly when you are nailed to the pillar of shame, and a Stalin Prize taken away? But Zhukovsky, the author of the opera *Heart and Soul*, did not steal this prize, he was given it by 70 people in the Committee, which consists of respectable people from all the arts! So it is they, the respectable people, who should have said: 'It's our fault! It's our oversight!' But they simply gathered, wiped the [government's] contemptuous spit from their faces, and decided to ask the government to take Zhukovsky's prize away from him! No one had the honesty to defend the composer from this shame – he's only guilty of having written an opera that wasn't liked at the top. What's going on? How can anyone go on living and creating?

And this was after a similar event had already taken the life of the historian Huseynov, the one who received a Stalin Prize for a historical work on the Caucasus. It was then found that he made an erroneous judgement on the significance of Shamil, representing him in a positive light when he should have represented him negatively. Well, fine, that's a huge mistake! But someone, in fact many people, the whole scientific committee had read this work and judged it to be outstanding. The government added its signature and gave the author a prize. And suddenly . . . And this 'suddenly' led to a man who had been rejected by everyone hanging himself from a tree in his own garden.[103]

Khrennikov on the Way Out?

The KSP had passed a work that no one believed in and no one liked. So who had 'sneaked it in', as one member put it? All eyes were on Khrennikov. Ivan Bolshakov, a KSP member and also the cinematography minister, who was feeling vulnerable after the government had made wholesale changes to the Film nominations list, all but suggested that Khrennikov should be removed from his position as Music Section chair, and seemed prepared to step down as the Film Section chair himself. KSP members began to realize how they had stopped thinking for themselves, and had meekly followed these leading, but very fallible, administrators.

Fadeyev was also one of these leading administrators, and although he had not recently committed any glaring errors, he could see his own position would be at risk if Khrennikov and Bolshakov had to stand down. Lest ordinary KSP members started to organize a recovery of their own powers (which had never officially been removed), he took this opportunity to speak up for the status quo. He reminded members that Khrennikov had been appointed by the government 'in the wake of the great event that brought about the destruction of formalism'. Khrennikov, he said, was himself a composer, and a good one at that (unlike Bolshakov who was not a filmmaker but just an administrator). There should be no rush to sack him for a single mistake.[104]

Indeed, the very fact that Khrennikov survived the Zhukovsky affair said much about his position in the high *nomenklatura*. He celebrated the New Year's holiday of 1952 at Shepilov's, singing songs for the entertainment of the prestigious invitees.[105] He still had some influence over the Stalin Prizes for music, since he was invited to the Politburo meetings that settled the final lists. But there was one candidate he could not help at these meetings, and that was himself. To be sure, he ended up a three-times laureate, but all of his prizes were for film scores, shared with several other crew members, and all of these were second class (*The Swine Girl and the Shepherd*, 1942; *At Six o'Clock after the War*, 1946; and *The Miners of Donetsk*, 1952). This, of course, was a paltry showing compared with the old formalists, and only an individual prize for a serious, large-scale work could raise him into the first rank of composers. After the failure of *Frol Skobeyev*, Khrennikov's only hope rested on the 1952 production of his opera *Into the Storm*, which he had written in the late 1930s, and premiered in 1939, but he revised the work for the new production, to be given at the same venue as before – the Stanislavsky and Nemirovich-Danchenko Opera in Moscow.

This is when Khrennikov found out that the Music Section, which he assumed was still under his control, was impatient to take revenge, since they threw out the nomination unanimously. Goldenweiser wondered why they should even be considering this 'reheated' dish from yesteryear, which, he said, was weak in its harmony and recitative writing, not to mention its counterpoint.[106] Golovanov said the same in more colourful language, expressing the hope that by now Khrennikov would have outgrown the 'short trousers' he was wearing thirteen years earlier.[107] Admittedly, these two musicians were known to be sceptical about the musical validity of Soviet opera in general, so to some extent their comments were predictable. It was a very different matter when Khrennikov's trusted adjutant, Zakharov, added a further layer of criticism. Since the old opera was by no means submerged under the revisions, Zakharov reminded members of the criticisms it had faced in 1939: its musical language lay in the aesthetically dubious urban popular-song genre rather than any more elevated sources. Zakharov also returned to the most controversial scene in the 1939 version, in which Lenin appeared, not singing (which would have been even worse), but speaking over a passage of rather bland orchestral music. This scene, he pointed out, was still present in the new version.

At the plenary, the decision was the same: the opera was dismissed out of hand (given the composer, the matter could not rest with the Music Section's rejection). The theatre director Alexei Popov, like Goldenweiser, was adamant that 'one cannot respond to the Resolution, five years later, by means of some old work'.[108] And yet a few days later *The Storm* brewed up again, owing to the ministrations of Fadeyev:

In my opinion, the production of *Into the Storm* should be awarded a prize. Given the poor state of our [Soviet] operas, this is an opera that was staged long ago, but now has been given a breath of new life, and it lives indeed, and the audience reacts to it. The music is good. This is a true people's drama with great passion and great class struggle.

Some said that Lenin shouldn't have appeared in this opera. Actually, his appearance is very apt, and it's right at the point where it should be. The audience's reaction to this is lively, and I felt like acting the same way myself.[109]

A chorus of protest erupted: 'But Lyonka [the central character] is just terrible'; 'Khrennikov wrote it when he was 23'; 'they sing out of tune' (the last comment was from Shostakovich). Gerasimov, the painter laureate, then pointed at the big white elephant in the room: someone must be pulling out all the stops to get this work awarded. This put Fadeyev on the defensive, yet he wasn't finished:

Here is something I simply cannot put out of my mind: the opera *Into the Storm* was written by a man who was not a formalist, but it was the formalists who trampled it, hoping that this work about class struggle would not reach its audience [...].[110]

Fadeyev was able to keep the production on the list, but the outcome was far from the individual first-class award that Khrennikov needed to raise his prestige as a composer. All that was on offer to him was a share in a third-class prize for the production. After Stalin's death, a KSP presidium was created to provide temporary oversight of KSP affairs out of session. They raised the prize for *Into the Storm* to the second class in August 1953. This decision failed to stand in the regular KSP session of 1954, which revisited all the nominations of the previous year (no prizes had actually been awarded in the year of Stalin's death). Khrennikov's miseries were only compounded when his beleaguered opera was attacked by another of his own trusted associates. This time it was the song composer Novikov, who saw scant evidence that Khrennikov had made exten-

sive revisions to the opera, contrary to his claims. The only novelty Novikov
had managed to detect was the addition of a rather pallid overture. By this stage
it was also clear that audiences were not showing any great enthusiasm for the
production. Zakharov then came to Khrennikov's defence (they must have
made amends in the intervening year), vouching for the fact that the opera had
been reworked significantly, otherwise it would not have been possible for it to
run again, seventeen years after its premiere. This did not quite make sense, and
Goldenweiser quipped, 'What about *Eugene Onegin*?' In the end, Khrennikov
kept his place in the production crew for the prize, but it was lowered back to
the third class. When the Stalin Prize fizzled out, with no further awards being
made, Khrennikov lost his shared prize and, of course, his position on the KSP
(although he was transferred to the more select Lenin Prize Committee). Still,
given that the prize was a humiliation for him rather than a real reward, he
must have been relieved that the matter could be forgotten.

Khrennikov survived this and many other hard times, and set an unbeat-
able record by serving as General Secretary of the Composers' Union for
forty-two years through to the end of that body in 1991. In the decade after
the failures we have just discussed, his political career took off: he ascended
to membership of the Party CC, and also became a member of the Supreme
Soviet. The 1960s and '70s saw the flourishing of his career as a composer, and
he won a list of high awards longer than anything he could have imagined in
the early 1950s (the highest was the Lenin Prize for his Second Piano Concerto
in 1974). A contradiction as ever, his activity in the 1970s included a twelve-
tone theme (in his prizewinning Concerto), but also a condemnation of seven
of the most distinctive Soviet composers of the younger generation.[111] He
continued composing and winning awards until his death in 2004. Various
details of his role in the late 1940s and early '50s were suddenly revealed to the
younger generation of musicians in an article from the late 1980s, a typical
glasnost event.[112] The older generation knew, of course, but for the majority,
their memories were filtered through the many years of knowing him as a facil-
itator, a source of favours and a useful organizer, and when the Composers'
Union was given a chance to vote on his chairmanship in 1986 and 1989, they
chose to retain him rather than throw him out (he continued in the position
until the Composers' Union was finally disbanded after the dissolution of the
Soviet Union, although lower-level composers' unions survived). Our documentary evidence, presented here and in the next chapter, offers a corrective
to recent literature that whitewashes his behaviour in the wake of the 1948
Resolution, when his involvement was much deeper than simply reading a
speech written by someone else, as he had professed.[113] He has been defended
as much as he has been accused, and the former trend seems to be winning, if

we are to judge by a volume dedicated to his centenary, edited by Khrennikov's grandson.[114] Returning to the years of late Stalinism, Khrennikov was already a formidable figure, feared and resented, but sometimes taunted. After Zhdanov's demise, the 1948 campaign was fully in Khrennikov's hands, and since it is usually acknowledged that he brought it to a resolute end,[115] then it should equally be true that he was responsible for how long it lasted.

CHAPTER ELEVEN

THE STALIN PRIZE WITHOUT STALIN

The authorities were deprived of their divine aura, but not completely: although they began to be judged as fallible humans, they were still expected to dole out gifts as formerly.

– *Elena Zubkova, Russia after the War*[1]

De-Stalinize, Really?

Anyone browsing through the card catalogues for Soviet music in the Russian State Library will notice an enormous corpus of songs and larger pieces written to mark Lenin's death. Even more glorify Stalin's life and toast his health. But what is striking is the apparent non-existence of any similar body of work marking the death of Stalin in 1953. Since we are looking only for earnest, contemporary tributes, we have to discount later pieces, such as the punk-style 'Stalin's Funeral' from the 2000s. There are poems, it is true, but nothing in music – no cantatas, not even a song. Even if a handful of songs were to be unearthed, the point would still hold – the contrast is startling. Were they suppressed? Are we to suppose that by the time the poems were available to composers, it was already unnecessary to mark the event?[2] How long did it take, indeed, for artists to feel a fresh wind on their cheeks?

Konstantin Simonov gives us a striking account of his own experiences. On 19 March 1953, he published an editorial in *Literaturnaya gazeta*, in which he appealed to all Soviet writers to perform their 'sacred duty' by devoting their efforts to the preservation of Stalin's image for posterity. Unexpectedly, a huge storm erupted: Khrushchev phoned the editorial board and threatened to sack Simonov as editor in chief for a backward-looking editorial. Fortunately for Simonov, he was not in his office at the time, and the storm blew over.[3] From that moment on, through the usual channels of leaks and rumours, the new policy of non-commemoration for Stalin started trickling down to the artists.

This was on 19 March, when only a fortnight had passed since Stalin's death. On the same day, the presidium of the Council of Ministers entrusted Khrushchev, Suslov and Pospelov to work out proposals for a radical reform of the Stalin Prize system.[4] The proposals (to which we shall return) were sketched and submitted, discussed at other meetings, sent back for reworking and, eventually, one department or another sat on them. No one demanded that the process be completed, and there was probably no consensus yet on whether the Stalin Prize could be ditched so soon, not out of respect for Stalin's memory (there was little of that commodity around now), but because the 1953 list of nominations represented hundreds of frustrated would-be laureates, with some big names among them. With so much money and prestige at stake, Stalin's memory was a relatively marginal issue.

Eventually a directive came for the list to be salvaged, although the details would all have to be subjected to a further round of scrutiny. To perform this task, the KSP gathered in the reduced form of a 'presidium', including the same Simonov, Tikhonov (Union of Writers), Popov (Drama Theatres), Chernyshev (Union of Architects), Bolshakov (Cinematography), Khrennikov (Music) and Kemenov (KSP secretary). It soon became clear what kind of 'reconsideration' was needed: there was no desire for a first-class prize or any prize to go to the last of Chiaureli's Stalin hagiographies, *The Unforgettable 1919* (with a score by Shostakovich, although the composer had withdrawn this from KSP consideration prior to Stalin's death). The formulation chosen by the presidium was euphemistic, but their meaning was clear enough: the film was accused of a one-sided portrayal of historical events that underestimated the role of Lenin in the 1919 defence of Petrograd (in other words, it overestimated the role of Stalin).[5] Three years later, at the 20th Party Congress, there was no more need for euphemism, and Khrushchev singled out this film for ridicule:

Stalin loved to watch the film *The Unforgettable 1919*, where he is portrayed travelling on the doorstep of an armoured train and all but striking the enemy down with his sabre. Let our dear friend Kliment Yefremovich [Voroshilov] pluck up the courage and write the truth about Stalin, since he knows how Stalin fought [they had fought together in the Civil War]. It will be hard for Comrade Voroshilov to get off the ground, but he would do well in this. It will be welcomed by everyone – by the people and the Party. And our grandchildren will be grateful. (Continuous applause.)[6]

But before such open mockery of Stalin was even conceivable, many artists and writers who had served the cult were in denial of the changes. Unsurprisingly, Chiaureli was one of these: unable to make sense of the new situation, he complained bitterly to the KSP about their change of mind, resenting, in particular, the hypocritical formulation of the reasons they had given for the withdrawal. Let the stated reason be something else, he demanded, like 'personality cult or whatever'. These words, spoken in desperation, were later deleted by Chiaureli from the transcript as his temper cooled (this was an option for KSP speakers).[7] Even so, his career was so enmeshed with the Stalin cult that it proved unsalvageable.

Euphemistic conversations about the art of the Stalin cult continued into the following year. A delicate formulation was needed next for the withdrawal of the intended prize for a gigantic, 54-metre-tall monument to Stalin on the Volga-Don canal (this had been erected in 1952 and was finally removed in 1961). After some discussion, Kemenov found the way to express it:

> A number of artworks that have been postponed from the previous years are now under our consideration in the setting of 1954, that is, when we have received a number of directives about past errors in propaganda works that are incompatible with Marxism. These were errors which both Comrade Lenin and Comrade Stalin had warned us against repeatedly. Of course, those sculptors didn't know all this when they created their works, but the discussion is taking place this year [. . .]. In a word, we have a deeper view of this issue today. This is also relevant to the criticism of a number of films, scenarios and theatre productions, where it is a little easier to correct things [!] – playwrights and directors can do that. In sculpture such revisions are not possible.
>
> We are making nominations in the setting of 1954, and we need to think whether these works correspond to the correct understanding of the leader's image as we would like to see it. I think if these monuments were made now, they would be made differently. First, some connection [of the leader] with the masses would be introduced. Second, this connection with the people would be found in a [certain kind of] gaze and the gesture, not like this upward gaze.[8]

This tortuous and equivocating explanation gives us a glimpse into the discourse of 1953–54, and tells us much about the KSP's bizarre afterlife. The members seem to have internalized the bizarre: when in January 1954 Khrennikov told the Music Section that among the nominations was a *Zdravitsa* (Good Health piece) for Comrade Stalin by Dvarionas, no one flinched. Shostakovich, deciding not to invoke Stalin when it was not necessary, simply told his fellow KSP members that the work had been auditioned at the Union and found very weak.[9]

Indeed, the KSP itself was enjoying a spell of good health after exaggerated rumours of its demise: the sinking of the Volga-Don monument and the *Zdravitsa* piece took place after a new round of KSP discussions had unexpectedly been convoked in December 1953. The KSP was to tie up the loose ends from 1952 as well as select new candidates. Both the name of the prize and the basic procedures were left unchanged.

A Bout of Soul-Searching

The deadline was tight (1 April 1954), but the government gave no clear instructions on how the committee should proceed, not even stipulating whether the 1952 and 1953 nominations should be treated separately or together. The 1952 list required yet more attention, since many items had clearly failed the test of time after just a year. It seemed foolish to give awards to plays that had already been removed from the repertoire for poor takings, or which had only been performed once during the eleven months since the last meeting.[10] Fadeyev was off duty because of ill health, and the committee was being steered by the poet Tikhonov and the actor and theatre director Popov. From the outset, though, it became clear that no serious work could be done before KSP members spoke their minds about the situation in which they found themselves.

Looking at a huge canvas devoted to the third centenary of the Ukraine-Russia Union, the painter Sergei Grigoryev remarked contemptuously: 'I must be a man of narrow horizons: I don't recognize or understand this kind of art, and I don't even understand the need for it.'[11] The playwright Boris Lavrenyov voiced his contempt for Soviet poetry: 'Everyone has learned to versify without difficulty, without thought, without images, without anything, just rhymed lines and that's all.'[12] As for cinematography, the architect Leonid Polyakov confessed that:

> [T]here was a host of films we found impossible to watch – we had had to close our eyes, that's how much lying and falsehood there was! [. . .] We have reached the point where our films are unwatchable, and the public shuns them, rushing to see any old foreign film, even if it isn't especially good.[13]

The poet Sergei Mikhalkov remarked that a classic form of Soviet architecture had still not been found: 'Even now they're still putting sculptures on the roof for the birds to look at; one day they'll start falling onto people's heads.'[14]

Mikhalkov, Polyakov, Lavrenyov, Grigoryev – these were well-established figures, not mavericks, but this is nevertheless how they spoke in 1954. Looking at their own creations, we recognize them as belonging to the very core of Socialist Realism they now seem to be indicting, although they more often point out flaws in the other arts rather than their own. 1953 already seems to have formed a gulf between their past careers and the present.

One thing that everyone agreed on was the excess of laureates. Particular scorn was poured on prize inflation and on the dubious value of multiple badges paraded by the fortunate but not always deserving few. The monetary value of the prize had lost its significance in many cases: a shared third-degree prize could bring each individual only three or four thousand roubles, which was roughly equivalent to a routine fee for an article or an internal report. But the number of medals had been invested with ever more significance, and the grotesque consequences were now brought to light. As Mikhalkov put it, 'An academician who had spent twenty-five years in a laboratory, injected himself with plague and nearly died, finally received a Stalin Prize and one medal, while the cameraman who filmed him had seven.'[15] The list of examples went on. The most respected Soviet writers, Sholokhov and Fadeyev, had only one medal each, while Simonov could boast six and Mikhalkov himself had three. The leading architect Ivan Zholtovsky, creator of Soviet neoclassicism (highly valued again in today's real-estate markets), only had one second-class prize to show for his years of effort, and even that was only awarded after a great argument among his fellow architects.[16]

Prize inflation had been exacerbated by the introduction of the third degree, KSP members agreed. Simonov recalled the fatal moment of their emergence:

> During one meeting with the government, a conversation started up about third-degree prizes, because that year we had particularly rich pickings of [literary] works. I remember then how Comrade Stalin said, 'Let us introduce third-class prizes and give them to a few people.' [...] And then in all the other arts, they started saying 'Why don't we have third-class prizes?' We started adding further third-degree prizes. There were no rich pickings in those years, but the number of prizes kept increasing endlessly. And because the total numbers were never specified, they just kept going up in every genre, without any restrictions.[17]

Simonov is right in implying that Stalin himself was partly to blame for the proliferation of third-class prizes. Stalin's desire to be inclusive and generous also led to awards being shared out among enormous crews of people for films and theatre productions. The previously unsayable was now uttered: third-class meant third-rate.[18] For the first time in the history of the Stalin Prize, the members even toyed with the radical idea of asking the government to reduce the total number of prizes (as it happened, the government was already considering such an idea).

Good-bye to Varnish

When the members picked up the nomination lists from the previous year, they saw them with new eyes. The list of films, for one, looked terribly out of date, even though the Stalin hagiographies had been already sifted out. A case in point was a masterpiece of late Stalinism, Grigory Aleksandrov's *Composer Glinka*, which had been voted through for the second-degree prize the previous year. But this time round, the bright colours and celebratory tone of the film seemed to have faded, revealing the shabbiness of its aesthetic.

The pre-history of *Composer Glinka* is revealing: the historical biography was one of the most common genres of the Stalin-period film industry, and within a period of five years, Glinka was the subject of two such films.[19] The original, black-and-white *Glinka*, directed by Leo Arnshtam in 1946, was much criticized. In an attempt to bring Glinka closer to the people, Arnshtam went for the demotic charm of Boris Chirkov, an actor best known for playing endearingly down-to-earth proletarians, most famously Maxim in *The Maxim Trilogy*. But at the same time, the film made it clear that Glinka was a nobleman, and the casting of Chirkov continually undermined the credibility of the character. Stalin himself remarked on this: 'What is this Glinka? This is Maxim, not Glinka.'[20] Pushkin, played by the celebrated comic actor Pyotr Aleynikov, was undermined in a different way: the public kept waiting for him to do something funny.[21] Despite failing to pass even the Film Section hurdle, *Glinka* ended up with a second-class prize (this decision was taken at the Politburo on 4 June 1947, most likely, at Stalin's behest). Stalin, as a lover of classic opera, was known to hold *Ivan Susanin* in very high regard and famously included Glinka in the list of national heroes in his historic speech on 6 November 1941.[22] Perhaps it was to this Glinka-hero that he wanted to give public prominence, rather than this particular film version of the composer's life. But from his complaint about the casting of the principal role, he did not see this film as a canonical depiction of the composer.

A new version, which became *Composer Glinka*, was commissioned, and an expert team was assembled. The script was by Pyotr Pavlenko, who had previously written *Alexander Nevsky* and two films canonizing Stalin (*The Vow* and *The Fall of Berlin*). The director was Grigory Aleksandrov, Stalin's personal favourite. The cameraman was the masterful Eduard Tisse, who had collaborated with Sergei Eisenstein on his silent masterpieces. The leading female role of Glinka's sister was given to Lyubov Orlova, the glamorous star actress of both screen and stage. The mistake of using a popular but unsuitable actor for Glinka himself would not be repeated, and the part was given to a little-known but plausible actor, Boris Smirnov, who was tall and sprightly, and well able to enunciate his lines in classic drama-school manner. The casting team had clearly looked for an actor who was the opposite of Chirkov in every respect (later he made a career of playing Lenin on stage and screen, and received a Lenin Prize for these efforts). Compared to the earlier *Glinka*, with its low wartime budget, its basic sets and poor lighting, no expense was spared this time to create beautiful backdrops, from the magnificent panoramic landscapes of Russia to the colourful carnival scenes in an almost believable Venice, and Orlova was draped in magnificent gowns. As well as Glinka himself, the other well-known cultural luminaries, Pushkin, Dargomyzhsky and Stasov, were also cast carefully, and looked very much like their standard Soviet portraits while they recited standard textbook quotations from themselves to ensure that no one could fail to recognize them.

Back in 1953, when *Composer Glinka* had first been discussed by the KSP, there were some complaints about the liberties taken with history, but defenders of the film had a ready answer: we know very well that Stalin never flew to Berlin in 1945, but does this place *The Fall of Berlin* outside Socialist Realism? (It was, of course, considered the last word in Socialist Realism at the time.) With few reservations, *Composer Glinka* was passed for a second-class prize.[23]

But a year later, in 1954, the KSP saw the film through new eyes. The meeting between Glinka and Pushkin, which in the film happens in a boat during the flood on the Neva, now struck members not only as a violation of history, but also of common sense. The saturation of the film with walking portraits of great men of the period now met with some mockery: young spectators allegedly placed bets on the more obscure cases – ah, here is the young Tolstoy being refused an audience with the great composer! The painter Grigoryev commented now on the predictable casting of the director's wife Orlova, who played Glinka's sister (known to be a modest woman) as a vamp in a startling red dress: 'And what about the morality of this? Glinka had a wife. But here he keeps embracing Orlova (God give every worker a sister like that!).'[24] The members laughed, but the general mood was not merry. Shostakovich not only found the film tedious but, as a musician, he was irritated by some aspects, and vented his frustration:

> The authors had the noble goal of demonstrating the greatness of this genius
> of Russian music, but his greatness is established by primitive means. He

behaves arrogantly, talks to his friends with his head held high – no, he doesn't talk so much as make trivial pronouncements.

[The filmmakers] wanted to demonstrate the superiority of Russian music over Italian, but they did so in a wretched, primitive manner. At one point, Glinka is rehearsing his own music [off stage], while Italian music is rehearsed on stage. Glinka is rehearsing very loudly, and I've heard people ask: Why is Russian music better than Italian, then? Just because it's much louder? [...]

What is completely unsatisfactory is the depiction of Glinka as a composer in the process of creating music. The torments of creation, we might say. This is shown unconvincingly, in a naive and dilettantish way: Glinka raps out a certain figure, then raps it out again, then walks over to the piano and plays the beginning of *Ruslan and Lyudmila*. [...] And there is a complete absence of personal life. Glinka appears before us like a statue, a monument.

[... T]he connection between Glinka and the people is also shown in a most primitive way. In one place, there is some kind of fair under way, in another, a kind of 'song and dance ensemble' is performing, and Glinka is inspired by these. It all seemed extremely naive and unsatisfactory to me.

[...] In one shot, [...] Dargomyzhsky looks at the score of *Ruslan* or *Ivan Susanin* with a magnifying glass. But the score exists so that it can be taken in at a glance, and to look at individual voices with a magnifying glass is so pointless! I was surprised that the composers Shebalin and Shaporin [who collaborated on the film] did not advise the filmmakers to get rid of this nonsensical shot.[25]

Shostakovich's point about the score is tendentious – professional musicians do indeed pore over the details in a score at times; Shostakovich could have made the mild point that Dargomyzhsky would probably not have done this on his first viewing of the score. At any rate, Shostakovich's opinion was received appreciatively by other members, but it was the Latvian writer Antanas Venclova who summarized the Glinka character: 'He doesn't eat or drink wine, and he doesn't love anyone – he just composes music and thinks of the Motherland.'[26]

But who had nominated the film; who had cast their votes for it in the secret ballot? Bolshakov, they recalled, used to bring a prepared list of films that everyone was expected to vote for (they could equally well have pointed out that Khrennikov did the same in Music). It was also recalled how the release of certain films was trumpeted so loudly by official sources that KSP members knew they were 'destined' to win – that is, the KSP knew its obedience was required when it came to the vote. As criticism began to turn into a rebellion, those who had headed the KSP over the past few years began to grow worried. Popov (the actor/director) appealed for the finger-pointing to stop, since members had only themselves to blame for the results of the previous year's vote. Gerasimov warned that such sharp U-turns could lose the committee its public credibility. Unexpectedly, Khrennikov broke ranks, and welcomed the frank and sincere conversation that was going on at the KSP: 'During the past year, negative attitudes to every kind of "varnishing of life" [*lakirovka zhizni*] have grown, and we [now] tend to reject works of art that lack true humanity.'[27] In the light of what we will hear from Khrennikov later in this chapter, his comment may have been hypocritical and opportunistic, but the colourful phrase described *Composer Glinka* perfectly (the metaphor came from the Russian lacquered-box tradition, with elaborate miniature scenes from folklore). The film wasn't about Stalin, or about Soviet life; it was beautifully shot, sometimes breathtakingly so, but it suffered from that common malaise of late Stalinist culture, the replacement of human beings with walking portraits, or 'statues', who uttered truisms crudely strung together. By rejecting even this comparatively benign example, the members attacked the very core of late Stalinist art.

New Trends: Satire and Psychology

It was one thing to criticize the old, but quite another to find a replacement. In those turbulent times, KSP members sometimes found that they were still showing conservative attitudes that lagged well behind the changes of artistic policy declared from the top. A case in point is Nikolai Okhlopkov's production of a classic Russian play, *The Storm*, which the KSP criticized for formalism in general, and for looking back to Meyerhold in particular, even though they would have been aware of a *Pravda* editorial extolling this production for its innovation and originality.[28] This cut two ways: the fact that they were confident enough to ignore a *Pravda* editorial was a sign of post-Stalin liberalization, but since that editorial was progressive in its views, their disregard for it was also a sign of their own conservatism, that is, their tendency to cling on to some late Stalinist values.[29]

The two works that provoked the most prolonged and heated debates in 1954 may not seem so groundbreaking to us, but for KSP members they represented something that had been missing from Stalinist art and which was about to make a return. One was a satirical play by Vasil Minko, *Without Naming Names*, whose production at the Moscow Drama Theatre was sold out months ahead of the opening night. The play depicted the moral decline of a highly placed Party bureaucrat, Karpo, who is a Ukrainian minister. Karpo is not a completely unsympathetic character, and he fails to notice how his own privileged family drags him further and further into the mire through their acquisitiveness. At the end of the play, he is dismissed from his post and rather endearingly lists his charges: 'One – for being a bureaucrat. Two – for moving sideways instead of upwards. Three – for becoming gullible and disorganized [*shlyapa i rotozey*]. Four – for surrounding myself with relatives and acquaintances.'[30] The members agreed that the artistic level of the play was not high enough for a Stalin Prize. But this was a public sensation, and it was bound to find its way to the stage in the wake of the 19th Party Congress, where satire was explicitly encouraged in Malenkov's speech.[31] The play was immediately staged in several theatres and enjoyed great public success everywhere, although KSP members suspected that some were driven by prurient interest in the details of the minister's decadent lifestyle (perhaps worrying that their own lifestyles, in some instances, might attract the same interest). In recognition of both the topicality and the public success of the play, the members agreed on a Stalin Prize, third class.

The second controversial work was also rather middlebrow, namely Sergei Grigoryev's painting 'He Returned' (*Vernulsya*), which recalls popular nineteenth-century book illustrations. But the subject matter was unusual and, from the title alone, dangerously opaque. 'He returned', but from where? From prison? From a labour camp? Or from a party meeting that had dismissed him from his post? These possibilities were all discussed but, in the end, they were rejected on the basis of the members' interpretation of the postures and facial expressions of the characters. They decided that it must be a portrayal of a man returning to the family he had once abandoned. The members spent hours debating the psycho-logical details of the presumed narrative, noting the man's clumsy intrusion into a peaceful scene (he was sitting on a small table right in the middle of his little daughter's play area), the woman's look of pity, the teenage son's eyes turned away, the little daughter's incomprehension and fear. The members even noticed a trace on the wall where the man's portrait had once hung. In the fourteen years of the KSP's existence, no painting had ever plunged them into the depths of human psychology, and now they were obsessed, rehearsing the details of the back story repeatedly. This sudden emergence of private life from the ruins of official art shook members to the core.[32]

The Opera that Came Late

The music world was not, of course, immune to the more general changes of mood. An important harbinger of the new times was an article by Khachaturian,

'On Creative Courage and Inspiration', published at the end of 1953 in the musicological journal *Sovetskaya muzïka*.[33] Khachaturian criticized works that seemed to be designed for 'average tastes', using 'grey, hackneyed musical phraseology'. 'A germ of musical progress', in his opinion, could not be found in 'works that are superficially smooth, well groomed, and streamlined to the point that one cannot be distinguished from another'.[34] And, most importantly, Khachaturian proposed a way forward:

> A creative problem cannot be solved by administrative, bureaucratic means.
> [. . .] We don't need to be chaperoned! It is the responsibility of the composer
> and the librettist alone to face the challenges of producing a given work.[35]

The article was noticed even by the foreign press and interpreted as a sign of change in Party policy towards the arts. However, in the climate of half-measures and contradictory moves so typical of 1953–54, the article prompted a negative reaction from Agitprop, which cited it as a sign of 'unhealthy tendencies among the artistic intelligentsia', which was the topic for their special report of 8 February 1954.[36]

In Music, more than in any other category, the disruption of the Stalin Prize cycle led to a drastic drop in output: while in 1952 there were 111 Music nominations, in 1953 the number went down to 36. Khrennikov explained that the main session of the Composers' Union usually took place just before the KSP began its work, and composers would rush to finish large-scale works in time for the list of nominations. This year, there was no such deadline, and the composers relaxed their creative schedules. The Composers' Union decided to hold its own Soviet-wide session on song composition only, with a series of public concerts featuring these works (there were too few large-scale works for the purpose).[37]

The main candidate for opera was Shaporin's *The Decembrists*, which was premiered at the Bolshoi in June 1953. Shaporin had been working on his magnum opus for more than a quarter of a century, to some extent out of sloth or indecision, but mainly because of the many demands for revision that came from above (Shaporin, it is worth recalling, was a solid establishment figure, not a beleaguered maverick). Everything had been prepared by September 1952; 'twice the artistes put their costumes on, the theatre waited for Stalin, but Stalin never came'.[38] In December 1952, the special run-through for the government took place, but permission was still not granted (Stalin was on holiday and did not attend).[39] The logjam was only cleared after Stalin's death, in March 1953. After the debacle of *Heart and Soul*, no one was prepared to allow Shaporin's major historical opera to run until Stalin had given his personal approval.

The Decembrists ran a course parallel to Prokofiev's War and Peace, not just because of the years of revisions, but also because both operas were transformed in the process from intimate dramas into national-historical epics guided by the principles of Stalin-era historiography. To pluck two examples out of thousands, the original hero, Pavel Annenkov, had to be replaced by a different Decembrist with the rather unsingable name of Dmitry Shchepin-Rostovsky; another, more radical Decembrist, Pavel Pestel, had to be added to the story even though this ran counter to historical fact (Pestel belonged to a branch of the secret society that was far from St Petersburg).[40] Shaporin, often infuriated by the level of intrusion and extra work involved, managed at last to reach the finish line, and it was clear to everyone that in both quality and scale it easily eclipsed any of the Soviet operas the KSP had discussed in recent times.

Despite this, the opera was not initially considered for a first-class prize. Some doubts remained about the characterization of Nicholas I, who seemed too benign on stage (Prokofiev had similar problems over his portrayal of Napoleon, who is humanized rather than portrayed as an outright villain). In general, characterization was not Shaporin's forte. As Goldenweiser quipped, 'Both Nicholas and [the Decembrist] Ryleyev sing nothing but Shaporin's fine music'.[41] Khrennikov was particularly lukewarm, refusing to admit that The Decembrists had so far outclassed other recent Soviet operas (after Frol Skobeyev and Into the Storm mark II, we might suppose his resistance to be personally rather than politically motivated). Shostakovich, who was hardly known for his admiration of Shaporin, felt it necessary to interfere in the interests of fairness:

[T]he quality of the music is very high. It's in good taste, melodious and very singable. I may be a little concerned that the characters are not clearly individuated, but I cannot deny that the composer has succeeded in his presentation of this collective portrait of the Decembrists. [...] I support a first-class prize, because it is of very high quality.[42]

Stepping outside the KSP discussion for a moment, we could well compare Shaporin's opera to the film Composer Glinka, since The Decembrists likewise presents a glossy surface and is beautifully executed, but the characters, especially those moulded in response to official demands, are walking statues once again. In opera, as opposed to film, the effect of slogan-filled exchanges between the characters is mitigated by the music, hence Shostakovich's different reaction to the two works (in Composer Glinka, the slogans were those of Soviet Glinka scholarship – music for the people, and so on). And yet, we can easily see that although *The Decembrists* was deserving of a prize, it was very much a relic of the Stalin years. Where, then, was all the controversial new work in music?

Shostakovich, Yet Again

It was hardly surprising that, in this uncertain year, the spotlight would again fall on Shostakovich. The dearth of large-scale works only placed his Tenth Symphony in higher relief. Audiences had heard nothing like this for a decade – since Shostakovich's Eighth, in fact. The plenary session of the KSP was quite aware of this, and members kept buttonholing Khrennikov: can we hear it, at least in a recording? What, they wanted to know, was the opinion of the Music Section? Khrennikov kept stalling: the work was at the centre of a controversy, and the Music Section had not yet discussed it.

Let us rewind a little. As is well known, Shostakovich did not stop writing large-scale, serious works after 1948, but he was prudent enough not to release them. After Stalin's death, sensing that a change for the better was in the air, he released the Fourth and Fifth Quartets in close succession. Goldenweiser, present at the audition of the Fifth at the Union of Composers on 29 September 1953, overheard Khrennikov and his retinue grumbling: 'This is rubbish! This is the old Shostakovich again. He hasn't learnt anything!'[43] But rather than attack the new piece openly, the leading group decided to postpone discussion of it, perhaps feeling that an open attack might not succeed. It appears that some arrangements were made behind the scenes in preparation for a bigger opportunity, because when Shostakovich's major new work, the Tenth Symphony, was due to be played through at the Conservatoire, there were suddenly no suitable rooms to hold it in. The Conservatoire director Sveshnikov refused the use of his capacious office space, where such auditions were normally held, then also ruled out the Chamber Hall and one other potential auditorium. 'He is afraid of something,' reflected Goldenweiser, 'I had no idea he was that stupid.' Under great pressure from colleagues, Sveshnikov settled for the option that would attract least attention, and held the audition in his own offices, where no more than fifty could attend.[44] The Symphony was played, spectacularly, by Shostakovich and Weinberg in a four-hand arrangement – even before the premiere under Mravinsky, listeners were able to sense the great power of the music[45] (a recording of this piano duet survived, allowing us to relive the moment). After hearing the orchestral performance, Goldenweiser surrendered to Shostakovich's artistry for once:

I cannot measure art by my own tastes. This is vivid, talented, courageous, original, powerful and constructed with the greatest mastery. He really has something to say, and he's not at all like those pitiful composers who are the leading politicians in the Union. Like a flock of geese, they are ready to peck to death a swan who finds himself in their midst.[46]

It seems that Goldenweiser, if only implicitly, now regretted the fact that he had taken the side of the very same 'pitiful composers' back in 1948. The scales had fallen from his eyes.[47]

Goldenweiser faced up to these 'geese' on 1 April 1954 – four days after he had made this diary entry – at the Music Section of the KSP. It was not Khrennikov, but Zakharov who hastened to take the lead with an expansive, rambling speech. He began by calling the Symphony 'interesting' and acknowledged the power of its tragic moments. But he still thought that this was a work immersed in the composer's own inner world, and a pessimistic inner world it seemed. This was a familiar charge. Just the previous day, at the discussion in the Composers' Union,[48] Zakharov reported, there were many who saw the Symphony as a work of genius, which they thought was the end of the matter. Others, he said, were trying to invent a topical programme for it, down to the exploration of unknown lands. But he, Zakharov, would not to be taken in by such word spinning:

[W]e have good people, a lot of good people, we have wonderful efforts, and sometimes on the path of progress, tragic things happen, even tragedies in the full sense of the word, but even so, we never entertain [this symphony's] pessimism without an exit, nor a perpetual lack of faith in ourselves, and so on. The whole country is living on its great energy, it is striving for joy and light. But the point is not that we cannot write tragic works at all, but rather that in our country, a tragic work would be painted in different colours and have a different conclusion. A tragic work written by an artist of ours cannot lead to hopelessness [...]. [W]hatever the tragedy, our people see light ahead of them and they have no doubt that light will win over darkness in the end. [... W]hat ideology will this work instil in the people? – a sense of fear.[49]

Goldenweiser was outraged: 'a vile speech from Zakharov about Shostakovich's symphony', he noted in his diary.[50] Central casting would never have chosen Goldenweiser as a passionate defender of Shostakovich, but here he was now, accusing Zakharov of inventing some personal, prejudicial programme for the work and then basing his criticisms on that (this is what we saw Zakharov doing just that with Prokofiev's Seventh, in Chapter 3). Well, he, Goldenweiser, could not imagine himself joining in the rejection of such a work. Zakharov was even wrong about the work being inaccessible, Goldenweiser continued, because at the premiere in the Grand Hall of the Conservatoire, where nine-tenths of the public were non-musicians, this Symphony, under Mravinsky, prompted a great ovation. Had the Symphony been depressing, as Zakharov suggested, could it really have caused such a reaction in the hall?[51] Goldenweiser asked members of the KSP to recall the second movement, which he described as 'vivid, bold and truly exciting', and also the superlative moments of lyricism in the third movement.[52] Goldenweiser's impassioned defence was seconded by Karayev, who argued that Zakharov had misread the Symphony, and that he had also chosen to ignore its convincingly optimistic ending.[53]

Khrennikov would have his say later, and so he could afford to act out his role as an impartial chair for the moment. He invited contributions from those who had not yet spoken. Georgy Nelepp, a celebrity tenor and Party secretary within the Bolshoi was blunt: 'I heard the Symphony. I didn't like it – it made no impression on me. But I am not a specialist. I'm against it being given a prize.'[54] The Ukrainian symphonist Shtoharenko was more expansive, but also negative: he rehearsed the old-hand theory of two Shostakoviches, the 'realist' of the First, Fifth and Seventh Symphonies and the individualist of the Eighth, Ninth and Tenth. And, although he had enjoyed the second movement of the Tenth, the wild and violent Scherzo, on balance he came out against. The slippery Shaporin then spoke in a manner that was so smoothly ambivalent that Khrennikov had to press him to make his conclusion clear. Forced to choose, Shaporin confessed that he 'liked it more than not'.[55]

With no more requests to speak, Khrennikov's turn had come, and he delivered a lengthy speech – who was going to stop him? Khrennikov came out against the Tenth, without the unctuousness of Zakharov's contribution, but expanding greatly on the same narrative of despair that Zakharov had suggested. He began by claiming that the Symphony was not just distant from, but even opposed to the ideals of Soviet music and even the whole of Russian music:

> I would imagine that the hero of this work is some frightened member of the intelligentsia, one who fears life. He sees life as some kind of terrible nightmare, and he cries and howls, because the symphony is full of neuropathic spasms, and he sees everything around him in such a light that there is absolutely no way out, while the isolated brighter moments in the symphony are of some infantile character.[56]

Before dismissing Khrennikov's narrative out of hand, we might pause to ask how far this is from narratives produced in our own time by those who imagine the Symphony as a fearful portrayal of life under Stalin. What Khrennikov condemns, these present-day commentators praise, but outside of the evaluation, is there not a substantial area of overlap? Still, in 1954 Khrennikov was

increasingly out of step with the cultural climate, and his power was waning. As
we have seen, an interest in psychology and private life was already burgeoning
in other arts, so why would KSP members wish to censure Shostakovich's music
for precisely this? It was as if Khrennikov (and Zakharov, if less stridently) was
holding on to the remnants of Stalinism, since it had given him power, while
his future under the new dispensation was not yet clear. 'This is not a reflection
of our reality, it's a skewed mirror of our reality.' In this way he hammered the
final nail in the Symphony's nomination.[57]

Yet, he did not wish to leave Shostakovich without an award altogether.
A possible alternative was to give a prize for the 24 Preludes and Fugues,
but Khrennikov thought this cycle was a mixed bag: six or seven good numbers
alongside the unacceptable majority of formalist pieces, which were merely
'Shostakovich's own technical exercises'.[58] He predicted that most of the
Preludes and Fugues would fall out of musical life just as the Poems for
Choir had done – he still regretted the award the KSP had made for these (see
Chapter 4). Despite an ardent defence from Goldenweiser, who was a connoisseur of contrapuntal writing, Khrennikov tried to talk members out of further
support for the Preludes and Fugues, and it seemed, for a while, that they would
go the same way as the Symphony. All that remained now was Shostakovich's
official work – his cantata, *The Sun Shines over Our Motherland* or, as it is
sometimes referred to, his 'Party cantata'.

No one really expected the 'Party cantata' to be pulled out of the bag at this
stage. Back in January 1953, when it had come up for consideration the first
time, Shostakovich insisted that it be withdrawn, in an attempt to protect his
reputation (the *Song of the Forests* had been equally Socialist Realist, but it was
musically much more ingenious than the 'Party cantata'). The Music Section's
discussion had taken a ridiculous turn, with Shostakovich attacking himself,
saying that 'he had not taken a single step forward in this work' and therefore
did not deserve to be awarded his sixth prize – *sixth* prize, he emphasized. His
attempts to withdraw the cantata were repeatedly rejected.

Returning to 1954, Khrennikov knew very well from that strange meeting
the previous year that an award for the cantata would be an insult to Shostakovich.
It would now even be much worse than in 1953, because the Tenth Symphony
had not been on offer then. Khrennikov's speech to the Music Section drips with
condescending praise. He had to suppress all outward signs of disdain now, lest
they undermine his purpose, which was to demonstrate a higher disdain later,
through the prize for the cantata. The strain shows in his repetitive phrases:

> Despite the fact that there isn't anything particularly new in the Cantata
> when it is compared to the *Song of the Forests*, it went off magnificently

when I heard it recently in the October concert at the Bolshoi. [...] And I am personally nominating it, because Shostakovich does indeed need to be supported; he works extremely hard – this is one of our most hardworking composers, he works all the time, writing a lot of music. It is another matter that much of what he writes is the kind of thing we don't like, but he is one of the most hardworking composers, a talented composer, and therefore we need to support him.[59]

Perhaps at any time during the preceding five years, this would have been allowed to round off the debate, but in 1954, the rank-and-file KSP members were no longer prepared to accept such manipulation. Karayev politely but firmly expressed his disagreement:

You see, no one here could fail to agree with all you say about tragedy, or the psychology of the Soviet man, or ideology. Only non-Soviet people and non-Soviet artists could disagree with this, and none of those are to be found here. So perhaps the real issue is that what I see and hear in this Symphony is not what you see and hear, and what you imagine to be there, I cannot see, and these must be the principal disagreements not just within our Section, but in general. [...] It seems that we perceive this music differently. We are all sincere, but everyone perceives it in his own way.

'And this is why reproaches are totally out of place here', replied Khrennikov, muddying the waters, to stop Karayev's comment from reviving further discussion of the Symphony.[60]

But it was too late, and now Goldenweiser spoke again, first in support of the Preludes and Fugues, and then in support of the Symphony (perhaps changing his mind, or perhaps even thinking of a prize for both works jointly). He reminded members that his own aesthetic was very different from Shostakovich's, and yet despite that (and he by now had heard the Symphony at least five times, once in the four-hand piano version, twice in rehearsal and twice in concert), he felt 'in thrall to this striking artist, this great, original artist who has a right to speak in his own language'. He did not hear the Symphony as decadent in the least; on the contrary, the second movement spoke to him of a heroic struggle with the forces of darkness.[61] When he mentioned the ovation the Symphony received at the concert in the Grand Hall of the Moscow Conservatoire, Zakharov felt he could show that this had no worthy implications for the Symphony. Since Zakharov reckoned he had special access to the thoughts of the people (*narod*), presumably via the folk choir he directed, he told KSP members that the people were not to be found applauding Shostakovich symphonies in the Conservatoire. The people were to be found on the collective farms, so the Symphony's reception had no purchase on a Stalin Prize vote.

Once again, Shostakovich's music was leading the KSP into a debate on the core issue of Socialist Realism: what is that much sought-after 'music for the people'? Goldenweiser firmly believed that, if properly prepared and 'enlightened', any social group could learn to appreciate serious music, although in the 1920s, this battle had been lost to popular song (which Goldenweiser clearly despised). Zakharov insisted that collective farmers should be given music that they enjoyed without any preparation (which was easy for him to argue, given his main line of work with the Pyatnitsky Folk Choir). Khrennikov, somewhat tangentially, added that the most requested piece of classical music on the radio was Tchaikovsky's First Piano Concerto. Zakharov now felt confident enough to launch into what was probably a set-piece speech, on the clarity of language:

> Why don't you read some Stalin [and try to appreciate] how much every phrase was polished, and that a given phrase would be understood everywhere, by the most backward person, somewhere beyond the Arctic Circle, or in the Chukotka, etc.[62]

This might have had the desired effect a couple of years earlier, but affectionate references to Stalin and his wisdom were now rather *mauvais ton*, as Russians like to put it. Like Khrennikov, Zakharov wanted to prolong the Stalinist past (their golden years, after all) and, not content with citing Stalin, he even rewarmed some of Zhdanov's pronouncements from six years back. The septuagenarian Goldenweiser demonstrated that he was much more up to date on official lore, and supported his next contribution by citing a recent *Pravda* article that saw Socialist Realism embracing different stylistic trends.[63] This article was seen as a concrete indication that artistic policy was being liberalized (artists did not have to rely on rumour any more), and it had been publicly discussed at the Conservatoire (Goldenweiser was likely to have attended that discussion). The article had encouraged some Conservatoire staff to refer back to the 1948 Resolution as an error.[64]

Khrennikov decided that his aims were best secured by tossing a compromise to the Music Section, promising them that they could return to the Tenth next year, when the debates would have died down and the Symphony's significance would have become clearer. But for now, the Cantata would take the prize. Shaporin added a compromise of his own: the Cantata (an empty trifle next to the Tenth) seemed rather slight, and if the nomination of the Tenth was to be postponed, then it was still possible to add a selection of the best Preludes and Fugues to the Cantata, submitting them jointly for the prize (he must have remembered that Khrennikov had liked some of these pieces). This was a strange combination, but it was what the Music Section presented to the plenary session nevertheless.

We have already noted the pattern that emerged when the Eighth Symphony and the Third Quartet were discussed: the non-musicians were prepared to come to the defence of Shostakovich even when the Music Section members spoke against him. The same happened this time: the painters Vasily Yefanov and Sergei Grigoryev and the theatre director Yury Zavadsky made impassioned pleas on behalf of the Tenth Symphony, in the hope that Khrennikov would back down. But he was adamant, and since there was no better deal that could be secured for Shostakovich that year, the KSP agreed to postpone further discussion of the Tenth until the following year. When the Shostakovich nomination was passed up to the KSP plenary, the members' sincere admiration for the Preludes and Fugues raised the potential award to the first class, despite a divided ballot (twenty for first class, twenty-two for second and three for third).

Several KSP members felt a responsibility before history. They wished to cast their votes in such a way that they would not be ashamed of themselves years later: they knew Shostakovich's Tenth to be not only a historic landmark, but also a litmus test of their conscience. Others – we have now named them – held on to the vanishing cloak of power that had fallen into their hands and that had allowed them to bully and humiliate their more illustrious colleagues.

Dissolution and Devaluation

As we saw at the beginning of this chapter, Khrushchev, Suslov and Pospelov were assigned by the presidium of the Council of Ministers on 19 March 1953 to reform the Stalin Prize system.[65] The main change they planned was that the KSP vote determined the prizes, and there would be no changes to the list by governmental or Party bodies. The arts and sciences KSP would meet together as a single body. It was indeed a radical change of thinking compared to Stalin's time, and the fact that this idea was introduced so quickly after Stalin's death is remarkable.

Another change was a drastic reduction in the number of prizes. The consensus was that the 1952 figure was nearly ten times larger than it should have been. One version of the Khrushchev proposal suggested triennial prize rounds for the sciences and literature, omitting the other arts altogether.[66] Membership of the integrated KSP was also to be kept low, with no more than twenty-six members. Only the actual personnel of the proposed KSP were predictable: they included the familiar names of Fadeyev, Surkov and Khrennikov (he alone would represent Music) and some cultural administrators – a list not unlike a list of invitees to the more recent Politburo sessions under Stalin.

As we know, the project to renew the Stalin Prize system stalled and inertia won. The matter was brought before the Politburo on 20 May 1954, and postponed indefinitely.[67] The list of 1952–53, which was completely ready, remained unimplemented.[68] We can judge the measure of frustration this caused from a letter written by one Andrianov, a scientist, to Kaganovich on 10 November 1954. He asked a pertinent question in a direct and even rude manner: 'Why is the CC admin putting the brakes on the award process? All this rubbish being spun around the Stalin Prizes – who needs it?' And then he arrived at his main concern: 'I am sure that any unbiased person can see that this only helps our enemies, who are starting to spread rumours about Stalin's good name being dragged through the mud.'[69] But the current Politburo had no such delicate concerns about Stalin's name; their only worry was where, when and how they could drag it through the mud without bringing too much trouble on themselves, Stalin's former collaborators. For now, at least, they could change the name of the prizes, and this, they thought, should be done soon, before the recalled KSP sat down to work.

While the prize system was still comatose, some of its past beneficiaries suffered an unexpected blow from the new regime. A surprising decision was taken on 4 November 1955: several architects had their Stalin Prizes withdrawn in line with the new policy on architecture, which was against superfluous decoration (*izlishestva*).[70] The titles were removed (there was no demand for the return of prize money) just because the times and aesthetic preferences had changed. Although the stylistic change was a very casual matter compared to the 1948 Resolution, it is notable that none of the formalist composers was stripped of any previous titles (even if some prizewinning works could not be played for a time). There were other reversals that took place in the late 1950s, including an admission of 'errors' in the 1948 Resolution on Music, and an admission that decisions on Zhukovsky's *Heart and Soul* and Dankevych's *Bohdan Khmelnytsky* were excessive.

On 15 November 1956, forty distinguished members of the Soviet cultural elite met in the Moscow Art Theatre. They were the newly appointed members of the Lenin Prize Committee, eager to start work on distributing eight prizes between five categories: Literature, Visual Arts, Film, Theatre and Music. For some of the members, this was a strange recapitulation of events sixteen years earlier, when they had first met as the KSP for the Arts; others had not been there at the beginning, but had still weathered years of KSP meetings. But a gulf lay between now and then – the 20th Party Congress and its demolition of Stalinism. The KSP's last chairman, Fadeyev, felt he no longer had a place in this new dispensation, and he shot himself in May, leaving an astonishing suicide note addressed to the Party CC (like the negative after-image of that other literary suicide, when Mayakovsky had taken his own life at the dawn of Stalinism). Others were better able to square their consciences with the changes, others again simply avoided pondering the matter as deeply as Fadeyev. The chairman, Tikhonov, found some solemn words to mark the independence of the new committee:

> Then it sometimes happened that works never discussed by the committee were included on the list at the last moment, after discussion by the government. Now there is no such possibility [...]. The selection of the works and their approval will be done by you, by your own will, conscience and reason.[71]

Indeed, added the playwright Nikolai Pogodin, 'Let us not hide the fact that the Stalin Prizes have been discredited, not only in the eyes of the people, but in our eyes too.' And, after all the business was done, in time for Lenin's birthday, the veteran KSP member, actor Nikolai Cherkasov felt that they had come full circle: it was like the very first KSP session, he said, before control from the top was established.

In the meantime, the hundreds and thousands of Stalin Prize laureates hid away their moustachioed medals. What did it mean to be a Stalin Prize laureate now, when the name of Stalin was becoming a rude word, and many artistic achievements of the past risked being tarnished by the awards? A bold solution was offered: on 16 November 1961, the CC presidium passed a resolution on the exchange of Stalin Prize medals for State Prize medals. Winners could still display their awards from the Stalin period on official occasions, but without the embarrassment. But in a twist that was characteristic of Khrushchev, who was opposed to the wealth of the Stalin-era elite, the material value of the new medals was much lower: the almost pure gold of Stalin's first class (.95) was to be replaced by standard jewellery gold of about half the value (.583). The silver of the second class was to be replaced by the cheaper alloy, nickel silver, while the third-class medals were now made from a brass alloy. This exercise was supposed to save the government 20 kilograms of gold and 64 kilograms of silver.[72] We have no statistics on how many former Stalin laureates chose to hold on to their relics of pure gold, as an heirloom that might help out grandchildren if times became hard, or as a memento of the times when the Soviet leader would dine with artists and bestow gold medals upon them.

CONCLUSION

Listening in the Stalin Prize Committee

It is often said that music suffered less from Stalinist oppression than any of the other arts. Although the list of musicians known to have been arrested, spent time in camps or been executed has grown as research becomes more extensive,[1] the reasons given for their arrest were not musical (Shostakovich's NKVD questioning in 1937, for example, was on account of his close acquaintance with Marshal Tukhachevsky). The Stalin Prize reinforces this sense of music being privileged: we can count on one hand the significant composers who were left without a prize. They are mainly 1920s modernists: Nikolai Roslavets and Alexander Krein had both descended into obscurity years before the Stalin Prizes were established; then there was Mosolov, who was due to receive a prize just at the moment when the awards were scrapped; and Shcherbachev, another 'reformed modernist', whose nominations reached the KSP plenary twice but were beaten by other works. Weinberg, politically compromised after the death of Mikhoels, as we have seen, was a special case – he alone was deliberately passed over for non-musical reasons. This is still very different from the situation in Literature, where some of the greatest names – Pasternak, Akhmatova and Zoshchenko – were frozen out of the award process.

One prominent feature that separated the Music category from the others was the general perception that special expertise was required for its evaluation. As Pierre Bourdieu has pointed out, the appreciation of classical music is a particularly elusive part of cultural capital, which is only gained through lengthy exposure and cultivation and is therefore most often dependent on family background.[2] We can say that it is rarer today among public intellectuals than it was among the KSP, but even so, its members routinely claimed ignorance, or said they could only speak from the perspective of the 'ordinary' listener, while no such caveats were given when judging literature or architecture. A typical remark came from Dovzhenko: 'Music is the only kind of art where I'm not such an expert [...].'[3] It was common, therefore, for the non-musicians of the KSP to accept the advice of the Music Section, which effectively pushed musical works back into a professional forum with its established hierarchies. It is all the more interesting for us, therefore, to isolate those rare occasions when non-musicians spoke confidently and forcefully about music. In what terms did they describe and evaluate the music in question, and how did they approach the vexed issue of Socialist Realism in music?

What we find is that even the most perceptive and eloquent non-musicians in the KSP still tended to slip from their customary professional discourse into more basic reports on immediate sensual impressions. The emphasis on music's immediate and visceral effects is quite striking when we put some of the Committee members' remarks side by side (author's emphasis added):

It was both elegant and profound, making me feel I'd entered *a trance-like state*. I felt cut off from everything around me.[4] [The poet Aseyev on Myaskovsky's Twenty-first Symphony]

When I was listening to Shostakovich's Quintet, I had the feeling that I was not among contemporary composers, but among the great masters. I was *completely shaken* – no, I was *crushed*. I had the feeling that I was back in Mozart's time [...].[5] [The painter Grabar]

The Shostakovich [Quintet] excited me to the same degree as some pieces by Beethoven or Tchaikovsky. I even had a kind of inward *physical trembling* – and this was a sign that something was right.[6] [The sculptor Mukhina]

The negative impressions were just as strikingly physical:

[Shostakovich's] Seventh Symphony shook me to the core, but here, when I listened [to the Eighth], nothing came of it but a headache.[7] [Aleksandrov, composer of the national anthem]

[U]nbearable cacophony – it's the most you can do just to stay put in your seat.[8] [The architect Mordvinov on Shostakovich's Second Quartet]

I've heard it and it found no response in my innermost being; it leaves me cold, and sometimes it unsettled and angered me, making me want to walk out just so that my nerves could recover.[9] [Fadeyev on Shostakovich's Eighth Symphony]

It was difficult for the non-musicians to translate these impressions into the kind of considered judgement they would express outside music. Instrumental music created the chief difficulty. Here they were 'timid', as Fadeyev put it, and this timidity and readiness to defer to the specialists' opinion meant that they were much less inclined to go hunting for formalism in music than they were in the other arts.[10] 'Music is obscure', said Moskvin, and it seemed that nothing short of a ritual-breaking outburst was needed (an outburst like Mordvinov's against Weinberg and Shostakovich)[11] to make members take the accusation of formalism in music seriously in the years prior to 1948.

Instrumental music also easily slipped out of memory: it was a performing art without a text and without any essential visual element. Scores were only of use to the professionals. This left the non-musicians with only their first impressions, short of listening to the piece again; there was nothing to ponder afterwards, no document to refer to, no vivid visual memory. They could take great pleasure in this or that piece, but still, the inability to 'take the music away' after the performance was their perennial complaint. The value of a catchy theme or some other easily memorable aspect could secure a prize for the whole work, as with Myaskovsky's Ninth Quartet and Shostakovich's Trio. The fact that Shostakovich's Quintet was played twice at the first audition must have raised its chances with the KSP.

As soon as words were attached to music, however, the KSP members regained their confidence. Opera librettos were taken apart and invariably found wanting, and even something apparently so slight as a dedication heading a textless piece could become a target and quickly unravel the good impression the piece had initially made (as we have seen in the case of Levitin's Quartet).[12] And even where no words at all could be found on the page, members were happy to rely on a kind of 'phantom programme', sometimes spread by rumours that could be traced back to the composer, sometimes the invention of hostile or friendly critics, and sometimes an ad hoc formulation arising from small details in the KSP discussion of the piece in question. This was not even limited to the non-musicians. Take Zakharov's stubborn translation of the *galop* theme in the finale of Prokofiev's Seventh into the image of little brats sticking their tongues out, simply because Prokofiev had been saying that the Symphony was in some way about childhood or youth. This visual image took over Zakharov's mind so completely that Shaporin could only counter him by displacing one visual image with another, and by telling Zakharov to think of the children enjoying themselves on a skating rink instead.[13] Mordvinov was right, in fact, when he claimed that a textless work produced during the war that made listeners think of Katyusha rockets would have a greater chance of success.[14] This, in fact, explains the reception of Shostakovich's Seventh Symphony: hooked by the 'invasion episode', listeners were able to enjoy (or endure) the rest of the lengthy piece, which offered no other easy opportunities for visualization or verbalization, as Mukhina's description of her own listening process suggested.[15]

The attachment of 'phantom programmes' to textless music was highly valued in Soviet criticism (the word *syuzhetnost'* was used, from *syuzhet*, a plot).[16] Shostakovich had been present at a discussion of the Tenth Symphony in the Conservatoire prior to the KSP's own discussion of the work. In the latter, Zakharov was infuriated by the labels friendly critics were attaching to the Symphony, such as 'the struggle of shadows' or 'the menacing forces', when those critics, he said, could simply have asked Shostakovich what he meant: 'What is going on here?! Let the composer come out and say: dear comrades, I had such-and-such a programme in mind here, I had such-and-such aims. Judge me – did I manage to do this or not?'[17]

Zakharov, despite having given Shostakovich some compliments about the Symphony during the discussion, did not want it to receive a prize. Seeing the device of the phantom programme working against his aims, Zakharov was calling for a return to the seemingly more solid ground of the composer's intentions (although he evidently had no interest in this principle when he was projecting his own ideas onto Prokofiev's Seventh Symphony). Zakharov was a professional musician, so we cannot imagine him unable to enjoy music without a text, so as a major player in the Soviet music world, he used this argument of principle in order to prevent his opponents from getting away with the kind of tricks he had used in the past.

There was a kind of higher-level text, so to speak, that also helped members to attach some external sense to the music, and this was the history of the composer (works, words and actions), or the critical and public reception of the composer's works. It is plausible that the communicative qualities KSP members found in Shostakovich's music were aided by the notoriety that had surrounded him since 1936, and the *Lady Macbeth* affair set a reference point for all subsequent criticism. A second reference point was set by his Seventh Symphony in 1942, and these poles of 'bad' and 'good' Shostakovich suggested a set of co-ordinates for listening and critiquing. This kind of reference point from the past was not uncommon in the other arts, but Shostakovich was unique in reaching such prominence and raising such controversy in the eye of the wider public. Prokofiev, by contrast, lacked such landmark pieces or critical points of reference to guide the ear of the uncertain listener. Is this why members often said nothing about his pieces – because they could not find any particular location for the music in the world around them? 1948 made life much easier for the non-musicians on the KSP, since it provided them with a frame of reference. Rather than leading members to dismiss pieces out of hand after a few bars, it enabled them, if anything, to listen much more closely. When they turned to Prokofiev's Seventh Symphony, even the non-musicians strove to identify melodies and follow the work's narrative drive.[18]

This close attention, however, applied to an ever-decreasing proportion of the submitted musical works in the last years of the Stalin Prize, since the overall numbers were increasing so steeply, especially with the introduction of the third-class prize division. Outside of a few prominent works, the non-musicians now tended to shy away from concerts and auditions, fearing that they would otherwise be overwhelmed. Shostakovich was unhappy about this:

> I have a question for all [non-musicians among the] KSP members. Why haven't they been listening to the music? There have been symphony concerts nearly every day. There was a Composers' Union plenary session recently where dozens of works were performed. Why weren't they listening?[19]

If the KSP would not go to the music, the music had to be brought to the KSP. And so auditions were held in the rooms they used for their discussions, and where this was not possible, recordings were played instead. At least many of the works were now heard, but some new problems were introduced. In these auditions, the performers were often overawed at performing in front of the Soviet artistic elite. The discussion rooms were unsuited to many of the performances, and the overall noise and reverberation could be confusing and unsettling for the listeners (we saw one such audition in the case of Sviridov's *My Fatherland*).[20] Poor recording quality was a further liability that the listeners sometimes had to separate from their fast-fading memories of the pieces that could not be given a live audition.

Given all these limitations – familiar to all of us – it becomes clear that only in a small minority of cases could the KSP judge a piece on the basis of a good performance which they had the ability to follow in an informed manner under conditions conducive to concentration. The proportion of extraneous ingredients in the decision-making had greater weight accordingly: reputation, rumour, the weight of professional opinion (sometimes heavily biased), the exigencies of the current nominations list and the past histories and current circumstances of the nominees. These considerations were even more significant at the higher levels, with the notable exception, in these later years, of Agitprop, which followed the practice of giving all the nominations a hearing; on average, therefore, Agitprop became considerably better informed than the KSP where music was concerned. Otherwise, musical works often travelled from level to level in the form of bland verbal descriptions (of the kind we have quoted), together with the numerical values produced by the KSP ballot. The nominees' personal dossiers also accompanied the selected works at these higher levels.

With all this in mind, can we really draw any conclusions about what kinds of works were most likely to be given a prize? If music was heard in such a haphazard manner, and sometimes not heard at all in the later years, did aesthetics, style and genre even matter? Can we make any connections between Stalin Prizes and the understanding of what Socialist Realism meant for music? It is, in fact, possible to draw reliable conclusions, because in spite of elements of chaos or arbitrariness, the Stalin Prize process was largely a consistent and rule-governed practice sustained over eleven annual cycles, and working through thousands of submitted works and productions from music and the other arts. With such a large statistical sample, significant patterns can be expected to emerge.

Musical Socialist Realism in Practice

To see what this practice tells us about musical Socialist Realism, we need a change in perspective: instead of looking at the small-scale details of the decision-making process, we will now examine the results, the published lists of prizewinners.[21] These lists (even without the leaks and rumours that usually accompanied them) transmitted a message to the Soviet art world that was bound to influence creative practice. As Zavadsky once admitted: 'In cinema, we have people trying to guess what kind of film is likely to receive a Stalin Prize, and whether their role in the film is Stalin Prize-worthy.'[22] Kemenov remarked on the same influence at work in the performance arts outside cinema:

> As soon as some production of a play, opera or ballet is awarded a prize in one of the central theatres, the next year, five or six productions of the same thing appear on the provincial stages. We award a prize for *Khovanshchina* at the Bolshoi, and so this year we have two more stagings of *Khovanshchina*; there are plenty of similar examples.[23]

For some of the arts, the message was quite transparent: if we look at the first batch of prizewinning works in Sculpture, the dominant genre is a full-size standing figure of a Party leader, its impact aided by an energetic gesture and often a flowing coat (see fig. 22). Mukhina's iconic sculpture of a worker and peasant woman, surprisingly, is the exception rather than the rule: not only does it belong to a different genre, but the figures are more stylized and pressed into service for the overall impression of movement her sculpture was intended to give. In Painting (see fig. 23), we see a trend towards huge, multi-figured narrative canvases, mostly in the nineteenth-century realist style, mildly updated with a smattering of Impressionist technique. In the same award cate-

Fig. 22. Winners of Stalin Prizes in Sculpture: first class (top row): Merkurov's Stalin; Mukhina's *Worker and Kolkhoz Woman*; second class (bottom row): Ingal's and Bogolyubov's Ordzhonikidze; Manizer's Lenin; Tomsky's Kirov.

gory, opera sets and book illustrations fit closely with this dominant trend. Nesterov's portrait of Ivan Pavlov was another exception: in style, colour and composition, it displays more modernist inclinations. The presence of these exceptions was not an aberration, however: in both cases, they were given to artists of the highest standing, and the spread of awards was designed to cover a breadth of genres and techniques, so that nothing was conspicuously absent, and so we sometimes find a lyrical landscape painting, an opera for children, or various literary translations. But the core genres and styles still predominated, giving artists a clear indication of what they should generally aim to do.

Fig. 23. 1941 winners in Painting: first class (top row): Gerasimov's *Stalin and Voroshilov in the Kremlin*; Ioganson's *Old Urals Factory*; Nesterov's portrait of Pavlov; second class (bottom two rows): Yefanov's *Unforgettable Meeting*; Saryan's sketch for the set design to *Almast*; Samokish's *Crossing of the Sivash*; Toidze's illustration to *The Knight in a Panther's Skin*.

As the case of visual arts suggests, we can viably speak of a Socialist Realist core of works that elicited the fullest consensus as canonical examples of Socialist Realism. This might seem platitudinous to some readers, but some commentators on Socialist Realism regard it as the sum of a purely arbitrary series of decisions handed down from the top, so that the search for any aesthetic doctrines or even large-scale trends is futile. The core shifted over time, it is true, but gradually, without any radical upsets. The genre of the historical novel, for example, which dominated the prose nominations at the outset of the Stalin Prize awards, produced increasingly tired and old-fashioned examples towards the final years, but the genre remained highly respectable. Works on the margins, by contrast, were in a much more precarious position: they elicited more doubt and sometimes found themselves excluded from Socialist Realism later, as the borders were redrawn. At the margins we find, for example, one of the greatest Russian sculptors of the twentieth century, Sergei Konenkov, whose prize nominations were repeatedly rejected, until he finally received a third-class prize in 1951 for two small-scale female heads, 'Marfinka' and 'Ninochka'.

Let us now approach the Music awards of the inaugural 1940–41 round as we have done with Sculpture and Painting, placing works side by side (see Table 4). Among the first-class awards we see a clear candidate for the core: namely, Shaporin's *On the Field of Kulikovo*, which was a monumental historical canvas written in a conservative musical idiom, a counterpart to the large historical novel or painting. If we look at the second-class awards, which were chosen to acknowledge the art of the five major national republics, we find more candidates for the core: here, there are pieces in national styles, and with subjects drawn from national myths or from Soviet revolutionary history. Myaskovsky's elegiac Symphony No. 21 and Shostakovich's neoclassical Quintet sit uneasily in this context.

Now let us look at the spread of Music awards in 1948 (see Table 5), when the bounds of the officially acceptable were at their narrowest. First-class prizes were given to Tallat-Kelpša's Stalin Cantata, and a quartet by Reinhold Glière. In the second-class bracket, there are three 'national' works (a cantata, an opera and a symphonic poem), a rousing march-like mass song, and a set of more lyrical popular songs that drew on a mix of folk and urban idioms. In comparison with the 1941 list, we can see two new features: the addition of mass and popular songs, and the appearance of a blatant 'Stalin' piece, the musical

Table 4. Prizewinning musical works of 1941.

I	Nikolai Myaskovsky	Symphony No. 21 (1940)
I	Yury Shaporin	Cantata *On the Field of Kulikovo* (1939)
I	Dmitry Shostakovich	Piano Quintet (1940)
II	Anatoly Bogatyrev	Opera *In the Forests of Polesye* (1940)
II	Uzeyir Hajibeyov	Opera *Koroğlu* (1937)
II	Grigor Kiladze	Symphonic poem *The Hermit* (1936)
II	Lev Revutsky	Symphony No. 2 (1940)
II	Aram Khachaturian	Violin Concerto (1940)

Table 5. Prizewinning musical works of 1948.

Opera, ballet, oratorio, cantata	I	Juozas Tallat–Kelpša	Stalin Cantata
	II	Yevgeny Brusilovsky	Cantata *Soviet Kazakhstan*
	II	Nazib Zhiganov	Opera *Altyn Chach*
Large instrumental works	I	Reinhold Glière	String Quartet No. 4
	II	Kara Karayev	Symphonic poem *Leyli and Majnun*
Small-scale works	II	Boris Mokrousov	Songs
	II	Anatoly Novikov	Song 'Anthem of the world's democratic youth'

counterpart of the Stalin monument, bust or portrait. The core, therefore, became more ideologized and populist, while increasing its national component. We find nothing on the 1948 list remotely comparable in artistic stature to the Shostakovich Quintet or Myaskovsky Symphony from seven years earlier, confirming the impression that such work existed on the margins of Socialist Realism. The 1948 Resolution trimmed off the margins, it would seem.

When we look at the general types among the award-winning works (such as the 'Stalin' work, the 'national' work and mass song), then if nothing else, we can appreciate the tidiness of the 1948 operation. However, at least one complication arises when we actually listen to Karayev's symphonic poem *Leyli and Majnun*: if we disregard the plot and some Orientalist writing, we hear very clearly that Karayev is a pupil of Shostakovich. The searing drama of the opening of the Fifth Symphony comes to mind: the texture is characteristically sparse, the melodies modally tense and even featuring figures distinctly reminiscent of Shostakovich. In other words, we have a modification of the Shostakovich style masquerading as a 'national' piece. In this case, it seems, the type the piece exemplified prevailed over its actual musical content (which could otherwise have been considered formalist). The type in question, the symphonic poem based on national myth or legend, is precisely the type to which the 1941 prizewinner, Kiladze's *The Hermit*, belongs. Within this context, the elements of Shostakovich's style acquire a different meaning: the tense unison melodies could be heard as stemming from the monodic nature of Azeri folk music; more importantly, the allegedly suspect content of Shostakovich's non-programmatic symphonies in Karayev is neutralized, defused, made safe by the appearance of a respectable programme. This is something that music can do particularly well: change its character in the listener's mind according to the verbal gloss that is offered alongside it. All these subtleties, however, matter only if Karayev's piece was actually heard by those responsible for awarding it a prize: we should not assume that this definitely happened in the haste and chaos of 1948.

Let us now see whether the same trends continued through to the longer list of 1949 awards (see Table 6). Interestingly, we find as many as three instrumental concertos on the list, two of them 'national', the other by Kabalevsky. 'National' works, as before, make a solid showing (six out of eleven prizewinners) and, as in the previous year, one of these even climbed to the first-class category (Arutiunian's Cantata). The populist strain was more diverse this year, with a work for Russian folk orchestra and a light symphonic suite designed for popular concerts in clubs or parks (Knipper).

The only standard symphony on the list was by Vladimir Bunin, a relatively unambitious piece in a conservative idiom, incorporating Russian folk themes, which Khrennikov particularly commended for its 'Russianness'.[24] We see here an example of the new tendency to treat Russian music under the same rubric of 'national in form, socialist in content', which had previously been directed towards the artists of the republics rather than to Russians. In Russia itself, of course, the nationalism of the Kuchka was already outmoded half a century earlier. In previous years, even the highly professional and technically polished

Table 6. Prizewinning musical works of 1949.

Opera, ballet, oratorio, cantata	I	Alexander Arutiunian	Motherland Cantata
	II	Eugen Kapp	Ballet *Kalevipoeg*
Large instrumental works	I	Balys Dvarionas	Violin Concerto
	II	Dmitry Kabalevsky	Violin Concerto
	II	Fikret Amirov	Azerbaijani mugams *Kurd ovshari* and *Shur* for symphony orchestra
	II	Vladimir Bunin	Symphony No. 2
	II	Gotfrid Hasanov	Piano Concerto
Small-scale works	I	Nikolai Budashkin	Works for folk orchestra
	II	Arkady Filippenko	String Quartet No. 2
	II	Lev Knipper	*Soldiers' Songs*, suite for symphony orchestra
	II	Yury Milyutin	Songs

works of Shaporin and Glière elicited the occasional sneer from some KSP members because of their hints of epigonism, but now the less accomplished Bunin Symphony could win an award because it fulfilled the 'national in form' criteria. We can compare this directly with a similar trend in architecture and design: while architectural styles that were 'national in form' were proudly developed in every one of the 'national' republics, any repetition of the pre-revolutionary Russian style ('pseudo-Russian', as it was usually called) was taboo until the 1940s.[25]

We can now say with greater certainty that the core of musical Socialist Realism was largely formed by pieces realizing Stalin's slogan of 'national in form, socialist in content': those were works in a national style, often based on folk themes, and following the principles of the Kuchka. In terms of genre, we see the domination of the monumental cantata (first-class prizes both in 1948 and '49), and two other important components: the concerto and the lighter, middlebrow works (such as folk-orchestra and symphonic suites). The life-affirming virtuosity of the concerto, an almost ineluctable attribute of the genre, made it a safe choice for composers, while the middlebrow pieces gave some extra weight to the populist end of the spectrum. Finally, we should not forget mass and popular songs, which Stalin Prizes elevated *almost* to the level of high-art, serious works. Their customary second-class prizes indicated that they could not quite reach that status. We should also mention the clear dominance of patriotic, historic and legendary extramusical themes or programmes, which supplied palpable 'content' for these musical works (such themes had progressively taken the place of the Stalin regime's vestigial socialist pretensions).

While in the 1948 list we were able to pick out a work that ostensibly belonged to the core, but was stylistically more marginal, namely Karayev's *Leyli and Majnun*, the 1949 list provides two works that fit this description. One was Amirov's Symphonic Mugams which, despite its unequivocally national and Orientalist sound, took a step away from the familiar Kuchka approach to folk music, seeking to reconceive the large-scale traditional genre of *mugam* in a symphonic context, which it did with great conviction and flair. The other work is Kabalevsky's Violin Concerto, which draws heavily from the music of Kabalevsky's idol, Prokofiev. While Prokofiev was still out of favour and could not be considered for any award, Kabalevsky managed to create a dilution of Prokofiev's style that was considered officially acceptable.

What do I mean by dilution? Both Prokofiev's and Shostakovich's musical styles were highly individual and recognizable; many of their stylistic aspects were aligned with modernism–for example, a high level of dissonance, highly unstable tonality, passages built from overlaid ostinatos or (at the other extreme) sprawling passages of seemingly unpatterned music that was difficult to follow.

They also frequently used certain musical 'topics' that were aesthetically alien to Socialist Realism, such as the 'grotesque' and so-called 'non-emotional lyricism'. Kabalevsky's 'dilution' means that Prokofievisms are restricted to small-scale detail, spicing up what is an essentially conservative nineteenth-century structure. Shostakovich's style was submitted to the same kind of dilution in Sviridov's Piano Trio, which was awarded a first-class prize in 1946 at a time when his teacher, Shostakovich, was unable to garner even a second-class prize for his controversial Ninth Symphony. Once again, Shostakovich is recognizable in the style, but it is 'Shostakovich lite', as the features of the style are fitted into the more reassuring emotional range and pacing of a nineteenth-century Romantic standard.

Shostakovich and Prokofiev evidently took the hint, diluting their own styles in the post-1948 works they wrote to regain favour with the authorities. This can be said of Shostakovich's cantata *Song of the Forests* and his Ten Poems on texts by Revolutionary poets, even though they manage to sound very different from each other. In the same vein were Prokofiev's *On Guard for Peace* and his orchestral suite for children *Winter Bonfire*. By this stage both composers evidently understood where the core of musical Socialist Realism lay and what needed to be done to gravitate towards it. We can compare this to the stylistic adjustment performed by the painter Alexander Gerasimov: when, in parallel to music, painting started to rid itself of Impressionist elements in 1948, Gerasimov abandoned his quasi-Impressionist brushstrokes in favour of a more detailed realism.[26] The difference in Gerasimov's case was that he acted as one of the initiators of the anti-Impressionist campaign, and single-handedly closed down the State Museum of New Western Art in March 1948.[27]

The most direct parallel to the marginality of Impressionism within Socialist Realism can be seen in musical neoclassicism: Impressionism was acceptable in 1940 but ruled out in 1948; musical neoclassicism was acceptable in 1940–41 (Shostakovich's Quintet), questionable in 1944–45 (Shostakovich's Eighth and Ninth) and impermissible after 1948. It is important to emphasize that neoclassicism never belonged to the core, but was already heard as dubious by the most perceptive listeners – not only by Grinberg, whose letter of complaint we explored in Chapter 2, but also, for example, by the critic Shlifshteyn, who warned back in 1941 against mistaking the Quintet for 'a portrait of our era'.[28] Whoever had ears heard: both Grinberg and Shlifshteyn listened out for style and narrative, and could not find Socialist Realism in the prizewinning work.

Myaskovsky's Twenty-first Symphony was marginal for a very different reason, that is, its lyricism and pessimism, and contemporaries were just as perceptive: Goldenweiser commented that this music was 'not of a kind that is needed by anyone these days',[29] while the same Shlifshteyn, who favoured

Myaskovsky, did his utmost to present the gloomy ending as a picture of utter serenity, and he insisted that the subjective feelings expressed in the work were somehow common to all.[30] And although Myaskovsky's music lay stylistically closer to the core than either Prokofiev's or Shostakovich's, his tendencies towards intellectualism and pessimism were always at odds with it. Today's listeners agree, wondering, for example, on an Internet forum how such a work could possibly have been awarded a Stalin Prize.[31]

Beyond the margins there were the boundaries: the extraordinary amount of attention received by Shostakovich's Eighth Symphony flags it up as an important test case for the boundaries of Socialist Realism in 1944–45.[32] The Symphony was at first acknowledged as a legitimate work on the margins, due to receive a second-class prize. The accusation of pessimism was countered by claims that Socialist Realism could include tragedy, especially when it was so intimately bound up with war experiences; the accusation of inaccessibility was tempered by the acknowledgement of the great immediate impression made by the two scherzos. And even the ideological shortcomings were almost over-looked because of Shostakovich's stature and because the quality of this partic-ular work made it tower over its rivals for the prize. And yet, in 1945, KSP members had second thoughts and decided it was not prizewinning material at all. This was still a very long way, though, from the banning of the Eighth from performance after the 1948 Resolution – even the work's original detractors in the KSP had never envisaged such an outcome back in the mid-1940s.

The case of Prokofiev's Seventh visibly demonstrates how the boundaries were gradually extended outwards in the years after 1948. It first appeared in the discussions as a marginal work, destined for the third class or possibly the second, then a year later it was definitely fit for the second, and possibly the first; it ended its prize journey in 1957 as a true Soviet 'classic'. Shostakovich's Tenth, in the same time period, moved from its position right on the boundary (the KSP could never completely reject it and chose to postpone their deci-sion), to well inside the acceptable but still marginal, as we can see from the 1957 Lenin Prize debates.[33]

The conclusion we must draw is this: while scholars often describe Socialist Realism as an arbitrary power game and essentially an empty concept, the prac-tice of the Stalin Prize awards allows us to see Socialist Realism within a coherent narrative framework, evolving slowly, never changing beyond recog-nition, with demarcations between core works, acceptable but marginal works and the unacceptable. Composers who wished to succeed preferred not to rack their brains over the impossible task of creating music that embodied 'ideology, Party-mindedness and *narodnost'*. It was much easier for them to look at the main trends in the awards and write pieces in a conservative 'national' style with some features that provided popular appeal, and then improve matters further by adding an appropriate programme. If they were to follow Prokofiev and Shostakovich, it was best to use their stylistic features sparingly and to place them within a more reassuring, conservative context. It was always best to steer clear of opera, for although the authorities encouraged it, the resulting works fell foul of numerous criticisms, followed by repeated demands for revision. A far more effective investment of time was a cantata on folk themes or a brilliant concerto.

But for the major figures of the Soviet musical landscape, these considerations could be brushed aside, since their stature within the Soviet Union and their international prestige generally mattered more than the content of their works – at least for some years. The three champion prizewinners – Shostakovich, Prokofiev and Myaskovsky – did not receive the majority of their awards on the grounds that their music was good Socialist Realism. On the contrary, they were aesthetically marginal. And this was plain to see for the young hopefuls who often resented the stylistic and aesthetic leeway allowed to these composers: as one said, what was allowed to Jupiter was not allowed to the bull.[34]

In the early 1950s, Socialist Realism reached its pinnacle, but there was little rejoicing. The KSP stopped reading and listening, resenting the stream of mediocrity that sloshed around them. Stalin complained about *Heart and Soul* because it was a poor opera. The people voted with their feet, shuffling out in the middle of tedious new plays. Many wrote letters of protest against *The Fall of Berlin*, a film they found inept and embarrassing.[35] Perhaps it was not only the Stalin Prize that lost momentum at this stage, but also the entire project of Socialist Realism. After Stalin's death, the Soviet artistic and political elites agreed without debate that the government's excessive generosity, just as the government's excessive interference, had to stop. In a return to artistic quality, as well as artistic independence, they saw hope for a long-awaited renewal.

MUSIC AWARDS IN COMPOSITION

Key to award cycles:

1941	for works from 1934–40
1942	for works from 1941
1943	for works from 1942
1946a	for works from 1943–44
1946b	for works from 1945
1947	for works from 1946
1948	for works from 1947
1949	for works from 1948
1950	for works from 1949
1951	for works from 1950
1952	for works from 1951

Not included here:

1953	for works from 1952, no awards made
1954	for works from 1952–53, no awards made (see Appendix IV)

Table 1. Awards in Composition by Genre

Unusually high numbers are in boldface

	'41	'42	'43	'46a	'46b	'47	'48	'49	'50	'51	'52
Opera	2		1		2	1	1		1	7	2
Cantata	1			2		1	2	1	**5**	3	2
Symphony	2	1	1	**4**			1		1	2	2
Symphonic poem	1	1							3	2	3
Suite					1	1	1	2	1	**6**	3
Concerto	1			3	1	1		3		**4**	3
Ballet			1		1		2	1	3	2	1
Chamber music	1		1	3	**4**	1	1	1	3	1	
Piano pieces			1	1							
Film scores	2	1		2	1	1	1		1		**4**

Songs		2	1	2	1	1	2	1		**6**	3
Art songs										1	2
Marches			1								
Incidental music				1							
Folk instruments						1		1		1	

Table 2. Composers in Alphabetical Order

Surnames are given in the most common transliteration (e.g. as in Wikipedia); first names are mostly given in the familiar anglicized form.

Name	Alternative Spellings/ Transliterations	Dates	Class and Year of Awards	Notes
1. Afanasyev, Leonid		1921–1995	III, 1952	
2. Aleksandrov, Alexander		1883–1946	I, 1942	see performers list for a further award (Appendix II)
3. Aleksandrov, Anatoly		1888–1982	II, 1951	
4. Amirov, Fikret		1922–1984	II, 1949	
5. Arakishvili, Dmitry		1873–1953	I, 1950	
6. Arutiunian, Alexander		1920–2012	I, 1949	
7. Ashrafiy, Mukhtor	Ashrafi, Mukhtar	1912–1975	II, 1943 III, 1952	
8. Babajanian, Arno	Babadjanian	1921–1983	III, 1951	
9. Balanchivadze, Andrei	Andria	1906–1992	II, 1946a I, 1947	
10. Balasanian, Sergei		1902–1982	II, 1949	
11. Bely, Viktor		1904–1983	III, 1951	
12. Blanter, Matvei		1903–1990	II, 1946b	
13. Bogatyrev, Anatoly	Bogatyryov	1913–2003	II, 1941	
14. Brusilovsky, Yevgeny		1905–1981	II, 1948	
15. Budashkin, Nikolai		1910–1988	II, 1947 I, 1949	
16. Bunin, Vladimir		1908–1970	II, 1949	
17. Chemberdzhi, Nikolai		1903–1948	II, 1946a	
18. Chulaki, Mikhail		1941–2002	II, 1947 II, 1948 II, 1950	
19. Dekhterev, Vasily	Dekhteryov	1910–1987	III, 1950	

20. Dunayevsky, Isaak	Dunaevsky, Isaac	1900–1955	I, 1941 II, 1951	
21. Dvarionas, Balys		1904–1974	I, 1949 II, 1952	
22. Dzerzhinsky, Ivan		1909–1978	III, 1950	
23. Ernesaks, Gustav		1908–1993	III, 1951	see performers list for a further award (Appendix II)
24. Feinberg, Samuil	Samuel	1890–1962	II, 1946a	
25. Filippenko, Arkady		1912–1983	II, 1949	
26. Galynin, German	Herman	1922–1966	II, 1951	
27. Glière, Reinhold	Glier, Gliyer	1875–1956	I, 1946a I, 1948 I, 1950	
28. Gnesin, Mikhail		1883–1957	II, 1946b	
29. Gomolyaka, Vadim	Gomoliaka	1914–1980	III, 1951	
30. Hajibeyov, Soltan	Hajibekov, Gajibekov, Gadzhibekov	1919–1974	II, 1952	
31. Hajibeyov, Uzeyir	Hajibekov, Gajibekov, Gadzhibekov	1885–1948	II, 1941 II, 1946b	
32. Hajiyev, Ahmed [Jovdat]	Cövdət Hacıyev; Gadjiev, Gadzhiev	1917–2002	II, 1946b III, 1952	
33. Hasanov, Gotfrid	Gasanov	1900–1965	II, 1949 III, 1951	
34. He, Shi-De (China)	Shide	1910–2000	I, 1951	
35. Ivanov-Radkevich, Nikolai		1904–1962	II, 1943	
36. Ivanovs, Jānis	Ivanov	1906–1983	II, 1950	
37. Jahangirov, Jahangir	Cahangirov, Djangirov, Jangirov	1921–1992	III, 1950	
38. Kabalevsky, Dmitry		1904–1987	I, 1946b II, 1949 II, 1951	
39. Kapp, Artur		1878–1952	II, 1950	
40. Kapp, Eugen		1908–1996	II, 1946b II, 1949 II, 1952	
41. Kapr, Jan (Czechoslovakia)		1914–1988	II, 1951	
42. Karayev, Kara	Garayev, Gara	1918–1982	II, 1946b II, 1948	
43. Kats, Sigizmund		1908–1984	III, 1950	
44. Khachaturian, Aram		1903–1978	II, 1941 I, 1943 I, 1946a I, 1950	

45. Khojamyarov, Quddus	Kuzhamyarov, Kuddus	1918–1994	III, 1951	
46. Khrennikov, Tikhon		1913–2007	II, 1942 II, 1946a II, 1952	
47. Kiladze, Grigor	Grigory, Grigol	1902–1962	II, 1941	see performers list for a further award (Appendix II)
48. Knipper, Lev		1898–1974	II, 1946b II, 1949	
49. Kochurov, Yury		1907–1952	III, 1952	
50. Korchmarev, Klimenty	Korchmariov, Korchmaryov	1899–1958	II, 1951	
51. Kõrver, Boris		1917–1994	III, 1951	
52. Kos-Anatolsky, Anatoly		1909–1983	III, 1951	
53. Koval [Kovalev], Marian		1907–1971	I, 1943	
54. Krasev, Mikhail		1897–1954	II, 1950	
55. Kryukov, Nikolai		1906–1961	I, 1947	
56. Leman, Albert		1915–1998	III, 1952	
57. Levitin, Yury		1912–1993	III, 1952	
58. Lukin, Filipp		1913–1994	III, 1952	
59. Lyatoshinsky, Boris	Lyatoshynsky	1895–1968	II, 1946b I, 1952	
60. Lyuban, Isaak		1906–1975	II, 1946a	
61. Machavariani, Alexei	Aleksi, Aleksandre	1913–1995	III, 1951	
62. Maiboroda, Platon		1918–1989	III, 1950	
63. Makarov, Valentin		1908–1952	II, 1950 II, 1951	
64. Manevich, Alexander		1908–1976	III, 1950	
65. Mazayev, Arkady	Mazaev	1909–1987	III, 1952	
66. Meitus, Yuly		1903–1997	II, 1951	
67. Milyutin, Georgy [Yury]		1903–1968	II, 1949	
68. Mokrousov, Boris		1909–1968	II, 1948	
69. Morozov, Igor		1913–1970	II, 1948	
70. Mshvelidze, Shalva		1904–1984	II, 1942 II, 1947	
71. Mukhatov, Velimukhamed	Muhatov, Velimuhamed, Veli	1916–2005	III, 1951 II, 1952	
72. Muradeli, Vano		1908–1970	II, 1946b II, 1951	
73. Muravlev, Alexei	Muravlyov	b. 1924	II, 1950	

74. Myaskovsky, Nikolai		1881–1950	I, 1941 I, 1946a I, 1946b II, 1950 I, 1951 (posth.)	
75. Neaga, Ștefan	Nyaga, Stepan	1900–1951	II, 1950	
76. Novikov, Anatoly		1896–1984	II, 1946a II, 1948	
77. Peyko, Nikolai	Peiko	1916–1995	II, 1947 II, 1951	
78. Pokrass, Dmitry		1899–1978	II, 1941	
79. Popov, Gavriil		1904–1972	II, 1946a	
80. Prokofiev, Sergei		1891–1953	II, 1943 I and I, 1946a I, 1946b I, 1947 II, 1951	
81. Rakov, Nikolai		1908–1990	II, 1946a	
82. Reimann, Villem		1906–1992	II, 1951	
83. Revutsky, Lev	Revutskyi, Levko	1889–1977	II, 1941	
84. Rustamov, Said		1907–1983	III, 1951	
85. Sadykov, Talib		1907–1957	III, 1951	this award was both for composition and conducting
86. Satian, Ashot		1906–1958	II, 1952	
87. Shaporin, Yury		1887–1966	I, 1941 I, 1946a II, 1952	
88. Shebalin, Vissarion		1902–1963	I, 1943 I, 1947	
89. Shostakovich, Dmitry		1906–1975	I, 1941 I, 1942 II, 1946a I, 1950 II, 1952	
90. Shtoharenko, Andriy	Shtogarenko, Andrei	1902–1992	II, 1946a II, 1952	
91. Skulte, Ādolfs	Adolf	1909–2000	II, 1950 II, 1951	
92. Solovyov-Sedoi, Vasily	Solovyov-Sedoy	1907–1979	II, 1943 II, 1947	
93. Starokadomsky, Mikhail		1901–1954	III, 1952	
94. Stepanian, Haro	Aro	1897–1966	III, 1951	
95. Stepanov, Lev		1908–1971	II, 1951	
96. Svechnikov, Anatoly		1908–1962	III, 1950	

97. Sviridov, Georgy (Yury)		1915–1998	I, 1946b	
98. Taktakishvili, Otar		1924–1989	III, 1951 II, 1952	
99. Tallat-Kelpša, Juozas		1889–1949	I, 1948	
100. Toradze, David		1922–1983	II, 1951	
101. Tsintsadze, Sulkhan		1925–1991	III, 1950	
102. Tulebaev, Mukan		1913–1960	II, 1949	
103. Tulikov, Serafim		1914–2004	III, 1951	
104. Vainiūnas, Stasys		1909–1982	III, 1951	
105. Vasilenko, Sergei		1872–1956	I, 1947	
106. Vasilyev-Buglai, Dmitry	Vasilyev-Buglay	1888–1956	III, 1951	
107. Yudakov, Solomon	Suleiman	1916–1990	III, 1951	
108. Zakharov, Vladimir		1901–1956	II, 1942 I, 1946a	see performers list for a further award (Appendix II)
109. Zariņš, Marģeris	Zarin, Marger	1910–1993	III, 1951	
110. Zhiganov, Nazib	Cihanov, Näcip	1911–1988	II, 1948 II, 1950	
111. Zhukovsky, Herman	German	1913–1976	II, 1950 III, 1951 (withdrawn)	
112. Zolotarev, Vasily	Zolotaryov	1872–1964	II, 1950	

APPENDIX II

OTHER MUSIC AWARDS (PERFORMANCE, NON-MUSICIANS IN PRODUCTION OR PERFORMANCE, MUSICOLOGY)

Key to award cycles:

1941	for works from 1934–40
1942	for works from 1941
1943	for works from 1942
1946a	for works from 1943–44
1946b	for works from 1945
1947	for works from 1946
1948	for works from 1947
1949	for works from 1948
1950	for works from 1949
1951	for works from 1950
1952	for works from 1951

Not included here:

1953	for works from 1952, no awards made
1954	for works from 1952–53, no awards made (see Appendix IV)

Table 3. Performers in Alphabetical Order

Surnames are given in the most common transliteration (e.g. as in Wikipedia); first names are mostly given in the familiar anglicized form.

Name	Alternative Spellings/ Transliterations	Dates	Class and Year of Awards	Notes
1. Abdullaev, Lutafali (operetta singer)	Abdullayev, Lütfəli	1914–1973	II, 1946b	
2. Abdurakhmanov, Gulyam (tenor)		1910–1987	III, 1951	
3. Aleksandrov, Alexander (choral conductor)		1883–1946	I, 1946b	see composers list for a further award (Appendix I)

4. Aleksandrov, Boris (choral conductor)		1905–1994	I, 1950	
5. Aleksandrovich, Mikhail (tenor)		1914–2002	II, 1948	
6. Aleksandrovskaya, Larisa (soprano)		1904–1980	II, 1941	
7. Almazov, Arkady (tenor)		1908–?	II, 1951	
8. Altunian, Tatul (choral conductor)	Altunyan	1902–1973	III, 1950	Armenian Song and Dance Ensemble
9. Aminarashvili, Pyotr (baritone)		1907–1976	I, 1947	
10. Andguladze, David (tenor)		1895–1973	I, 1947	
11. Anikeyev, Serafim (operetta singer)		1904–1962	II, 1950	
12. Antonova, Yelizaveta (contralto)		1904–1994	I, 1942	
13. Aslamazian, Sergei (cellist)	Aslamazyan	1897–1978	II, 1946a	Komitas Quartet
14. Azmayparashvili, Shalva (conductor)		1903–1957	I, 1947	
15. Azrikan, Arnold (tenor)		1906–1976	II, 1946b	
16. Babaev, Georgy (soloist)		?	I, 1950	Red Army Song and Dance Ensemble
17. Baiseitova, Kulyash (soprano)		1912–1957	II, 1948 II, 1949	
18. Balabanian, Nikita (violinist)	Balabanyan	?	II, 1946a	Komitas Quartet
19. Barinova, Galina (violinist)		1910–2006	II, 1949	
20. Barnabishvili, Georgy (cellist)		?	III, 1952	Georgian Quartet
21. Barsova, Valeria (soprano)		1892–1967	I, 1941	
22. Batalbekova, Isbat (mezzo-soprano)		1922–1999	III, 1952	
23. Baturin, Alexander (bass-baritone)		1904–1983	I, 1943	
24. Begalishvili, Alexander (violist)		?	III, 1952	Georgian Quartet
25. Behbudov, Rashid (tenor)	Beybutov	1915–1989	II, 1946b	
26. Beysekova, Shabal (soprano)		1919–1997	II, 1949	
27. Bezrodny, Igor (violinist)		1930–1997	III, 1951	

28. Bolshakov, Grigory (baritone)		1904–1974	I, 1942 II, 1950	
29. Borisenko, Vera [Veronika] (mezzo-soprano)		1918–1995	I, 1948	
30. Borisovsky, Vadim (violist)		1900–1972	I, 1946a	Beethoven Quartet
31. Boykinya, Nikifor (baritone)		1901–?	II, 1951	
32. Bronzov, Ivan (baritone)		1896–1963	III, 1952	
33. Butkov, Boris (opera singer)		?	III, 1952	
34. Chernetsky, Semyon (military band conductor)		1881–1950	II, 1946b	
35. Chiaureli, Boris (violinist)		?	III, 1952	Georgian Quartet
36. Ciobanu, Tamara (soprano)	Cheban	1914–1990	III, 1950	
37. Danielian, Aikanush (soprano)		1893–1958	I, 1946a	
38. Dashkov, Alexander (bass)		1914–2004	II, 1950	
39. Dautartas, Jonas (choir master)		1905–1984	III, 1951	
40. Davydova, Vera (soprano)		1906–1993	I, 1946a I, 1950 I, 1951	
41. Delitsiyev, Sergei (conductor)		1903–1981	III, 1951	
42. Derzhinskaya, Xenia (soprano)	Ksenia	1889–1951	I, 1943	
43. Dikopolskaya, Vera (soprano)		1919–?	III, 1951	
44. Dolukhanova, Zara (mezzo-soprano)	Zarui	1918–2007	II, 1951	
45. Dosymzhanov, Baigali (tenor)		1920–1998	II, 1949	
46. Dybcho, Sergei (operetta singer)		1894–1952	II, 1946a	
47. Ernesaks, Gustav (choral conductor)		1908–1993	II, 1947	see composers list for a further award (Appendix I)
48. Fayer, Yury (conductor)	Faier, Feuer	1890–1971	I, 1941 I, 1946b I, 1947 II, 1950	
49. Feldt, Pavel (conductor)		1905–1960	II, 1951	

50. Freydkov, Boris (bass)	Freidkov	1904–1966	I, 1942	
51. Frinbergs, Artūrs (tenor)	Frinberg, Artur	1916–1984	II, 1950	
52. Gaidai, Zoya (soprano)	Gayday	1902–1965	II, 1941	
53. Galperin, Samson (conductor)		1906–1962	I, 1952	
54. Gasparyan, Gohar (soprano)	Gasparian	1924–2007	III, 1951	
55. Gilels, Emil (pianist)		1916–1985	I, 1946a	
56. Ginzburg, Grigory (pianist)		1904–1961	II, 1949	
57. Gmyrya, Boris (bass)	Gmyria	1903–1969	II, 1952	
58. Goedike, Alexander (organist)	Gedike	1877–1957	I, 1948	
59. Goldenweiser, Alexander (pianist)	Goldenveyzer	1875–1961	I, 1947	
60. Golovanov, Nikolai (conductor)		1891–1953	I, 1946a I, 1949 I, 1950 I, 1951	
61. Golovina, Olga (mezzo-soprano)		1904–1975	II, 1951	
62. Grigorian, Vagram (baritone)		?	III, 1951	
63. Grikurov, Edouard (conductor)	Eduard	1907–1982	II, 1951	
64. Guseyn-zade, Alekper (operetta singer)	Hüseynzadə, ələkpər	1887–1967	II, 1946b	
65. Igumnov, Konstantin (pianist)		1873–1948	I, 1946b	
66. Ivanov, Alexei (baritone)		1904–1982	II, 1946a I, 1948 II, 1950	
67. Ivanov, Konstantin (conductor)		1907–1984	II, 1949	
68. Ivanovsky, Vladimir (tenor)		1912–2004	II, 1951	
69. Izmaylova, Natalya (mezzo-soprano)		1899–1968	II, 1947	
70. Jansons, Arvīds (conductor)		1914–1984	II, 1951	
71. Javanshirova, Leyla (operetta singer)	Cavanşirova	1920–1999	I, 1946b	
72. Kalantarli, Munavvar (operetta singer)	Kələntərli, Münəvvər	1912–1962	II, 1946b	
73. Kalinina, Olga (soprano)		1907–1959	II, 1947	
74. Kalyada, Bella (soprano)		1928–2003	II, 1951	

75. Kandelaki, Vladimir (bass-baritone)		1908–1994	II, 1952	
76. Kashevarova, Olga (soprano)		1905–1977	I, 1942	
77. Katulskaya, Elena (soprano)		1888–1966	II, 1950	
78. Kazantseva, Nadezhda (soprano)		1911–2000	III, 1950	
79. Kazmin, Pyotr (choir director)		1892–1964	I, 1952	
80. Khanaev, Nikandr (tenor)	Khanayev	1890–1974	II, 1943 I, 1949 I, 1950	
81. Khatiashvili, Givi (violinist)		?	III, 1952	Georgian Quartet
82. Khaykin, Boris (conductor)		1904–1978	II, 1946a I, 1946b II, 1951	
83. Khvatov, Vasily (folk orchestra director)		1891–1975	I, 1952	
84. Kiladze, Grigor (conductor)	Grigory, Grigol	1902–1962	I, 1948	see composers list for a further award (Appendix I)
85. Kiporenko-Damansky, Yury (tenor)		1988–1955	II, 1949	
86. Kiselevskaya, Natalya (soprano)		1906–1964	II, 1946b	
87. Klodnina, Valentina (singer)		1912–?	I, 1952	Pyatnitsky Choir
88. Knushevitsky, Svyatoslav (cellist)		1907/8–1963	III, 1950	
89. Kodanipork, Meta (soprano)		1904–1983	II, 1950	
90. Kokurin, Boris (tenor)		1921–1983	III, 1951	
91. Kolotilova, Antonina (choir director)		1890–1962	II, 1949	Russian Folk Choir of Northern Song
92. Kondrashin, Kirill (conductor)		1914–1981	I, 1948 II, 1949	
93. Kotenkov, Georgy (singer)		?	I, 1950	Red Army Song and Dance Ensemble
94. Kozinets, Dmitry (opera singer)		?	III, 1952	
95. Kozlova-Vladimirova, Anna (singer)		?	I, 1952	Pyatnitsky Choir
96. Kozlovsky, Ivan (tenor)		1900–1993	I, 1941 I, 1949	
97. Krampe, Vera (soprano)		1907–1977	II, 1950	
98. Krivchenya, Alexei (bass)		1910–1974	I, 1951	

99. Kruglikova, Elena (soprano)		1907–1982	I, 1943	
100. Kuusik, Tiit (baritone)	Dietrich	1911–1990	II, 1950 II, 1952	
101. Kuznetsova, Ekaterina (singer)		?	I, 1952	Pyatnitsky Choir
102. Lavrova, Tatyana (soprano)		1911–2004	I, 1947 II, 1951	
103. Lazovskaya, Agniya (soprano)		1907–2000	II, 1951	
104. Lebedeva, Yevdokiya (operetta singer)		1903–1987	II, 1950	
105. Lemeshev, Sergei (tenor)		1902–1977	II, 1941	
106. Litvinenko-Volgemut, Maria (soprano)	Wollgemuth	1892–1966	I, 1946a	
107. Lubentsov, Vasily (bass)		1886–1975	I, 1951	
108. Ludynia-Pabian, Anna (mezzo-soprano)		1906–?	II, 1950	
109. Lund, Olga (mezzo-soprano)		1912–1998	III, 1951	
110. Lyudmilin, Anatoly (conductor)		1903–1966	II, 1947 II, 1951	
111. Maasik, Elsa (soprano)		1908–1991	II, 1952	
112. Maksakova, Maria (mezzo-soprano)		1902–1974	I, 1946a I, 1949 I, 1951	
113. Mamedov, Bulbul (tenor)	Bülbül, Byul-Byul	1897–1961	II, 1950	
114. Margulian, Arnold (conductor)		1879–1950	II, 1946b	
115. Maslennikova, Leokadia (soprano)	Leocadia	1918–1995	II, 1949	
116. Massalitinov, Konstantin (choir director)		1905–1979	II, 1949	
117. Melik-Pashayev, Alexander (conductor)		1905–1964	I, 1942 I, 1943	
118. Mikhailov, Maxim (bass)		1893–1971	I, 1941 I, 1942	
119. Mirtskhulava, Didim (conductor)		1912–?	II, 1951	
120. Mravinsky, Yevgeny (conductor)		1903–1988	I, 1946a	
121. Mshanskaya, Olga (mezzo-soprano)		1899–1983	II, 1951	

122. Nasyrova, Khalima (soprano)		1913–2003	II, 1942 III, 1951	
123. Nebolsin, Vasily (conductor)		1898–1958	II, 1950	
124. Nechayev, Ivan (tenor)		1900–1963	II, 1951	
125. Necheporenko, Pavel (balalaika player)		1916–2009	III, 1952	
126. Nelepp, Georgy (tenor)		1904–1957	I, 1942 II, 1949 I, 1950	
127. Nezhdanova, Antonina (soprano)		1873–1950	I, 1943	
128. Nikolayeva, Tatyana (pianist)		1924–1993	I, 1951	this award was both for performance and composition
129. Niyazi, Tagizade (conductor)		1912–1984	II, 1951 II, 1952	
130. Nortsov, Panteleimon (tenor)		1900–1993	I, 1942	
131. Oborin, Lev (pianist)		1907–1974	II, 1943	
132. Obukhova, Nadezhda (mezzo-soprano)		1886–1961	I, 1943	
133. Ognivtsev, Alexander (bass)		1920–1981	I, 1951	
134. Oistrakh, David (violinist)		1908–1974	I, 1943	
135. Orfenov, Anatoly (tenor)	Orfionov	1908–1987	II, 1949	
136. Osipov, Dmitry (folk orchestra director)		1909–1954	II, 1950	
137. Ots, Georg (baritone)		1920–1975	II, 1950	
138. Pakul, Elfrida (soprano)		1912–1991	II, 1946b	
139. Pantofel-Nechetskaya, Debora (soprano)	Pantoffel	1904/5–1998	II, 1946a	
140. Pärn, August (singer)		?	II, 1952	
141. Patorzhinsky, Ivan (bass)	Patorzhynsky	1896–1960	II, 1942	
142. Pazovsky, Ary (conductor)		1887–1953	II, 1941 I, 1942 II, 1943	
143. Peregudov, Alexander (tenor)		1894–1952	I, 1951	
144. Petraškevičiūtė, Jadvyga (soprano)	Petrashkevichute, Yadviga; Pietraszkiewicz, Jadwiga	1919–2013	III, 1951	
145. Petrauskas, Kipras (tenor)		1885–1968	III, 1951	

146. Petrosian, Avak (tenor)	Petrosyan	1912–?	III, 1951	
147. Petrosiants, Ashot (folk orchestra director)		1910–1978	III, 1951	
148. Petrov (Krause), Ivan (bass)		1920–2003	II, 1950 I, 1951	
149. Pirogov, Alexander (bass)		1899–1964	I, 1943 I, 1949	
150. Podlatova, Maria (singer)		?	I, 1952	Pyatnitsky Choir
151. Popov, Valentin (bass)		1907–1987	II, 1951	
152. Preobrazhenskaya, Sofia (soprano)	Sofya	1904–1966	II, 1946b II, 1951	
153. Preobrazhensky, Alexander (tenor)		1925–2002	II, 1946b	
154. Prokoshina, Alexandra (singer)		1918–2005	I, 1952	Pyatnitsky Choir
155. Rakhlin, Nathan (conductor)		1906–1979	II, 1952	
156. Raudsepp, Kirill (conductor)		1915–2006	III, 1951 II, 1952	
157. Reizen, Mark (bass)	Reyzen	1895–1992	I, 1941 I, 1949 I, 1951	
158. Richter, Svyatoslav (pianist)		1915–1997	I, 1950	
159. Romensky, Mikhail (bass)		1887–1971	II, 1949	
160. Rostropovich, Mstislav (cellist)		1927–2007	II, 1951	
161. Ruban, Nikolai (tenor)		1913–1987	II, 1950	
162. Rusin, Mikhail (tenor)		1902–1974	II, 1951	
163. Rybnov, Alexander (choir master)		1906–1992	II, 1950	
164. Samosud, Samuil (conductor)		1884–1964	II, 1941 I, 1947 II, 1952	
165. Sazandarian, Tatevik (mezzo-soprano)	Sazandaryan	1916–1999	III, 1951	
166. Serebrovsky, Gleb (bass)		1896–1975	I, 1947 III, 1951	
167. Shafran, Daniil (cellist)		1923–1997	III, 1952	
168. Shaposhnikov, Sergei (baritone)		1911–1973	II, 1951	
169. Shchegolkov, Nikolai (bass)		1905–1981	I, 1948 II, 1949	

170. Shirinsky, Sergei (cellist)		1903–1974	I, 1946a	Beethoven Quartet
171. Shirinsky, Vasily (violinist)		1901–1965	I, 1946a	Beethoven Quartet
172. Shkarovsky, Nisson (conductor)		1904–1964	III, 1951	
173. Sholina, Galina (soprano)		1918–2006	II, 1949	
174. Shorin, Mikhail (choir master)		1904–1965	I, 1949 I, 1951	
175. Shpiller, Natalya (soprano)		1909–1995	II, 1941 I, 1943 I, 1950	
176. Shumilova, Elena (soprano)		1913–1994	II, 1949	
177. Shumskaya, Yelizaveta (soprano)		1905–1988	I, 1950	
178. Silvestrova, Nadezha (soprano)		1920–1971	II, 1947	
179. Siparis, Rimantas (bass)		1927–1990	III, 1951	
180. Skorobohatko, Pavel (tenor)	Skorobohat'ko	?	III, 1952	
181. Sofronitsky, Vladimir (pianist)		1901–1961	I, 1943	
182. Sokhadze, Ekaterina (soprano)		1907–1984	I, 1947	
183. Stasiūnas, Jonas (baritone)		1919–1987	III, 1951	
184. Stepanov, Vladimir (choir master)		1890–1954	I, 1946b	
185. Stepulis, Pranas (kanklės player)		1913–2007	III, 1950	Lithuanian Song and Dance Ensemble
186. Stupalskaya, Antonina (mezzo-soprano)		1906–1988	II, 1951	
187. Švedas, Jonas (choral conductor)		1908–1971	III, 1950	Lithuanian Song and Dance Ensemble
188. Sveshnikov, Alexander (choral conductor)		1890–1980	II, 1946b	
189. Taleš, Georg (baritone)	Talesh, Georgy	1912–1997	III, 1951	
190. Talyan, Shara (tenor/baritone)	Talian	1893–1965	II, 1946b	
191. Taras, Martin (tenor)		1899–1968	II, 1950 III, 1951	
192. Targama, Tiiu (choir master)		1907–1994	II, 1952	

193. Tavrizian, Mikhail (conductor)		1907–1957	II, 1946b III, 1951	
194. Ter-Gabrielian, Avet (violinist)		1899–1983	II, 1946a	Komitas Quartet
195. Terian, Michael (violist)	Mikael, Mikhail	1905–1987	II, 1946a	Komitas Quartet
196. Tolba, Veniamin (conductor)		1909–1984	II, 1949	
197. Tomm, Eleonora (mezzo-soprano)		1915–1988	II, 1949	
198. Tsenin, Sergei (tenor)		1903–1978	II, 1952	
199. Tsyganov, Dmitry (violinist)		1903–1992	I, 1946a	Beethoven Quartet
200. Ulyanov, Vladimir (tenor)		1908–?	II, 1951	
201. Umbetbaev, Anvarbek (tenor)		1914–1973	II, 1949	
202. Ureche, Eugeniu (bass)	Ureke, Yevgeny	1917–2005	III, 1950	
203. Vanags, Rudolfs (choir master)		1892–1977	II, 1950	
204. Veikat, Vootele (baritone)		1907–1980	III, 1951	
205. Verevka, Grigory (choral conductor)	Veryovka	1895–1964	I, 1948	
206. Viks, Maria (soprano)		1910–1990	II, 1946a	
207. Viliumanis, Alexander (baritone)	Viluman	1910–1980	II, 1950	
208. Vinogradov, Konstantin (choir master)		1899–1980	I, 1950	Red Army Song and Dance Ensemble
209. Yanko, Tamara (mezzo-soprano)		1912–1988	II, 1952	
210. Yaroshenko, Lavrenty (bass)		1909–1975	II, 1951	
211. Yashugin, Ivan (bass)		1907–?	II, 1951	
212. Yemelyanova, Polina (operetta singer)		1907–1983	II, 1946a	
213. Yudina, Tatyana (soprano)		?	II, 1952	
214. Yunitsky, Yury (baritone)		1906–1963	II, 1952	
215. Zaichkin, Gennady (operetta singer)		1908–?	II, 1950	
216. Zakharov, Vladimir (choir director)		1901–1956	I, 1952	see composers list for a further award (Appendix I)
217. Zhukov, Mikhail (conductor)		1901–1969	II, 1950	

Table 4. Non-musicians Involved in the Production of Opera and Musical Film etc.

Name	Alternative Spellings/ Transliterations	Dates	Class and Year of Awards	Notes
1. Ajemian, Vardan (director)	Vartan	1905–1977	III, 1951	
2. Baratov, Leonid (director)		1895–1964	II, 1943 I, 1949 II, 1950 I, 1951 II, 1952	
3. Brill, Yefim (director)		1896–1959	II, 1946b	
4. Cydynjapov, Gombojap (director)	Tsydynzhapov, Gombozhap	1905–80	II, 1949	
5. Dmitriyev, Vladimir (designer)		1900–1948	I, 1946b I, 1948 II, 1949 (posth.)	one more prize for drama theatre: I, 1946a
6. Fedorovsky, Fyodor (designer)		1883–1955	II, 1941 II, 1943 I, 1949 I, 1950 I, 1951	
7. Grybauskas, Juozas (director)		1906–1964	III, 1951	
8. Gulakian, Armen (director)		1899–1960	II, 1946b	
9. Haas, Voldemar (designer)		1898–1982	III, 1951	
10. Jandarbekov, Kurmanbek (director)		1905–1973	II, 1949	
11. Keller, Iosif (director)		1903–1977	II, 1949	
12. Kemarskaya, Nadezhda (director)		1899–1984	II, 1952	
13. Khvostov-Khvostenko, Alexander (designer)	Oleksandr	1895–1967	II, 1951	
14. Kobuladze, Sergei (designer)		1909–1978	I, 1947	
15. Kugushev, Georgy (director)		1896–1971	II, 1946a	
16. Lapiņš, Arturs (designer)		1911–1983	II, 1950	
17. Lebedev-Kumach Vasily, (poet)		1898–1949	II, 1941	for writing the lyrics of several popular songs
18. Leonov, Rodion (designer)		?	II, 1951	
19. Leshchenko, Nikolai (film director)		1908–1954	II, 1946b	
20. Malyavin, Savely (director)		1892–1967	II, 1950	

21. Mirzoyan, Ashot (designer)		1913–1986	III, 1951	
22. Musaev, Meli (designer)		1914–1961	III, 1951	
23. Nenashev, Anatoly (designer)		1903–1967	II, 1949	
24. Okhlopkov, Nikolai (director)		1900–1967	II, 1951	five more prizes for acting and directing drama
25. Ozhigova, Margarita (director)		1908–1987	III, 1951	
26. Parilov, Nikolai (designer)		1891–1962	II, 1947	
27. Pokrovsky, Boris (director)		1912–2009	I, 1947 I, 1948 II, 1949 I, 1950	
28. Shlepyanov, Ilya (director)		1900–1951	I, 1946b II, 1951	
29. Sokovnin, Yevgeny (director)		1904–1973	I, 1947	
30. Stefanovich, Mikhail (director)		1898–1970	II, 1949	
31. Tahmasib, Rza (film director)		1894–1990	II, 1946b	
32. Tsutsunava, Alexander (director)		1881–1955	I, 1947	
33. Tumanov (Tumanishvili), Iosif (director)		1909–1981	II, 1950	
34. Uuli, Eino (director)		1906–1976	III, 1951	
35. Vainonen, Vasily (choreographer)		1901–1964	II, 1949	
36. Vilyams, Pyotr (designer)		1902–1947	I, 1943	
37. Viner, Alexander (director)		1896–1984	II, 1950 II, 1952	
38. Virsaladze, Simon (designer)		1909–1989	II, 1951	
39. Volkov, Boris (designer)		1900–1970	II, 1952	
40. Yashen (Nugmanov), Kamil (librettist)		1909–1997	III, 1951	
41. Zakharov, Rostislav (director)		1907–1984	I, 1943	

Table 5. Musicologist

1. Boris Asafyev		1884–1949	II, 1943 I, 1948	

ALL MUSIC AWARDS YEAR BY YEAR

Within each year, names are listed in the order in which they were originally published. Titles of songs appear here in English translation; the original Russian titles can be found in Appendix VII.

Table 6. 1941 (for 1934–40)

Nomination	Class	Name(s)	Awarded for
Music [composition]	I	Nikolai Myaskovsky	Symphony No. 21 (1940)
	I	Yury Shaporin	Cantata *On the Field of Kulikovo* (1939)
	I	Dmitry Shostakovich	Piano Quintet (1940)
	II	Anatoly Bogatyrev	Opera *In the Forests of Polesye* (1940)
	II	Uzeyir Hajibeyov	Opera *Koroğlu* (1937)
	II	Grigor Kiladze	Symphonic poem *The Hermit* (1936)
	II	Lev Revutsky	Symphony No. 2 (1940)
	II	Aram Khachaturian	Violin Concerto (1940)
Opera [performance and production]	I	Valeria Barsova (soprano)	Outstanding achievements
	I	Maxim Mikhailov (bass)	Outstanding achievements
	I	Mark Reizen (bass)	Outstanding achievements
	I	Ivan Kozlovsky (tenor)	Outstanding achievements
	II	Larisa Aleksandrovskaya (soprano)	Great achievements
	II	Zoya Gaidai (soprano)	Great achievements
	II	Sergei Lemeshev (tenor)	Great achievements in music theatre and cinematography
	II	Ary Pazovsky (conductor)	Great achievements
	II	Samuil Samosud (conductor)	Great achievements
	II	Natalya Shpiller (soprano)	Great achievements

Ballet [musical performance and production]	I	Yury Fayer (conductor)	High mastery in ballet conducting
Film	I	Isaak Dunayevsky (shared with other team members)	Music for *The Circus* (1936) and *Volga-Volga* (1938)
	II	Dmitry Pokrass (shared with 1 other team member)	Music for *We Are from Kronstadt* (1936) and *If There's War Tomorrow* (1938)
Painting	II	Fyodor Fedorovsky	Design for Borodin's *Prince Igor*, Bolshoi production (1934)
	II	Martiros Saryan	Design for Spendiarov's *Almast*, Yerevan Opera production (1939)
Poetry	II	Vasily Lebedev-Kumach	The lyrics of several popular songs

Total: 10 composers, 11 performers (8 singers, 3 conductors), 2 set designers for opera, 1 poet

Table 7. 1942 (for 1941)

Nomination	Class	Name(s)	Awarded for
Music [composition]	I	Alexander Aleksandrov	Bolshevik Party Anthem and Red Army songs
	I	Dmitry Shostakovich (second time)	Symphony No. 7
	II	Vladimir Zakharov	Songs: And who knows why; The pathway; Two falcons; and other songs
	II	Shalva Mshvelidze	Symphonic poem *Zviadauri*
Opera [performance and production]	I	Alexander Melik-Pashayev (conductor); Maxim Mikhailov (bass; second time); Grigory Bolshakov (baritone); Panteleimon Nortsov (tenor); Yelizaveta Antonova (contralto)	Tchaikovsky's *Cherevichki* at the Bolshoi
	I	Ary Pazovsky (conductor; second time); Georgy Nelepp (tenor); Boris Freydkov (bass); Olga Kashevarova (soprano)	Tchaikovsky's *The Enchantress* at the Kirov Opera
	II	Khalima Nasyrova (soprano)	Role of Leyli in Glière/Sadykov's *Leyli and Majnun* at the Uzbek Opera
	II	Ivan Patorzhinsky (bass)	Role of Taras Bulba in Lysenko's *Taras Bulba* at the Kiev Opera
Film	II	Tikhon Khrennikov (shared with 4 other team members)	Music for *The Swine Girl and the Shepherd*

Total: 5 composers and 11 performers (9 singers, 2 conductors)

Table 8. 1943 (for 1942)

Nomination	Class	Name(s)	Awarded for
Music [opera, ballet, oratorio, cantata]	I	Marian Koval (Kovalyov)	Oratorio *Yemelyan Pugachev*
	I	Aram Khachaturian (second time)	Ballet *Gayaneh*
Music [large instrumental works]	I	Vissarion Shebalin	'Slavonic' Quartet
	II	Sergei Prokofiev	Piano Sonata No. 7
	II	Mukhtor Ashrafiy	'Heroic' Symphony
Music [small-scale works]	II	Nikolai Ivanov-Radkevich	Military marches
	II	Vasily Solovyov-Sedoi	Songs: Evening patrol; Play, bayan, play!; A song of revenge
Music [performance]	I	Vladimir Sofronitsky (pianist)	[no formulation]
	I	David Oistrakh (violinist)	[no formulation]
	II	Lev Oborin (pianist)	[no formulation]
Opera [performance and production]	I	Alexander Melik-Pashayev (conductor; second time); Rostislav Zakharov (director); Pyotr Vilyams (designer); Alexander Baturin (bass-baritone); Elena Kruglikova (soprano); Natalya Shpiller (soprano; second time)	Rossini's *William Tell* at the Bolshoi (in Kuybyshev, now Samara)
	II	Ary Pazovsky (conductor; third time); Leonid Baratov (director); Fyodor Fedorovsky (designer)	Koval's *Yemelyan Pugachev* at the Kirov Opera (in Molotov, now Perm)
Lifetime achievement	I	Antonina Nezhdanova (soprano)	Outstanding achievements
	I	Xenia Derzhinskaya (soprano)	Outstanding achievements
	I	Alexander Pirogov (bass)	Outstanding achievements
	I	Nadezhda Obukhova (mezzo-soprano)	Outstanding achievements
	II	Boris Asafyev (musicologist)	Outstanding achievements
	II	Nikandr Khanaev (tenor)	Outstanding achievements

Total: 7 composers, 13 performers (2 pianists, 1 violinist, 8 singers, 2 conductors), 2 opera directors and 2 set designers, 1 musicologist

Table 9. 1946a (for 1943–44)

Nomination	Class	Name(s)	Awarded for
Music [opera, ballet, oratorio, cantata]	I	Yury Shaporin (second time)	Oratorio *A Tale of the Battle for the Russian Land*
	II	Andriy Shtoharenko	Cantata *My Ukraine*
Music [large instrumental works]	I	Nikolai Myaskovsky (second time)	Quartet No. 9
	I	Sergei Prokofiev (second time)	Symphony No. 5 and Piano Sonata No. 8
	I	Aram Khachaturian (third time)	Symphony No. 2

	II	Andrei Balanchivadze	Symphony No. 1
	II	Gavriil Popov	Symphony No. 2
	II	Nikolai Rakov	Violin Concerto
	II	Samuil Feinberg	Piano Concerto
Music [small-scale works]	I	Reinhold Glière	Concerto for Voice and Orchestra
	I	Vladimir Zakharov (second time)	Songs: Glory to the Soviet state; A paean to Stalin; The infantry; No matter where I'd go; Turn to face the West; A paean to Molotov; Katyusha
	II	Dmitry Shostakovich (third time)	Piano Trio [No. 2]
	II	Nikolai Chemberdzhi	String Quartet
	II	Anatoly Novikov	Songs: Vasya-Vasilyok; Where the eagle spread his wings; A chill wind; A lyrical song of the partisans; Five bullets; and other songs
Music [performance]	I	Nikolai Golovanov (conductor)	[no formulation]
	I	Emil Gilels (pianist)	[no formulation]
	I	Beethoven Quartet: Vadim Borisovsky (viola); Dmitry Tsyganov (violin); Vasily Shirinsky (violin); Sergei Shirinsky (cello)	[no formulation]
	I	Yevgeny Mravinsky (conductor)	[no formulation]
	II	Komitas Quartet: Sergei Aslamazian (cello); Nikita Balabanian (violin); Avet Ter-Gabrielian (violin); Michael Terian (viola)	[no formulation]
	II	Debora Pantofel-Nechetskaya (soprano)	[no formulation]
Drama Theatre	II	Isaak Lyuban (shared with 4 other team members)	Music for *Nesterka* at the Vitebsk Drama Theatre
Film	I	Sergei Prokofiev (third time) (shared with 5 other team members)	Music for *Ivan the Terrible* (Part I)
	II	Tikhon Khrennikov (second time) (shared with 4 other team members)	Music for *At Six O' Clock after the War*
Opera [performance and production]	I	Vera Davydova (soprano)	Outstanding achievements in opera and concert performance
	I	Aikanush Danielian (soprano)	Roles of Antonida in Glinka's *Ivan Susanin* and Marguerite Valois in *Les Huguenots* at the Yerevan Opera
	I	Maria Litvinenko-Volgemut (soprano)	Outstanding achievements in opera performance

	I	Maria Maksakova (mezzo-soprano)	Outstanding achievements in opera and concert performance
	II	Boris Khaykin (conductor)	Tchaikovsky's *Iolanta* at the Leningrad Maly Opera
	II	Georgy Kugushev (director); Maria Viks (soprano); Sergei Dybcho (operetta singer); Polina Yemelyanova (soprano)	Shcherbachev's *The Tobacco Captain* at the Sverdlovsk Musical Comedy Theatre
	II	Alexei Ivanov (baritone)	Roles of the Demon in Rubinstein's *Demon*, Rigoletto in Verdi's *Rigoletto*, the Devil in Tchaikovsky's *Cherevichki* and the Commissar in Kabalevsky's *In the Fire*

Total: 16 composers (one twice), 21 performers (9 singers, 3 conductors, 1 pianist, 2 string quartets), 1 opera director

Table 10. 1946b (for 1945)

Nomination	Class	Name(s)	Awarded for
Music [opera, ballet, oratorio, cantata]	I	Sergei Prokofiev (fourth time)	Ballet *Cinderella*
	II	Eugen Kapp	Opera *The Flames of Revenge*
	II	Kara Karayev; Ahmed Hajiyev	Opera *Veten* (*Motherland*)
Music [large instrumental works]	I	Dmitry Kabalevsky	Quartet No. 2
	I	Nikolai Myaskovsky (third time)	Cello Concerto
	II	Boris Lyatoshinsky	Ukrainian Quintet
	II	Vano Muradeli	Symphony No. 2
Music [small-scale works]	I	Georgy Sviridov	Piano Trio
	II	Mikhail Gnesin	Sonata-Fantasia for piano and strings
	II	Matvei Blanter	Songs: Under Balkan stars; The long way ahead; My beloved; In a forest at the front
	II	Lev Knipper	Serenade for strings
Music [performance]	I	Alexander Aleksandrov (choral conductor; second time)	[no formulation]
	I	Konstantin Igumnov (pianist)	[no formulation]
	II	Alexander Sveshnikov (choral conductor)	[no formulation]
	II	Semyon Chernetsky (military band conductor)	[no formulation]
	II	Elfrida Pakul (soprano)	[no formulation]

Opera [performance and production]	I	Boris Khaykin (conductor; second time); Sofia Preobrazhenskaya (soprano); Vladimir Stepanov (choir master); Ilya Shlepyanov (director); Vladimir Dmitriyev (designer; second time)	Tchaikovsky's *The Maid of Orleans* at the Kirov Opera
	II	Armen Gulakian (director); Mikhail Tavrizian (conductor); Shara Talyan (tenor/baritone)	Tchoukhajian's *Arshak II* at the Yerevan Opera
	II	Arnold Margulian (conductor); Alexander Preobrazhensky (tenor); Arnold Azrikan (tenor); Natalya Kiselevskaya (soprano); Yefim Brill (director)	Verdi's *Otello* at the Sverdlovsk Opera
Ballet [musical performance and production]	I	Yury Fayer (conductor; second time) (shared with 7 other team members)	Prokofiev's *Cinderella* at the Bolshoi
Film	II	Uzeyir Hajibeyov (composer; second time); Rza Tahmasib (director); Nikolai Leshchenko (director); Rashid Behbudov (tenor); Leyla Javanshirova; Alekper Guseyn-zade; Lutafali Abdullaev; Munavvar Kalantarli (operetta singers)	*Arşın mal alan*

Total: 13 composers, 18 performers (11 singers, 4 conductors, 2 choral conductors, 1 military band conductor, 1 pianist), 3 opera directors, 1 set designer, 1 choir master, 2 musical film directors

Table 11. 1947 (for 1946)

Nomination	Class	Name(s)	Awarded for
Music [opera, ballet, oratorio cantata]	I	Vissarion Shebalin (second time)	Cantata *Moscow*
	II	Shalva Mshvelidze (second time)	Opera *The Tale of Tariel*
Music [large instrumental works]	I	Sergei Prokofiev (fifth time)	Violin Sonata
	I	Andrei Balanchivadze (second time)	Piano Concerto
	II	Nikolai Peyko	Symphony No. 1
	II	Mikhail Chulaki	Symphony No. 2
Music [small-scale works]	I	Sergei Vasilenko	Ballet Suite
	II	Nikolai Budashkin	Works for folk orchestra: Russian Rhapsody; Fantasy on a Russian Folk Song; Musical picture *At the Fair*
	II	Vasily Solovyov-Sedoi (second time)	Songs: It's a long time since we saw home; It's time to go; Lad on a cart; The nights have grown brighter

Music [performance]	I	Alexander Goldenweiser (pianist)	[no formulation]
	II	Gustav Ernesaks (choral conductor)	[no formulation]
Opera [performance and production]	I	Samuil Samosud (conductor; second time); Boris Pokrovsky (director); Tatyana Lavrova (soprano)	Prokofiev's *War and Peace* at the Leningrad Maly Opera
	I	Shalva Azmayparashvili (conductor); Alexander Tsutsunava (director); David Andguladze (tenor); Pyotr Aminarashvili (baritone); Ekaterina Sokhadze (soprano); Sergei Kobuladze (designer)	Mshvelidze's *The Tale of Tariel* at the Tbilisi Opera
	II	Anatoly Lyudmilin (conductor); Yevgeny Sokovnin (director); Natalya Izmaylova (mezzo-soprano); Nadezhda Silvestrova (soprano)	Koval's *People of Sevastopol* at the Molotov [now Perm] Opera
	II	Olga Kalinina (soprano); Gleb Serebrovsky (bass); Nikolai Parilov (designer)	Rimsky-Korsakov's *The Golden Cockerel* at the Saratov Opera
Ballet [musical performance and production]	II	Yury Fayer (conductor; third time) (shared with 3 other team members)	Prokofiev's *Romeo and Juliet* at the Bolshoi
Film	I	Nikolai Kryukov (shared with 7 other team members)	Music to *Admiral Nakhimov*

Total: 10 composers, 14 performers (8 singers, 4 conductors, 1 choral conductor, 1 pianist), 3 opera directors and 2 set designers

Table 12. 1948 (for 1947)

Nomination	Class	Name(s)	Awarded for
Literature [literary and arts criticism]	I	Boris Asafyev (second time)	*Glinka*
Music [opera, ballet, oratorio, cantata]	I	Juozas Tallat-Kelpša	Stalin Cantata
	II	Yevgeny Brusilovsky	Cantata *Soviet Kazakhstan*
	II	Nazib Zhiganov	Opera *Altyn Chach*
Music [large instrumental works]	I	Reinhold Glière (second time)	Quartet No. 4
	II	Kara Karayev (second time)	Symphonic poem *Leyli and Majnun*
Music [small-scale works]	II	Boris Mokrousov	Songs: The sacred stone; My native land; A lonely accordion; Beautiful spring flowers in the garden
	II	Anatoly Novikov (second time)	Song: Anthem of the world's democratic youth
Music [performance]	I	Alexander Goedike (organist)	[no formulation]
	I	Grigory Verevka (choral conductor)	[no formulation]

	II	Mikhail Aleksandrovich (tenor)	[no formulation]
	II	Kulyash Baiseitova (soprano)	[no formulation]
Opera [performance and production]	I	Boris Pokrovsky (director; second time); Vladimir Dmitriyev (designer; third time); Kirill Kondrashin (conductor); Alexei Ivanov (baritone; second time); Nikolai Shchegolkov (bass); Vera Borisenko (mezzo-soprano)	Serov's *The Power of the Fiend* at the Bolshoi
Ballet [musical performance and production]	I	Grigor Kiladze (conductor; shared with 4 other team members)	Kiladze's *Sinatle* at the Tbilisi Opera
	II	Mikhail Chulaki (composer; second time) (shared with 6 other team members)	Chulaki's *The False Bridegroom* at the Leningrad Maly Opera
	II	Igor Morozov (composer; shared with 5 other team members)	Morozov's *Doctor Aybolit* at the Novosibirsk Opera

Total: 9 composers, 9 performers (5 singers, 2 conductors, 1 choral conductor, 1 organist), 1 opera director and 1 set designer

Table 13. 1949 (for 1948)

Nomination	Class	Name(s)	Awarded for
Music [opera, ballet, oratorio, cantata]	I	Alexander Arutiunian	Motherland Cantata
	II	Eugen Kapp (second time)	Ballet *Kalevipoeg*
Music [large instrumental works]	I	Balys Dvarionas	Violin Concerto
	II	Dmitry Kabalevsky (second time)	Violin Concerto
	II	Fikret Amirov	Azerbaijani mugams *Kurd ovshari* and *Shur* for symphony orchestra
	II	Vladimir Bunin	Symphony No. 2
	II	Gotfrid Hasanov	Piano Concerto
Music [small-scale works]	I	Nikolai Budashkin (second time)	Works for folk orchestra: Russian Fantasia; Second Rhapsody, *Dumka*
	II	Arkady Filippenko	Quartet No. 2
	II	Lev Knipper (second time)	*Soldiers' Songs*, suite for symphony orchestra
	II	Georgy [Yury] Milyutin	Songs: The Lenin Hills; Lilac and cherry-tree; The marine corps
Music [performance]	II	Konstantin Massalitinov (director of the Voronezh Russian Folk Choir)	[no formulation]
	II	Antonina Kolotilova (director of the Russian Folk Choir of Northern Song)	[no formulation]

	II	Konstantin Ivanov (chief conductor of the State Symphony Orchestra)	[no formulation]
	II	Grigory Ginzburg (pianist)	[no formulation]
	II	Galina Barinova (violinist)	[no formulation]
Opera [performance and production]	I	Nikolai Golovanov (conductor; second time); Leonid Baratov (director; second time); Fyodor Fedorovsky (designer; third time); Mikhail Shorin (choir master); Alexander Pirogov (bass; second time); Mark Reizen (bass; second time); Maria Maksakova (mezzo-soprano; second time); Ivan Kozlovsky (tenor; second time); Nikandr Khanaev (tenor; second time)	Musorgsky's *Boris Godunov* at the Bolshoi
	II	Mikhail Stefanovich (director); Veniamin Tolba (conductor); Alexander Khvostov-Khvostenko (designer); Mikhail Romensky (bass); Galina Sholina (soprano); Eleonora Tomm (mezzo-soprano); Yury Kiporenko-Damansky (tenor)	Glinka's *Ivan Susanin* at the Kiev Opera
	II	Boris Pokrovsky (director; third time); Vladimir Dmitriyev (designer; fourth time); Kirill Kondrashin (conductor; second time); Vasily Vainonen (choreographer); Leokadia Maslennikova (soprano); Elena Shumilova (soprano); Georgy Nelepp (tenor; second time); Nikolai Shchegolkov (bass; second time); Anatoly Orfenov (tenor)	Smetana's *The Bartered Bride* at the Bolshoi
	II	Mukan Tulebaev (composer); Kurmanbek Jandarbekov (director); Anvarbek Umbetbaev (tenor); Kulyash Baiseitova (soprano; second time); Shabal Beysekova (soprano); Baigali Dosymzhanov (tenor); Anatoly Nenashev (designer)	Tulebaev's *Birzhan and Sara* at the Kazakh Opera
	II	Gombojap Cydynjapov, (director)	Achievements in the development of Buryat-Mongol theatre
Ballet [musical performance and production]	II	Sergei Balasanian (composer; shared with 4 other team members)	Balasanian's *Leyli and Majnun* at the Tajik Opera

Total: 13 composers, 26 performers (18 singers, 4 conductors, 2 choral conductors, 1 pianist, 1 violinist), 5 opera directors and 4 set designers, 1 choir master

Table 14. 1950 (for 1949)

Nomination	Class	Name(s)	Awarded for
Music (Opera, ballet, oratorio, cantata)	I	Reinhold Glière (third time)	Ballet *The Bronze Horseman*
	I	Dmitry Shostakovich (fourth time)	Oratorio *Song of the Forests* and music for the film *The Fall of Berlin*
	II	Herman Zhukovsky	Cantata *Glory to the Fatherland*
	II	Ştefan Neaga	Cantata for the 25th Anniversary of the Moldavian SSR; Stalin Song
	II	Mikhail Krasev	Children's opera *Morozko* and children's songs: Lenin song; Stalin song of Moscow's children; Festive morning; Cuckoo; Uncle Yegor
	III	Jahangir Jahangirov	Symphonic poem with chorus *Beyond the Aras River*
	III	Vasily Dekhterev	Cantata *The Russian Land*
	III	Alexander Manevich	Cantata *For Peace*
Music (Large instrumental works)	II	Alexei Muravlev	Symphonic poem *Azov Mountain*
	II	Artur Kapp	Symphony No. 4 ('Youth')
	II	Jānis Ivanovs	Symphony No. 6
	II	Nazib Zhiganov (second time)	Suite on Tatar Themes for symphony orchestra
	III	Sulkhan Tsintsadze	Quartet No. 2 and three miniatures for string quartet: 'Lale', 'Indi-Mindi', 'Sachidao'
	III	Anatoly Svechnikov	Symphonic poem *Shchors*
Music (Small-scale works)	II	Nikolai Myaskovsky (fourth time)	Cello Sonata
	II	Valentin Makarov	Song cycle *A Sunlit Path* and songs: Wide are the fields around Stalingrad; Dear old Sevastopol
	III	Platon Maiboroda	Songs: Mark Ozyorny; Olena Khobta; Maria Lysenko
	III	Ivan Dzerzhinsky	Song cycle *The New Village*
	III	Sigizmund Kats	Songs: Lilac in bloom; A stiff wind blew through the Bryansk forest; By the old oaktree; A toast; There stands a rock
Music (Performance)	I	Boris Aleksandrov (director of the Red Army Song and Dance Ensemble); Pavel Virsky (choreographer); Konstantin Vinogradov (choir master); Georgy Babaev (soloist); Georgy Kotenkov (soloist)	[no formulation]
	I	Svyatoslav Richter (pianist)	[no formulation]

	II	Elena Katulskaya (soprano)	[no formulation]
	II	Bulbul Mamedov (tenor)	performance of Azerbaijani folk songs
	II	Dmitry Osipov (artistic director and head conductor of the N. P. Osipov Russian Folk Orchestra)	[no formulation]
	III	Svyatoslav Knushevitsky (cellist)	[no formulation]
	III	Nadezhda Kazantseva (soprano)	[no formulation]
	III	Tatul Altunian (director of the Armenian Song and Dance Ensemble)	[no formulation]
	III	Tamara Ciobanu (soprano); Eugeniu Ureche (bass)	Performance of Moldavian folk songs
	III	Jonas Švedas (director of the Lithuanian Song and Dance Ensemble); Juozas Lingys (choreographer); Pranas Stepulis (kanklès player and director of the instrumental group)	[no formulation]
Opera [performance and production]	I	Nikolai Golovanov (conductor; third time); Boris Pokrovsky (director; fourth time); Fyodor Fedorovsky (designer; fourth time); Nikandr Khanaev (tenor; third time); Georgy Nelepp (tenor; third time); Vera Davydova (soprano; second time); Yelizaveta Shumskaya (soprano); Natalya Shpiller (soprano; third time)	Rimsky-Korsakov's *Sadko* at the Bolshoi
	II	Mikhail Zhukov (conductor); Savely Malyavin (director); Rudolfs Vanags (choir master); Arturs Lapiņš (designer); Alexander Viliumanis (baritone); Alexander Dashkov (bass); Anna Ludynia-Pabian (mezzo-soprano); Vera Krampe (soprano); Artūrs Frinbergs (tenor)	Musorgsky's *Boris Godunov* at the Latvian Opera
	II	Vasily Nebolsin (conductor); Leonid Baratov (director; third time); Alexei Ivanov (baritone; third time); Nina Pokrovskaya (soprano); Ivan Petrov (Krause) (bass); Grigory Bolshakov (baritone; second time); Alexander Rybnov (choir master)	Tchaikovsky's *Mazeppa* at the Bolshoi (second stage)
	II	Tiit Kuusik (baritone); Meta Kodanipork (soprano); Georg Ots (baritone); Martin Taras (tenor); Alexander Viner (director)	Tchaikovsky's *Eugene Onegin* at the Estonian Opera
	II	Iosif Tumanov (Tumanishvili) (director); Nikolai Ruban (tenor); Yevdokiya Lebedeva (soprano); Serafim Anikeyev (operetta singer); Gennady Zaichkin (operetta singer)	Milyutin's *The Trembita* at the Moscow Operetta

Ballet [musical performance and production]	II	Yury Fayer (conductor; fourth time) (shared with 9 other team members)	Glière's *The Red Poppy* at the Bolshoi
	II	Vasily Zolotarev (composer; shared with 4 other team members)	Zolotarev's *The Lake Prince* at the Belorussian Opera
	II	Mikhail Chulaki (composer; third time) (shared with 5 other team members)	Chulaki's *Youth* at the Leningrad Maly Opera
Film	I	Aram Khachaturian (fourth time) (shared with 10 other team members)	Music to *The Battle of Stalingrad*
	II	Ādolfs Skulte (shared with 4 other team members)	Music to *Rainis*
Film (awarded separately)	I	Dmitry Arakishvili (shared with 4 other team members)	Music to *Jurgai's Shield*

Total: 23 composers, 42 performers (28 singers, 4 conductors, 2 directors of folk orchestras, 1 cellist, 1 pianist, 3 choral directors, 3 choir masters), 5 opera directors and 2 set designers

Table 15. 1951 (for 1950)

Nomination	Class	Name(s)	Awarded for
Feature film	I	He Shi-De (composer; shared with 13 other team members)	Music for *China Liberated*
	II	Isaak Dunayevsky (composer; second time) (shared with 8 other team members)	Music for *The Kuban Cossacks*
Documentary film	II	Jan Kapr (composer; shared with 5 other team members)	Music for *The New Czechoslovakia*
	II	Villem Reimann (composer; shared with 4 other team members)	Music for *Soviet Estonia*
Music (Opera, ballet, oratorio, cantata)	II	Dmitry Kabalevsky (third time)	Opera *Taras's Family*
	II	Yuly Meitus	Opera *The Young Guard*
	II	Ādolfs Skulte (second time)	Ballet *The Sakta of Freedom*
	II	Lev Stepanov	Opera *Ivan Bolotnikov*
	II	Sergei Prokofiev (sixth time)	Vocal-symphonic suite *Winter Bonfire* and oratorio *On Guard for Peace*
	III	Gotfrid Hasanov (second time)	Daghestani Stalin Cantata
	III	Herman Zhukovsky (second time; later withdrawn)	Opera *Heart and Soul*
	III	Marģeris Zariņš	Oratorio *Heroes of Valmiera*
	III	Gustav Ernesaks (second time, but first time as a composer)	Opera *Stormy Shores*
	I	Nikolai Myaskovsky (fifth time)	Symphony No. 27 and Quartet No. 13 (posth.)
Music (Large instrumental works)	II	German Galynin	Epic Poem on Russian Themes for symphony orchestra
	II	Nikolai Peyko (second time)	Moldavian Suite for symphony orchestra

		III	Arno Babajanian	*Heroic Ballad* for piano and orchestra
		III	Stasys Vainiūnas	Rhapsody on Lithuanian Themes for violin and orchestra
		III	Vadim Gomolyaka	Symphonic suite *Trans-Carpathian Sketches*
		III	Quddus Khojamyarov	Symphonic poem *Rizvangul*
		III	Alexei Machavariani	Violin Concerto
		III	Velimukhamed Mukhatov	Turkmen Suite
		III	Otar Taktakishvili	Symphony No. 1
Music (Small-scale works)		II	Anatoly Aleksandrov	Song cycle *Loyalty*; cycle of Pushkin songs; piano pieces for children
		II	Klimenty Korchmarev	*China is Free*, suite for choir and symphony orchestra
		II	Valentin Makarov (second time)	*The Mighty River*, suite for choir and folk orchestra
		II	Vano Muradeli (second time)	Songs: Anthem of the international union of students; The will of Stalin led us; Those who struggle for peace; Moscow–Peking; Hymn to Moscow
		III	Dmitry Vasilyev-Buglai	Songs: Fly nightingale, fly to Moscow; In the wastes of the Barents Sea; A mountain eagle; The death of Chapayev; Harvest dance
		III	Anatoly Kos-Anatolsky	Songs: From Moscow to the Carpathians; New Verkhovina; Meeting in a field
		III	Boris Kõrver	Songs: In our kolkhoz; The swings are calling; After work
		III	Said Rustamov	Songs: Komsomol; Sureya; I vote for peace; Sumgait
		III	Serafim Tulikov	Songs: We are for peace; Song of the Volga; Come out in bloom, land of the kolkhozes; They came on leave; The mighty forest
		III	Solomon Yudakov	Vocal-orchestral suite *Mirzachul*
Music (Performance)		I	Tatyana Nikolayeva (pianist)	Concert performances and the composition of the Piano Concerto
		II	Zara Dolukhanova (mezzo-soprano)	[no formulation]
		II	Tagizade Niyazi (conductor)	[no formulation]
		II	Mstislav Rostropovich (cellist)	[no formulation]
		III	Igor Bezrodny (violinist)	[no formulation]
		III	Ashot Petrosiants (director of the Uzbek Folk Orchestra)	[no formulation]

Opera [performance and production]	I	Nikolai Golovanov (conductor; fourth time); Fyodor Fedorovsky (designer; fourth time); Leonid Baratov (director; fourth time); Mikhail Shorin (choir master; second time); Mark Reizen (bass; third time); Vera Davydova (soprano; third time); Alexei Krivchenya (bass); Maria Maksakova (mezzo-soprano; third time); Vasily Lubentsov (bass); Alexander Peregudov (tenor); Ivan Petrov (bass; second time); Alexander Ognivtsev (bass)	Musorgsky's *Khovanshchina* at the Bolshoi
	II	Boris Khaykin (conductor; third time); Ilya Shlepyanov (director; second time); Simon Virsaladze (designer); Ivan Yashugin (bass); Sofia Preobrazhenskaya (soprano; second time); Lavrenty Yaroshenko (bass); Olga Mshanskaya (mezzo-soprano); Vladimir Ulyanov (tenor); Ivan Nechayev (tenor); Vladimir Ivanovsky (tenor); Bella Kalyada (soprano)	Kabalevsky's *Taras's Family* at the Kirov Opera
	II	Nikolai Okhlopkov (director; sixth time, but first for directing opera); Edouard Grikurov (conductor); Sergei Shaposhnikov (baritone); Tatyana Lavrova (soprano; second time); Arkady Almazov (tenor); Antonina Stupalskaya (mezzo-soprano); Olga Golovina (mezzo-soprano)	Meitus's *The Young Guard* at the Leningrad Maly Opera
	II	Anatoly Lyudmilin (conductor; second time); Iosif Keller (director); Rodion Leonov (designer); Nikifor Boykinya (baritone); Agniya Lazovskaya (soprano); Valentin Popov (bass); Mikhail Rusin (tenor)	Stepanov's *Ivan Bolotnikov* at the Molotov [now Perm] Opera
	III	Haro Stepanian (composer); Mikhail Tavrizian (conductor; second time); Vardan Ajemian (director); Ashot Mirzoyan (designer); Tatevik Sazandarian (mezzo-soprano); Gohar Gasparyan (soprano); Avak Petrosian (tenor); Vagram Grigorian (baritone)	Stepanian's *A Heroine* at the 'Yerevan' Opera
	III	Sergei Delitsiyev (conductor); Juozas Grybauskas (director); Jonas Stasiūnas (baritone); Kipras Petrauskas (tenor); Jadvyga Petraškevičiūtė (soprano); Jonas Dautartas (choir master); Rimantas Siparis (bass)	Musorgsky's *Boris Godunov* at the Lithuanian Opera

	III	Nisson Shkarovsky (conductor); Margarita Ozhigova (director); Gleb Serebrovsky (bass; second time); Vera Dikopolskaya (soprano); Boris Kokurin (tenor)	Zhukovsky's *Heart and Soul* at the Saratov Opera
	III	Kirill Raudsepp (conductor); Eino Uuli (director); Voldemar Haas (designer); Olga Lund (mezzo-soprano); Georg Taleš (baritone); Vootele Veikat (baritone); Martin Taras (tenor; second time)	Ernesaks' s *Stormy Shores* at the Estonian Opera
	III	Talib Sadykov (composer and conductor); Kamil Yashen (Nugmanov) (librettist); Meli Musaev (designer); Khalima Nasyrova (soprano; second time); Gulyam Abdurakhmanov (tenor); Mukarram Turgunbaeva (dancer)	Glière/Sadykov's *Gyulsara* at the Uzbek Opera
Ballet [musical performance and production]	II	David Toradze (composer); Didim Mirtskhulava (conductor; shared with 6 other team members)	Toradze's *Gorda* at the Tbilisi Opera
	II	Arvīds Jansons (conductor; shared with 6 other team members)	Skulte's *The Sakta of Freedom* at the Latvian Opera
	II	Pavel Feldt (conductor; shared with 9 other team members)	Yarullin's *Ali-batyr* at the Kirov Opera

Total: 2 composer/performers, 36 composers (1 withdrawn), 45 performers (30 singers, 11 conductors, 1 folk orchestra director, 1 violinist, 1 cellist, 1 opera choir master), 7 opera directors and 6 set designers, 1 librettist

Table 16. 1952 (for 1951)

Nomination	Class	Name(s)	Awarded for
Feature film	I	Boris Lyatoshinsky (composer; second time (shared with 7 other team members)	Music for *Taras Shevchenko*
	II	Tikhon Khrennikov (composer; third time shared with 9 other team members)	Music for *The Miners of Donetsk*
Documentary film	II	Balys Dvarionas (composer; second time shared with 4 other team members)	Music for *Soviet Lithuania*
Music (Opera, ballet, oratorio, cantata)	II	Eugen Kapp (third time)	Opera *Freedom's Bard*
	II	Dmitry Shostakovich (fifth time)	Ten Poems for Choir
	III	Mukhtor Ashrafiy (second time)	Cantata *Song of Joy*
	III	Yury Levitin	Cantata *Lights upon the Volga*

Music (Large instrumental works)	II	Velimukhamed Mukhatov (second time)	Symphonic poem *My Motherland*
	II	Otar Taktakishvili (second time)	Piano Concerto
	II	Andriy Shtoharenko (second time)	Symphonic suite *In Memory of Lesya Ukrainka*
	III	Leonid Afanasyev	Violin Concerto
	III	Ahmed Hajiyev (second time)	Symphonic poem *For Peace*
	III	Albert Leman	Violin Concerto
	III	Arkady Mazayev	Symphonic poem *Krasnodontsy*
Music (Small-scale works)	II	Ashot Satian	Orchestral song cycle *Songs of the Ararat Valley*
	II	Yury Shaporin (third time)	Art songs: Under blue skies; Incantation; Autumn festival; By evening the sounds of war died down. Arrangements of Russian folk songs: Nothing stirs in the fields; The boatmen's song; There's more than one path across the field
	III	Viktor Bely	Songs: In defence of peace; Alexander Matrosov
	III	Yury Kochurov	Art songs: Dedication; Life's joys; Spring; After the rain; Love; The spring
	III	Filipp Lukin	Songs: Stalin gave us happiness; Moscow song; A song of youth; Drinking song; A song to the joy of friendship
	III	Mikhail Starokadomsky	Children's songs: Under the banner of peace; Songs of the older brothers; A song about morning exercises; Merry travellers
Music (Performance)	I	Vladimir Zakharov (director of the Pyatnitsky Choir; third time, but previous two as a composer); Pyotr Kazmin (co-director); Tatyana Ustinova (choreographer); Vasily Khvatov (orchestra director); Anna Kozlova-Vladimirova; Valentina Klodnina; Alexandra; Prokoshina; Maria Podlatova; Ekaterina Kuznetsova (singers); Ivan Turchenkov; Andrei Klimov; Alexandra Danilina; Maria Moskvitina; Pyotr Sorokin (dancers)	[no formulation]
	I	Samson Galperin (conductor of the Moiseyev Dance Ensemble; shared with 10 other team members)	[no formulation]
	II	Boris Gmyrya (bass)	[no formulation]

	II	Nathan Rakhlin (conductor)	[no formulation]
	III	Isbat Batalbekova (mezzo-soprano)	[no formulation]
	III	Pavel Necheporenko (balalaika player)	[no formulation]
	III	Daniil Shafran (cellist)	[no formulation]
	III	Boris Chiaureli (violinist); Givi Khatiashvili (violinist); Alexander Begalishvili (violist); Georgy Barnabishvili (cellist)	[Georgian Quartet]
Opera [performance and production]	II	Kirill Raudsepp (conductor; second time); Alexander Viner (director; second time); Tiit Kuusik (baritone; second time); Elsa Maasik (soprano); August Pärn (singer); Tiiu Targama (choir master)	Eugen Kapp's *Freedom's Bard* at the Estonian Opera
	II	Samuil Samosud (conductor; third time); Leonid Baratov (director; fifth time); Nadezhda Kemarskaya (director); Boris Volkov (designer); Vladimir Kandelaki (bass-baritone); Tamara Yanko (mezzo-soprano); Yury Yunitsky (baritone); Tatyana Yudina (soprano); Sergei Tsenin (tenor)	Kabalevsky's *Taras's Family* at the Stanislavsky and Nemirovich-Danchenko Opera
	III	Ivan Bronzov (baritone); Dmitry Kozinets (singer); Boris Butkov (singer); Pavel Skorobohatko (tenor)	Musorgsky's *Boris Godunov* at the Kharkov Opera
Ballet [musical performance and production]	II	Soltan Hajibeyov (composer); Tagizade Niyazi (conductor; second time) (shared with 3 other team members)	Soltan Hajibeyov's *Gyulshen* at the Azerbaijani Opera

Total (dancers and choreographers not included here): 21 composers, 34 performers (19 singers, 5 conductors, 1 folk orchestra director, 2 choral directors, 1 string quartet, 1 cellist, 1 balalaika player, 1 opera choir master), 3 opera directors and 1 set designer

Appendices IV–VIII are available at: http://yalebooks.co.uk/frolova_walker_appendix.asp

NOTES

Introduction

1. Maretskaya's acceptance speech, 27 or 28 December 1951. RGALI, fond 2073, op. 1, ye. kh. 50, ll. 97–8.
2. Georgiy Sviridov, *Muzïka kak sud'ba* (Moscow: Molodaya gvardiya, 2002), 563.
3. For the narrative of persecution see, for example, Solomon Volkov's *Shostakovich and Stalin: The Extraordinary Relationship between the Great Composer and the Brutal Dictator*, trans. Antonina W. Bouis (London: Little, Brown, 2004). For the narrative of reward, see Leonid Maksimenkov's 'Stalin and Shostakovich: Letters to a "Friend" ', in Laurel Fay (ed.), *Shostakovich and His World* (Princeton and Oxford: Princeton University Press, 2004), 43–58.
4. Simon Morrison, *The People's Artist: Prokofiev's Soviet Years* (Oxford: Oxford University Press, 2008) and *The Love and Wars of Lina Prokofiev* (London: Harvill Secker, 2013).
5. Kiril Tomoff, *Creative Union: The Professional Organization of Soviet Composers, 1939-1953* (Ithaca and London: Cornell University Press, 2006). Other volumes on institutional history of Soviet music include Simo Mikkonen's *Music and Power in the 1930s: A History of Composers' Bureaucracy* (Lewiston, Queenston and Lampeter: The Edwin Mellen Press, 2009) and Meri E. Herrala's *The Struggle for Control of Soviet Music from 1932 to 1948: Socialist Realism vs. Western Formalism* (Lewiston, Queenston and Lampeter: The Edwin Mellen Press, 2012).
6. Alexander Gerasimov at the plenary session of 4 April 1947. RGALI, fond 2073, op. 1, ye. kh. 21, l. 235.
7. Mainly RGASPI and GARF, partly also RGALI.
8. Dmitriy Shepilov, *Neprimknuvshiy* (Moscow: Vagrius, 2001); Konstantin Simonov, *Glazami cheloveka moyego pokoleniya: razmïshleniya o I. V. Staline* (Moscow: Kniga, 1990).
9. V. F. Svin'yin and K. A. Oseyev (eds), *Stalinskiye premii: dve storonï odnoy medali. Sbornik dokumentov i khudozhestvenno–publitsisticheskikh materialov* (Novosibirsk: Svin'yin i sïnov'ya, 2007).
10. An example of Ivkin's publication on the subject is 'Kak otmenyali Stalinskiye premii: Dokumentï TsK KPSS i Soveta ministrov SSSR, 1953–1967 gg', *Istoricheskiy Arkhiv* (2013), no. 6, 3–49.
11. V. V. Perkhin (ed.), *Deyateli russkogo iskusstva i M. B. Khrapchenko, predsedatel' Vsesoyuznogo komiteta po delam iskusstv: aprel' 1939–yanvar' 1948: svod pisem* (Moscow: Nauka, 2007).
12. Oliver Johnson, 'The Stalin Prize and the Soviet Artist – Status Symbol or Stigma?', *Slavic Review* (2011), vol. 70, no. 4, 819–43; Joan Neuberger, 'The Politics of Bewilderment: Eisenstein's "Ivan the Terrible" in 1945', in Al LaValley and Barry P. Scherr (eds), *Eisenstein at 100: A Reconsideration* (New Brunswick: Rutgers University Press, 2001), 227–52.
13. Blazhennïy Ioann, *Fortepiannoye yevangeliye Marii Veniaminovnï Yudinoy* (Kiev: Mir Sofii, 2010).
14. Ibid., 74–6.
15. Solomon Volkov, *Testimony: The Memoirs of Dmitri Shostakovich*, trans. Antonina W. Bouis (London: Hamish Hamilton, 1979), 148–9. Daniil Granin believes that he heard the same story from Shostakovich himself, but it is still within the bounds of possibility that he had first read it in *Testimony*. Daniil Granin, Listopad http://magazines.russ.ru/zvezda/2008/1/gra6.html (accessed 5 February 2015).
16. 'Beifallssturm um eine sowjetische Pianistin. Stalinpreisträgerin Maria Judina im "Haus der Kultur der Sowjetunion" ', *Tägliche Rundschau* (1 August 1950). The reference comes from Gabriele

Leupold's piece that appears on a Russian website: Gabriele Loypold, 'Yudinu v Germaniyu!', www. owl.ru/avangard/myslitelnitsaur.html (accessed 25 September 2014).

17. Aleksandr Minkin, 'Kabala svyatosh: Razgovorï s Yuriyem Petrovichem Lyubimovïm 25 let nazad', http://echo.msk.ru/blog/minkin/1417896-echo (accessed 9 February 2015).

18. Oleg Khlevniuk, *Khozyain: Stalin i utverzhdeniye stalinskoy diktaturï* (Moscow: ROSSPEN, 2010), 200.

Chapter 1: How It All Worked

1. N. S. Khrushchev, 'O kul'te lichnosti i yego posledstviyakh' [speech at the 20th Party Congress on 25 February 1956], first published in *Izvestiya TsK KPSS* (1989), no. 3, 128–66 (159).

2. This story passed through several pairs of hands. Alexander Poskrebyshev, Stalin's chief secretary, allegedly told it to Lev Kandinov, a writer who was an aide to the Tajik prime minister, when they met at a VIP retreat near Moscow in 1965. Three decades later, Kandinov, who had ended up in New Jersey, passed it on to the journalist Raisa Silver, who published it in an émigré newspaper. The story lacks corroboration from any other source; even so, it is unlikely that any evidence to the contrary will emerge. Raisa Silver, 'Istorii novogodney nochi', *Russkiy bazar* (1998), no. 1/351, http://russian-bazaar.com/en/content/1998.htm (accessed 28 March 2013). Reprinted in V. F. Svin'yin and K. A. Oseyev (eds), *Stalinskiye premii: dve storonï odnoy medali. Sbornik dokumentov i khudozhestvenno–publitsisticheskikh materialov* (Novosibirsk: Svin'yin i sïnov'ya, 2007), 57–60.

3. This is in keeping with the concept of the gift economy under Stalin, where labour itself could be viewed as a gift to the leader. See Jeffrey Brooks, *Thank You, Comrade Stalin!: Soviet Public Culture from Revolution to Cold War* (Princeton: Princeton University Press, 2000; also Nikolai Ssorin-Chaikov, 'On Heterochrony: Birthday Gifts to Stalin, 1949', *Journal of the Royal Anthropological Institute* (2006), vol. 12, issue 2, 355–75.

4. Zakharov's telegram to Stalin of 18 April 1942. RGANI, fond 3, op. 53a, ye. kh. 5, l. 181.

5. RGANI, fond 3, op. 53a, ye. kh. 1, l. 31.

6. Among the most famous prizewinners were geneticist Nikolai Vavilov, engineer Vladimir Shukhov and chemist Nikolai Zelinsky.

7. 'Spravka o premii im. V. I. Lenina' (Report on the Lenin Prize). RGASPI, fond 82 (Molotov), op. 2, ye. kh. 468, l. 5.

8. From 1942 onwards, the top prize for scientists was set at 200,000 roubles.

9. Aleksandr Il'yukhov, *Kak platili bol'sheviki: Politika sovetskoy vlasti v sfere oplatï truda v 1917–1941 gg.* (Moscow: ROSSPEN, 2010), 369.

10. This rumour comes from Samuil Samosud's conversation with Lev Mekhlis in 1936 (Mekhlis was then *Pravda*'s editor in chief), RGASPI, fond 82, op. 2, ye. kh. 951, l. 10. Although the figures may well be exaggerated, Kozlovsky's unique status in the Soviet artistic hierarchy is beyond doubt.

11. From a report by a commission created by the Politburo to investigate 'serious mishandling of the remuneration of authors'. RGASPI, fond 82, op. 2, ye. kh. 949, ll. 133–9.

12. Ibid., l. 135.

13. Ibid., l. 136.

14. Report by P. Daniel'yants (deputy director of the Gorky Film Studio) to Agitprop, RGASPI, fond 17, op. 132, ye. kh. 251, l. 66. The episode took place in 1947, by which time Bogolyubov was already four-times laureate (he would receive six Stalin Prizes altogether), and Samoilov had been awarded three times.

15. Letter from Bespalov to Shepilov of 13 April 1949. RGASPI, fond 17, op. 132, ye. kh. 238, ll. 39–40.

16. Nikolai Aseyev proposed Pasternak for a first-class prize for both original poetry and translations, but Khrapchenko took advantage of KSP members' uncertainty over the eligibility of literary translations, and simply blocked the nomination. Plenary session of 1 March 1943. RGALI, fond 2073, op.1, ye. kh. 7, ll. 69 and 70v.

17. Letter from Pasternak to Shcherbakov of 16 July 1943. RGASPI, fond 17, op. 125, ye. kh. 212, l. 73.

18. Pasternak's letter to Fadeyev, end of June 1947, in N. Dikushina (ed.), *Aleksandr Fadeyev: Pis'ma i dokumentï iz fondov Rossiyskogo Gosudarstvennogo Arkhiva literaturï i iskusstva* (Moscow: Izdatel'stvo Literaturnogo Instituta im. A. M. Gor'kogo, 2001), 55.

19. Pasternak's letter to Fadeyev of 20 July 1949, ibid., 267–8.

20. Vasil' Minko, *Ne nazïvaya familiy* (Moscow: Gosudarstvennoye izdatel'stvo 'Iskusstvo', 1953), 95–8. This play, which was a great hit in Moscow, was itself in the running for a Stalin Prize, although already after Stalin's death. At that point, it was seen as a perfect response to Molotov's appeal to nurture Soviet satire, which he made in his speech at the 19th Party Congress in October 1952. See more on this in Chapter 11.

21. Bokshanskaya herself was a figure of some note: Stanislavsky dictated his memoirs to her; she was Mikhail Bulgakov's sister-in-law, and she inspired the character of Poliksena Toropetskaya in

Bulgakov's *Theatrical Novel*. See V. Vilenkin's entry on her on the theatre's history pages, www.mxat. ru/history/persons/bokshanskaya (accessed 5 June 2013).

22. The complete list, and also the changes to the membership over the subsequent years, can be found in Appendix VIII.

23. Gurvich lost his seat as early as 1943, in the first reshuffle; Aseyev lost his in the second, in September 1944. Dovzhenko's exit was more dramatic: a special resolution was passed on 25 February 1944 to remove him for 'crude political errors of an anti-Lenin nature' in his works. GARF, fond 5446, op. 46, ye. kh. 2437, ll. 2–3.

24. The killing of Mikhoels, who was chairman of the Jewish Anti-Fascist Committee and the recognized leader of the Soviet Union's Jewish community, anticipated the 'anti-cosmopolitanism' campaign which was unleashed a year later, at the beginning of 1949.

25. The Music Section of the Artistic Council was created in March 1939 and included the composers Hajibeyov, Glière, Myaskovsky and Dunayevsky, the conductor Samosud (all five later became members of the KSP), as well as the opera singer Barsova (not in the KSP). The personnel of the visual arts and theatre sections of the same council also reappeared on the KSP membership lists. Information on the Artistic Council is supplied in Vladimir Nevezhin, *Zastol'ya Iosifa Stalina: Bol'shiye kremlevskiye priyomï*, vol. 1 (Moscow: Novïy khronograf, 2011), 215.

26. Plenary session of 16 September 1940. RGALI, fond 2073, op. 1, ye. kh. 1, l. 22.

27. Plenary session of 26 November 1940. Ibid., l. 262.

28. Ibid., l. 266.

29. Nemirovich-Danchenko's speech at the award ceremony on 21 April 1941. RGALI, fond 2073, op. 1, ye. kh. 2, ll. 269–71.

30. RGANI, fond 3, op. 53a, ye. kh. 1, l. 7. The statutes were published in *Pravda* (2 April 1940).

31. From 1939 to 1948, it was called the Administration for Agitation and Propaganda of the Communist Party CC (*Upravleniye agitatsii i propagandï TsK VKP(b)*; from 1948 to 1956, it was retitled a 'Department' instead of an 'Administration' (*Otdel agitatsii i propagandï TsK VKP(b)–KPSS*).

32. The relevant published volume of Politburo agendas contains references only to those meetings on the Stalin Prize that altered rules and regulations, but not those that simply discussed the allocation of awards. See G. M. Adibekov, K. M. Anderson and L. A. Rogovaya (eds), *Politbyuro TsK RKP(b) – VKP(b): Povestki dnya zasedaniy. Katalog*, vol. 3 (Moscow: ROSSPEN, 2001).

33. Khrapchenko was married to Tamara Tsytovich (1907–92).

34. Fadeyev's diary entry of 16 March 1937, in Dikushina, *Aleksandr Fadeyev*, 55. Quoted in Benedict Sarnov, *Stalin i pisateli*, vol. 4 (Moscow: EKSMO, 2011), 263.

35. Chukovsky's diary entry of 11 November 1962; see K. Chukovskiy, *Dnevnik*, vol. 2 (1930–1969), ed. Ye. Chukovskaya (Moscow: PROZAiK, 2012), 351.

36. There is a copy of Khrapchenko's letter to Shcherbakov (1943) that contains Shcherbakov's markings in RGASPI, fond 17, op. 125, ye. kh. 127, ll. 25–8. Andreyev's copy of the same letter is in the same document, ll. 116–19. Among their collective decisions was the second-class award to Vladimir Zakharov, composer of songs for the Pyatnitsky Choir and its director (see more on this in Chapter 8).

37. More on Aleksandrov's downfall in Alexei Kojevnikov, 'Games of Stalinist Democracy: Ideological Discussions in Soviet Sciences, 1947–52', in Sheila Fitzpatrick (ed.), *Stalinism: New Directions: A Reader* (London and New York: Routledge, 2000), 142–75.

38. Letter from Kaftanov and Khrapchenko to Molotov of 12 June 1944, with Molotov's resolution. RGASPI, fond 82 (Molotov), op. 2, ye. kh. 458, l. 14.

39. Letter to Stalin from the Politburo Commission (Malenkov, Zhdanov, Tikhonov, Aleksandrov, Bolshakov, Khrapchenko). RGANI, fond 3, op. 53a, ye. kh. 9, ll. 2–7.

40. Khrushchev, in his memoirs, tells us that 'Zhdanov was a jolly fellow. Once he had a few drinks with us, and he'd already had a few before. In short, he climbed onto the stage and drew out an accordion [*dvukhryadnuyu garmon'*]. He could play the accordion and the piano well enough. I liked that. Kaganovich, however, spoke of him with contempt: "A simple accordion player" [*garmonist*]. But I didn't see anything wrong with that. I'd tried to learn the accordion myself, and I had my own instrument. I never played well, but he did play well. Later, when Zhdanov started circulating in the Politburo milieu, it was obvious that Stalin gave him every attention. We started to hear much more of Kaganovich's grumbling about Zhdanov, and he would often say sarcastically: "You don't need any great capacity for work here [in the Politburo], but what you do need is the gift of the gab, to be able to crack a few good jokes, and make up scurrilous songs [*pet' chastushki*]; then you'll do very well for yourself." I must admit that when I got to see Zhdanov up close, working alongside him, I began to agree with Kaganovich.' N. S. Khrushchev, *Vremya, lyudi, vlast'*, vol. 1 (Moscow: Moskovskiye novosti, 1999), 109–10.

41. Draft resolution of the CC on the creation of the Politburo Commission, 3 June 1946. RGASPI, fond 17, op. 163, ye. kh.1482, l. 209; CC Resolution of 30 April 1947. RGASPI, fond 17, op. 163, ye. kh. 1498, l. 46.
42. Dmitriy Shepilov, *Neprimknuvshiy* (Moscow: Vagrius, 2001), 108.
43. Konstantin Simonov, *Glazami cheloveka moyego pokoleniya: razmïshleniya o I.V. Staline* (Moscow: Kniga, 1990), 137.
44. Ibid., 158.
45. Here is the complete list of PB members and CC secretaries present: 1) Stalin; 2) Molotov; 3) Mikoyan; 4) Beria; 5) Malenkov; 6) Kaganovich; 7) Voroshilov; 8) Kosygin; 9) Shvernik; 10) Suslov; 11) Popov; 12) Ponomarenko. RGANI, fond 3, op. 53a, ye. kh. 16, l. 54.
46. Tikhonov was Fadeyev's deputy at the KSP, while Simonov and Sofronov were his deputies in the Writers' Union. See Fadeyev's letter to Stalin written five days before the Politburo meeting, on 14 March 1949. RGASPI, fond 82, op. 2, ye. kh. 458, l. 57. Fadeyev's preparations for the Politburo meeting were of some importance: his biographer says that he would have a private discussion of the nominations with Stalin one or two days prior to the meeting. See Dmitriy Buzin, *Aleksandr Fadeyev: Taynï zhizni i smerti* (Moscow: Algoritm, 2008), 234–5.
47. Shepilov, *Neprimknuvshiy*, 108–9.
48. Compared with the previous meeting (note 45), Ponomarenko was absent while Bulganin was present. Also, the list includes Stalin's secretary Poskrebyshev and a certain Yagmadjanov, whose identity I have not managed to establish. RGANI, fond 3, op. 53a, l. 17.
49. In 1950 (Politburo meeting on 6 March) we find the same principle of selection for invitees: Lebedev and his deputy Nikolai Bespalov (Committee for Arts Affairs), Fadeyev and his deputy Kemenov (KSP); once again, Fadeyev's literary guard from the Union of Writers: Simonov, Sofronov and Surkov; Bolshakov (Cinema), Khrennikov (Music), Mordvinov (Architecture), and Kruzhkov (Agitprop). This time, there were only five Politburo members present: Stalin, Molotov, Malenkov, Bulganin and Khrushchev. RGANI, fond 3, op. 53a, ye. kh. 22, l. 1.
    In 1951 the discussion was split into two meetings, on 19 February and 9 March. The first was devoted to literature and cinema and attended by twelve Politburo members and candidates and two CC secretaries (Ponomarenko and Suslov). The invitees were Lebedev (CAA), Tikhonov and Kemenov (KSP), Surkov (Union of Writers), Bolshakov (Cinema), Nesmeyanov (Head of Moscow University and the KSP for sciences), Stoletov (minister for higher education), and Kruzhkov and Tarasov from Agitprop. Fadeyev and Simonov were invited but could not attend. RGANI, fond 3, op. 53a, ye. kh. 24, l. 87. It is possible (if unlikely) that Stalin was absent from the meeting of 9 March, as his name does not appear on the list. We have ten PB members and two CC members plus fourteen invitees here: once again Lebedev and Bespalov, Fadeyev, Tikhonov and Kemenov, Nesmeyanov and Stoletov, Kruzhkov and Tarasov (Agitprop), then Bolshakov (Cinema), Khrennikov (Music), Gerasimov (Visual Arts), and Alexei Popov (Drama Theatre). RGANI, fond 3, op. 53a, ye. kh. 27, l. 67.
    The last meeting of this kind, on 25 February 1952, was the most populous: twelve Politburo members and seventeen invitees, including Shkiryatov from the CC presidium, chief editor of *Pravda* Leonid Ilyichev and many familiar names: Bespalov who now became the minister (Committee for Arts Affairs), Tikhonov and Kemenov (KSP; Fadeyev ill?), Nesmeyanov and Stoletov, Kruzhkov and Tarasov, and then Bolshakov, Khrennikov, Mordvinov (Architecture), Gerasimov (Painting) and Simonov (Writers). RGANI, fond 3, op. 53a, ye. kh. 30, l. 78. Simonov tells us that Stalin, unusually, delegated the chairing of this meeting to Malenkov, who was unnerved by the task (Simonov, *Glazami cheloveka*, 176). Some unfinished business was left in Painting and Drawing, which was taken up on 3 March with fewer invitees. RGANI, fond 3, op. 53a, ye. kh. 32, l. 7.
50. Simonov, *Glazami cheloveka*, 159.
51. Simonov provides a story about one such meeting of the Central Committee and select members of the intelligentsia. The writer Orest Maltsev was proposed for a prize. Stalin began objecting vigorously to the presentation of the writer's name on the prize list. Beside the writer's familiar literary pseudonym, 'Maltsev', was his original family name 'Rovinsky' (see Chapter 7, fig. 15). Stalin claimed that this was a clear anti-Semitic gesture, needlessly advertising Maltsev's Jewish roots. Simonov went on to interpret this as a façade for the benefit of the invited guests, to impress on them the idea that Stalin was rigorously opposed to all manifestations of anti-Semitism. Whether or not the outburst was sincere, the story takes a bizarre turn, as Simonov mentions, because, in spite of the Jewish-sounding surname 'Rovinsky', the writer wasn't actually Jewish anyway. Ibid., 288–90.
52. Shepilov, *Neprimknuvshiy*, 109.
53. Simonov, *Glazami cheloveka*, 145–6.

54. Ibid., 146.
55. Shepilov, *Neprimknuvshiy*, 110. It is most likely that Shepilov is talking here about the Politburo meeting in 1949, and the novella in question was *Light in Koordi* (*Valgus Koordis*) by the Estonian writer Hans Leberecht; this novella was indeed published in the December 1948 issue of *Zvezda*, while Leberecht's name appears several times in Stalin's marginalia. If I am right, then Shepilov was mistaken about the type of prize, since Leberecht received a third-class prize, not a second.
56. Ibid., 110–20.
57. Simonov, *Glazami cheloveka*, 157–8.
58. Ibid., 183.
59. Ibid., 171. The novel in question was *Ivan Ivanovich*, by Antonina Koptyayeva; it received a third-class prize in 1950.
60. A. I. Kokarev (ed.), *Tikhon Nikolayevich Khrennikov: K 100-letiyu so dnya rozhdeniya (stat'yi i vospominaniya)* (Moscow: Kompozitor, 2013), 168–9. Boris Troyanovsky (1881–1953) was a soloist in the Great-Russian Orchestra founded by Vasily Andreyev (1891–1918).
61. Most of these are held in RGANI, fond 3, op. 53a.
62. Fadeyev's letter to the CC Secretariat (Stalin, Malenkov, Zhdanov, Kuznetsov and Popov) of 12 April 1946. RGASPI, fond 17, op. 125, ye. kh. 399, ll. 1–11.
63. Fadeyev's letter to the CC of 17 April 1946, ibid., ll. 67–9.
64. RGASPI, fond 17, op. 117, ye. kh. 689, l. 22; also fond 17, op. 125, ye. kh. 400, ll. 33–4. Fadeyev's proposal was discussed by the CC Secretariat, and then handed over to Agitprop and the Committee for Arts Affairs, so that they could work out the details and report to the Politburo.
65. In Music, for example, Sofronitsky and Maldybaev lost their membership because they never attended; Samosud lost his after he was dismissed from his post at the Bolshoi; most curiously, Dunayevsky was removed for reasons of insufficient authority – a rather opaque formulation that might have had something to do with the genre of popular music that he represented. Letter from the CC Secretariat to Stalin [January 1947]. RGASPI, fond 17, op. 125, ye. kh. 400, l. 34.
66. Aleksandrov's handwritten note of 6 January 1947. RGASPI, fond 17, op. 117, ye. kh. 689, l. 23.
67. See Chapter 10.
68. Fadeyev's letter to Stalin of 14 March 1949. RGASPI, fond 82 (Molotov), op. 2, ye. kh. 458, l. 55.
69. Ibid., l. 57.
70. Plenary session of 4 January 1950. RGALI, fond 2073, op. 1, ye. kh. 35, ll. 237–9.
71. Extraordinary plenary session of 11 May 1950. RGALI, fond 2073, op. 1, ye. kh. 36, l. 244.
72. Ibid., ll. 239–40.
73. Ibid.
74. Extraordinary plenary session of 5 June 1950. RGALI, fond 2073, op. 1, ye. kh. 40, l. 2.
75. *Jurgai's Shield* was set in the Caucasus during the Second World War. A flimsy plotline was stitched around concert numbers featuring well-loved Georgian artistes.
76. Plenary session of 5 June 1950. RGALI, fond 2073, op. 1, ye. kh. 40, l. 4.
77. Ibid., l. 7.
78. G. B. Mar'yamov, *Kremlevskiy tsenzor: Stalin smotrit kino* (Moscow: Konfederatsiya Soyuzov Kinematografistov 'Kinotsentr', 1992), 103.
79. Plenary session of 5 May 1951. RGALI, fond 2073, op. 1, ye. kh. 47, l. 50.
80. RGANI, fond 3, op. 53a, ye. kh. 30, l. 42.
81. Entry of 15 March 1952. Typescript of Goldenweiser's Diaries, VMOMK, fond 162, notebook 33, l. 119.
82. Kruzhkov's report on the work of the KSP. RGASPI, fond 17, op. 133, ye. kh. 387, ll. 21–8.
83. Letter from Kruzhkov and Tarasov to Malenkov of 5 January 1952. RGASPI, fond 17, op.133, ye. kh. 345, ll. 3–5.
84. Fadeyev's letter to Suslov of 18 July 1952. RGASPI, fond 17, op.133, ye. kh. 345, ll. 6–8.

Chapter 2: The First Year

1. Solomon Volkov, *Shostakovich and Stalin: The Extraordinary Relationship between the Great Composer and the Brutal Dictator*, trans. Antonina W. Bouis (London: Little, Brown, 2004), 199.
2. V. Lebedev, S. Mel'chin, A. Stepanov and A. Chernev (eds), 'Proizvedeniye Shostakovicha – gluboko zapadnoy oriyentatsii', *Istochnik: Vestnik Arkhiva Prezidenta Rossiyskoy Federatsii* (Moscow, 1995), no. 5, 156–9.
3. Volkov's interview with Irina Chaykovskaya. Solomon Volkov, 'Umer on velikim sovetskim kompozitorom', *Chastniy korrespondent* (1 October 2011), www.chaskor.ru/article/solomon_volkov_umer_on_velikim_sovetskim_kompozitorom_25043 (accessed 9 January 2013). Volkov expresses similar ideas in his conversation with Anatoly Rybakov, 'Razgovor s Anatoliyem

Rïbakovïm', *Druzhba narodov*, no. 1 (2000), p. 10, http://shevkunenko.ru/rybakov/about/16info_9. htm (accessed 9 January 2013).

4. See on this M. Frolova-Walker and J. Walker, *Music and Soviet Power, 1917–32* (Woodbridge: The Boydell Press, 2012), 262–3.

5. Goldenweiser notes this in his diary entry of 12 November 1940, Typescript of Goldenweiser's Diaries, VMOMK, fond 162, notebook 17, l. 73.

6. Plenary session of 21 November 1940. RGALI, fond 2073, op. 1, ye. kh. 1, ll. 178–9.

7. Ibid., l. 189.

8. Ibid., l. 185.

9. Plenary session of 11 November 1940. RGALI, fond 2073, op. 1, ye. kh. 1, l. 32.

10. Plenary session of 24 November 1940. RGALI, fond 2073, op. 1, ye. kh. 1, l. 254.

11. The KSP's voting system was a secret ballot in which each committee member present was supplied with a list of all the nominations. There was no restriction on the number of works each member could vote for. This system made no distinction between enthusiastic and merely dutiful endorsement, and thus had a built-in bias towards consensus.

12. Report on the KSP's work. GARF, fond 5446, op. 25a, ye. kh 769, ll. 224–33 (233v).

13. A. Shaverdyan, 'Kvintet D. Shostakovicha', *Pravda* (25 November 1940), no. 327, 4. This article was supported by a long review of the piece, again entirely positive, in the 1 December edition of *Sovetskoye iskusstvo* itself. See D. Zhitomirskiy, 'Kvintet Shostakovicha', *Sovetskoye iskusstvo*, no. 61 (1 December 1940), 2.

14. Plenary session of 26 November 1940. RGALI, fond 2073, op. 1, ye. kh. 1, l. 269.

15. Plenary session of 18 November 1940. RGALI, fond 2073, op. 1, ye. kh. 1, l. 110.

16. Ibid., ll. 120–21 and 127.

17. Gerasimov's separate written report on Fine Arts nominations of 10 November 1940. RGALI, fond 2073, op. 1, ye. kh. 4, l. 22.

18. As Nemirovich-Danchenko reported to the KSP at the second plenary session, on 11 November 1940. RGALI, fond 2073, op.1, ye. kh. 1, l. 32.

19. Khrapchenko's letter to Stalin and Molotov of 30 November 1940. GARF, fond 5446, op. 25a, ye. kh. 769, ll. 177–9.

20. Kukryniksy was a conflation of three names, Mikhail Kupriyanov, Porfiry Krylov and Nikolai Sokolov. The artists collaborated on many political cartoons and posters, occasionally venturing into producing more 'high-art' paintings.

21. Plenary session of 13 November 1940. RGALI, fond 2073, op. 1, ye. kh. 1, l. 94.

22. At the meeting on 9 December 1940, Khrapchenko was instructed to submit his proposals by 15 December. GARF, fond 5446, op. 25a, ye. kh. 769.

23. GARF, fond 5446, op. 25a, ye. kh. 769, ll. 33–4.

24. Plenary session of 3 January 1941. RGALI, fond 2073, op. 1, ye. kh. 2, ll. 147–8.

25. Note Myaskovsky's private thoughts of Shaporin's Cantata: 'a strange impression: everything is superlative – themes, narrative character, but it doesn't move one almost at all'. See O. P. Lamm, *Stranitsï tvorcheskoy biografii Myaskovskogo* (Moscow: Sovetskiy kompozitor, 1989), 276.

26. Plenary session of 30 December 1940. RGALI, fond 2073, op. 1, ye. kh. 2, l. 43.

27. Ibid., l. 42.

28. Khrapchenko's letter to Stalin and Molotov of 6 January 1941. RGALI, fond 962 (Komitet po delam iskusstv), op. 10, ye. kh. 44, ll. 38–43.

29. Among those dissatisfied with Ballot 2 was Dunayevsky, who complained to Khrapchenko both about the procedure and about the results (he was particularly unhappy that his own genre, the mass song, was effectively being excluded from serious consideration). His letter of 6 January 1941 was published in V. V. Perkhin (ed.), *Deyateli russkogo iskusstva i M.B. Khrapchenko, predsedatel' Vsesoyuznogo komiteta po delam iskusstv: aprel' 1939–yanvar' 1948: svod pisem* (Moscow: Nauka, 2007), 580–81.

30. Grinberg's letter to Stalin of 7 January 1941. RGASPI, fond 82 (Molotov), op. 2, ye. kh. 950, ll. 104–7.

31. RGALI, fond 962, op. 10, ye. kh. 136, ll. 23–6.

32. Grinberg's letter to Stalin, ll. 104–7 (104).

33. Ibid., ll. 104–5.

34. Cf. note 13.

35. Valerian Bogdanov-Berezovsky's position paper at the plenary session of the Composers' Union in May 1941 contains the following passage: 'Stylistic variety, as well as generic variety, has wonderfully enriched Soviet symphonic music. It is sufficient to point to the completely legitimate co-existence of such [disparate] works as Shaporin's First Symphony, with its romanticization of the traditions of Kuchka symphonism and *pesennost'* [songfulness], and, say, Starokadomsky's Concerto grosso, whose three movements – an overture, passacaglia and toccata – establish a style

characteristic of contemporary Western contrapuntalists, a style that modernizes the old masters of the 17th and 18th centuries.' RGALI, fond 2077 (Union of Soviet Composer), op. 1, ye. kh. 42, l. 72. For an explanation of 'Kuchka', see note 47.

36. Grinberg's letter to Stalin, l. 105.
37. Prokofiev did not give up when his Cantata was not performed for the twentieth anniversary of the October Revolution, for which it was written. He continued to send letters to the arts ministry throughout 1938, including to Grinberg personally. See, for example, the letter to Grinberg of 10 August 1938, in which Prokofiev once again requests that rehearsals for the Cantata should begin immediately. RGALI, fond 1929 (Prokofiev), op. 2, ye. kh. 327, l. 6. I thank Vladimir Orlov for providing me with this reference.
38. Grinberg's letter to Stalin, ll. 105–6.
39. Stalin's positive impressions of the opera were expressed in a meeting with the production team, which was publicized by TASS; see 'Beseda tovarishchey Stalina i Molotova s avtorami opernogo spektaklya "Tikhiy Don"', Pravda (20 January 1936), 1.
40. RAPM (Russian Association of Proletarian Musicians, 1923–32) was an organization of musicians who sought for an alternative both to the elite music culture of the opera houses and concert halls, and also to much popular music, whether home-grown or imported from the West. Their favoured genre was the rousing mass song. In 1929–32, RAPM, with some (arm's-length) support from the Party, became very powerful, temporarily sidelining many prominent musical figures, especially members of the organization ASM (Association for Contemporary Music).
41. Grinberg's letter to Stalin, l. 107.
42. Diary entry of 18 February 1941. Lamm, Stranitsi, 279.
43. Diary entry of 15 May 1941. Ibid., 280.
44. The main document here is Khrapchenko's letter to Stalin and Molotov of 16 January 1941, in two copies, with handwritten changes and comments in different hands. RGALI, fond 962, op. 10, ye. kh. 44, ll. 1–18a. I thank Kevin Bartig for introducing me to this document.
45. GARF, fond 5446, op. 25a, ye. kh. 769, l. 175.
46. Khrapchenko's letter to Stalin and Molotov of 8 March 1941. GARF, fond 5446, op. 25a, ye. kh. 769, ll. 192–4 (193).
47. Khrapchenko's letter to Stalin and Molotov of 16 March 1941. RGALI, fond 962, op. 10, ye. kh. 44, l. 5.
48. The Mighty Handful (Moguchaya kuchka, also known as The Five) was a group of composers whose members came together in the 1860s under the leadership of the arts and music critic Vladimir Stasov and composer Mily Balakirev. The four other composers were Modest Musorgsky, Nikolai Rimsky-Korsakov, Alexander Borodin and César Cui. For at least a decade, they espoused common ideas of musical nationalism.
49. Myaskovsky's excerpts from Diary, entries for 4 July 1940 and 15 May 1941. RGALI, fond 2040, op. 1, ye. kh. 65, ll. 52v and 54.
50. Khrapchenko turned against Shostakovich nominations from the Eighth Symphony onwards, insisting that the government should accept neither the Eighth nor the Ninth, despite the positive vote of the KSP. The Eighth and the Ninth represented to him the undesirable, individualistic Shostakovich, while he recognized the broader appeal of the Quintet and the Seventh Symphony, which he commended. See, for example, the discussions transcript in RGALI, fond 2073, op. 1, ye. kh. 9, l. 221.

Chapter 3: Prokofiev: The Unlikely Champion

1. Diary entry of 4 June 1940. RGALI, fond 2040, op. 1, ye. kh. 65, l. 52v.
2. Vyshinsky's letter to Molotov. RGASPI, fond 82 (Molotov), op. 2, ye. kh. 950, l. 99. This was not an overreaction: indeed Hitler and Goebbels seem to have monitored the Soviet press for any sign of anti-German sentiment and reacted strongly to every suspected violation of friendly relations. V. A. Nevezhin, 'Yesli zavtra v pokhod': Podgotovka k voyne i ideologicheskaya propaganda v 30-kh–40kh godakh (Moscow: Yauza, Eksmo, 2007), 262–4.
3. The draft of Myaskovsky's letter (7 September 1940), in which he nominates the opera, is preserved in RGALI, fond 2040, op. 1, ye. kh. 62, ll. 35 and 35v.
4. Plenary session of 21 November 1940. RGALI, fond 2073, op. 1, ye. kh. 1, l. 174.
5. I. Nest'yev, ' "Semyon Kotko" S. Prokof'yeva', Sovetskaya muzïka (1940), no. 9, 7–26; L. Khristiansen, 'Voplotit' chuvstva sovetskogo cheloveka', Sovetskaya muzïka (1940), no. 10, 25–6, among others.
6. Cf. note 4, l. 190.
7. Plenary session of 3 January 1941. RGALI, fond 2073, op. 1, ye. kh. 2, ll. 153–4.
8. Ibid., l. 155.
9. Ibid., l. 156.
10. See more on this slogan in Chapter 7, note 2.
11. Plenary meeting in Tbilisi, 19 February 1942. RGALI, fond 2073, op. 1, ye. kh. 6, ll. 59–60.

12. Ibid., l. 60.
13. Ibid., ll. 60–61.
14. Ibid., l. 61.
15. Ibid., ll. 61–2.
16. Ibid., l. 71.
17. Ibid., l. 70.
18. This is particularly obvious from remarks by Mikhoels at the plenary session of 11 November 1940. RGALI, fond 2073, op. 1, ye. kh. 1, ll. 60, 228.
19. Natal'ya Gromova, *Raspad: Sud'ba sovetskogo kritika: 40-ye–50-ye godï* (Moscow: Ellis Lak, 2009).
20. Plenary meeting in Tbilisi, 19 February 1942. RGALI, fond 2073, op. 1, ye. kh. 6, ll. 66–7.
21. Ibid., l. 69.
22. GARF, fond 5446, op. 43a, ye. kh. 4499, ll. 12–19.
23. Susan Lockwood Smith, *Soviet Arts Policy, Folk Music, and National Identity: The Piatnitskii State Russian Folk Choir, 1927–1945*. PhD thesis, University of Minnesota, 1997, 183.
24. I would suggest that the abundance of Georgian works on the 1942 award list has more to do with the KSP's residence in Tbilisi than with the paying of 'feudal homage' to Stalin, which is how his daughter Svetlana Alliluyeva described ritual gestures from fellow Georgians. Alliluyeva, *Twenty Letters to a Friend*, trans. P. Johnson (London: Hutchinson & Co., 1967), 210–11.
25. Irina Medvedeva, 'Istoriya prokof'yevskogo aftografa, ili GURK v deystvii', *Sergey Prokof'yev, k 110-letiyu so dnya rozhdeniya: Pis'ma, vospominaniya, stat'yi* (Moscow: Gosudarstvennïy tsentral'nïy muzey imeni M. I. Glinki, 2001), 216–39 (218–19).
26. Nemirovich-Danchenko's letter to Bokshanskaya of 17 February 1942. Vl. I. Nemirovich-Danchenko, *Tvorcheskoye naslediye: Pis'ma, 1938–43*, ed. I. N. Solov'yov, vol. 4 (Moscow: Moskovskiy Khudozhestvennïy Teatr, 2003), 113.
27. Ibid., 220.
28. Ibid., 221–2.
29. Both Khrapchenko's and Shlifshteyn's letters are published in full in Medvedeva, 'Istoriya prokof'yevskogo aftografa', 223–6.
30. Prokofiev was still an evacuee from Moscow at the time. Since he had left his family two years previously, he had no flat of his own in Moscow. The flat, in the end, did not live up to Prokofiev's expectations. See Nelli Kravets, *Ryadom s velikimi: Atovmyan i yego vremya* (Moscow: GITIS, 2012), 100 and 106.
31. T. Tsïtovich, 'Novïy balet S. Prokof'yeva', *Sovetskoye iskusstvo* (30 November 1945), no. 48, 3.
32. Letter to Myaskovsky of 4 April 1943, in S. S. Prokof'yev and N. Ya. Myaskovskiy, *Perepiska* (Moscow: Sovetskiy kompozitor, 1977), 466.
33. 'Novïye proizvedeniya sovetskikh kompozitorov', *Literatura i iskusstvo* (16 January 1943), no. 2, 1.
34. Bruno Monsenzhon [Monsaingeon] (ed.), *Rikhter: Dialogi, dnevniki* (Moscow: Klassika–XXI, 2007), 75.
35. Plenary session of 1 March 1943. RGALI, fond 2073, op. 1, ye. kh. 7, l. 76.
36. Shcherbakov's(?) letter to Stalin of 15 March 1943. RGASPI, fond 17, op. 125, ye. kh. 127, ll. 22–5.
37. Levon Atovmyan (1901–73) was an important figure in Soviet music, particularly during his years as the director of Muzfond, the financial division of the Composers' Union (1939–48). He was close to both Prokofiev and Shostakovich, routinely making arrangements of their works for piano and compiling suites out of their larger works.
38. Kravets, *Ryadom s velikimi*, 87. All of the listed candidates were confirmed for the prizes.
39. Ibid, 88.
40. Ibid., 89.
41. Simon Morrison, *The People's Artist: Prokofiev's Soviet Years* (Oxford: Oxford University Press, 2009), 16–19.
42. RGASPI, fond 82, op. 2, ye. kh. 956, ll. 34–5. In the same cohort were composers Vasilenko, Shaporin, Shcherbachev and Anatoly Aleksandrov (not to be confused with the future author of the national anthem). In the same letter a higher order is requested for Myaskovsky, the Order of Lenin.
43. He was accompanied by Richter, who did not mark out the performance as a failure, and went on to perform the Sonata with Kharkovsky several times, enjoying great public success. Monsenzhon, *Rikhter*, 77.
44. Plenary meeting of 16 March 1944. RGALI, fond 2073, op. 1, ye. kh. 9, ll. 146–7.
45. Plenary meeting of 24 March 1944. RGALI, fond 2073, op. 1, ye. kh. 9, l. 228.
46. Letter to the Council of Ministers of 31 March 1944, signed by Myaskovsky, Shaporin, Samosud, Glière and Moskvin. GARF, fond 5446, op. 48, ye. kh. 2195, l. 40.
47. Plenary session of 3 April 1945. RGALI, fond 2073, op. 1, ye. kh. 11, l. 198.
48. I. Nest'yev, 'Sonatnaya triada', *Sovetskoye iskusstvo*, no. 11 (15 March 1945), 2.
49. In this round of awards, approval of the nominations by the higher bodies took a particularly long time: the KSP had voted on 9 April 1945, but the final decision was published only on 26 January

1946. Perhaps the key to the delay is contained in the Politburo Commission's letter to Stalin of 23 June 1945 [?], reporting on a decision to wait until the end of the year with the arts and literature nominations (although the final film list was ready), as the most recent works, the 1944 batch, had not yet been given enough time to succeed or fail in making an impression on the public. RGASPI, fond 77, op. 3, ye. kh. 28, ll. 19–34 (19).

50. Plenary session of 29 March 1945. RGALI, fond 2073, op. 1, ye. kh. 11, l. 158.
51. See more on this in David Brandenberger, *National Bolshevism: Stalinist Mass Culture and the Formation of Modern Russian National Identity, 1931-56* (Cambridge, MA and London: Harvard University Press, 2002), 57–8.
52. Ibid., ll. 150–58. See also Joan Neuberger, 'The Politics of Bewilderment: Eisenstein's "Ivan the Terrible" in 1945', in Al LaValley and Barry P. Scherr (eds), *Eisenstein at 100: A Reconsideration* (New Brunswick, NJ: Rutgers University Press, 2001), 227–52.
53. Diary entry of 10 January 1945. RGALI, fond 2040, op. 1, ye. kh. 65, l. 75v.
54. Politburo Commission's letter to Stalin of 23 June 1945[?]. RGASPI, fond 77, op. 3, ye. kh. 28, ll. 19–34 (20).
55. Plenary session of 14 April 1946. RGALI, fond 2073, op. 1, ye. kh.16, l. 202.
56. Fadeyev's letter to the CC Secretariat (Stalin, Malenkov, Zhdanov, Kuznetsov, Popov) on the preliminary results of KSP discussions of 12 April 1946. RGASPI, fond 17, op. 125, ye. kh. 399, ll. 1–11 (5).
57. GARF, fond 5446, op. 48, ye. kh. 2194, l. 89.
58. Plenary session of 4 April 1947. RGALI, 2073, fond 1, op. 1, ye. kh. 21, l. 238.
59. GARF, fond 5446, op. 49, ye. kh. 2842, l. 105.
60. Morrison, *The People's Artist*, 277.
61. Monsenzhon, *Rikhter*, 77.
62. Plenary session of 21 October 1947. RGALI, fond 2073, op. 1, ye. kh. 25, l. 8.
63. A. K. San'ko, *Ye. K. Golubev: kompozitor, pedagog, muzïkal'nïy deyatel'* (dissertatsiya na soiskaniye uchyonoy stepeni kandidata iskusstvovedeniyaï) (Moscow: Moskovskaya konservatoriya, 2000), 19.
64. This haunting story is told fully in Simon Morrison, *The Love and Wars of Lina Prokofiev* (London: Harvill Secker, 2013).
65. Vladimir Orlov traced the genesis of *On Guard for Peace* and its early reception in his paper ' "Did He Make a Step toward Rebirth?" Prokofiev's Pursuits of Self-Rehabilitation after 1948', which was delivered at the conference *Musical Legacies of State Socialism: Revisiting Narratives about Post-World War II Europe* (Belgrade, September 2015).
66. Music Section meeting of 30 January 1951. RGALI, fond 2073, op. 1, ye. kh. 43, ll. 8–9.
67. Kruzhkov's report of 2 March 1951. RGASPI, fond 17, op. 133, ye. kh. 307, l. 60.
68. RGASPI, fond 117, op. 133, ye. kh. 307, ll. 91–112 and 126–36.
69. Meeting of the Music Section of 21 February 1953. RGALI, fond 2073, op. 2, ye. kh. 10, l. 299.
70. Meeting of the Music Section of 8 January 1953. RGALI, fond 2073, op. 2, ye. kh. 10, l. 72.
71. Plenary session of 15 January 1953. RGALI, fond 2073, op. 2, ye. kh.1, l. 148.
72. Ibid.
73. Ibid., l. 150.
74. Ibid., l. 149.
75. Ibid., ll. 150–51.
76. Ibid., l. 153.
77. Ibid., l. 154.
78. Meeting of the Music Section of 3 February 1953. RGALI, fond 2073, op. 2, ye. kh. 10, l. 224.
79. According to Rostropovich, Prokofiev initially intended to entitle the Seventh 'A Children's Symphony' but he, Rostropovich, talked him out of it. See Morrison, *The People's Artist*, 373.
80. Meeting of the Music Section of 3 February 1953. RGALI, fond 2073, op. 2, ye. kh. 10, l. 225.
81. Ibid., ll. 225–6.
82. Vladlen Chistyakov (1929–2011) was a young composer from Leningrad who was represented on the 1953 nominations list by his cantata *Song of Labour and Struggle*.
83. Meeting of the Music Section of 4 February 1953. RGALI, fond 2073, op. 2, ye. kh. 10, l. 236.
84. Ibid., ll. 237–8.
85. Meeting of the Music Section of 30 March 1954. RGALI, fond 2073, op. 2, ye. kh. 30, ll. 146–7.
86. Plenary session of 7 April 1954. RGALI, fond 2073, op. 2, ye. kh. 28, l. 35.
87. Minutes of the counting commission, 10 April 1954. RGANI, fond 3, op. 53a, ye. kh. 38, l. 18.
88. Interview with Olga Manulkina, *Kommersant*, no. 153 (14 September 1996), 12.
89. Morrison, *The People's Artist*, 373.
90. Plenary session of 15 January 1953. RGALI, fond 2073, op. 2, ye. kh.1, l. 152.
91. Plenary session of the Lenin Prize Committee, 1 February 1957. RGALI, fond 2916, op. 1, ye. kh. 5, l. 77.

92. Meeting of the Music Section of the Lenin Prize Committee, 31 January 1957. RGALI, fond 2916, op. 1, ye. kh. 14 and 15.
93. Plenary session of the Lenin Prize Committee, 6 April 1957. RGALI, fond 2916, op. 1, ye. kh. 8, l. 31.
94. Plenary session of the Lenin Prize Committee, 9 April 1957. RGALI, fond 2916, op. 1, ye. kh. 8, l. 87. There were only five winners across the arts: Prokofiev, the Tatar poet Musa Jalil (also deceased), the writer Leonid Leonov (for his novel *Russian Forest*), the sculptor Sergei Konenkov (for his self-portrait) and the ballerina Galina Ulanova.

Chapter 4: Shostakovich: Hits and Misses

1. On 18 February 1942, Goldenweiser reported in his diary: 'I cannot say that I made sense of the symphony [by playing through the orchestral score], but this work immediately makes an impression of being very significant. Some episodes are amazing.' Typescript of Goldenweiser's Diaries, VMOMK, fond 162, notebook 20, l. 99.
2. A. N. Tolstoy, 'Na repetitsii sed'moy simfonii Shostakovicha', *Pravda* (16 February 1942), 3.
3. Plenary meeting in Tbilisi on 19 February 1942. RGALI, fond 2073, op. 1, ye. kh. 6, l. 44.
4. 'We shall rest', the final phrase in Chekhov's *Uncle Vanya*, was used to characterize Shostakovich's finale by L. Danilevich in 'Vos'maya simfoniya Shostakovicha', *Sovetskaya muzïka*, no. 12 (1946), 56–64 (64).
5. O. P. Lamm, *Stranitsï tvorcheskoy biografii Myaskovskogo* (Moscow: Sovetskiy kompozitor, 1989), 302–3.
6. Plenary session of 16 March 1944. RGALI, fond 2073, op. 1, ye. kh. 9, ll. 140–41. Fragments of the KSP discussion of the Eighth Symphony were published in V. V. Perkhin (ed.), *Deyateli russkogo iskusstva i M. B. Khrapchenko, predsedatel' Vsesoyuznogo komiteta po delam iskusstv: aprel' 1939–yanvar' 1948: svod pisem* (Moscow: Nauka, 2007), 627–9. A complete transcript of the discussions on 24 March and 3 April 1945 can be found at http://sglavatskih.narod.ru/ (personal site of Sergei Glavatskikh, accessed 17 September 2015), partially reprinted in V. F. Svin'yin and K. A. Oseyev (eds), *Stalinskiye premii: dve storonï odnoy medali. Sbornik dokumentov i khudozhestvenno-publitsisticheskikh materialov* (Novosibirsk: Svin'yin i sïnov'ya, 2007), 148–56.
7. Plenary session of 16 March 1944. RGALI, fond 2073, op. 1, ye. kh. 9, ll. 140–41 and 142.
8. Ibid., l. 143.
9. Ibid., l. 143.
10. Ibid., ll. 143–4.
11. Ibid., l. 149.
12. Plenary session of 21 March 1944. RGALI, fond 2073, op. 1, ye. kh. 9, ll. 221–2.
13. Ibid., l. 223.
14. Ibid., l. 224.
15. Plenary session of 27 March 1944. RGALI, fond 2073, op. 1, ye. kh. 9, ll. 289–90.
16. Khrapchenko's letter to Stalin and Molotov of 1 April 1944. GARF, fond 5446, op. 48, ye. kh. 2195, l. 32.
17. Letter from Aleksandrov and Zuyeva to Malenkov and Shcherbakov (spring 1944). RGASPI, fond 17, op. 125, ye. kh. 234, ll. 34–6.
18. Yu. Shaporin, 'Novoye v tvorchestve Shostakovicha', *Sovetskoye iskusstvo*, no. 4 (28 November 1944), 3. In this article Shaporin also coined the label 'little Shostakoviches', referring to Shostakovich's disciples.
19. Plenary session of 3 April 1945. RGALI, fond 2073, op. 1, ye. kh. 11, l. 186.
20. Mordvinov won a Stalin Prize for residential buildings on Gorky Street.
21. Mordvinov is most likely referring to passages where pizzicato and arco alternate in quick succession.
22. Plenary session of 3 April 1945. RGALI, fond 2073, op. 1, ye. kh. 11, ll. 186–7.
23. Ibid., ll. 188–9.
24. Ibid., l. 189.
25. Ibid., l. 191.
26. KSP minutes of 1945. RGALI, fond 2073, op. 1, ye. kh. 14, l. 56.
27. As, for example, in Joachim Braun, 'The Double Meaning of Jewish Elements in Dmitri Shostakovich's Music', *Music Quarterly* (1985), no. 71, 68–80.
28. 'Proslushivaniya novoy simfonii Shostakovicha', *Sovetskoye iskusstvo*, no. 37 (14 September 1945), 4.
29. I. Nest'yev, 'Zametki o tvorchestve D. Shostakovicha: neskol'ko mïsley, vïzvannïkh Devyatoy simfoniyey', *Kul'tura i zhizn'*, no. 10 (30 September 1946), 4.
30. Olga Digonskaya, 'Simfonicheskiy fragment 1945 goda: k istorii pervogo neokonchennogo varianta Devyatoy simfonii D.D. Shostakovicha', *Muzïkal'naya akademiya*, no. 2 (2006), 97–102.

31. S. Shlifshteyn, 'Devyataya simfoniya Shostakovicha', *Sovetskoye iskusstvo*, no. 43 (26 October 1945), 3.

32. D. Zhitomirskiy, 'Pervïye ispolneniya Devyatoy simfonii D. Shostakovicha', *Sovetskoye iskusstvo* (30 November 1945), no. 48, 4.

33. Discussion of Shostakovich's Ninth Symphony by the Musicology Commission of the Composers' Union on 4 December 1945. RGALI, fond 2077 (Union of Soviet Composers), op. 1, ye. kh. 129, ll. 86–147.

34. Plenary session of 14 April 1946. RGALI, fond 2073, op. 1, ye. kh. 16, ll. 213–14.

35. Ibid., l. 214.

36. Fadeyev's letter to the CC Secretariat (Stalin, Malenkov, Zhdanov, Kuznetsov, Popov) of 12 April 1946. RGASPI, fond 17, op. 125, ye. kh. 399, ll. 1–11.

37. GARF, fond 5446, op. 47, ye. kh. 2163, l. 74.

38. Plenary session of 4 April 1947. RGALI, fond 2073, op. 1, ye. kh. 21, l. 233.

39. Ibid., ll. 233–4.

40. Ibid., l. 234.

41. *Narodnost'*, literally 'people-ness', variously translated as 'people-mindedness', 'populism' or 'folk character', was a much-vaunted ingredient of Socialist Realism.

42. Ibid., ll. 234–5.

43. A facsimile of the ban in question, 'Order No. 17', is published in Friedrich Geiger, *Musik in zwei Diktaturen: Verfolgung von Komponisten unter Hitler und Stalin* (Kassel: Bärenreiter, 2004), 130. An English translation can be found in Jonathan Walker and Marina Frolova-Walker, *Music and Dictatorship: Russia under Stalin. Newly Translated Source Documents* (New York: Carnegie Hall, 2003), 16.

44. Yury Levitin's memoir in Elizabeth Wilson (ed.), *Shostakovich: A Life Remembered* (London: Faber and Faber, 2004), 244–6.

45. Terry Klefstad, 'Shostakovich and the Peace Conference', *Music and Politics*, vol. 6 (2012), no. 2, http://quod.lib.umich.edu/m/mp (accessed 8 July 2013).

46. A. Kryukov, 'Shostakovich i Lenfil'm: koe-chto v obshchuyu kopilku', in L. Kovnatskaya and M. Yakubov (eds), *Dmitriy Shostakovich: Issledovaniya i materialï*, vol. 1 (Moscow: DSCH, 2005), 33. I thank Olga Digonskaya for providing me with this reference.

47. See more on this in Marina Frolova-Walker, 'A Birthday Present for Stalin: Shostakovich's *Song of the Forests*', in Esteban Buch, Igor Contreras Zubillaga and Manuel Deniz Silva (eds), *Composing for the State: Music in Twentieth-Century Dictatorships* (Aldershot: Ashgate, forthcoming).

48. Plenary session of 23 December 1949. RGALI, fond 2073, op. 1, ye. kh. 35, l. 102.

49. Ibid., l. 106.

50. Plenary session of 25 December 1949. RGALI, fond 2073, op.1, ye. kh. 35, l. 181.

51. Plenary session of 19 January 1950. RGALI, fond 2073, op. 1, ye. kh. 36, l. 165.

52. *History of the All-Union Communist Party (Bolsheviks): Short Course*, a 1938 textbook prepared under the direct supervision of Stalin. It was a catechism no one could question.

53. Music Section meeting of 26 December 1951. RGALI, fond 2073, op. 1, ye. kh. 54, ll. 51–2.

54. Plenary session of 25 January 1952. RGALI, fond 2073, op. 1, ye. kh. 52, l. 252.

55. Ibid., l. 254.

56. Ibid., l. 255.

57. Ibid., l. 252.

58. Ibid., ll. 256–7.

59. Meeting of the Music Section of 14 January 1953. RGALI, fond 2073, op. 2, ye. kh. 10, ll. 95–6.

60. Meeting of the Music Section of 3 February 1953. RGALI, fond 2073, op. 2, ye. kh. 10, ll. 228–9.

61. Plenary session of 24 February 1953. RGALI, fond 2073, op. 2, ye. kh. 7, l. 25.

62. Ibid., ll. 23–6.

Chapter 5: Shostakovich as a Committee Member

1. Nelli Kravets, *Ryadom s velikimi: Atovmyan i yego vremya* (Moscow: GITIS, 2012), 256.

2. Diary entry of 7 March 1947. Typescript of Goldenweiser's Diaries, VMOMK, fond 162, notebook 28, l. 74.

3. O. P. Lamm, *Stranitsï tvorcheskoy biografii Myaskovskogo* (Moscow: Sovetskiy kompozitor, 1989), 320.

4. My interest in the Golubev affair was awakened by Laurel Fay, who brought both the quoted accounts to my attention, and for this I am immensely grateful.

5. Sviridov's interview from 1996. See S. Biryukov, 'Dusha kompozitora – raskalyonnaya pech'', *Trud*, no. 175 (22 September 2006), 5.

6. Kravets, *Ryadom s velikimi*, 282.

7. Lamm, *Stranitsï*, 271. A biographer claims that Shostakovich's criticism of the Second Symphony was the cause of Golubev's nervous breakdown. A. K. San'ko, *Ye. K. Golubev: kompozitor, pedagog, muzïkal'nïy deyatel'* (dissertatsiya na soiskaniye uchyonoy stepeni kandidata iskusstvovedeniya) [PhD diss.] (Moscow: Moskovskaya konservatoriya, 2000), 31.

8. Plenary session of 4 April 1947. RGALI, fond 2073, op. 1 ye. kh. 21, ll. 225–6.

9. Ibid., l. 225.

10. Diary entry of 5 April 1947. Typescript of Goldenweiser's Diaries, notebook 28, l. 90. Khrapchenko might well have expressed some dissatisfaction to Goldenweiser at the end of the meeting. Others might have written this off as a mere difference of opinion, but Goldenweiser was rather sycophantic in his relations with Khrapchenko. Whatever the immediate cause, Goldenweiser evidently thought that, in this case, a written apology was appropriate: 'I'm very unhappy about what took place [in the meeting]. I always try to be objective and tactful. I've always said the same thing about Golubev, and I didn't support him at the [Music] Section either. What I said about him wasn't harsh.' Goldenweiser also apologized for some approving remarks he had directed at Shostakovich's Third Quartet: 'With Shostakovich it's even worse. When speaking against his Quartet, I blurted out the word "genius" in relation to the last two movements, which in my opinion are very fine. That was stupid, as I readily admit, and I do apologize for it'. See V. V. Perkhin (ed.), *Deyateli russkogo iskusstva i M. B. Khrapchenko, predsedatel' Vsesoyuznogo komiteta po delam iskusstv: aprel' 1939–yanvar' 1948: svod pisem* (Moscow: Nauka, 2007), 573.

11. Golubev received two votes for the first class (from Khrapchenko and Myaskovsky, perhaps), and eighteen for the second. RGALI, fond 2073, op. 1, ye. kh. 23, l. 11.

12. Khrapchenko's letter to Stalin (copy to Malenkov) of 13 April 1947. GARF, fond 5446, op. 48, ed. khr. 2196, ll. 66–70.

13. RGASPI, fond 77, op. 3, ed. khr. 143, l. 1.

14. Golubev, 'Alogizmï', typescript held in RGALI, fond 2798, op. 2, ye. kh. 23, ll. 65–70. I am immensely grateful to Patrick Zuk for sharing this source with me.

15. RGASPI, fond 77 (Zhdanov), op. 3, ye. kh. 17, ll. 81–2. This is a rare, and perhaps even unique, example of an extant transcript of the meeting of the Politburo Commission; I have not been able to locate any similar documents. Partially published in Perkhin, *Deyateli russkogo iskusstva i M. B. Khrapchenko*, 107.

16. 'Gorodetsky [one of the authors of the text] asked me whether the name of the Generalissimo should be included in the text. I replied that my main hero is the people. Gorodetsky understood my hint: Stalin was not mentioned.' And further: 'My hunch proved to be more correct than the lists. At the very last moment, my name was struck off. Absolutism could not bear to recognize the true role of the people, of the people's spirit, seeing it instead as building material for "the great architect".' Golubev, 'Alogizmï', l. 70. Also quoted in A. K. San'ko, 'Nesokrushimaya eticheskaya konstanta', *Rossiyskiy muzïkant* (February 2010), no. 2, 1; http://rm.mosconsv.ru/?p=2521 (accessed 2 August 2012).

17. Perkhin, *Deyateli russkogo iskusstva i M. B. Khrapchenko*, 640.

18. Letter of 27 May 1946, published in Leonid Maximenkov, 'Stalin and Shostakovich: Letters to a "Friend"', in Laurel Fay (ed.), *Shostakovich and His World* (Princeton and Oxford: Princeton University Press, 2004), 43–58 (43).

19. Letter of 31 January 1947, ibid., 44.

20. Meeting of the Music Section of 7 February 1951. RGALI, fond 2073, op. 1, ye. kh. 43, l. 49.

21. *Bela* was premiered at the Bolshoi *filial* (second stage) on 10 December 1946.

22. Plenary session of 4 April 1947. RGALI, fond 2073, op. 1, ye. kh. 21, ll. 220–21.

23. Plenary session of 2 April 1947. RGALI, fond 2073, op. 1, ye. kh. 21, ll. 188–9.

24. Ibid., l. 179.

25. Ibid., l. 206.

26. A number of Party resolutions addressed the dangers of 'prettifying the feudal past'; the first of these was addressed to the Tatar Party organization (9 August 1944), then followed a similar one for Bashkiria (27 January 1945). This urgent issue for national literatures was discussed more broadly at the tenth plenary session of the Writers' Union Board in May 1945.

27. Plenary session of 4 April 1947. RGALI, fond 2073, op. 1, ye. kh. 21, l. 229.

28. VMOMK, fond 32, ye. kh. 261, l. 11v. I thank Olga Digonskaya for providing me with this information.

29. Meeting of the Music Section of 12 January 1952. RGALI, fond 2073, op.1, ye. kh. 54, l. 57.

30. See Marina Frolova-Walker and Jonathan Walker, *Music and Soviet Power, 1917–32* (Woodbridge: The Boydell Press, 2012), 202.

31. Cf. note 29, l. 58.

32. Plenary session of 18 January 1952. RGALI, fond 2073, op. 1, ye. kh. 51, l. 166.

33. I. A. Barsova, 'Sem'desyat vosem' dney i nochey v zastenke: kompozitor Mechislav Vaynberg', *Nauchnïy vestnik Moskovskoy konservatorii* (2014), no. 2, 90–104.
34. Meeting of the Music Section of 6 February 1954. RGALI, fond 2073, op. 2, ye. kh. 30, l. 50.
35. Shostakovich had supported Levitin in the press before: D. Shostakovich, 'Oratoriya "Svyashchennaya voyna" ' (*The Holy War*), *Sovetskoye iskusstvo* (5 June 1943), no. 23, 4. At that point, the oratorio in question had only been performed on the piano. Shostakovich also used this opportunity to commend Levitin's Second Quartet.
36. Plenary session of 25 January 1952. RGALI, fond 2073, op. 1, ye. kh. 52, l. 259.
37. Ibid., l. 260.
38. Ibid., l. 261.
39. Lyalya (Elena) Ubiyvovk (1918–1942) played an important role in the resistance movement during the Nazi occupation of Poltava in Ukraine.
40. Meeting of the Music Section of 14 January 1953. RGALI, fond 2073, op. 2, ye. kh 10, ll. 79–80.
41. Ibid., l. 81.
42. Meeting of the Music Section of 4 February 1953. RGALI, fond 2073, op. 2, ye. kh. 10, l. 246.
43. Meeting of the Music Section of 10 February 1953. RGALI, fond 2073, op. 2, ye. kh. 10, l. 271.
44. Georgiy Sviridov, *Muzïka kak sud'ba* (Moscow: Molodaya gvardiya, 2002), 87.
45. Meeting of the Music Section of 6 February 1954. RGALI, fond 2073, op. 2, ye. kh. 30, l. 50.
46. Hristo Botev (1847/8–76), Bulgarian poet and revolutionary who spent most of his life in exile in Romania.
47. Plenary session of 31 March 1954. RGALI, fond 2073, op. 2, ye. kh. 24, l. 198.
48. Nelepp was appointed to the KSP only a short time before this, at the start of the 1954 session.
49. Cf. note 47, l. 202.
50. Plenary session of 10 April 1954. RGALI, fond 2073, op. 2, ye. kh. 28, ll. 164–6.
51. Meeting of the Music Section of 1 April 1954. RGALI, fond 2073, op. 2, ye. kh. 30, l. 199.
52. Shostakovich's letter to the KSP and the Council of Ministers, 5 April 1954. RGALI, fond 2073, op. 2, ye. kh. 43, ll. 4–5.
53. Plenary session of 18 January 1952. RGALI, fond 2073, op. 1, ye. kh. 51, l. 176.
54. Meeting of the Music Section of 26 December 1951. RGALI, fond 2073, op. 1, ye. kh. 54, l. 18.
55. See M. Sabinina, 'V groznïy god: ob opere G. Kreytnera, *Sovetskaya muzïka* (1953), no. 6, 29–32; D. Shostakovich 'Yeshcho raz ob opere "V groznïy god" ', *Sovetskaya muzïka* (1953), no. 10, 30–31; M. Sabinina, 'Otkrïtoye pis'mo D. D. Shostakovichu', ibid., 32–3.
56. Marian Koval', 'Tvorcheskiy uspekh', *Ogonyok* (22 August 1954), no. 34, 18–19.
57. Plenary session of 7 February 1953. RGALI, fond 2073, op. 2, ye. kh. 4, ll. 164–5.
58. Ibid., l. 170.
59. Plenary session of 21 January 1953. RGALI, fond 2073, op. 2, ye. kh. 2, l. 20.
60. Plenary session of 15 January 1952. RGALI, fond 2073, op. 1, ye. kh. 51, l. 147.
61. Plenary session of 17 January 1953. RGALI, fond 2073, op. 2, ye. kh. 1, ll. 183–5.
62. Plenary session of 26 February 1953. RGALI, fond 2073, op. 2, ye. kh. 7, ll. 166–8.
63. D. Shostakovich, 'Gruzinskiye muzïkantï', *Sovetskoye iskusstvo* (15 March 1945), no. 11, 2.
64. Plenary session of 25 January 1952. RGALI, fond 2073, op. 1, ye. kh. 52, l. 267.
65. Gulbat Toradze, *Shostakovich i gruzinskiye kompozitorï* (Tbilisi: Mezhdunarodnïy kulturno-prosvetitel'skiy soyuz 'Russkii klub', 2006), 80–82.
66. Meeting of the Music Section of 21 February 1953. RGALI, fond 2073, op. 2 ye. kh. 10, l. 299.
67. Plenary session of 25 February 1953. RGALI, fond 2073, op. 2, ye. kh. 7, l. 157.
68. Meeting of the Music Section of 6 February 1954. RGALI, fond 2073, op. 2, ye. kh. 30, l. 59.

Chapter 6: Myaskovsky and his School

1. Pavel (Paul) Lamm (1882–1951) was an eminent musicologist and lifelong friend of Myaskovsky. He had an apartment in the Moscow Conservatoire building, where he held regular musical evenings; old and new symphonic works were regularly played there in Lamm's own eight-hand arrangements. Lamm was nominated for a Stalin Prize posthumously, in 1952, for his editorial work on Russian classical operas. The KSP vote went in his favour, but his name was later deleted from the list (with Stalin's emphatic 'no!' in the margins), see RGANI, fond 3, op. 53a, ye. kh. 28, l. 74. Perhaps no particular significance should be attached to this, as posthumous nominations only succeeded in exceptional cases (such as Myaskovsky's). It may be worth noting, even so, that Fadeyev's letter to Stalin of 25 July 1952, reflecting on the KSP's most recent proceedings, contained a complaint that Goldenweiser had been promoting his friends in an unprincipled manner, citing as examples his support for Lamm and for the pianist Grigory Ginzburg, who was Goldenweiser's pupil (Ginzburg had won a prize in 1949). RGANI, fond 3, op. 53a, ye. kh. 2, 39–46.

2. O. P. Lamm, *Stranitsï tvorcheskoy biografii Myaskovskogo* (Moscow: Sovetskiy kompozitor, 1989), 328.

3. See more on this in Marina Frolova-Walker and Jonathan Walker, *Music and Soviet Power, 1917–32* (Woodbridge: The Boydell Press, 2012), 264 and 284–6.

4. Diary entry of 17 September 1940. Typescript of Goldenweiser's Diaries, VMOMK, fond 161, notebook 19, l. 38.

5. S. Shlifshteyn, 'Simfoniya–elegiya', *Sovetskoye iskusstvo*, no. 62 (8 December 1940), 2.

6. It is interesting to note that the Sixth, which was quite explicitly a pained reaction to the Russian Revolution, was by no means an outcast in Soviet symphonic repertoire. Suffice it to point to a performance on 18 November 1944 in Moscow, where it was aptly matched with Rachmaninov's *Bells* by the conductor Boris Khaikin. Moreover, the Symphony was performed in the original version with the final chorus on a funeral spiritual verse. In a review that followed, these 'pinnacles of Russian symphonic music' received much praise. See Igor' Belza, 'Dve simfonii', *Sovetskoye iskusstvo*, no. 3 (21 November 1944), 3.

7. D. Zhitomirskiy, 'Myaskovskiy–simfonist', *Sovetskoye iskusstvo*, no. 16 (20 April 1941), 3.

8. Plenary session of 21 November 1940. RGALI, fond 2073, op. 1 ye. kh. 1, l. 177.

9. Ibid., l. 196.

10. Ibid., ll. 196–7.

11. Cf. note 7.

12. Music lost its pride of place in Stalin Prize listings as a result of the 1948 embarrassment.

13. The card (*udostovereniye*) is preserved in RGALI, fond 2040, op. 2, ye. kh. 348, ll. 6 and 6v.

14. L. T. Atovmyan, 'Vospominaniya', in Nelli Kravets, *Ryadom s velikimi: Atovmyan i yego vremya* (Moscow: GITIS, 2012), 257.

15. Meeting of the presidium of the Organizational Committee (Orgkomitet) of the Composers' Union of 25 January 1941. RGALI, fond 2077 (Union of Soviet Composers), op. 1, ye. kh. 36, ll. 3–4.

16. Meeting of the presidium of the Organizational Committee (Orgkomitet) of the Composers' Union of 6 February 1941. Ibid., l. 17.

17. Ibid.

18. Diary entry of 25 December 1940. Typescript of Goldenweiser's Diaries, notebook 19, l. 87.

19. Cf. note 16, ll. 21–2.

20. Ibid., l. 24.

21. These rumours were not completely unfounded: Maria Yudina, for example, remembered that the oratorio was started in 1918, and that Alexander Blok himself changed some of the lines of his poetry for Shaporin. A. M. Kuznetsov (ed.), *Mariya Yudina. Vïsokiy stoykiy dukh: perepiska 1918–45 gg.* (Moscow: ROSSPEN, 2006), 137.

22. Cf. note 16, l. 22.

23. Diary entry of 11 November 1941. Lamm, *Stranitsï*, 282.

24. Shostakovich mentions this fact when recommending Stasevich for a Stalin Prize in 1947. GARF, fond 5446, op. 49, ye. kh. 2823, l. 2.

25. Diary entry of 13 January 1942. Lamm, *Stranitsï*, 283.

26. Khrapchenko's letter to Stalin, Molotov and Voznesensky of March (?) 1942. GARF, fond 5446, op. 43a, ye. kh. 4499, ll. 24–5.

27. Plenary session of 16 March 1944. RGALI, fond 2073, op. 1, ye. kh. 9, l. 146.

28. Myaskovsky's letter to Pavel Lamm of 28 May 1943. Lamm, *Stranitsï*, 298.

29. Plenary session of 14 April 1946. RGALI, fond 2073, op. 1, ye. kh. 16, ll. 212–13.

30. Diary entry of 15 December 1947. RGALI, fond 2040, op. 1, ye. kh. 65, l. 87v.

31. Patrick Zuk emphasizes the importance of the negative view of Myaskovsky presented by Shepilov in his 1947 report 'O nedostatkakh v razvitii sovetskoy muzïki' [On shortcomings in the development of Soviet music]. See Patrick Zuk, 'Nikolay Myaskovsky and the Events of 1948', *Music and Letters*, vol. 93 (2012), no. 1, 61–85. Shepilov's report is published in V. Rubtsova (ed.), *Tak eto bïlo: Tikhon Khrennikov o vremeni i o sebe* (Moscow: Muzïka, 1994), 140–47.

32. Sherman's letter to Lebedev of 13 January 1948. RGASPI, fond 17, op. 125, ye. kh. 637, ll. 38–89. This letter received a detailed analysis in Patrick Zuk, 'Nikolay Myaskovsky and the Events of 1948'.

33. Altogether, Myaskovsky wrote twenty-seven songs on her texts: eighteen songs, op. 4 collected under the title 'Na grani' (On the Edge, 1904–08), three songs 'From Zina Gippius', op. 5 (1905–08) and 'Premonitions', op. 16 (1913–14).

34. Sherman's letter, cf. note 32, ll. 63–4.

35. ASM (Association for Contemporary Music, 1923–32, active 1923–29) was an organization of composers and musicologists that promoted close links with progressive Western composers. It ran an annual concert series and published a journal.

36. See Zuk's account of Myaskovsky's resistant behaviour in 'Nikolay Myaskovsky and the Events of 1948'.

37. Knushevitsky premiered Myaskovsky's Cello Concerto on 17 March 1945 with the Radio Orchestra under Orlov.
38. Plenary session of 21 February 1948. RGALI, fond 2073, op. 1, ye. kh. 25, ll. 299–300.
39. Undated letter from Khrennikov and Asafyev to Zhdanov (most likely of late February or early March 1948). RGASPI, fond 17, op. 132, ye. kh. 84, l. 1.
40. Shepilov's letter to Zhdanov of 24 March 1948, with Zhdanov's resolution. Ibid., ll. 3–4.
41. Diary entry of 26 August 1948. Lamm, *Stranitsï*, 327.
42. In his diary entry of 19 March 1949, Goldenweiser records a conversation on the subject with Yefim Galanter, director of the Conservatoire's Grand Hall. Typescript of Goldenweiser's Diaries, notebook 31, l. 47.
43. Diary entry of 18 January 1950. RGALI, fond 2040, op. 1, ye. kh. 65, l. 97.
44. Khachaturian's letter to Myaskovsky of 14 February 1949, in A. Khachaturyan, *Pis'ma*, ed. G. A. Arutyunyan et al. (Moscow: Kompozitor, 2005), 51.
45. Plenary session of 23 December 1949. RGALI, fond 2073, op. 1, ye. kh. 35, l. 116.
46. Ibid., l. 122.
47. Agitprop's comments on the KSP proposals. RGASPI, fond 17, op. 132, ye. kh. 271, l. 175.
48. Letter from Kruzhkov and Tarasov to Suslov about the Composers' Union plenary session (end 1949). RGASPI, fond 17, op. 132, ye. kh. 271, l. 64.
49. Agitprop's report. RGASPI, fond 17, op. 132, ye. kh. 271, l. 209.
50. Lamm, *Stranitsï*, 332.
51. Plenary session of 12 February 1951. RGALI, fond 2073, op. 1, ye. kh. 41, ll. 207–8.
52. Osip Chyornïy, *Opera Snegina* (Moscow: Sovetskiy pisatel', 1953). The book is discussed in detail in Yevgeniy Dobrenko, 'Realästhetik, ili narod v bukval'nom smïsle: oratoriya v pyati chastyakh s prologom i epilogom', *Novoye literaturnoye obozreniye* (2006), no. 82, 183–242 (228–40). See also http://magazines.russ.ru/nlo/2006/82/ (accessed 5 December 2014). Dobrenko, however, does not identify Myaskovsky among the characters of the novel.
53. Plenary session of 21 November 1940. RGALI, fond 2073, op. 1, ye. kh.1, l. 181.
54. Ibid., l. 192.
55. Letters to V. I. Khachaturian of 9 February 1942 and to Z. A. Gayamova (autumn 1942), in A. Khachaturyan, *Pis'ma*, 31–4.
56. Letter to Gayamova, ibid., 34.
57. Plenary session of 21 February 1943. RGALI, fond 2073, op. 1, ye. kh. 7, l. 9v.
58. Letter to A. Ya. Gayamov of 3 June 1945, in A. Khachaturyan, *Pis'ma*, 38.
59. Plenary session of 16 March 1944. RGALI, fond 2073, op. 1, ye. kh. 9, l. 146.
60. Ibid., l. 145.
61. Ibid., l. 146.
62. Rodion Shchedrin, *Avtobiograficheskiye zapisi* (Moscow: AST, 2008), 40.
63. Plenary session of 16 March 1944. RGALI, fond 2073, op. 1, ye. kh. 9, l. 135.
64. Annotations to the KSP proposals on Stalin Prizes for 1945. RGASPI, fond 17, op. 125, ye. kh. 399, l. 119.
65. Materials of the Politburo Commission (1946). GARF, fond 5446, op. 48, ye. kh. 2194, l. 74.
66. Goldenweiser's letter to the government of 19 January 1948. RGASPI, fond 17, op. 125, ye. kh. 637, ll. 11–36 (16). Goldenweiser mistakenly refers to this work as having won a Stalin Prize.
67. For example, in Khrapchenko's report of 3 February 1948 (a week before the Resolution), Kabalevsky is still mentioned among the main formalist composers. Khrapchenko's letter to Suslov of 3 February 1948, RGASPI, fond 17, op. 125, ye. kh. 633, 20–34 (21). Leonid Maksimenkov discusses this issue in his 'Partiya – nash rulevoy', *Muzïkal'naya zhizn'*, 15–16 (1993), 8–10, but does not offer an explanation of how and why it happened. Nelli Kravets, when providing a commentary to Atovmyan's memoirs, claimed that Kabalevsky was saved owing to his influential wife, Larisa Chegodayeva, 'closely allied with the security organs'. Kravets, *Ryadom s velikimi*, 283 and 435.
68. Letter from Ogolevets to Suslov and Malenkov [1950?]. RGASPI, fond 17, op. 132, ye. kh. 243, ll. 82–3.
69. Livanova's letter to Stalin [1950?]. RGASPI, fond 17, op. 132, ye. kh. 243, ll. 79–81.
70. Shepilov's report to Zhdanov and Suslov of 13 February 1948. RGASPI, fond 77, op. 3, ye. kh. 142, ll. 4–8 (4).
71. Diary entry of 19 March 1948. Lamm, *Stranitsï*, 324.
72. Plenary session of 31 January 1949. RGALI, fond 2073, op.1, ye. kh. 30, l. 27.
73. See the ministry's comments on the KSP's proposals for 1948. GARF, fond 5446, op. 41, ye. kh. 2988, l. 78.
74. This was Kabalevsky's third opera. Diary entry of 4 December 1947. Lamm, *Stranitsï*, 323.
75. Meeting of the Music Section of 10 February 1951. RGALI, fond 2073, op. 1, ye. kh. 43, ll. 81–3.
76. Plenary session of 11 February 1951. RGALI, fond 2073, op. 1, ye. kh. 41, ll. 105–6.
77. See Livanova's letter to Stalin (already cited). Livanova also spoke openly against Kabalevsky in public forums, although in different terms. See ibid., ll. 84–94.

78. A. Shebalina (ed.), *V. Ya. Shebalin: godï zhizni i tvorchestva* (Moscow: Sovetskiy kompozitor, 1990), 166.
79. Plenary sesssion of 17 January 1943. RGALI, fond 2073, op. 1, ye. kh. 7, l. 12.
80. Letter to M. G. Gube of 12 March 1943, quoted in Shebalina, *V. Ya. Shebalin*, 127.
81. Plenary session of 16 March 1944. RGALI, fond 2073, op. 1, ye. kh. 9, l. 153.
82. *Moscow* was premiered on 14 December 1946, in a concert marking the eightieth anniversary of the Moscow Conservatoire, by the Conservatoire's soloists, choir and orchestra under the direction of Nikolai Anosov, and broadcast on the radio. See Shebalina, *V. Ya. Shebalin*, 317.
83. Plenary session of 4 April 1947. RGALI, fond 2073, op. 1, ye. kh. 21, l. 228.

Chapter 7: Checks and Balances

1. F. Chuyev (ed.), *Sto sorok besed s Molotovïm: iz dnevnika F. Chuyeva* (Moscow: Terra, 1991), 278–9.
2. Stalin, it seems, first used this phrase in his speech before the Joint Plenary Session of the CC and CCC of the Communist Party on 5 August 1927: 'We now support the development of the national cultures of the peoples of the USSR, their national languages, their schools, press and so on, on the basis of the Soviets. And what does this caveat "on the basis of the Soviets" mean? It means that in its content, the culture of the peoples of the USSR, developed by the Soviet authorities, must be common to all working people, it must be a socialist culture; however, in its form, it will be different for each of the peoples of the USSR; it will be a national culture in keeping with linguistic distinctions and national peculiarities.' 'Ob'yedinyonnïy plenum TsK i TsKK VKP (b): Rech' 5 avgusta', in Stalin, *Sochineniya*, in 13 vols, vol. 10 (Moscow: Gosudarstvennoye izdatel'stvo politicheskoy literatury, 1950). It was a modification of his 1925 slogan: 'Proletarian in content, national in form – such is the universal culture towards which socialism is heading', 'O politicheskikh zadachakh universiteta narodov Vostoka', same edition, vol. 7 (1947), 138.
         See more on this in Marina Frolova-Walker, '"National in Form, Socialist in Content": Musical Nation-Building in the Soviet Republics', *Journal of the American Musicological Society*, (1998), vol. 51, no. 2, 331–71.
3. Vladimir Nevezhin, *Zastol'ya Iosifa Stalina: Bol'shiye kremlevskiye priyomï*, vol. 1 (Moscow: Novïy khronograf, 2011), 254.
4. Ibid., 122.
5. *Arşın mal alan* was Stalin's favourite, and he personally commissioned the screen version.
6. V. V. Ivanov, *Dnevniki* (Moscow: IMLI RAN, 2001), 28. Entry for 13 August 1936. Quoted in Nevezhin, *Zastol'ya Iosifa Stalina*, 118.
7. At some point in early 1945, Khachaturian wrote a letter to Anastas Mikoyan in support of Glière's nomination for a Stalin Prize. He reminded Mikoyan of their personal meeting back in 1944, when Khachaturian was receiving his own Stalin Prize for *Gayaneh*, and of their conversation at the time. Khachaturian, back then, expressed his regret that Glière had failed to win a prize that year, and now he reminded Mikoyan again of Glière's achievements, including works written for Azerbaijan, Uzbekistan and the Buryat-Mongol autonomous republic. Letter to A. I. Mikoyan (undated) from 1945, A. Khachaturyan, *Pis'ma*, ed. G. A. Arutyunyan et al. (Moscow: Kompozitor, 2005), 39–40.
8. Meeting of the Theatre and Cinema Section of 15 November 1946. RGALI, fond 2073, op. 1, ye. kh. 22, l. 13.
9. Ibid., l. 22. This is what they saw in the ballet scenes of *Manas*.
10. Ibid., l. 14.
11. Ibid., l. 18.
12. Plenary session of 4 April 1947. RGALI, fond 2073, op. 1, ye. kh. 21, l. 222.
13. Cf. note 8, ll. 10–15.
14. Khrapchenko's letter to Stalin of 13 April 1947. GARF, fond 5446, op. 49, ye. kh. 2842, ll. 66–70.
15. Plenary session of 24 January 1952. RGALI, fond 2073, op. 1, ye. kh. 52, l. 202.
16. Ibid.
17. Plenary sessions of 24 and 25 January 1952. RGALI, fond 2073, op. 1, ye. kh. 52, ll. 205 and 294.
18. Plenary session of 24 January 1952. RGALI, fond 2073, op. 1, ye. kh. 52, l. 203.
19. RGALI, fond 2073, op. 1, ye. kh. 6, l. 10v.
20. Letter from F. Kaloshin to P. Tarasov (undated). RGASPI, fond 17, op. 132, ye. kh. 241, ll. 55–6.
21. Letter from D. Popov and P. Tarasov to M. Suslov of 14 December 1949. Ibid., ll. 57–9.
22. Ibid., ll. 58–9.
23. Kiril Tomoff gives an exhaustive account of the brigade's investigation in his article 'Uzbek Music's Separate Path: Interpreting "Anticosmopolitanism" in Stalinist Central Asia, 1949–52', *Russian Review*, (2004), vol. 63, no. 2, 212–40. He constructs an elaborate argument presenting the 'separatist' movement in Uzbek music as a local interpretation of the 'anti-cosmopolitanism' campaign of 1949. I do not fully agree with him: in my view, the ever-present tensions between the Westernizing

and separatist tendencies flared up once again in the wake of the 1948 Resolution, which opened up opportunities for a shift of power from one group of composers to another.

24. Plenary session of 24 March 1945. RGALI, fond 2073, op. 1, ye. kh. 11, ll. 100–01.
25. Plenary session of 19 December 1949. RGALI, fond 2073, op.1, ye. kh. 35, l. 50.
26. Plenary session of 20 December 1949. RGALI, fond 2073, op. 1, ye. kh. 35, ll. 86–90.
27. RGASPI, fond 17, op. 132, ye. kh. 422, l. 47.
28. Plenary session of 13 April 1946. RGALI, fond 2073, op. 1, ye. kh. 16, ll. 171–4.
29. Ibid., ll. 175–6.
30. The Theatre Section decided to give an award to Baiseitova alone (ibid., l. 188); the Section was overruled, but she did receive a prize the following year.
31. Plenary session of 24 January 1953. RGALI, fond 2073, op. 2, ye. kh. 2, l. 243. Plenary session of 10 February 1953. RGALI, fond 2073, op. 2, ye. kh. 4, l. 203.
32. Ibid. (10 February), l. 205.
33. Translation from Jonathan Walker and Marina Frolova-Walker, *Music and Dictatorship: Russia under Stalin*. Newly Translated Source Documents (New York: Carnegie Hall, 2003), 12.
34. More on this in Tomoff, 'Uzbek Music's Separate Path', 212–40.
35. Tulebaev's open letter with accusations against Zhubanov was published in a Kazakh newspaper on 28 February 1951. Baubek Nogerbek on Zhubanov's 100th anniversary, *Kinoman*, 2007, no. 1, http://kk.convdocs.org/docs/index-48333.html?page=8 (accessed 27 March 2013). See also interview with the filmmaker Kalila Ukhmarov who made a documentary about Zhubanov, www.np.kz/old/2007/01/rkino.html (accessed 27 March 2013).
36. Plenary session of 10 February 1953. RGALI, fond 2073, op. 2, ye. kh. 4, l. 207.
37. Yu. V. Keldïsh (ed.), *Istoriya muzïki narodov SSSR*, vol. 3 (Moscow: Sovetskiy kompozitor, 1972), 376.
38. Plenary session of 14 April 1946. RGALI, fond 2073, op. 1, ye. kh. 16, l. 206.
39. Yu. Paletskis (the head of the pro-Soviet government of 1940 who signed the annexation agreement) on Salomėja Nėris, a radio programme from 1972, available at http://svidetel.su/audio/190 (accessed 26 November 2013).
40. Plenary session of 22 February 1948. RGALI, fond 2073, op. 1, ye. kh. 25, l. 336.
41. See 'Pered novïm kontsertnïm sezonom', *Sovetskoye iskusstvo* (21 August 1948), 1.
42. RGANI, fond 3, op. 53a, ye. kh. 13, ll. 125–53.
43. On a folder cover preserved in RGANI, Stalin wrote in red pencil: 'Zhdanov. Norms of representation (music prizes, etc.)', and placed a tick next to it. Although the meaning is not entirely clear, this inscription would seem to indicate that Stalin discussed the music prizes in a meeting with Zhdanov. RGANI, fond 3, op. 53a, ye. kh. 13, l. 154.
44. In this speech, he criticized the highly formalist works of Vytautas Bacevičius (the brother of Grażyna Bacewicz) and Jeronimas Kačinskas, both already émigrés, comparing them unfavourably with promising realists such as Dvarionas and Stasys Vainiūnas (although he warned that the latter also displayed formalist tendencies towards excessive stylistic refinement). See *Pervïy vsesoyuznïy s'yezd sovetskikh kompozitorov: stenograficheskiy otchyot* (Moscow: Izdaniye Soyuza Sovetskikh Kompozitorov, 1948), 95–8.
45. A. Tauragis, *Lithuanian Music* (Vilnius: Gintaras, 1971), 119. Also, author's interview with Saulus Sondeckis (8 September 2013, Vilnius).
46. I am much indebted to the conductor Saulus Sondeckis for his elucidation of the Dvarionas episode, and largely rely on his version of events (to which he was, at least in part, a direct witness), as presented to me in the interview on 8 September 2013 in Vilnius. Sondeckis claims that Dvarionas's nomination was blocked at the local Composers' Union due to professional jealousies, and so the nomination should not have been taken up in Moscow again. The minutes and transcripts of the relevant meetings, however, say quite the reverse: there was enthusiastic support for the piece (even though some criticisms are indeed mentioned). I am most grateful to Rūta Stanevičiūtė, who, at my request, consulted these documents in the Lithuanian Archive for Literature and the Arts (LLMA), fund 21, list 1, folders 16 and 20.
47. Plenary session of 22 February 1949. RGALI, fond 2073, op.1, ye. kh. 30, l. 117.
48. Author's interview with Sondeckis; this is also corroborated by the documents referenced in note 46.
49. Terry Martin, 'Modernization or Neo-Traditionalism?: Ascribed Nationality and Soviet primordialism', in S. Fitzpatrick (ed.), *Stalinism: New Directions: A Reader*, (London and New York: Routledge, 2000), 348–67 (355).

Chapter 8: High and Low

1. Dunayevsky's letter to Khrapchenko of 6 January 1941. V. V. Perkhin (ed.), *Deyateli russkogo iskusstva i M. B. Khrapchenko, predsedatel' Vsesoyuznogo komiteta po delam iskusstv: aprel' 1939–yanvar' 1948: svod pisem* (Moscow: Nauka, 2007), 580.

2. Kirill Tomoff addressed this issue in his unpublished paper 'Agents of Empire: Soviet Concert Tours and Cultural Empire in Eastern Europe, 1945–1958', delivered at the annual convention of ASEEES, New Orleans, 18 November 2012.

3. As Aleksandrov recalled, 'Comrades Stalin and Voroshilov took an active part in shaping the ensemble's repertoire, and even chose individual songs. The ensemble owes it to them that the repertoire came to include a number of folk songs and classical works. Thus, for example, "Kalinushka", "The grey cuckoo began to sing", "Unsaddle the horses, lads!", were introduced into the repertoire on the personal instructions of comrades Stalin and Voroshilov, and it was comrade Stalin personally who recommended the inclusion of folk instruments in the accompanying group. One favourite of comrades Stalin and Voroshilov, and of all our listeners too, was the Song of the Volga Boatmen, which is an excellent song but lacks a proper ending. "As a composer yourself," said comrade Stalin, "you will need to devise a proper ending for it." Comrades Stalin and Voroshilov also made a lot of correctives to our dances, removing everything that was superfluous, everything that struck one as pseudo-folk or pseudo-Red-Army.' A. I. Revyakin, 'Stalin i teatr', Teatr (1939), nos 11–12, 95–107 (100–01).

4. Ibid., 100.

5. Susan Lockwood Smith, Soviet Arts Policy, Folk Music, and National Identity: The Piatnitskii State Russian Folk Choir, 1927–1945. PhD thesis at the University of Minnesota (1997), 123. This is a comprehensive investigation into the progression of the Pyatnitsky from folk choir to state-sponsored choir.

6. Yu. A. Mansfel'd, 'Russkiye v Anglii (istoriya odnoy poyezdki)', in A. V. Tikhonov (ed.), Sozdatel' Velikorusskogo orkestra V. V. Andreyev v zerkale russkoy pressï (St Petersburg: Soyuz Khudozhnikov, 2000), 193–222 (222).

7. L. Sesilkina (ed.), 'V. V. Andreyev i yego velikorusskiy orkestr', Rossiyskiy Arkhiv: Istoriya Otechestva v svidetel'stvakh i dokumentakh XVIII–XX vv (Moscow: Studiya TRITE, 2007), vol. 15, 491–538.

8. See www.youtube.com/watch?v=sP3B-2DZWjs (accessed 13 January 2015). The confusion is discussed on www.sovmusic.ru/forum/c_read.php?fname=budtezd2 (accessed 13 January 2015).

9. Plenary session of 21 February 1943. RGALI, fond 2073, op. 1, ye. kh. 7, l. 14.

10. Plenary session of 5 April 1947. RGALI, fond 2073, op. 1, ye. kh. 21, ll. 245–6.

11. Plenary session of 3 April 1945. RGALI, fond 2073, op. 1, ye. kh. 11, l. 203.

12. Ibid., l. 204.

13. Plenary session of 14 April 1946. RGALI, fond 2073, op. 1, ye. kh. 16, ll. 219–20.

14. Ibid., ll. 219–20.

15. Plenary session of 23 December 1949. RGALI, fond 2073, op. 1, ye. kh. 35, l. 120.

16. Ibid., l. 125.

17. RGANI, fond 3, op. 53a, ye. kh. 13, ll. 125–53.

18. Plenary session of 24 March 1945. RGALI, fond 2073, op. 1, ye. kh. 11, l. 92.

19. Ruslanova was arrested in 1948, together with her husband, the army general Kryukov, and was released only in 1953 (this also resulted in a temporary ban on her songs).

20. Letter from Utyosov to Stalin of 18 April 1944 and related letter from Khrapchenko to Molotov. RGASPI, fond 17, op. 125, ye. kh. 234, ll. 37–8.

21. Plenary session of 24 March 1945. RGALI, fond 2073, op. 1, ye. kh. 11, l. 92.

22. Complete list of nominees with annotations from 1945. RGALI, fond 2073, op. 1, ye. kh. 20, l. 28.

23. Plenary session of 14 April 1946. RGALI, fond 2073, op. 1, ye. kh. 16, l. 226.

24. Plenary session of 14 April 1946. RGALI, fond 2073, op. 1, ye. kh. 16, ll. 226–31.

25. Plenary session of 5 April 1947. RGALI, fond 2073, op. 1, ye. kh. 21, ll. 256–7.

26. RGASPI, fond 17, op. 132, ye. kh. 84, ll. 79–80 and 85–6.

27. Vladimir Nevezhin, Zastol'ya Iosifa Stalina: Bol'shiye kremlevskiye priyomï, vol. 1 (Moscow: Novïy khronograf, 2011), 299. Utyosov claimed that he was no longer invited after 1936, but Nevezhin dates his last appearance at a Kremlin banquet to 2 May 1938.

28. Plenary session of 4 April 1945. RGALI, fond 2073, op. 1, ye. kh. 11, l. 228.

29. Plenary session of 18 February 1948. RGALI, fond 2073, op. 1, ye. kh. 25, ll. 201–10.

30. Ibid., l. 202.

31. Ibid., l. 203.

32. Ibid., l. 212.

33. Plenary session of 21 February 1948. RGALI, fond 2073, op. 1, ye. kh. 25, ll. 283–4.

34. Letter from Dunayevsky to Lyudmila Raynl of 11 April 1948. I. Dunayevskiy and L. Raynl', Pochtovïy roman, ed. N. Shafer (Moscow: Kompozitor, 2001), 62–3.

35. Letter from Dunayevsky to Lyudmila Raynl of 2 May 1948, ibid., 67–8.

36. Plenary session of 29 December 1949. RGALI, fond 2073, op. 1, ye. kh. 35, ll. 93–4.

37. RGASPI, fond 17, op. 132, ye. kh. 271.

38. Antony Beevor, The Mystery of Olga Chekhova (London: Penguin Books, 2005), 176–7.

39. Plenary session of 5 April 1947. RGALI, fond 2073, op. 1, ye. kh. 21, ll. 243–4.

40. Plenary session of 16 March 1944. RGALI, fond 2073, op. 1, ye. kh. 9, ll. 153–4.

41. Plenary session of 9 March 1944. RGALI, fond 2073, op. 1, ye. kh. 7, l. 13v.

42. Plenary session of 5 April 1947. RGALI, fond 2073, op. 1, ye. kh. 21, ll. 242-3.

43. Plenary session of 1 March 1943. RGALI, fond 2073, op. 1, ye. kh. 7, l. 76.

44. Plenary session of 16 March 1944. RGALI, fond 2073, op. 1, ye. kh. 9, ll. 155-7.

45. Ibid., l. 156.

46. Among many other popular songs, Kruchinin was the author of 'The Brick Factory' (*Kirpichiki*), which in the 1920s became a symbolic target of RAPM's castigation of bourgeois-decadent melancholy.

47. Music Section meeting of 21 February 1953. RGALI, fond 2073, op. 2, ye. kh. 10, l. 300.

48. Plenary session of 25 January 1952. RGALI, fond 2073, op. 1, ye. kh. 52, ll. 261-3.

49. Plenary session of 28 January 1952. RGALI, fond 2073, op. 1, ye. kh. 53, ll. 80-82.

50. Plenary session of 22 February 1943. RGALI, fond 2073, op. 1, ye. kh. 7, l. 26. In 1941, *Sovetskoye iskusstvo* reported on the 100th performance of *Po rodnoy zemle*. The ensemble was then directed by the composer Zinovy Dunayevsky, brother of the famous Isaak. *Sovetskoye iskusstvo* (27 April 1941), no. 17, 4.

51. Plenary session of 4 April 1945. RGALI, fond 2073, op. 1, ye. kh. 11, l. 222.

52. Plenary sessions of 29 January and 14 February 1952. RGALI, fond 2073, op.1, ye. kh. 53, ll. 195 and 236.

53. Plenary session of 29 January 1952. RGALI, fond 2073, op. 1, ye. kh. 53, ll. 172-3.

54. Plenary session of 25 February 1943. RGALI, fond 2073, op. 1, ye. kh. 7, l. 42.

55. Igor Vorob'yov, *Sotsrealicheskiy 'bol'shoy stil'' v sovetskoy muzïke, 1930-1950-ye godï* (St Petersburg: Kompozitor-Sankt-Peterburg, 2013), 117.

Chapter 9: Awards for Performers

1. R. Pikhoy (ed.), 'Perepiska Alliluyevoy i Stalina', *Rodina* (1992), no. 10, http://bagira.guru/zhurnaly/rodina/1992-10/perepiska-alliluevoy-i-stalina.html (accessed 18 September 2015).

2. Zavadsky's summary at the plenary session of 25 December 1949. RGALI, fond 2073, op. 1, ye. kh. 35, l. 151.

3. See more on this in M. Frolova-Walker, *Russian Music and Nationalism from Glinka to Stalin* (New Haven and London: Yale University Press, 2007), 61-70.

4. Mikhoels's comment at the plenary session of 29 December 1940. RGALI, fond 2073, op. 1, ye. kh. 2, l. 2.

5. Plenary session of 29 December 1940. Ibid., l. 19.

6. Vladimir Nevezhin, *Zastol'ya Iosifa Stalina: Bol'shiye kremlevskiye priyomï*, vol. 1 (Moscow: Novïy khronograf, 2011), 385-400.

7. Leonard Gendlin published a piece in the style of a confessional memoir, *Behind the Kremlin Wall* (London: R. Trevers, 1983), attributing it to Davydova; she disowned the publication vehemently, but the scandal, it seems, helped to bring on her final decline. Afterwards, her relatives presented the story that Stalin had proposed to Davydova, but that she rejected him. There were also various rumours about Barsova, Shpiller and Maksakova, but none has been corroborated by any evidence. See Geliy Kleymenov, *O lichnoy zhizni Iosifa Stalina*, www.proza.ru/2013/05/11/872 (accessed 1 August 2014).

8. Plenary session of 27 February 1943. RGALI, fond 2073, op. 1, ye. kh. 7, ll. 45-6.

9. See more on this in Marina Frolova-Walker and Jonathan Walker, *Music and Soviet Power, 1917-32* (Woodbridge: The Boydell Press, 2012), 285.

10. D. Rabinovich, 'Yemel'yan Pugachyov', *Sovetskoye iskusstvo*, no. 10 (6 March 1943), 4.

11. Plenary session of 27 February 1943. RGALI, fond 2073, op. 1, ye. kh. 7, ll. 48.

12. Meeting of the Theatre/Cinema and Literature sessions of 3 March 1947. RGALI, fond 2073, op. 1, ye. kh. 22, ll. 37-8. *People of Sevastopol*, strangely enough, was revived in 2014 as the basis of a patriotic show to mark Crimea's entry into the Russian Federation.

13. The original libretto by Tovmas Terzian was rewritten by Armen Gulakian, who staged the opera; the musical revision was accomplished by Alexander Shaverdyan and Leon Khodja-Einatov. See Georgiy Geodakyan, *Puti formirovaniya armyanskoy muzïkal'noy klassiki* (Yerevan: Izdatel'stvo Instituta iskusstv NAN RA, 2006).

14. Georgiy Geodakyan mistakenly reports this award as being first-class in his *Puti formirovaniya*.

15. Plenary sessions of 2 and 4 April 1947. RGALI, fond 2073, op. 1, ye. kh. 21, ll. 182 and 224.

16. Letter from Pazovsky, Baratov and Fedorovsky to Zhdanov of 31 October 1946. RGASPI, fond 17, op. 125, ye. kh. 465, ll. 228-9.

17. Letter from Aleksandrov to Zhdanov of 12 February 1947. RGASPI, fond 17, op. 125, ye. kh. 465, l. 231.

18. ' "Boris Godunov": Narodnaya muzïkal'naya drama na stsene Bol'shogo teatra', *Kul'tura i zhizn'*, no. 14 (21 May 1947), 4.

19. Ibid. Mikhail Pokrovsky (1868-1932) was a Marxist historian who held a leading position in Soviet historical scholarship of the 1920s and early 1930s, but was posthumously denounced in 1936 and afterwards referred to as 'anti-Marxist'.

20. 'Yeshcho raz o "Borise Godunove"', *Pravda* (13 July 1947).
21. 'Narod – glavnoye deystvuyushcheye litso', *Sovetskiy artist* (22 October 1948).
22. Letter from Shepilov and Kuznetsov to Malenkov of 9 December 1948. RGASPI, fond 17, op. 132, ye. kh. 84, ll. 87–8.
23. Plenary session of 28 February 1949. RGALI, fond 2073, op. 1, ye. kh. 30, ll. 295–6.
24. Ibid., ll. 296–7.
25. GARF, fond 5446, op. 51, ye. kh. 2988, l. 78.
26. In 1930, the Bolshoi was placed under the direct control of the Central Executive Committee (TsIK SSSR). A. A. Artizov and O. Naumov (eds), *Vlast' i khudozhestvennaya intelligentsiya: dokumentï TsK RKP(b) – VKP(b) – VChK – OGPU – NKVD o kul'turnoy politike, 1917–1953* (Moscow: Mezhdunarodnïy fond 'Demokratiya', 1999), 128.
27. Letter from Kruzhkov and Tarasov to Suslov of 26 April 1950. RGASPI, fond 17, op. 132, ye. kh. 419, ll. 144–6.
28. In the end, these changes were not implemented. See B. Yarustovskiy, ' "Khovanshchina" na stsene Bol'shogo teatra', *Kul'tura i zhizn'*, no. 29 (21 October 1950), 3.
29. Plenary session of 11 February 1951. RGALI, fond 2073, op. 1, ye. kh. 41, l. 96.
30. Ibid., l. 97.
31. At one of the 1954 KSP sessions, the writer Alexei Surkov pointed out how easy it was for documentary cameramen to win a string of awards: 'It turns out that the greatest genius in the Soviet Union is the cameraman [Mikhail] Oshurkov, because no one has more Stalin Prizes than him. This is very odd, very odd indeed! It reminds me of the juggler who toured everywhere during the war – it was said of him that he had defended every Russian city.' Plenary Session of 10 April 1954. RGALI, fond 2073, op. 2, ye. kh. 28, l. 136. Oshurkov, however, had only four prizes; Surkov must have confused him with Ilya Kopalin who had six.
32. Plenary session of 20 December 1949. RGALI, fond 2073, op. 1, ye. kh. 35, l. 80.
33. Boris Pokrovsky, the Bolshoi's young star producer, it seems, owed his meteoric rise to the KSP: back in 1943, the literary critic Gurvich suggested that he should be given a prize for his direction of Serov's *Judith* in Gorky (now Nizhny Novgorod). Khrapchenko baulked at the idea that the director alone could win a prize for an opera production, but those who had seen it insisted that it was exciting as theatre, even though the level of musical performance was low. Dovzhenko proposed that the best prize for the young director would be a transfer to Moscow; this must have been heard by Khrapchenko, because from the next season, Pokrovsky started his new job at the Bolshoi Opera. RGALI, fond 2073, op. 1, ye. kh. 7, l. 54.
34. Plenary session of 20 December 1949. RGALI, fond 2073, op. 1, ye. kh. 35, l. 81.
35. Plenary session of 16 January 1950. RGALI, fond 2073, op. 1, ye. kh. 36, l. 138.
36. Plenary session of 27 February 1943. RGALI, fond 2073, op. 1, ye. kh. 7, l. 48v.
37. Plenary session of 15 January 1941. RGALI, fond 2073, op. 1, ye. kh. 2, l. 264.
38. Plenary session of 16 March 1944. RGALI, fond 2073, op. 1, ye. kh. 9, ll. 161.
39. Khrapchenko's letter to Stalin and Molotov of 1 April 1944. GARF, fond 5446, op. 48, ye. kh. 2195, l. 32.
40. Plenary session of 24 March 1945. RGALI, fond 2073, op. 1, ye. kh. 11, l. 77.
41. Golovanov's letter to Agitprop of 4 February 1950. RGASPI, fond 17, op. 132, ye. kh. 420, l. 14.
42. Plenary session of 2 March 1943. RGALI, fond 2073, op. 1, ye. kh. 7, l. 88v.
43. Khrapchenko's letter to Stalin and Molotov of 1 April 1944. GARF, fond 5446, op. 48, ye. kh. 2195, l. 32.
44. Plenary session of 24 March 1944. RGALI, fond 2073, op. 1, ye. kh. 9, l. 232.
45. Shepilov's letter to Zhdanov of 23 March 1948. RGASPI, fond 17, op. 132, ye. kh. 82, ll. 31–2.
46. Plenary session of 16 March 1944. RGALI, fond 2073, op. 1, ye. kh. 9, ll. 159–60. Vyacheslav (Václav) Suk (1861–1933) was conductor at the Bolshoi Opera in the 1920s and early 1930s. Arthur Nikisch (1855–1922) and Otto Klemperer (1885–1973) were conductors of international renown.
47. Plenary session of 31 January 1951. RGALI, fond 2073, op. 1, ye. kh. 43, ll. 25 and 39.
48. Plenary sessions of 31 January 1951 and 11 January 1950. RGALI, fond 2073, op. 1, ye. kh. 43, ll. 25–6 and ye. kh. 36, ll. 58–9.
49. Plenary session of 24 March 1945. RGALI, fond 2073, op. 1, ye. kh. 11, ll. 84 and 86.
50. Plenary sessions of 24 March 1944 and 3 April 1945. RGALI, fond 2073, op. 1, ye kh. 9, l. 234 and ye. kh. 11, l. 207. In 1949, a hand injury interrupted Flier's solo career for ten years.

Chapter 10: 1948 and Khrennikov's Rule

1. The phrase, referring to the period ushered in by the 1948 Resolution, allegedly belongs to the composer Kosababov, one of those 'overlooked' people who, he thought, stood to benefit from the 1948 Resolution. See Shepilov's report to Zhdanov and Suslov on the closed Party meeting of the Composers' Union, sent 13 February 1948. RGASPI, fond 77, op. 3, ye. kh. 142, ll. 4–8 (4).

2. The Politburo Resolution 'On Muradeli's Opera *The Great Friendship*' was published on 10 February 1948. The Russian text is available at www.hist.msu.ru/ER/Etext/USSR/music.htm (accessed 11 January 2015). Translated by Jonathan Walker and Marina Frolova-Walker in *Music and Dictatorship: Russia under Stalin. Newly Translated Source Documents* (New York: Carnegie Hall, 2003), 10–15.

3. Yekaterina Vlasova points to the fact that Muradeli was born in the same town as Stalin (Gori), but under the Armenian name Ovanes Muradian, which he changed to the Georgian version Vano Muradeli. See her *1948 god v sovetskoy muzïke* (Moscow: Klassika-XXI, 2010), 221. In the light of this, his many songs and cantatas for Stalin may be seen more as personal gifts from one son of Gori to another. For example, his cantata *For the Leader* (*Vozhdyu*, 1937) is written in the style of Georgian folk polyphony, and ends with exclamations, 'You are our brother! You are our dearest! You are our father!', which seem to be Muradeli's additions to Vladimir Lugovskoy's source poem. His 1941 'Song of the Leader's Youth' specifically refers to Stalin's Gori period.

4. Oleg Khlevniuk, *In Stalin's Shadow: The Career of 'Sergo' Ordzhonikidze*, ed. Donald J. Raleigh, trans. David J. Nordlander (Armonk, NY and London: M. E. Sharpe, 1995), 173–4.

5. Zhdanov's notebooks. RGASPI, fond 77 (Zhdanov), op. 3, ye. kh. 177, notebook 4, l. 41.

6. Ibid., l. 42.

7. The fact that the three most important people in the Union of Composers happened to be Armenians must have been widely commented upon. See, for example, how Khachaturian referred to this fact ironically. At a successful premiere of a piece by Alexander Arutiunian in early 1949, someone remarked that 'Armenians are putting right the situation at the music front'. Khachaturian quipped: 'Armenians messed up the music front, and now they are putting it right'. See Khachaturian's letter to M. G. Arutiunian, in A. Khachaturian, *Pis'ma*, ed. G. A. Arutyunyan et al. (Moscow: Kompozitor, 2005), 50.

8. Ibid., ll. 43, 46, 48, 52. Partially published in V. V. Perkhin (ed.), *Deyateli russkogo iskusstva i M. B. Khrapchenko, predsedatel' Vsesoyuznogo komiteta po delam iskusstv: aprel' 1939–yanvar' 1948: svod pisem* (Moscow: Nauka, 2007), 123.

9. Yoram Gorlizki and Oleg Khlevniuk, *Cold Peace: Stalin and the Soviet Ruling Circle, 1945–1953* (Oxford and New York: Oxford University Press, 2004), 31.

10. Ibid., 33–41.

11. Ibid., 43.

12. N. S. Khrushchev, *Vremya, lyudi, vlast'*, vol. 2 (Moscow: Moskovskiye novosti, 1999), 91. Elsewhere in the memoirs, he puts it even more strongly: 'With regard to [the resolutions on literature and music], Zhdanov was only an appointed speaker: he said what he was told to say. What he himself thought is hard to find out. Perhaps it was exactly what he said, but I doubt that. Not likely. At the time, Zhdanov was in complete disfavour. [Stalin's] relationship to him changed during the war'. Ibid., vol. 1, 111.

13. Report from Leningrad of 19 February 1948, signed by the head of the Leningrad City and Region Party Committee Pyotr Popkov. RGASPI, fond 17, op. 125, ye. kh. 637, l. 167.

14. Grinberg's report of 13 January 1948. RGASPI, fond 17, op. 125, ye. kh. 637, l. 92.

15. *Soveshchaniye deyateley sovetskoy muzïki v TsK VKP(b)* (Moscow: Pravda, 1948).

16. Nelli Kravets, *Ryadom s velikimi: Atovmyan i yego vremya* (Moscow: GITIS, 2012), 288. Muzfond was the Union of Composers' financial division.

17. Yu. Shaporin, 'Novoye v tvorchestve Shostakovicha', *Sovetskoye iskusstvo* (28 November 1944), no. 4, 3.

18. *Soveshchaniye deyateley sovetskoy muzïki v TsK VKP(b)*, 10–17.

19. O. P. Lamm, 'Vospominaniya (fragment: 1948–1951 godï)', in M. P. Rakhmanova (ed.), *Sergey Prokof'yev: Vospominaniya, pis'ma, stat'yi* (Moscow: Deka-VS, 2004), 227–73 (243).

20. Goldenweiser's letter to Zhdanov of 19 January 1948. RGASPI, fond 17, op. 125, ye. kh. 637, ll. 11–36.

21. Diary entry of 6 March 1947. Typescript of Goldenweiser's Diaries, notebook 28, 73.

22. Fragments from Goldenweiser's letter were published in Vlasova, *1948 god*, 250–2.

23. Mikhail Meyerovich (1920–93) was one of the younger targets of Goldenweiser's criticism. 'Woe to them who cause the little ones to stumble', he wrote, claiming that Meyerovich used to compose 'ultramodernist music even when he was at school, [...] and now writes music that frightens even the Composers' Union'. Cf. n. 20, ll. 14–15.

24. Plenary session of 13 February 1948. RGALI, fond 2073, op. 1, ye. kh. 25, l. 62.

25. Plenary session of 21 February 1948. RGALI, fond 2073, op. 1, ye. kh. 25, l. 289.

26. Letter to Stalin, Molotov et al. signed by Shepilov and Ilyichev, [late March or early April] 1948. GARF, fond 5446, op. 50, ye. kh. 2815, ll. 1–5.

27. Yu. Keldïsh, 'Porochnïye metodï rabotï Moskovskoy konservatorii', *Sovetskoye iskusstvo*, no. 9 (28 February 1948), 3.

28. See Chapter 7, n. 43.

29. Although the Composers' Union existed on paper from 1932 onwards, it had never actually been given a Union-wide inaugural congress by its governing body, the Orgkomitet, although it had functioned perfectly well through Sections (art composers, song composers, musicologists and so on) and through branches that met on the level of cities and republics.

30. The transcripts of the proceedings were published in *Pervïy vsesoyuznïy s'yezd sovetskikh kompozitorov: stenograficheskiy otchyot*, ed. M. Koval et al. (Moscow: Izdaniye Soyuza sovetskikh kompozitorov, 1948). Asafyev received a first-class Stalin Prize that year himself, for his monograph on Glinka, alongside his elevation to new posts in the Union of Composers and the KSP (although due to his illness he never performed any of his new duties). This was in great contrast with his problematic nominations in the past: in 1941, he was rejected because he had published too little in the immediately preceding years; in 1943, this was still true, but Myaskovsky and Shaporin both spoke vigorously in defence of his nomination (noting that Asafyev wrote over 2,500 pages during the Leningrad siege), convincing Khrapchenko that it was worth taking a vote, and so Asafyev received a second-class prize for lifetime achievement in 1943. RGALI, fond 2073, op. 1, ye. kh. 7, ll. 93v–94. Note that Asafyev was the only musicologist to be awarded a Stalin Prize.

31. Phrase used by Ilyichev in his letter to Zhdanov, Kuznetsov, Suslov and Popov [shortly after 25 April 1948]. RGASPI, fond 17, op. 125, ye. kh. 637, l. 254.

32. Letter from Shepilov to Zhdanov, Kuznetsov, Suslov and Popov of 21 April 1948. RGASPI, fond 17, op. 125, ye. kh. 637, ll. 229–32.

33. Ibid.

34. Plenary session of 31 January 1949. RGALI, fond 2073, op. 1, ye. kh. 30, l. 27.

35. Ibid., l. 121. In 1951, Khrennikov, on the contrary, supported the revised version of Shcherbachev's Fifth Symphony for a third-class prize, but the award was postponed instead. RGALI, fond 2073, op. 1, ye. kh. 41, l. 202.

36. Plenary session of 28 February 1949. RGALI, fond 2073, op. 1, ye. kh. 41, ll. 356–7.

37. Myaskovsky's diary entry of 15 December 1949. RGALI, fond 2040, op. 1, ye. kh. 65, l. 95.

38. Plenary session of 23 December 1949. RGALI, fond 2073, op. 1, ye. kh. 35, l. 110.

39. Plenary session of 12 February 1951. RGALI, fond 2073, op. 1, ye. kh. 41, l. 218.

40. Ibid., l. 220.

41. Ibid., l. 222.

42. Letter from Lebedev to Stalin of 31 January 1950. RGASPI, fond 17, op. 132, ye. kh. 272, l. 137.

43. Agitprop report signed by Kruzhkov. RGASPI, fond 17, op. 132, ye. kh. 271, l. 59.

44. RGASPI, fond 17, op. 132, ye. kh. 271, l. 175. Suslov's marginalia: 'Khrennikov is for a 2nd (gloomy)'.

45. Olga Lamm remarks that Shaporin managed to take credit for supervising Muravlev's work, although the piece was written when Muravlev was still a student under Shebalin. Lamm, 'Vospominaniya', 243.

46. Kruzhkov's report to Suslov of 11 March 1950. RGASPI, fond 17, op. 132, ye. kh. 272, ll. 130–36.

47. A summary of the play's content and its brief discussion can be found in Yevgeniy Dobrenko, 'Realästhetik, ili narod v bukval'nom smïsle: oratoriya v pyati chastyakh s prologom i epilogom', *Novoye literaturnoye obozreniye* (2006), no. 82, 183–242 (223–8). See also http://magazines.russ.ru/nlo/2006/82/ (accessed 5 December 2014).

48. Plenary session of 16 January 1950. RGALI, fond 2073, op. 1, ye. kh. 36, l. 125. *Ilya Golovin* was directed by Vasily Toporkov who also played the starring role.

49. Plenary session of 25 December 1949. RGALI, fond 2073, op. 1, ye. kh. 35, l. 166.

50. Plenary session of 5 January 1950. RGALI, fond 2073, op. 1, ye. kh. 36, ll. 7–9.

51. Meri Herrala touches on this story in *The Struggle for Control of Soviet Music from 1932 to 1948: Socialist Realism vs. Western Formalism* (Lewiston, Queenston and Lampeter: The Edwin Mellen Press, 2012), 357–71.

52. The two main literary sources of *Frol Skobeyev* were the 1869 play by Dmitry Averkiyev and an anonymous work of seventeenth-century literature.

53. Myaskovsky's diary entry of 5 March 1950. RGALI, fond 2040, op. 1, ye. kh. 65, l. 97v.

54. The instigators of this 'rayok' were Professor Viktor Berkov and the students Liana Genina, (?) Fradkin and Mikhail Tarakanov. Report sent to Suslov (signed by Kruzhkov and Tarasov), RGASPI, fond 17, op. 132, ye. kh. 419, ll. 31–3.

55. Letter from Kruzhkov and Tarasov to Suslov [end of March 1950]. RGASPI, fond 17, op. 132, ye. kh. 419, ll. 31–3.

56. RGASPI, fond 17, op. 132, ye. kh. 419, ll. 41–3. Khrennikov himself describes the content of the letter in V. Rubtsova (ed.), *Tak eto bïlo: Tikhon Khrennikov o vremeni i o sebe* (Moscow: Muzïka, 1994), 109.

57. Negative letters (mixed with some cautiously positive) were presented in 'O novoy opere T. Khrennikova "Frol Skobeyev"', *Sovetskoye iskusstvo*, no. 24 (6 May 1950), 2 and no. 26 (13 May 1950), 2. A more balanced critique appeared in the Agitprop organ: G. Khubov, 'Komicheskaya opera "Frol Skobeyev"', *Kul'tura i zhizn'*, no. 14 (21 May 1950), 3.

58. Tarasov's letter to Suslov of 1 July 1950. RGASPI, fond 17, op. 132, ye. kh. 411, ll. 123–9.

59. Ibid., l. 125.

60. Ibid., l. 128. This information is attributed to Yarustovsky.

61. Plenary Session of 28 February 1949. RGALI, fond 2073, op. 1, ye. kh. 30, l. 323.
62. This compared favourably with the casting of the corpulent Bolshakov as hero (Rodion) of *Heart and Soul* at the Bolshoi. Plenary session of 11 February 1951. RGALI, fond 2073, op. 1, ye. kh. 41, l. 99. In Saratov, Rodion was sung by Boris Kokurin, who was still a student at the time and therefore deemed ineligible for an award. Plenary session of 11 February 1951. RGALI, fond 2073, op. 1, ye. kh. 41, l. 102.
63. Plenary session of 12 February 1951. RGALI, fond 2073, op. 1, ye. kh. 41, l. 196.
64. Minutes of the Counting Commission. RGALI, fond 2073, op. 1, ye. kh. 46, l. 50.
65. Plenary session of 11 February 1951. RGALI, fond 2073, op. 1, ye. kh. 41, l. 114.
66. Ibid.
67. Ibid., l. 119.
68. Plenary session of 12 February 1951. RGALI, fond 2083, op. 1, ye. kh. 41, l. 197.
69. Ibid., l. 198.
70. Ibid., l. 199.
71. Plenary session of 24 January 1952. RGALI, fond 2073, op. 1, ye. kh. 52, l. 194.
72. Leah Goldman devotes a chapter to Zhukovsky's opera in her *The Art of Intransigence: Soviet Composers and Art Music Censorship, 1945–1957*, PhD diss. (University of Chicago, 2015). I read this chapter after my own account had already been written; it uses a slightly different set of sources and thus creates a story which both complements and intersects with mine. It was a privilege to discuss this rather obscure subject with Leah Goldman whenever we had a chance.
73. The second was Kabalevsky's *Taras's Family*, the third Enke's *The Wealthy Bride*. Khrennikov's own *Frol Skobeyev* was on the list, too, but as a work of secondary importance, because it was not on a Soviet theme. Kruzhkov and Tarasov's report to Suslov (on the plenary meeting of the Composers' Union at the end of 1949). RGASPI, fond 17, op. 132, ye. kh. 244, ll. 123–6.
74. Letter from Kruzhkov and Tarasov to Suslov of 23 February 1950. RGASPI, fond 17, op. 132, ye. kh. 419, ll. 21–5.
75. 'Ob opere "Bogdan Khmel'nitskiy"', *Pravda* (20 July 1951), 2. On the circumstances of this scandal, see Serhy Yekelchyk, 'Diktat and Dialogue in Stalinist Culture: Staging Patriotic Historical Opera in Soviet Ukraine', *Slavic Review* (2000), vol. 59, no. 3, 597–624.
76. Report from the secretary of the CC of the Communist Party of Ukraine, I. Nazarenko. RGASPI, fond 17, op. 132, ye. kh. 418, ll. 37–42.
77. Anonymous letter of 30 May 1950. Ibid., ll. 44–5.
78. Report from Kruzhkov and Tarasov. Ibid, ll. 48–9.
79. Letter from Kruzhkov and Tarasov to Suslov of 18 October 1950. RGASPI, fond 17, op. 132, ye. kh. 419, ll. 253–4.
80. Transcript of the meeting of the presidium of the CC of the Art Workers' Trade Union, 'On the production at the Bolshoi Theatre of the unsuccessful opera *Heart and Soul*', 27 April 1951. GARF, fond 5508, op. 2, ye. kh. 1011, l. 39.
81. Zhukovsky's insertions into the opera *Heart and Soul*, Bolshoi Theatre's Rare Music Fund, no. 4115.
82. 'Delo chesti vsego kollektiva – vïpustit' v srok spektakl' "Ot vsego serdtsa"', *Sovetskiy artist* (8 December 1950), 4.
83. Letter from Kruzhkov and Kiselev to Suslov. RGASPI, fond 17, op. 132, ye. kh. 419, ll. 259–61.
84. Transcript of the post run-through meeting at the Bolshoi Theatre, 30 December 1950. The Bolshoi Theatre Museum, folder on *Heart and Soul*, l. 2.
85. Ibid., l. 4.
86. Ibid., l. 5.
87. Letter from Lebedev to Stalin of 18 January 1951. RGASPI, fond 17, op. 133, ye. kh. 325, ll. 16–17.
88. Letter to Stalin from Zhukovsky, Pokrovsky and Kondrashin of 24 January 1951. RGASPI, fond 17, op. 133, ye. kh. 325, l. 14.
89. Meeting of the Music Section of 10 February 1951. RGALI, fond 2073, op. 1, ye. kh. 43, l. 95.
90. Ibid., l. 96.
91. Plenary session of 11 February 1951. RGALI, fond 2073, op. 1, ye. kh. 41, l. 114.
92. Leah Goldman, after a thorough search, found no documentary evidence of Stalin's visit: see *The Art of Intransigence*, 275. Svinyin and Oseyev are confident that the visit did take place, but do not supply any source: see V. F. Svin'yin and K. A. Oseyev (eds), *Stalinskiye premii: dve storonï odnoy medali. Sbornik dokumentov i khudozhestvenno–publitsisticheskikh materialov* (Novosibirsk: Svin'yin i sïnov'ya, 2007), 229.
93. 'Neudachnaya opera: O postanovke operï "Ot vsego serdtsa" v Bol'shom teatre', *Pravda* (19 April 1951), 2.
94. Goldenweiser's letter to Suslov of 26 April 1951 (it was forwarded to Khrushchev, Ponomarenko, Kruzhkov). RGASPI, fond 17, op. 133, ye. kh. 325, ll. 19–20.
95. Ibid.

96. Plenary session of 8 May 1951. RGALI, fond 2073, op. 1, ye. kh. 43, l. 16.

97. Ibid., l. 28.

98. Ibid., ll. 8–9.

99. Plenary session of 23 February 1953. RGALI, fond 2073, op. 2, ye. kh. 6, l. 223.

100. Leonid Maximenkov, 'The Rise and Fall of the 1948 Central Committee Resolution on Music', *Three Oranges* (November 2008), no. 16, 14–20 (19).

101. Gorlizki and Khlevniuk, *Cold Peace*, 108.

102. B. A. Pokrovskiy, ' "Spektakl'" ' o nashikh sovremennikakh: k postanovke operï G. Zhukovskogo "Ot vsego serdtsa" ', *Sovetskiy artist* (8 September 1950), no. 28, 3.

103. Letter from Dunayevsky to Lyudmila Raynl of 22 June 1951. I. Dunayevskiy and L. Raynl', *Pochtovïy roman*, ed. N. Shafer (Moscow: Kompozitor, 2001), 207–8.

104. Plenary session of 8 May 1951. RGALI, fond 2073, op. 1, ye. kh. 47, ll. 33 and 52–3.

105. Dmitriy Shepilov, *Neprimknuvshiy* (Moscow: Vagrius, 2001), 178.

106. Meeting of the Music Section of 2 February 1953. RGALI, fond 2073, op. 2, ye. kh. 10, l. 190.

107. Meeting of the Music Section of 21 February 1953. RGALI, fond 2073, op. 2, ye. kh. 10, ll. 304 and 307.

108. Plenary session of 11 February 1953. RGALI, fond 2073, op. 2, ye. kh. 4.

109. Plenary session of 23 February 1953. RGALI, fond 2073, op. 2, ye. kh. 6, l. 214.

110. Ibid., l. 227.

111. 'Khrennikov's Seven' were Elena Firsova, Dmitry Smirnov, Alexander Knaifel, Viktor Suslin, Vyacheslav Artyomov, Sofia Gubaidulina and Edison Denisov (following the order in Khrennikov's speech) – the Sixth Congress of the USSR Composers' Union (November 1979).

112. Vera Gornostayeva, 'Komu prinadlezhit iskusstvo?', *Sovetskaya kultura* (12 May 1988), 5.

113. Rubtsova (ed.), *Tak eto bïlo*, 130.

114. A. I. Kokarev (ed.), *Tikhon Nikolayevich Khrennikov: K 100-letiyu so dnya rozhdeniya (stat'yi i vospominaniya)* (Moscow: Kompozitor, 2013).

115. Khrennikov is usually given credit for initiating the CC Resolution 'On the correction of mistakes in the evaluation of the operas *The Great Friendship*, *Bohdan Khmelnytsky* and *Heart and Soul*', which was passed on 28 May 1958.

Chapter 11: The Stalin Prize without Stalin

1. Elena Zubkova, *Russia after the War: Hopes, Illusions, and Disappointments, 1945–1957*, trans. and ed. Hugh Ragsdale (Armonk and London: M. E. Sharpe, 1998), 154.

2. Goldenweiser mentions in his diary Feinberg's Five Pieces in Memory of Stalin, which were played to him by the author on 10 May 1953. Typescript of Goldenweiser's Diaries, VMOMK, fond 161, notebook 34, l. 122.

3. Konstantin Simonov, *Glazami cheloveka moyego pokoleniya: razmïshleniya o I.V. Staline* (Moscow: Kniga, 1990), 249–51.

4. GARF, fond 5446, op. 87, ye. kh. 1323, l. 91.

5. KSP presidium meeting of 1 August 1953. RGALI, fond 2073, op. 2, ye. kh. 7, l. 253.

6. N. S. Khrushchev, 'O kul'te lichnosti i yego posledstviyakh' [speech at the 20th Party Congress on 25 February 1956], first published in *Izvestiya TsK KPSS*, no. 3 (1989), 159–60.

7. Plenary session of 16 March 1954. RGALI, fond 2073, op. 2, ye. kh. 22, ll. 49 and 124–5.

8. Plenary session of 17 March 1954. RGALI, fond 2073, op. 2, ye. kh. 22, l. 238.

9. Meeting of the Music Section of 21 January 1954. RGALI, fond 2073, op. 2, ye. kh. 30, l. 17.

10. Plenary session of 14 January 1954. RGALI, fond 2073, op. 2, ye. kh. 20, l. 45.

11. Plenary session of 8 February 1954. RGALI, fond 2073, op. 2, ye. kh. 20, l. 156.

12. Plenary session of 10 March 1954. RGALI, fond 2073, op. 2, ye. kh. 21, l. 62.

13. Plenary session of 6 April 1954. RGALI, fond 2073, op. 2, ye. kh. 27, l. 18.

14. Plenary session of 25 March 1954. RGALI, fond 2073, op. 2, ye. kh. 24, l. 68.

15. Plenary session of 10 March 1954. RGALI, fond 2073, op. 2, ye. kh. 21, l. 73. The cameraman in question was most likely Ilya Kopalin, who had six (not seven) prizes. Stalin was usually very generous where documentary films were concerned, as they constituted a vital propaganda tool.

16. Ibid., l. 109.

17. Plenary session of 10 April 1954. RGALI, fond 2073, op. 2, ye. kh. 28, l. 130.

18. Lavrenyov at the plenary session of 10 March 1954. RGALI, fond 2073, op. 2, ye. kh. 21, ll. 62–3.

19. See more on this in Marina Raku, *Muzïkal'naya klassika v mifotvorchestve sovetskoy epokhi* (Moscow: Novoye literaturnoye obozreniye, 2014), 451–554.

20. G. B. Mar'yamov, *Kremlevskiy tsenzor: Stalin smotrit kino* (Moscow: Konfederatsiya Soyuzov Kinematografistov 'Kinotsentr', 1992), 87.

21. Plenary session of 2 April 1947. RGALI, fond 2073, op. 1, ye. kh. 21, l. 204.

22. On 6 November 1941, Stalin made a patriotic speech in Moscow when the German army was only a few dozen miles away. Alexei Tolstoy is usually cited as its ghost-writer.
23. Plenary session of 2 February 1953. RGALI, fond 2073, op. 2, ye. kh. 3, ll. 191–200. Many of the criticisms the film faced at the KSP discussions, both in 1953 and 1954, were anticipated in the pre-release debates at Mosfilm's studios, as established by Kevin Bartig in his paper 'Music History for the Masses: Reinventing Glinka in Post-War Soviet Russia', which he delivered at the international conference *Musical Legacies of State Socialism: Revisiting Narratives about Post-World War II Europe* (Belgrade, September 2015). Bartig also shows that Aleksandrov, a powerful figure, ignored the criticism and disregarded the demands for changes.
24. Plenary session of 6 April 1954. RGALI, fond 2073, op. 2, ye. kh. 27, l. 10.
25. Ibid., ll. 10–12 and 14.
26. Ibid., ll. 12–13.
27. Ibid., ll. 21–2.
28. Zritel', 'Pravo i dolg teatra', *Pravda*, (27 November 1953).
29. Plenary session of 12 March 1954. RGALI, fond 2073, op. 2, ye. kh. 21, ll. 184 and 192–3.
30. Vasil' Minko, *Ne nazïvaya familiy* (Moscow: Gosudarstvennoye izdatel'stvo 'Iskusstvo', 1953), 92.
31. 'It would be a mistake to think that our Soviet reality does not offer material for satire. We need Soviet Gogols and Shchedrins who would use the flame of satire to burn out from our life everything that is negative, rotten, ossified, everything that hinders our progress.' Georgy Malenkov's speech at the 19th Party Congress, 'Otchyotnïy doklad Tsentral'nogo Komiteta VKP(b) XIX-mu syezdu partii', *Pravda*, no. 280 (6 October 1952), 6.
32. After a lengthy debate, the KSP voted on Grigoryev's painting and it was proposed for a second-class Stalin Prize.
33. Aram Khachaturyan, 'O tvorcheskoy smelosti i vdokhnovenii', *Sovetskaya muzïka* no. 11, (November 1953), 7–13.
34. Ibid., 7 and 9.
35. Ibid., 10.
36. V. Yu. Afiani (ed.), *Apparat TsK KPSS i kul'tura. 1953–1957: Dokumentï* (Moscow: ROSSPEN, 2001), 198–201 (199).
37. RGALI, fond 2073, op. 2, ye. kh. 20, ll. 35–6. The plenary session on songs took place from 19 to 29 December 1953, and consisted of ten concerts devoted to individual songwriters, where 90 percent of the songs performed were old ones. The 'theoretical' part of the plenary was apparently a complete flop: Zakharov proved unable to write any kind of position paper, and the paper hastily compiled by his helpers was still found wanting. Agitprop did not miss this, and reported on the poor performance of Khrennikov's Union to the CC secretary, P. Pospelov. See *Apparat TsK KPSS i kul'tura*, 195–7.
38. Lyubov' Shaporina, *Dnevnik* (Moscow: Novoye literaturnoye obozreniye, 2012), vol. 2, 219.
39. Ibid., 221.
40. RGALI holds more than a dozen versions of the libretto, e.g. fond 2642, op. 1, ye. kh. 14–18; Leah Goldman devotes a whole chapter to the convoluted genesis of Shaporin's *Decembrists*, see *The Art of Intransigence: Soviet Composers and Art Music Censorship, 1945–1957*, PhD diss. (University of Chicago, 2015).
41. Meeting of the Music Section of 10 March 1954. RGALI, fond 2073, op. 2, ye. kh. 30, l. 102.
42. Ibid.
43. Entry of 29 September 1953. Typescript of Goldenweiser's Diaries, notebook 35, l. 16.
44. Entry of 8 December 1953, ibid., l. 42.
45. Entry of 9 December 1953, ibid., l. 43.
46. Entry of 27 March 1954, ibid., l. 82.
47. Thanks to Goldenweiser's Diaries of 1950–51, we can trace how his attitude to Shostakovich's music becomes ever more positive, the Preludes and Fugues op. 87 eliciting his particular admiration. In 1951, he also began to feel better disposed towards the man himself, when Shostakovich attempted to secure a prize nomination for Goldenweiser's Piano Trio (albeit unsuccessfully). See Typescript of Goldenweiser's Diaries, notebook 33, ll. 57, 67, 70, 71, 73.
48. The discussion at the Moscow House of Composers took place over several days in March and April 1954. A report was written up by the Agitprop employees, Tarasov and Yarustovsky, and sent to Khrushchev. They expressed their concern that too many of the speakers at the discussion mentioned 'the new times', which supposedly made the 1948 Resolution outdated, and called for the rehabilitation of Shostakovich's formalist works. Tarasov and Yarustovsky also criticized the conduct of Khrennikov, Zakharov and Vasily Kukharsky (one of the younger generation of music bureaucrats), who, while panning the Symphony in the corridors, chose not to say anything in public. *Apparat TsK KPSS i kul'tura*, 212–13.
49. Meeting of the Music Section of 30 March 1954. RGALI, fond 2073, op. 2, ye. kh. 30, ll. 155–8.

50. Diary entry of 30 March 1954. Typescript of Goldenweiser's Diaries, notebook 35, l. 82.
51. Meeting of the Music Section of 1 April 1954. RGALI, fond 2073, op. 2, ye. kh. 30, l. 208.
52. Meeting of the Music Section of 30 March 1954. Ibid., ll. 159–60.
53. Ibid., ll. 161–2.
54. Meeting of the Music Section of 1 April 1954. Ibid., l. 195.
55. Ibid., ll. 196–9.
56. Ibid., l. 201.
57. Ibid.
58. Ibid., l. 203.
59. Ibid., l. 204.
60. Ibid.
61. Ibid., l. 209.
62. Ibid., l. 211.
63. Zritel', 'Pravo i dolg teatra', *Pravda* (27 November 1953). This was the article on Okhlopkov's production of Ostrovsky's play *The Storm*.
64. Letter of the Department for Science and Culture of the CC CPSU (Agitprop) on 'unhealthy' moods among the artistic intelligentsia, 8 February 1954. RGASPI, fond 5, op. 17, ye. kh. 454, ll. 33–6. http://doc20vek.ru/node/595 (accessed 31 December 2014).
65. Cf. n. 4.
66. Undated draft of a resolution produced by Khrushchev, Suslov and Pospelov. GARF, fond 5446, op. 87, ye. kh. 1323, l. 95.
67. RGANI, fond 3, op. 53a, ye. kh. 2, l. 142.
68. This list was published in V. F. Svin'yin and K. A. Oseyev (eds), *Stalinskiye premii: dve storoni odnoy medali. Sbornik dokumentov i khudozhestvenno-publitsisticheskikh materialov* (Novosibirsk: Svin'yin i sinov'ya, 2007), 633–50.
69. Letter from Andrianov to Kaganovich of 10 November 1954. Ibid., l. 144. The author of the letter is most likely the chemist Kuzma Andrianov (1904–1987), quadruple Stalin Prizewinner.
70. The architects Leonid Polyakov and Alexander Boretsky were stripped of their laureate titles (awarded for their work on the *Leningradskaya* Hotel); the architect Yevgeny Rybitsky also lost his title (awarded for a building in Chkalov Street in Moscow). Resolution of the CC and the Council of Ministers of 4 November 1955 on the removal of superfluous decoration in building design. RGANI, fond 3, op. 53a, ye. kh. 22, l. 154.
71. Session of the Lenin Prize Committee of 15 November 1956. RGALI, fond 2916 (Komitet po Leninskim Premiyam), op. 1, ye. kh. 3, ll. 8–9.
72. RGANI, fond 3, op. 53a, ye. kh. 2, ll. 148 and 159.

Conclusion

1. See, for example, Caroline Brooke, 'Soviet Musicians and the Great Terror', *Europe–Asia Studies* (2002), vol. 54, no. 3, 397–413; I. A. Barsova (ed.), *Nikolay Sergeyevich Zhilyayev: trudi, dni i gibel'* (Moscow: Muzïka, 2008); Inna Klause, 'Composers in the Gulag: An Initial Survey', in Patrick Zuk and Marina Frolova-Walker (eds), *Russian Music since 1917* (Oxford: Oxford University Press, forthcoming).
2. Pierre Bourdieu, *Distinction: A Social Critique of the Judgement of Taste*, trans. R. Nice (Cambridge, MA: Harvard University Press, 1984), 19, 75, etc.
3. Plenary session of 25 February 1943. RGALI, fond 2073, op. 1, ye. kh. 7, l. 31.
4. Plenary session of 21 November 1940. RGALI, fond 2073, op. 1, ye. kh. 1, l. 184.
5. Ibid., l. 185.
6. Ibid., l. 189.
7. Plenary session of 24 March 1944. RGALI, fond 2073, op. 1, ye. kh. 9, l. 221.
8. Plenary session of 3 April 1945. RGALI, fond 2073, op. 1, ye. kh. 11, ll. 186–7.
9. Ibid., fond 189.
10. Ibid.
11. See Chapter 4.
12. See Chapter 5.
13. See Chapter 3.
14. Plenary session of 3 April 1945. RGALI, fond 2073, op. 1, ye. kh. 11, ll. 186–7.
15. See Chapter 4.
16. I introduce the term 'phantom programmes' in ' "Music is Obscure": Textless Soviet Works and their Phantom Programmes', in *Representation and Meaning in Western Music*, ed. Joshua S. Walden (Cambridge, MA: Cambridge University Press, 2013), 47–63.
17. Meeting of the Music Section of 1 April 1954. RGALI, fond 2073, op. 2, ye. kh. 30, l. 212.

18. See Chapter 3.
19. Plenary session of 15 January 1952. RGALI, fond 2073, op. 1, ye. kh. 51, l. 94.
20. See Chapter 5.
21. An attempt to analyse the literary Stalin Prizes in a similar way was made by Alla Latynina in 'The Stalin Prizes for Literature as the Quintessence of Socialist Realism', in Hilary Chung et al. (eds), *In the Party Spirit: Socialist Realism and Literary Practice in the Soviet Union, East Germany and China*, Critical Studies, vol. 6 (Amsterdam, Atlanta, GA: Rodopi, 1996), 106–28. Igor Vorob'yov also uses Stalin Prizes as a guide, in his attempt to trace canon-formation in Soviet music, see *Sotsrealisticheskiy 'bol'shoy stil'' v sovetskoy muzïke, 1930–1950-ye godï* (St Petersburg: Kompozitor-Sankt-Peterburg, 2013), 235–56. Vorobyov's emphasis is on lengthy lists of pieces, rather than analysis.
22. Plenary session of 10 March 1954. RGALI, fond 2073, op. 2, ye. kh. 21, l. 79.
23. Plenary session of 21 January 1953. RGALI, fond 2073, op. 2, ye. kh. 2, l. 23.
24. See Chapter 10.
25. Even at the 1954 All-Union Agriculture Exhibition, the Russian pavilion was the only one without any national design elements. Greg Castillo, 'Peoples at an Exhibition: Soviet Architecture and the National Question', in Thomas Lahusen and Evgeny Dobrenko (eds), *Socialist Realism without Shores* (Durham and London: Duke University Press, 1997), 91–119 (112).
26. Jørn Guldberg, 'Socialist Realism as Institutional Practice: Observations on the Interpretation of the Works of Art in the Stalin Period', in Hans Günther (ed.), *The Culture of the Stalin Period* (New York: St Martin's Press, 1990), 166–7.
27. GARF, fond 5446, op. 50, ye. kh. 2812.
28. These were the words of Marietta Shaginian, one of Shostakovich's consistent admirers.
29. See Chapter 6.
30. S. Shlifshteyn, '21-ya simfoniya Myaskovskogo', *Sovetskaya muzïka* (1941), no. 1, 27–32 (32).
31. See http://classic-online.ru/ru/production/1222 (accessed 18 November 2014).
32. See Chapter 4.
33. See Chapter 11.
34. This was the sense of Konstantyn Dankevych's Ukrainian proverb, 'what's allowed for the priest is forbidden for the clerk', which he used to criticize Shostakovich's Ninth Symphony at the Composers' Union plenary session in October 1946. RGALI, fond 2077 (Union of Soviet Composers), op. 1, ye. kh. 136 [l. ref is missing].
35. Agitprop collected and analysed dozens of these letters. RGASPI, fond 17, op. 132, ye. kh. 427, ll. 17–61.

BIBLIOGRAPHY

Archives

The Bolshoi Theatre Manuscript Collection
The Bolshoi Theatre Museum
GARF (Gosudarstvennïy arkhiv Rossiyskoy Federatsii) – State Archive of the Russian Federation, Moscow
RGALI (Rossiyskiy gosudarstvennïy arkhiv literaturï i iskusstva) – Russian State Archive for Literature and Art, Moscow
RGANI (Rossiyskiy gosudarstvennïy arkhiv novoy istorii) – Russian State Archive of New [Recent] History, Moscow
RGASPI (Rossiyskiy gosudarstvennïy arkhiv sotsial'no-politicheskoy istorii) – Russian State Archive of Social and Political History, Moscow
VMOMK, formerly GtSMMK (Vserossiyskoye muzeynoye obyedineniye muzïkal'noy kul'turï im. Glinki) – All-Russian Consortium of Museums of Musical Culture, formerly the Glinka Museum; including the Goldenweiser Museum, Moscow

Periodicals

Kul'tura i zhizn'
Pravda
Sovetskaya muzïka
Sovetskiy artist
Sovetskoye iskusstvo
Teatr

Books and Articles

Adibekov, G. M., Anderson, K. M. and Rogovaya, L. A. (eds), *Politbyuro TsK RKP(b) – VKP(b): Povestki dnya zasedaniy. Katalog*, vol. 3 (Moscow: ROSSPEN, 2001)
Afiani, V. Yu. (ed.), *Apparat TsK KPSS i kul'tura, 1953–1957: Dokumentï* (Moscow: ROSSPEN, 2001)
Alliluyeva, Svetlana, *Twenty Letters to a Friend*, trans. P. Johnson (London: Hutchinson & Co., 1967)
Anderson, K. M., *RGASPI: Kratkiy spravochnik*, vol. 3 (Moscow: ROSSPEN, 2004)
Anderson, K. M., Maksimenkov, L. et al. (eds), *Kremlyovskiy kinoteatr, 1928–53: Dokumentï* (Moscow: ROSSPEN, 2005).
Bakhtarov, G. Yu., *Zapiski aktyora: genii i podletsï* (Moscow: OLMA Press, 2002)
Barsova, I. A., 'Iz neopublikovannogo arkhiva A.V. Mosolova', *Sovetskaya muzïka* (1989), no. 7, 80–92 and no. 8, 69–75
—, 'Sem'desyat vosem' dney i nochey v zastenke: kompozitor Mechislav Vaynberg', *Nauchnïy vestnik Moskovskoy konservatorii* (2014), no. 2, 90–104
— (ed.), *Nikolay Sergeyevich Zhilyayev: trudï, dni i gibel'* (Moscow: Muzïka, 2008)
Bartig, Kevin, *Composing for the Red Screen: Prokofiev and Soviet Film* (New York and Oxford: Oxford University Press, 2013)

—, 'Music History for the Masses: Reinventing Glinka in Post-War Soviet Russia', conference paper delivered at *Musical Legacies of State Socialism: Revisiting Narratives about Post-World War II Europe* (Belgrade, September 2015)

Beevor, Antony, *The Mystery of Olga Chekhova* (London: Penguin Books, 2005)

Blagoy, D. D. (ed.), *A. B. Gol'denveyzer: Staty'i, materialï, vospominaniya* (Moscow: Gosudarstvennïy tsentral'nïy muzey muzïkal'noy kul'turï imeni M. I. Glinki, 1969)

Blazhennïy Ioann, *Fortepiannoye yevangeliye Marii Veniaminovnï Yudinoy* (Kiev: Mir Sofii, 2010)

Borisov, S. B., *Andrey Aleksandrovich Zhdanov: opït politicheskoy biografii* (Shadrinsk: Iset', 1998)

Bourdieu, Pierre, *Distinction: A Social Critique of the Judgement of Taste*, trans. R. Nice (Cambridge, MA: Harvard University Press, 1984)

Bown, Matthew Cullerne and Taylor, Brandon (eds), *Art of the Soviets: Painting, Sculpture, and Architecture in a One-Party State, 1917–1992* (Manchester: Manchester University Press, 1993)

Brandenberger, David, *National Bolshevism: Stalinist Mass Culture and the Formation of Modern Russian National Identity, 1931–56* (Cambridge, MA and London: Harvard University Press, 2002)

Brooke, Caroline, 'Soviet Musicians and the Great Terror', *Europe–Asia Studies* (2002), vol. 54, no. 3, 397–413

Brooks, Jeffrey, *Thank You, Comrade Stalin!: Soviet Public Culture from Revolution to Cold War* (Princeton: Princeton University Press, 2000)

—, 'Stalin's Politics of Obligation', in Harold Shukman (ed.), *Redefining Stalinism* (London, Portland: Frank Cass Publishers, 2003), 47–68

Bugay, N. F. (ed.), *Narodï stran Baltii v usloviyakh stalinizma (1940-ye–1950-ye godï): dokumentirovannaya istorya* (Stuttgart: ibidem-Verlag, 2005)

—, 'Osobennosti organizatsii dekadï belorusskogo iskusstva v Moskve, Natsional'nïy teatr v kontekste mnogonatsional'noy kul'turï', *Shestïye mezhdunarodnïye Mikhoelsovskiye chteniya: dokladï, soobshcheniya* (Moscow: Rossiyskaya gosudarstvennaya biblioteka iskusstv, 2010), 262–9

Chernobayev, A. A. (ed.), *Na priyome u Stalina: Tetradi (zhurnalï) zapisey lits, prinyatïkh I. V. Stalinïm (1924–1953 gg.)* (Moscow: Novïy khronograf, 2008)

Chukovskiy, Korney, *Dnevnik*, vol. 2 (1930–1969), ed. Ye. Chukovskaya (Moscow: PROZAiK, 2012)

Chuyev, F. (ed.), *Sto sorok besed s Molotovïm: iz dnevnika F. Chuyeva* (Moscow: Terra, 1991)

Clark, Katerina, *The Soviet Novel: History as Ritual* (Chicago: University of Chicago Press, 1981)

Crankshaw, Edward, *Russia without Stalin: The Emerging Pattern* (London: Michael Joseph, 1956)

Digonskaya, Olga, 'Simfonicheskiy fragment 1945 goda: k istorii pervogo neokonchennogo varianta Devyatoy simfonii D. D. Shostakovicha', *Muzïkal'naya akademiya* (2006), no. 2, 97–102

Dikushina, N. (ed.), *Aleksandr Fadeyev: Pis'ma i dokumentï iz fondov Rossiyskogo Gosudarstvennogo Arkhiva literaturï i iskusstva* (Moscow: Izdatel'stvo Literaturnogo Instituta im. A.M. Gor'kogo, 2001)

Dobrenko, Yevgeniy, 'Realästhetik, ili narod v bukval'nom smïsle: oratoriya v pyati chastyakh s prologom i epilogom', *Novoye literaturnoye obozreniye* (2006), no. 82, 183–242

—, *Muzey Revolyutsii: Sovetskoye kino i stalinskiy istoricheskiy narrativ* (Moscow: Novoye literaturnoye obozreniye, 2008)

— and Eric Naiman (eds), *The Landscape of Stalinism: The Art and Ideology of Soviet Space* (Seattle: University of Washington, 2003)

Dunayevskiy, I. and Raynl', L., *Pochtovïy roman*, ed. N. Shafer (Moscow: Kompozitor, 2001)

Dunham, Vera, *In Stalin's Time: Middleclass Values in Soviet Fiction* (Durham and London: Duke University Press, 1990)

Dunmore, Timothy, *The Stalinist Command Economy: The Soviet State Apparatus and Economic Policy, 1945–53* (London and Basingstoke: Macmillan, 1980)

—, *Soviet Politics, 1945–53* (London and Basingstoke: Macmillan, 1984)

Edmunds, Neil (ed.), *Soviet Music and Society under Lenin and Stalin: The Baton and Sickle* (London and New York: Routledge Curzon, 2004)

English, James F., *The Economy of Prestige: Prizes, Awards, and the Circulation of Cultural Value* (Cambridge, MA and London: Harvard University Press, 2005)

Fairclough, Pauline, *Classics for the Masses: Shaping Soviet Musical Identity under Lenin and Stalin* (New Haven and London: Yale University Press, forthcoming)

Fay, Laurel, *Shostakovich: A Life* (Oxford: Oxford University Press, 2000)

Fitzpatrick, Sheila (ed.), *Stalinism: New Directions: A Reader* (London and New York: Routledge, 2000)

—, *On Stalin's Team: The Years of Living Dangerously in Soviet Politics* (Princeton and Oxford: Princeton University Press), 2015

Frolova-Walker, M., ' "National in Form, Socialist in Content": Musical Nation-Building in the Soviet Republics', *Journal of the American Musicological Society* (1998), vol. 51, no. 2, 331–71

—, *Russian Music and Nationalism from Glinka to Stalin* (New Haven and London: Yale University Press, 2007)

— and Walker, J., *Music and Soviet Power, 1917–32* (Woodbridge: The Boydell Press, 2012)

—, '"Music is Obscure": Textless Soviet Works and their Phantom Programmes', in *Representation and Meaning in Western Music*, ed. Joshua S. Walden (Cambridge, MA: Cambridge University Press, 2013), 47–63

—, 'A Birthday Present for Stalin: Shostakovich's *Song of the Forests*', in Esteban Buch, Igor Contreras Zubillaga and Manuel Deniz Silva (eds), *Composing for the State: Music in Twentieth-Century Dictatorships* (Aldershot: Ashgate, forthcoming)

Geodakyan, Georgiy, *Puti formirovaniya armyanskoy muzïkal'noy klassiki* (Yerevan: Izdatel'stvo Instituta iskusstv NAN RA, 2006)

Gershzon, M. M., 'Ministerstvo kul'turï SSSR v 1953–1963 godakh', *Russkiy sbornik: Issledovaniya po istorii Rossii,* vol. 8, ed. O. R. Ayrapetov et al. (Moscow: Modest Kolerov, 2010), 274–388

Goldman, Leah, *The Art of Intransigence: Soviet Composers and Art Music Censorship, 1945–1957*, PhD diss. (University of Chicago, 2015)

Goleyzovskiy, Kas'yan, *Zhizn' i tvorchestvo: stat'yi, vospominaniya, dokumentï* (Moscow, 1984)

Golovanov, N. S., *Literaturnoye naslediye, perepiska, vospominaniya sovremennikov* (Moscow, Sovetskiy kompozitor, 1982)

Gorlizki, Yoram, 'Stalin's Cabinet: The Politburo and Decision-Making in the Post-war Years', *Europe–Asia Studies* (2001), vol. 53, no. 2, 291–312

— and Oleg Khlevniuk, *Cold Peace: Stalin and the Soviet Ruling Circle, 1945–1953* (Oxford and New York: Oxford University Press, 2004)

Granin, Daniil, *Prichudy moyey pamyati* (Moscow and St Petersburg: Tsentrpoligraf, MiM-Del'ta, 2009)

Gregory, Paul R. and Naimark, Norman (eds), *Lost Politburo Transcripts: From Collective Rule to Stalin's Dictatorship* (New Haven and London: Yale University Press, 2008)

Gromov, Yevgeniy, *Stalin: Vlast' i iskusstvo* (Moscow: Respublika, 1998)

Gromova, Natal'ya, *Raspad: Sud'ba sovetskogo kritika: 40-ye–50-ye godï* (Moscow: Ellis Lak, 2009)

Guldberg, Jørn, 'Socialist Realism as Institutional Practice: Observations on the Interpretation of the Works of Art in the Stalin Period', in Hans Günther (ed.), *The Culture of the Stalin Period* (New York: St Martin's Press, 1990), 149–77

Gyunter, Khans and Dobrenko, Yevgeniy (eds), *Sotsrealisticheskiy kanon* (St Petersburg: Gumanitarnoye agentstvo 'Akademicheskiy proyekt', 2000)

Heller, Leonid and Baudin, Antoine, 'Le réalisme socialiste comme organisation du champ culturel', *Cahiers du monde russe et soviétique*, 34 (1993), no. 3, 307–44

Herrala, Meri E., *The Struggle for Control of Soviet Music from 1932 to 1948: Socialist Realism vs. Western Formalism* (Lewiston, Queenston and Lampeter: The Edwin Mellen Press, 2012)

Iğmen, Ali, *Speaking Soviet with an Accent: Culture and Power in Kyrgyzstan* (Pittsburgh, PA: University of Pittsburgh Press, 2012)

Il'yukhov, Aleksandr, *Kak platili bol'sheviki: Politika sovetskoy vlasti v sfere oplatï truda v 1917–1941 gg.* (Moscow: ROSSPEN, 2010)

Ivanov, V. V., *Dnevniki* (Moscow: IMLI RAN, 2001)

Ivkin, V. I., 'Kak otmenyali Stalinskiye premii: Dokumentï TsK KPSS i Soveta ministrov SSSR, 1953–1967 gg.', *Istoricheskiy Arkhiv* (2013), no. 6, 3–49

Johnson, Oliver, 'The Stalin Prize and the Soviet Artist – Status Symbol or Stigma?', *Slavic Review* (2011), vol. 70, no. 4, 819–43

Keldïsh, Yu. V. (ed.), *Istoriya muzïki narodov SSSR*, vols 2 and 3 (Moscow: Sovetskiy kompozitor, 1970 and 1972)

Kenez, Peter, *Cinema and Soviet Society from the Revolution to the Death of Stalin* (London and New York: I. B. Tauris Publishers, 2001)

Khachaturyan, Aram, *Pis'ma*, ed. G. A. Arutyunyan et al. (Moscow: Kompozitor, 2005)

Khederer, Vladislav and Ditssh, Shteffen, *1940: Schastliviy god Stalina* (Moscow: ROSSPEN, 2011)

Khlevniuk, Oleg V., *In Stalin's Shadow: The Career of 'Sergo' Ordzhonikidze*, ed. Donald J. Raleigh, trans. David J. Nordlander (Armonk, NY and London: M. E. Sharpe, 1995)

—, *Khozyain: Stalin i utverzhdeniye stalinskoy diktaturï* (Moscow: ROSSPEN, 2010)

Khrushchev, N. S., 'O kul'te lichnosti i yego posledstviyakh', *Izvestiya TsK KPSS* (1989), no. 3, 128–66

—, *Vremya, lyudi, vlast'* (Moscow: Moskovskiye novosti, 1999)

Klause, Inna, 'Composers in the Gulag: An Initial Survey', in Patrick Zuk and Marina Frolova-Walker (eds), *Russian Music since 1917* (Oxford: Oxford University Press, forthcoming)

Klefstad, Terry, 'Shostakovich and the Peace Conference', *Music and Politics* (2012), vol. 6, no. 2, http://quod.lib.umich.edu/m/mp/ (accessed 8 July 2013)

Kokarev, A. I. (ed.), *Tikhon Nikolayevich Khrennikov: K 100-letiyu so dnya rozhdeniya (stat'yi i vospominaniya)* (Moscow: Kompozitor, 2013)

Köll, Anu Mai (ed.), *The Baltic Countries Under Occupation: Soviet and Nazi Rule, 1939–1991*, Acta universitatis stockholmiensis, Studia Baltica Stockholmiensia, 23, (Stockholm: Almqvist & Wiksell International, 2003)

Koval', M., *S pesney skvoz' godï* (Moscow: Sovetskiy kompozitor, 1968)

Kovnatskaya, L. and Yakubov, M. (eds), *Dmitriy Shostakovich: Issledovaniya i materialï*, vol. 1 (Moscow: DSCH, 2005)

— et al. (eds), *Shostakovich v Leningradskoy konservatorii, 1919-1930*, 3 vols (St Petersburg: Kompozitor, 2013)

Kravets, Nelli, *Ryadom s velikimi: Atovmyan i yego vremya* (Moscow: GITIS, 2012)

Kuznetsov, A. M. (ed.), *Mariya Yudina. Vïsokiy stoykiy dukh: perepiska 1918–45 gg.* (Moscow: ROSSPEN, 2006)

Lahusen, Thomas and Evgeny Dobrenko (eds), *Socialist Realism without Shores* (Durham and London: Duke University Press, 1997)

Lamm, O. P., *Stranitsï tvorcheskoy biografii Myaskovskogo* (Moscow: Sovetskiy kompozitor, 1989)

—, 'Vospominaniya (fragment: 1948-1951 godï)', in M. P. Rakhmanova (ed.), *Sergey Prokof'yev: Vospominaniya, pis'ma, stat'yi* (Moscow: Deka-VS, 2004), 227–73

Latynina, Alla, 'The Stalin Prizes for Literature as the Quintessence of Socialist Realism', in Hilary Chung at al. (eds), *In the Party Spirit: Socialist Realism and Literary Practice in the Soviet Union, East Germany and China*, Critical Studies, vol. 6 (Amsterdam, Atlanta, GA: Rodopi, 1996), 106–28

Lebedev, V., Mel'chin, S., Stepanov, A. and Chernev, A. (eds), 'Proizvedeniye Shostakovicha – gluboko zapadnoy oriyentatsii', *Istochnik: Vestnik Arkhiva Prezidenta Rossiyskoy Federatsii* (Moscow, 1995), no. 5, 156–9

Liber, George O., 'Adapting to the Stalinist Order: Alexander Dovzhenko's Psychological Journey, 1933–1953', *Europe–Asia Studies* (2001), vol. 53, no. 7, 109–116

Lyatoshinskiy, Boris, *Vospominaniya, pis'ma i materialï*, ed. L. N. Grisenko, 2 vols (Kiev: Muzïchna Ukraina, 1985–86)

Maksimenkov, Leonid, 'Partiya – nash rulevoy', *Muzïkal'naya zhizn'*, 13–14 (1993), 6–8; 15–16 (1993), 8–10

—, *Sumbur vmesto muzïki: Stalinskaya kul'turnaya revolyutsiya, 1936–38* (Moscow: Yuridicheskaya kniga, 1997)

— (ed.), *Muzïka vmesto sumbura: Kompozitorï i muzïkantï v strane sovetov, 1917–1991* (Moscow: Mezhdunarodnïy fond 'Demokratiya', 2013)

Mariya Yudina: Obrechennaya abstraktsii, simvolike i besplotnosti muzïki: Perepiska 1946–1955 gg. (Moscow: ROSSPEN, 2008)

Martin, Terry, 'Modernization or neo-Traditionalism?: Ascribed Nationality and Soviet primordialism', in S. Fitzpatrick (ed.), *Stalinism: New Directions: A Reader* (London and New York: Routledge, 2000), 348–67

Mar'yamov, G. B., *Kremlevskiy tsenzor: Stalin smotrit kino* (Moscow: Konfederatsiya Soyuzov Kinematografistov 'Kinotsentr', 1992)

Maximenkov, Leonid, 'Stalin and Shostakovich: Letters to a "Friend"', in Laurel Fay (ed.), *Shostakovich and His World* (Princeton and Oxford: Princeton University Press, 2004), 43–58

—, 'The Rise and Fall of the 1948 Central Committee Resolution on Music', *Three Oranges* (November 2008), no. 16, 14–20

McCagg, Jr., William O., *Stalin Embattled, 1943–1948* (Detroit, Michigan: Wayne State University Press, 1978)

Medvedeva, Irina, 'Istoriya prokof'yevskogo aftografa, ili GURK v deystvii', *Sergey Prokof'yev, k 110-letiyu so dnya rozhdeniya: Pis'ma, vospominaniya, stat'yi* (Moscow: Gosudarstvennïy tsentral'nïy muzey imeni M. I. Glinki, 2001), 216–39

Merchant, Tanya, 'Revived Musical Practices within Uzbekistan's Evolving National Project', *The Oxford Handbook of Music Revival*, ed. Caroline Bithell and Juniper Hill (Oxford and New York: Oxford University Press, 2014)

Mikkonen, Simo, *Music and Power in the 1930s: A History of Composers' Bureaucracy* (Lewiston, Queenston and Lampeter: The Edwin Mellen Press, 2009)

Monsenzhon, Bruno (ed.), *Rikhter: Dialogi, dnevniki* (Moscow: Klassika-XXI, 2007)

Morrison, Simon, *The People's Artist: Prokofiev's Soviet Years* (Oxford: Oxford University Press, 2008)

—, *The Love and Wars of Lina Prokofiev* (London: Harvill Secker, 2013)

Naroditskaya, Inna, *Song from the Land of Fire: Azerbaijanian Mugam in the Soviet and Post-Soviet Periods* (New York: Routledge, 2003)

Nemirovich-Danchenko, Vl. I., *Tvorcheskoye naslediye: Pis'ma, 1938–43*, ed. I. N. Solov'yov, vol. 4 (Moscow: Moskovskiy Khudozhestvennïy teatr, 2003)

Neuberger, Joan, 'The Politics of Bewilderment: Eisenstein's "Ivan the Terrible" in 1945', in Al LaValley and Barry P. Scherr (eds), *Eisenstein at 100: A Reconsideration* (New Brunswick, NJ: Rutgers University Press, 2001), 227–52

Nevezhin, Vladimir, 'Yesli zavtra v pokhod': Podgotovka k voyne i ideologicheskaya propaganda v 30-kh–40kh godakh (Moscow: Yauza, Eksmo, 2007)
—, Zastol'ya Iosifa Stalina: Bol'shiye kremlevskiye priyomï, vol. 1 (Moscow: Novïy khronograf, 2011)
Norman, John O. (ed.), New Perspectives on Russian and Soviet Artistic Culture: Selected Papers from the 4th World Congress for Soviet and European Studies (Harrogate: Palgrave Macmillan, 1990)
Olson, Laura J., Performing Russia: Folk Revival and Russian Identity (New York: Routledge, 2004)
Orlov, Vladimir, Soviet Cantatas and Oratorios by Sergei Prokofiev in their Social and Cultural Context, PhD diss. (University of Cambridge, 2011)
—, ' "Did He Make a Step toward Rebirth?" Prokofiev's Pursuits of Self-Rehabilitation after 1948', conference paper delivered at Musical Legacies of State Socialism: Revisiting Narratives about Post-World War II Europe (Belgrade, September 2015)
Perkhin, V. V. (ed.), Deyateli russkogo iskusstva i M. B. Khrapchenko, predsedatel' Vsesoyuznogo komiteta po delam iskusstv: aprel' 1939–yanvar' 1948: svod pisem (Moscow: Nauka, 2007)
Pervïy vsesoyuznïy s'yezd sovetskikh kompozitorov: stenograficheskiy otchyot, ed. M. Koval et al. (Moscow: Izdaniye Soyuza sovetskikh kompozitorov, 1948)
Politbyuro TsK VKP(b) i Sovet Ministrov SSSR, 1945–1953, compiled by O. V. Khlevnyuk et al. (Moscow: ROSSPEN, 2002)
Pomerantsev, V. M., 'Ob iskrennosti v literature', Novïy mir (1953), no. 12, 218–45
Poponov, V., Orkestr khora imeni Pyatnitskogo (Moscow: Sovetskiy kompozitor, 1979)
Raku, Marina, Muzïkal'naya klassika v mifotvorchestve sovetskoy epokhi (Moscow: Novoye literaturnoye obozreniye, 2014)
Rasmussen, Mikkel Bolt and Wamberg, Jacob (eds), Totalitarian Art and Modernity (Aarhus: Aarhus University Press, 2010)
Reid, Susan E., 'Destalinization and Taste, 1953–63', Journal of Design History (1997), vol. 10, no. 2, 180–82
Romashchuk, I., Gavriil Nikolayevich Popov: Tvorchestvo. Vremya. Sud'ba (Moscow: GMPI im. Ippolitova–Ivanova, 2000)
Rubtsova, V. (ed.), Tak eto bïlo: Tikhon Khrennikov o vremeni i o sebe (Moscow: Muzïka, 1994)
San'ko, A. K., Ye. K. Golubev: kompozitor, pedagog, muzïkal'nïy deyatel' (dissertatsiya na soiskaniye uchyonoy stepeni kandidata iskusstvovedeniya) (Moscow: Moskovskaya konservatoriya, 2000)
Sesilkina, L. (ed.), 'V. V. Andreyev i yego velikorusskiy orkestr', Rossiyskiy Arkhiv: Istoriya Otechestva v svidetel'stvakh i dokumentakh XVIII–XX vv (Moscow: Studiya TRITE, 2007), vol. 15, 491–538
Shaporina, Lyubov', Dnevnik, 2 vols (Moscow: Novoye literaturnoye obozreniye, 2012)
Shchedrin, Rodion, Avtobiograficheskiye zapisi (Moscow: AST, 2008)
Shebalina, A. (ed.), V.Ya. Shebalin: godï zhizni i tvorchestva (Moscow: Sovetskiy kompozitor, 1990)
Shepilov, Dmitriy, Neprimknuvshiy (Moscow: Vagrius, 2001)
Shlapentokh, Vladimir, Soviet Intellectuals and Political Power: The Post-Stalin Era (Princeton: Princeton University Press, 1990)
Simonov, Konstantin, Glazami cheloveka moyego pokoleniya: razmïshleniya o I.V. Staline (Moscow: Kniga, 1990)
Smith, Susan Lockwood, Soviet Arts Policy, Folk Music, and National Identity: The Piatnitskii State Russian Folk Choir, 1927–1945. PhD diss. (University of Minnesota, 1997)
Smrž, Jiří, Symphonic Stalinism: Claiming Russian Musical Classics for the New Soviet Listener, 1932–1953 (Berlin: Lit Verlag, 2011)
Solodovnikov, A. V., 'Mï bïli molodï togda', in Yu. S. Rïbakov and M. D. Sedïkh (eds), Teatral'nïye stranitsï: sbornik statey (Moscow: Iskusstvo, 1979), 186–223
Soveshchaniye deyateley sovetskoy muzïki v TsK VKP(b) (Moscow: Pravda, 1948)
Sovetskaya opera: Sbornik kriticheskikh statey, ed. M. Grinberg and N. Polyakova (Moscow: GMI, 1953)
Ssorin-Chaikov, Nikolai, 'On Heterochrony: Birthday Gifts to Stalin, 1949', Journal of the Royal Anthropological Institute (2006), vol. 12, issue 2, 355–75
Svin'yin, V. F., and Oseyev, K. A. (eds), Stalinskiye premii: dve storonï odnoy medali. Sbornik dokumentov i khudozhestvenno–publitsisticheskikh materialov (Novosibirsk: Svin'yin i sïnov'ya, 2007)
Sviridov, Georgiy, Muzïka kak sud'ba (Moscow: Molodaya gvardiya, 2002)
Taruskin, Richard, 'The Ghetto and the Imperium', keynote lecture delivered at Nationalism in Music in the Totalitarian State (1945–89) (Budapest, 2015)
—, 'Two Serendipities: Keynoting a Conference, "Music and Power"', Journal of Musicology (forthcoming)
Tauragis, A., Lithuanian Music (Vilnius: Gintaras, 1971)
Terent'yev, B. M., Vospominaniya o V. G. Zakharove (Moscow: Muzïka, 1947)
Tikhonov, A. V. (ed.), Sozdatel' Velikorusskogo orkestra V. V. Andreyev v zerkale russkoy pressï (St Petersburg: Soyuz Khudozhnikov, 2000)
Tomilina, N. I. et al. (eds), Otdel kul'turï TsK KPSS (1953–1966): annotirovannïye opisi (Moscow: ROSSPEN, 2004)

Tomoff, Kiril, 'Most Respected Comrade: Patrons, Clients, Brokers, and Unofficial Networks in the Stalinist Music World', *Contemporary European History* (2002), vol. 11, no. 1, 33–65

—, *Creative Union: The Professional Organization of Soviet Composers, 1939–1953* (Ithaca and London: Cornell University Press, 2006)

—, 'Uzbek Music's Separate Path: Interpreting "Anticosmopolitanism" in Stalinist Central Asia, 1949–52', *Russian Review* (2004), vol. 63, no. 2, 212–40

—, *Virtuosi Abroad: Soviet Music and Imperial Competition and Integration during the Early Cold War, 1945–1958* (Ithaca: Cornell University Press, 2015)

Toradze, Gulbat, *Shostakovich i gruzinskiye kompozitorï* (Tbilisi: Mezhdunarodnïy kulturno-prosvetitel'skiy soyuz 'Russkii klub', 2006)

Tromly, Benjamin, 'The Leningrad Affair and Soviet Patronage Politics, 1949–1950', *Europe–Asia Studies* (2004), vol. 56, no. 5, 707–29

Unger, Heinz, *Hammer, Sickle and Baton: The Soviet Memoirs of a Musician* (London: The Cresset Press Ltd, 1939)

Vaughan, James C., *Soviet Socialist Realism: Origins and Theory* (London: Macmillan, 1975)

Vlasova, Ye., *1948 god v sovetskoy muzïke* (Moscow: Klassika-XXI, 2010)

Vodop'yanova, Z. et al., *Mezhdu molotom i nakoval'ney: Soyuz sovetskikh pisateley SSSR. Dokumentï i kommentarii*, vol. 1, ed. RGALI (Moscow: ROSSPEN, 2011)

Volkov, Solomon, *Testimony: The Memoirs of Dmitri Shostakovich*, trans. Antonina W. Bouis (London: Hamish Hamilton, 1979)

—, *Shostakovich and Stalin: The Extraordinary Relationship between the Great Composer and the Brutal Dictator*, trans. Antonina W. Bouis (London: Little, Brown, 2004)

Vorob'yov, Igor, *Sotsrealisticheskiy 'bol'shoy stil'' v sovetskoy muzïke, 1930–1950-ye godï* (St Petersburg: Kompozitor-Sankt-Peterburg, 2013)

Walker, Jonathan and Frolova-Walker, Marina, *Music and Dictatorship: Russia under Stalin. Newly Translated Source Documents* (New York: Carnegie Hall, 2003)

Ward, Chris, *Stalin's Russia* (London, Sydney and Auckland: Arnold, 1999)

Wilson, Elizabeth (ed.), *Shostakovich: A Life Remembered* (London: Faber and Faber, 2004)

Yekelchyk, Serhy, '*Diktat* and Dialogue in Stalinist Culture: Staging Patriotic Historical Opera in Soviet Ukraine', *Slavic Review* (2000), vol. 59, no. 3, 597–624

Zubkova, Elena, *Russia after the War: Hopes, Illusions, and Disappointments, 1945–1957*, trans. and ed. Hugh Ragsdale (Armonk and London: M. E. Sharpe, 1998)

Zuk, Patrick, 'Nikolay Myaskovsky and the Events of 1948', *Music and Letters* (2012), vol. 93, no. 1, 61–85

INDEX